# From the Pages of Emma

Emma Woodhouse, handsome, clever, and rich, with a comfortable home and happy disposition, seemed to unite some of the best blessings of existence; and had lived nearly twenty-one years in the world with very little to distress or vex her.                                                                   (page 3)

Matrimony, as the origin of change, was always disagreeable.
(page 5)

"Success supposes endeavour."                               (page 10)

"The attentions of a certain person can hardly be among the tittle-tattle of Highbury yet. Hitherto I fancy you and I are the only people to whom his looks and manners have explained themselves."                                     (page 51)

"One half of the world cannot understand the pleasures of the other."                                                        (page 77)

"I shall not be a poor old maid; and it is poverty only which makes celibacy contemptible to a generous public!"
(page 80)

There are people, who the more you do for them, the less they will do for themselves.                              (page 86)

"The truth is, that in London it is always a sickly season. Nobody is healthy in London, nobody can be."          (page 97)

It was a delightful visit;—perfect, in being much too short.
(page 101)

"There is, I believe, in many men, especially single men, such an inclination—such a passion for dining out; a dinner engagement is so high in the class of their pleasures, their employments, their dignities, almost their duties, that any thing gives way to it—and this must be the case with Mr. Elton: a most valuable, amiable, pleasing young man undoubtedly, and very much in love with Harriet; but still he cannot refuse an invitation, he must dine out wherever he is asked."  (page 104)

Human nature is so well disposed towards those who are in interesting situations, that a young person, who either marries or dies, is sure of being kindly spoken of.  (page 170)

"I cannot separate Miss Fairfax and her complexion."
(page 188)

Perfect happiness, even in memory, is not common.
(page 217)

"Business, you know, may bring money, but friendship hardly ever does."  (page 276)

"If other children are at all like what I remember to have been myself, I should think five times the amount of what I have ever yet heard named as a salary on such occasions dearly earned."  (page 364)

Seldom, very seldom, does complete truth belong to any human disclosure; seldom can it happen that something is not a little disguised, or a little mistaken.  (page 411)

"I always deserve the best treatment, because I never put up with any other."  (page 452)

# Emma

Jane Austen

*With an Introduction
by Steven Marcus
Notes by Victoria Blake*

**George Stade
Consulting Editorial Director**

**BARNES & NOBLE CLASSICS**
**NEW YORK**

*JB*

## BARNES & NOBLE CLASSICS
### NEW YORK

Begun in 1814, *Emma* was first published in 1816.

Introduction, Notes, and For Further Reading
Copyright © 2004 by Steven Marcus.

Note on Jane Austen, The World of Jane Austen and *Emma*, Notes,
Inspired by *Emma*, Comments & Questions, and For Further Reading
Copyright © 2004 by Fine Creative Media, Inc.

*Emma*
ISBN 1-59308-089-1
LC Control Number 2003116499

Produced and Published in conjunction with:
Fine Creative Media, Inc.
322 Eighth Avenue
New York, NY 10001

Michael J. Fine, President and Publisher

Printed in the United States of America
QB
1 3 5 7 9 10 8 6 4 2
First Printing

# Jane Austen

The English novelist Jane Austen was born on December 16, 1775, the seventh of eight children, in the Parsonage House of Steventon, Hampshire, where she spent her first twenty-five years. During her relatively brief lifetime Austen witnessed political unrest, revolution, war, and industrialization, yet these momentous events are not the central or explicit subjects of her finely focused novels. Rather, Austen wrote out of her immediate experience: the world of the country gentry and middle-class professional and business families. Jane's father, the Reverend George Austen, was the well-read country rector of Steventon, and her mother, Cassandra (née Leigh), was descended from a well-connected line of learned clergymen. By no means wealthy, the Austens nonetheless enjoyed a comfortable and socially respectable life.

Jane and her beloved elder (and only) sister, Cassandra, were schooled in Southampton and Reading for short periods, but most of their education took place at home. Private theatrical performances in the barn at Steventon complemented Jane's studies of French, Italian, history, music, and eighteenth-century fiction. An avid reader from earliest childhood, she began writing at age twelve, no doubt encouraged by her highly literate and affectionate family. Indeed, family and writing were her great loves. Despite a momentary engagement in 1802, Jane Austen never married. Her first two extended narratives, "Elinor and Marianne" and "First Impressions," were written while she was at Steventon but were never published in their original form.

Following her father's retirement, Jane moved in 1801 with her parents and sister to Bath. That popular watering hole, removed from the country life Jane preferred, presented the observant young writer with a wealth of events and experiences that would later be put to good use in her novels. Austen moved to Southampton with her mother and sister after the death of her father in 1805. Several years later the three women settled in Chawton Cottage in Hampshire, where Austen resided until the end of her life. She welcomed her return to the countryside and, with it, there came a renewed artistic vigor that led to the revision of her early novels. *Sense and Sensibility*, a reworking of "Elinor and Marianne," was published in 1811, followed by *Pride and Prejudice*, a reworking of "First Impressions," two years later.

Austen completed three more novels (*Mansfield Park*, *Emma*, and *Persuasion*) in the Chawton sitting room. Productive and discreet, she was not widely known to be the author of her published work. All of her novels were published anonymously, including the posthumous appearance, thanks to her brother Henry, of *Northanger Abbey* and *Persuasion*.

The last years of Austen's life were relatively quiet and comfortable. Her final, unfinished work, *Sanditon*, was put aside in the spring of 1817, when her health sharply declined and she was taken to Winchester for medical treatment of what appears to have been Addison's disease or a form of lymphoma. Jane Austen died there on July 18, 1817, and is buried in Winchester Cathedral.

# Table of Contents

# The World of Jane Austen
# *and* Emma

**1775**  The American Revolution begins in April. Jane Austen is born on December 16 in the Parsonage House in Steventon, Hampshire, England, the seventh of eight children (two girls and six boys).

**1778**  Frances (Fanny) Burney publishes *Evelina*, a seminal work in the development of the novel of manners.

**1781**  German philosopher Immanuel Kant publishes the *Critique of Pure Reason*.

**1782**  The American Revolution ends. Fanny Burney's novel *Cecilia* is published.

**1783**  Cassandra and Jane Austen begin their formal education in Southampton, followed by study in Reading.

**1788**  King George III of England suffers his first attack of mental illness, leaving the country in a state of uncertainty and anxiety. George Gordon, Lord Byron, is born.

**1789**  George III recuperates. The French Revolution begins. William Blake's *Songs of Innocence* is published.

**1791**  American political writer Thomas Paine publishes the first part of *The Rights of Man*.

**1792**  Percy Bysshe Shelley is born. Mary Wollstonecraft publishes *A Vindication of the Rights of Woman*.

**1793**  Europe is shocked by the execution of King Louis XVI of France and, some months later, his wife, Marie-Antoinette; the Reign of Terror begins. England declares war on France. Two of Austen's brothers, Francis (1774–1865) and Charles (1779–1852), serve in the Royal Navy, but life in the countryside at Steventon remains relatively tranquil.

**1795**    Austen begins her first novel, "Elinor and Marianne," written as letters (this early version is now lost); she will later revise the material as *Sense and Sensibility*. John Keats is born.

**1796–**   Austen drafts a second novel, "First Impressions,"
**1797**    which was also never published; it will later be rewritten as *Pride and Prejudice*.

**1798**    Poets William Wordsworth and Samuel Taylor Coleridge publish *Lyrical Ballads*.

**1801**    Jane's father, the Reverend George Austen, retires. He and his wife and two daughters leave the quiet country life of Steventon and move to the bustling, fashionable town of Bath.

**1803**    Austen's novel "Susan" is accepted for publication but does not see the light of day. The manuscript is eventually returned by the publisher. It will be revised and released posthumously as *Northanger Abbey*. The United States buys Louisiana from France. Ralph Waldo Emerson is born.

**1804**    Napoleon crowns himself emperor of France. Spain declares war on Britain.

**1805**    Jane's father dies. Jane and her mother and sister subsequently move to Southampton. Sir Walter Scott publishes *The Lay of the Last Minstrel*.

**1809**    After several years of moving about and short-term stays in various towns, the Austen women settle in Chawton Cottage in Hampshire; in the parlor of this house Austen writes her most famous works. Charles Darwin and Alfred, Lord Tennyson, are born.

**1811**    Austen begins *Mansfield Park* in February. In November *Sense and Sensibility* is published with the notation "By a Lady"; all of Austen's subsequent novels are also brought out anonymously. George III is declared insane, and the Prince of Wales (the future King George IV) becomes regent.

**1812**    *Fairy Tales* by the Brothers Grimm and the first parts of Lord Byron's *Childe Harold* are published. The United States declares war on Great Britain.

**1813**   *Pride and Prejudice* is published. Napoleon is exiled to Elba, and the Bourbons are restored to power.

**1814**   *Mansfield Park* is published.

**1815**   Napoleon is finally defeated at Waterloo.

**1816**   *Emma* is published. Charlotte Brontë is born.

**1817**   Austen begins the satiric novel *Sanditon*, but puts it aside because of declining health. She dies on July 18 in Winchester and is buried in Winchester Cathedral.

**1818**   *Northanger Abbey* and *Persuasion* are published under Austen's brother Henry's supervision.

# Introduction

*Emma*, first published in 1816, is Jane Austen's masterpiece. It is also one of the greatest novels in the English language. There is, and has been for some time, general agreement on these conclusions, but that consensus has in recent years remained largely tacit and unspoken, since judgments of value and relative merit in literary studies have as a category become contested ground, a site of principled dubiety. Still, it is difficult to deny that Jane Austen is a writer of exceptional interest, perhaps even of singular gifts, and that her writing has been steadily regarded as special and distinctive from the time of its original appearance to the present.

Simple reflection yields the observation that the very conception of judgments—of people making differing and differential estimates of value, of better and worse, or good and bad or better, of right and wrong and neither, of each other and themselves—is a central concern and undeviating activity of and in Austen's novels. The characters in these narratives are uninterruptedly involved in efforts to discriminate better from worse, and so is Jane Austen as narrator and architect of these fictions. Hence the contemporary student of literature is confronted with a paradox: In order to read Jane Austen appropriately, in order to achieve that willing suspension of disbelief that constitutes poetic faith and enables us to enter into fictive projections and imagined situations and problems as if they were, for the moment, "real" and we were experiencing them on a plane adjacent to that on which narrator and characters are assumed or proposed to exist—to do this we have to enter fully into the activities of judging, evaluating, and discriminating, as if they were as binding for us as they were for the author and her characters and their perplexities.

Another consideration along these lines has to do with the circumstance that, despite the clarity of line of its narrative, prose, and dialogue, *Emma* is an exceptionally dense and complex novel. So tightly woven is the intertexture of its thematic expressions, images, and representations that one can enter into it at almost any point or juncture in the narrative and begin to take up an analysis of the whole from there. It is almost as if no single strand or theme were exclusive of any of the others; each of them, by a strict economy of expressive means, leads to the center, which is at the same time a differentiated whole or totality. But that totality is equally neither stable nor self-identical but is continually shifting and permutating while we read, changing through each cumulative episode and detail, yet remaining somehow recognizably also itself.

What this complexity and variability require of us as readers, therefore, if we want to grasp what is taking place in this novel, is that we arouse our awareness and perceptiveness as collaborating intelligences to an intensity and subtlety of feeling, and a discrimination of existential distinctions and moral differences more focused and unremitting than most of us bring to our own everyday experience. The dramatic representation of characters in motion, speech, inner reflection, and intercourse, and the judgments of value that are rendered on each—and that we in our turn must also imagine—are simultaneous and inseparable. They take place in the same behavior (whether as narrative, speech, or dialogue) which is by that very token the writing that we read.

This is in part what older literary critics meant when they insisted upon the existence of a moral function or purpose in literature, and in particular in the novel. That function is disclosed to a degree in how—in the cause we undertake of trying fully to understand a story—the novel prompts and even compels us to exercise, more actively and purposefully than we ordinarily do, intellect, feeling, self-conscious reflection, and judgmental discrimination. In reading better we momentarily improve ourselves.

*Emma* is an exemplary instantiation of these processes. How and in what ways, for the purposes of explanation, do we locate its achieved originality? We can single out three general categories that will serve to organize discussion.

1. It is an extraordinary inward and detailed and coherent account of the circumstances, thoughts, and emotions—both conscious and otherwise—of a single complex character—in this instance a young woman of almost twenty-one.

2. It is a concrete realization of astonishing formal and technical creative originality, in which the narrative and dramatic possibilities and capacities of the novel as a genre are exponentially enlarged—as we observe, for the largest measure, in the fluid and continuously modulating relations between the authorial narrator and the chief characters—exploring and disclosing simultaneously shifting and evolving perspectives.

3. It constructs a succinct, telling, and detailed social and cultural context: Set in the first fifteen years of the nineteenth century, it focuses on a country village located sixteen miles from London. This confined world is very largely concerned with itself and its internal goings-on; yet in it the weight and density of rapid, uncontrollable social change is registered in and through the lives of its carefully distributed array of characters.

Most of the almost innumerable critical discussions of *Emma* undertake to explore or analyze one or another of these general areas. But a central part of *Emma*'s greatness has to do with its rendering of all three into interanimated coherence. It does so (to continue for another moment at this pitch of schematic simplicity and abstraction) by dramatically juxtaposing and integrating the interests and questions set out in numbers 1 and 3—the personal and inward with the impingements of social and cultural circumstances. It achieves this interpenetration and transformation of both largely, though not exclusively, by such innovations as are adverted to in number 2. It dramatizes such interfusions through the deployment of original representational means—in prose, in style and idiom, in narrative voice and dialogue, and through the juxtaposition of a range of narrative discourses. That is to say, it represents with unprecedented fullness the interpenetration of these large, stipulated spheres of existence—the domain of individual, reflective consciousness and emotions as it engages, mediates, and is modified by external and public pressures. These pressures are exerted for the most part by other persons—family members, friends, and acquaintances—as well as by the familiar constraints imposed by gender, money, situation, fortune, age, accident, and other circumstances. How this is done and what it suggests about the registration and elaboration of meaning in narrative comprises one side of *Emma*'s extraordinary claim as a novel, an achieved textual totality, and it is the purpose of this introduction to explore how this complex, heterogeneous whole is put together.

The first sentence of *Emma* is only less well known than the legendary opening of *Pride and Prejudice*. "Emma Woodhouse, handsome, clever, and rich, with a comfortable home and happy disposition, seemed to unite some of the best blessings of existence; and had lived nearly twenty-one years in the world with very little to distress or vex her." The immediate effect of this statement is to stop us, we readers, in our tracks. It is also a heads-up or alert, signaling to us as the narrator's adherents and collaborators to step up the volume and fine-tune the attentiveness that we direct toward the page. It begins with a broadside of affirmations and modulates into a conclusion that intimates serious problems may exist in the offing. Emma is very good looking in a rather striking and forceful way (not pretty or, here, beautiful); she is intelligent and quick-witted; and she is more than affluent when it comes to material means. She takes pleasure as well in the amenities of an established place in which to live, the establishment being part of a settled order in which she also feels at home. And best of all, perhaps, she is blessed with a "happy" temperament or general tone of well-being. With all these fortunate and combined bestowals, is there anything else to ask for? Well, yes—since they amount, the narrator remarks without pausing, to no more than "seemed." The dubiety carried in that ironic reservation turns the sentence around and prepares us for vexation and distress.

Emma has also reached a conventional juncture or locus of passage in the life cycle of European women and men. And this reference to numbers leads to a series of statements that informs us about how, in turn, those twenty-one years are to be regarded. Emma's mother has been dead for about sixteen years, since that is the interval during which Miss Taylor has been employed as her beloved governess—Emma's memory of her goes back to the age of five. Emma's older married sister, Isabella, is at least six years her senior, since we soon learn that she has been married for seven years and already has five children, the youngest of whom is less than a year old. It is reasonable to assume that Emma "had been mistress" of her father's house since she was about thirteen (a number that will come up later). Her father's age we will get to in a bit.

Her father and governess have raised Emma with great affection and equal indulgence. Restraint and authority have been close to absent from her experience, and she has, within this atmosphere of tenderness, permissiveness, and admiration, grown up "doing just what she liked; highly esteeming Miss Taylor's judgment, but directed chiefly by her own." The consequent disadvantages of Emma's situation were "the power of having rather too much her own way, and a disposition to think a little too much of herself." These "real evils" are at once modulated by "rather" and "a little too much." There may be forebodings, but they are neither very dark nor desperate.

The novel begins, however, with Miss Taylor's departure from the Woodhouse home of Hartfield. She has become Mrs. Weston, having just married a prosperous widower neighbor and taken up residence at Randalls, his recently purchased "little estate," only a half-mile from the Woodhouses (p. 13). The wedding guests have gone, and Emma and her father are left to themselves "to dine together, with no prospect of a third to cheer a long evening." Miss Taylor's wedding precipitates in Emma a "gentle sorrow." She understandably experiences Mrs. Weston's happiness as a "loss" as well, and sits in "mournful thought" pondering "what she had lost" (p. 4). The good fortune of her dear friend is both a source of "satisfaction" to her and yet, more questionably, "a black morning's work." The lightly stressed irony is that Emma is responding to her idealized surrogate mother's marriage as if it were an echo or shadow reenactment of her natural mother's death sixteen years before. Even more, in recent years the two of them have stood on "equal footing" and in "perfect unreserve"; to Emma, Miss Taylor has been that most rare "friend and companion," someone "peculiarly interested in herself, in every pleasure, every scheme of hers;—one to whom she could speak every thought as it arose, and . . . could never find fault."

With this approving mirror of another consciousness, another affirming yet senior female self, moving away into separateness and independence, Emma recognizes in herself the sense that things can never be the same for her again. "How was she to bear the change?" (p. 4). Indeed.

The "melancholy change" is compounded by Emma's awareness that "she was now in great danger of suffering from intellectual solitude. She dearly loved her father, but he was no companion for her. He could not meet her in conversation, rational or playful" (p. 5). Mr. Woodhouse is somewhere between sixty-five and seventy years old.[i] Yet

> the evil of the actual disparity in their ages . . . was much increased by his constitution and habits; for having been a valetudinarian all his life, without activity of mind or body, he was a much older man in ways than in years; and though every where beloved for the friendliness of his heart and his amiable temper, his talents could not have recommended him at any time (p. 5).

Although Emma dearly loves her father, they don't have interests or resources in common. Emma loves talk, the back and forth of conversation, the playfulness of wit and the bite of argument; her father is somewhere else. He is obsessed to the point of looniness with his health; he lives in terror of the weather; drafts, heat, cold and colds, damp, snow, the dews of a summer evening all imperil him and everyone he can warn. And he is equally endangered by food: His fearful admonitions on thin gruel, pork, boiled eggs, and baked apples are the stuff of unforgettable comic turns. He has behaved as "quite an invalid" all his life (p. 198) and has in fact become one. He claims that he goes "no where" and is torpid and inert. He exists at such a depressed level of vitality that he seems to be far older than his years. Friendly, affectionate, and amiable as he may be, he is neither brainy nor energetic. Mr. Woodhouse is effectively old enough to be Emma's grandfather, and in the far-distant resolution of this novel he partially fills that functional role.

Emma is responsive to these striking differences between her father and herself, as she is also mindful of her responsibilities as a daughter. Her melancholy musings end as her father awakens from his postprandial repose:

> and made it necessary to be cheerful. His spirits required support. He was a nervous man, easily depressed; fond of every body that he was used to, and hating to part with them; hating change of every kind. Matrimony, as the origin of change, was always disagreeable; and he was by no means yet reconciled to his own daughter's marrying, nor could ever speak of her but with compassion (p. 5).

Although Emma is neither nervous nor easily depressed, she is nonetheless her father's daughter. And in no characteristic is she more tellingly aligned with him than in her resistance to change—both change in general and in particular as it touches upon her own life circumstances, especially when it comes to marriage, marriage for herself, against which she has resolutely set her face. Her father's opposition to change, which takes on epic and mythical comic proportions, focuses with phobic intensity on marriage. Change equals separation and loss; and marriage—"the origin of change"—is for him, no matter what the circumstances, always exogamous.[ii] Moreover, that babies largely come about by means of marriage is an idea that has never found a secure lodging in his mind. It remains something of an unexplained wonder how it is that he ever married; and it is even more of a challenge to imagine how he himself ever came to father two thriving daughters. It is part of Jane Austen's comic genius and tact that she prompts such questions from her readers but utterly declines to undertake the provision of simple, rationalistic answers.

Mr. Woodhouse lives by his "habits of gentle selfishness," and these behaviors include his being "never able to suppose that other people could feel differently from himself" (p. 6). Emma too, in a more differentiated sense, suffers from habitual, sustained self-reference. And although she is intermittently aware that this practice may not be the best way to understand and negotiate with both the world and herself, she does not at the outset and far beyond actually question its rightness for herself. Nor does she seriously examine her own disinclination to the idea of marriage for herself. Although she too is saddened by the "loss" of Miss Taylor, she feels obliged to be cheerful as her father emerges from somnolence to resume his lament over "Poor Miss Taylor."

Emma is interrupted in her efforts to turn her father's attention to less doleful matters by the entrance of Mr. Knightley, just returned from London, where he has been visiting with his brother's family: John, his younger brother, Isabella, Emma's older sister, and their five children. He has brought back good news of their uninterrupted good health, and his "cheerful manner" also always does Mr. Woodhouse good. He is part of the family, connected to them by marriage and long friendship, as well as by rank, class, status, propinquity, and the common interests that arise from them. He declines to commiserate with the "Poor Miss Taylor" of Mr. Woodhouse or even with Emma's sense of loss—"'How did you all behave? Who cried most?'" He jollies them along with irony and good sense, remarking on the great improvement of Mrs. Weston's new circumstances. Emma answers this observation by turning the conversation in her own self-referring direction, and Mr. Woodhouse mistakenly responds to Emma with further self-reference on his own part. In the service of momentary clarification, Emma then exclaims: "'Oh, no! I meant only myself. Mr. Knightley loves to find fault with me, you know—in a joke—it is all a joke. We always say what we like to one another'" (p. 8). Whether Knightley "loves" to find faults with Emma remains moot, as does all of it being a joke. And although both Emma and Knightley have the highest regard for openness of temperament and relatively uninhibited personal communication, they do not *always* say what they like, or feel, to one another. Still, what Emma has cheerfully asserted is more true than false, and it tends, additionally, in the right direction.

The narrator concurs:

> Mr. Knightley, in fact, was one of the few people who could see faults in Emma Woodhouse, and the only one who ever told her of them; and though this was not particularly agreeable to Emma herself, she knew it would be so much less so to her father, that she would not have him really suspect such a circumstance as her not being thought perfect by every body.
>
> "Emma knows I never flatter her," said Mr. Knightley (pp. 8–9).

Having administered this semi-neutral and cooling dose, Knightley backs off, as does Emma. This reestablishing of dialectical balance permits him to continue his little lecture on Miss Taylor's good fortune. First, she has emancipated herself from her condition of "dependence." There can be no doubt of the correctness of her choice, both for herself and everyone else. "'Every friend of Miss Taylor must be glad to have her so happily married.'" Next, it is entirely to her "'advantage . . . at [her] time of life to be settled in a home of her own, and how important to her to be secure of a comfortable provision'" (p. 9). Knightley is here standing in for the narrator, as he recurs to the "comfortable home" of the novel's opening sentence.[iii] Emma knows all this, he goes on, addressing both father and daughter, and hence "'cannot allow herself to feel so much pain as pleasure.'"

Emma gaily changes gears and counters Knightley's pedagogy by affirming that she is also happy on the occasion, and moreover Knightley has "'forgotten'" one important element in her "'joy'"—namely that she "'made the match'" herself "'four years ago,'" in the face of general disbelief in the prospect that Mr. Weston would ever marry again. When her father pleads with her to desist from exercising her prophetic powers again, Emma replies: "'I promise you to make none for myself, papa; but I must, indeed, for other people. It is the greatest amusement in the world! And after such a success, you know!'" (p. 10). And she goes on to elaborate on how only she foresaw the happy resolution so long ago, "'planned the match'" from the outset, and should consequently be allowed to enjoy her "'success.'"

Knightley responds to the jibes in both "forgotten" and "success" by sharply observing that there was nothing for him to forget since Emma's "success" had been at best "'a lucky guess,'" a purely mental operation. And Emma comes back with an utterance that is worthy of the novelist *manqué* that she turns out to be. Lucky guesses in human relations "'are never merely luck.'" What passes between men and women is more subtle and complex than Knightley's blunt logic accounts for.

Rather than pursuing this branch of disagreement further, Knightley ascends to a higher plane of generality. "'A straight-forward, open-hearted man, like Weston, and a rational unaffected woman, like Miss Taylor, may be safely left to manage their own concerns. You are more likely to have

done harm to yourself, than good to them, by interference'"
(p. 11). It isn't self-evidently clear what harm to herself
Knightley may have in mind. However, when Emma answers
her father's repeated pleadings that she desist on the
grounds that marriages "'break up one's family circle grievously,'" and remarks that she must in any case first find a wife
for the relatively newly arrived clergyman, Mr. Elton, her father gamely and vainly tries to head her off by suggesting
that they invite him to dinner along with Knightley instead.
Knightley laughingly declares time-out and brings to a close
this bit of serial dispute and the first chapter itself. "'Invite
him to dinner, Emma, and help him to the best of the fish
and the chicken, but leave him to choose his own wife. Depend upon it, a man of six or seven and twenty can take care
of himself'" (p. 12).

It is worth recalling that the language or diction in which
Knightley couches most of his assertions in this opening
episode—from dependence/independence, to home/com-
fortable provision, to straightforward/rational and self-
management/interference, to choose your own wife/take care
of yourself—is associated with or belongs to the idiom of indi-
vidualism and individual choice and autonomy. This idiom is
also common to (if not identical with) the ideals and ideology
of the free market, of *laissez-faire* and noninterference, of a system of self-acting regulation and rational choice.[iv]

Knightley is the leading personage in the district (which
includes at least two parishes). As an elder son, he has inherited Donwell Abbey, the extensive family estate. On its acres
he rents out at least one (and possibly two) substantial farms.
He also cultivates, for sale and profit, a home farm, which is
large enough to require the services of a full-time steward.
He is in addition a magistrate, or justice of the peace, for this
local region. He is responsible for public order (see the
episode of the gypsies on page 316) and is actively involved in
the business affairs of the other men of substance and their
families of the district, as well as the public responsibilities of
the two parishes that the demographic geography of this

novel includes. He keeps current with agricultural reports and developments, and keeps a weather eye open for the respectably needy (the Bateses)—that is, for those on the way down—as well for those on the way up (Robert Martin and his family). He belongs both to the social group or ranking of the landed gentry, and he is very much a modern capitalist. He devotes considerable energy in balancing the "free," meritocratic claims made by the ideological adherents of the capitalist open market, and the counterclaims of ascribed status, social privileges, and inherited hierarchies exerted by the complex and traditional institutional matrix into which the newer capitalist agricultural economic order has to also fit. As this undertaking of adjusting and adapting two disparate and sometimes contradictory arrays of value and conceptual formulations develops throughout the novel, we can observe that such key terms as "independence" and "interference" are neither univalent nor stable. They vary in signification with context and character and can sometimes be applied to describe both identical and different phenomena in a single conceptual field.

These introductory pages amount to no more than a cursory traversal of the novel's first chapter, but they are intended to suggest something of the complexity and depth of conception at which Jane Austen's imagination is employed. That chapter also introduces a considerable number of the novel's store of interconnected themes and provides a useful sample of how they arise out of concretely represented individual characters whose interests and relations generate the several levels of interest and discourse that *Emma* keeps continually in play.

## I

As for Emma herself, Jane Austen famously declared that "I am going to take a heroine whom no one but myself will much like." Although one should on principle never trust the teller instead of the tale, she had, as usual, a point. There is considerably much about Emma to put one off: Her presumption, her snobberies, her maneuverings and manipulations have all served to mobilize a company of critical detractors. These disapproving voices often fail to take into account that Emma's shortcomings are not, at least at first, easily separable from her attractive qualities: her high spirits, her intelligence and wit, her genuine thoughtfulness and capacity for generosity. Jane Austen goes out of her way to foreground Emma's formidable endowment of personal and intellectual force and charm. When Harriet Smith is first introduced at Hartfield, Emma at once takes to her very good looks and to her deference and artless simplicity and falls to plotting an imagined future for Harriet that will elevate her place in the society of Highbury. Emma will take her in hand and "improve" her; she will "form her opinions and her manners." It will certainly be for Emma "an interesting . . . a very kind undertaking." Newly energized by the prospect of having something in the way of purposefulness to occupy her, Emma turns to organizing the supper table.

> With an alacrity beyond the common impulse of a spirit which yet was never indifferent to the credit of doing every thing well and attentively, with the real good-will of a mind delighted with its own ideas, did she then do all the honours of the meal, and help and recommend the minced chicken and scalloped oysters (p. 21).

Emma is simultaneously pleased by her skills and competence as a hostess and by her fledgling scheme for managing Harriet's future. Her behavior here is not private or covert (not yet), and she is never indifferent to recognition of her accomplishments and of the style in which she carries out "everything." She is very much "on stage" a good deal of the time and is sensible of the opinions and judgments of others on her performances in her diverse range of roles. But she is also experiencing substantial self-approval; her "real good-will" is an expression of "a mind delighted with its own ideas." If such a locution puts us in mind of a writer, artist, or novelist happily brooding over what she is about to put into action or execute, then we have only Jane Austen—or the narrator, if we insist—to blame. The ideas in question are also for the most part fantasies about couples and pairings, the very stuff of Jane Austen's novels themselves, and hence by moderately strong implication metafictional comments or representations.

In chapter V of the first volume, Knightley and Mrs. Weston discuss, among other things, Emma's new project of Harriet Smith, on which Knightley holds a very dim opinion. It is, according to him, only another installment of Emma's sense of superiority; no one (except himself) ever resists her. She has been "mistress of the house and of you all since she was twelve." Mrs. Weston responds by noting that Knightley must have thought her a bust at being a governess. "'I am sure you always thought me unfit for the office I held.'" Knightley agrees and remarks that Mrs. Weston, during her years with Emma, was really being trained to be a wife rather than a teacher or governess. "'You might not give Emma such a complete education as your powers would seem to promise; but you were receiving a very good education from *her*, on the very material matrimonial point of submitting your own will, and doing as you were bid'" (p. 34). It was Emma who was the governess and authority. It was Emma who exercised the commanding will, who gave orders, and who was obeyed. She occupied the adult position in this dyad; in gendered terms, she filled the male role; it was her ego that was in charge.

Both Knightley and Mrs. Weston admire and care for Emma, despite these excesses. Knightley expresses himself on this topic in a strikingly salient observation. "'I have a very sincere interest in Emma. . . . There is an anxiety, a curiosity in what one feels for Emma. I wonder what will become of her'" (p. 37). How will Emma turn out? The question has an interest of its own which goes quite beyond the matter of will Emma marry. Emma is someone with an as yet unspecified future, a fate or destiny, a set of possibilities that might find expression in some alternative structure. It is almost as if she were a narrative or a novel herself—with a probable but uncertain line of development, a *Bildung*, a contingent resolution. She has, in other words, the capacity for creating an identity for herself; and if her career in life includes marriage (and what follows from it), it will in any event be a strongly individuated choice and arrangement.

Knightley cannot restrain himself for long. When he learns from Emma that she has persuaded Harriet to turn down a proposal of marriage from Robert Martin—Knightley's tenant farmer—in the hope (and, to Emma, the certain likelihood) of an offer from Mr. Elton, he explodes in exasperation at Emma's misguided scheme. The two battle it out, with Emma getting decidedly the worse part. He breaks off the conversation and walks out without ceremony and in a state of high annoyance. Emma is momentarily shaken by their disagreement, but quickly recovers her composure and self-confidence. Knightley, she rather ruefully observes, has "walked off in more complete self-approbation than he left for her." Moreover, she goes on, Knightley could have observed Elton "neither with the interest nor . . . with the skill of such an observer on such a question as herself." He is resentful, ignorant, and prejudiced. He did not "make due allowance for the influence of a strong passion at war with all interested motives. Mr. Knightley saw no such passion, and of course thought nothing of its effects; but she saw too much of it to feel a doubt of its overcoming any hesitations that a reasonable prudence might originally suggest" (p. 63).

Emma is, of course, talking through her hat. In her fantasy of a passionate courtship between Elton and Harriet she is unconsciously projecting some of her own unacknowledged wishes and desires onto both members of the pair; and in her repudiation of Knightley's disapproval she is displacing her own misperceptions and misapprehensions onto his "conventional" moral authority. But what chiefly deflects her vision and confounds her observations here is that she is denying the palpable reality of Elton's desire for her. Still further, she is denying desire in general and altogether so far as she herself is concerned. This denial runs deep and is one of the principal sources of the cognitive (and comic) distortions that characterize Emma's schemes and plans for others.

"Mr. Knightley might quarrel with her, but Emma could not quarrel with herself. . . . She was sorry, but could not repent" (p. 64). She is in fact high on herself, and although she cannot be angry at herself at this point in the narrative, she will soon to her chagrin learn to be increasingly self-critical. Although Emma has to be educated and "cured" of her infatuation with herself, her self-love and narcissism do not at the same time, however much trouble and grief they precipitate for her and others, seem in the end to be irremediable and pathological.[v] There is also something winning and untutored about her narcissism—it is part of her immaturity, part of the unachieved and uneven development of the emotions that we find her contending with throughout the narrative.

One of the technical devices that Jane Austen deploys to express and investigate this inner matrix is free indirect discourse, the narrator's entry into Emma's consciousness. Situated flexibly somewhere between narration and direct speech and fluidly shifting its properties, vectors, and psychic distances, this style of narrative permits the represented consciousnesses of both Emma and the narrator to permeate one another, sometimes to fuse, sometimes to be held distinct, sometimes to be both a mingling of the two and something else at the same time. It is part of the experience the novel provides us with, of "getting to know" with intimacy and in copious and fulminating detail the imagined inner life of a represented character. To this end, Jane Austen represents Emma as habitually talking to herself. We eavesdrop on Emma's silent conversations with herself. And one of the things we quickly come to learn is how much Emma enjoys the sound of her own (inner) voice. She is regularly aware of how delightful it is to be Emma. She talks to herself so much because she is such good company. And if this incessant silent chatter is further evidence of her narcissism, we might also recall that Knightley and Mrs. Weston agree that Emma is the very picture of "health," an ascription that is repeated more than once in the narrative. And even though the health here is primarily physical and refers to Emma's beauty and bloom, her "firm and upright figure," her robust comportment and energetic bearing, there is an overflow or carry-over into a more general assessment. Knightley remarks, "'I love to look at her; and I will add this praise, that I do not think her personally vain. Considering how very handsome she is, she appears to be little occupied with it; her vanity lies another way'" (p. 36). He means, to be sure, that Emma's vanity lies in her preposterous overestimation of her powers of insight and judgment, her unshaken faith in her own capacity of "penetration." This conventionally male metaphorical attribute is referred to ironically throughout the narrative (p. 23, p. 126, p. 314, and throughout). What Knightley leaves unsaid is that despite this silly and troublesome characteristic, he loves to listen to her as well. Even when she is spouting rubbish, Emma's talk is a genuine pleasure to hear.

Part of that pleasure is incurred through Emma's "playfulness." She relishes the rapid stab of wit and paradoxical opposition; she plays uninterruptedly at "imaginistic" matchmaking. She is exceptionally skillful at games, particularly verbal ones: puzzles, riddles, and ciphers, "enigmas, charades, . . . [and] conundrums" (p. 66), Scrabble *avant la lettre* are all integral to the ways she occupies her considerable spare time, engaged for the most part in self-amusement. She reads codes and encryptions with accomplished ease, even as she cannot recognize or interpret correctly matters that are passing in front of her nose. She thinks of Jane Fairfax's behavior as "quite a separate puzzle" (p. 268). Frank Churchill is Emma's superior at playing make-believe; his entire relation to her can be thought of as a kind of game of pretending, an exercise in frivolity, bluffing, and fakery, while his treatment of Jane has a distinct element of teasing, of sadistic playfulness and rule-breaking license to it. Emma also likes to "play" the piano, and she loves to dance—steps and rituals and elaborate patterns all appeal to her sense of "the rigour of the game."[vi]

Emma's playfulness, however, is carefully "placed" by her in a specific context of requirements: She must be "always first and always right." And although she qualifies this by saying that the demand applies to her relations to men, it equally includes Mrs. Weston and Harriet as well as most of the lesser female lights of Highbury. When it does not, as it does not with Jane Fairfax and Mrs. Elton, Emma responds with coldness and remoteness. The form that her principal exercise of playfulness takes is that of romantic fantasy, of "match-making," as she calls it. These fantasies reveal a singular and simple structure. They are almost all of them triangles, with Emma at one of the points performing as the managing director of the other two—and hence as a kind of displaced center. First there is Emma and Mr. and Mrs. Weston, a completed pairing that Emma believes she has brought about. Then there is Emma, Elton, and Harriet, which Emma totally misinterprets, denying Elton's undisguised designs on herself and deflecting them onto Harriet—Harriet figuring here as the clearest instance of Emma's constructing an imaginary and unconscious sexual life by proxy. Then there is Emma, Harriet, and Robert Martin—something unambiguously actual and ready, which Emma heads off, blocks, and tries to destroy. She behaves in this instance out of several motives: She enlists her always-handy snobbery to lower Martin in Harriet's estimation; she absurdly elevates Harriet's status simply by virtue of Emma's having taken her up— that is, by her patronage. In effect, she keeps Harriet for herself by pursuing a fantastic and impossible object (Elton) and rejecting a plausible and logical one (Martin). The fantasticated triangle of Emma, Frank Churchill, and

Jane Fairfax is a parody of Emma-Elton-Harriet. The symmetry in this second instance is to be found in Emma's mistaken belief that Frank is in love with her, while he is all along secretly engaged to Jane. Indeed Emma never once suspects that anything at all exists between the two lovers. Emma's fantasies are additionally and understandably set going full blast by the highly attractive Jane, and Emma rapidly cooks up another imaginary three-sided figure involving Jane and the invisible Mr. and Mrs. Dixon, which includes illicit love and a possibly adulterous affair. Then there are Emma's off-the-wall fabrications about Harriet and Frank and, at the end, Harriet and Knightley, this latter helped along by Harriet herself. Finally there is the climactic triangle of Emma, her father, and Knightley, a fantasy that is also an actuality which will be resolved by extraordinary and even slightly magical measures.

These triangles represent among other things the classic unconscious fantasies of children about both familial and parental relations and the familiar sexual patterns or scenarios that such imaginations both trace out and figure forth. Their unpremeditated self-referential nature is to be observed in the manner in which the child is always the central figure in the pattern and also in the ways in which the child is both included in and walled out of the sexual activities of the parental figures. Emma's lively curiosity about the affairs of others combines her impulse to be "first," to be always centrally in on the action (in both fantasy and intellectual activity), with her actual repudiation and denial of personal, sexual desire.

This repudiation is brought forward in a number of passages in which Emma is prompted (mostly by herself) to enlarge upon her early arrived-at decision never to marry. When the innocent and slightly airheaded Harriet asks her in alarm: "'Dear me! but what shall you do? how shall you employ yourself when you grow old?'" Emma begins her reply as follows:

"If I know myself, Harriet, mine is an active, busy mind,
with a great many independent resources; and I do not
perceive why I should be more in want of employment at
forty or fifty than one-and-twenty. Women's usual occupations of eye, and hand, and mind will be as open to me
then as they are now; or with no important variation. If I
draw less, I shall read more; if I give up music, I shall take
to carpet-work" (p. 81).

Of course she does not know herself in any acceptable sense,
and the parody fuses high comedy with pathos. The lame-
ness of her protestations about self-sufficiency is accentuated
by the circumstance that the detestable Mrs. Elton is also
given to prating about her "resources," both mental and
otherwise. Mrs. Elton is one of several fractionated and split-
off representations of parts of Emma. She is in genuine degree a caricature and parody of Emma, and some degree of
our understanding of Emma and *Emma* is derived from our
reading off from these subsidiary characters back onto
Emma herself. The pathos of Emma's reply is disclosed in
the limp alternatives and vague specifications of her legion
of independent resources.

Emma's rejection of the idea of her marrying is also articulated in her resistance to change. "'I cannot really
change for the better. If I were to marry, I must expect to repent it'" (p. 80). Like so many of Emma's categorical cer-
tainties, this "must" covers over doubt, anxiety, and
uncertainty. It is a characteristic bit of Emma's bravado,
which is, however, and in its turn, connected with both her
chutzpah and her courage. But her aversion to change is not
restricted to her personal life. It is expressed in a global
sense in her snobbery. The Woodhouses, along with the
Knightleys, are at the top of the heap in Highbury. Emma, in
addition, can add social privilege and superiority of inherited status to her personal claims to ascendancy and power.
We have observed this already in her treatment of Harriet
and Robert Martin. Harriet, an illegitimate child with no

known family, is raised above her "appropriate" plane simply by virtue of her personal connection with Emma; and Martin, a prosperous and upwardly mobile young farmer, is correspondingly demoted by Emma to being "Hodge," illiterate, unmannerly, and uncouth simply because he *is* a farmer and labors for his livelihood—and is hence unworthy of any young woman whom Emma has stooped to "notice."

The absurd comedy of Emma's snootiness is admirably dramatized in the dinner party proposed by the Coles. The Coles, relative newcomers to Highbury, and personally "friendly, liberal and unpretending," are also unfortunately "of low origin, in trade, and only moderately genteel." The last few years, however, have "brought them a considerable increase of means—the house in town[vii] had yielded greater profits, and fortune in general had smiled on them"—unlike Highbury itself, which seems to have had both ups and downs. Accordingly they undertake to enlarge their circumstances and improve their amenities. They add to their house, increase their number of servants, purchase a grand piano, and "in fortune and style of living" were by this time "second only to the family at Hartfield." Donwell Abbey is out of the parish as well as out of range, but they have surpassed in material and consumerist terms the Westons at Randalls. Their sociability plus their new dining room add up to expectations of a dinner party. They have already had some trial runs at parties "chiefly among single men." Emma from on high pontificates that the Coles would "hardly presume to invite" the "regular and best families"—"neither Donwell, nor Hartfield, nor Randalls. Nothing should tempt *her* to go, if they did."

> The Coles were very respectable in their way, but they ought to be taught that it was not for them to arrange the terms on which the superior families would visit them. This lesson, she very much feared, they would receive only from herself; she had little hope of Mr. Knightley, none of Mr. Weston (p. 195).

Only she is capable of reminding them of their proper place and of the propriety of their staying fixed in that station. In the event, however, both Knightley and the Westons (along with almost everyone else Emma is friendly with) are invited and accept, but no invitation arrives for the Woodhouses. Mrs. Weston's consoling effort to account for the omission—"'I suppose they will not take the liberty with you; they know you do not dine out,'"—makes no dent on the disappointed, disgruntled, and offended Emma. "She felt that she should like to have had the power of refusal." And the presence of all her friends and the possibility of after-dinner dancing leave her paradoxically stranded: "Her being left in solitary grandeur, even supposing the omission to be intended as a compliment, was but poor comfort" (p. 196).

It turns out that the invitation arrives belatedly. And though Emma at once declares "'of course it must be declined,'" she just as quickly asks the Westons "what they advised her to do . . . their advice for her going was most prompt and successful." The final ironic rub is delivered in the Coles' explanation for the delayed arrival of the invitation. They had been "waiting the arrival of a folding-screen from London, which they hoped might keep Mr. Woodhouse from any draught of air, and therefore induce him the more readily to give them the honour of his company" (p. 196). Emma is obliged to admit that the Coles have "expressed themselves so properly," that there was "so much real attention in the manner" of their explanation and "so much consideration for her father," that she allows the Westons to "persuade" her of what she has already decided to do. And it is unmistakably not the Coles' prose (let alone the Westons' eloquence) that has done it, but Emma's desire not to high-hat herself out of a pleasant, sociable, and even possibly exciting evening.

There is an unpleasantly tough, hard, and callous streak running through Emma's character; that hardness is expressed in her snobbery and in a number of her other social responses. But it is expressed as well in her attitudes toward marriage. As Knightley first observes, Emma has never been in love: Despite her matchmaking impulse, she has no experience of romantic or sexual love and hence can know little about it. Emma concurs, but takes the account one step further: "'I never have been in love: it is not my way, or my nature; and I do not think I ever shall'" (p. 80). This is another of her declarative certitudes that is bound to be falsified. What is implied in this utterance, among much else, is that Emma has thus far in her young life only been in love with herself; or to rotate the formulation slightly, she has never yet fallen out of favor with herself. She has still to experience that abrupt precipitation into passionate dependency that is one of the genuine markers of sexual, romantic love. She conflates the economic dependency (and humiliation) of Miss Bates and her family with dependency in general and claims that her own, Emma's, immunity from poverty will be sufficient to keep or preserve her "'as sensible and pleasant as any body else'" (p. 81).

But Emma is "clever" and knows that as an unmarried woman she will not have "objects for the affections" that only marriage can supply. One thinks, almost naturally, of a husband, a mate, and an intimate companion, and then of children. But Emma makes it quite clear that she has isolated and distanced the idea of a husband and is thinking only about babies and children when she refers to objects of interest and objects for the affections. Moreover, she has prepared a line of defense against that deprivation. She will be the loving aunt of her sister's children.

"There will be enough of them, in all probability, to supply every sort of sensation that declining life can need. There will be enough for every hope and every fear; and though my attachment to none can equal that of a parent, it suits my ideas of comfort better than what is warmer and blinder" (p. 81).

As it frequently happens with Emma, smugness and self-conceit consort with genuine, telling insight into herself. At the age of twenty, Emma is speaking with fatuous confidence about "declining life" and referring with gnomic compression to "every fear." But she also brings forward the notion of comfort, which refers in this novel to a broad range of meanings—in this instance, to an inner state, a state of the emotions in which ease, equilibrium, and relaxation are foregrounded. "Warmer" will figure with increasingly manifest sense in the latter part of the narrative. And "blinder" also refers to another matrix of ideas. Emma will repeatedly indict herself for blindness, meaning self-deception, misreading, and misinterpreting. But she will also accuse Frank Churchill of using his extended flirtation with her as

> "merely a blind to conceal his real situation with another. It was his object to blind all about him; and no one, I am sure, could be more effectually blinded than myself—except that I was *not* blinded—that it was my good fortune—that, in short, I was somehow or other safe from him" (p. 407).

She was, and then again she wasn't. Emma, who regards herself as sharp-eyed and penetrating, has been both used and blinded (or deceived) by Frank. Love is blind, so it is said. *A Midsummer Night's Dream* is one of Shakespeare's comedies that Jane Austen seems to have had in mind when she was writing, in *Emma*, about multiple deceptions, mismatches, and gross errors of perception. "Love looks not with the eyes, but with the mind, / And therefore is wing'd Cupid painted blind" (act 1, scene 1). And Cupid figures as one of the possible answers to the riddle that begins, "Kitty, a fair but frozen maid." Cupid turns out not to be the correct answer, but the riddle itself is laden with references to love—that is, to sex—and its likely injurious consequences for health.[viii] When Elton is about to return to Highbury, bringing his bride with him, Emma observes that Harriet is still re-

pining over her loss. In order, as she believes, to jolt Harriet
out of her fruitless moping, Emma cleverly and not very
scrupulously or subtly accuses her of ingratitude. Harriet is
duly shocked and falls all over herself in hyperbolic protestations to Emma of love, thankfulness, and subservience.
Emma's self-conceit is touched, and as Harriet leaves, she
silently reflects that "she had never loved Harriet so well, nor
valued her affection so highly before." She then gives herself
a "serious" talking-to.

> There is no charm equal to tenderness of heart. . . .
> There is nothing to be compared to it. Warmth and ten-
> derness of heart, with an affectionate, open manner, will
> beat all the clearness of head in the world, for attraction:
> I am sure it will. It is tenderness of heart which makes my
> dear father so generally beloved—which gives Isabella all
> her popularity.—I have it not; but I know how to prize
> and respect it. Harriet is my superior in all the charm and
> all the felicity it gives. . . . happy the man who changes
> Emma for Harriet (pp. 252–253).

This splendid passage characteristically welds together
Emma's acute, if momentary, sense of personal shortcoming
with her contrived, sustained self-bamboozlement. It is not
an either/or proposition, as if one might conceivably make
an exchange of one for the other—it never is. Emma's supposed "clearness of head" also includes her cloudy pipe
dreams of glorious triangularities; "for attraction" begins a
detour that takes her away from her temporary, dispassion-
ate self-analysis; and Isabella's popularity is, as far as the text
bears evidence, an assertion concocted out of pure wind.
Nevertheless, she has touched on a sensitive if not excessively painful spot. Warmth and tenderness of heart are what
she recognizes as being missing or undeveloped parts of her
being. In other words, there is something inadequate or de-
fective in her affections—her emotions or affects, as we
would rather portentously say today. If for her Jane Fairfax

embodies "coldness," then Emma, even in her own estimation, is definitely cool. In other words, she may have to
change, perhaps even to grow up. How such a development
is to be brought about is a consideration that we will defer
for the present.

## II

If we examine Jane Austen's detailed representation of the
society in which she sets *Emma*, one of the things that is likely
to strike us as readers almost two hundred years later is that
for all its traditional rural inertia, the local social world of
this narrative and the larger world that is its context are in
the course of going through complex, uneven, and even
contradictory processes of change. The era of European-
wide wars brought on by the epoch-making French Revolution, and its Napoleonic succession is coming to a final end.
In Britain the sense of national emergency has subsided; restrictions on such activities as travel to the Continent have
been lifted, and a bumpy and unpredictable transition to a
peacetime yet rapidly changing economy has begun to set in.

   Highbury itself, where all the dramatized action of the
novel takes place, is "a large and populous village, almost
amounting to a town" (p. 5). Such a description seems to
suggest growth and increase. And when Frank Churchill is
first introduced to this local scene, he notes that it appears
"airy, cheerful, happy-looking." He has his own reasons for
producing this characterization, but he and his companions
make their first pause

   at the Crown Inn, an inconsiderable house, though the
   principal one of the sort, where a couple of pair of post-
   horses were kept, more for the convenience of the neighbourhood than from any run on the road; and his
   companions had not expected to be detained by any interest excited there; but in passing it they gave the history
   of the large room visibly added. It had been built many

> years ago for a ball-room, and while the neighbourhood had been in a particularly populous, dancing state, had been occasionally used as such: but such brilliant days had long passed away; and now the highest purpose for which it was ever wanted was to accommodate a whist club established among the gentlemen and half gentlemen of the place (p. 186).

The village has more than one inn, but its principal stopping place is nothing to boast about. Although it is only sixteen miles from London, it seems not to be located on a road that is directly connected to the city or, for that matter, is much used. The post-horses are the Regency equivalent of the village taxi. At some time in the past, the place was livelier than it now appears to be. There has been a visible downward demographic shift. Population has been lost, along with the leading and more prosperous social luminaries. At present the most notable social activity at the Crown is cardplaying among the mixed bag of gentlemen and half gentlemen. With that unique English genius for ever-finer distinctions of class and status, Jane Austen leaves it to the reader to define what a half gentleman might be.

Frank Churchill wants to dance and good-naturedly challenges Emma to "'revive the good old days of the room.'" After all, she is the presiding and authorizing female center of social activity. Frank's companions point out to him "the want of proper families in the place, and . . . that none beyond the place and its immediate environs could be tempted to attend." He remains unpersuaded and argues that the well-kept houses that he sees around him could surely

> furnish numbers enough for such a meeting; and even when particulars were given and families described, he was still unwilling to admit that the inconvenience of such a mixture would be any thing, or that there would be the smallest difficulty in every body's returning into their proper place the next morning (p. 186).

The ratio of genteel or respectable families per acre has gone downhill. We are not told anything about the causes or meanings of this change. But Emma observes to herself that Frank seems to have inherited the indiscriminate sociability of his father. And she silently huffs and puffs that Frank's "indifference to a confusion of rank bordered too much on inelegance of mind. He could be no judge . . . of the evil he was holding cheap" (p. 187). It is as if the relation between peerless Emma and the illegitimate, fatherless and motherless, and effectively anonymous Harriet Smith portends nothing confused or inelegant. The stilted awkwardness of Emma's formulations suggests their anachronistic inappropriateness, as she will duly learn.

But there are also counter-indications to this apprehension of downwardness. When John Knightley comes down to Hartfield to leave his two oldest boys with their grandfather and aunt for a holiday visit of "some weeks" in the spring (p. 274), their arrival coincides with a welcoming dinner for the Eltons that Emma feels obliged to hold. John Knightley represents in some degree a departure in social sensibility. It is fair to say that he is in general unsociable, unlike his brother and even his father-in-law. He prefers the excluding and private domestic circle of his considerable and growing nuclear family. He is one of the extreme partisans of "home" in this novel and is never comfortable when separated from wife, children, and their dwelling in Brunswick Square. He can also be peevish and a considerable grouch; in particular, he has to control his irritable temper when he is confronted with the perseverated anxieties, phobias, and obsessions of Mr. Woodhouse, a duty at whose performance he is only moderately successful. Ironically, however, he resembles his father-in-law in his own easily disturbed equilibrium, his insecurity and anxiety when the restricted family circumstances that he has established for himself are broken into. At the dinner party, he charges Emma with the care of his boys and enjoins her to send them home if "'you find them troublesome.'" He is of course needling their affectionate aunt in his annoyance at the supposed exponential intensification of her social life.

> "Here am I come down for only one day, and you are engaged with a dinner-party! When did it happen before? or any thing like it? Your neighbourhood is increasing, and you mix more with it . . . every letter to Isabella [has] brought an account of fresh gaieties" (p. 294).

This semi-facetious account is in large measure hyperbole, and Emma fires back a sensible and convincing confutation. John Knightley has also, however, atypically expressed himself with some ambiguity when he remarks that "your neighbourhood is increasing." He may simply imply that Emma's rate of socializing has grown; but he may also mean that Highbury is also growing, or even that the range of those admitted into the precincts of the upper social circles has been enlarged. In any case, it is useful to recall Emma's remark that "there was no denying that those brothers had penetration" (p. 126), meaning that their observations as a rule have some non-incidental point. Here the point suggests that the representation of Highbury's situation as far as demographic circumstances and socio-economic changes are concerned is a mixed and uncertain picture, with indications and pointers going in more than one direction.

Such complexities and equivocalities are borne out in the life histories of most of the narrative's significant characters. Mr. Weston is one of the sources for such impacted significations. A native of Highbury, he comes from a respectable family that for several generations "had been rising into gentility and property." Well-educated, he was at the same time disinclined as a young man to enter into the "more homely pursuits" of profession or trade that engaged his brothers. He took advantage of the urgencies brought on by England's response to the French Revolution and joined the county militia, which had been activated. The "chances of . . . military life" had led Captain Weston to meeting Miss Churchill, "of a great Yorkshire family." She fell in love with him, and they married. Her brother and his wife, however, were offended, indeed mortified, by the lowness of her choice, and "they threw her off with due decorum." Though the young couple were in love, the marriage proved to be "an unsuitable connection, and did not produce much happiness." Mrs. Weston, willful, resolute, and independent enough to defy her family's interdictions, could not "refrain from unreasonable regrets at . . . [their] unreasonable anger." She missed the opulence of the family estate, and although she never "ceased to love her husband . . . she wanted to be at once the wife of Captain Weston and Miss Churchill of Enscombe." After three years of living "beyond their income," she died, leaving Mr. Weston a rather poorer man than before along with a young son. Her death from "a lingering illness" and the little boy's half-deserted existence had led the forbidding brother and sister-in-law to soften. Childless themselves, they offered to take over entirely the rearing of the boy. Mr. Weston, having given up his son to these resources of wealth and opportunity, now "had only his own comfort to seek and his own situation to improve as he could."

He resigned from the militia and went into trade with his brothers in London. He did not work with exceptional ardor at his business and divided his time between employment in the city and "a small house in Highbury" where he enjoyed his leisure hours. After eighteen or twenty years of this not very strenuous existence, he discovered that he had "realized an easy competence"—he was a beneficiary, like many others in the middling ranks at the time, of an economy that prospered in wartime, and that was simultaneously expanding at an unheard-of rate. He had achieved independence. He could now purchase "a little estate adjoining Highbury, which he had always longed for." He was free to marry without hindrance or second thoughts a woman "as portionless even as Miss Taylor," a gentlewoman whose resources were so reduced that she had had to hire herself out as a governess.

And he was now able "to live according to the wishes of his own friendly and social disposition" (p. 14).

For Weston the phases of the life cycle and the social cycle have happily coincided. In his mid-forties, he "had made his fortune, bought his house, and obtained his wife"—in that order. He was "beginning a new period of existence with every probability of greater happiness" (p. 14). On this occasion he was aware that "he had only himself to please in his choice." Even more, in the person of Miss Taylor he had "the pleasantest proof of its being a great deal better to choose than to be chosen, to excite gratitude than to feel it" (p. 14). His trajectory in life is clearly meant to be paradigmatic of major tendencies of social change in the densely contextualized world of this novel. It is characterized by moderate but genuine mobility upward, and to a lesser degree by obstacles and detours along that route. Weston has augmented his freedom by means of the working of a growing commercial and market economy. In terms of social class he has achieved freedom from trade through his successful application to trade.

Nevertheless, this depiction of open possibilities is modified by the shadow cast by prohibitions and restrictions. On the whole, it is a representation of progress, but this progress includes deep inequalities. It is defined by broadly increasing life-chances, which means increasing freedom of choice. Still this progression toward increased latitude and amplitude of individual freedom of choice is not simply a one-way street. It is better to be active than passive, independent than dependent, choosing rather than being chosen. This asymmetry applies not only to money and rank or social status; it applies to differences in gender as well. One of Emma's objections to marriage is that she has no inclination to be dependent, or to be anything other, or less, than "first."

Robert Martin seems, on first inspection, a less elaborate case. He is a comfortably situated and hopeful young farmer (the principal tenant of Knightley) who works the Abbey-Mill Farm. He is literate and alert, and his sisters have been to school with Harriet at Mrs. Goddard's. He is doing very well with his sheep, selling their wool at a premium in a market whose processing and manufacture of woolens was in the first stages of industrialization and was to expand massively. He is ambitious, sensible, and without affectation; he reads "the Agricultural Reports," keeps up on both improvements in farming technology and the states of the various markets. He owns a copy of *Elegant Extracts*, the anthology of miscellaneous pieces that both Emma and her father are familiar with, and from which Emma claims she has copied out the riddle "Kitty, a fair but frozen maid." He has read *The Vicar of Wakefield* but is unacquainted with the popular Gothic romances that Harriet recommends. He travels on horseback to do business in a nearby town, although he also makes his way about the neighborhood on foot. His "appearance" is "very neat," and he is by all reports a solid and stable young man of twenty-four—seven years older than Harriet. He writes a straightforward and coherent letter and maintains an attractive and comfortable home.

None of this cuts any ice with Emma. She waves him out of consideration and declares that the "'yeomanry are precisely the order of people with whom I feel I can have nothing to do'" (p. 26). Although yeomen was one of the terms used for the local militias raised for defense against possible invasion during the wars of the French Revolution, the term itself was commonly, if loosely, applied to free-holding farmers. In her put-down of Martin, Emma seems unwittingly, through an almost anachronistic usage, also to have raised him up—at least formally—since he rents his farm (which has very little to do with his relative prosperity).[ix] And, she goes on to say to Harriet, when Robert Martin is Mr. Weston's age, he "'will be a completely gross, vulgar farmer,'" unattractive, slovenly, obsessed with money. He may become rich, but he will remain "'clownish,'" a local mechanic and yokel, "'illiterate and coarse'" (pp. 29–30).

Leaving to one side Emma's personal motives for behaving in this crude and nasty way, we understand that she has done a number on both Harriet and Robert Martin. She has reproduced by analogy (and in parody again) the situation of the young Captain Weston and Miss Churchill, grotesquely inflating Harriet to a great Yorkshire heiress far beyond the social possibilities of the lowly Captain of Yeomanry (or Militia, or Volunteers). Emma herself occupies the place of the Churchill brother and sister-in-law; and she threatens Harriet with the fate Miss Churchill incurred when she insisted on choosing Weston (p. 57). Harriet sends Martin a letter of rejection—largely composed by Emma (p. 50). The next morning Knightley promptly appears to tell Emma the good news that Martin has consulted him before writing his letter of proposal to Harriet. Knightley is a great champion of Martin, and Martin "'considers me as one of his best friends'" (p. 55). Knightley recommends him highly in terms we are already familiar with, and adds that Martin can afford to marry and that he, Knightley, has happily encouraged him to go ahead. Emma, smiling to herself that she is far ahead of Knightley, informs him of what he doesn't know. Knightley cannot believe his ears, and Emma has to repeat herself. He goes red, stands up, and hits the ceiling. He sees at once that Emma has schemed this whole thing through. He is furious at her for her failure of intelligence, for her narcissism, for her self-referential and mistaken interfering, for her irresponsibility. Emma, as yet unshaken, saucily replies that it is inconceivable that Martin could be "'a good match for my intimate friend! . . . It would be a degradation.'" At this, Knightley more or less jumps out of his skin. "'A degradation to illegitimacy and ignorance, to be married to a respectable, intelligent gentleman-farmer'" (p. 57). And he proceeds to commend Martin's manners for their "'sense, sincerity and good-humour'" and concludes with the more salient "'and his mind has more true gentility than Harriet Smith could understand'" (p. 61).

Emma admits that although legally Harriet is a "Nobody" there can be no doubt that her father is both a gentleman and rich, thereby providing her with everything that Emma believes she needs. She and Knightley have a regular verbal brawl, with Knightley landing the best blows, and Emma "playfully" and energetically defending a bad cause. A number of slippery and disputable terms have also been put into play: yeomanry, gentleman-farmer, Nobody, gentility.

A recollection or recurrence of this spirited exchange takes place toward the end. Knightley, this time unbeknown to Emma, has "interfered," has taken charge of the match-making, and has arranged for a meeting of Harriet and Martin in London; Martin has again proposed and this time been accepted. And this time Knightley breaks the news to Emma, although he is unduly anxious that she will still be adamantly opposed. He now calls Martin "'my friend Robert.'" In his solicitude toward Emma, Knightly acknowledges that—

> "His situation is an evil; but you must consider it as what satisfies your friend. . . . As far as the man is concerned, you could not wish your friend in better hands. His rank in society I would alter if I could; which is saying a great deal, I assure you, Emma. You laugh at me about William Larkins; but I could quite as ill spare Robert Martin" (p. 451).[x]

Martin's character remains unblemished. His place or status in an inherited, customary social hierarchy is a circumstance that Knightley would like to change but cannot. Knightley would, in this instance, be happy to depart from the social regime of a market economy that in its turn is embedded in and constrained by a traditional, semi-feudal order of ranking. This disposition of legitimate authority allows for gradual, progressive change and the rising of worthy persons through the traditional grades or categories: from farmer to gentleman-farmer to bona fide gentleman. Knightley would be willing, for Robert Martin, to bypass the noninterference policy that guides doctrinally the social economy of a market-driven system, which has in turn been mixed into a supervening context of historical, inherited socio-political institutions. It would be close to violating his ideological principles (he has, ironically, already done so in master-minding the match of Martin and Harriet), and he would if he could, but he can't.[xi] Still he relies as much on Martin as he does on his steward, William Larkins (along with Martin, one of the considerable group of enumerated and signifi-cant symbolically silent characters in *Emma*). The laughter that Knightley refers to has to do with Larkins giving Knight-ley "permission" to keep back some extra apples (which he will doubtless give away), but the purport of his remark is that he depends on Martin and that his tenant's Abbey-Mill Farm and Knightley's home farm are connected by more than geographical proximity. In sum, the shiftings and ir-regularities or inconsistencies that are observable in Emma's and Knightley's statements about Robert Martin are refrac-tions from an actual historical world of social changes and contradictions.

The Bates family is a counterpart to Weston and Martin, but going in the opposite direction. (As George Orwell de-scribed his own Anglo-Indian family, they are downstarts.) Mrs. Bates is the very old widow of "a former vicar of High-bury." While Mr. Bates was alive, we are prompted to assume, the family occupied the same social position as Mr. and Mrs. Elton. But the defunct vicar left his family in a very poor way, almost without resources. Miss Bates, the unmarried daugh-ter, is neither young, handsome, clever, or rich.[xii] She takes care of her "failing" parent and also does whatever she can for her niece, Jane Fairfax, the orphaned child of a sister— and also as good as penniless. Miss Bates is all goodwill and "contented temper," simplicity and cheerfulness, "a recom-mendation to every body, and a mine of felicity to herself" (pp. 18–19). She is a lesson in Christian acceptance and gladness and buoyancy in the midst of adversity and loss. She keeps herself spiritually afloat through an endless stream of talk, gossip, and scattered recollections. Her uninterrupted and harmless monologues form her chief defense against the poverty, emptiness, and subordination into which the family has descended.

The Bateses live in Highbury itself, in a house belonging to "people in business." They rent two rooms up a flight of stairs, and "love to be called on" and included in almost any social occasion. They are dependent on Knightley and the Woodhouses for little luxuries of meat and fruit. Although they are in constant danger of falling through the cracks in the economic floor, their secure and well-cared-for neighbors undertake to support them through marginal assistance and by involving them in communal life by means of steady invitations and visits. Emma has been negligent in her attentions to them, and she is aware that she has behaved grudgingly and as "not contributing what she ought to the stock of their scanty comforts" (p. 145). Both Knightley, her external conscience, and "her own heart" have tweaked her over such "deficiency," but Emma cannot overcome her distaste for applying herself to what is self-evidently her duty (the performance of what used to be called duty was unvaryingly unpleasant). It was to her all "very disagreeable,—a waste of time—tiresome women—and all the horror of being in danger of falling in with the second rate and third rate of Highbury, who were calling on them for ever, and therefore she seldom went near them" (p. 145). Emma regards genteel poverty as spiritually sordid and even contaminating. She also forgets that as the family of a clergyman, the Bateses were perforce well acquainted with the fourth and fifth rate as well, though perhaps not as friendly callers. The point is that there is no social safety net strung beneath the Bates women (or anyone else). They are the dependent objects of charity administered personally by members of their own social rank and local neighborhood; and Miss Bates' Christian denials and self-denials as well as her mother's fortuitous insensibility act as buffers against the perpetual abradings of their middle-class sensibilities that poverty and dependency remorselessly inflict. Jane Fairfax, by contrast, handsome, clever, and poor, is rubbed raw by these circumstances. And it is no surprise that Emma's surpassing act of thoughtless cruelty, hardness, and irresponsibility should be dramatized in the personal insult she delivers, in the form of a witty remark, to Miss Bates in public, and within the hearing of others.

The Bates women are, then, illustrations of counter-tendencies in the inclusive representation of the social world in *Emma*. They are casualties of the larger circumstances of change and accident that move almost everyone in this novel around. The arc of Jane Fairfax's life and fortune traces out one of the social movements taken by these under-lying forces of inscrutable complexity. She is the orphaned niece and granddaughter of her two surviving relatives. Her father was a lieutenant of infantry who died "in action abroad." Her mother sank "under consumption and grief soon afterwards" (p. 153). She has inherited from her mother a disposition that is easily upset and susceptible to suffering, as well as a delicate and unstable physical consti-tution (unlike Emma). She became at the age of three "the fondling of her grandmother and aunt," and in their re-duced and straitened situation there appeared to be "every possibility of her being permanently fixed there," with scanty means and no advantages of "connection or improvement." A former fellow officer of her dead father, Colonel Campbell, who felt much indebted to him, returned eventually to England and sought out the orphaned girl. Married and with one daughter Jane's age, he took Jane up and assumed responsibility for her education. She became part of his fam-ily and "had lived with them entirely, only visiting her grand-mother from time to time" (p. 154). She is another one of the homeless people among the population of *Emma*.

But Colonel Campbell's fortune was no more than "mod-erate," and so Jane was prepared by means of her excellent education to earn a "respectable subsistence hereafter" (p. 154). Her "heart and understanding had received every ad-vantage of discipline and culture." As she approaches major-ity she has become an elegant, cultivated, and accomplished young woman, "qualified for the care of children, fully competent to the office of instruction herself" (p. 154). An evil future looms ahead of her, since she will as a governess enter into a situation of semi-permanent homelessness. She will also descend in status—a gentlewoman, educated but without means, enters a respectable, affluent family to be employed, ambiguously, as a semi-member of the family who is also an upper servant. Her companionship and deep friendship with Miss Campbell continue until "that chance, that luck which so often defies anticipation in matrimonial affairs" leads Miss Campbell (rather than the superior Jane) to engage the affections of a rich young man and finds herself "happily settled," while Jane "had yet her bread to earn." And so with "the fortitude of a devoted noviciate, she had resolved at one-and-twenty to complete the sacrifice, and retire from all the pleasures of life, of rational intercourse, equal society, peace and hope, to penance and mortification for ever" (p. 155). There is some question of how we are to take such a passage. Are we to read it in the sense that Emma's avowal never to marry is to be read? We are persuaded that Emma will eventually marry—heroines who are handsome, clever, and rich almost invariably do. The question of interest in this connection is how Emma will find her way toward deciding to marry, how she will change, grow, and develop so that marriage becomes not merely her contingent but her appropriate, indeed her inevitable choice. I do not think that the passage about Jane is ironic in quite that way. There is nothing playful about Jane; she is straight and sober all the way. She thinks of herself as a nun entering a convent and sealing herself away from ampler life, resolved to do penance for the sin of poverty and to mortify herself for having desired to live fully, in accordance with her personal possibilities and gifts, as well as her desires. Later on, she compares the employment offices for governesses in London to slave markets: "'offices for the sale, not quite of human flesh, but of human intellect'" (p. 283). She feels acutely that she is a victim of a mysterious and far from benevolent set of forces.

This cheerless prospect is suddenly lightened; chance leads her to meet Frank Churchill at a seaside resort and watering hole. The two fall quickly and deeply in love, and Frank, in his youthful and passionate impulsiveness, successfully importunes her to undertake a secret engagement. This agreement, in violation of the protocols that governed courtship among the upper orders at the time, weighs heavily on Jane's sense of propriety and acceptable conduct. The two lovers have also agreed to conduct a secret correspondence, and this covert behavior, along with the deception of others that it unavoidably involves, adds to the stress and constraint, the recessiveness and "restraint" that is so notable a feature of Jane's manner of conducting herself. Her burdens are only made heavier by Emma's dislike, envy, and rivalry, and by Frank's impossible behavior when he comes to Highbury—he doesn't even tell her that it is he who has bought the piano for her. As a crowning imposition of misery, Jane has been "taken over" by Mrs. Elton, who with sadistic glee keeps urging her to get on with it and allow Mrs. Elton to procure for her a "superior" situation, among her acquaintances near Bristol, as a governess.[xiii] It is no wonder that Jane's health begins to break down, her nerves to crack, and her composure to falter. She is rescued from being ground up by the forces of social circumstance, which also propel social change, only through the intervening exigencies of comic conventions, including the comic plot.

In *Emma* Jane Austen enlarges her social imagination in the direction of downward inclusiveness. When Emma takes Harriet along with her to visit a "poor sick family," she is on a mission of charitable obligation and behaves with compassion and tact. She gives relief to these poor people in the form of money, along with her "personal attention and kindness." She enters into "their troubles with ready sympathy" but does not idealize them; she could "allow for their ignorance and their temptations, had no romantic expectations of extraordinary virtue from those for whom education had done so little" (p. 82). As they leave the cottage, she moralizes to Harriet to the effect that such scenes serve to restore one's sense of moral proportion; they make everything else appear "trifling." At the moment, her consciousness is flooded with impressions brought about by squalor and misery; and, she goes on, she feels as if she could think about "'these poor creatures all the rest of the day; and yet, who can say how soon it may all vanish from my mind?'" This morsel of easily won and easily understood self-critical reflection is parroted by Harriet, and Emma then proceeds to assert that she does not think "'the impression will soon be over.'" She offers this self-correction as "she crossed the low hedge, and tottering footstep which ended the narrow, slippery path through the cottage garden." Emma then repeats herself once again, as she pauses "to look once more at all the outward wretchedness of the place, and recall the still greater within" (p. 83).

As they walk down the lane, Mr. Elton appears, and Emma realizes that her "stability in good thoughts" is about to vanish. But, she resiliently continues, "'If we feel for the wretched, enough to do all we can for them, the rest is empty sympathy, only distressing to ourselves'" (p. 83). And she at once resumes her imaginings and matchmaking. In such a passage, Jane Austen directs attention to the incompatibilities and cross-purposes, registered in personal attitudes and responsiveness, that cannot in this historical world be undone. Emma is self-consciously cognizant of the constraints that bind them all, and the narrator is a touch more aware of dissonances and overtones than Emma. These poor are of course among the Nobodies. They remain nameless and are swallowed up in the conventional abstractions of "sickness and poverty." There is no hint of an imagination of possible social improvement, much less of structural change. It is Jane Austen and not Emma who puts us in the way of inferring such defects and fallings short.

*Emma* also takes brief notice of those who are external to

the context of English society altogether. These are the gypsies, nomadic people who are both homeless and seek no home. They harass and terrify Harriet with their importunate begging, and Frank Churchill's fortunate appearance turns "the terror" they had been creating in Harriet into "their own portion." He half-carries the fainting Harriet to Hartfield, where she collapses; and he entrusts Emma to bring "notice of there being such a set of people in the neighbourhood to Mr. Knightley" (p. 318). These "trampers" may reduce Harriet to fear and trembling, but they are no more than a nuisance to individual persons. They represent nothing really dangerous, since they are an alien and external agency and signify no endogenous threat, precisely because they are so utterly exterior. The local magistrate will shoo them off. One of the better-known myths about gypsies was that they inveterately steal babies. Harriet Smith (Smith being the equivalent of X) does not know who her parents are and might be, for all she knows, a changeling as well as a foundling. Perhaps to her terrorized state of mind they were attempting to steal her back![xiv]

There is nothing to do about the gypsies but move them on. They are there, inexplicably, outside the boundaries of full social intelligibility. But there are other anomalies as well. In *Emma*, Jane Austen goes to considerable lengths to name and particularize both outlying members of the respectable Highbury community and the servants who are omnipresent throughout and make comfortable life possible for their masters and mistresses. Among others, we learn about Mr. Perry and Mr. Coxe, whose son and daughter have mysteriously dropped the "e" from the spelling of their surname. We also hear of Mrs. Wallis, who runs the village bakery and who is supposed to be uncivil, and about James the coachman as well as his daughter, and Hannah and Patty and Mrs. Hodges, Knightley's housekeeper, who frets over apple tart. These are all figures imagined in an effort to flesh out the representation (and our impression) of an actual functioning community, of a textured social world, including specified and individuated minor and subminor characters (as Dickens would shortly do). But this very effort paradoxically serves to bring into sudden relief instances in which the opposite occurs. When Frank Churchill brings Harriet to Hartfield, she is collapsing and leaning on his arm. Emma is outdoors and is surprised "when the great iron sweep-gate opened, and two persons entered" (p. 316). The great iron sweep-gate did not open by itself. Somebody pushed it open and pulled it to. This is a genuine reification in the sense that the servant who opens the gate has become invisible and been absorbed in the gate itself: The gate has been correspondingly endowed with human will and agency. Frank's chance meeting with Harriet is represented in a similar mode. He has been on his way out of the village, but the "pleasantness of the morning had induced him to walk forward, and leave his horses to meet him by another road, a mile or two beyond Highbury" (p. 317). What has happened, to be sure, is that Frank has left his horse with the mounted servant who has accompanied him and has agreed to meet up with the servant and the horses again later on. But the servant's identity, his human being, has been eclipsed; he has been erased and banished from the scene and from narrative consciousness, and the horses, intelligent creatures that they are, will no doubt find their way to the appointed meeting all by themselves.[xv]

Before we jump all over Jane Austen for having committed a false consciousness, we might reflect that such lapses are connected with the endeavor she is making to be more inclusive. She is, I believe, intuitively aware that the course of her own development (as well as that of the novel) requires the progressive and individualized incorporation of the Nobodies and Nothings who largely make up our and her world. These Nobodies include the Eltons and Mrs. Churchill before she was married; they embrace Weston and Frank Churchill as soon as he is compared to Knightley; they explicitly account for everyone in this novel except for the Knightleys and the Woodhouses (and the far-away Yorkshire

Churchills). These gentry and lower gentry and less distinguished middling families are the experiential base out of which Jane Austen's imagination rose, which it neither abandoned nor affirmed uncritically. As she enhanced the social range and creative reach of her novelistic intelligence, she concomitantly opened herself to including the lapses, contradictions, illogicalities, and even inhumanity that were constituent elements of the social and cultural world that she lived in, and of the larger consciousness that she both expressed and worked successfully to alter.

Another realization of how Jane Austen's impulse to be extensive, exact, and complex can lead her into small but perceptible lapses occurs as Emma arrives at the Coles' dinner party.

> She followed another carriage to Mr. Cole's door; and was pleased to see that it was Mr. Knightley's; for Mr. Knightley keeping no horses, having little spare money and a great deal of health, activity, and independence, was too apt, in Emma's opinion, to get about as he could, and not use his carriage so often as became the owner of Donwell Abbey (p. 201).

It is a fine, compact little passage, which (as usual in Jane Austen) serves multiple purposes. It sets up the comic exchange between Emma and Knightley on how Emma can infallibly, and by simple inspection, discern whether a gentleman is living up to his rank.[xvi] Her absurdity and comic boastfulness, however, also include warm praise of Knightley's unaffected naturalness of bearing. He responds by saying, either to Emma herself or to himself or to the air or even to the reader, "'Nonsensical girl!'"—but the reply, the narrator assures us, was not at all in anger. He has learned long since to accept and even to bear with humor Emma's willful self-assertion, her aggressive determination to be herself (which means principally to be on top and in command on all occasions) as part of her interest and charm, along with the nonsensicalities and even mischief that it entails.

Emma's praise, however, is also part of the continued irony trained against her. For unbeknown to herself, Knightley has put his carriage in use in order to send it out again to pick up and deliver Miss Bates and Jane Fairfax, who have been invited along with "the less worthy females" to join the company after dinner. And it will also take them back. The ever-considerate Mrs. Weston has also thought of putting their family carriage to this service in view of Jane's delicate health and the cold weather, but Knightley has forestalled her. In any case, Knightley does not choose to treat them as "less worthy females" or less worthy anything else. Emma, we know, cordially dislikes both Miss Bates and Jane, though each of them for different reasons, and her class-bound appraisal of Knightley's appearance as being solely motivated by equally class-bound self-approval is at once shot down. Mrs. Weston has been cultivating her own "plans"—which consist of the scenario that Knightley is going to be smitten by Jane's beauty, elegance, and finished accomplishments, and that this will leave the way clear for a "match" between Emma and her stepson, Frank Churchill. She observes, knowing Knightley as they all do, that it is likely "'that it was for their accommodation the carriage was used at all. I do suspect he would not have had a pair of horses for himself, and that it was only an excuse for assisting them'" (p. 211).

Emma covers her slight surprise by praising Knightley's habitual "'unostentatious kindness'" and noting that when she was ribbing him about the carriage and the gentleman he "'said not a word that could betray'" (p. 211). Mrs. Weston then discloses to Emma her suspicion, which is also a wish that Knightley and Jane are going to get together. At which point, Emma explodes in alarm: "'Mr. Knightley must not marry! . . . I cannot at all consent to Mr. Knightley's marrying. . . . I have never had such an idea, and I cannot adopt it now.'" On top of that, there is her secondary, defensive fantasy about her little nephew, Henry, Isabella and John

Knightley's oldest son, inheriting the estate—"'I could not bear to have Henry supplanted'" (pp. 211–212). This wild idea, we will eventually learn, is part of Emma's self-mystification, and she will part with it without pain.

Two reasons are given for Knightley's "keeping no horses." One is that he has "a great deal of health, activity and independence" and is apt "to get about as he could." He prefers being on his feet and moving around freely.[xvii] He likes to mingle and also to go off spontaneously in unexpected directions. As the chief landowner and personage in the neighborhood, he chooses to be present and on the scene. He is direct, practical, prudent, and down to earth. The second reason is that he has "little spare money." This detail, one supposes, is there to suggest to us the uneven, uncertain, and rapidly fluctuating character of the state of both national and regional economies: Some are rising and some are falling. Knightley is trying with success to hold his own at Donwell. He even feels constrained to keep no horses, not even for his carriage, if Mrs. Weston, when she says, "'he would not have had a pair of horses for himself,'" agrees with Emma and means that he rented, borrowed, or otherwise procured two horses for the specific occasion. We know that the Crown Inn keeps "a couple of pair of post-horses" to be used "for the convenience of the neighbourhood." There may be horses to rent at the other, lesser inns of the village; there may even be a village stables, but we are not told. What we do know is that people do get around, even the super-sedentary Mr. Woodhouse. He owns a carriage and horses, and we even know the name of his trusty coachman. John Knightley also has a carriage for his family, into which he invites Elton on their way to dinner and Mr. Weston's good wine. The Westons have a carriage too. Mr. Weston also rides on horseback to London and back in one fatiguing day. Mr. Elton rides his horse to London to get Harriet's portrait framed, and after his marriage he also commands a "new" carriage. Mr. Perry performs his medical rounds with the help of a horse; and his unrealized plan of "setting up his carriage," conveyed as news in the letter secretly sent Frank, almost causes that worthy to blow the cover on his engagement to Jane (p. 327ff). Frank in his turn hires a chaise to get to London for a haircut and surreptitiously to buy a Broadwood for Jane; otherwise he travels back and forth between Richmond and Highbury or Donwell on horseback. Emma fancies seeing "Mr. Cole's carriage horses returning from exercise" as she stands idly in the doorway at Ford's— newly gained affluence requires a show. Only the women and Knightley and the anonymous Nobodies and the gypsies, who are called "trampers," go on foot; and even the gypsies have horses to pull their caravans. Or so it seems, until Miss Bates, "passing near the window" of one of her two rooms, "descried Mr. Knightley on horseback not far off" (p. 230). After that, Knightley appears either on horseback or without specification of his means of transportation. But when they all go to Box Hill for an outdoor party, the narrator inclusively notes "the gentlemen on horseback" (p. 349). Unless they were all leasing from Avis, there seems to be something to explain.

What is this apparent rigmarole all about? In the first place we can remark that those commentators who have criticized Jane Austen for omitting the details of daily, material, and historical life have not read her novels with sufficient care. Those works are, on the contrary, dense with such notations. The exceptional economy and steady flow of her prose make it very easy to overlook what she is actually doing. Knightley is the leading gentleman and chief agricultural man of business in this miniature society. Why make such a point of depriving him of his own horses and ready cash and then apparently contradict it? For when we finally get to Donwell Abbey, we find no signs of economic distress or strain.

> . . . its ample gardens stretching down to meadows washed by a stream, of which the Abbey, with all the old neglect of prospect, had scarcely a sight,—and its abun-

dance of timber in rows and avenues, which neither fashion nor extravagance had rooted up. The house was
larger than Hartfield, and totally unlike it, covering a good
deal of ground, rambling and irregular, with many comfortable and one or two handsome rooms. It was just what
it ought to be, and it looked what it was (pp. 340–341).

In this representation of a portion of the civilized world in
which appearance and reality seem as closely allied as they
are ever likely to be, Mrs. Elton characteristically introduces
contradictory impulses and discordant tendencies. Gotten
up "in all the apparatus of her happiness," she leads the way
in the ritual ceremony of gathering strawberries.

"The best fruit in England—every body's favourite—always wholesome. . . . Delightful to gather for one's self—
the only way of really enjoying them. Morning decidedly
the best time—never tired. . . . delicious fruit—only too
rich to be eaten much of—inferior to cherries—currants
more refreshing—only objection to gathering strawberries the stooping—glaring sun—tired to death—could
bear it no longer—must go and sit in the shade" (p. 341).

The rhythmic trajectory of ideas in this virtuoso passage
moves from inflated expectations of pleasure to disappointment, frustration, distress, and complaint. And what happens immediately thereafter is similar, or analogous, but in
reverse. Mrs. Elton has just received word of an available
"situation" for Jane. She is "in raptures."

Delightful, charming, superior, first circles, spheres, lines,
ranks, every thing: and Mrs. Elton was wild to have the
offer closed with immediately. On her side, all was
warmth, energy, and triumph (p. 342).

Mrs. Elton's ecstatic expressiveness might be right out of
*Songs of Experience*, as she exults in her power to exploit the

misery and pain of another human creature and finds her
happiness in this form of antagonistic cooperation.

The morning is hot and still, and the party scatters and
disperses itself out of the gardens and

> to the delicious shade of a broad short avenue of limes,
> which, stretching beyond the garden at an equal distance
> from the river, seemed the finish of the pleasure grounds.
> It led to nothing; nothing but a view at the end . . . which
> seemed intended . . . to give the appearance of an ap-
> proach to the house, which never had been there . . . it
> was in itself a charming walk, and the view which closed it
> extremely pretty. The considerable slope, at nearly the
> foot of which the Abbey stood, gradually acquired a
> steeper form beyond its grounds; and at half a mile dis-
> tant was a bank of considerable abruptness and grandeur,
> well clothed with wood; and at the bottom of this bank,
> favourably placed and sheltered, rose the Abbey-Mill
> Farm, with meadows in front, and the river making a
> close and handsome curve around it.
>
> It was a sweet view—sweet to the eye and the mind.
> English verdure, English culture, English comfort, seen
> under a sun bright, without being oppressive (pp. 342–343).

And the Abbey-Mill Farm itself is viewed, "with all its appendages of prosperity and beauty, its rich pastures, spreading flocks, orchard in blossom, and light column of smoke
ascending" (p. 343).

Throughout this scene, and through its shifting field of
view, we are solicited to perceive the harmonious elements
in a complex, irregular conceptual and material group of
structures—culture and comfort resonate and consort
equably together.[xviii] Donwell Abbey itself remains true to its
historical identity—its unmodern yet becoming siting, "low
and sheltered," its unplanned and rather haphazard development through time—its avenue of limes and pleasure
grounds leading to "nothing," and an "approach to the

house, which never had been there." Knightley is both a "preserver" and an "improver." The improvements are clearly focused on what has been done to improve the use of the land—including its appearance. The owner has taken advantage of recent advances in science and agricultural technology: with meadows going down to the water and rich pastures and the river coming around and through the estate, there has had to be considerable investment in ditching and drainage to control the degree of moisture in the soil and to maintain its level. Those "spreading flocks" whose wool commands top prices must come from one or another of the newly developed and much improved breeds that were being created at this time—breeds whose names, taken from the British locations where they were said to be first developed, still exist today. And the same holds true for the steady increase of seasonal yields in fruits and vegetables (although fruit trees are not in bloom when strawberries are ripe).

But all these traces and suggestions of how such diversities of interests and activities are integrated into the sustaining life of an actual, imagined community are by those very tokens connected as well to such dissonances as are typically embodied in Mrs. Elton's behavior and that have, in the first place, also prompted the narrator and Emma to "note" that Knightley keeps no horses and is strapped for cash. In a general cultural situation whose manifest properties are experienced, at different moments, as pulling one's judgment in divergent and contraposed directions, it is not a surprise to find that tendencies of change and resistances to change, of both expansion and dislocation, are registered as, in, and through conceptual lapses or inconsistencies in an otherwise exquisitely coherent text. Our female Homer may occasionally nod, but what she is in her advanced modern way undertaking to create is an imagined world in which there are several orders, grades, and categories of change, both for good and for ill, and several equally diverse and equivocal kinds of stability or permanence.

One further figuration of this submatrix of minor discrepancies and inconsistencies in *Emma* is salient to this line of analysis and explanation. Chapter VIII of the third volume begins immediately after the fiasco of Box Hill and Knightley's severe reproof of Emma for her rude and brutal behavior to Miss Bates. Emma is miserable, and she regards a "whole evening of backgammon with her father" as a pleasant relief from her abhorrent recollections of a "completely misspent" day. Her penitence has begun, and she quickly resolves to call on Miss Bates in a contrite, friendly, and "equal" spirit. Next morning she enters into a scene of confusion and disarray. Jane "looking extremely ill" is "escaping" along with her aunt into the next room. Miss Bates reenters and, struggling both to keep back her tears and maintain her "happy" face to the world, explains that Jane, who has been writing letters and crying all morning, has decided to accept at once the offered employment as governess—she has been putting off such a resolution for some time.

> "One cannot wonder. . . . It is a great change; and though she is amazingly fortunate— . . . do not think us ungrateful, Miss Woodhouse, for such surprising good fortune . . . but, poor dear soul; if you were to see what a headache she has. When one is in great pain, you know one cannot feel any blessing quite as it may deserve. She is as low as possible. To look at her, nobody would think how delightful and happy she is to have secured such a situation" (p. 361).

Miss Bates seems unconsciously to be trying to literalize the traditional Christian notion of the grace of affliction—and is having a hard time of it. It was all decided at the Eltons', to which the Bateses were conveyed after leaving Box Hill. Mrs. Elton has naturally been the activating agent of the offer and has been pressing Jane to accept the situation at Mrs. Smallridge's—"'only four miles from Maple Grove'" to have "'the charge of her three little girls.'" Mrs. Elton

"'would not take a denial . . . would not let Jane say 'No.'"
She had been harrying Jane about it for several days, as "in-defatigable" good friends do. Unknown to Mrs. Elton, Miss Bates, or Emma, Jane has had enough of Frank's offensive and intolerable teasing, flirtatiousness, and semi-hysterical carrying-on and has decided that self-immolation is prefer-able to patient, protracted torture. While the Bateses were at the Eltons' something else occurred.

> "Mr. Elton was called out of the room before tea, old John Abdy's son wanted to speak with him. Poor old John, I have a great regard for him; he was clerk to my poor father twenty-seven years; and now, poor old man, he is bed-ridden, and very poorly with the rheumatic gout in his joints—I must go and see him to-day; and so will Jane, I am sure, if she gets out at all. And poor John's son came to talk to Mr. Elton about relief from the parish: he is very well to do himself, you know, being head man at the Crown, ostler, and every thing of that sort, but still he cannot keep his father without some help . . ." (p. 365).

In the course of this reported interview or petition, the younger Abdy informs Elton that Frank Churchill has been summoned back to Richmond (to be with his ailing aunt) with some urgency and that he has left promptly.

Emma has been only half-listening to this latter part of Miss Bates' monologue:

> There was nothing in all this either to astonish or inter-est, and it caught Emma's attention only as it united with the subject which already engaged her mind. The con-trast between Mrs. Churchill's importance in the world, and Jane Fairfax's struck her; one was every thing; the other nothing—and she sat musing on the difference of woman's destiny (p. 366).

The chapter concludes after two further paragraphs. It is a marvel of compactness, and everyone in it seems to be talking past everyone else. Miss Bates readily accepts Emma's contrition and goodwill as if it were another confirming blow dealt to her by fate itself. Emma herself, in her subdued mood, listens at first with sympathy, then with diminishing attention, and finally "quite unconscious on what her eyes were fixed" (p. 366). Mrs. Churchill, tyrannical, arbitrary, capricious, was before she married "'nobody . . . barely the daughter of a gentleman; but ever since her being turned into a Churchill, she has out-Churchill'd them all in high and mighty claims: but in herself, I assure you, she is an upstart'" (p. 292). Sufficient wealth will inevitably transform a Nobody into "everything," while the Jane Fairfaxes, whom we all know, will remain to be reminded that nothing will come of "nothing."

Yet if Jane Fairfax is nothing, then what is old John Abdy, or even his son? Old John was parish clerk, employed under Mr. Bates for more than a quarter of a century. He has been turned out in his old age and is now infirm and helpless. Miss Bates will visit him, but in her depleted state she surely has little except good wishes to give. His son is ostler at the Crown, itself slightly run-down, on a relatively unfrequented road, keeping only "a couple of pair of post-horses." If Miss Bates has it right, "'he is also head man . . . and everything of that sort,'" which implies that he is a man of all work, which is what one might expect at an "inconsiderable house." Yet Miss Bates runs on in her hyperbolic and virtually pathological cheerfulness to assert that "'he is very well to do himself.'" So well to do that he has come to request relief from the parish because he cannot support his aged father on what he earns.[xix] If Jane Fairfax is nothing, then what is he, let alone his aged father? It puts one in mind of the notorious question featured in the arithmetic of political economy: What is a man worth? Is he worth more or less than nothing?

Emma recurs to her critical reflections shortly thereafter,

when she has learned, to her utter surprise, about the secret engagement of Frank and Jane. She hears the news, to be sure, from the generous-hearted Mrs. Weston, who is always willing to take the extra step and make allowances and exceptions. She continues to affirm Jane's

> "steadiness of character and good judgment . . . in spite of this one great deviation from the strict rule of right. And how much may be said in her situation for even that error!"
>
> "Much indeed!" cried Emma feelingly. "If a woman can ever be excused for thinking only of herself, it is in a situation like Jane Fairfax's.—Of such, one may almost say, that 'the world is not theirs, nor the world's law'" (p. 382).

Jane Austen among all our novelists is unsurpassed in pursuing arguments to logically consequent ends. It is part of her genius that such pressure often leads to comically absurd conclusions. But this is not such an instance. For we as readers are prompted by thematic continuities and densities, by proximity of occurrence within an unfolding narrative, and by analogical reasoning—all of these being cognitive habits by whose means Jane Austen herself has been tutoring us to read and reflect closely and coherently. Can such a claim as Emma is asserting here be extended to old John Abdy and his son? The answer is self-evident. And if a counterclaim of defense is raised that there are categorical distinctions to be maintained between the personal and the social and political, we must recall that it is just such conventional and convenient distinctions that Jane Austen often takes pleasure in overriding, that she persistently observes both the connections and disjunctions between the personal and the political or cultural, and that in precisely such asymmetrical and unpredictable appositions does she find the moral energies that justify the claims of both.[xx]

Still, if the determinations, judgments, and measurements of value put forward by political arithmetic remain outside the cultural and historical spectrum of terms available to Jane Austen—that is to say, outside the conceptual categories that she found enabling to her decisive narrative imagination—she is certainly not very far removed from bringing them into saliency and bearing. In any case, and to return to the earlier scene, the narrator and Emma are off somewhere musing about the contrasts in "woman's destiny." Miss Bates brings Emma back to focused awareness by observing that she is staring at Jane's beloved pianoforte.

> "Ay, I see what you are thinking of, the piano-forte. What is to become of that? Very true. Poor dear Jane was talking of it just now. 'You must go,' said she. 'You and I must part. You will have no business here. Let it stay, however,' said she" (p. 366).

Emma talks to herself; Jane talks to her pianoforte. It comes as no alarming surprise that Jane Austen was closely percipient of—or at least attuned to—the characteristic phases of the growth of mind in the early nineteenth century. On the one hand, an expansion and deepening of self-consciousness through interior reflection and silent speech; on the other, an expansion and deepening of the self in its life of feeling through the expressive agencies of music and art.[xxi] On the whole, both of these amount to a growing apprehension that in order to make actual the grand priority of self-realization and development, individual persons, the outward and material manifestations of those spiritual selves, would have to contend forcefully against the impersonal might of circumstances.

Emma is deeply implicated in these antagonistic tendencies of impulse and attitude. Although, like her father, she is averse to change in both her personal life and in society at large, she is also vexed and distressed by the built-in inertia and confinements of the world that she at the same time dominates. After the disastrous outcome of her flight-to-the-moon scenario involving Elton and Harriet, Emma turns, for the first time in the narrative, to confront herself adversarially. Her own embarrassment and repugnance at Elton's heated, tipsy advances are compounded in her compelled admission that she had been "grossly mistaken and misjudging in all her ideas on one subject" (p. 132). These sobering assessments are not as acute, however, as the shame she feels at having actively misled Harriet and caused her grief. She promises herself to be in the future "humble and discreet" and confirms her resolve to "[repress] imagination all the rest of her life." The unlikelihood of her adhering to that vow is underscored by how rapidly she bypasses any reflection on serious wrongdoing or on the damage possibly inflicted on Harriet, who, Emma breezily estimates, will recover her "composure" by the time Elton returns from Bath. As for Elton himself, she has no compassion to spare, except in one sense: "Their being fixed, so absolutely fixed, in the same place, was bad for each, for all three. Not one of them had the power of removal, or of effecting any material change of society. They must encounter each other, and make the best of it" (p. 134). Although the principal meaning of this passage is evident enough—a country village has its disadvantages with which one must put up—its generalizing extension is equally plain. The pleasant familiarity of such a world has as its concomitant, in addition to its own permanence, the absolute fixity of those who are consigned or sentenced to live in it. They lack the resources to move away—let alone light out for the Territory—in the literal sense of relocation. Moreover, there is no possibility of their behavior effecting "any material change of society." In this last phrase one detects impaction of meaning and a soliciting of interpretation. Such a world is not merely stable; it may also be apparently static, frozen, paralyzed—at least when it is regarded from a particular point of view.[xxii]

It is notable that Jane Austen, in common with the other great novelists of the nineteenth century, resists ascribing certainty and inevitability to the narrativized social and historical world of her novels. That world, despite its textual inhabitation of the unalterable past tense, is also comparatively open and unpredictable—the future before it is uncertain, occluded, and contingent. The characters in it make choices that are "real" in the sense that they are neither predetermined, inescapable, nor uniformly irrevocable. The obverse can also be true. Hence no sooner does Emma begin, quite validly, to complain about absolute fixity than the narrator also begins to undermine not merely the "absolutely" but the "fixed" as well. The great novelists had the capacity of representing contemporary life as being simultaneously comparatively stable and yet charged with the tension and threat of the eruption of immanent antagonistic forces. These unresolved antagonisms find partial expression in the less-than-coherent utterances, attitudes, and assertions of principle, along with their contraventions, that the characters in *Emma*—most notably Emma herself—meaningfully but unconsciously dramatize.

Once Emma has made this admission of being limited and "fixed" to herself, she is prepared to try out the attitude it leads to. Mrs. Weston informs her that Frank Churchill has had to postpone his maiden trip to Highbury. Emma in turn announces this news to Knightley, and "proceed[s] to say a good deal more than she [feels] of the advantage of such an addition to their confined society in Surrey" (p. 135). Her attitude toward change is so compromised that two pages after her lamentation about their being absolutely fixed she has to pump herself up to express pleasure at the idea of a newcomer to their world. Yet even Mr. Woodhouse, who embodies the principle of stasis and immobility, is able, when the Bateses are being discussed, of expressing himself to the effect that "'It is a great pity that their circumstances should be so confined'" (p. 162). And Mrs. Weston comments on Jane's accepting of the Eltons' invitation along the same line:

"We cannot suppose that she has any great enjoyment at the Vicarage, my dear Emma—but it is better than being always at home. Her aunt is a good creature; but, as a constant companion, must be very tiresome. We must consider what Miss Fairfax quits, before we condemn her taste for what she goes to" (p. 268).

And when Emma at Donwell Abbey suddenly runs into Jane, she observes "a look of escape" in her expression (p. 345). Jane is indeed narratively conceived of as one of the candidates for absolute fixity, and her situation is compared not merely to that of a nun or a slave but to that of a prisoner as well.

Frank Churchill, whose path through life is marked by a progression toward increasing amplitude and latitude of choice, complains steadily about narrowness, tedium, and restriction. As for life at Enscombe, the considerable estate in Yorkshire, he tells Emma that "there was very little going on." Mrs. Churchill's alleged ill health and her general social indisposition result in their making "a point of visiting no fresh person." Frank has wanted very much to travel, "to go abroad." But Mrs. Churchill "would not hear of it."[xxiii] She keeps him on a short leash, largely, we are led to conclude, for her own convenience. But Frank's youthfulness is also expressed in impatience and impulsiveness. "'Ah! that ball!— why did we wait for any thing?—why not seize the pleasure at once?—How often is happiness destroyed by preparation, foolish preparation!'" (p. 244). When he drives off to London for a haircut, Emma primly comments to herself: "Vanity, extravagance, love of change, restlessness of temper, which must be doing something, good or bad" (p. 193). At Donwell Abbey, where Frank joins the group late, hot, and in ill humor, matters begin rapidly to come to a head. Frank again expresses his restless need to go abroad: "'I ought to travel. I am tired of doing nothing. I want a change. . . . I am sick of England—and would leave it to-morrow, if I could'" (p. 348). This passage comes almost immediately after

Emma's (or the narrator's) reflections on "English culture, English comfort," and the juxtaposition itself renders the critical point.

But Emma herself can also feel the genuine need for something new. When the Westons know that Frank is finally coming to visit, Emma sincerely "rejoice[d] in their joy. It was a most delightful re-animation of exhausted spirits. The worn-out past was sunk in the freshness of what was coming" (p. 178). And Emma's vivacity and energy require forms of expression. One such means is dancing—she loves to feel "the felicities of rapid motion" (p. 232). She may be confined, but she is not sedentary. As spring ripens into summer, the "state of schemes, and hopes, and connivance" continue to move at Hartfield—that is to say they continue to germinate and bubble in Emma's head. As to "Highbury, in general, it brought no material change" (p. 326). Emma's aversion to innovation has not deterred her from introducing a "large modern circular table . . . which none but Emma could have had power to place there and persuade her father to use, instead of the small sized Pembroke, on which two of his daily meals had, for forty years, been crowded" (p. 330). In the cause of middle-class comfort Emma has brought in a table at which there is no "natural" head. Comfort has trumped inconvenience, even though rank has been bypassed.[xxiv] Nevertheless, such narrative details serve to point toward the subtextual conflict and ambivalence in which for most of the novel Emma is suspended.

One partial representation of this state of mind occurs when Emma accompanies Harriet to Ford's, the village's combined drapery shop and haberdashery. While Harriet is "hanging over muslins" and being indecisive

> Emma went to the door for amusement. Much could not be hoped from the traffic of even the busiest part of Highbury;—Mr. Perry walking hastily by; Mr. William Cox letting himself in at the office door; Mr. Cole's carriage-horses returning from exercise; or a stray letter-boy on an obsti-

nate mule, were the liveliest objects she could presume to expect; and when her eyes fell only on the butcher with his tray, a tidy old woman travelling homewards from shop with her full basket, two curs quarrelling over a dirty bone, and a string of dawdling children round the baker's little bow-window eyeing the gingerbread, she knew she had no reason to complain, and was amused enough; quite enough still to stand at the door. A mind lively and at ease can do with seeing nothing, and can see nothing that does not answer (pp. 219–220).

It is one of Jane Austen's incomparable passages. In it Emma is represented in close alignment with her creator—both of them being simultaneously at this juncture "imaginists." Emma is only occasionally bored; the workings of her own mind are frequently a source of amusement to her. The world of Highbury is pretty "fixed" when it comes to action or novelty. The "liveliest objects" Emma can imagine are fragments of ordinary movement; even these are more endowed with vitality than what she does actually see. She imagines an ordinary social scene, and then she perceives another one. The narrator is imagining Emma doing both—and both (along with the counterpart activity of the narrator herself) are represented on the level of the narrative as epistemologically equivalent. On this plane of metafictional discourse there is neither difference nor distinction between perception and imagination. The narrator, to be sure, is creatively in charge of both processes. Emma, who can complain about being "absolutely fixed," is both amused and content with what she has imagined and what she perceives. She herself, "still to stand," becomes for the moment fixed as well. Yet her mind is "lively," active, self-sustaining, at ease with itself. It sees nothing but makes something out of it—"seeing nothing" itself becomes the source of mental activity and pleasure. And nothing, including everything in the perceived world, answers—answers back, responds. At this moment, Emma, like her creator, is at home in the world. Their

minds and the perceived/imagined universe are represented as naturally yet miraculously fitting together.

But the forces of change are as relentless in their urgings
as the countervailing impulses that gravitate toward stability
and solidity. And this complication bears upon Emma's personal destiny as well as on the social world represented in
*Emma* with such deftness and economy. How is Jane Austen
going to get Emma to move off the dime on which she pirou-
ettes while going nowhere?

### III

Emma is averse to change; she vows never to marry; she cannot envision leaving her father and their home; she is obsessed with reveries of matchmaking, and projects imaginary
romantic engagements and marital entanglements, for others, among the people she knows and doesn't know (Mr.
Dixon, for example). She largely ignores, avoids, and bypasses questions of sex; she explicitly rejects the idea of her
having babies, and her idea of her own future is vaguely
specified.

At the same time she wants to be "first" in the eyes of an
admiring world, particularly of the men in it. Yet she blinds
herself to Elton's patent sexual designs on her until it is too
late for her to recover anything. She embarks upon a semi-
serious flirtation with Frank Churchill and sustains it far beyond the point where it yields her pleasure, and almost,
indeed, to the very end. Her management of this flirtation is
such that she keeps Frank always at arms' length. Moreover,
when Frank is on the verge of confessing to her about his
engagement to Jane (believing that Emma, with her famous
powers of penetration, has seen through their pretense)
she prepares herself to withstand a proposal to herself
(pp. 275ff). How she behaves in the Frank-Jane-Emma triangle is the unbecoming inversion of her even more unseemly
procedures in the Elton-Emma-Harriet confusion.

At the Coles' dinner-party, when Mrs. Weston reveals to

Emma her "discovery" that Knightley is very attracted to Jane, Emma goes into a protracted flap of consternation (I have cited part of this aria-like flurry earlier):

> "How could you think of such a thing? . . . Mr. Knightley must not marry!—You would not have little Henry cut out from Donwell? . . . I cannot at all consent to Mr. Knightley's marrying. . . . Mr. Knightley marry! No, I have never had such an idea, and I cannot adopt it now . . . every feeling revolts. For his own sake, I would not have him do so mad a thing. . . .
>
> But Mr. Knightley does not want to marry. I am sure he has not the least idea of it. Do not put it into his head. Why should he marry? He is as happy as possible by himself. . . . He has no occasion to marry, either to fill up his time or his heart" (pp. 211–212).

A better defense by denial might be difficult to locate. And shortly thereafter when Frank and Jane make music together, when Emma hears "the sweet sounds of the united voices," Emma can only think of babies, of "a most mortifying change" in which little Henry would be ejected as "the heir of Donwell" (p. 215). Frank and Jane are expressing themselves erotically before her, but Emma, deaf and blind to what is obvious, displaces her response onto the unacceptable, abhorrent fantasy of Knightley and Jane producing at least one male baby while she continues to repudiate, as far as she herself is concerned, any personal connection with such affairs.

In fact, Emma seems at least on one occasion not to be on the easiest terms with her body. When the heated discussion about where to hold a ball gets underway, Mr. Woodhouse has a panic about drafts, and Emma is concerned with adequate space in which to dance. "'It would be dreadful to be standing so close. Nothing can be farther from pleasure than to be dancing in a crowd—and a crowd in a little room'" (p. 235). Emma loves to dance, and Mrs. Weston, "capital in her country-dances," is seated, and a waltz is beginning. Frank Churchill takes Emma's hand "and [leads] her up to the top" (p. 216); the dance itself, however, seems less a combination of the two styles than a British domestication of the still notorious waltz. It is in any case not to be confused with the sexual arousal and turmoil reportedly induced by the waltz and represented as such by Goethe, in *The Sorrows of Young Werther* (1774), by Byron in *The Waltz: An Apostrophic Hymn* (1813), and in the testimony of numberless others.

Similarly Emma's response to Harriet is also in part deflected. She is at first attracted to Harriet "on account of her beauty." Harriet's lovely good looks "happened to be of a sort which Emma particularly admired. She was short, plump, and fair, with a fine bloom, blue eyes, light hair, regular features, and a look of great sweetness." And Emma spends the evening "admiring those soft blue eyes" (p. 21). In recent years a number of feminist and gay commentators have taken such remarks (along with others) to suggest a lesbian interest on the part of Emma and Jane Austen. Whatever the merit of this contention (and I believe that there is quite a bit of merit to it), it seems to me that Emma's warm response to Harriet is also an expression of her suspended state of affective development and of her narcissism.[xxv] In being physically attracted to Harriet, she is in effect also admiring and arousing herself. For Harriet throughout the novel functions as Emma's sexual stand-in. Her imaginings juxtapose Harriet sexually with the available but, for her, socially ineligible men in the novel—Elton, Frank, Knightley—while Harriet's one real opportunity, Robert Martin, is fiercely embargoed by Emma herself.

When Frank has to leave Highbury to attend to the caprices of his sick aunt, Emma reflects that Frank has "*almost* told her that he loved her" and that this persuasion, plus everything else,

> made her think that she *must* be a little in love with him, in spite of every previous determination against it.

"I certainly must," said she. "This sensation of listlessness, weariness, stupidity, this disinclination to sit
down and employ myself, this feeling of every thing being
dull and insipid about the house!—I must be in love"
(pp. 246–247).

Knightley's remark early on that Emma has never been in
love was closer to home than even he might have reckoned.
Emma feels let down after two exciting weeks, and she is also
for the moment bored and at loose ends. That she mistakes
boredom and momentary tedium for being in love suggests
to us where she is. Her imagination of being in love at this
moment intimates some negative inner state, some condition that compounds loss, frustration, and disappointment.
It does not propose the ardent desire and yearning for the
object, for the presence of another, that we ordinarily associate with romantic love. That desire and longing Emma
tends to regard as "mania," which is how she describes
Harriet's infatuation with Elton (p. 318).

When Frank rescues Harriet from the gypsies, Emma
happily succumbs to her fantasy-work again. She feels "on
fire with speculation and foresight!—especially with such a
ground-work of anticipation as her mind had already made."
In her heightened state, she thinks of what she is doing as
analogous to the activities of "a linguist . . . a grammarian . . .
even a mathematician" (p. 318). These occupations have in
common a concern with language, with codes and encryptions, with the interpretation of symbols, and with formulae
that conjure up other worlds. She thinks of herself as "an
imaginist," and this arresting coinage suggests her shadow or
secondary identity as a crypto- or pseudo-novelist, a proto-
novelist, or novelist *manqué*. But she is also a constructivist
and fantasticator—she simply makes things up, but considers such fabrications on her part as clever and penetrating
interpretations.[xxvi] When it comes to matters of romance and
adventure, her readings, despite her cleverness, are almost
always wrong. Some unacknowledged source in her, some

embedded contrariety of wishes, feelings, desires, and ideas, distorts her perceptions and judgments, the faculties of intelligence on which she sets particularly high store. This unresolved or unintegrated mental state impels her to perceive falsely what isn't there (invention in this context is a failure of imagination) and to further deny or misperceive what is staring her in the face. The upshot is that she repeatedly substitutes unmoored fantasy for imaginative inference or genuine interpretation.

Emma had determined quite early that she was not in love with Frank Churchill. After he departs from Highbury, "she could not admit herself to be unhappy." And although she continues to daydream about herself and Frank,

> the conclusion of every imaginary declaration on his side was that she *refused him* . . . "I do not find myself making any use of the word *sacrifice*. . . . In not one of all my clever replies, my delicate negatives, is there any allusion to making a sacrifice. I do suspect that he is not really necessary to my happiness. So much the better. I certainly will not persuade myself to feel more than I do" (p. 248).

Admirable to a fault. And yet she continues to flirt with Frank long after she has come to this conclusion. She does so partly out of tedium—or the lack of anything more purposeful for her to do—partly out of mischievous high spirits, and partly, I suspect, out of her rivalrous dislike for Jane Fairfax. She continues to do so right up to the breaking point, which occurs at Box Hill.

The excursion begins and ends badly. Out of doors, the party disperses and never gets back together in either physical or social senses. There is no concord but only separateness and estrangement among the members of the outing. Even Frank is "silent . . . stupid . . . and dull," at least in Emma's eyes. Eventually he becomes talkative by turning to Emma and flirting with her intensely, openly, "and excessively." Although to Emma this now "meant nothing," she nonetheless responds in kind. At the same time, she is aware of a counter-tendency in herself. "Not that Emma was gay and thoughtless from any real felicity; it was rather because she felt less happy than she had expected. She laughed because she was disappointed" (p. 350). They exchange sallies of wit, and Emma comments that Frank is currently in "command" of his temper, although he had not been the day before at Donwell Abbey, where his behavior had "'broken bounds.'" He then turns to the sulky and silent gathering, and "with lively impudence" tries to get them talking; he announces that Emma, as the presiding presence, "'desires to know what you are all thinking of.'" Among the mixed replies is Knightley's query whether Emma is really sure that she wants to know this. Emma at once answers, laughingly, of course not: "'It is the very last thing I would stand the brunt of just now. Let me hear any thing rather than what you are all thinking of'" (p. 352).

Mrs. Elton is incoherently affronted, as are some others, so Frank changes his tack and proclaims that Emma wants instead to hear from each of them one "very clever" thing, or two "things moderately clever," or "'three things very dull indeed.'" Miss Bates, with her eternal humility and good humor, observes that this is just right for her, for as soon as she opens her mouth three dull things will surely pop out. "Emma could not resist. 'Ah! ma'am, but there may be a difficulty. Pardon me—but you will be limited as to number,—only three at once'" (p. 353). Miss Bates does not at first get it, but she does a double take, and is clearly hurt, and says to Knightley that she must really "'make myself very disagreeable, or she would not have said such a thing to an old friend'" (p. 353). Emma has been teasing Frank about losing his "self-command," but it is she who cannot control herself and lets herself go in order to turn a cruel piece of wit, in order not to pass up a one-liner.[xxvii] It was Emma who said that she did not want to hear what people were thinking, but it is she who gives uncensored expression to her private and hypercritical opinion of Miss Bates. Instead of talking to her-

self as she customarily does, Emma has turned off that inner
interlocutor, and out has come frigid wit and withering resentment and aggression. Catastrophe.

The party continues to fall apart. Mr. Weston makes a
well-meaning ass of himself, Mrs. Elton carries on as usual,
and Frank goes on in his deplorable way. (At this point, Jane
silently decides to pack it in and go for martyrdom as a governess.) The party breaks up as raggedly as it began. As
Emma is waiting for her carriage, Knightley comes up to her
and, seeing that they are alone, lets her have it. "'How could
you be so unfeeling to Miss Bates? How could you be so insolent in your wit to a woman of her character, age, and situation? Emma, I had not thought it possible'" (p. 357).
Emma at first tries to "laugh it off," but Knightley pursues
her relentlessly and advances a full bill of particulars about
Miss Bates and Emma that is both irresistible and crushing.
For Miss Bates does represent a principle; in Emma's mistreatment of her, the personal and the moral, the social and
the cultural-political, are fused. Emma is for once utterly silenced.

She feels virtually undone. She weeps uncontrollably almost all the way home. She is "agitated, mortified, grieved"
as never before. For the first time she really feels guilt about
something she has done. She cannot shrug it off, nor will she
feel better about it later on. "The truth of his [Knightley's]
representation there was no denying. She felt it at her heart.
How could she have been so brutal, so cruel to Miss Bates!"
(p. 358). What Knightley has said is *true.* How does she *know*
that it is true? How do we? Because she *feels* it "at her heart."
It is a feeling cognition, a knowledge made possible and rat-
ified by the emotions that accompany and are inseparable
from it. It bears witness to its own truth by the depth of feeling to which it penetrates, which it disturbs and stirs. It is an
axiom in philosophy being proved upon the pulses. Here
Jane Austen joins the company of the great romantics, of
Wordsworth, Coleridge, and Keats.

From this moment onward the language that Emma uses

about herself changes—the leading or operating words now become warmth, heart, feeling, open, contrition, and a cluster of related idioms. Knightley's reprimand has been so sharp and fundamental, so drastically true, that Emma feels imperiled. It is almost as if he had threatened to expel Emma from her privileged place in his life and affections. Emma's inner evolution and the movement of the narrative, the structural falling into place of narrative detail, now rapidly accelerate. It immediately follows that Mrs. Churchill expires and that the engagement of Frank and Jane is almost simultaneously revealed. Emma has been entirely taken in, and at first she feels general outrage. Mrs. Weston, who breaks the news to her, sympathetically reminds Emma that the two lovers must both have suffered greatly "'under such a system of secresy and concealment.'" Emma is not quite forthcoming in her well-wishes, especially when she thinks of her inventions about Mr. Dixon, and she improves upon Mrs. Weston's account by declaring the whole complication or imbroglio

> "a very abominable sort of proceeding. What has it been but a system of hypocrisy and deceit,—espionage, and treachery?—To come among us with professions of openness and simplicity; and such a league in secret to judge us all!—Here have we been . . . completely duped, fancying ourselves on an equal footing of truth and honour, with two people in the midst of us. . . ." (p. 381).

Emma, as they say, goes over the top. The language that she finds to describe Frank and Jane's secret engagement would be more appropriate if it were applied to the Gunpowder Plot or the French Revolution. She is of course blowing off steam, but the words that first occur to her describe a capital crime, as if England itself were being betrayed. But the speech is also theatrical, and Emma's hyperbolic ranting is slightly farcical. It was bad behavior, to be sure, but it was neither fatal nor unforgivable—in *Emma* only illness is fatal.

Emma turns this same language on herself. When she reflects on her friendly offer to take the ailing Jane for a
carriage-ride and on her sending arrowroot to comfort
her—both of which amicable gestures were turned down—it
now appears to her that "an airing in the Hartfield carriage
would have been the rack, and arrow-root from the Hartfield
store-room must have been poison" (p. 384). We are now
dealing with a tragedy-queen, and Emma's observations on
her own role in this drama is accordingly elevated.

> Of all the sources of evil surrounding [Jane] . . . she was
> persuaded that she must herself have been the worst. She
> must have been a perpetual enemy. They never could
> have been all three together, without her having stabbed
> Jane Fairfax's peace in a thousand instances (p. 401).

When Jane Austen was fifteen she wrote a short, satirical
history of England. She regarded Queen Elizabeth with de-
testation and called her "that disgrace to humanity, that pest
of society." Her persecution, confinement, and execution of
Mary Queen of Scots who was guilty of nothing more "than
Imprudencies into which she was betrayed by the openness
of her Heart, her Youth, and her Education," is a shadowed
anticipation of Emma's description of how she has abused
poor Jane.[xxviii]

Emma still has miles to go before she can catch up with
herself. She thinks immediately of "'poor Harriet,'" who has
been the continued object of yet another of Emma's fantasticated manipulations. She thinks of Harriet and is angry
with Frank. "Frank Churchill had behaved very ill by herself
[that is, Emma]—very ill in many ways,—but it was not so
much *his* behaviour as her *own*, which made her so angry
with him" (p. 383). This is a neat instance of double-entry
moral bookkeeping. Emma then turns to confess her culpa-
bility to Harriet, who has already learned the news from Mr.
Weston. Harriet believes that Emma "'can see into every-

body's heart,'" but Emma is rapidly learning that she has seen into no one's heart, least of all her own.

She has got it all wrong again. She has misconstrued Harriet's sweetness as docile compliance with Emma's pipe dream about a match with Frank, and has overlooked altogether Harriet's infatuation with Knightley, an affection that, Harriet believes, Knightley returns. Emma directs her attention inward for a few minutes. This interval was

> sufficient for making her acquainted with her own heart. A mind like hers, once opening to suspicion, made rapid progress: she touched . . . she acknowledged the whole truth. Why was it so much worse that Harriet should be in love with Mr. Knightley, than with Frank Churchill? . . . It darted through her with the speed of an arrow, that Mr. Knightley must marry no one but herself! (p. 389).

Once again, her heart and her capacities of drawing consequent and rational conclusions are put into dynamic correlation. The penetrating Emma is, in her turn, penetrated by the arrow of the god of love. And although the arrow flies straight and true, Emma's recognition of its meaning is obliquely formulated. And once more it appears to her in the form of a negation—as a prohibition, injunction, or interdiction. Emma acknowledges her love for Knightley by, so to speak, backing into it. This admission is followed by another: How unconscionably she has treated Harriet. "How inconsiderate, how indelicate, how irrational, how unfeeling, had been her conduct!" (p. 389). At Box Hill Knightley had reproved her conduct to Miss Bates for its lack of feeling—its hardness and disregard. Now Emma remorsefully does it herself: It isn't so much that her feelings are inappropriate or misdirected; it is that they aren't quite there. Emma has already recognized earlier that she is neither tenderhearted nor easily susceptible to the warmer and blinder affections; now she has to realize that there has been an actual absence in her—that she has been unfeeling, armored, indifferent, even more than slightly anesthetized in her responses to life as it appears in the form of other people, and even as it is manifested in herself. Her defenses against emotion, particularly the emotions of sexuality, have been so prepotent that they have warped her intelligence and deformed her perceptions as to what she and other people think and feel.

Emma has a great deal to learn and as much to overcome. Flooded by a "confusion of sudden and perplexing emotions," by all the "perturbation" brought about by "such a development of self" (p. 390), she must begin to face up to the circumstances of how little she understands about herself, how she has deceived, deluded, duped, and imposed upon herself, and how "totally ignorant of her own heart" and utterly bereft of "knowledge of herself" she has been (p. 393). Her "insufferable vanity" has encouraged her to believe "herself in the secret of everybody's feelings" and to act with a high hand on such unfounded beliefs. "She was proved to have been universally mistaken" (p. 394). How could she have been anything else when she had such impaired and impoverished communications with her own deeper feelings. Her prolonged flirtation with Frank had been at once an introduction to romantic urgings and sexual impulses, and a contrivance or tactic to keep her feelings about Knightley at a secure distance. She has isolated her intimations of sexual attraction from her deeper affections and love. She has in doing so also disengaged her feelings about both men from each other and has carefully avoided instituting any "comparison" between them in her own affections. In this splitting away of one group of elemental affections from another equally powerful and primitive range of needs and desires, she has adapted herself to a familiar and disabling structural economy of the psyche. She has done so at the cost of inner integration and intelligence and by forfeiting, at least temporarily, her own further evolution. In her long-term resistance to change, it is she who has become fixed.

In this abrupt disclosure of herself to self-examination, it is instructive to observe that Emma never asks herself why she has behaved in this way, why she has done all these strange and even perverse things, what remote causes have impelled her to contrive such strategies. It is sufficient for now, for the time being, that she has perceived this much: "Till now that she was threatened with its loss Emma had never known how much of her happiness depended on being *first* with Mr. Knightley, first in interest and affection" (p. 395). Repeatedly and again she comes to a larger perception of what she feels by means of negative or contravening ideas and possibilities. It is the prospect of loss, "the dread of being supplanted," that drives her to realize how dependent she is on Knightley's attention and love. Nevertheless, she is still ready to settle happily for the "compromise" that Knightley remain "single all his life. Could she be secure of . . . his never marrying at all, she believed she should be perfectly satisfied. Let him but continue the same Mr. Knightley. . . . Marriage, in fact, would not do for her. It would be incompatible with what she owed to her father, and with what she felt for him. Nothing should separate her from her father" (p. 396). But she also begins to sense that all this inner palaver is slightly delusionary, as she talks with Mrs. Weston about Frank and Jane and their future together elsewhere, as she thinks about the baby that Mrs. Weston is to give birth to, and how this new rival will also entail a loss on Emma's part, and how the most unbearable deprivation of all would be Knightley's marriage to Harriet. And although she is devastatingly candid about her failings, Emma remains throughout incurably friendly to herself: As she remarks about her mistreatment of Jane, "'this is all to be forgotten.'" She forgives the trespasses of others generously and leads the way in forgiving herself. (And as she later remarks to Jane, "'let us forgive each other at once'" (p. 439). Her basic trust in her own goodness prompts her to conclude, not without warrant, that when she looks inside herself she is not likely to find anything that is very bad.

She is in need of all her self-propelling goodwill in the episode that follows. It is the great comic scene of misperception, crisis, revelation, reversal, self-confrontation, proposal, and reconciliation between Emma and Knightley. He suspects that Emma is heartbroken over the news about Frank and Jane. ("'Abominable scoundrel. . . . a disgrace to the name of man'" are his memorable eruptions of rivalry [p. 405]). Emma disabuses him and unflinchingly confesses to her vanity in pointlessly extending the flirtation and her folly in becoming so easily Frank's dupe and his blind (p. 406). They commune over the undeserved good luck of Frank, "the favourite of fortune"; he is able, reflects Knightley, to fulfill every man's wish, "'to give a woman a better home than the one he takes her from'" (p. 408). He speaks of how in one respect he envies Frank, and Emma fears that he is on the point of bringing up Harriet. She thinks of changing the subject, but Knightley forges ahead and says that he must speak even though he may regret it at once. Emma, following her own fever chart of pain and pleasure, eagerly responds: "'Oh, then, don't speak it. . . . Take a little time, consider, do not commit yourself'" (p. 408) Knightley thanks her hollowly and, mortified, lapses into the deep, unbroken silence of rejection. At this moment, the comedy of errors comes to an end.

> Emma could not bear to give him pain. He was wishing to confide in her—perhaps to consult her;—cost her what it would, she would listen. She might assist his resolution, or reconcile him to it; she might give just praise to Harriet, or, by representing to him his own independence, relieve him from that state of indecision, which must be more intolerable than any alternative to such a mind as his. . . .
>
> "I stopped you ungraciously, just now . . . and, I am afraid, gave you pain. But if you have any wish to speak openly to me as a friend, or to ask my opinion of any thing that you may have in contemplation . . . indeed, you

> may command me. I will hear whatever you like. I will tell
> you exactly what I think" (p. 409).

In her exquisitely protracted obtuseness and denial, Emma persists in misreading the signs. But her comic misinterpretation of Knightley's intentions and remarks is transformed by her sudden sense that by distancing herself from him she has also caused him pain. In her own urgency to avoid what she is convinced is the awful news about Knightley's passion for Harriet, she has also cut herself off from his confidence and intimacy. Spontaneously she sacrifices her own peace of mind to relieve Knightley of his pain—which she is causing by not permitting him to speak, though she thoroughly misconceives what it is that he is bursting to say. She will suffer anything, endure any "cost" if it helps him to overcome the terrible state of indecision that she imagines him to be in because, as she believes, he is so reluctant to inflict the pain on her that the revelation about himself and Harriet will incur, the pain of his final turning away from her, and of her final loss of him. And so she says, in effect, Go on, tell me about it. "'I will hear whatever you like'" (p. 409). Whatever it may be, I will endeavor to take it. The rest is all surprise and delight—for both of them.

Emma had realized that she was not in love with Frank Churchill because the idea of sacrifice played no part in her thoughts about him or in her projections of the contingencies that a joint future for the two of them might involve. She finds herself more than prepared to make such a sacrifice for Knightley. And yet once more Emma comes upon the disclosure of love in an act that entails loss, pain, and negation. One of the possibilities started by this repeated occurrence focuses on how much Emma has to overcome before she is able actively to open herself to love, before she can commit herself to surrendering to desire and want and hence dependency. But Knightley, pursuing his lovemaking, detours her in an tangential direction. "'You hear nothing but truth from me. I have blamed you, and lectured you, and you have borne it as no other woman in England would have borne it. Bear with the truths I would tell you now, dearest Emma, as well as you have borne with them'" (p. 410). He all but says, "Emma, you can take it like a man."[xxix] And Emma's busy mind follows this congenial line of explanation "without losing a word," catching and comprehending "the exact truth of the whole." The exact truth is succinctly articulated: "'That Harriet was nothing; that she was every thing herself'" (p. 410). Harriet is, after all, a Nobody, a cipher, a zero. And Emma, "everything herself," is exalted as a young goddess, solitary in her narcissistic splendor and at the same time the central object of the universe—Her majesty the baby, as well as the best beloved of women. She is "first" for both Knightley and her father, "everything" to them and to herself too.[xxx]

## IV

Having gotten this far, the narrator takes a step backward and sideways. "Seldom, very seldom does complete truth belong to any human disclosure."[xxxi] Although she is referring literally to Emma's withholding from Knightley an account of the double delusion of both herself and Harriet, there remains, as is customary with such narratorial comments in Jane Austen, a residue of generalizing extension. For Emma, who has passed from inner distress to "something so like perfect happiness," has undergone a momentous "change" (p. 412). That change is not yet complete. Emma still cannot marry Knightley. "While her dear father lived, any change of condition must be impossible for her." Knightley agrees that Emma cannot leave her father, nor can Mr. Woodhouse suffer a "transplantation." His comfort, his very life, would be at hazard. But Knightley can move in with the Woodhouses at Hartfield, which will be his home as long as Mr. Woodhouse lives. This solution turns out to be not merely negotiable but irresistible, and we can bring a long-delayed conclusion forward while unpacking some of its meanings. Knightley has known Emma since she was a child. His closer attention to her dates from her twelfth or thirteenth year. He has been her guide and mentor, the monitor of her conduct and voice of her conscience. He has also, in the absence of any strong, positive personal authority among her intimate family circle, functioned as her ego ideal. He is sixteen years older than she, about the same age as Miss Taylor/Mrs. Weston, who figured for Emma as a loving but insufficiently assertive surrogate mother. He is a surrogate father to Emma, but he is just as much an older, very senior brother and a literal brother-in-law. He might as well be a benevolent uncle, too. He is a whole spectrum of male imagoes wrapped up in one. Although Emma dearly loves her father, Mr. Woodhouse, despite all his sweetness and old-fashioned politeness of manner, is weak, fretful, selfish, and utterly incompetent as a father. What could be more "natural," then, that Emma, unknown to herself, should want and love a much-improved version of a man so important to her entire life? And what could be more natural as well that she should isolate, conceal, and encapsulate that love, banish it from conscious awareness, since it is so close to violating fundamental taboos?

But Knightley also modulates the blunt force of his masculine identity. In volunteering to live at Hartfield after they are married, he is undertaking to behave in what was conventionally regarded as a woman's role: He elects symbolically to feminize himself, although we are simultaneously and silently reassured to take heart, for he has plenty of masculinity to spare. Emma realizes that "in quitting Donwell, he must be sacrificing a great deal of independence . . . that in living constantly with her father, and in no house of his own, there would be much, very much, to be borne with" (p. 428). She understands very well by now what sacrifice means *to her*. And although Knightley will have to postpone indefinitely the gratification of giving "'a woman a better home than the one he takes her from'" (p. 408), he suffers no anxiety about having to forgo a late-in-life Oedipal triumph, nor is he at all concerned about supplanting Mr. Woodhouse. In short, Emma is succeeding at what was hitherto regarded as impossible. The ill-fated marriage between Mr. Weston and Miss Churchill went wrong, we recall, because of her vain desire "at once to be the wife of Captain Weston, and Miss Churchill of Enscombe" (p. 13). Emma will be at once the wife of Mr. Knightley and Miss Woodhouse of Hartfield. Here we enter upon the grand sweep of wish fulfillments with which the comedy closes. There will be for Emma dramatic change and no change at all. She will have it all.

But having it all brings into account a number of experiences that Emma has also tried not to contemplate. These include sex, babies, illness, and death, the fulfilling and downward curves of the life cycle. Emma is conscious in a semi-distinct way of some of this. For example, her first big quarrel with Knightley—the Harriet-Elton-Martin debacle—is quickly resolved after Isabella and her family arrive for Christmas. Emma senses that she can dispel Knightley's anger by arranging to meet him with one of Isabella's children. She chooses "the youngest, a nice little girl about eight months old, who was . . . very happy to be danced about in her aunt's arms." Knightley's gravity and reserve melt away, and he is delighted "to take the child out of her arms with all the unceremoniousness of perfect amity" (pp. 92–93). However aware (or otherwise) she may be of what she is doing, Emma's intuitions in this instance are directly on the mark. Knightley responds to this tableau of Emma and an infant in her arms with his own fantasy (conscious or not) of Emma as the mother of their baby. It helps matters along that this eight-month-old is also named Emma, and we begin to be prepared this early in the narrative for a perpetuation of Emma into the distant future. Knightley then counsels Emma to be "'guided by nature'" rather than fancy or whim, and although this sentiment is at the time lost on her, he does go on to check himself and moderate his sternness by reminding himself and Emma that he is sixteen years older than she and has the "advantage" of "'not being a pretty young woman and a spoiled child'" (p. 93). They shake hands and make things up.

This theme is recurred to in the grand finale of forgiveness, reconciliation, and resolution. Mrs. Weston is safely delivered of her child, a girl. Emma is delighted by the event, for it is again as if she were being reborn yet once more—Mrs. Weston, after all, took the place of her mother for many years, beginning when Emma was five. She immediately falls silently to planning a match between the newborn infant and little Henry or his brother. And she also imagines the growing young girl caring for Mr. Weston, her father, as he grows older, enlivening her father's life and her own with "the fancies of a child never banished from home" (p. 440). It is, for a second time, a reduplication of Emma. She is like the first Catherine in *Wuthering Heights*, preparing herself for immortality while beginning to contemplate, with some seriousness, her actual mortality. As she imagines the happy life before herself and Knightley, she must also take other matters into account: "Such a companion for herself in the periods of anxiety and cheerlessness before her! Such a partner in all those duties and cares to which time must be giving increase of melancholy!" (p. 429). It is not only the decline and death of her father that she must be prepared for. It is the dangers of childbirth and of infant and maternal mortality, both of which were ever-present and almost daily perils in Jane Austen's time, and to both of which her life and letters bear full testimony.[xxxii]

Emma will go on imagining, matchmaking, and amusing herself. Redeemed but by no means entirely regenerate, she will persist as what she is: lively, willful, difficult, self-referring, complicated, resistant, and stubborn. She did not want to marry, and her married life with Knightley will be strenuous with minor differences. It will not be like the marriage of Frank Churchill and Jane Fairfax, which is based on the full-blooded chemistry of youth, physical beauty, and sexual passion. Emma retains her ambivalence along with her desires to dominate, lead, and exercise her personal gifts and powers. In her masterpiece, Jane Austen created a social world in which a number of lines of conflict, dissonance, and contradiction are foregrounded, and a heroine of whom something similar may be claimed. If she was not able to transcend and resolve such differences and discords, she gave expression to them in a memorable narrative structure and the dramatic and inward representation of a heroine so full and rich and inexhaustible that they may be equaled, but it is unlikely that they will be surpassed.

---

STEVEN MARCUS is Professor of English and Comparative Literature and George Delacorte Professor in the Humanities at Columbia University and a specialist in nineteenth-century literature and culture. A fellow of both the American Academy of Arts and Sciences and the Academy of Literary Studies, he has received Fulbright, American Council of Learned Societies, Guggenheim, Center for Advanced Study in the Behavioral Sciences, Rockefeller, and Mellon grants. He is the author of more than 200 publications.

# Notes to Introduction

i. He "had not married early." Knightley is thirty-seven or thirty-eight; we can use this datum as a relevant marker for not marrying early. Isabella is near thirty. Somewhere in the upper sixties seems a workable estimate for Mr. Woodhouse.

ii. That both his daughters—two sisters, in fact—marry two brothers seems to provide him with no perceptible consolation, despite the implied endogamy.

iii. Indeed, he parses it. A home of her own is a place to be settled in, to let down roots and think of permanency and rest. And "comfortable" entails here provision—that is, resources and amenities and a certain style of life.

iv. None of this implies that Knightley is not perfectly capable of contradicting himself in both speech and behavior—which, in due course, he does.

v. Lionel Trilling seems to have been among the first to draw attention to Emma's profound self-approval. He calls it self-love and does not adduce the noxious side of it that is commonly thought of as narcissism. He regards it as almost wholly beneficent and absolves it of any responsibility for the harm and damage that Emma inflicts on Harriet, Jane Fairfax, or Miss Bates. See *Beyond Culture*, New York: Harcourt Brace Jovanovich, 1979, pp. 28–49.

vi. See Charles Lamb's essay, "Mrs. Battle's Opinions on Whist," in *Essays of Elia*, Iowa City, University of Iowa Press, 2003.

vii. The term refers to the place of business and even to the business itself, regardless of place. It is not a town house, an investment in city real estate, or, necessarily, a residence, although the historical identity of an urban merchant's place of business and his domicile accounts for the origin of the idiom.

viii. A closer occurrence of blindness as a theme is found in
     Wordsworth's great poem "Michael," first published in
     1800; it is at least possible that Jane Austen read it. This
     "pastoral poem" is about social change and its conse-
     quences for a traditional shepherd's way of life and cul-
     ture. Michael, childless until a very late age, loves the land
     on which his family has for generations worked and lived
     with passionate intensity.

> Those fields, those hills . . . had laid
> Strong hold on his affections, were to him
> A pleasurable feeling of blind love,
> The pleasure which there is in life itself.

When a child is born to him and his wife long after they
had any right to expect such an event, Michael responds
again with passionate intensity. Although he of course
loves his "Helpmate" of many years—

> to Michael's heart
> This son of his old age was yet more dear—
> Less from instinctive tenderness, the same
> Fond spirit that blindly works in the blood of all—
> Than that a child, more than all other gifts
> That earth can offer to declining man,
> Brings hope with it, and forward-looking thoughts,
> And stirrings of inquietude, when they
> By tendency of nature needs must fail.

The convergence of theme and diction seems to me more
than coincidental. The double emphasis on blindness,
the declining years of life, the tenderness of instinct, the
implied warmth of blood all tend toward commonality.
And what Emma's idea of "comfort" defends her against
is regarded in "Michael" as "stirrings of inquietude." For
Wordsworth the pleasurable feeling of "blind love" is virtually identical with the pleasure that life itself entails. It

is instinctive and blind and good. But it also exposes us to tragic injury and bereavement when that love fails us or is lost. It is just such tragic intensity that Emma wants most to avoid. Hence her choice of comfort over the possibility of a love that brings tragic suffering and loss.

ix. Since Martin has inherited the farm from his father (p. 27), one can suppose that the lease on the property was for life, a circumstance that enhanced his status and justifies Knightley's referring to him as "a gentleman-farmer."

x. Knightley deploys the word "evil" in a sense that is different from our modern and almost exclusively moral usage. We largely reserve it for only the most dreadful, heinous actions or persons—for example, Hitler was evil. In Jane Austen it tends also to mean disadvantageous, unfavorable, troublesome. On the first page of *Emma*, the narrator remarks that Emma's life of having her own way and thinking too well of herself constitute "the real evils" of her situation, and then goes on to call such evils "disadvantages." And later on, Mr. Weston speaks of Highbury's distance from Enscombe in Yorkshire as an "evil"—it is difficult and awkward for Frank to get away while his aunt is ill.

Tony Tanner has, from a different perspective, also taken note of this usage. See *Jane Austen*, Cambridge, MA: Harvard University Press, 1986, p. 203.

xi. Knightley is echoing the sentiments of Burke. In *Reflections on the Revolution in France*, Burke comes to discuss the confiscation of church property and the expulsion of monks from their former precincts:

> The monks are lazy. Be it so. Suppose them no otherwise employed than by singing in the choir. . . . They are as usefully employed as if they worked from dawn to dark in the innumerable servile, degrading, unseemly, unmanly, and often most unwholesome and pestiferous occupations, to which by the social oeconomy so many wretches are in-

evitably doomed. If it were not generally perni-
cious to disturb the natural course of things, and to
impede, in any degree, the great wheel of circula-
tion which is turned by the strangely-directed
labour of these unhappy people, I should be infinitely more inclined forcibly to rescue them from
their miserable industry, than violently to disturb
the tranquil repose of monastic quietude. Humanity, and perhaps policy, might better justify me in
one than in the other. It is a subject on which I
have often reflected, and never reflected without
feeling from it. I am sure that no consideration, except the necessity of submitting to the yoke of luxury, and the despotism of fancy, who in their own
imperious way will distribute the surplus product of
the soil, can justify the toleration of such trades
and employments in a well-regulated state (*Reflections on the Revolution in France*, New York: Penguin,
1968, p. 271).

xii. She is also one of the split-off and partial anti-types of
Jane Austen herself. The daughter of a deceased clergyman who looks after her widowed mother, Miss Bates
"had no intellectual superiority to make atonement to
herself, or frighten those who might hate her, into outward respect" (p. 18).

xiii. Mrs. Elton's efforts to commandeer and appropriate Jane
constitute a grim parody of Emma's manipulations of
Harriet Smith.

xiv. Such legends persist with extraordinary tenacity. In 1944,
in Auschwitz, Primo Levi ran across a nineteen-year-old illiterate gypsy. Born in Spain, he had "wandered about" in
central Europe and been swept up in Hungary by the
Nazi dragnets. He begged Levi to write a letter for him to
his fiancée. He showed Levi a photograph of her: "She
was almost a child, with laughing eyes, a little white kitten
by her side." He explained, as if in justification, that she
"had not been picked by him but by his father. She was an

official fianceé, not a girl abducted unceremoniously" (*Moments of Reprieve*, New York: Penguin, 1987, pp. 68–69).

xv. An episode of instructive similarity occurs in *Sense and Sensibility* (vol. 1, chapter 16). The sisters are out of doors; in the distance they see a horseman riding toward them. As he comes closer they can "distinguish him to be a gentleman." A bit closer and Marianne concludes that it must be Wllloughby; Elinor, who is both calmer and may have sharper sight, disagrees. When he gets to within thirty yards, Marianne gives up and turns away, only to be called back by her sisters and by the horseman's voice, which she at once recognizes as belonging to Edward Ferrars. "He dismounted, and giving his horse to his servant, walked back with them to Barton, whither he was purposely come to visit them."

The scene is exemplary. It concentrates on a distant figure who gradually comes into focus as he gets nearer to the point of narrative perspective. We see him at several moments in his approach, as additional details become visible. Finally he is close enough to identify and to recognize his voice. He then dismounts and gives his horse to his servant, who has suddenly materialized. Up to that moment, the servant who is accompanying his master has been invisible and nonexistent to both the characters and the narrator.

xvi. She contends that "'when people come in a way which they know to be beneath them,'" they invariably betray themselves by "'a look of consciousness or bustle'" (p. 201).

xvii. In *Emma*, men move about and across distances easily and with regularity. Women are much more confined and restricted in their physical movements through space and geography.

xviii. Both of these keywords have a substantial history of usage in the nineteenth century. In *Emma* we observe in the two appearances made by "culture" the evolutionary shift from physical and agricultural cultivation to the prevailing sense of inner or mental cultivation, with its decided emphasis on literature, the arts, and languages. In "comfort," repeatedly put into play throughout *Emma*, one can make out the emergence into hegemony of what one has to call a middle-class set of values. The aristocratic values or noble qualities that comfort supplants are conveyed on one side in such terms as "grandeur" (still in use in this passage to describe the abruptly sloping, wooded bank that at the distance of a half-mile, makes up the frame for the view from the Abbey to the Farm), "large," "imposing," "splendor," "magnificent," and "majestic"; and on another and equally important side by "luxury" and its long series of related words and expressions. "Comfort," like "culture," is increasingly interiorized as the century progresses and, in the end, expresses as much a mental and spiritual state of being as "culture" does—"I'm comfortable with that" or "That fits into my comfort zone" are among the latest, and very soggy, postmodern manifestations. See Raymond Williams, *Keywords: A Vocabulary of Culture and Society*, New York: Oxford University Press, 1976, and Norbert Elias, *The Civilizing Process*, New York: Urizen Books, 1978.

xix. How to support the poor and indigent was very much a matter of heated public discussion and debate. See, among many others, Gertrude Himmelfarb, *The Idea of Poverty: England in the Early Industrial Age*, New York: Alfred A. Knopf, 1984.

xx. Emma's quotation from *Romeo and Juliet* (act 5, scene 1) drives home the point. Romeo has just been falsely informed that Juliet is dead. He seeks a quick means to join her and recalls having seen an apothecary nearby: "Meagre were his looks, / Sharp misery had worn him to the bones." He offers the poor man gold for a "dram of poison." The apothecary hesitates because of the law that forbids on pain of death the dispensing of such agents. Romeo scornfully replies:

Art thou so bare and full of wretchedness,
And fear'st to die? famine is in thy cheeks,

Need and oppression starveth in thine eyes,
Contempt and beggary hangs upon thy back.
The world is not thy friend nor the world's law;
The world affords no law to make thee rich.
Then be not poor, but break it, and take this.

It can hardly be denied that the passage from *Romeo and Juliet* bears more relevantly on the Abdys, father and son, than it does on Jane. It may moreover be suggested that it is by means of such a displacement that this powerful and negative analogy, or disanalogy, is constructed here—that is to say, the unconscious defenses of displacement and denial, the very means by which the contradictions in question are put aside and pushed away, are at the same time the means by which those same contradictions are brought forward and revealed. The same defenses are also in action when the narrator causes Emma to effectively nod off while Miss Bates is recounting the incident of old John Abdy and his son.

xxi. It was Hegel who characteristically affirmed that music enhanced the listener's awareness of the workings of the inner self. By means of the emotions evoked by music, the modern self—through deepening and enlarging the subjectivity of the ego—sustains its relation to the abstract, philosophical consciousness.

xxii. Emma has in this connection anticipated herself. When Elton has handed over his charade, Emma has confidently misconstrued it as being directed to Harriet: "'It is a certainty. Receive it on my judgment'" (p. 70). However, she also cautions Harriet not to "'refine too much upon this charade.'" She is using "refine" in the sense of building or leaning on, freely interpreting or extrapolating to premature conclusions. "'You will betray your feelings improperly, if you are too conscious and too quick, and appear to *affix* more meaning, or even quite all the meaning which may be *affixed* to it'" (p. 73, emphasis added). In the verbal games that Emma expertly plays, meanings keep shifting around. This destabilization of the established and conventional relations between words and meanings is, for Emma, an entry-way to a world of relative freedom—which can also be understood as both pseudo-freedom and the enabling freedom, limited but nonetheless actual, of an imaginative literary and linguistic creative force. Her advice to Harriet boils down to this: When verbal puzzles and ambiguities are in play, as they are in "courtship," play it loose.

xxiii. The coming of peace to the Continent in 1814 and 1815 made travel there, after nearly twenty years of war, a practicable choice.

xxiv. On the other hand, there is this countervailing observation from Virginia Woolf's autobiographical "A Sketch of the Past": "The tea table rather than the dinner table was the centre of Victorian family life—in our family at least. Savages I suppose have some tree, or fire place, round which they congregate; the round table marked that focal, that sacred spot in our house" (*Moments of Being*, New York, 1985, p. 118). I owe this reference to Vicki Tromenhauser.

xxv. See, especially, Claudia L. Johnson, *Jane Austen: Women, Politics and the Novel*, Chicago: University of Chicago Press, 1988; "The Divine Miss Jane: Jane Austen, Janeites, and the Discipline of Novel Studies," in *Janeites: Austen Disciples and Devotees*, edited by Diedre Lynch, Princeton, NJ: Princeton University Press, 2000, pp. 25–44; and "Austen Cults and Cultures," in *The Cambridge Companion to Jane Austen*, edited by Edward Copeland and Juliet McMaster, Cambridge, MA: Cambridge University Press, 1997, pp. 211–226; and Terry Castle, "Was Jane Austen Gay?" *London Review of Books*, August 3, 1995.

In any event, the ambiguous valence of Emma's gender identity may owe as much to her uncertainty about the nature of inner sexual objects as it does to her desire for any specific sexual or gender configuration.

xxvi. If she had "lived" in the twentieth century, she might have taken a hint from the candor of P. G. Wodehouse who observed of the cast of characters in his Blandings narratives: "I thought them all up, starting from scratch."

xxvii. Nietzsche observed that "a witty remark is an epigram on the death of a feeling" *Human, All Too Human* (1880), vol. 2, part 1, number 202.

xxviii. R. W. Chapman, ed. *The Works of Jane Austen*, vol. 6, London: Oxford University Press, 1954, p. 146.

xxix. When John Knightley remarks that Isabella and Emma have handwritings that are "'very much alike,'" his older brother responds, "'I know what you mean—but Emma's hand is the strongest.'" Emma observes, in turn, that Frank Churchill "'writes one of the best gentlemen's hands I ever saw.'" To which Knightley promptly rejoins, "'I do not admire it. . . . It is too small—wants strength. It is like a woman's writing'" (p. 280). Although Knightley suffers from nonstop jealousy of Frank and rarely passes up an opportunity to put him down or comment on his "puppydom," the juxtaposition he implicitly makes of Emma's and Frank's handwriting also speaks for itself—at least in terms of conventional gender categories. In other words, such details bolster the supposition that Emma's gender identity remains unresolved and slightly ambiguous.

In *The Mayor of Casterbridge*, chapter 20, Hardy puts to use the same conventional belief about the gendered character of handwriting, to the painful discreditation of Elizabeth in the eyes of her father.

xxx. This ringing conclusion is to be traced back to its first iteration in Emma's mind, when she compared Mrs. Churchill with Jane Fairfax: "one was every thing, the other nothing." (p. 366)

xxxi. One of Jane Austen's collateral descendants—if not her "lawful issue"—took her up on this epigram and added: "Truth is rarely pure and never simple" (Oscar Wilde, *The Importance of Being Earnest*, act 1).

xxxii. Two of Jane Austen's sisters-in-law died shortly after childbirth—one of them, suddenly, soon after giving birth to her eleventh child. This sister-in-law, Elizabeth Knight, was married to Jane Austen's older brother, Edward, from whose circumstances she took certain external details of Frank Churchill's life—that is, adoption by a rich family connection, change of name, etc. (And from whom as well she derived the first part of Knightley's name.) The other sister-in-law, the wife of Jane Austen's younger naval brother, died, along with her baby, after giving birth to her fourth child.

# Volume the First.

# Chapter I.

Emma Woodhouse, handsome, clever, and rich, with a comfortable home and happy disposition, seemed to unite some of the best blessings of existence; and had lived nearly twenty-one years in the world with very little to distress or vex her.

She was the youngest of the two daughters of a most affectionate, indulgent father; and had, in consequence of her sister's marriage, been mistress of his house from a very early period. Her mother had died too long ago for her to have more than an indistinct remembrance of her caresses, and her place had been supplied by an excellent woman as governess, who had fallen little short of a mother in affection.

Sixteen years had Miss Taylor been in Mr. Woodhouse's family, less as a governess than a friend, very fond of both daughters, but particularly of Emma. Between *them* it was more the intimacy of sisters. Even before Miss Taylor had ceased to hold the nominal office of governess, the mildness of her temper had hardly allowed her to impose any restraint; and the shadow of authority being now long passed away, they had been living together as friend and friend very mutually attached, and Emma doing just what she liked; highly esteeming Miss Taylor's judgment, but directed chiefly by her own.

The real evils indeed of Emma's situation were the power of having rather too much of her own way, and a disposition to think a little too well of herself: these were the disadvantages which threatened alloy to her many enjoyments. The danger, however, was at present so unperceived, that they did not by any means rank as misfortunes with her.

Sorrow came—a gentle sorrow—but not at all in the shape of any disagreeable consciousness. Miss Taylor mar-

ried. It was Miss Taylor's loss which first brought grief. It was
on the wedding-day of this beloved friend, that Emma first
sat in mournful thought of any continuance. The wedding
over, and the bride-people gone, her father and herself were
left to dine together, with no prospect of a third to cheer a
long evening. Her father composed himself to sleep after
dinner, as usual, and she had then only to sit and think of
what she had lost.

The event had every promise of happiness for her friend.
Mr. Weston was a man of unexceptionable character, easy
fortune, suitable age, and pleasant manners; and there was
some satisfaction in considering with what self-denying, generous friendship, she had always wished and promoted the
match; but it was a black morning's work for her. The want
of Miss Taylor would be felt every hour of every day. She recalled her past kindness—the kindness, the affection of sixteen years—how she had taught and how she had played
with her from five years old—how she had devoted all her
powers to attach and amuse her in health—and how nursed
her through the various illnesses of childhood. A large debt
of gratitude was owing here; but the intercourse of the last
seven years, the equal footing and perfect unreserve which
had soon followed Isabella's marriage on their being left to
each other, was yet a dearer, tenderer recollection. It had
been a friend and companion such as few possessed: intelligent, well-informed, useful, gentle, knowing all the ways of
the family, interested in all its concerns, and peculiarly interested in herself, in every pleasure, every scheme of
hers;—one to whom she could speak every thought as it
arose, and who had such an affection for her as could never
find fault.

How was she to bear the change? It was true, that her
friend was going only half a mile from them; but Emma was
aware that great must be the difference between a Mrs.
Weston, only half a mile from them, and a Miss Taylor in the
house; and with all her advantages, natural and domestic,
she was now in great danger of suffering from intellectual

solitude. She dearly loved her father, but he was no companion for her. He could not meet her in conversation, rational or playful.

The evil of the actual disparity in their ages (and Mr. Woodhouse had not married early) was much increased by his constitution and habits; for having been a valetudinarian all his life, without activity of mind or body, he was a much older man in ways than in years; and though every where beloved for the friendliness of his heart and his amiable temper, his talents could not have recommended him at any time.

Her sister, though comparatively but little removed by matrimony, being settled in London, only sixteen miles off, was much beyond her daily reach; and many a long October and November evening must be struggled through at Hartfield, before Christmas brought the next visit from Isabella and her husband, and their little children, to fill the house, and give her pleasant society again.

Highbury, the large and populous village almost amounting to a town, to which Hartfield, in spite of its separate lawn, and shrubberies, and name, did really belong, afforded her no equals. The Woodhouses were first in consequence there. All looked up to them. She had many acquaintance in the place; for her father was universally civil, but not one among them who could be accepted in lieu of Miss Taylor for even half a day. It was a melancholy change; and Emma could not but sigh over it, and wish for impossible things, till her father awoke, and made it necessary to be cheerful. His spirits required support. He was a nervous man, easily depressed; fond of every body that he was used to, and hating to part with them; hating change of every kind. Matrimony, as the origin of change, was always disagreeable; and he was by no means yet reconciled to his own daughter's marrying, nor could ever speak of her but with compassion, though it had been entirely a match of affection, when he was now obliged to part with Miss Taylor too; and from his habits of gentle selfishness, and of being never able to suppose that other people could feel differently from himself, he was very much disposed to think Miss Taylor had done as sad a thing for herself as for them, and would have been a great deal happier if she had spent all the rest of her life at Hartfield. Emma smiled and chatted as cheerfully as she could, to keep him from such thoughts; but when tea came, it was impossible for him not to say exactly as he had said at dinner.

"Poor Miss Taylor!—I wish she were here again. What a pity it is that Mr. Weston ever thought of her!"

"I cannot agree with you, papa; you know I cannot. Mr. Weston is such a good humoured, pleasant, excellent man, that he thoroughly deserves a good wife;—and you would not have had Miss Taylor live with us for ever, and bear all my odd humours, when she might have a house of her own?"

"A house of her own!—but where is the advantage of a house of her own? This is three times as large;—and you have never any odd humours, my dear."

"How often we shall be going to see them, and they coming to see us!—We shall be always meeting! *We* must begin; we must go and pay our wedding-visit very soon."

"My dear, how am I to get so far? Randalls is such a distance. I could not walk half so far."

"No, papa; nobody thought of your walking. *We* must go in the carriage, to be sure."

"The carriage! But James will not like to put the horses to for such a little way;—and where are the poor horses to be while we are paying our visit?"

"They are to be put into Mr. Weston's stable, papa. You know we have settled all that already. We talked it all over with Mr. Weston last night. And as for James, you may be very sure he will always like going to Randalls, because of his daughter's being housemaid there. I only doubt whether he will ever take us anywhere else. That was your doing, papa. You got Hannah that good place. Nobody thought of Hannah till you mentioned her—James is so obliged to you!"

"I am very glad I did think of her. It was very lucky, for I would not have had poor James think himself slighted upon any account; and I am sure she will make a very good servant; she is a civil, pretty spoken girl; I have a great opinion of her. Whenever I see her, she always courtesies and asks me how I do, in a very pretty manner; and when you have had her here to do needlework, I observe she always turns the lock of the door the right way and never bangs it. I am sure she will be an excellent servant; and it will be a great comfort to poor Miss Taylor to have somebody about her that she is used to see. Whenever James goes over to see his daughter, you know, she will be hearing of us. He will be able to tell her how we all are."

Emma spared no exertions to maintain this happier flow of ideas, and hoped, by the help of backgammon, to get her father tolerably through the evening, and be attacked by no regrets but her own. The backgammon-table was placed; but a visiter immediately afterwards walked in and made it unnecessary.

Mr. Knightley, a sensible man about seven or eight and thirty, was not only a very old and intimate friend of the family, but particularly connected with it as the elder brother of Isabella's husband. He lived about a mile from Highbury, was a frequent visiter, and always welcome, and at this time more welcome than usual, as coming directly from their mutual connections in London. He had returned to a late dinner after some days' absence, and now walked up to Hartfield to say that all were well in Brunswick Square. It was a happy circumstance, and animated Mr. Woodhouse for some time. Mr. Knightley had a cheerful manner which always did him good; and his many enquiries after "poor Isabella" and her children were answered most satisfactorily. When this was over, Mr. Woodhouse gratefully observed,—

"It is very kind of you, Mr. Knightley, to come out at this late hour to call upon us. I am afraid you must have had a shocking walk."

"Not at all, sir. It is a beautiful moonlight night; and so mild that I must draw back from your great fire."

"But you must have found it very damp and dirty. I wish you may not catch cold."

"Dirty, sir! Look at my shoes. Not a speck on them."

"Well! That is quite surprising, for we have had a vast deal of rain here. It rained dreadfully hard for half an hour, while we were at breakfast. I wanted them to put off the wedding."

"By the by, I have not wished you joy. Being pretty well aware of what sort of joy you must both be feeling, I have been in no hurry with my congratulations; but I hope it all went off tolerably well. How did you all behave? Who cried most."

"Ah! poor Miss Taylor! 'tis a sad business."

"Poor Mr. and Miss Woodhouse, if you please; but I cannot possibly say 'poor Miss Taylor.' I have a great regard for you and Emma; but when it comes to the question of dependence or independence! At any rate, it must be better to have only one to please than two."

"Especially when *one* of those two is such a fanciful, troublesome creature!" said Emma playfully. "That is what you have in your head, I know—and what you would certainly say if my father were not by."

"I believe it is very true, my dear, indeed," said Mr. Woodhouse with a sigh. "I am afraid I am sometimes very fanciful and troublesome."

"My dearest papa! You do not think I could mean *you*, or suppose Mr. Knightley to mean *you*. What a horrible idea! Oh, no! I meant only myself. Mr. Knightley loves to find fault with me, you know—in a joke—it is all a joke. We always say what we like to one another."

Mr. Knightley, in fact, was one of the few people who could see faults in Emma Woodhouse, and the only one who ever told her of them; and though this was not particularly agreeable to Emma herself, she knew it would be so much less so to her father, that she would not have him really suspect such a circumstance as her not being thought perfect by every body.

"Emma knows I never flatter her," said Mr. Knightley; "but I meant no reflection on any body. Miss Taylor has been used to have two persons to please; she will now have but one. The chances are that she must be a gainer."

"Well," said Emma, willing to let it pass, "you want to hear about the wedding; and I shall be happy to tell you, for we all behaved charmingly. Every body was punctual, every body in their best looks: not a tear, and hardly a long face to be seen. Oh, no; we all felt that we were going to be only half a mile apart, and were sure of meeting every day."

"Dear Emma bears every thing so well," said her father. "But, Mr. Knightley, she is really very sorry to lose poor Miss Taylor, and I am sure she *will* miss her more than she thinks for."

Emma turned away her head, divided between tears and smiles.

"It is impossible that Emma should not miss such a companion," said Mr. Knightley. "We should not like her so well as we do, sir, if we could suppose it: but she knows how much the marriage is to Miss Taylor's advantage; she knows how very acceptable it must be at Miss Taylor's time of life to be settled in a home of her own, and how important to her to be secure of a comfortable provision, and therefore cannot allow herself to feel so much pain as pleasure. Every friend of Miss Taylor must be glad to have her so happily married."

"And you have forgotten one matter of joy to me," said Emma, "and a very considerable one—that I made the match myself. I made the match, you know, four years ago; and to have it take place, and be proved in the right, when so many people said Mr. Weston would never marry again, may comfort me for any thing."

Mr. Knightley shook his head at her. Her father fondly replied, "Ah! my dear, I wish you would not make matches and foretell things, for whatever you say always comes to pass. Pray do not make any more matches."

"I promise you to make none for myself, papa; but I must, indeed, for other people. It is the greatest amusement in the world! And after such success, you know! Every body said that Mr. Weston would never marry again. Oh dear, no! Mr. Weston, who had been a widower so long, and who seemed so perfectly comfortable without a wife, so constantly occupied either in his business in town or among his friends here, always acceptable wherever he went, always cheerful— Mr. Weston need not spend a single evening in the year alone if he did not like it. Oh, no! Mr. Weston certainly would never marry again. Some people even talked of a promise to his wife on her death-bed, and others of the son and the uncle not letting him. All manner of solemn nonsense was talked on the subject, but I believed none of it. Ever since the day (about four years ago) that Miss Taylor and I met with him in Broadway Lane, when, because it began to mizzle, he darted away with so much gallantry, and borrowed two umbrellas for us from Farmer Mitchell's, I made up my mind on the subject. I planned the match from that hour; and when such success has blessed me in this instance, dear papa, you cannot think that I shall leave off match-making."

"I do not understand what you mean by 'success,'" said Mr. Knightley. "Success supposes endeavour. Your time has been properly and delicately spent, if you have been endeavouring for the last four years to bring about this marriage. A worthy employment for a young lady's mind! but if, which I rather imagine, your making the match, as you call it, means only your planning it, your saying to yourself one idle day, 'I think it would be a very good thing for Miss Taylor if Mr. Weston were to marry her,' and saying it again to yourself every now and then afterwards,—why do you talk of success? where is your merit? What are you proud of? You made a lucky guess; and *that* is all that can be said."

"And have you never known the pleasure and triumph of

a lucky guess? I pity you. I thought you cleverer; for depend upon it, a lucky guess is never merely luck. There is always some talent in it. And as to my poor word 'success,' which you quarrel with, I do not know that I am so entirely without any claim to it. You have drawn two pretty pictures; but I think there may be a third,—a something between the do-nothing and the do-all. If I had not promoted Mr. Weston's visits here, and given many little encouragements, and smoothed many little matters, it might not have come to any thing after all. I think you must know Hartfield enough to comprehend that."

"A straight-forward, open-hearted man, like Weston, and a rational unaffected woman, like Miss Taylor, may be safely left to manage their own concerns. You are more likely to have done harm to yourself, than good to them, by interference."

"Emma never thinks of herself, if she can do good to others," rejoined Mr. Woodhouse, understanding but in part. "But, my dear, pray do not make any more matches, they are silly things, and break up one's family circle grievously."

"Only one more, papa; only for Mr. Elton. Poor Mr. Elton! You like Mr. Elton, papa; I must look about for a wife for him. There is nobody in Highbury who deserves him,— and he has been here a whole year, and has fitted up his house so comfortably, that it would be a shame to have him single any longer; and I thought when he was joining their hands to-day, he looked so very much as if he would like to have the same kind office done for him! I think very well of Mr. Elton, and this is the only way I have of doing him a service."

"Mr. Elton is a very pretty young man, to be sure, and a very good young man, and I have a great regard for him. But if you want to show him any attention, my dear, ask him to come and dine with us some day. That will be a much better thing. I dare say Mr. Knightley will be so kind as to meet him."

"With a great deal of pleasure, sir, at any time," said Mr.

Knightley, laughing; "and I agree with you entirely, that it will be a much better thing. Invite him to dinner, Emma, and help him to the best of the fish and the chicken, but leave him to choose his own wife. Depend upon it, a man of six or seven and twenty can take care of himself."

## Chapter II.

M r. Weston was a native of Highbury, and born of a respectable family, which for the last two or three generations had been rising into gentility and property. He had received a good education, but on succeeding early in life to a small independence, had become indisposed for any of the more homely pursuits in which his brothers were engaged; and had satisfied an active cheerful mind and social temper by entering into the militia of his county, then embodied.

Captain Weston was a general favourite; and when the chances of his military life had introduced him to Miss Churchill, of a great Yorkshire family, and Miss Churchill fell in love with him, nobody was surprised except her brother and his wife, who had never seen him, and who were full of pride and importance, which the connection would offend.

Miss Churchill, however, being of age, and with the full command of her fortune—though her fortune bore no proportion to the family-estate—was not to be dissuaded from the marriage, and it took place to the infinite mortification of Mr. and Mrs. Churchill, who threw her off with due decorum. It was an unsuitable connection, and did not produce much happiness. Mrs. Weston ought to have found more in it, for she had a husband whose warm heart and sweet temper made him think every thing due to her in return for the great goodness of being in love with him; but though she had one sort of spirit, she had not the best. She had resolution enough to pursue her own will in spite of her brother, but not enough to refrain from unreasonable regrets at that brother's unreasonable anger, nor from missing the luxuries of her former home. They lived beyond their income, but still it was nothing in comparison of Enscombe: she did not cease to love her husband; but she wanted at once to be the wife of Captain Weston, and Miss Churchill of Enscombe.

Captain Weston, who had been considered, especially by the Churchills, as making such an amazing match, was proved to have much the worst of the bargain; for when his wife died, after a three years' marriage, he was rather a poorer man than at first, and with a child to maintain. From the expense of the child, however, he was soon relieved. The boy had, with the additional softening claim of a lingering illness of his mother's, been the means of a sort of reconciliation; and Mr. and Mrs. Churchill, having no children of their own, nor any other young creature of equal kindred to care for, offered to take the whole charge of the little Frank soon after her decease. Some scruples and some reluctance the widower-father may be supposed to have felt; but as they were overcome by other considerations, the child was given up to the care and the wealth of the Churchills, and he had only his own comfort to seek, and his own situation to improve as he could.

A complete change of life became desirable. He quitted the militia and engaged in trade, having brothers already established in a good way in London, which afforded him a favourable opening. It was a concern which brought just employment enough. He had still a small house in Highbury, where most of his leisure days were spent; and between useful occupation and the pleasures of society, the next eighteen or twenty years of his life passed cheerfully away. He had, by that time, realised an easy competence—enough to secure the purchase of a little estate adjoining Highbury,

which he had always longed for—enough to marry a woman
as portionless even as Miss Taylor, and to live according to
the wishes of his own friendly and social disposition.

It was now some time since Miss Taylor had begun to influence his schemes; but as it was not the tyrannic influence
of youth on youth, it had not shaken his determination of
never settling till he could purchase Randalls, and the sale of
Randalls was long looked forward to; but he had gone
steadily on, with these objects in view, till they were accomplished. He had made his fortune, bought his house, and obtained his wife; and was beginning a new period of existence
with every probability of greater happiness than in any yet
passed through. He had never been an unhappy man; his
own temper had secured him from that, even in his first marriage; but his second must show him how delightful a well-
judging and truly amiable woman could be, and must give
him the pleasantest proof of its being a great deal better to
choose than to be chosen, to excite gratitude than to feel it.

He had only himself to please in his choice: his fortune
was his own; for as to Frank, it was more than being tacitly
brought up as his uncle's heir, it had become so avowed an
adoption as to have him assume the name of Churchill on
coming of age. It was most unlikely, therefore, that he should
ever want his father's assistance. His father had no apprehension of it. The aunt was a capricious woman, and governed her husband entirely; but it was not in Mr. Weston's
nature to imagine that any caprice could be strong enough
to affect one so dear, and, as he believed, so deservedly dear.
He saw his son every year in London, and was proud of him;
and his fond report of him as a very fine young man had
made Highbury feel a sort of pride in him too. He was
looked on as sufficiently belonging to the place to make his
merits and prospects a kind of common concern.

Mr. Frank Churchill was one of the boasts of Highbury,
and a lively curiosity to see him prevailed, though the compliment was so little returned that he had never been there

in his life. His coming to visit his father had been often talked of but never achieved.

Now, upon his father's marriage, it was very generally proposed, as a most proper attention, that the visit should take place. There was not a dissentient voice on the subject, either when Mrs. Perry drank tea with Mrs. and Miss Bates, or when Mrs. and Miss Bates returned the visit. Now was the time for Mr. Frank Churchill to come among them; and the hope strengthened when it was understood that he had written to his new mother on the occasion. For a few days every morning visit in Highbury included some mention of the handsome letter Mrs. Weston had received. "I suppose you have heard of the handsome letter Mr. Frank Churchill had written to Mrs. Weston? I understood it was a very handsome letter, indeed. Mr. Woodhouse told me of it. Mr. Woodhouse saw the letter, and he says he never saw such a handsome letter in his life."

It was, indeed, a highly-prized letter. Mrs. Weston had, of course, formed a very favourable idea of the young man; and such a pleasing attention was an irresistible proof of his great good sense, and a most welcome addition to every source and every expression of congratulation which her marriage had already secured. She felt herself a most fortunate woman; and she had lived long enough to know how fortunate she might well be thought, where the only regret was for a partial separation from friends, whose friendship for her had never cooled, and who could ill bear to part with her.

She knew that at times she must be missed; and could not think, without pain, of Emma's losing a single pleasure, or suffering an hour's ennui, from the want of her companionableness: but dear Emma was of no feeble character; she was more equal to her situation than most girls would have been, and had sense, and energy, and spirits that might be hoped would bear her well and happily through its little difficulties and privations. And then there was such comfort in the very easy distance of Randalls from Hartfield, so convenient for even solitary female walking, and in Mr. Weston's disposition and circumstances, which would make the approaching season no hinderance to their spending half the evenings in the week together.

Her situation was altogether the subject of hours of gratitude to Mrs. Weston, and of moments only of regret; and her satisfaction—her more than satisfaction—her cheerful enjoyment was so just and so apparent, that Emma, well as she knew her father, was sometimes taken by surprise at his being still able to pity "poor Miss Taylor," when they left her at Randalls in the centre of every domestic comfort, or saw her go away in the evening attended by her pleasant husband to a carriage of her own. But never did she go without Mr. Woodhouse's giving a gentle sigh, and saying,—

"Ah, poor Miss Taylor! She would be very glad to stay."

There was no recovering Miss Taylor—nor much likelihood of ceasing to pity her; but a few weeks brought some alleviation to Mr. Woodhouse. The compliments of his neighbours were over: he was no longer teased by being wished joy of so sorrowful an event; and the wedding-cake, which had been a great distress to him, was all ate up. His own stomach could bear nothing rich, and he could never believe other people to be different from himself. What was unwholesome to him, he regarded as unfit for any body; and he had, therefore, earnestly tried to dissuade them from having any wedding-cake at all; and when that proved vain, as earnestly tried to prevent any body's eating it. He had been at the pains of consulting Mr. Perry, the apothecary, on the subject. Mr. Perry was an intelligent, gentlemanlike man, whose frequent visits were one of the comforts of Mr. Woodhouse's life; and, upon being applied to, he could not but acknowledge (though it seemed rather against the bias of inclination), that wedding-cake might certainly disagree with many—perhaps with most people, unless taken moderately. With such an opinion, in confirmation of his own, Mr. Woodhouse hoped to influence every visiter of the new-married pair; but still the cake was eaten; and there was no rest for his benevolent nerves till it was all gone.

There was a strange rumour in Highbury of all the little Perrys being seen with a slice of Mrs. Weston's wedding-cake in their hands; but Mr. Woodhouse would never believe it.

## Chapter III.

Mr. Woodhouse was fond of society in his own way. He liked very much to have his friends come and see him; and from various united causes, from his long residence at Hartfield, and his good nature, from his fortune, his house, and his daughter, he could command the visits of his own little circle, in a great measure, as he liked. He had not much intercourse with any families beyond that circle: his horror of late hours, and large dinner-parties, made him unfit for any acquaintance, but such as would visit him on his own terms. Fortunately for him, Highbury, including Randalls in the same parish, and Donwell Abbey in the parish adjoining, the seat of Mr. Knightley, comprehended many such. Not unfrequently, through Emma's persuasion, he had some of the chosen and the best to dine with him: but evening parties were what he preferred; and, unless he fancied himself at any time unequal to company, there was scarcely an evening in the week in which Emma could not make up a card-table for him.

Real, long standing regard brought the Westons and Mr. Knightley; and by Mr. Elton, a young man living alone without liking it, the privilege of exchanging any vacant evening of his own blank solitude for the elegancies and society of

Mr. Woodhouse's drawing-room, and the smiles of his lovely daughter, was in no danger of being thrown away.

After these came a second set: among the most come-at-able of whom were Mrs. and Miss Bates, and Mrs. Goddard, three ladies almost always at the service of an invitation from Hartfield, and who were fetched and carried home so often, that Mr. Woodhouse thought it no hardship for either James or the horses. Had it taken place only once a year, it would have been a grievance.

Mrs. Bates, the widow of a former vicar of Highbury, was a very old lady, almost past every thing but tea and quadrille.* She lived with her single daughter in a very small way, and was considered with all the regard and respect which a harmless old lady, under such untoward circumstances, can excite. Her daughter enjoyed a most uncommon degree of popularity for a woman neither young, handsome, rich, nor married. Miss Bates stood in the very worst predicament in the world for having much of the public favour; and she had no intellectual superiority to make atonement to herself, or frighten those who might hate her, into outward respect. She had never boasted either beauty or cleverness. Her youth had passed without distinction, and her middle of life was devoted to the care of a failing mother, and the endeavour to make a small income go as far as possible. And yet she was a happy woman, and a woman whom no one named without good-will. It was her own universal good-will and contented temper which worked such wonders. She loved every body, was interested in every body's happiness, quicksighted to every body's merits; thought herself a most fortunate creature, and surrounded with blessings in such an excellent mother, and so many good neighbours and friends, and a home that wanted for nothing. The simplicity and cheerfulness of her nature, her contented and grateful spirit, were a recommendation to every

---

*Four-person card game.

body, and a mine of felicity to herself. She was a great talker upon little matters, which exactly suited Mr. Woodhouse, full of trivial communications and harmless gossip.

Mrs. Goddard was the mistress of a school,—not of a seminary, or an establishment, or any thing which professed, in long sentences of refined nonsense, to combine liberal acquirements with elegant morality, upon new principles and new systems,—and where young ladies for enormous pay might be screwed out of health and into vanity,—but a real, honest, old fashioned boarding-school, where a reasonable quantity of accomplishments were sold at a reasonable price, and where girls might be sent to be out of the way, and scramble themselves into a little education, without any danger of coming back prodigies. Mrs. Goddard's school was in high repute, and very deservedly; for Highbury was reckoned a particularly healthy spot: she had an ample house and garden, gave the children plenty of wholesome food, let them run about a great deal in the summer, and in winter dressed their chilblains* with her own hands. It was no wonder that a train of twenty young couple now walked after her to church. She was a plain, motherly kind of woman, who had worked hard in her youth, and now thought herself entitled to the occasional holiday of a tea-visit; and having formerly owed much to Mr. Woodhouse's kindness, felt his particular claim on her to leave her neat parlour, hung round with fancy work, whenever she could, and win or lose a few sixpences by his fireside.

These were the ladies whom Emma found herself very frequently able to collect; and happy was she, for her father's sake, in the power; though, as far as she was herself concerned, it was no remedy for the absence of Mrs. Weston. She was delighted to see her father look comfortable, and very much pleased with herself for contriving things so well;

---

*Mild form of frostbite in which the hands and feet swell from excessive exposure to cold.

but the quiet prosings of three such women made her feel that every evening so spent was indeed one of the long evenings she had fearfully anticipated.

As she sat one morning, looking forward to exactly such a close of the present day, a note was brought from Mrs. Goddard, requesting, in most respectful terms, to be allowed to bring Miss Smith with her: a most welcome request; for Miss Smith was a girl of seventeen, whom Emma knew very well by sight, and had long felt an interest in, on account of her beauty. A very gracious invitation was returned, and the evening no longer dreaded by the fair mistress of the mansion.

Harriet Smith was the natural daughter of somebody. Somebody had placed her, several years back, at Mrs. Goddard's school, and somebody had lately raised her from the condition of scholar to that of parlour boarder. This was all that was generally known of her history. She had no visible friends but what had been acquired at Highbury, and was now just returned from a long visit in the country to some young ladies who had been at school there with her.

She was a very pretty girl, and her beauty happened to be of a sort which Emma particularly admired. She was short, plump, and fair, with a fine bloom, blue eyes, light hair, regular features, and a look of great sweetness; and before the end of the evening, Emma was as much pleased with her manners as her person, and quite determined to continue the acquaintance.

She was not struck by any thing remarkably clever in Miss Smith's conversation, but she found her altogether very engaging,—not inconveniently shy, not unwilling to talk,—and yet so far from pushing, showing so proper and becoming a deference, seeming so pleasantly grateful for being admitted to Hartfield, and so artlessly impressed by the appearance of every thing in so superior a style to what she had been used to, that she must have good sense, and deserve encouragement. Encouragement should be given. Those soft blue eyes, and all those natural graces, should not be wasted on the in-

ferior society of Highbury, and its connections. The acquaintance she had already formed were unworthy of her.
The friends from whom she had just parted, though very
good sort of people, must be doing her harm. They were a
family of the name of Martin, whom Emma well knew by
character, as renting a large farm of Mr. Knightley, and residing in the parish of Donwell,—very creditably, she believed: she knew Mr. Knightley thought highly of them; but
they must be coarse and unpolished, and very unfit to be the
intimates of a girl who wanted only a little more knowledge
and elegance to be quite perfect. *She* would notice her; she
would improve her; she would detach her from her bad acquaintance, and introduce her into good society; she would
form her opinions and her manners. It would be an interesting and certainly a very kind undertaking; highly becoming her own situation in life, her leisure, and powers.

She was so busy in admiring those soft blue eyes, in talking and listening, and forming all these schemes in the in-
betweens, that the evening flew away at a very unusual rate;
and the supper table, which always closed such parties, and
for which she had been used to sit and watch the due time,
was all set out and ready, and moved forwards to the fire, before she was aware. With an alacrity beyond the common impulse of a spirit which yet was never indifferent to the credit
of doing every thing well and attentively, with the real good-
will of a mind delighted with its own ideas, did she then do
all the honours of the meal, and help and recommend the
minced chicken and scalloped oysters, with an urgency
which she knew would be acceptable to the early hours and
civil scruples of their guests.

Upon such occasions poor Mr. Woodhouse's feelings
were in sad warfare. He loved to have the cloth laid, because
it had been the fashion of his youth: but his conviction of
suppers being very unwholesome made him rather sorry to
see any thing put on it; and while his hospitality would have
welcomed his visiters to every thing, his care for their health
made him grieve that they would eat.

Such another small basin of thin gruel as his own was all that he could, with thorough self-approbation, recommend; though he might constrain himself, while the ladies were comfortably clearing the nicer things, to say,—

"Mrs. Bates, let me propose your venturing on one of these eggs. An egg boiled very soft is not unwholesome. Serle understands boiling an egg better than any body. I would not recommend an egg boiled by any body else,—but you need not be afraid, they are very small, you see,—one of our small eggs will not hurt you. Miss Bates, let Emma help you to a *little* bit of tart—a *very* little bit. Ours are all apple tarts. You need not be afraid of unwholesome preserves here. I do not advise the custard. Mrs. Goddard, what say you to *half* a glass of wine? A *small* half glass, put into a tumbler of water? I do not think it could disagree with you."

Emma allowed her father to talk—but supplied her visiters in a much more satisfactory style; and on the present evening had particular pleasure in sending them away happy. The happiness of Miss Smith was quite equal to her intentions. Miss Woodhouse was so great a personage in Highbury, that the prospect of the introduction had given as much panic as pleasure; but the humble, grateful little girl went off with highly gratified feelings, delighted with the affability with which Miss Woodhouse had treated her all the evening, and actually shaken hands with her at last!

## Chapter IV.

Harriet Smith's intimacy at Hartfield was soon a settled thing. Quick and decided in her ways, Emma lost no time in inviting, encouraging, and telling her to come very often; and as their acquaintance increased, so did their satisfaction in each other. As a walking companion, Emma had very early foreseen how useful she might find her. In that respect Mrs. Weston's loss had been important. Her father never went beyond the shrubbery, where two divisions of the ground sufficed him for his long walk, or his short, as the year varied; and since Mrs. Weston's marriage her exercise had been too much confined. She had ventured once alone to Randalls, but it was not pleasant; and a Harriet Smith, therefore, one whom she could summon at any time to a walk, would be a valuable addition to her privileges. But in every respect as she saw more of her, she approved her, and was confirmed in all her kind designs.

Harriet certainly was not clever, but she had a sweet, docile, grateful disposition; was totally free from conceit; and only desiring to be guided by any one she looked up to. Her early attachment to herself was very amiable; and her inclination for good company, and power of appreciating what was elegant and clever, showed that there was no want of taste, though strength of understanding must not be expected. Altogether she was quite convinced of Harriet Smith's being exactly the young friend she wanted,—exactly the something which her home required. Such a friend as Mrs. Weston was out of the question. Two such could never be granted. Two such she did not want. It was quite a different sort of thing,—a sentiment distinct and independent. Mrs. Weston was the object of a regard which had its basis in gratitude and esteem. Harriet would be loved as one to whom she could be useful. For Mrs. Weston there was nothing to be done; for Harriet every thing.

Her first attempts at usefulness were in an endeavour to find out who were the parents; but Harriet could not tell. She was ready to tell every thing in her power, but on this subject questions were vain. Emma was obliged to fancy what she liked; but she could never believe that in the same situation *she* should not have discovered the truth. Harriet had no penetration. She had been satisfied to hear and believe just what Mrs. Goddard chose to tell her; and looked no farther.

Mrs. Goddard, and the teachers, and the girls, and the affairs of the school in general, formed naturally a great part of her conversation,—and but for her acquaintance with the Martins of Abbey-Mill Farm, it must have been the whole. But the Martins occupied her thoughts a good deal: she had spent two very happy months with them, and now loved to talk of the pleasures of her visit, and describe the many comforts and wonders of the place. Emma encouraged her talkativeness,—amused by such a picture of another set of beings, and enjoying the youthful simplicity which could speak with so much exultation of Mrs. Martin's having "*two* parlours, two very good parlours, indeed; one of them quite as large as Mrs. Goddard's drawing-room; and of her having an upper maid who had lived five-and-twenty years with her; and of their having eight cows, two of them Alderneys, and one a little Welsh cow, a very pretty little Welsh cow, indeed; and of Mrs. Martin's saying, as she was so fond of it, it should be called *her* cow; and of their having a very handsome summer-house in their garden, where some day next year they were all to drink tea,—a very handsome summerhouse, large enough to hold a dozen people."

For some time she was amused, without thinking beyond the immediate cause; but as she came to understand the family better, other feelings arose. She had taken up a wrong idea, fancying it was a mother and daughter, a son and son's wife, who all lived together; but when it appeared that the Mr. Martin, who bore a part in the narrative, and was always mentioned with approbation for his great good-nature in doing something or other, was a single man; that there was no young Mrs. Martin, no wife in the case; she did suspect danger to her poor little friend from all this hospitality and kindness,—and that if she were not taken care of, she might be required to sink herself for ever.

With this inspiriting notion, her questions increased in number and meaning; and she particularly led Harriet to

talk more of Mr. Martin,—and there was evidently no dislike
to it. Harriet was very ready to speak of the share he had had
in their moonlight walks and merry evening games; and
dwelt a good deal upon his being so very good-humoured
and obliging. "He had gone three miles round one day, in
order to bring her some walnuts, because she had said how
fond she was of them,—and in every thing else he was so
very obliging. He had his shepherd's son into the parlour
one night on purpose to sing to her. She was very fond of
singing. He could sing a little himself. She believed he was
very clever, and understood every thing. He had a very fine
flock; and, while she was with them, he had been bid more
for his wool than any body in the country. She believed every
body spoke well of him. His mother and sisters were very
fond of him. Mrs. Martin had told her one day (and there
was a blush as she said it), that it was impossible for any body
to be a better son; and therefore she was sure whenever he
married he would make a good husband. Not that she
*wanted* him to marry. She was in no hurry at all."

"Well done, Mrs. Martin!" thought Emma. "You know
what you are about."

"And when she had come away, Mrs. Martin was so very
kind as to send Mrs. Goddard a beautiful goose: the finest
goose Mrs. Goddard had ever seen. Mrs. Goddard had
dressed it on a Sunday, and asked all the three teachers, Miss
Nach, and Miss Prince, and Miss Richardson, to sup with
her."

"Mr. Martin, I suppose, is not a man of information beyond the line of his own business. He does not read?"

"Oh, yes!—that is, no—I do not know—but I believe he
has read a good deal—but not what you would think any
thing of. He reads the Agricultural Reports, and some
other books that lie in one of the window seats—but he
reads all *them* to himself. But sometimes of an evening, before we went to cards, he would read something aloud out
of the Elegant Extracts, very entertaining. And I know he
has read the Vicar of Wakefield. He never read the Ro-

mance of the Forest, nor the Children of the Abbey.[1] He had never heard of such books before I mentioned them, but he is determined to get them now as soon as ever he can."

The next question was,—

"What sort of looking man is Mr. Martin?"

"Oh! not handsome—not at all handsome. I thought him very plain at first, but I do not think him so plain now. One does not, you know, after a time. But did you never see him? He is in Highbury every now and then, and he is sure to ride through every week in his way to Kingston. He has passed you very often."

"That may be, and I may have seen him fifty times, but without having any idea of his name. A young farmer, whether on horseback or on foot, is the very last sort of person to raise my curiosity. The yeomanry are precisely the order of people with whom I feel I can have nothing to do. A degree or two lower, and a creditable appearance might interest me; I might hope to be useful to their families in some way or other. But a farmer can need none of my help, and is therefore, in one sense, as much above my notice, as in every other he is below it."

"To be sure. Oh, yes, it is not likely you should ever have observed him; but he knows you very well, indeed—I mean by sight."

"I have no doubt of his being a very respectable young man. I know, indeed, that he is so; and, as such, wish him well. What do you imagine his age to be?"

"He was four-and-twenty the 8th of last June, and my birthday is the 23d: just a fortnight and a day's difference; which is very odd."

"Only four-and-twenty. That is too young to settle. His mother is perfectly right not to be in a hurry. They seem very comfortable as they are, and if she were to take any pains to marry him, she would probably repent it. Six years hence, if he could meet with a good sort of young woman in the same rank as his own, with a little money, it might be very desirable."

"Six years hence! dear Miss Woodhouse, he would be thirty years old."

"Well, and that is as early as most men can afford to marry, who are not born to an independence. Mr. Martin, I imagine, has his fortune entirely to make—cannot be at all beforehand with the world. Whatever money he might come into when his father died, whatever his share of the family property, it is, I dare say, all afloat, all employed in his stock, and so forth; and though, with diligence and good luck, he may be rich in time, it is next to impossible that he should have realised any thing yet."

"To be sure, so it is. But they live very comfortably. They have no in-doors man—else they do not want for any thing; and Mrs. Martin talks of taking a boy another year."

"I wish you may not get into a scrape, Harriet, whenever he does marry,—I mean, as to being acquainted with his wife; for though his sisters, from a superior education, are not to be altogether objected to, it does not follow that he might marry any body at all fit for you to notice. The misfortune of your birth ought to make you particularly careful as to your associates. There can be no doubt of your being a gentleman's daughter, and you must support your claim to that station by every thing within your own power, or there will be plenty of people who would take pleasure in degrading you."

"Yes, to be sure, I suppose there are. But while I visit at Hartfield, and you are so kind to me, Miss Woodhouse, I am not afraid of what any body can do."

"You understand the force of influence pretty well, Harriet; but I would have you so firmly established in good society, as to be independent even of Hartfield and Miss Woodhouse. I want to see you permanently well connected,—and to that end it will be advisable to have as few odd acquaintance as may be; and, therefore, I say, that if you should still be in this country when Mr. Martin marries, I wish you may not be drawn in by your intimacy with the sisters, to be acquainted with the wife, who will probably be some mere farmer's daughter, without education."

"To be sure. Yes. Not that I think Mr. Martin would ever marry any body but what had had some education, and been very well brought up. However, I do not mean to set up my opinion against yours,—and I am sure I shall not wish for the acquaintance of his wife. I shall always have a great regard for the Miss Martins, especially Elizabeth, and should be very sorry to give them up, for they are quite as well educated as me. But if he marries a very ignorant, vulgar woman, certainly I had better not visit her, if I can help it."

Emma watched her through the fluctuations of this speech, and saw no alarming symptoms of love. The young man had been the first admirer, but she trusted there was no other hold, and that there would be no serious difficulty on Harriet's side to oppose any friendly arrangement of her own.

They met Mr. Martin the very next day, as they were walking on the Donwell road. He was on foot, and after looking very respectfully at her, looked with most unfeigned satisfaction at her companion. Emma was not sorry to have such an opportunity of survey; and walking a few yards forward, while they talked together, soon made her quick eye sufficiently acquainted with Mr. Robert Martin. His appearance was very neat, and he looked like a sensible young man, but his person had no other advantage; and when he came to be contrasted with gentlemen, she thought he must lose all the ground he had gained in Harriet's inclination. Harriet was not insensible of manner; she had voluntarily noticed her father's gentleness with admiration as well as wonder. Mr. Martin looked as if he did not know what manner was.

They remained but a few minutes together, as Miss Woodhouse must not be kept waiting; and Harriet then came running to her with a smiling face, and in a flutter of spirits, which Miss Woodhouse hoped very soon to compose.

"Only think of our happening to meet him! How very odd! It was quite a chance, he said, that he had not gone round by Randalls. He did not think we ever walked this road. He thought we walked towards Randalls most days. He has not been able to get the Romance of the Forest yet. He was so busy the last time he was at Kingston that he quite forgot it, but he goes again to-morrow. So very odd we should happen to meet! Well, Miss Woodhouse, is he like what you expected? What do you think of him? Do you think him so very plain?"

"He is very plain, undoubtedly, remarkably plain; but that is nothing, compared with his entire want of gentility. I had no right to expect much, and I did not expect much; but I had no idea that he could be so very clownish, so totally without air. I had imagined him, I confess, a degree or two nearer gentility."

"To be sure," said Harriet, in a mortified voice, "he is not so genteel as real gentlemen."

"I think, Harriet, since your acquaintance with us, you have been repeatedly in the company of some, such very real gentlemen, that you must yourself be struck with the difference in Mr. Martin. At Hartfield, you have had very good specimens of well educated, well bred men. I should be surprised if, after seeing them, you could be in company with Mr. Martin again without perceiving him to be a very inferior creature,—and rather wondering at yourself for having ever thought him at all agreeable before. Do not you begin to feel that now? Were not you struck? I am sure you must have been struck by his awkward look and abrupt manner; and the uncouthness of a voice, which I heard to be wholly unmodulated as I stood here."

"Certainly, he is not like Mr. Knightley. He has not such a fine air and way of walking as Mr. Knightley. I see the difference plain enough. But Mr. Knightley is so very fine a man!"

"Mr. Knightley's air is so remarkably good that it is not fair to compare Mr. Martin with *him*. You might not see one in a hundred, with *gentleman* so plainly written as in Mr.

Knightley. But he is not the only gentleman you have been lately used to. What say you to Mr. Weston and Mr. Elton? Compare Mr. Martin with either of *them*. Compare their manner of carrying themselves; of walking; of speaking; of being silent. You must see the difference."

"Oh, yes, there is a great difference. But Mr. Weston is almost an old man. Mr. Weston must be between forty and fifty."

"Which makes his good manners the more valuable. The older a person grows, Harriet, the more important it is that their manners should not be bad,—the more glaring and disgusting any loudness, or coarseness, or awkwardness becomes. What is passable in youth is detestable in later age. Mr. Martin is now awkward and abrupt; what will he be at Mr. Weston's time of life?"

"There is no saying, indeed," replied Harriet, rather solemnly.

"But there may be pretty good guessing. He will be a completely gross, vulgar farmer,—totally inattentive to appearances, and thinking of nothing but profit and loss."

"Will he, indeed? that will be very bad."

"How much his business engrosses him already, is very plain from the circumstance of his forgetting to enquire for the book you recommended. He was a great deal too full of the market to think of anything else,—which is just as it should be, for a thriving man. What has he to do with books? And I have no doubt that he *will* thrive and be a very rich man in time,—and his being illiterate and coarse need not disturb *us*."

"I wonder he did not remember the book," was all Harriet's answer, and spoken with a degree of grave displeasure which Emma thought might be safely left to itself. She, therefore, said no more for some time. Her next beginning was,—

"In one respect, perhaps, Mr. Elton's manners are superior to Mr. Knightley's or Mr. Weston's. They have more gentleness. They might be more safely held up as a pattern. There is an openness, a quickness, almost a bluntness in Mr.

Weston, which every body likes in *him*, because there is so much good humour with it—but that would not do to be copied. Neither would Mr. Knightley's downright, decided, commanding sort of manner—though it suits *him* very well: his figure, and look, and situation in life seem to allow it; but if any young man were to set about copying him, he would not be sufferable. On the contrary, I think a young man might be very safely recommended to take Mr. Elton as a model. Mr. Elton is good humoured, cheerful, obliging, and gentle. He seems to me to be grown particularly gentle of late. I do not know whether he had any design of ingratiating himself with either of us, Harriet, by additional softness, but it strikes me that his manners are softer than they used to be. If he means any thing, it must be to please you. Did not I tell you what he said of you the other day?"

She then repeated some warm personal praise which she had drawn from Mr. Elton, and now did full justice to; and Harriet blushed and smiled, and said she had always thought Mr. Elton very agreeable.

Mr. Elton was the very person fixed on by Emma for driving the young farmer out of Harriet's head. She thought it would be an excellent match; and only too palpably desirable, natural and probable, for her to have much merit in planning it. She feared it was what every body else must think of and predict. It was not likely, however, that any body should have equalled her in the date of the plan, as it had entered her brain during the very first evening of Harriet's coming to Hartfield. The longer she considered it, the greater was her sense of its expediency. Mr. Elton's situation was most suitable, quite the gentleman himself and without low connections; at the same time not of any family that could fairly object to the doubtful birth of Harriet. He had a comfortable home for her, and Emma imagined a very sufficient income; for though the vicarage of Highbury was not large, he was known to have some independent property; and she thought very highly of him as a good-humoured,

well-meaning, respectable young man, without any deficiency of useful understanding or knowledge of the world.

She had already satisfied herself that he thought Harriet
a beautiful girl, which she trusted, with such frequent meetings at Hartfield, was foundation enough on his side; and on
Harriet's there could be little doubt that the idea of being
preferred by him would have all the usual weight and effi-
cacy. And he was really a very pleasing young man, a young
man whom any woman not fastidious might like. He was
reckoned very handsome; his person much admired in general, though not by her, there being a want of elegance of
feature which she could not dispense with: but the girl who
could be gratified by a Robert Martin's riding about the
country to get walnuts for her might very well be conquered
by Mr. Elton's admiration.

## *Chapter V.*

"I do not know what your opinion may be, Mrs. Weston,"
said Mr. Knightley, "of this great intimacy between
Emma and Harriet Smith, but I think it a bad thing."

"A bad thing! Do you really think it a bad thing?—why
so?"

"I think they will neither of them do the other any good."

"You surprise me! Emma must do Harriet good; and by
supplying her with a new object of interest, Harriet may be
said to do Emma good. I have been seeing their intimacy
with the greatest pleasure. How very differently we feel! Not
think they will do each other any good! This will certainly be
the beginning of one of our quarrels about Emma, Mr.
Knightley."

"Perhaps you think I am come on purpose to quarrel with you, knowing Weston to be out, and that you must still fight your own battle."

"Mr. Weston would undoubtedly support me, if he were here, for he thinks exactly as I do on the subject. We were speaking of it only yesterday, and agreeing how fortunate it was for Emma, that there should be such a girl in Highbury for her to associate with. Mr. Knightley, I shall not allow you to be a fair judge in this case. You are so much used to live alone, that you do not know the value of a companion; and, perhaps, no man can be a good judge of the comforts a woman feels in the society of one of her own sex, after being used to it all her life. I can imagine your objection to Harriet Smith. She is not the superior young woman which Emma's friend ought to be. But, on the other hand, as Emma wants to see her better informed, it will be an inducement to her to read more herself. They will read together. She means it, I know."

"Emma has been meaning to read more ever since she was twelve years old. I have seen a great many lists of her drawing up at various times of books that she meant to read regularly through—and very good lists they were—very well chosen, and very neatly arranged—sometimes alphabetically, and sometimes by some other rule. The list she drew up when only fourteen—I remember thinking it did her judgment so much credit, that I preserved it some time; and I dare say she may have made out a very good list now. But I have done with expecting any course of steady reading from Emma. She will never submit to any thing requiring industry and patience, and a subjection of the fancy to the understanding. Where Miss Taylor failed to stimulate, I may safely affirm that Harriet Smith will do nothing. You never could persuade her to read half so much as you wished. You know you could not."

"I dare say," replied Mrs. Weston, smiling, "that I thought so *then*; but since we have parted, I can never remember Emma's omitting to do any thing I wished."

"There is hardly any desiring to refresh such a memory as *that*," said Mr. Knightley, feelingly; and for a moment or two he had done. "But I," he soon added, "who have had no such charm thrown over my senses, must still see, hear, and remember. Emma is spoiled by being the cleverest of her family. At ten years old she had the misfortune of being able to answer questions which puzzled her sister at seventeen. She was always quick and assured; Isabella slow and diffident. And ever since she was twelve, Emma has been mistress of the house and of you all. In her mother she lost the only person able to cope with her. She inherits her mother's talents, and must have been under subjection to her."

"I should have been sorry, Mr. Knightley, to be dependent on *your* recommendation, had I quitted Mr. Woodhouse's family and wanted another situation; I do not think you would have spoken a good word for me to any body. I am sure you always thought me unfit for the office I held."

"Yes," said he smiling. "You are better placed *here*; very fit for a wife, but not at all for a governess. But you were preparing yourself to be an excellent wife all the time you were at Hartfield. You might not give Emma such a complete education as your powers would seem to promise; but you were receiving a very good education from *her*, on the very material matrimonial point of submitting your own will, and doing as you were bid; and if Weston had asked me to recommend him a wife, I should certainly have named Miss Taylor."

"Thank you. There will be very little merit in making a good wife to such a man as Mr. Weston."

"Why, to own the truth, I am afraid you are rather thrown away, and that with every disposition to bear, there will be nothing to be borne. We will not despair, however. Weston may grow cross from the wantonness of comfort, or his son may plague him."

"I hope not *that*. It is not likely. No, Mr. Knightley, do not foretell vexation from that quarter."

"Not I, indeed. I only name possibilities. I do not pretend

to Emma's genius for foretelling and guessing. I hope, with all my heart, the young man may be a Weston in merit, and a Churchill in fortune. But Harriet Smith,—I have not half done about Harriet Smith. I think her the very worst sort of companion that Emma could possibly have. She knows nothing herself, and looks upon Emma as knowing every thing. She is a flatterer in all her ways; and so much the worse, because undesigned. Her ignorance is hourly flattery. How can Emma imagine she has any thing to learn herself, while Harriet is presenting such a delightful inferiority? And as for Harriet, I will venture to say that *she* cannot gain by the acquaintance. Hartfield will only put her out of conceit with all the other places she belongs to. She will grow just refined enough to be uncomfortable with those among whom birth and circumstances have placed her home. I am much mistaken if Emma's doctrines give any strength of mind, or tend at all to make a girl adapt herself rationally to the varieties of her situation in life. They only give a little polish."

"I either depend more upon Emma's good sense than you do, or am more anxious for her present comfort; for I cannot lament the acquaintance. How well she looked last night."

"Oh, you would rather talk of her person than her mind, would you? Very well; I shall not attempt to deny Emma's being pretty."

"Pretty! say beautiful rather. Can you imagine any thing nearer perfect beauty than Emma altogether—face and figure?"

"I do not know what I could imagine, but I confess that I have seldom seen a face or figure more pleasing to me than hers. But I am a partial old friend."

"Such an eye!—the true hazel eye—and so brilliant! regular features, open countenance, with a complexion—oh, what a bloom of full health, and such a pretty height and size; such a firm and upright figure. There is health, not merely in her bloom, but in her air, her head, her glance. One hears sometimes of a child being 'the picture of health;'

now Emma always gives me the idea of being the complete picture of grown-up health. She is loveliness itself. Mr. Knightley, is not she?"

"I have not a fault to find with her person," he replied. "I think her all you describe. I love to look at her; and I will add this praise, that I do not think her personally vain. Considering how very handsome she is, she appears to be little occupied with it; her vanity lies another way. Mrs. Weston, I am not to be talked out of my dislike of her intimacy with Harriet Smith, or my dread of its doing them both harm."

"And I, Mr. Knightley, am equally stout in my confidence of its not doing them any harm. With all dear Emma's little faults, she is an excellent creature. Where shall we see a better daughter, or a kinder sister, or a truer friend? No, no; she has qualities which may be trusted; she will never lead any one really wrong; she will make no lasting blunder; where Emma errs once, she is in the right a hundred times."

"Very well; I will not plague you any more. Emma shall be an angel, and I will keep my spleen to myself till Christmas brings John and Isabella. John loves Emma with a reasonable and therefore not a blind affection, and Isabella always thinks as he does, except when he is not quite frightened enough about the children. I am sure of having their opinions with me."

"I know that you all love her really too well to be unjust or unkind; but excuse me, Mr. Knightley, if I take the liberty, (I consider myself, you know, as having somewhat of the privilege of speech that Emma's mother might have had,) the liberty of hinting, that I do not think any possible good can arise from Harriet Smith's intimacy being made a matter of much discussion among you. Pray excuse me; but supposing any little inconvenience may be apprehended from the intimacy, it cannot be expected that Emma, accountable to nobody but her father, who perfectly approves the acquaintance, should put an end to it, so long as it is a source of pleasure to herself. It has been so many years my province to give advice, that you cannot be surprised, Mr. Knightley, at this little remains of office."

"Not at all," cried he; "I am much obliged to you for it. It is very good advice, and it shall have a better fate than your advice has often found; for it shall be attended to."

"Mrs. John Knightley is easily alarmed, and might be made unhappy about her sister."

"Be satisfied," said he, "I will not raise any outcry. I will keep my ill-humour to myself. I have a very sincere interest in Emma. Isabella does not seem more my sister: has never excited a greater interest; perhaps hardly so great. There is an anxiety, a curiosity in what one feels for Emma. I wonder what will become of her."

"So do I," said Mrs. Weston, gently, "very much."

"She always declares she will never marry, which, of course, means just nothing at all. But I have no idea that she has yet ever seen a man she cared for. It would not be a bad thing for her to be very much in love with a proper object. I should like to see Emma in love, and in some doubt of a return: it would do her good. But there is nobody hereabouts to attach her; and she goes so seldom from home."

"There does, indeed, seem as little to tempt her to break her resolution at present," said Mrs. Weston, "as can well be; and while she is so happy at Hartfield, I cannot wish her to be forming any attachment which would be creating such difficulties, on poor Mr. Woodhouse's account. I do not recommend matrimony at present to Emma, though I mean no slight to the state, I assure you."

Part of her meaning was to conceal some favorite thoughts of her own and Mr. Weston's on the subject as much as possible. There were wishes at Randalls respecting Emma's destiny, but it was not desirable to have them suspected; and the quiet transition which Mr. Knightley soon afterwards made to

"What does Weston think of the weather?—shall we have rain?"—convinced her that he had nothing more to say or surmise about Hartfield.

# *Chapter VI.*

E
mma could not feel a doubt of having given Harriet's fancy a proper direction, and raised the gratitude of her young vanity to a very good purpose; for she found her decidedly more sensible than before of Mr. Elton's being a remarkably handsome man, with most agreeable manners; and as she had no hesitation in following up the assurance of his admiration by agreeable hints, she was soon pretty confident of creating as much liking on Harriet's side as there could be any occasion for. She was quite convinced of Mr. Elton's being in the fairest way of falling in love, if not in love already. She had no scruple with regard to him. He talked of Harriet; and praised her so warmly, that she could not suppose any thing wanting which a little time would not add. His perception of the striking improvement of Harriet's manner, since her introduction at Hartfield, was not one of the least agreeable proofs of his growing attachment.

"You have given Miss Smith all that she required," said he: "you have made her graceful and easy. She was a beautiful creature when she came to you; but, in my opinion, the attractions you have added are infinitely superior to what she received from nature."

"I am glad you think I have been useful to her; but Harriet only wanted drawing out, and receiving a few, very few, hints. She had all the natural grace of sweetness of temper and artlessness in herself. I have done very little."

"If it were admissible to contradict a lady——" said gallant Mr. Elton.

"I have, perhaps, given her a little more decision of character,—have taught her to think on points which had not fallen in her way before."

"Exactly so; that is what principally strikes me. So much superadded decision of character! Skilful has been the hand."

"Great has been the pleasure, I am sure. I never met with a disposition more truly amiable."

"I have no doubt of it." And it was spoken with a sort of sighing animation which had a vast deal of the lover. She was not less pleased, another day, with the manner in which he seconded a sudden wish of hers—to have Harriet's picture.

"Did you ever have your likeness taken, Harriet?" said she: "did you ever sit for your picture?"

Harriet was on the point of leaving the room, and only stopped to say, with a very interesting *naïveté*,—

"Oh, dear, no,—never."

No sooner was she out of sight than Emma exclaimed,—

"What an exquisite possession a good picture of her would be! I would give any money for it. I almost long to attempt her likeness myself. You do not know it, I dare say; but, two or three years ago, I had a great passion for taking likenesses, and attempted several of my friends, and was thought to have a tolerable eye in general; but, from one cause or another, I gave it up in disgust. But, really, I could almost venture, if Harriet would sit to me. It would be such a delight to have her picture!"

"Let me entreat you," cried Mr. Elton,—"it would indeed be a delight: let me entreat you, Miss Woodhouse, to exercise so charming a talent in favour of your friend. I know what your drawings are. How could you suppose me ignorant? Is not this room rich in specimens of your landscapes and flowers? and has not Mrs. Weston some inimitable figure-pieces in her drawing-room at Randalls?"

Yes, good man!—thought Emma—but what has all that to do with taking likenesses? You know nothing of drawing. Don't pretend to be in raptures about mine. Keep your raptures for Harriet's face. "Well, if you give me such kind encouragement, Mr. Elton, I believe I shall try what I can do. Harriet's features are very delicate, which makes a likeness difficult; and yet there is a peculiarity in the shape of the eye and the lines about the mouth which one ought to catch."

"Exactly so,—the shape of the eye and the lines about the mouth,—I have not a doubt of your success. Pray, pray attempt it. As you will do it, it will indeed, to use your own words, be an exquisite possession."

"But I am afraid, Mr. Elton, Harriet will not like to sit,— she thinks so little of her own beauty. Did not you observe her manner of answering me? How completely it meant, 'Why should my picture be drawn?'"

"Oh, yes, I observed it, I assure you. It was not lost on me. But still I cannot imagine she would not be persuaded."

Harriet was soon back again, and the proposal almost immediately made; and she had no scruples which could stand many minutes against the earnest pressing of both the others. Emma wished to go to work directly, and therefore produced the portfolio containing her various attempts at portraits, for not one of them had ever been finished, that they might decide together on the best size for Harriet. Her many beginnings were displayed. Miniatures, half-lengths, whole-lengths, pencil, crayon, and water-colours had been all tried in turn. She had always wanted to do every thing, and had made more progress both in drawing and music than many might have done with so little labour as she would ever submit to. She played and sang, and drew in almost every style; but steadiness had always been wanting; and in nothing had she approached the degree of excellence which she would have been glad to command, and ought not to have failed of. She was not much deceived as to her own skill, either as an artist or a musician; but she was not unwilling to have others deceived, or sorry to know her reputation for accomplishment often higher than it deserved.

There was merit in every drawing,—in the least finished, perhaps the most. Her style was spirited; but had there been

much less, or had there been ten times more, the delight
and admiration of her two companions would have been the
same. They were both in ecstasies. A likeness pleases every
body; and Miss Woodhouse's performances must be capital.

"No great variety of faces for you," said Emma. "I had only
my own family to study from. There is my father,—another
of my father;—but the idea of sitting for his picture made
him so nervous, that I could only take him by stealth; neither
of them very like, therefore. Mrs. Weston again, and again,
and again, you see. Dear Mrs. Weston—always my kindest
friend on every occasion. She would sit whenever I asked
her. There is my sister; and really quite her own little elegant
figure—and the face not unlike. I should have made a good
likeness of her, if she would have sat longer; but she was in
such a hurry to have me draw her four children that she
would not be quiet. Then, here come all my attempts at
three of those four children:—there they are, Henry, and
John, and Bella, from one end of the sheet to the other, and
any one of them might do for any one of the rest. She was so
eager to have them drawn that I could not refuse; but there
is no making children of three or four years old stand still,
you know; nor can it be very easy to take any likeness of
them, beyond the air and complexion, unless they are
coarser featured than any of mamma's children ever were.
Here is my sketch of the fourth, who was a baby. I took him
as he was sleeping on the sofa, and it is as strong a likeness
of his cockade* as you would wish to see. He had nestled
down his head most conveniently:—that's very like. I am
rather proud of little George. The corner of the sofa is very
good. Then here is my last,"—unclosing a pretty sketch of a
gentleman in small size, whole-length,—"my last and my
best,—my brother, Mr. John Knightley. This did not want
much of being finished, when I put it away in a pet, and
vowed I would never take another likeness. I could not help

---

*Ornamental ribbon or rosette worn on a hat.

being provoked; for after all my pains, and when I had really made a very good likeness of it—(Mrs. Weston and I were quite agreed in thinking it *very* like)—only too handsome— too flattering—but that was a fault on the right side;—after all this, came poor dear Isabella's cold approbation of—'Yes, it was a little like; but to be sure it did not do him justice.' We had had a great deal of trouble in persuading him to sit at all. It was made a great favour of; and altogether it was more than I could bear; and so I never would finish it, to have it apologised over as an unfavourable likeness, to every morning visiter in Brunswick Square; and, as I said, I did then forswear ever drawing any body again. But for Harriet's sake, or rather for my own, and as there are no husbands and wives in the case at present, I will break my resolution now."

Mr. Elton seemed very properly struck and delighted by the idea, and was repeating, "No husbands and wives in the case *at present*, indeed, as you observe. Exactly so. No husbands and wives," with so interesting a consciousness, that Emma began to consider whether she had not better leave them together at once. But as she wanted to be drawing, the declaration must wait a little longer.

She had soon fixed on the size and sort of portrait. It was to be a whole-length in water-colours, like Mr. John Knightley's, and was destined, if she could please herself, to hold a very honourable station over the mantle-piece.

The sitting began; and Harriet, smiling and blushing, and afraid of not keeping her attitude and countenance, presented a very sweet mixture of youthful expression to the steady eyes of the artist. But there was no doing any thing, with Mr. Elton fidgeting behind her, and watching every touch. She gave him credit for stationing himself where he might gaze and gaze again without offence; but was really obliged to put an end to it, and request him to place himself elsewhere. It then occurred to her to employ him in reading.

"If he would be so good as to read to them, it would be a kindness indeed! It would amuse away the difficulties of her part, and lessen the irksomeness of Miss Smith's."

Mr. Elton was only too happy. Harriet listened, and Emma drew in peace. She must allow him to be still frequently coming to look; any thing less would certainly have been too little in a lover; and he was ready at the smallest intermission of the pencil to jump up and see the progress, and be charmed. There was no being displeased with such an encourager, for his admiration made him discern a likeness almost before it was possible. She could not respect his eye, but his love and his complaisance were unexceptionable.

The sitting was altogether very satisfactory: she was quite enough pleased with the first day's sketch to wish to go on. There was no want of likeness: she had been fortunate in the attitude; and as she meant to throw in a little improvement to the figure, to give a little more height, and considerably more elegance, she had great confidence of its being in every way a pretty drawing at last, and of its filling its destined place with credit to them both;—a standing memorial of the beauty of one, the skill of the other, and the friendship of both; with as many other agreeable associations as Mr. Elton's very promising attachment was likely to add.

Harriet was to sit again the next day; and Mr. Elton, just as he ought, entreated for the permission of attending and reading to them again.

"By all means. We shall be most happy to consider you as one of the party."

The same civilities and courtesies, the same success and satisfaction, took place on the morrow, and accompanied the whole progress of the picture, which was rapid and happy. Every body who saw it was pleased, but Mr. Elton was in continual raptures, and defended it through every criticism.

"Miss Woodhouse has given her friend the only beauty she wanted," observed Mrs. Weston to him, not in the least suspecting that she was addressing a lover. "The expression of the eye is most correct, but Miss Smith has not those eyebrows and eyelashes. It is the fault of her face that she has them not."

"Do you think so?" replied he. "I cannot agree with you. It appears to me a most perfect resemblance in every feature. I never saw such a likeness in my life. We must allow for the effect of shade, you know."

"You have made her too tall, Emma," said Mr. Knightley.

Emma knew that she had, but would not own it; and Mr. Elton warmly added,—

"Oh, no—certainly not too tall—not in the least too tall. Consider she is sitting down, which naturally presents a different—which in short gives exactly the idea;—and the proportions must be preserved, you know. Proportions, fore-shortening:—oh no: it gives one exactly the idea of such a height as Miss Smith's;—exactly so, indeed."

"It is very pretty," said Mr. Woodhouse. "So prettily done! Just as your drawings always are, my dear. I do not know any body who draws so well as you do. The only thing I do not thoroughly like is, that she seems to be sitting out of doors, with only a little shawl over her shoulders; and it makes one think she must catch cold."

"But, my dear papa, it is supposed to be summer; a warm day in summer. Look at the tree."

"But it is never safe to sit out of doors, my dear."

"You, sir, may say any thing," cried Mr. Elton; "but I must confess that I regard it as a most happy thought, the placing Miss Smith out of doors; and the tree is touched with such inimitable spirit! Any other situation would have been much less in character. The *naïveté* of Miss Smith's manners,—and altogether—oh, it is most admirable! I cannot keep my eyes from it. I never saw such a likeness."

The next thing wanted was to get the picture framed; and here were a few difficulties. It must be done directly; it must be done in London; the order must go through the hands of some intelligent person whose taste could be depended on; and Isabella, the usual doer of all commissions, must not be applied to, because it was December, and Mr. Woodhouse could not bear the idea of her stirring out of her house in the fogs of December. But no sooner was the distress known to Mr. Elton than it was removed. His gallantry was always on the alert. "Might he be trusted with the commission, what infinite pleasure should he have in executing it! he could ride to London at any time. It was impossible to say how much he should be gratified by being employed on such an errand."

"He was too good!—she could not endure the thought!—she would not give him such a troublesome office for the world,"—brought on the desired repetition of entreaties and assurances,—and a very few minutes settled the business.

Mr. Elton was to take the drawing to London, choose the frame, and give the directions; and Emma thought she could so pack it as to ensure its safety without much incommoding him, while he seemed mostly fearful of not being incommoded enough.

"What a precious deposit!" said he, with a tender sigh, as he received it.

"This man is almost too gallant to be in love," thought Emma. "I should say so, but that I suppose there may be a hundred different ways of being in love. He is an excellent young man, and will suit Harriet exactly: it will be an 'exactly so,' as he says himself; but he does sigh and languish, and study for compliments rather more than I could endure as a principal. I come in for a pretty good share as a second. But it is his gratitude on Harriet's account."

## Chapter VII.

The very day of Mr. Elton's going to London produced a fresh occasion for Emma's services towards her friend. Harriet had been at Hartfield, as usual, soon after breakfast; and after a time, had gone home to return again to dinner: she returned, and sooner than had been talked of, and with an agitated, hurried look, announcing

something extraordinary to have happened which she was
longing to tell. Half a minute brought it all out. She had
heard, as soon as she got back to Mrs. Goddard's, that Mr.
Martin had been there an hour before, and finding she was
not at home, nor particularly expected, had left a little parcel for her from one of his sisters, and gone away; and on
opening this parcel, she had actually found, besides the two
songs which she had lent Elizabeth to copy, a letter to herself; and this letter was from him, from Mr. Martin, and contained a direct proposal of marriage. "Who could have
thought it! She was so surprised she did not know what to do.
Yes, quite a proposal of marriage; and a very good letter, at
least she thought so. And he wrote as if he really loved her
very much—but she did not know—and so, she was come as
fast as she could to ask Miss Woodhouse what she should
do." Emma was half ashamed of her friend for seeming so
pleased and so doubtful.

"Upon my word," she cried, "the young man is determined not to lose any thing for want of asking. He will connect himself well if he can."

"Will you read the letter?" cried Harriet. "Pray do. I'd
rather you would."

Emma was not sorry to be pressed. She read, and was surprised. The style of the letter was much above her expectation. There were not merely no grammatical errors, but as a
composition it would not have disgraced a gentleman: the
language, though plain, was strong and unaffected, and the
sentiments it conveyed very much to the credit of the writer.
It was short, but expressed good sense, warm attachment,
liberality, propriety, even delicacy of feeling. She paused
over it, while Harriet stood anxiously watching for her opinion, with a "Well, well," and was at last forced to add, "Is it a
good letter? or is it too short?"

"Yes, indeed, a very good letter," replied Emma, rather
slowly;—"so good a letter, Harriet, that, every thing considered, I think one of his sisters must have helped him. I can
hardly imagine the young man whom I saw talking with you

the other day could express himself so well, if left quite to his own powers, and yet it is not the style of a woman; no, certainly, it is too strong and concise; not diffuse enough for a woman. No doubt he is a sensible man, and I suppose may have a natural talent for—thinks strongly and clearly—and when he takes a pen in hand, his thoughts naturally find proper words. It is so with some men. Yes, I understand the sort of mind. Vigorous, decided, with sentiments to a certain point, not coarse. A better written letter, Harriet (returning it), than I had expected."

"Well," said the still waiting Harriet;—"well—and—and what shall I do?"

"What shall you do! In what respect? Do you mean with regard to this letter?"

"Yes."

"But what are you in doubt of? You must answer it of course—and speedily."

"Yes. But what shall I say? Dear Miss Woodhouse, do advise me."

"Oh, no, no: the letter had much better be all your own. You will express yourself very properly, I am sure. There is no danger of your not being intelligible, which is the first thing. Your meaning must be unequivocal: no doubts or demurs; and such expressions of gratitude and concern for the pain you are inflicting as propriety requires, will present themselves unbidden to *your* mind, I am persuaded. *You* need not be prompted to write with the appearance of sorrow for his disappointment."

"You think I ought to refuse him, then?" said Harriet, looking down.

"Ought to refuse him! My dear Harriet, what do you mean? Are you in any doubt as to that? I thought—but I beg your pardon, perhaps I have been under a mistake. I certainly have been misunderstanding you, if you feel in doubt as to the *purport* of your answer. I had imagined you were consulting me only as to the wording of it."

Harriet was silent. With a little reserve of manner, Emma continued,—

"You mean to return a favourable answer, I collect."

"No, I do not; that is I do not mean—What shall I do? What would you advise me to do? Pray, dear Miss Woodhouse, tell me what I ought to do?"

"I shall not give you any advice, Harriet. I will have nothing to do with it. This is a point which you must settle with your own feelings."

"I had no notion that he liked me so very much," said Harriet, contemplating the letter. For a little while Emma persevered in her silence; but beginning to apprehend the bewitching flattery of that letter might be too powerful, she thought it best to say,—

"I lay it down as a general rule, Harriet, that if a woman *doubts* as to whether she should accept a man or not, she certainly ought to refuse him. If she can hesitate as to 'Yes,' she ought to say 'No' directly. It is not a state to be safely entered into with doubtful feelings, with half a heart. I thought it my duty as a friend, and older than yourself, to say thus much to you. But do not imagine that I want to influence you."

"Oh, no, I am sure you are a great deal too kind to—— but if you would just advise me what I had best do:—no, no, I do not mean that:—as you say one's mind ought to be quite made up—one should not be hesitating:—it is a very serious thing. It will be safer to say 'No,' perhaps. Do you think I had better say 'No?'"

"Not for the world," said Emma, smiling graciously, "would I advise you either way. You must be the best judge of your own happiness. If you prefer Mr. Martin to every other person; if you think him the most agreeable man you have ever been in company with, why should you hesitate? You blush, Harriet. Does any body else occur to you at this moment under such a definition? Harriet, Harriet, do not deceive yourself; do not be run away with by gratitude and compassion. At this moment whom are you thinking of?"

The symptoms were favourable. Instead of answering,

Harriet turned away confused, and stood thoughtfully by the fire; and though the letter was still in her hand, it was now mechanically twisted about without regard. Emma waited the result with impatience, but not without strong hopes. At last, with some hesitation, Harriet said,—

"Miss Woodhouse, as you will not give me your opinion, I must do as well as I can by myself; and I have now quite determined, and really almost made up my mind, to refuse Mr. Martin. Do you think I am right?"

"Perfectly, perfectly right, my dearest Harriet; you are doing just what you ought. While you were at all in suspense, I kept my feelings to myself, but now that you are so completely decided I have no hesitation in approving. Dear Harriet, I give myself joy of this. It would have grieved me to lose your acquaintance, which must have been the consequence of your marrying Mr. Martin. While you were in the smallest degree wavering, I said nothing about it, because I would not influence; but it would have been the loss of a friend to me. I could not have visited Mrs. Robert Martin, of Abbey-Mill Farm. Now I am secure of you for ever."

Harriet had not surmised her own danger, but the idea of it struck her forcibly.

"You could not have visited me!" she cried, looking aghast. "No, to be sure you could not; but I never thought of that before. That would have been too dreadful! What an escape! Dear Miss Woodhouse, I would not give up the pleasure and honour of being intimate with you for any thing in the world."

"Indeed, Harriet, it would have been a severe pang to lose you; but it must have been. You would have thrown yourself out of all good society. I must have given you up."

"Dear me! How should I ever have borne it? It would have killed me never to come to Hartfield any more."

"Dear, affectionate creature! *You* banished to Abbey-Mill Farm! *You* confined to the society of the illiterate and vulgar all your life! I wonder how the young man could have the assurance to ask it. He must have a pretty good opinion of himself."

"I do not think he is conceited either, in general," said Harriet, her conscience opposing such censure; "at least he is very good natured, and I shall always feel much obliged to him, and have a great regard for—but that is quite a different thing from—and you know, though he may like me, it does not follow that I should—and, certainly, I must confess that since my visiting here I have seen people—and if one comes to compare them, person and manners, there is no comparison at all, *one* is so very handsome and agreeable. However, I do really think Mr. Martin a very amiable young man, and have a great opinion of him; and his being so much attached to me—and his writing such a letter—but as to leaving you, it is what I would not do upon any consideration."

"Thank you, thank you, my own sweet little friend. We will not be parted. A woman is not to marry a man merely because she is asked, or because he is attached to her, and can write a tolerable letter."

"Oh, no;—and it is but a short letter, too."

Emma felt the bad taste of her friend, but let it pass with a "very true; and it would be a small consolation to her, for the clownish manner which might be offending her every hour of the day, to know that her husband could write a good letter."

"Oh yes, very. Nobody cares for a letter: the thing is, to be always happy with pleasant companions. I am quite determined to refuse him. But how shall I do? What shall I say?"

Emma assured her there would be no difficulty in the answer, and advised its being written directly, which was agreed to, in the hope of her assistance; and though Emma continued to protest against any assistance being wanted, it was in fact given in the formation of every sentence. The looking over his letter again, in replying to it, had such a softening tendency, that it was particularly necessary to brace her up with a few decisive expressions; and she was so very much concerned at the idea of making him unhappy, and thought so much of what his mother and sisters would think and say, and was so anxious that they should not fancy her ungrateful, that Emma believed if the young man had come in her way at that moment, he would have been accepted after all.

This letter, however, was written, and sealed, and sent. The business was finished, and Harriet safe. She was rather low all the evening; but Emma could allow for her amiable regrets, and sometimes relieved them by speaking of her own affection, sometimes by bringing forward the idea of Mr. Elton.

"I shall never be invited to Abbey-Mill again," was said in rather a sorrowful tone.

"Nor, if you were, could I ever bear to part with you, my Harriet. You are a great deal too necessary at Hartfield to be spared to Abbey-Mill."

"And I am sure I should never want to go there; for I am never happy but at Hartfield."

Some time afterwards it was, "I think Mrs. Goddard would be very much surprised if she knew what had happened. I am sure Miss Nash would—for Miss Nash thinks her own sister very well married, and it is only a linen-draper."*

"One should be sorry to see greater pride or refinement in the teacher of a school, Harriet. I dare say Miss Nash would envy you such an opportunity as this of being married. Even this conquest would appear valuable in her eyes. As to any thing superior for you, I suppose she is quite in the dark. The attentions of a certain person can hardly be among the tittle-tattle† of Highbury yet. Hitherto I fancy you and I are the only people to whom his looks and manners have explained themselves."

Harriet blushed and smiled, and said something about wondering that people should like her so much. The idea of

---

*Person who sells cloth.
†Gossip.

Mr. Elton was certainly cheering; but still, after a time, she was tender-hearted again towards the rejected Mr. Martin.

"Now he has got my letter," said she softly. "I wonder what they are all doing—whether his sisters know—if he is unhappy, they will be unhappy too. I hope he will not mind it so very much."

"Let us think of those among our absent friends who are more cheerfully employed," cried Emma. "At this moment, perhaps, Mr. Elton is showing your picture to his mother and sisters, telling how much more beautiful is the original, and after being asked for it five or six times, allowing them to hear your name, your own dear name."

"My picture! But he has left my picture in Bond Street."

"Has he so! Then I know nothing of Mr. Elton. No, my dear little modest Harriet, depend upon it, the picture will not be in Bond Street till just before he mounts his horse tomorrow. It is his companion all this evening, his solace, his delight. It opens his designs to his family, it introduces you among them, it diffuses through the party those pleasantest feelings of our nature, eager curiosity and warm prepossession. How cheerful, how animated, how suspicious, how busy their imaginations all are!"

Harriet smiled again, and her smiles grew stronger.

## Chapter VIII.

Harriet slept at Hartfield that night. For some weeks past she had been spending more than half her time there, and gradually getting to have a bed-room appropriated to herself; and Emma judged it best in every respect, safest and kindest, to keep her with them as much as possible just at present. She was obliged to go the next morning for an hour or two to Mrs. Goddard's, but it was then to be settled that she should return to Hartfield, to make a regular visit of some days.

While she was gone, Mr. Knightley called, and sat some time with Mr. Woodhouse and Emma, till Mr. Woodhouse, who had previously made up his mind to walk out, was persuaded by his daughter not to defer it, and was induced by the entreaties of both, though against the scruples of his own civility, to leave Mr. Knightley for that purpose. Mr. Knightley, who had nothing of ceremony about him, was offering, by his short, decided answers, an amusing contrast to the protracted apologies and civil hesitations of the other.

"Well, I believe, if you will excuse me, Mr. Knightley, if you will not consider me as doing a very rude thing, I shall take Emma's advice and go out for a quarter of an hour. As the sun is out, I believe I had better take my three turns while I can. I treat you without ceremony, Mr. Knightley. We invalids think we are privileged people."

"My dear sir, do not make a stranger of me."

"I leave an excellent substitute in my daughter. Emma will be happy to entertain you. And therefore I think I will beg your excuse, and take my three turns—my winter walk."

"You cannot do better, sir."

"I would ask for the pleasure of your company, Mr. Knightley, but I am a very slow walker, and my pace would be tedious to you; and, besides, you have another long walk before you, to Donwell Abbey."

"Thank you, sir, thank you; I am going this moment myself; and I think the sooner *you* go the better. I will fetch your great coat and open the garden door for you."

Mr. Woodhouse at last was off; but Mr. Knightley, instead of being immediately off likewise, sat down again, seemingly inclined for more chat. He began speaking of Harriet, and speaking of her with more voluntary praise than Emma had ever heard before.

"I cannot rate her beauty as you do," said he; "but she is

a pretty little creature, and I am inclined to think very well of her disposition. Her character depends upon those she is with; but in good hands she will turn out a valuable woman."

"I am glad you think so; and the good hands, I hope, may not be wanting."

"Come," said he, "you are anxious for a compliment, so I will tell you that you have improved her. You have cured her of her school-girl's giggle; she really does you credit."

"Thank you. I should be mortified, indeed, if I did not believe I had been of some use; but it is not every body who will bestow praise where they may. *You* do not often overpower me with it."

"You are expecting her again, you say, this morning?"

"Almost every moment. She has been gone longer already than she intended."

"Something has happened to delay her; some visiters, perhaps."

"Highbury gossips! Tiresome wretches!"

"Harriet may not consider every body tiresome that you would."

Emma knew this was too true for contradiction, and, therefore, said nothing. He presently added, with a smile,—

"I do not pretend to fix on times or places, but I must tell you that I have good reason to believe your little friend will soon hear of something to her advantage."

"Indeed! how so? of what sort?"

"A very serious sort, I assure you," still smiling.

"Very serious! I can think of but one thing:—who is in love with her? Who makes you their confidant?"

Emma was more than half in hopes of Mr. Elton's having dropped a hint. Mr. Knightley was a sort of general friend and adviser, and she knew Mr. Elton looked up to him.

"I have reason to think," he replied, "that Harriet Smith will soon have an offer of marriage, and from a most unexceptionable quarter:—Robert Martin is the man. Her visit to Abbey-Mill, this summer, seems to have done his business. He is desperately in love, and means to marry her."

"He is very obliging," said Emma; "but is he sure that Harriet means to marry him?"

"Well, well, means to make her an offer then. Will that do? He came to the Abbey two evenings ago, on purpose to consult me about it. He knows I have a thorough regard for him and all his family, and, I believe, considers me as one of his best friends. He came to ask me whether I thought it would be imprudent in him to settle so early; whether I thought her too young: in short, whether I approved his choice altogether; having some apprehension, perhaps, of her being considered (especially since *your* making so much of her) as in a line of society above him. I was very much pleased with all that he said. I never hear better sense from any one than Robert Martin. He always speaks to the purpose; open, straight-forward, and very well judging. He told me every thing; his circumstances and plans, and what they all proposed doing in the event of his marriage. He is an excellent young man, both as son and brother. I had no hesitation in advising him to marry. He proved to me that he could afford it; and that being the case, I was convinced he could not do better. I praised the fair lady too, and altogether sent him away very happy. If he had never esteemed my opinion before, he would have thought highly of me then; and, I dare say, left the house thinking me the best friend and counsellor man ever had. This happened the night before last. Now, as we may fairly suppose, he would not allow much time to pass before he spoke to the lady, and as he does not appear to have spoken yesterday, it is not unlikely that he should be at Mrs. Goddard's to-day: and she may be detained by a visiter, without thinking him at all a tiresome wretch."

"Pray, Mr. Knightley," said Emma, who had been smiling to herself through a great part of this speech, "how do you know that Mr. Martin did not speak yesterday?"

"Certainly," replied he, surprised, "I do not absolutely know it; but it may be inferred. Was not she the whole day with you?"

"Come," said she, "I will tell you something, in return for what you have told me. He did speak yesterday—that is, he wrote, and was refused."

This was obliged to be repeated before it could be believed; and Mr. Knightley actually looked red with surprise and displeasure, as he stood up, in tall indignation, and said,—

"Then she is a greater simpleton than I ever believed her. What is the foolish girl about?"

"Oh, to be sure," cried Emma, "it is always incomprehensible to a man that a woman should ever refuse an offer of marriage. A man always imagines a woman to be ready for any body who asks her."

"Nonsense! a man does not imagine any such thing. But what is the meaning of this? Harriet Smith refuse Robert Martin! Madness, if it is so; but I hope you are mistaken."

"I saw her answer; nothing could be clearer."

"You saw her answer! you wrote her answer too. Emma, this is your doing. You persuaded her to refuse him."

"And if I did, (which, however, I am far from allowing,) I should not feel that I had done wrong. Mr. Martin is a very respectable young man, but I cannot admit him to be Harriet's equal; and am rather surprised, indeed, that he should have ventured to address her. By your account, he does seem to have had some scruples. It is a pity that they were ever got over."

"Not Harriet's equal!" exclaimed Mr. Knightley, loudly and warmly; and with calmer asperity added, a few moments afterwards, "No, he is not her equal, indeed, for he is as much her superior in sense as in situation. Emma, your infatuation about that girl blinds you. What are Harriet Smith's claims, either of birth, nature, or education, to any connection higher than Robert Martin? She is the natural daughter of nobody knows whom, with probably no settled provision at all, and certainly no respectable relations. She is known only as parlour-boarder at a common school. She is not a sensible girl, nor a girl of any information. She has been taught nothing useful, and is too young and too simple to have acquired any thing herself. At her age she can have no experience; and, with her little wit, is not very likely ever to have any that can avail her. She is pretty, and she is good tempered, and that is all. My only scruple in advising the match was on his account, as being beneath his deserts, and a bad connection for him. I felt that, as to fortune, in all probability he might do much better; and that, as to a rational companion or useful helpmate, he could not do worse. But I could not reason so to a man in love, and was willing to trust to there being no harm in her; to her having that sort of disposition which, in good hands like his, might be easily led aright, and turn out very well. The advantage of the match I felt to be all on her side; and had not the smallest doubt (nor have I now) that there would be a general cryout upon her extreme good luck. Even *your* satisfaction I made sure of. It crossed my mind immediately that you would not regret your friend's leaving Highbury, for the sake of her being settled so well. I remember saying to myself, 'Even Emma, with all her partiality for Harriet, will think this a good match.'"

"I cannot help wondering at your knowing so little of Emma as to say any such thing. What! think a farmer (and with all his sense and all his merit Mr. Martin is nothing more) a good match for my intimate friend! Not regret her leaving Highbury for the sake of marrying a man whom I could never admit as an acquaintance of my own! I wonder you should think it possible for me to have such feelings. I assure you mine are very different. I must think your statement by no means fair. You are not just to Harriet's claims. They would be estimated very differently by others as well as myself; Mr. Martin may be the richest of the two, but he is undoubtedly her inferior as to rank in society. The sphere in which she moves is much above his. It would be a degradation."

"A degradation to illegitimacy and ignorance, to be married to a respectable, intelligent gentleman-farmer!"

"As to the circumstances of her birth, though in a legal sense she may be called Nobody, it will not hold in common sense. She is not to pay for the offence of others, by being held below the level of those with whom she is brought up. There can scarcely be a doubt that her father is a gentleman—and a gentleman of fortune. Her allowance is very liberal; nothing has ever been grudged for her improvement or comfort. That she is a gentleman's daughter is indubitable to me; that she associates with gentlemen's daughters, no one, I apprehend, will deny. She is superior to Mr. Robert Martin."

"Whoever might be her parents," said Mr. Knightley, "whoever may have had the charge of her, it does not appear to have been any part of their plan to introduce her into what you would call good society. After receiving a very indifferent education, she is left in Mrs. Goddard's hands to shift as she can;—to move, in short, in Mrs. Goddard's line, to have Mrs. Goddard's acquaintance. Her friends evidently thought this good enough for her; and it *was* good enough. She desired nothing better herself. Till you chose to turn her into a friend, her mind had no distaste for her own set, nor any ambition beyond it. She was as happy as possible with the Martins in the summer. She had no sense of superiority then. If she has it now, you have given it. You have been no friend to Harriet Smith, Emma. Robert Martin would never have proceeded so far, if he had not felt persuaded of her not being disinclined to him. I know him well. He has too much real feeling to address any woman on the hap-hazard of selfish passion. And as to conceit, he is the farthest from it of any man I know. Depend upon it, he had encouragement."

It was most convenient to Emma not to make a direct reply to this assertion; she chose rather to take up her own line of the subject again.

"You are a very warm friend to Mr. Martin; but, as I said before, are unjust to Harriet. Harriet's claims to marry well are not so contemptible as you represent them. She is not a clever girl, but she has better sense than you are aware of, and does not deserve to have her understanding spoken of so slightingly. Waving that point, however, and supposing her to be, as you describe her, only pretty and good natured, let me tell you, that in the degree she possesses them, they are not trivial recommendations to the world in general, for she is, in fact, a beautiful girl, and must be thought so by ninety-nine people out of a hundred; and till it appears that men are much more philosophic on the subject of beauty than they are generally supposed; till they do fall in love with well-informed minds instead of handsome faces, a girl, with such loveliness as Harriet, has a certainty of being admired and sought after, of having the power of choosing from among many, consequently a claim to be nice.* Her good nature, too, is not so very slight a claim, comprehending, as it does, real, thorough sweetness of temper and manner, a very humble opinion of herself, and a great readiness to be pleased with other people. I am very much mistaken if your sex in general would not think such beauty, and such temper, the highest claims a woman could possess."

"Upon my word, Emma, to hear you abusing the reason you have is almost enough to make me think so too. Better be without sense, than misapply it as you do."

"To be sure," cried she playfully. "I know *that* is the feeling of you all. I know that such a girl as Harriet is exactly what every man delights in—what at once bewitches his senses and satisfies his judgment. Oh, Harriet may pick and choose. Were you, yourself, ever to marry, she is the very woman for you. And is she, at seventeen, just entering into life, just beginning to be known, to be wondered at because she does not accept the first offer she receives? No—pray let her have time to look about her."

"I have always thought it a very foolish intimacy," said Mr. Knightley presently, "though I have kept my thoughts to my-

---

*Cultured, refined.

self; but I now perceive that it will be a very unfortunate one for Harriet. You will puff her up with such ideas of her own beauty, and of what she has a claim to, that, in a little while, nobody within her reach will be good enough for her. Vanity working on a weak head produces every sort of mischief. Nothing so easy as for a young lady to raise her expectations too high. Miss Harriet Smith may not find offers of marriage flow in so fast, though she is a very pretty girl. Men of sense, whatever you may choose to say, do not want silly wives. Men of family would not be very fond of connecting themselves with a girl of such obscurity,—and most prudent men would be afraid of the inconvenience and disgrace they might be involved in, when the mystery of her parentage came to be revealed. Let her marry Robert Martin, and she is safe, respectable, and happy for ever; but if you encourage her to expect to marry greatly, and teach her to be satisfied with nothing less than a man of consequence and large fortune, she may be a parlour-boarder at Mrs. Goddard's all the rest of her life,—or, at least (for Harriet Smith is a girl who will marry somebody or other), till she grow desperate, and is glad to catch at the old writing master's son."

"We think so very differently on this point, Mr. Knightley, that there can be no use in canvassing it. We shall only be making each other more angry. But as to my *letting* her marry Robert Martin, it is impossible: she has refused him, and so decidedly, I think, as must prevent any second application. She must abide by the evil of having refused him, whatever it may be; and as to the refusal itself, I will not pretend to say that I might not influence her a little; but I assure you there was very little for me or for any body to do. His appearance is so much against him, and his manner so bad, that if she ever were disposed to favour him, she is not now. I can imagine, that before she had seen any body superior, she might tolerate him. He was the brother of her friends, and he took pains to please her; and altogether, having seen nobody better (that must have been his great assistant), she might not, while she was at Abbey-Mill, find him disagreeable. But the case is altered now. She knows now what gentlemen are; and nothing but a gentleman in education and manner has any chance with Harriet."

"Nonsense, arrant nonsense, as ever was talked!" cried Mr. Knightley. "Robert Martin's manners have sense, sincerity, and good-humour to recommend them; and his mind has more true gentility than Harriet Smith could understand."

Emma made no answer, and tried to look cheerfully unconcerned, but was really feeling uncomfortable, and wanting him very much to be gone. She did not repent what she had done; she still thought herself a better judge of such a point of female right and refinement than he could be: but yet she had a sort of habitual respect for his judgment in general, which made her dislike having it so loudly against her; and to have him sitting just opposite to her in angry state, was very disagreeable. Some minutes passed in this unpleasant silence, with only one attempt on Emma's side to talk of the weather, but he made no answer. He was thinking. The result of his thoughts appeared at last in these words,—

"Robert Martin has no great loss—if he can but think so; and I hope it will not be long before he does. Your views for Harriet are best known to yourself; but as you make no secret of your love of match-making, it is fair to suppose that views, and plans, and projects you have;—and as a friend I shall just hint to you, that if Elton is the man, I think it will be all labour in vain."

Emma laughed and disclaimed. He continued,—

"Depend upon it, Elton will not do. Elton is a good sort of man, and a very respectable vicar of Highbury, but not at all likely to make an imprudent match. He knows the value of a good income as well as any body. Elton may talk sentimentally but he will act rationally. He is as well acquainted with his own claims as you can be with Harriet's. He knows that he is a very handsome young man, and a great favourite wherever he goes; and from his general way of talking in unreserved moments, when there are only men present, I am convinced that he does not mean to throw himself away. I have heard him speak with great animation of a large family of young ladies that his sisters are intimate with, who have all twenty thousand pounds apiece."

"I am very much obliged to you," said Emma, laughing again. "If I had set my heart on Mr. Elton's marrying Harriet, it would have been very kind to open my eyes; but at present I only want to keep Harriet to myself. I have done with match-making, indeed. I could never hope to equal my own doings at Randalls. I shall leave off while I am well."

"Good morning to you," said he, rising and walking off abruptly. He was very much vexed. He felt the disappointment of the young man, and was mortified to have been the means of promoting it, by the sanction he had given; and the part which he was persuaded Emma had taken in the affair was provoking him exceedingly.

Emma remained in a state of vexation too; but there was more indistinctness in the cause of hers than in his. She did not always feel so absolutely satisfied with herself, so entirely convinced that her opinions were right and her adversary's wrong, as Mr. Knightley. He walked off in more complete self-approbation than he left for her. She was not so materially cast down, however, but that a little time and the return of Harriet were very adequate restoratives. Harriet's staying away so long was beginning to make her uneasy. The possibility of the young man's coming to Mrs. Goddard's that morning, and meeting with Harriet, and pleading his own cause, gave alarming ideas. The dread of such a failure, after all, became the prominent uneasiness; and when Harriet appeared, and in very good spirits, and without having any such reason to give for her long absence, she felt a satisfaction which settled her with her own mind; and convinced her, that, let Mr. Knightley think or say what he would, she had done nothing which woman's friendship and woman's feelings would not justify.

He had frightened her a little about Mr. Elton; but when she considered that Mr. Knightley could not have observed him as she had done, neither with the interest nor (she must

be allowed to tell herself, in spite of Mr. Knightley's pretensions) with the skill of such an observer on such a question
as herself, that he had spoken it hastily and in anger, she was
able to believe, that he had rather said what he wished re-
sentfully to be true, than what he knew any thing about. He
certainly might have heard Mr. Elton speak with more unreserve than she had ever done, and Mr. Elton might not be of
an imprudent, inconsiderate disposition, as to money matters: he might naturally be rather attentive than otherwise to
them; but then, Mr. Knightley did not make due allowance
for the influence of a strong passion at war with all interested
motives. Mr. Knightley saw no such passion, and of course
thought nothing of its effects; but she saw too much of it to
feel a doubt of its overcoming any hesitations that a reasonable prudence might originally suggest; and more than a
reasonable, becoming degree of prudence, she was very sure
did not belong to Mr. Elton.

Harriet's cheerful look and manner established hers: she
came back, not to think of Mr. Martin, but to talk of Mr.
Elton. Miss Nash had been telling her something, which she
repeated immediately with great delight. Mr. Perry had been
to Mrs. Goddard's to attend a sick child, and Miss Nash had
seen him; and he had told Miss Nash, that as he was coming
back yesterday from Clayton Park he had met Mr. Elton, and
found, to his great surprise, that Mr. Elton was actually on his
road to London, and not meaning to return till the morrow,
though it was the whist-club* night, which he had been
never known to miss before; and Mr. Perry had remon-
strated with him about it, and told him how shabby it was in
him, their best player, to absent himself, and tried very much
to persuade him to put off his journey only one day; but it
would not do: Mr. Elton had been determined to go on, and
had said, in a *very particular* way indeed, that he was going on
business which he would not put off for any inducement in

---

*Whist is a four-person card game.

the world; and something about a very enviable commission, and being the bearer of something exceedingly precious. Mr. Perry could not quite understand him, but he was very sure there must be a *lady* in the case, and he told him so; and Mr. Elton only looked very conscious and smiling, and rode off in great spirits. Miss Nash had told her all this, and had talked a great deal more about Mr. Elton; and said, looking so very significantly at her, "that she did not pretend to understand what his business might be, but she only knew, that any woman whom Mr. Elton could prefer she should think the luckiest woman in the world; for, beyond a doubt, Mr. Elton had not his equal for beauty or agreeableness."

## Chapter IX.

M r. Knightley might quarrel with her, but Emma could not quarrel with herself. He was so much displeased, that it was longer than usual before he came to Hartfield again; and when they did meet, his grave looks showed that she was not forgiven. She was sorry, but could not repent. On the contrary, her plans and proceedings were more and more justified, and endeared to her by the general appearances of the next few days.

The picture, elegantly framed, came safely to hand soon after Mr. Elton's return, and being hung over the mantlepiece of the common sitting-room, he got up to look at it, and sighed out his half sentences of admiration just as he ought; and as for Harriet's feelings, they were visibly forming themselves into as strong an attachment as her youth and sort of mind admitted. Emma was soon perfectly satisfied of Mr. Martin's being no otherwise remembered, than as he furnished a contrast with Mr. Elton, of the utmost advantage to the latter.

Her views of improving her little friend's mind, by a great deal of useful reading and conversation, had never yet led to more than a few first chapters, and the intention of going on to-morrow. It was much easier to chat than to study; much pleasanter to let her imagination range and work at Harriet's fortune, than to be labouring to enlarge her comprehension, or exercise it on sober facts; and the only literary pursuit which engaged Harriet at present, the only mental provision she was making for the evening of life, was the collecting and transcribing all the riddles of every sort that she could meet with, into a thin quarto* of hot-pressed paper, made up by her friend, and ornamented with ciphers and trophies.

In this age of literature, such collections on a very grand scale are not uncommon. Miss Nash, head teacher at Mrs. Goddard's, had written out at least three hundred; and Harriet, who had taken the first hint of it from her, hoped, with Miss Woodhouse's help, to get a great many more. Emma assisted with her invention, memory, and taste; and as Harriet wrote a very pretty hand, it was likely to be an arrangement of the first order, in form as well as quantity.

Mr. Woodhouse was almost as much interested in the business as the girls, and tried very often to recollect something worth their putting in. "So many clever riddles as there used to be when he was young—he wondered he could not remember them; but he hoped he should in time." And it always ended in "Kitty, a fair but frozen maid."†

His good friend Perry, too, whom he had spoken to on the subject, did not at present recollect any thing of the riddle kind; but he had desired Perry to be upon the watch, and

---

*Book made by folding whole sheets of paper twice to produce four leaves out of each original sheet.

†See page 74 and endnote 5.

as he went about so much, something, he thought, might come from that quarter.

It was by no means his daughter's wish that the intellects of Highbury in general should be put under requisition. Mr. Elton was the only one whose assistance she asked. He was invited to contribute any really good enigmas, charades, or conundrums, that he might recollect; and she had the pleasure of seeing him most intently at work with his recollections; and at the same time, as she could perceive, most earnestly careful that nothing ungallant, nothing that did not breathe a compliment to the sex, should pass his lips. They owed to him their two or three politest puzzles; and the joy and exultation with which at last he recalled, and rather sentimentally recited, that well-known charade,—

> My first doth affliction denote,
> Which my second is destin'd to feel;
> And my whole is the best antidote
> That affliction to soften and heal,—[2]

made her quite sorry to acknowledge that they had transcribed it some pages ago already.

"Why will you not write one yourself for us, Mr. Elton?" said she; "that is the only security for its freshness; and nothing could be easier to you."

"Oh, no; he had never written, hardly ever, any thing of the kind in his life. The stupidest fellow! He was afraid not even Miss Woodhouse"—he stopped a moment—"or Miss Smith could inspire him."

The very next day, however, produced some proof of inspiration. He called for a few moments, just to leave a piece of paper on the table containing, as he said, a charade which a friend of his had addressed to a young lady, the object of his admiration; but which, from his manner, Emma was immediately convinced must be his own.

"I do not offer it for Miss Smith's collection," said he. "Being my friend's, I have no right to expose it in any de-

gree to the public eye, but perhaps you may not dislike looking at it."

The speech was more to Emma than to Harriet, which
Emma could understand. There was deep consciousness
about him, and he found it easier to meet her eye than her
friend's. He was gone the next moment:—after another moment's pause,—

"Take it,"—said Emma, smiling, and pushing the paper
towards Harriet,—"it is for you. Take your own."

But Harriet was in a tremour, and could not touch it; and
Emma, never loth to be first, was obliged to examine it herself.

### To Miss———

#### CHARADE.

My first displays the wealth and pomp of kings,
    Lords of the earth! their luxury and ease.
Another view of man, my second brings,
    Behold him there, the monarch of the seas!

But ah! united, what reverse we have!
    Man's boasted power and freedom, all are flown;
Lord of the earth and sea, he bends a slave,
    And woman, lovely woman, reigns alone.

    Thy ready wit the word will soon supply,
    May its approval beam in that soft eye!

She cast her eye over it, pondered, caught the meaning,
read it through again to be quite certain, and quite mistress
of the lines, and then passing it to Harriet, sat happily, smiling, and saying to herself, while Harriet was puzzling over
the paper in all the confusion of hope and dulness, "Very
well, Mr. Eton, very well, indeed. I have read worse charades.
*Courtship*—a very good hint. I give you credit for it. This is
feeling your way. This is saying very plainly—'Pray, Miss

Smith, give me leave to pay my addresses to you. Approve my charade and my intentions in the same glance.'

> May its approval beam in that soft eye!

Harriet exactly. Soft is the very word for her eye—of all epithets, the justest that could be given.

> Thy ready wit the word will soon supply.

Humph—Harriet's ready wit! All the better. A man must be very much in love, indeed, to describe her so. Ah! Mr. Knightley, I wish you had the benefit of this; I think this would convince you. For once in your life you would be obliged to own yourself mistaken. An excellent charade, indeed—and very much to the purpose. Things must come to a crisis soon now."

She was obliged to break off from these very pleasant observations, which were otherwise of a sort to run into great length, by the eagerness of Harriet's wondering opinions.

"What can it be, Miss Woodhouse?—what can it be? I have not an idea—I cannot guess it in the least. What can it possibly be? Do try to find it out, Miss Woodhouse. Do help me. I never saw any thing so hard. Is it kindgom? I wonder who the friend was—and who could be the young lady. Do you think it is a good one? Can it be woman?

> And woman, lovely woman, reigns alone.

Can it be Neptune?

> Behold him there, this monarch of the seas!

Or a trident? or a mermaid? or a shark? Oh, no: shark is only one syllable. It must be very clever, or he would not have brought it. Oh, Miss Woodhouse, do you think we shall ever find it out?"

"Mermaids and sharks! Nonsense! My dear Harriet, what are you thinking of? Where would be the use of his bringing us a charade made by a friend upon a mermaid or a shark? Give me the paper, and listen.

**"For Miss——, read Miss Smith.**

My first displays the wealth and pomp of kings,
    Lords of the earth! their luxury and ease.

That is *court*.

Another view of man, my second brings;
    Behold him there, the monarch of the seas!

That is *ship*,—plain as he can be.—Now for the cream.

But ah! united (*courtship*, you know,) what reverse we have!
    Man's boasted power and freedom, all are flown.
Lord of the earth and sea, he bends a slave,
    And woman, lovely woman, reigns alone.

A very proper compliment!—and then follows the application, which I think, my dear Harriet, you cannot find much difficulty in comprehending. Read it in comfort to yourself. There can be no doubt of its being written for you and to you."

Harriet could not long resist so delightful a persuasion. She read the concluding lines, and was all flutter and happiness. She could not speak. But she was not wanted to speak. It was enough for her to feel. Emma spoke for her.

"There is so pointed, and so particular a meaning in this compliment," said she, "that I cannot have a moment's doubt as to Mr. Elton's intentions. You are his object,—and you will soon receive the completest proof of it. I thought it must be so. I thought I could not be so deceived; but now it is clear: the state of his mind is as clear and decided as my wishes on the subject have been ever since I knew you. Yes, Harriet, just so long have I been wanting the very circumstance to happen which has happened. I could never tell whether an attachment between you and Mr. Elton were most desirable or most natural. Its probability and its eligibility have really so equalled each other! I am very happy. I congratulate you, my dear Harriet, with all my heart. This is an attachment which a woman may well feel pride in creating. This is a connection which offers nothing but good. It will give you every thing that you want,—consideration, independence, a proper home,—it will fix you in the centre of all your real friends, close to Hartfield and to me, and confirm our intimacy for ever. This, Harriet, is an alliance which can never raise a blush in either of us."

"Dear Miss Woodhouse," and "Dear Miss Woodhouse," was all that Harriet, with many tender embraces, could articulate at first; but when they did arrive at something more like conversation, it was sufficiently clear to her friend that she saw, felt, anticipated, and remembered just as she ought. Mr. Elton's superiority had very ample acknowledgment.

"Whatever you say is always right," cried Harriet, "and therefore I suppose, and believe, and hope it must be so; but otherwise I could not have imagined it. It is so much beyond any thing I deserve. Mr. Elton, who might marry any body! There cannot be two opinions about *him*. He is so very superior. Only think of those sweet verses—'To Miss———.' Dear me, how clever! Could it really be meant for me?"

"I cannot make a question, or listen to a question about that. It is a certainty. Receive it on my judgment. It is a sort of prologue to the play, a motto to the chapter; and will be soon followed by matter-of-fact prose."

"It is a sort of thing which nobody could have expected. I am sure, a month ago, I had no more idea myself!—The strangest things do take place!"

"When Miss Smiths and Mr. Eltons get acquainted—they do indeed—and really it is strange; it is out of the common course that what is so evidently, so palpably desirable—what courts the pre-arrangement of other people—should so immediately shape itself into the proper form. You and Mr. Elton are by situation called together; you belong to one another by every circumstance of your respective homes. Your marrying will be equal to the match at Randalls. There does seem to be a something in the air of Hartfield which gives love exactly the right direction, and sends it into the very channel where it ought to flow.

The course of true love never did run smooth—[3]

A Hartfield edition of Shakspeare would have a long note on that passage."

"That Mr. Elton should really be in love with me,—me, of all people, who did not know him, to speak to him, at Michaelmas![4] And he, the very handsomest man that ever was, and a man that every body looks up to, quite like Mr. Knightley! His company so sought after, that every body says he need not eat a single meal by himself if he does not choose it; that he has more invitations than there are days in the week. And so excellent in the church! Miss Nash has put down all the texts he has ever preached from since he came to Highbury. Dear me! When I look back to the first time I saw him! How little did I think! The two Abbotts and I ran into the front room and peeped through the blind when we heard he was going by, and Miss Nash came and scolded us away, and staid* to look through herself; however, she called me back presently, and let me look too, which was very good-natured. And how beautiful we thought he looked! He was arm in arm with Mr. Cole."

"This is an alliance which, whoever—whatever your friends may be, must be agreeable to them, provided at least they have common sense; and we are not to be addressing our conduct to fools. If they are anxious to see you *happily* married, here is a man whose amiable character gives every

---

*Stayed.

assurance of it: if they wish to have you settled in the same country and circle which they have chosen to place you in, here it will be accomplished; and if their only object is that you should, in the common phrase, be *well* married, here is the comfortable fortune, the respectable establishment, the rise in the world which must satisfy them."

"Yes, very true. How nicely you talk! I love to hear you. You understand every thing. You and Mr. Elton are one as clever as the other. This charade! If I had studied a twelve-month, I could never have made any thing like it."

"I thought he meant to try his skill, by his manner of declining it yesterday."

"I do think it is, without exception, the best charade I ever read."

"I never read one more to the purpose, certainly."

"It is as long again as almost all we have had before."

"I do not consider its length as particularly in its favour. Such things in general cannot be too short."

Harriet was too intent on the lines to hear. The most satisfactory comparisons were rising in her mind.

"It is one thing," said she, presently, her cheeks in a glow, "to have very good sense in a common way, like every body else, and if there is any thing to say, to sit down and write a letter, and say just what you must, in a short way; and another, to write verses and charades like this."

Emma could not have desired a more spirited rejection of Mr. Martin's prose.

"Such sweet lines!" continued Harriet—"these two last! But how shall I ever be able to return the paper, or say I have found it out? Oh, Miss Woodhouse what can we do about that?"

"Leave it to me. You do nothing. He will be here this evening, I dare say, and then I will give it him back, and some nonsense or other will pass between us, and you shall not be committed. Your soft eyes shall choose their own time for beaming. Trust to me."

"Oh, Miss Woodhouse, what a pity that I must not write

this beautiful charade into my book! I am sure I have not got one half so good."

"Leave out the two last lines, and there is no reason why you should not write it into your book."

"Oh, but those two lines are——"—"The best of all. Granted;—for private enjoyment; and for private enjoyment keep them. They are not at all the less written you know, because you divide them. The couplet does not cease to be, nor does its meaning change. But take it away, and all *appropriation* ceases, and a very pretty gallant charade remains, fit for any collection. Depend upon it, he would not like to have his charade slighted much better than his passion. A poet in love must be encouraged in both capacities, or neither. Give me the book, I will write it down, and then there can be no possible reflection on you."

Harriet submitted, though her mind could hardly separate the parts, so as to feel quite sure that her friend were not writing down a declaration of love. It seemed too precious an offering for any degree of publicity.

"I shall never let that book go out of my own hands," said she.

"Very well," replied Emma, "a most natural feeling, and the longer it lasts, the better I shall be pleased. But here is my father coming: you will not object to my reading the charade to him. It will be giving him so much pleasure. He loves any thing of the sort, and especially any thing that pays woman a compliment. He has the tenderest spirit of gallantry towards us all. You must let me read it to him."

Harriet looked grave.

"My dear Harriet, you must not refine too much upon this charade. You will betray your feelings improperly, if you are too conscious and too quick, and appear to affix more meaning, or even quite all the meaning which may be affixed to it. Do not be overpowered by such a little tribute of admiration. If he had been anxious for secrecy, he would not have left the paper while I was by; but he rather pushed it towards me than towards you. Do not let us be too solemn on the business. He has encouragement enough to proceed, without our sighing out our souls over this charade."

"Oh no: I hope I shall not be ridiculous about it. Do as you please."

Mr. Woodhouse came in, and very soon led to the subject again, by the recurrence of his very frequent enquiry of "Well, my dears, how does your book go on? Have you got any thing fresh?"

"Yes, papa; we have something to read you, something quite fresh. A piece of paper was found on the table this morning—(dropped, we suppose, by a fairy)—containing a very pretty charade, and we have just copied it in."

She read it to him, just as he liked to have any thing read, slowly and distinctly, and two or three times over, with explanations of every part as she proceeded; and he was very much pleased, and, as she had foreseen, especially struck with the complimentary conclusion.

"Ay, that's very just, indeed; that's very properly said. Very true. 'Woman, lovely woman.' It is such a pretty charade, my dear, that I can easily guess what fairy brought it. Nobody could have written so prettily but you, Emma."

Emma only nodded, and smiled. After a little thinking, and a very tender sigh, he added,—

"Ah, it is no difficulty to see who you take after. Your dear mother was so clever at all those things. If I had but her memory. But I can remember nothing; not even that particular riddle which you have heard me mention: I can only recollect the first stanza; and there are several.

> Kitty, a fair but frozen maid,
>     Kindled a flame I yet deplore;
> The hoodwink'd boy I called to aid,
> Though of his near approach afraid,
>     So fatal to my suit before.[5]

And that is all that I can recollect of it; but it is very clever all the way through. But I think, my dear, you said you had got it."

"Yes, papa, it is written out in our second page. We copied it from the Elegant Extracts. It was Garrick's, you know."

"Ay, very true:—I wish I could recollect more of it.

> Kitty, a fair but frozen maid,

The name makes me think of poor Isabella; for she was very near being christened Catherine after her grand-mamma. I hope we shall have her here next week. Have you thought, my dear, where you shall put her, and what room there will be for the children?

"Oh yes—she will have her own room, of course; the room she always has;—and there is the nursery for the children,—just as usual, you know. Why should there be any change?"

"I do not know, my dear—but it is so long since she was here:—not since last Easter, and then only for a few days. Mr. John Knightley's being a lawyer is very inconvenient. Poor Isabella!—she is sadly taken away from us all;—and how sorry she will be when she comes, not to see Miss Taylor here."

"She will not be surprised, papa, at least."

"I do not know, my dear. I am sure I was very much surprised when I first heard she was going to be married."

"We must ask Mr. and Mrs. Weston to dine with us, while Isabella is here."

"Yes, my dear, if there is time. But—(in a very depressed tone)—she is coming for only one week. There will not be time for any thing."

"It is unfortunate that they cannot stay longer,—but it seems a case of necessity. Mr. John Knightley must be in town again on the 28th; and we ought to be thankful, papa, that we are to have the whole of the time they can give to the country, that two or three days are not to be taken out for the Abbey. Mr. Knightley promises to give up his claim this Christmas, though you know it is longer since they were with him than with us."

"It would be very hard, indeed, my dear, if poor Isabella were to be any where but at Hartfield."

Mr. Woodhouse could never allow for Mr. Knightley's claims on his brother, or any body's claims on Isabella, except his own. He sat musing a little while, and then said,—

"But I do not see why poor Isabella should be obliged to go back so soon, though he does. I think, Emma, I shall try and persuade her to stay longer with us. She and the children might stay very well."

"Ah, papa, that is what you never have been able to accomplish, and I do not think you ever will. Isabella cannot bear to stay behind her husband."

This was too true for contradiction. Unwelcome as it was, Mr. Woodhouse could only give a submissive sigh; and as Emma saw his spirits affected by the idea of his daughter's attachment to her husband, she immediately led to such a branch of the subject as must raise them.

"Harriet must give us as much of her company as she can while my brother and sister are here. I am sure she will be pleased with the children. We are very proud of the children, are not we, papa? I wonder which she will think the handsomest, Henry or John?"

"Ay, I wonder which she will. Poor little dears, how glad they will be to come. They are very fond of being at Hartfield, Harriet."

"I dare say they are, sir. I am sure I do not know who is not."

"Henry is a fine boy, but John is very like his mamma. Henry is the eldest, he was named after me, not after his father. John, the second, is named after his father. Some people are surprised, I believe, that the eldest was not, but Isabella would have him called Henry, which I thought very pretty of her. And he is a very clever boy, indeed. They are all remarkably clever; and they have so many pretty ways. They will come and stand by my chair and say, 'Grandpapa, can you give me a bit of string?' and once Henry asked me for a knife, but I told him knives were only made for grandpapas. I think their father is too rough with them very often."

"He appears rough to you," said Emma, "because you are so very gentle yourself; but if you could compare him with other papas, you would not think him rough. He wishes his boys to be active and hardy; and if they misbehave, can give them a sharp word now and then: but he is an affectionate father—certainly Mr. John Knightley is an affectionate father. The children are all fond of him."

"And then their uncle comes in, and tosses them up to the ceiling in a very frightful way."

"But they like it, papa; there is nothing they like so much. It is such enjoyment to them, that if their uncle did not lay down the rule of their taking turns, which ever began would never give way to the other."

"Well, I cannot understand it."

"That is the case with us all, papa. One half of the world cannot understand the pleasures of the other."

Later in the morning, and just as the girls were going to separate in preparation for the regular four o'clock dinner, the hero of this inimitable charade walked in again. Harriet turned away: but Emma could receive him with the usual smile, and her quick eye soon discerned in his the consciousness of having made a push—of having thrown a die; and she imagined he was come to see how it might turn up. His ostensible reason, however, was to ask whether Mr. Woodhouse's party could be made up in the evening without him, or whether he should be in the smallest degree necessary at Hartfield. If he were, every thing else must give way; but otherwise his friend Cole had been saying so much about his dining with him—had made such a point of it— that he had promised him conditionally to come.

Emma thanked him, but could not allow of his disappointing his friend on their account; her father was sure of his rubber. He re-urged—she re-declined; and he seemed then about to make his bow, when, taking the paper from the table, she returned it.

"Oh, here is the charade you were so obliging as to leave with us; thank you for the sight of it. We admired it so much, that I have ventured to write it into Miss Smith's collection.

Your friend will not take it amiss I hope. Of course I have not transcribed beyond the eight first lines."

Mr. Elton certainly did not very well know what to say. He looked rather doubtingly—rather confused; said something about "honour;"—glanced at Emma and at Harriet, and then seeing the book open on the table, took it up, and examined it very attentively. With the view of passing off an awkward moment, Emma smilingly said,—

"You must make my apologies to your friend; but so good a charade must not be confined to one or two. He may be sure of every woman's approbation while he writes with such gallantry."

"I have no hesitation in saying," replied Mr. Elton, though hesitating a good deal while he spoke,—"I have no hesitation in saying—at least if my friend feels at all as *I* do—I have not the smallest doubt that, could he see his little effusion honoured as *I* see it, (looking at the book again, and replacing it on the table,) he would consider it as the proudest moment of his life."

After this speech he was gone as soon as possible. Emma could not think it too soon; for with all his good and agreeable qualities there was a sort of parade in his speeches which was very apt to incline her to laugh. She ran away to indulge the inclination, leaving the tender and the sublime of pleasure to Harriet's share.

# Chapter X.

Though now the middle of December, there had yet been no weather to prevent the young ladies from tolerably regular exercise; and on the morrow, Emma had a charitable visit to pay to a poor sick family who lived a little way out of Highbury.

Their road to this detached cottage was down Vicarage Lane, a lane leading at right-angles from the broad, though irregular, main street of the place; and, as may be inferred, containing the blessed abode of Mr. Elton. A few inferior dwellings were first to be passed, and then, about a quarter of a mile down the lane, rose the vicarage; an old and not very good house, almost as close to the road as it could be. It had no advantage of situation: but had been very much smartened up by the present proprietor; and, such as it was, there could be no possibility of the two friends passing it without a slackened pace and observing eyes. Emma's remark was,—

"There it is. There go you and your riddle-book one of these days." Harriet's was,—

"Oh, what a sweet house! How very beautiful! There are the yellow curtains that Miss Nash admires so much."

"I do not often walk this way *now*," said Emma, as they proceeded, "but *then* there will be an inducement, and I shall gradually get intimately acquainted with all the hedges, gates, pools, and pollards of this part of Highbury."

Harriet, she found, had never in her life been within-side the vicarage; and her curiosity to see it was so extreme, that, considering exteriors and probabilities, Emma could only class it, as a proof of love, with Mr. Elton's seeing ready wit in her.

"I wish we could contrive it," said she; "but I cannot think of any tolerable pretence for going in;—no servant that I want to enquire about of his housekeeper—no message from my father."

She pondered, but could think of nothing. After a mutual silence of some minutes, Harriet thus began again,

"I do so wonder, Miss Woodhouse, that you should not be married, or going to be married—so charming as you are."

Emma laughed, and replied,—

"My being charming, Harriet, is not quite enough to induce me to marry; I must find other people charming—one other person at least. And I am not only not going to be married at present, but have very little intention of ever marrying at all."

"Ah, so you say; but I cannot believe it."

"I must see somebody very superior to any one I have seen yet, to be tempted: Mr. Elton, you know (recollecting herself), is out of the question; and I do *not* wish to see any such person. I would rather not be tempted. I cannot really change for the better. If I were to marry, I must expect to repent it."

"Dear me!—it is so odd to hear a woman talk so!"

"I have none of the usual inducements of women to marry. Were I to fall in love, indeed, it would be a different thing; but I never have been in love: it is not my way, or my nature; and I do not think I ever shall. And, without love, I am sure I should be a fool to change such a situation as mine. Fortune I do not want; employment I do not want; consequence I do not want: I believe few married women are half as much mistress of their husband's house as I am of Hartfield; and never, never could I expect to be so truly beloved and important; so always first and always right in any man's eyes as I am in my father's."

"But then, to be an old maid at last, like Miss Bates!"

"That is as formidable an image as you could present, Harriet; and if I thought I should ever be like Miss Bates—so silly, so satisfied, so smiling, so prosing, so undistinguishing and unfastidious, and so apt to tell every thing relative to every body about me, I would marry to-morrow. But between *us*, I am convinced there never can be any likeness, except in being unmarried."

"But still, you will be an old maid—and that's so dreadful!"

"Never mind, Harriet, I shall not be a poor old maid; and it is poverty only which makes celibacy contemptible to a generous public! A single woman with a very narrow income must be a ridiculous, disagreeable old maid! the proper sport of boys and girls; but a single woman of good fortune is always respectable, and may be as sensible and pleasant as any body else! And the distinction is not quite so much against the candour and common sense of the world as appears at first; for a very narrow income has a tendency to contract the mind, and sour the temper. Those who can barely live, and who live perforce in a very small, and generally very inferior, society, may well be illiberal and cross. This does not apply, however, to Miss Bates: she is only too good natured and too silly to suit me; but, in general, she is very much to the taste of every body, though single and though poor. Poverty certainly has not contracted her mind: I really believe, if she had only a shilling in the world she would be very likely to give away sixpence of it; and nobody is afraid of her: that is a great charm."

"Dear me! but what shall you do? How shall you employ yourself when you grow old?"

"If I know myself, Harriet, mine is an active, busy mind, with a great many independent resources; and I do not perceive why I should be more in want of employment at forty or fifty than one-and-twenty. Woman's usual occupations of eye, and hand, and mind, will be as open to me then as they are now, or with no important variation. If I draw less, I shall read more; if I give up music, I shall take to carpet-work. And as for objects of interest, objects for the affections, which is, in truth, the great point of inferiority, the want of which is really the great evil to be avoided in *not* marrying, I shall be very well off, with all the children of a sister I love so much to care about. There will be enough of them, in all probability, to supply every sort of sensation that declining life can need. There will be enough for every hope and every fear; and though my attachment to none can equal that of a parent, it suits my ideas of comfort better than what is warmer and blinder. My nephews and nieces: I shall often have a niece with me."

"Do you know Miss Bates's niece? That is, I know you

must have seen her a hundred times—but are you acquainted?"

"Oh yes; we are always forced to be acquainted whenever she comes to Highbury. By the by, *that* is almost enough to put one out of conceit with a niece. Heaven forbid, at least, that I should ever bore people half so much about all the Knightleys together as she does about Jane Fairfax. One is sick of the very name of Jane Fairfax. Every letter from her is read forty times over: her compliments to all friends go round and round again; and if she does but send her aunt the pattern of a stomacher, or knit a pair of garters for her grandmother, one hears of nothing else for a month. I wish Jane Fairfax very well; but she tires me to death."

They were now approaching the cottage, and all idle topics were superseded. Emma was very compassionate; and the distresses of the poor were as sure of relief from her personal attention and kindness, her counsel and her patience, as from her purse. She understood their ways, could allow for their ignorance and their temptations, had no romantic expectations of extraordinary virtue from those for whom education had done so little, entered into their troubles with ready sympathy, and always gave her assistance with as much intelligence as good will. In the present instance, it was sickness and poverty together which she came to visit; and after remaining there as long as she could give comfort or advice, she quitted the cottage with such an impression of the scene as made her say to Harriet, as they walked away,—

"These are the sights, Harriet, to do one good. How trifling they make every thing else appear! I feel now as if I could think of nothing but these poor creatures all the rest of the day; and yet who can say how soon it may all vanish from my mind?"

"Very true," said Harriet. "Poor creatures! one can think of nothing else."

"And really, I do not think the impression will soon be over," said Emma, as she crossed the low hedge, and tottering footstep which ended the narrow, slippery path through the cottage garden, and brought them into the lane again. "I do not think it will," stopping to look once more at all the outward wretchedness of the place, and recall the still greater within.

"Oh dear, no," said her companion.

They walked on. The lane made a slight bend; and when that bend was passed, Mr. Elton was immediately in sight; and so near as to give Emma time only to say farther,—

"Ah, Harriet, here comes a very sudden trial of our stability in good thoughts. Well (smiling), I hope it may be allowed that if compassion has produced exertion and relief to the sufferers, it has done all that is truly important. If we feel for the wretched, enough to do all we can for them, the rest is empty sympathy, only distressing to ourselves."

Harriet could just answer, "Oh dear, yes," before the gentleman joined them. The wants and sufferings of the poor family, however, were the first subject on meeting. He had been going to call on them. His visit he would now defer; but they had a very interesting parley about what could be done and should be done. Mr. Elton then turned back to accompany them.

"To fall in with each other on such an errand as this," thought Emma; "to meet in a charitable scheme; this will bring a great increase of love on each side. I should not wonder if it were to bring on the declaration. It must, if I were not here. I wish I were any where else."

Anxious to separate herself from them as far as she could, she soon afterwards took possession of a narrow footpath, a little raised on one side of the lane, leaving them together in the main road. But she had not been there two minutes when she found that Harriet's habits of dependence and imitation were bringing her up too, and that, in short, they would both be soon after her. This would not do; she immediately stopped, under pretence of having some alteration to make in the lacing of her half-boot, and stooping down in complete occupation of the footpath, begged them to have the goodness to walk on, and she would follow in half a minute. They did as they were desired; and by the time she judged it reasonable to have done with her boot, she had the comfort of further delay in her power, being overtaken by a child from the cottage, setting out, according to orders, with her pitcher, to fetch broth from Hartfield. To walk by the side of this child, and talk to and question her, was the most natural thing in the world, or would have been the most natural, had she been acting just then without design; and by this means the others were still able to keep ahead, without any obligation of waiting for her. She gained on them, however, involuntarily: the child's pace was quick, and theirs rather slow; and she was the more concerned at it, from their being evidently in a conversation which interested them. Mr. Elton was speaking with animation, Harriet listening with a very pleased attention; and Emma having sent the child on, was beginning to think how she might draw back a little more, when they both looked around, and she was obliged to join them.

Mr. Elton was still talking, still engaged in some interesting detail; and Emma experienced some disappointment when she found that he was only giving his fair companion an account of the yesterday's party at his friend Cole's, and that she was come in herself for the Stilton cheese, the north Wiltshire, the butter, the celery, the beet-root, and all the dessert.

"This would soon have led to something better, of course," was her consoling reflection; "any thing interests between those who love; and any thing will serve as introduction to what is near the heart. If I could but have kept longer away."

They now walked on together quietly till within view of the vicarage pales, when a sudden resolution, of at least getting Harriet into the house, made her again find something very much amiss about her boot, and fall behind to arrange it once more. She then broke the lace off short, and dexterously throwing it into a ditch, was presently obliged to entreat them to stop, and acknowledge her inability to put herself to rights so as to be able to walk home in tolerable comfort.

"Part of my lace is gone," said she, "and I do not know how I am to contrive. I really am a most troublesome companion to you both, but I hope I am not often so ill-equipped. Mr. Elton, I must beg leave to stop at your house, and ask your housekeeper for a bit of riband or string, or any thing just to keep my boot on."

Mr. Elton looked all happiness at this proposition; and nothing could exceed his alertness and attention in conducting them into his house, and endeavouring to make every thing appear to advantage. The room they were taken into was the one he chiefly occupied, and looking forwards; behind it was another with which it immediately communicated: the door between them was open, and Emma passed into it with the housekeeper, to receive her assistance in the most comfortable manner. She was obliged to leave the door ajar as she found it; but she fully intended that Mr. Elton should close it. It was not closed, however, it still remained ajar; but by engaging the housekeeper in incessant conversation, she hoped to make it practicable for him to choose his own subject in the adjoining room. For ten minutes she could hear nothing but herself. It could be protracted no longer. She was then obliged to be finished, and make her appearance.

The lovers were standing together at one of the windows. It had a most favourable aspect; and, for half a minute, Emma felt the glory of having schemed successfully. But it would not do; he had not come to the point. He had been most agreeable, most delightful: he had told Harriet that he had seen them go by, and had purposely followed them; other little gallantries and allusions had been dropped, but nothing serious.

"Cautious, very cautious," thought Emma: "he advances inch by inch, and will hazard nothing till he believes himself secure."

Still, however, though every thing had not been accomplished by her ingenious device, she could not but flatter herself that it had been the occasion of much present enjoyment to both, and must be leading them forward to the great event.

## Chapter XI.

Mr. Elton must now be left to himself. It was no longer in Emma's power to superintend his happiness, or quicken his measures. The coming of her sister's family was so very near at hand, that first in anticipation, and then in reality, it became henceforth the prime object of interest; and during the ten days of their stay at Hartfield it was not to be expected—she did not herself expect—that any thing beyond occasional, fortuitous assistance could be afforded by her to the lovers. They might advance rapidly if they would, however; they must advance somehow or other, whether they would or no. She hardly wished to have more leisure for them. There are people, who the more you do for them, the less they will do for themselves.

Mr. and Mrs. John Knightley, from having been longer than usual absent from Surrey, were exciting, of course, rather more than the usual interest. Till this year, every long vacation since their marriage had been divided between Hartfield and Donwell Abbey: but all the holidays of this autumn had been given to sea-bathing for the children; and it was therefore many months since they had been seen in a regular way by their Surrey connections, or seen at all by Mr. Woodhouse, who could not be induced to get so far as London, even for poor Isabella's sake; and who, consequently, was now most nervously and apprehensively happy in fore-stalling this too short visit.

He thought much of the evils of the journey for her, and not a little of the fatigues of his own horses and coachman who were to bring some of the party the last half of the way; but his alarms were needless: the sixteen miles being happily accomplished, and Mr. and Mrs. John Knightley, their five children, and a competent number of nursery-maids, all reaching Hartfield in safety. The bustle and joy of such an ar-rival, the many to be talked to, welcomed, encouraged, and variously dispersed and disposed of, produced a noise and confusion which his nerves could not have borne under any other cause, nor have endured much longer even for this; but the ways of Hartfield and the feelings of her father were so respected by Mrs. John Knightley, that in spite of mater-nal solicitude for the immediate enjoyment of her little ones, and for their having instantly all the liberty and attendance, all the eating and drinking, and sleeping and playing, which they could possibly wish for, without the smallest delay, the children were never allowed to be long a disturbance to him, either in themselves or in any restless attendance on them.

Mrs. John Knightley was a pretty, elegant little woman, of gentle, quiet manners, and a disposition remarkably amiable and affectionate, wrapt up in her family, a devoted wife, a doting mother, and so tenderly attached to her father and sister that, but for these higher ties, a warmer love might have seemed impossible. She could never see a fault in any of them. She was not a woman of strong understanding or any quickness; and with this resemblance of her father, she inherited also much of his constitution; was delicate in her own health, over-careful of that of her children, had many fears and many nerves, and was as fond of her own Mr. Wing-field in town as her father could be of Mr. Perry. They were alike, too, in a general benevolence of temper, and a strong habit of regard for every old acquaintance.

Mr. John Knightley was a tall, gentleman-like, and very clever man; rising in his profession, domestic, and respectable in his private character: but with reserved manners which prevented his being generally pleasing; and capable of being sometimes out of humour. He was not an ill-tempered man, not so often unreasonably cross as to deserve such a reproach: but his temper was not his great perfection; and, indeed, with such a worshipping wife, it was hardly possible that any natural defects in it should not be increased. The extreme sweetness of her temper must hurt his. He had all the clearness and quickness of mind which she wanted; and he could sometimes act an ungracious, or say a severe thing. He was not a great favourite with his fair sister-in-law. Nothing wrong in him escaped her. She was quick in feeling the little injuries to Isabella, which Isabella never felt herself. Perhaps she might have passed over more had his manners been flattering to Isabella's sister, but they were only those of a calmly kind brother and friend, without praise and without blindness; but hardly any degree of personal compliment could have made her regardless of that greatest fault of all in her eyes which he sometimes fell into, the want of respectful forbearance towards her father. There he had not always the patience that could have been wished. Mr. Woodhouse's peculiarities and fidgetiness were sometimes provoking him to a rational remonstrance or sharp retort equally ill bestowed. It did not often happen; for Mr. John Knightley had really a great regard for his father-in-law, and generally a strong sense of what was due to him: but it was too often for Emma's charity, especially as there was all the pain of apprehension frequently to be endured, though the offence came not. The beginning, however, of every visit displayed none but the properest feelings, and this being of necessity so short might be hoped to pass away in unsullied cordiality. They had not been long seated and composed when Mr. Woodhouse, with a melancholy shake of the head and a sigh, called his daughter's attention to the sad change at Hartfield since she had been there last.

"Ah, my dear," said he, "poor Miss Taylor. It is a grievous business."

"Oh yes, sir," cried she, with ready sympathy, "how you must miss her! And dear Emma too. What a dreadful loss to you both! I have been so grieved for you. I could not imagine how you could possibly do without her. It is a sad change, indeed; but I hope she is pretty well, sir."

"Pretty well, my dear,—I hope,—pretty well. I do not know but that the place agrees with her tolerably."

Mr. John Knightley here asked Emma, quietly, whether there were any doubts of the air of Randalls.

"Oh no: none in the least. I never saw Mrs. Weston better in my life,—never looking so well. Papa is only speaking his own regret."

"Very much to the honour of both," was the handsome reply.

"And do you see her, sir, tolerably often?" asked Isabella in the plaintive tone which just suited her father.

Mr. Woodhouse hesitated. "Not near so often, my dear, as I could wish."

"Oh, papa, we have missed seeing them but one entire day since they married. Either in the morning or evening of every day, excepting one, have we seen either Mr. Weston or Mrs. Weston, and generally both, either at Randalls or here; and as you may suppose, Isabella, most frequently here. They are very, very kind in their visits. Mr. Weston is really as kind as herself. Papa, if you speak in that melancholy way, you will be giving Isabella a false idea of us all. Every body must be aware that Miss Taylor must be missed; but every body ought also to be assured that Mr. and Mrs. Weston do really prevent our missing her by any means to the extent we ourselves anticipated,—which is the exact truth."

"Just as it should be," said Mr. John Knightley, "and just as I hoped it was from your letters. Her wish of showing you attention could not be doubted, and his being a disengaged and social man makes it all easy. I have been always telling you, my love, that I had no idea of the change being so very material to Hartfield as you apprehended; and now you have Emma's account, I hope you will be satisfied."

"Why, to be sure," said Mr. Woodhouse,—"yes, certainly. I cannot deny that Mrs. Weston,—poor Mrs. Weston,—does come and see us pretty often; but then, she is always obliged to go away again."

"It would be very hard upon Mr. Weston if she did not, papa. You quite forget poor Mr. Weston."

"I think, indeed," said John Knightley, pleasantly, "that Mr. Weston has some little claim. You and I, Emma, will venture to take the part of the poor husband. I being a husband, and you not being a wife, the claims of the man may very likely strike us with equal force. As for Isabella, she has been married long enough to see the convenience of putting all the Mr. Westons aside as much as she can."

"Me, my love," cried his wife, hearing and understanding only in part. "Are you talking about me? I am sure nobody ought to be, or can be, a greater advocate for matrimony than I am; and if it had not been for the misery of her leaving Hartfield, I should never have thought of Miss Taylor but as the most fortunate woman in the world; and as to slighting Mr. Weston,—that excellent Mr. Weston,—I think there is nothing he does not deserve. I believe he is one of the very best tempered men that ever existed. Excepting yourself and your brother, I do not know his equal for temper. I shall never forget his flying Henry's kite for him that very windy day last Easter; and ever since his particular kindness last September twelvemonth in writing that note, at twelve o'clock at night, on purpose to assure me that there was no scarlet fever at Cobham,[6] I have been convinced there could not be a more feeling heart nor a better man in existence. If any body can deserve him, it must be Miss Taylor."

"Where is the young man?" said John Knightley. "Has he been here on this occasion, or has he not?"

"He has not been here yet," replied Emma. "There was a strong expectation of his coming soon after the marriage, but it ended in nothing; and I have not heard him mentioned lately."

"But you should tell them of the letter, my dear," said her

father. "He wrote a letter to poor Mrs. Weston, to congratulate her, and a very proper, handsome letter it was. She showed it to me. I thought it very well done of him, indeed. Whether it was his own idea, you know, one cannot tell. He is but young, and his uncle, perhaps——"

"My dear papa, he is three-and-twenty. You forget how time passes."

"Three-and-twenty! is he, indeed? Well, I could not have thought it; and he was but two years old when he lost his poor mother. Well, time does fly indeed! and my memory is very bad. However, it was an exceeding good, pretty letter, and gave Mr. and Mrs. Weston a great deal of pleasure. I remember it was written from Weymouth, and dated Sept. 28th, and began 'My dear Madam,' but I forget how it went on; and it was signed 'F. C. Weston Churchill.' I remember that perfectly."

"How very p easing and proper of him!" cried the good-hearted Mrs. John Knightley. "I have no doubt of his being a most amiable young man. But how sad it is that he should not live at home with his father! There is something so shocking in a child's being taken away from his parents and natural home! I never can comprehend how Mr. Weston could part with him. To give up one's child! I really never could think well of any body who proposed such a thing to any body else."

"Nobody ever did think well of the Churchills, I fancy," observed Mr. John Knightley, coolly. "But you need not imagine Mr. Weston to have felt what you would feel in giving up Henry or John. Mr. Weston is rather an easy, cheerful tempered man, than a man of strong feelings: he takes things as he finds them, and makes enjoyment of them somehow or other, depending, I suspect, much more upon what is called *society* for his comforts, that is, upon the power of eating and drinking, and playing whist with his neighbours five times a week, than upon family affection, or any thing that home affords."

Emma could not like what bordered on a reflection on

Mr. Weston, and had half a mind to take it up; but she struggled, and let it pass. She would keep the peace if possible;
and there was something honourable and valuable in the
strong domestic habits, the all-sufficiency of home to himself, whence resulted her brother's disposition to look down
on the common rate of social intercourse, and those to
whom it was important. It had a high claim to forbearance.

## Chapter XII.

M r. Knightley was to dine with them, rather against
the inclination of Mr. Woodhouse, who did not like
that any one should share with him in Isabella's
first day. Emma's sense of right, however, had decided it;
and, besides the consideration of what was due to each
brother, she had particular pleasure, from the circumstance
of the late disagreement between Mr. Knightley and herself,
in procuring him the proper invitation.

She hoped they might now become friends again. She
thought it was time to make up. Making-up, indeed, would
not do. *She* certainly had not been in the wrong, and *he*
would never own that he had. Concession must be out of the
question: but it was time to appear to forget that they had
ever quarrelled; and she hoped it might rather assist the
restoration of friendship, that when he came into the room
she had one of the children with her,—the youngest, a nice
little girl about eight months old, who was now making her
first visit to Hartfield, and very happy to be danced about in
her aunt's arms. It did assist; for though he began with grave
looks and short questions, he was soon led on to talk of them
all in the usual way, and to take the child out of her arms

with all the unceremoniousness of perfect amity. Emma felt they were friends again; and the conviction giving her at first great satisfaction, and then a little sauciness, she could not help saying, as he was admiring the baby,—

"What a comfort it is, that we think alike about our nephews and nieces. As to men and women, our opinions are sometimes very different; but with regard to these children, I observe we never disagree."

"If you were as much guided by nature in your estimate of men and women, and as little under the power of fancy and whim in your dealings with them, as you are where these children are concerned, we might always think alike."

"To be sure—our discordances must always arise from my being in the wrong."

"Yes," said he, smiling, "and reason good. I was sixteen years old when you were born."

"A material difference, then," she replied; "and no doubt you were much my superior in judgment at that period of our lives; but does not the lapse of one-and-twenty years bring our understandings a good deal nearer?"

"Yes, a good deal *nearer.*"

"But still, not near enough to give me a chance of being right, if we think differently."

"I have still the advantage of you by sixteen years' experience, and by not being a pretty young woman and a spoiled child. Come, my dear Emma, let us be friends, and say no more about it. Tell your aunt, little Emma, that she ought to set you a better example than to be renewing old grievances, and that if she were not wrong before, she is now."

"That's true," she cried, "very true. Little Emma, grow up a better woman than your aunt. Be infinitely cleverer and not half so conceited. Now, Mr. Knightley, a word or two more, and I have done. As far as good intentions went, we were *both* right, and I must say, that no effects on my side of the argument have yet proved wrong. I only want to know that Mr. Martin is not very, very bitterly disappointed."

"A man cannot be more so," was his short, full answer.

"Ah! Indeed I am very sorry. Come, shake hands with me."

This had just taken place, and with great cordiality, when John Knightley made his appearance; and "How d'ye do, George?" and "John, how are you?" succeeded in the true English style, burying under a calmness that seemed all but indifference the real attachment which would have led either of them, if requisite, to do every thing for the good of the other.

The evening was quiet and conversible, as Mr. Woodhouse declined cards entirely for the sake of comfortable talk with his dear Isabella, and the little party made two natural divisions: on one side he and his daughter; on the other the two Mr. Knightleys; their subjects totally distinct, or very rarely mixing, and Emma only occasionally joining in one or the other.

The brothers talked of their own concerns and pursuits, but principally of those of the elder, whose temper was by much the most communicative, and who was always the greater talker. As a magistrate, he had generally some point of law to consult John about, or, at least, some curious anecdote to give; and as a farmer, as keeping in hand the home-farm at Donwell, he had to tell what every field was to bear next year, and to give all such local information as could not fail of being interesting to a brother, whose home it had equally been the longest part of his life, and whose attachments were strong. The plan of a drain, the change of a fence, the felling of a tree, and the destination of every acre for wheat, turnips, or spring corn, was entered into with as much equality of interest by John as his cooler manners rendered possible; and if his willing brother ever left him any thing to enquire about, his enquiries even approached a tone of eagerness.

While they were thus comfortably occupied, Mr. Woodhouse was enjoying a full flow of happy regrets and fearful affection with his daughter.

"My poor dear Isabella," said he, fondly taking her hand,

and interrupting, for a few moments, her busy labours for some one of her five children, "how long it is, how terribly long since you were here! And how tired you must be after your journey! You must go to bed early, my dear,—and I recommend a little gruel to you before you go. You and I will have a nice basin of gruel together. My dear Emma, suppose we all have a little gruel."

Emma could not suppose any such thing, knowing, as she did, that both the Mr. Knightleys were as unpersuadable on that article as herself, and two basins only were ordered. After a little more discourse in praise of gruel, with some wondering at its not being taken every evening by every body, he proceeded to say, with an air of grave reflection,—

"It was an awkward business, my dear, your spending the autumn at South End instead of coming here. I never had much opinion of the sea air."

"Mr. Wingfield most strenuously recommended it, sir, or we should not have gone. He recommended it for all the children, but particularly for the weakness in little Bella's throat,—both sea air and bathing."

"Ah, my dear, but Perry had many doubts about the sea doing her any good; and as to myself, I have been long perfectly convinced, though perhaps I never told you so before, that the sea is very rarely of use to any body. I am sure it almost killed me once."

"Come, come," cried Emma, feeling this to be an unsafe subject, "I must beg you not to talk of the sea. It makes me envious and miserable; I who have never seen it! South End is prohibited, if you please. My dear Isabella, I have not heard you make one enquiry after Mr. Perry yet; and he never forgets you."

"Oh, good Mr. Perry, how is he, sir?"

"Why, pretty well; but not quite well. Poor Perry is bilious, and he has not time to take care of himself; he tells me he has not time to take care of himself—which is very sad—but he is always wanted all round the country. I suppose there is not a man in such practice any where. But then, there is not so clever a man any where."

"And Mrs. Perry and the children, how are they? Do the children grow? I have a great regard for Mr. Perry. I hope he will be calling soon. He will be so pleased to see my little ones."

"I hope he will be here to-morrow, for I have a question or two to ask him about myself of some consequence. And, my dear, whenever he comes, you had better let him look at little Bella's throat."

"Oh, my dear sir, her throat is so much better that I have hardly any uneasiness about it. Either bathing has been of the greatest service to her, or else it is to be attributed to an excellent embrocation of Mr. Wingfield's, which we have been applying at times ever since August."

"It is not very likely, my dear, that bathing should have been of use to her; and if I had known you were wanting an embrocation, I would have spoken to——"

"You seem to me to have forgotten Mrs. and Miss Bates," said Emma; "I have not heard one enquiry after them."

"Oh, the good Bateses—I am quite ashamed of myself; but you mention them in most of your letters. I hope they are quite well. Good old Mrs. Bates. I will call upon her to-morrow, and take my children. They are always so pleased to see my children. And that excellent Miss Bates!—such thorough worthy people! How are they, sir?"

"Why, pretty well, my dear, upon the whole. But poor Mrs. Bates had a bad cold about a month ago."

"How sorry I am! but colds were never so prevalent as they have been this autumn. Mr. Wingfield told me that he had never known them more general or heavy, except when it has been quite an influenza."

"That has been a good deal the case, my dear, but not to the degree you mention. Perry says that colds have been very general, but not so heavy as he has very often known them in November. Perry does not call it altogether a sickly season."

"No, I do not know that Mr. Wingfield considers it *very* sickly, except——"

"Ah, my poor dear child, the truth is, that in London it is always a sickly season. Nobody is healthy in London, nobody can be. It is a dreadful thing to have you forced to live there;—so far off!—and the air so bad!"

"No, indeed, *we* are not at all in a bad air. Our part of London is so very superior to most others. You must not confound us with London in general, my dear sir. The neighbourhood of Brunswick Square is very different from almost all the rest. We are so very airy! I should be unwilling, I own, to live in any other part of the town; there is hardly any other that I could be satisfied to have my children in: but *we* are so remarkably airy! Mr. Wingfield thinks the vicinity of Brunswick Square decidedly the most favourable as to air."

"Ah, my dear, it is not like Hartfield. You make the best of it—but after you have been a week at Hartfield, you are all of you different creatures; you do not look like the same. Now I cannot say that I think you are any of you looking well at present."

"I am sorry to hear you say so, sir: but I assure you, excepting those little nervous headaches and palpitations which I am never entirely free from any where, I am quite well myself; and if the children were rather pale before they went to bed, it was only because they were a little more tired than usual, from their journey and the happiness of coming. I hope you will think better of their looks to-morrow; for I assure you Mr. Wingfield told me, that he did not believe he had ever sent us off, altogether, in such good case. I trust, at least, that you do not think Mr. Knightley looking ill," turning her eyes with affectionate anxiety towards her husband.

"Middling, my dear; I cannot compliment you. I think Mr. John Knightley very far from looking well."

"What is the matter, sir? Did you speak to me?" cried Mr. John Knightley, hearing his own name.

"I am sorry to find, my love, that my father does not think you looking well; but I hope it is only from being a little fatigued. I could have wished, however, as you know, that you had seen Mr. Wingfield before you left home."

"My dear Isabella," exclaimed he, hastily, "pray do not concern yourself about my looks. Be satisfied with doctoring and coddling yourself and the children, and let me look as I choose."

"I did not thoroughly understand what you were telling your brother," cried Emma, "about your friend Mr. Graham's intending to have a bailiff from Scotland, to look after his new estate. But will it answer? Will not the old prejudice be too strong?"

And she talked in this way so long and successfully that, when forced to give her attention again to her father and sister, she had nothing worse to hear than Isabella's kind enquiry after Jane Fairfax; and Jane Fairfax, though no great favourite with her in general, she was, at that moment, very happy to assist in praising.

"That sweet, amiable Jane Fairfax!" said Mrs. John Knightley. "It is so long since I have seen her, except now and then for a moment accidentally in town. What happiness it must be to her good old grandmother and excellent aunt, when she comes to visit them! I always regret excessively, on dear Emma's account, that she cannot be more at Highbury; but now their daughter is married, I suppose Colonel and Mrs. Campbell will not be able to part with her at all. She would be such a delightful companion for Emma."

Mr. Woodhouse agreed to it all, but added,—

"Our little friend, Harriet Smith, however, is just such another pretty kind of young person. You will like Harriet. Emma could not have a better companion than Harriet."

"I am most happy to hear it; but only Jane Fairfax one knows to be so very accomplished and superior, and exactly Emma's age."

This topic was discussed very happily, and others succeeded of similar moment, and passed away with similar harmony; but the evening did not close without a little return of agitation. The gruel came, and supplied a great deal to be said—much praise and many comments—undoubting decision of its wholesomeness for every constitution, and pretty severe philippics[7] upon the many houses where it was never met with tolerable; but, unfortunately, among the failures which the daughter had to instance, the most recent, and therefore most prominent, was in her own cook at South End, a young woman hired for the time, who never had been able to understand what she meant by a basin of nice smooth gruel, thin, but not too thin. Often as she had wished for and ordered it, she had never been able to get any thing tolerable. Here was a dangerous opening.

"Ah," said Mr. Woodhouse, shaking his head, and fixing his eyes on her with tender concern. The ejaculation in Emma's ear expressed, "Ah, there is no end of the sad consequences of your going to South End. It does not bear talking of." And for a little while she hoped he would not talk of it, and that a silent rumination might suffice to restore him to the relish of his own smooth gruel. After an interval of some minutes, however, he began with,—

"I shall always be very sorry that you went to the sea this autumn, instead of coming here."

"But why should you be sorry, sir? I assure you, it did the children a great deal of good."

"And, moreover, if you must go to the sea, it had better not have been to South End. South End is an unhealthy place. Perry was surprised to hear you had fixed upon South End."

"I know there is such an idea with many people, but indeed it is quite a mistake, sir. We all had our health perfectly well there, never found the least inconvenience from the mud, and Mr. Wingfield says it is entirely a mistake to suppose the place unhealthy; and I am sure he may be depended on, for he thoroughly understands the nature of the air, and his own brother and family have been there repeatedly."

"You should have gone to Cromer,* my dear, if you went any where. Perry was a week at Cromer once, and he holds it to be the best of all the sea-bathing places. A fine open sea, he says, and very pure air. And, by what I understand, you might have had lodgings there quite away from the sea—a quarter of a mile off—very comfortable. You should have consulted Perry."

"But, my dear sir, the difference of the journey; only consider how great it would have been. A hundred miles, perhaps, instead of forty."

"Ah, my dear," as Perry says, "where health is at stake, nothing else should be considered; and if one is to travel, there is not much to choose between forty miles and a hundred. Better not move at all, better stay in London altogether, than travel forty miles to get into a worse air. This is just what Perry said. It seemed to him a very ill-judged measure."

Emma's attempts to stop her father had been vain; and when he had reached such a point as this, she could not wonder at her brother-in-law's breaking out.

"Mr. Perry," said he, in a voice of very strong displeasure, "would do as well to keep his opinion till it is asked for. Why does he make it any business of his to wonder at what I do?—at my taking my family to one part of the coast or another? I may be allowed, I hope, the use of my judgment as well as Mr. Perry. I want his directions no more than his drugs." He paused, and growing cooler in a moment, added, with only sarcastic dryness, "If Mr. Perry can tell me how to convey a wife and five children a distance of a hundred and thirty miles with no greater expense or inconvenience than a distance of forty, I should be as willing to prefer Cromer to South End as he could himself."

"True, true," cried Mr. Knightley, with most ready interposition,—"very true. That's a consideration, indeed. But,

---

*Health and vacation resort on England's North Sea coast.

John, as to what I was telling you of my idea of moving the path to Langham, of turning it more to the right that it may not cut through the home meadows, I cannot conceive any difficulty. I should not attempt it, if it were to be the means of inconvenience to the Highbury people, but if you call to mind exactly the present line of the path. . . . The only way of proving it, however, will be to turn to our maps. I shall see you at the Abbey to-morrow morning I hope, and then we will look them over, and you shall give me your opinion."

Mr. Woodhouse was rather agitated by such harsh reflections on his friend Perry, to whom he had, in fact, though unconsciously, been attributing many of his own feelings and expressions; but the soothing attentions of his daughters gradually removed the present evil, and the immediate alertness of one brother, and better recollections of the other, prevented any renewal of it.

## Chapter XIII.

There could hardly be a happier creature in the world than Mrs. John Knightley, in this short visit to Hartfield, going about every morning among her old acquaintance with her five children, and talking over what she had done every evening with her father and sister. She had nothing to wish otherwise, but that the days did not pass so swiftly. It was a delightful visit;—perfect, in being much too short.

In general their evenings were less engaged with friends than their mornings: but one complete dinner engagement, and out of the house too, there was no avoiding, though at Christmas. Mr. Weston would take no denial: they must all dine at Randalls one day;—even Mr. Woodhouse was persuaded to think it a possible thing in preference to a division of the party.

How they were all to be conveyed, he would have made a difficulty if he could, but as his son and daughter's carriage and horses were actually at Hartfield, he was not able to make more than a simple question on that head; it hardly amounted to a doubt; nor did it occupy Emma long to convince him that they might in one of the carriages find room for Harriet also.

Harriet, Mr. Elton, and Mr. Knightley, their own especial set, were the only persons invited to meet them:—the hours were to be early as well as the numbers few; Mr. Woodhouse's habits and inclination being consulted in every thing.

The evening before this great event (for it was a very great event that Mr. Woodhouse should dine out on the 24th of December) had been spent by Harriet at Hartfield, and she had gone home so much indisposed with a cold, that, but for her own earnest wish of being nursed by Mrs. Goddard, Emma could not have allowed her to leave the house. Emma called on her the next day, and found her doom already signed with regard to Randalls. She was very feverish and had a bad sore-throat: Mrs. Goddard was full of care and affection, Mr. Perry was talked of, and Harriet herself was too ill and low to resist the authority which excluded her from this delightful engagement, though she could not speak of her loss without many tears.

Emma sat with her as long as she could, to attend her in Mrs. Goddard's unavoidable absences, and raise her spirits by representing how much Mr. Elton's would be depressed when he knew her state; and left her at last tolerably comfortable, in the sweet dependence of his having a most comfortless visit, and of their all missing her very much. She had not advanced many yards from Mrs. Goddard's door, when she was met by Mr. Elton himself, evidently coming towards it, and as they walked on slowly together in conversation about the invalid,—of whom he, on the rumour of considerable illness, had been going to enquire, that he might carry some report of her to Hartfield,—they were overtaken by Mr. John Knightley returning from the daily visit to Donwell, with his two eldest boys, whose healthy, glowing faces showed all the benefit of a country run, and seemed to ensure a quick despatch of the roast mutton and rice pudding they were hastening home for. They joined company and proceeded together. Emma was just describing the nature of her friend's complaint:—"a throat very much inflamed, with a great deal of heat about her, a quick low pulse, &c.,* and she was sorry to find from Mrs. Goddard that Harriet was liable to very bad sore throats, and had often alarmed her with them." Mr. Elton looked all alarm on the occasion, as he exclaimed,—

"A sore throat!—I hope not infectious. I hope not of a putrid infectious sort. Has Perry seen her? Indeed you should take care of yourself as well as of your friend. Let me entreat you to run no risks. Why does not Perry see her?"

Emma, who was not really at all frightened herself, tranquillised this excess of apprehension by assurances of Mrs. Goddard's experience and care; but as there must still remain a degree of uneasiness which she could not wish to reason away, which she would rather feed and assist than not, she added soon afterwards—as if quite another subject,—

"It is so cold, so very cold, and looks and feels so very much like snow, that if it were to any other place or with any other party, I should really try not to go out to-day, and dissuade my father from venturing; but as he has made up his mind, and does not seem to feel the cold himself, I do not like to interfere, as I know it would be so great a disappointment to Mr. and Mrs. Weston. But upon my word, Mr. Elton, in your case, I should certainly excuse myself. You appear to me a little hoarse already; and when you consider what demand of voice and what fatigues to-morrow will bring, I

---

*Et cetera.

think it would be no more than common prudence to stay at home and take care of yourself to-night."

Mr. Elton looked as if he did not very well know what answer to make; which was exactly the case; for though very much gratified by the kind care of such a fair lady, and not liking to resist any advice of hers, he had not really the least inclination to give up the visit; but Emma, too eager and busy in her own previous conceptions and views to hear him impartially, or see him with clear vision, was very well satisfied with his muttering acknowledgment of its being "very cold, certainly very cold," and walked on, rejoicing in having extricated himself from Randalls, and secured him the power of sending to enquire after Harriet every hour of the evening.

"You do quite right," said she:—"we will make your apologies to Mr. and Mrs. Weston."

But hardly had she so spoken when she found her brother was civilly offering a seat in his carriage, if the weather were Mr. Elton's only objection, and Mr. Elton actually accepting the offer with much prompt satisfaction. It was a done thing: Mr. Elton was to go; and never had his broad handsome face expressed more pleasure than at this moment; never had his smile been stronger; nor his eyes more exulting than when he next looked at her.

"Well," said she to herself, "this is most strange! After I had gotten him off so well, to choose to go into company, and leave Harriet ill behind! Most strange indeed! But there is, I believe, in many men, especially single men, such an inclination—such a passion for dining out; a dinner engagement is so high in the class of their pleasures, their employments, their dignities, almost their duties, that any thing gives way to it—and this must be the case with Mr. Elton: a most valuable, amiable, pleasing young man undoubtedly, and very much in love with Harriet; but still, he cannot refuse an invitation, he must dine out wherever he is asked. What a strange thing love is! he can see ready wit in Harriet, but will not dine alone for her."

Soon afterwards Mr. Elton quitted them, and she could not but do him the justice of feeling that there was a great deal of sentiment in his manner of naming Harriet at parting; in the tone of his voice while assuring her that he should call at Mrs. Goddard's for news of her fair friend, the last thing before he prepared for the happiness of meeting her again, when he hoped to be able to give a better report; and he sighed and smiled himself off in a way that left the balance of approbation much in his favour.

After a few minutes of entire silence between them, John Knightley began with,—

"I never in my life saw a man more intent on being agreeable than Mr. Elton. It is downright labour to him where ladies are concerned. With men he can be rational and unaffected, but when he has ladies to please every feature works."

"Mr. Elton's manners are not perfect," replied Emma; "but where there is a wish to please, one ought to overlook, and one does overlook a great deal. Where a man does his best with only moderate powers, he will have the advantage over negligent superiority. There is such perfect good temper and good will in Mr. Elton as one cannot but value."

"Yes," said Mr. John Knightley presently, with some slyness, "he seems to have a great deal of good will towards *you*."

"Me!" she replied, with a smile of astonishment; "are you imagining me to be Mr. Elton's object?"

"Such an imagination has crossed me, I own, Emma; and if it never occurred to you before, you may as well take it into consideration now."

"Mr. Elton in love with me! What an idea!"

"I do not say it is so; but you will do well to consider whether it is so or not, and to regulate your behaviour accordingly. I think your manners to him encouraging. I speak as a friend, Emma. You had better look about you, and ascertain what you do, and what you mean to do."

"I thank you; but I assure you you are quite mistaken. Mr. Elton and I are very good friends, and nothing more;" and she walked on, amusing herself in the consideration of the blunders which often arise from a partial knowledge of circumstances, of the mistakes which people of high pretensions to judgment are for ever falling into; and not very well pleased with her brother for imagining her blind and ignorant, and in want of counsel. He said no more.

Mr. Woodhouse had so completely made up his mind to the visit, that in spite of the increasing coldness, he seemed to have no idea of shrinking from it, and set forward at last most punctually with his eldest daughter in his own carriage, with less apparent consciousness of the weather than either of the others; too full of the wonder of his own going, and the pleasure it was to afford at Randalls to see that it was cold, and too well wrapt up to feel it. The cold, however, was severe; and by the time the second carriage was in motion, a few flakes of snow were finding their way down, and the sky had the appearance of being so overcharged as to want only a milder air to produce a very white world in a very short time.

Emma soon saw that her companion was not in the happiest humour. The preparing and the going abroad in such weather, with the sacrifice of his children after dinner, were evils, were disagreeables at least, which Mr. John Knightley did not by any means like: he anticipated nothing in the visit that could be at all worth the purchase; and the whole of their drive to the vicarage was spent by him in expressing his discontent.

"A man," said he, "must have a very good opinion of himself when he asks people to leave their own fire-side, and encounter such a day as this, for the sake of coming to see him. He must think himself a most agreeable fellow; I could not do such a thing. It is the greatest absurdity—actually snowing at this moment! The folly of not allowing people to be comfortable at home—and the folly of people's not staying comfortably at home when they can! If we were obliged to go out such an evening as this, by any call of duty or business, what a hardship we should deem it;—and here are we, probably with rather thinner clothing than usual, setting forward voluntarily, without excuse, in defiance of the voice of nature, which tells man, in every thing given to his view or his feelings, to stay at home himself, and keep all under shelter that he can;—here are we setting forward to spend five dull hours in another man's house, with nothing to say or to hear that was not said and heard yesterday, and may not be said and heard again to-morrow. Going in dismal weather, to return probably in worse;—four horses and four servants taken out for nothing but to convey five idle, shivering creatures into colder rooms and worse company than they might have had at home.

Emma did not find herself equal to give the pleased assent, which no doubt he was in the habit of receiving, to emulate the "Very true, my love," which must have been usually administered by his travelling companion; but she had resolution enough to refrain from making any answer at all. She could not be complying; she dreaded being quarrelsome; her heroism reached only to silence. She allowed him to talk, and arranged the glasses, and wrapped herself up, without opening her lips.

They arrived, the carriage turned, the step was let down, and Mr. Elton, spruce, black, and smiling, was with them instantly. Emma thought with pleasure of some change of subject. Mr. Elton was all obligation and cheerfulness; he was so very cheerful in his civilities indeed, that she began to think he must have received a different account of Harriet from what had reached her. She had sent while dressing, and the answer had been, "Much the same—not better."

"*My* report from Mrs. Goddard's," said she, presently, "was not so pleasant as I had hoped:—'Not better,' was *my* answer."

His face lengthened immediately; and his voice was the voice of sentiment as he answered,—

"Oh no—I am grieved to find—I was on the point of telling you that when I called at Mrs. Goddard's door, which I did the very last thing before I returned to dress, I was told that Miss Smith was not better, by no means better, rather worse. Very much grieved and concerned—I had flattered myself that she must be better after such a cordial as I knew had been given in the morning."

Emma smiled, and answered,—"My visit was of use to the nervous part of her complaint, I hope; but not even I can charm away a sore throat; it is a most severe cold, indeed. Mr. Perry has been with her, as you probably heard."

"Yes—I imagined—that is—I did not——"

"He has been used to her in these complaints, and I hope to-morrow morning will bring us both a more comfortable report. But it is impossible not to feel uneasiness. Such a sad loss to our party to-day!"

"Dreadful! Exactly so, indeed. She will be missed every moment."

This was very proper; the sigh which accompanied it was really estimable; but it should have lasted longer. Emma was rather in dismay when only half a minute afterwards he began to speak of other things, and in a voice of the greatest alacrity and enjoyment.

"What an excellent device," said he, "the use of a sheep-skin for carriages. How very comfortable they make it;—impossible to feel cold with such precautions. The contrivances of modern days, indeed, have rendered a gentleman's carriage perfectly complete. One is so fenced and guarded from the weather, that not a breath of air can find its way unpermitted. Weather becomes absolutely of no consequence. It is a very cold afternoon—but in this carriage we know nothing of the matter. Ha! snows a little, I see."

"Yes," said John Knightley, "and I think we shall have a good deal of it."

"Christmas weather," observed Mr. Elton. "Quite season-able; and extremely fortunate we may think ourselves that it did not begin yesterday, and prevent this day's party, which it might very possibly have done, for Mr. Woodhouse would hardly have ventured had there been much snow on the ground; but now it is of no consequence. This is quite the season, indeed, for friendly meetings. At Christmas every body invites their friends about them, and people think little of even the worst weather. I was snowed up at a friend's house once for a week. Nothing could be pleasanter. I went for only one night, and could not get away till that very day se'nnight."*

Mr. John Knightley looked as if he did not comprehend the pleasure, but said only, coolly,—

"I cannot wish to be snowed up a week at Randalls."

At another time Emma might have been amused, but she was too much astonished now at Mr. Elton's spirits for other feelings. Harriet seemed quite forgotten in the expectation of a pleasant party.

"We are sure of excellent fires," continued he, "and every thing in the greatest comfort. Charming people, Mr. and Mrs. Weston;—Mrs. Weston indeed is much beyond praise, and he is exactly what one values, so hospitable, and so fond of society;—it will be a small party, but where small parties are select, they are, perhaps, the most agreeable of any. Mr. Weston's dining-room does not accommodate more than ten comfortably; and for my part, I would rather, under such circumstances, fall short by two than exceed by two. I think you will agree with me (turning with a soft air to Emma), I think I shall certainly have your approbation, though Mr. Knightley, perhaps, from being used to the large parties of London, may not quite enter into our feelings."

"I know nothing of the large parties of London, sir—I never dine with any body."

"Indeed! (in a tone of wonder and pity,) I had no idea that the law had been so great a slavery. Well, sir, the time must come when you will be paid for all this, when you will have little labour and great enjoyment."

---

*Seven nights, or a week.

"My first enjoyment," replied John Knightley, as they passed through the sweep-gate, "will be to find myself safe at Hartfield again."

## Chapter XIV.

Some change of countenance was necessary for each gentleman as they walked into Mrs. Weston's drawing-room;—Mr. Elton must compose his joyous looks, and Mr. John Knightley disperse his ill-humour. Mr. Elton must smile less, and Mr. John Knightley more, to fit them for the place. Emma only might be as nature prompted, and show herself just as happy as she was. To her, it was real enjoyment to be with the Westons. Mr. Weston was a great favourite, and there was not a creature in the world to whom she spoke with such unreserve as to his wife; not any one, to whom she related with such conviction of being listened to and understood, of being always interesting and always intelligible, the little affairs, arrangements, perplexities, and pleasures of her father and herself. She could tell nothing of Hartfield, in which Mrs. Weston had not a lively concern; and half an hour's uninterrupted communication of all those little matters on which the daily happiness of private life depends, was one of the first gratifications of each.

This was a pleasure which perhaps the whole day's visit might not afford, which certainly did not belong to the present half hour; but the very sight of Mrs. Weston, her smile, her touch, her voice, was grateful to Emma, and she determined to think as little as possible of Mr. Elton's oddities, or of any thing else unpleasant, and enjoy all that was enjoyable to the utmost.

The misfortune of Harriet's cold had been pretty well gone through before her arrival. Mr. Woodhouse had been safely seated long enough to give the history of it, besides all the history of his own and Isabella's coming, and of Emma's being to follow; and had, indeed, just got to the end of his satisfaction that James should come and see his daughter, when the others appeared, and Mrs. Weston, who had been almost wholly engrossed by her attentions to him, was able to turn away and welcome her dear Emma.

Emma's project of forgetting Mr. Elton for a while made her rather sorry to find, when they had all taken their places, that he was close to her. The difficulty was great of driving his strange insensibility towards Harriet from her mind, while he not only sat at her elbow, but was continually obtruding his happy countenance on her notice, and solicitously addressing her upon every occasion. Instead of forgetting him, his behaviour was such that she could not avoid the internal suggestion of "Can it really be as my brother imagined? can it be possible for this man to be beginning to transfer his affections from Harriet to me?—Absurd and insufferable!"—Yet he would be so anxious for her being perfectly warm, would be so interested about her father, and so delighted with Mrs. Weston; and, at last, would begin admiring her drawings with so much zeal and so little knowledge, as seemed terribly like a would-be lover, and made it some effort with her to preserve her good manners. For her own sake she could not be rude; and for Harriet's, in the hope that all would yet turn out right, she was even positively civil: but it was an effort; especially as something was going on amongst the others, in the most overpowering period of Mr. Elton's nonsense, which she particularly wished to listen to. She heard enough to know that Mr. Weston was giving some information about his son: she heard the words "my son," and "Frank," and "my son," repeated several times over; and, from a few other half syllables, very much suspected that he was announcing an early visit from his son; but before she could quiet Mr. Elton, the subject was so completely past, that any reviving question from her would have been awkward.

Now it so happened, that, in spite of Emma's resolution of never marrying, there was something in the name, in the idea, of Mr. Frank Churchill, which always interested her. She had frequently thought,—especially since his father's marriage with Miss Taylor,—that if she *were* to marry, he was the very person to suit her in age, character, and condition. He seemed, by this connection between the families, quite to belong to her. She could not but suppose it to be a match that every body who knew them must think of. That Mr. and Mrs. Weston did think of it, she was very strongly persuaded; and though not meaning to be induced by him, or by any body else, to give up a situation which she believed more replete with good than any she could change it for, she had a great curiosity to see him, a decided intention of finding him pleasant, of being liked by him to a certain degree, and a sort of pleasure in the idea of their being coupled in their friends' imaginations.

With such sensations, Mr. Elton's civilities were dreadfully ill-timed; but she had the comfort of appearing very polite, while feeling very cross;—and of thinking that the rest of the visit could not possibly pass without bringing forward the same information again, or the substance of it, from the open-hearted Mr. Weston. So it proved;—for, when happily released from Mr. Elton, and seated by Mr. Weston at dinner, he made use of the very first interval in the cares of hospitality, the very first leisure from the saddle of mutton, to say to her,—

"We want only two more to be just the right number. I should like to see two more here,—your pretty little friend, Miss Smith, and my son,—and then I should say we were quite complete. I believe you did not hear me telling the others in the drawing-room that we are expecting Frank. I had a letter from him this morning, and he will be with us within a fortnight."

Emma spoke with a very proper degree of pleasure, and fully assented to his proposition, of Mr. Frank Churchill and Miss Smith making their party quite complete.

"He has been wanting to come to us," continued Mr. Weston, "ever since September: every letter has been full of it; but he cannot command his own time. He has those to please who must be pleased, and who (between ourselves) are sometimes to be pleased only by a good many sacrifices. But now I have no doubt of seeing him here about the second week in January."

"What a very great pleasure it will be to you! and Mrs. Weston is so anxious to be acquainted with him, that she must be almost as happy as yourself."

"Yes, she would be, but that she thinks there will be another put-off. She does not depend upon his coming so much as I do; but she does not know the parties so well as I do. The case, you see, is—(but this is quite between ourselves: I did not mention a syllable of it in the other room. There are secrets in all families, you know)—the case is, that a party of friends are invited to pay a visit at Enscombe in January, and that Frank's coming depends upon their being put off. If they are not put off, he cannot stir. But I know they will, because it is a family that a certain lady, of some consequence at Enscombe, has a particular dislike to; and though it is thought necessary to invite them once in two or three years, they always are put off when it comes to the point. I have not the smallest doubt of the issue. I am as confident of seeing Frank here before the middle of January, as I am of being here myself: but your good friend there (nodding towards the upper end of the table) has so few vagaries herself, and has been so little used to them at Hartfield, that she cannot calculate on their effects, as I have been long in the practice of doing."

"I am sorry there should be any thing like doubt in the case," replied Emma; "but am disposed to side with you, Mr. Weston. If you think he will come, I shall think so too; for you know Enscombe."

"Yes—I have some right to that knowledge; though I have never been at the place in my life. She is an odd woman! But I never allow myself to speak ill of her, on Frank's account; for I do believe her to be very fond of him. I used to think she was not capable of being fond of any body except herself: but she has always been kind to him (in her way—allowing for little whims and caprices, and expecting every thing to be as she likes). And it is no small credit, in my opinion, to him, that he should excite such an affection; for, though I would not say it to any body else, she has no more heart than a stone to people in general, and the devil of a temper."

Emma liked the subject so well, that she began upon it, to Mrs. Weston, very soon after their moving into the drawing-room; wishing her joy,—yet observing, that she knew the first meeting must be rather alarming. Mrs. Weston agreed to it; but added, that she should be very glad to be secure of undergoing the anxiety of a first meeting at the time talked of; "for I cannot depend upon his coming. I cannot be so sanguine as Mr. Weston. I am very much afraid that it will all end in nothing. Mr. Weston, I dare say, has been telling you exactly how the matter stands."

"Yes—it seems to depend upon nothing but the ill-humour of Mrs. Churchill, which I imagine to be the most certain thing in the world."

"My Emma!" replied Mrs. Weston, smiling, "what is the certainty of caprice?" Then turning to Isabella, who had not been attending before,—"You must know, my dear Mrs. Knightley, that we are by no means so sure of seeing Mr. Frank Churchill, in any opinion, as his father thinks. It depends entirely upon his aunt's spirits and pleasure; in short, upon her temper. To you—to my two daughters—I may venture on the truth. Mrs. Churchill rules at Enscombe, and is a very odd-tempered woman; and his coming now depends upon her being willing to spare him."

"Oh, Mrs. Churchill, every body knows Mrs. Churchill," replied Isabella; "and I am sure I never think of that poor young man without the greatest compassion. To be constantly living with an ill-tempered person must be dreadful. It is what we happily have never known any thing of; but it must be a life of misery. What a blessing, that she never had any children! Poor little creatures, how unhappy she would have made them!"

Emma wished she had been alone with Mrs. Weston. She should then have heard more: Mrs. Weston would speak to her with a degree of unreserve which she would not hazard with Isabella; and, she really believed, would scarcely try to conceal any thing relative to the Churchills from her, excepting those views on the young man, of which her own imagination had already given her such instinctive knowledge. But at present there was nothing more to be said. Mr. Woodhouse very soon followed them into the drawing-room. To be sitting long after dinner was a confinement that he could not endure. Neither wine nor conversation was any thing to him; and gladly did he move to those with whom he was always comfortable.

While he talked to Isabella, however, Emma found an opportunity of saying,—

"And so you do not consider this visit from your son as by any means certain. I am sorry for it. The introduction must be unpleasant, whenever it takes place; and the sooner it could be over the better."

"Yes; and every delay makes one more apprehensive of other delays. Even if this family, the Braithwaites, are put off, I am still afraid that some excuse may be found for disappointing us. I cannot bear to imagine any reluctance on his side; but I am sure there is a great wish on the Churchills to keep him to themselves. There is jealousy. They are jealous even of his regard for his father. In short, I can feel no dependence on his coming, and I wish Mr. Weston were less sanguine."

"He ought to come," said Emma. "If he could stay only a couple of days, he ought to come; and one can hardly conceive a young man's not having it in his power to do as much as that. A young *woman*, if she fall into bad hands, may be teazed, and kept at a distance from those she wants to be with; but one cannot comprehend a young *man*'s being under such restraint, as not to be able to spend a week with his father, if he likes it."

"One ought to be at Enscombe, and know the ways of the

family, before one decides upon what he can do," replied Mrs. Weston. "One ought to use the same caution, perhaps, in judging of the conduct of any one individual of any one family; but Enscombe, I believe, certainly must not be judged by general rules: *she* is so very unreasonable; and every thing gives way to her."

"But she is so fond of the nephew: he is so very great a favourite. Now, according to my idea of Mrs. Churchill, it would be most natural, that while she makes no sacrifice for the comfort of the husband, to whom she owes every thing, while she exercises incessant caprice towards *him*, she should frequently be governed by the nephew, to whom she owes nothing at all."

"My dearest Emma, do not pretend, with your sweet temper, to understand a bad one, or to lay down rules for it: you must let it go its own way. I have no doubt of his having, at times, considerable influence; but it may be perfectly impossible for him to know beforehand *when* it will be."

Emma listened, and then coolly said, "I shall not be satisfied, unless he comes."

"He may have a great deal of influence on some points," continued Mrs. Weston, "and on others, very little; and among those, on which she is beyond his reach, it is but too likely may be this very circumstance of his coming away from them to visit us."

## Chapter XV.

Mr. Woodhouse was soon ready for his tea; and when he had drank his tea he was quite ready to go home; and it was as much as his three companions could do, to entertain away his notice of the lateness of the hour, before the other gentlemen appeared. Mr. Weston was chatty and convivial, and no friend to early separations of any sort; but at last the drawing-room party did receive an augmentation. Mr. Elton, in very good spirits, was one of the first to walk in. Mrs. Weston and Emma were sitting together on a sofa. He joined them immediately, and with scarcely an invitation, seated himself between them.

Emma, in good spirits too, from the amusement afforded her mind by the expectation of Mr. Frank Churchill, was willing to forget his late improprieties, and be as well satisfied with him as before, and on his making Harriet his very first subject, was ready to listen with most friendly smiles.

He professed himself extremely anxious about her fair friend—her fair, lovely, amiable friend. "Did she know?—had she heard any thing about her, since their being at Randalls?—he felt much anxiety—he must confess that the nature of her complaint alarmed him considerably." And in this style he talked on for some time very properly, not much attending to any answer, but altogether sufficiently awake to the terror of a bad sore throat; and Emma was quite in charity with him.

But at last there seemed a perverse turn; it seemed all at once as if he were more afraid of its being a bad sore throat on her account than on Harriet's—more anxious that she should escape the infection, than that there should be no infection in the complaint. He began with great earnestness to entreat her to refrain from visiting the sick chamber again, for the present—to entreat her to *promise him* not to venture into such hazard till he had seen Mr. Perry and learned his opinion; and though she tried to laugh it off and bring the subject back into its proper course, there was no putting an end to his extreme solicitude about her. She was vexed. It did appear—there was no concealing it—exactly like the pretence of being in love with her, instead of Harriet; an inconstancy, if real, the most contemptible and abominable! and she had difficulty in behaving with temper. He turned to Mrs. Weston to implore her assistance: "Would not she give him her support?—would not she add her persuasions to his, to induce Miss Woodhouse not to go to Mrs. Goddard's, till it were certain that Miss Smith's disorder had no infection? He could not be satisfied without a promise—would not she give him her influence in procuring it?

"So scrupulous for others," he continued, "and yet so careless for herself! She wanted me to nurse my cold by staying at home to-day, and yet will not promise to avoid the danger of catching an ulcerated sore throat herself. Is this fair, Mrs. Weston? Judge between us. Have not I some right to complain? I am sure of your kind support and aid."

Emma saw Mrs. Weston's surprise, and felt that it must be great, at an address which, in words and manner, was assuming to himself the right of first interest in her; and as for herself, she was too much provoked and offended to have the power of directly saying any thing to the purpose. She could only give him a look; but it was such a look as she thought must restore him to his senses; and then left the sofa, removing to a seat by her sister, and giving her all her attention.

She had not time to know how Mr. Elton took the reproof, so rapidly did another subject succeed; for Mr. John Knightley now came into the room from examining the weather, and opened on them all with the information of the ground being covered with snow, and of its still snowing fast, with a strong drifting wind; concluding with these words to Mr. Woodhouse;—

"This will prove a spirited beginning of your winter engagements, sir. Something new for your coachman and horses to be making their way through a storm of snow."

Poor Mr. Woodhouse was silent from consternation; but every body else had something to say; every body was either surprised, or not surprised, and had some question to ask, or some comfort to offer. Mrs. Weston and Emma tried earnestly to cheer him and turn his attention from his son-in-law, who was pursuing his triumph rather unfeelingly.

"I admired your resolution very much, sir," said he, "in venturing out in such weather, for of course you saw there would be snow very soon. Every body must have seen the snow coming on. I admired your spirit; and I dare say we shall get home very well. Another hour or two's snow can hardly make the road impassable; and we are two carriages; if *one* is blown over in the bleak part of the common field there will be the other at hand. I dare say we shall be all safe at Hartfield before midnight."

Mr. Weston, with triumph of a different sort, was confessing that he had known it to be snowing some time, but had not said a word, lest it should make Mr. Woodhouse uncomfortable, and be an excuse for his hurrying away. As to there being any quantity of snow fallen or likely to fall to impede their return, that was a mere joke; he was afraid they would find no difficulty. He wished the road might be impassable, that he might be able to keep them all at Randalls; and with the utmost good-will was sure that accommodation might be found for every body, calling on his wife to agree with him, that, with a little contrivance, every body might be lodged, which she hardly knew how to do, from the consciousness of there being but two spare rooms in the house.

"What is to be done, my dear Emma? what is to be done?" was Mr. Woodhouse's first exclamation, and all that he could say for some time. To her he looked for comfort; and her assurances of safety, her representation of the excellence of the horses, and of James, and of their having so many friends about them, revived him a little.

His eldest daughter's alarm was equal to his own. The horror of being blocked up at Randalls, while her children were at Hartfield, was full in her imagination; and fancying the road to be now just passable for adventurous people, but in a state that admitted no delay, she was eager to have it settled, that her father and Emma should remain at Randalls while she and her husband set forward instantly through all the possible accumulations of drifted snow that might impede them.

"You had better order the carriage directly, my love," said she: "I dare say we shall be able to get along, if we set off directly; and if we do come to any thing very bad, I can get out and walk. I am not at all afraid. I should not mind walking half the way. I could change my shoes, you know, the moment I got home; and it is not the sort of thing that gives me cold."

"Indeed!" replied he. "Then, my dear Isabella, it is the most extraordinary sort of thing in the world, for in general every thing does give you cold. Walk home!—you are prettily shod for walking home, I dare say. It will be bad enough for the horses."

Isabella turned to Mrs. Weston for her approbation of the plan. Mrs. Weston could only approve. Isabella then went to Emma; but Emma could not so entirely give up the hope of their being all able to get away; and they were still discussing the point, when Mr. Knightley, who had left the room immediately after his brother's first report of the snow, came back again, and told them that he had been out of doors to examine, and could answer for there not being the smallest difficulty in their getting home, whenever they liked it, either now or an hour hence. He had gone beyond the sweep—some way along the Highbury road—the snow was no where above half an inch deep—in many places hardly enough to whiten the ground; a very few flakes were falling at present, but the clouds were parting, and there was every appearance of its being soon over. He had seen the coachmen, and they both agreed with him in there being nothing to apprehend.

To Isabella, the relief of such tidings was very great, and they were scarcely less acceptable to Emma on her father's account, who was immediately set as much at ease on the subject as his nervous constitution allowed; but the alarm that had been raised could not be appeased so as to admit of any comfort for him while he continued at Randalls. He was satisfied of there being no present danger in returning home, but no assurance could convince him that it was safe to stay; and while the others were variously urging and recommending, Mr. Knightley and Emma settled it in a few brief sentences: thus,—

"Your father will not be easy; why do not you go?"

"I am ready, if the others are."

"Shall I ring the bell?"

"Yes, do."

And the bell was rung, and the carriages spoken for. A few minutes more, and Emma hoped to see one troublesome companion deposited in his own house, to get sober and cool, and the other recover his temper and happiness when this visit of hardship were over.

The carriage came; and Mr. Woodhouse, always the first object on such occasions, was carefully attended to his own by Mr. Knightley and Mr. Weston; but not all that either could say could prevent some renewal of alarm at the sight of the snow which had actually fallen, and the discovery of a much darker night than he had been prepared for. "He was afraid they should have a very bad drive. He was afraid poor Isabella would not like it. And there would be poor Emma in the carriage behind. He did not know what they had best do. They must keep as much together as they could;" and James was talked to, and given a charge to go very slow, and wait for the other carriage.

Isabella stept in after her father; John Knightley, forgetting that he did not belong to their party, stept in after his wife very naturally; so that Emma found, on being escorted and followed into the second carriage by Mr. Elton, that the door was to be lawfully shut on them, and that they were to have a tête-à-tête drive. It would not have been the awkwardness of a moment, it would have been rather a pleasure, previous to the suspicions of this very day; she could have talked to him of Harriet, and the three quarters of a mile would have seemed but one. But how, she would rather it had not happened. She believed he had been drinking too much of Mr. Weston's good wine; and felt sure that he would want to be talking nonsense.

To restrain him as much as might be, by her own manners, she was immediately preparing to speak with exquisite calmness and gravity of the weather and the night; but scarcely had she begun, scarcely had they passed the sweep-gate and joined the other carriage, than she found her subject cut up—her hand seized—her attention demanded, and Mr. Elton actually making violent love to her: availing himself of the precious opportunity, declaring sentiments which must be already well known, hoping—fearing—adoring—ready to die if she refused him; but flattering himself that his ardent attachment and unequalled love and unexampled passion could not fail of having some effect, and in short, very much resolved on being seriously accepted as soon as possible. It really was so. Without scruple—without apology—without much apparent diffidence, Mr. Elton, the lover of Harriet, was professing himself *her* lover. She tried to stop him; but vainly; he would go on, and say it all. Angry as she was, the thought of the moment made her resolve to restrain herself when she did speak. She felt that half this folly must be drunkenness, and therefore could hope that it might belong only to the passing hour. Accordingly, with a mixture of the serious and the playful, which she hoped would best suit his half and half state, she replied,—

"I am very much astonished, Mr. Elton. This to *me*, you forget yourself—you take me for my friend—any message to Miss Smith I shall be happy to deliver; but no more of this to *me*, if you please."

"Miss Smith!—Message to Miss Smith!—What could she possibly mean!"—And he repeated her words with such assurance of accent, such boastful pretence of amazement, that she could not help replying with quickness,—

"Mr. Elton, this is the most extraordinary conduct! and I can account for it only in one way; you are not yourself, or you could not speak either to me, or of Harriet, in such a manner. Command yourself enough to say no more, and I will endeavour to forget it."

But Mr. Elton had only drunk wine enough to elevate his spirits, not at all to confuse his intellects. He perfectly knew his own meaning; and having warmly protested against her suspicion as most injurious, and slightly touched upon his respect for Miss Smith as her friend,—but acknowledging his wonder that Miss Smith should be mentioned at all,—he resumed the subject of his own passion, and was very urgent for a favourable answer.

As she thought less of his inebriety, she thought more of his inconstancy and presumption; and with fewer struggles for politeness, replied,—

"It is impossible for me to doubt any longer. You have made yourself too clear. Mr. Elton, my astonishment is much beyond any thing I can express. After such behaviour, as I have witnessed during the last month, to Miss Smith—such attentions as I have been in the daily habit of observing—to be addressing me in this manner—this is an unsteadiness of character, indeed, which I had not supposed possible! Believe me, sir, I am far—very far—from gratified in being the object of such professions."

"Good heaven!" cried Mr. Elton, "what can be the meaning of this? Miss Smith! I never thought of Miss Smith in the whole course of my existence—never paid her any attentions, but as your friend: never cared whether she were dead or alive, but as your friend. If she has fancied otherwise, her own wishes have misled her, and I am very sorry—extremely sorry. But, Miss Smith, indeed! Oh, Miss Woodhouse, who can think of Miss Smith when Miss Woodhouse is near? No, upon my honour, there is no unsteadiness of character. I have thought only of you. I protest against having paid the smallest attention to any one else. Every thing that I have said or done, for many weeks past, has been with the sole view of marking my adoration of yourself. You cannot really, seriously doubt it. No! (in an accent meant to be insinuating) I am sure you have seen and understood me."

It would be impossible to say what Emma felt on hearing this; which of all her unpleasant sensations was uppermost. She was too completely overpowered to be immediately able to reply; and two moments of silence being ample encouragement for Mr. Elton's sanguine state of mind, he tried to take her hand again, as he joyously exclaimed.—

"Charming Miss Woodhouse! allow me to interpret this interesting silence. It confesses that you have long understood me."

"No, sir," cried Emma, "it confesses no such thing. So far

from having long understood you, I have been in a most complete error with respect to your views till this moment. As to myself I am very sorry that you should have been giving way to any feelings——Nothing could be farther from my wishes—your attachment to my friend Harriet—your pursuit of her (pursuit it appeared)—gave me great pleasure, and I have been very earnestly wishing you success; but had I supposed that she were not your attraction to Hartfield, I should certainly have thought you judged ill in making your visits so frequent. Am I to believe that you have never sought to recommend yourself particularly to Miss Smith? that you have never thought seriously of her?"

"Never, madam," cried he, affronted in his turn: "never, I assure you. *I* think seriously of Miss Smith!—Miss Smith is a very good sort of girl; and I should be happy to see her respectably settled. I wish her extremely well; and, no doubt, there are men who might not object to——Every body has their level; but as for myself, I am not, I think, quite so much at a loss. I need not so totally despair of an equal alliance as to be addressing myself to Miss Smith! No, madam, my visits to Hartfield have been for yourself only; and the encouragement I received——"

"Encouragement! I give you encouragement!—sir, you have been entirely mistaken in supposing it. I have seen you only as the admirer of my friend. In no other light could you have been more to me than a common acquaintance. I am exceedingly sorry; but it is well that the mistake ends where it does. Had the same behaviour continued, Miss Smith might have been led into a misconception of your views; not being aware, probably, any more than myself, of the very great inequality which you are so sensible of. But, as it is, the disappointment is single, and, I trust, will not be lasting. I have no thoughts of matrimony at present."

He was too angry to say another word; her manner too decided to invite supplication: and in this state of swelling resentment, and mutually deep mortification, they had to continue together a few minutes longer, for the fears of Mr. Woodhouse had confined them to a foot pace. If there had not been so much anger, there would have been desperate awkwardness; but their straight-forward emotions left no room for the little zigzags of embarrassment. Without knowing when the carriage turned into Vicarage Lane, or when it stopped, they found themselves, all at once, at the door of his house; and he was out before another syllable passed. Emma then felt it indispensable to wish him a good night. The compliment was just returned, coldly and proudly; and, under indescribable irritation of spirits, she was then conveyed to Hartfield.

There she was welcomed, with the utmost delight, by her father, who had been trembling for the dangers of a solitary drive from Vicarage Lane—turning a corner which he could never bear to think of—and in strange hands—a mere common coachman—no James; and there it seemed as if her return only were wanted to make every thing go well: for Mr. John Knightley, ashamed of his ill-humour, was now all kindness and attention; and so particularly solicitous for the comfort of her father, as to seem—if not quite ready to join him in a basin of gruel—perfectly sensible of its being exceedingly wholesome; and the day was concluding in peace and comfort to all their little party, except herself. But her mind had never been in such perturbation; and it needed a very strong effort to appear attentive and cheerful till the usual hour of separating allowed her the relief of quiet reflection.

## Chapter XVI.

The hair was curled, and the maid sent away, and Emma sat down to think and be miserable. It was a wretched business, indeed. Such an overthrow of every thing she had been wishing for! Such a development

of every thing most unwelcome! Such a blow for Harriet!—
that was the worst of all. Every part of it brought pain and
humiliation of some sort or other; but, compared with the
evil to Harriet, all was light; and she would gladly have submitted to feel yet more mistaken—more in error—more disgraced by mis-judgment than she actually was,—could the
effects of her blunders have been confined to herself.

"If I had not persuaded Harriet into liking the man, I
could have borne any thing. He might have doubled his presumption to me—but poor Harriet!"

How she could have been so deceived! He protested that
he had never thought seriously of Harriet—never! She
looked back as well as she could; but it was all confusion. She
had taken up the idea, she supposed, and made every thing
bend to it. His manners, however, must have been un-
marked, wavering, dubious, or she could not have been so
misled.

The picture! How eager he had been about the picture!—and the charade!—and a hundred other circumstances;—how clearly they had seemed to point at Harriet.
To be sure, the charade, with its "ready wit"—but then, the
"soft eyes"—in fact it suited neither; it was a jumble without
taste or truth. Who could have seen through such thick-
headed nonsense?

Certainly she had often, especially of late, thought his
manners to herself unnecessarily gallant; but it had passed as
his way, as a mere error of judgment, of knowledge, of taste,
as one proof, among others, that he had not always lived in
the best society; that with all the gentleness of his address,
true elegance was sometimes wanting; but, till this very day,
she had never for an instant suspected it to mean any thing
but grateful respect to her as Harriet's friend.

To Mr. John Knightley was she indebted for her first idea
on the subject, for the first start of its possibility. There was
no denying that those brothers had penetration. She remembered what Mr. Knightley had once said to her about
Mr. Elton, the caution he had given the conviction he had

professed that Mr. Elton would never marry indiscreetly; and blushed to think how much truer a knowledge of his character had been there shown than any she had reached herself. It was dreadfully mortifying; but Mr. Elton was proving himself, in many respects, the very reverse of what she had meant and believed him; proud, assuming, conceited: very full of his own claims, and little concerned about the feelings of others.

Contrary to the usual course of things, Mr. Elton's wanting to pay his addresses to her had sunk him in her opinion. His professions and his proposals did him no service. She thought nothing of his attachment, and was insulted by his hopes. He wanted to marry well, and having the arrogance to raise his eyes to her, pretended to be in love; but she was perfectly easy as to his not suffering any disappointment that need be cared for. There had been no real affection either in his language or manners. Sighs and fine words had been given in abundance; but she could hardly devise any set of expressions, or fancy any tone of voice, less allied with real love. She need not trouble herself to pity him. He only wanted to aggrandise and enrich himself; and if Miss Woodhouse of Hartfield, the heiress of thirty thousand pounds, were not quite so easily obtained as he had fancied, he would soon try for Miss Somebody else with twenty, or with ten.

But, that he should talk of encouragement, should consider her as aware of his views, accepting his intentions, meaning, in short, to marry him!—should suppose himself her equal in connection or mind!—look down upon her friend, so well understanding the gradations of rank below him, and be so blind to what rose above, as to fancy himself showing no presumption in addressing her!—it was most provoking.

Perhaps it was not fair to expect him to feel how very much he was her inferior in talent, and all the elegancies of mind. The very want of such equality might prevent his perception of it; but he must know that in fortune and consequence she was greatly his superior. He must know that the

Woodhouses had been settled for several generations at Hartfield, the younger branch of a very ancient family,—and that the Eltons were nobody. The landed property of Hartfield certainly was inconsiderable, being but a sort of notch in the Donwell Abbey estate, to which all the rest of Highbury belonged; but their fortune, from other sources, was such as to make them scarcely secondary to Donwell Abbey itself, in every other kind of consequence; and the Woodhouses had long held a high place in the consideration of the neighbourhood which Mr. Elton had first entered not two years ago, to make his way as he could, without any alliances but in trade, or any thing to recommend him to notice but his situation and his civility. But he had fancied her in love with him; that evidently must have been his dependence; and after raving a little about the seeming incongruity of gentle manners and a conceited head, Emma was obliged, in common honesty, to stop and admit, that her own behaviour to him had been so complaisant and obliging, so full of courtesy and attention, as (supposing her real motive unperceived) might warrant a man of ordinary observation and delicacy, like Mr. Elton, in fancying himself a very decided favourite. If *she* had so misinterpreted his feelings, she had little right to wonder that *he*, with self-interest to blind him, should have mistaken hers.

The first error, and the worst, lay at her door. It was foolish, it was wrong, to take so active a part in bringing any two people together. It was adventuring too far, assuming too much, making light of what ought to be serious, a trick of what ought to be simple. She was quite concerned and ashamed, and resolved to do such things no more.

"Here have I," said she, "actually talked poor Harriet into being very much attached to this man. She might never have thought of him but for me; and certainly never would have thought of him with hope, if I had not assured her of his attachment, for she is as modest and humble as I used to think him. Oh that I had been satisfied with persuading her not to accept young Martin! There I was quite right: that was well

done of me; but there I should have stopped, and left the
rest to time and chance. I was introducing her into good
company, and giving her the opportunity of pleasing some
one worth having; I ought not to have attempted more. But
now, poor girl, her peace is cut up for some time. I have
been but half a friend to her; and if she were *not* to feel this
disappointment so very much, I am sure I have not an idea
of any body else who would be at all desirable for her:—
William Coxe—oh no, I could not endure William Coxe,—a
pert young lawyer."

She stopped to blush and laugh at her own relapse, and
then resumed a more serious, more dispiriting cogitation
upon what had been, and might be, and must be. The distressing explanation she had to make to Harriet, and all that
poor Harriet would be suffering, with the awkwardness of future meetings, the difficulties of continuing or discontinu-
ing the acquaintance, of subduing feelings, concealing
resentment, and avoiding éclat, were enough to occupy her
in most unmirthful reflections some time longer, and she
went to bed at last with nothing settled but the conviction of
her having blundered most dreadfully.

To youth and natural cheerfulness like Emma's, though
under temporary gloom at night, the return of day will
hardly fail to bring return of spirits. The youth and cheerfulness of morning are in happy analogy, and of powerful
operation; and if the distress be not poignant enough to
keep the eyes unclosed, they will be sure to open to sensations of softened pain and brighter hope.

Emma got up on the morrow more disposed for comfort
than she had gone to bed; more ready to see alleviations of
the evil before her, and to depend on getting tolerably out
of it.

It was a great consolation that Mr. Elton should not be really in love with her, or so particularly amiable as to make it
shocking to disappoint him; that Harriet's nature should not
be of that superior sort in which the feelings are most acute
and retentive; and that there could be no necessity for any

body's knowing what had passed except the three principals, and especially for her father's being given a moment's uneasiness about it.

These were very cheering thoughts; and the sight of a great deal of snow on the ground did her further service, for any thing was welcome that might justify their all three being quite asunder at present.

The weather was most favourable for her; though Christmas-day, she could not go to church. Mr. Woodhouse would have been miserable had his daughter attempted it, and she was therefore safe from either exciting or receiving unpleasant and most unsuitable ideas. The ground covered with snow, and the atmosphere in that unsettled state between frost and thaw, which is of all others the most unfriendly for exercise, every morning beginning in rain or snow, and every evening setting in to freeze, she was for many days a most honourable prisoner. No intercourse with Harriet possible but by note; no church for her on Sunday any more than on Christmas-day; and no need to find excuses for Mr. Elton's absenting himself.

It was weather which might fairly confine every body at home; and though she hoped and believed him to be really taking comfort in some society or other, it was very pleasant to have her father so well satisfied with his being all alone in his own house, too wise to stir out; and to hear him say to Mr. Knightley, whom no weather could keep entirely from them,—

"Ah, Mr. Knightley, why do not you stay at home like poor Mr. Elton?"

These days of confinement would have been, but for her private perplexities, remarkably comfortable, as such seclusion exactly suited her brother, whose feelings must always be of great importance to his companions; and he had, besides, so thoroughly cleared off his ill-humour at Randalls, that his amiableness never failed him during the rest of his stay at Hartfield. He was always agreeable and obliging, and speaking pleasantly of every body. But with all the hopes of cheerfulness, and all the present comfort of delay, there was still such an evil hanging over her in the hour of explanation with Harriet, as made it impossible for Emma to be ever perfectly at ease.

## Chapter XVII.

Mr. and Mrs. John Knightley were not detained long at Hartfield. The weather soon improved enough for those to move who must move; and Mr. Woodhouse having, as usual, tried to persuade his daughter to stay behind with all her children, was obliged to see the whole party set off, and return to his lamentations over the destiny of poor Isabella;—which poor Isabella, passing her life with those she doted on, full of their merits, blind to their faults, and always innocently busy, might have been a model of right feminine happiness.

The evening of the very day on which they went brought a note from Mr. Elton to Mr. Woodhouse, a long, civil, ceremonious note, to say, with Mr. Elton's best compliments, "that he was proposing to leave Highbury the following morning in his way to Bath; where, in compliance with the pressing entreaties of some friends, he had engaged to spend a few weeks; and very much regretted the impossibility he was under, from various circumstances of weather and business, of taking a personal leave of Mr. Woodhouse, of whose friendly civilities he should ever retain a grateful sense; and had Mr. Woodhouse any commands, should be happy to attend to them."

Emma was most agreeably surprised. Mr. Elton's absence just at this time was the very thing to be desired. She admired him for contriving it, though not able to give him much credit for the manner in which it was announced. Resentment could not have been more plainly spoken than in a civility to her father, from which she was so pointedly excluded. She had not even a share in his opening compliments. Her name was not mentioned; and there was so striking a change in all this, and such an ill-judged solemnity of leave-taking in his grateful acknowledgments, as she thought, at first, could not escape her father's suspicion.

It did, however. Her father was quite taken up with the surprise of so sudden a journey, and his fears that Mr. Elton might never get safely to the end of it, and saw nothing extraordinary in his language. It was a very useful note, for it supplied them with fresh matter for thought and conversation during the rest of their lonely evening. Mr. Woodhouse talked over his alarms, and Emma was in spirits to persuade them away with all her usual promptitude.

She now resolved to keep Harriet no longer in the dark. She had reason to believe her nearly recovered from her cold, and it was desirable that she should have as much time as possible for getting the better of her other complaint before the gentleman's return. She went to Mrs. Goddard's accordingly the very next day, to undergo the necessary penance of communication; and a severe one it was. She had to destroy all the hopes which she had been so industriously feeding, to appear in the ungracious character of the one preferred, and acknowledge herself grossly mistaken and misjudging in all her ideas on one subject, all her observations, all her convictions, all her prophecies for the last six weeks.

The confession completely renewed her first shame, and the sight of Harriet's tears made her think that she should never be in charity with herself again.

Harriet bore the intelligence very well, blaming nobody, and in every thing testifying such an ingenuousness of disposition and lowly opinion of herself, as must appear with particular advantage at that moment to her friend.

Emma was in the humour to value simplicity and modesty to the utmost; and all that was amiable, all that ought to be attaching, seemed on Harriet's side, not her own. Harriet did not consider herself as having any thing to complain of. The affection of such a man as Mr. Elton would have been too great a distinction. She never could have deserved him; and nobody but so partial and kind a friend as Miss Woodhouse would have thought it possible.

Her tears fell abundantly; but her grief was so truly art-less, that no dignity could have made it more respectable in Emma's eyes; and she listened to her, and tried to console her with all her heart and understanding,—really for the time convinced that Harriet was the superior creature of the two, and that to resemble her would be more for her own welfare and happiness than all that genius or intelligence could do.

It was rather too late in the day to set about being simple-minded and ignorant; but she left her with every previous resolution confirmed of being humble and discreet, and re-pressing imagination all the rest of her life. Her second duty now, inferior only to her father's claims, was to promote Harriet's comfort, and endeavour to prove her own affection in some better method than by match-making. She got her to Hartfield, and showed her the most unvarying kindness, striving to occupy and amuse her, and by books and conver-sation to drive Mr. Elton from her thoughts.

Time, she knew, must be allowed for this being thor-oughly done; and she could suppose herself but an indiffer-ent judge of such matters in general, and very inadequate to sympathise in an attachment to Mr. Elton in particular; but it seemed to her reasonable that at Harriet's age, and with the entire extinction of all hope, such a progress might be made towards a state of composure by the time of Mr. Elton's return, as to allow them all to meet again in the common routine of acquaintance, without any danger of betraying sentiments or increasing them.

Harriet did think him all perfection, and maintain the

non-existence of any body equal to him in person or goodness, and did, in truth, prove herself more resolutely in love than Emma had foreseen; but yet it appeared to her so natural, so inevitable to strive against an inclination of that sort *unrequited*, that she could not comprehend its continuing very long in equal force.

If Mr. Elton, on his return, made his own indifference as evident and indubitable as she could not doubt he would anxiously do, she could not imagine Harriet's persisting to place her happiness in the sight or the recollection of him.

Their being fixed, so absolutely fixed, in the same place, was bad for each, for all three. Not one of them had the power of removal, or of effecting any material change of society. They must encounter each other, and make the best of it.

Harriet was further unfortunate in the tone of her companions at Mrs. Goddard's, Mr. Elton being the adoration of all the teachers and great girls in the school; and it must be at Hartfield only that she could have any chance of hearing him spoken of with cooling moderation or repellant truth. Where the wound had been given, there must the cure be found, if any where; and Emma felt that, till she saw her in the way of cure, there could be no true peace for herself.

## Chapter XVIII.

Mr. Frank Churchill did not come. When the time proposed drew near, Mrs. Weston's fears were justified in the arrival of a letter of excuse. For the present, he could not be spared, to his "very great mortification and regret; but still he looked forward with the hope of coming to Randalls at no distant period."

Mrs. Weston was exceedingly disappointed,—much more disappointed, in fact, than her husband, though her dependence on seeing the young man had been so much more sober; but a sanguine temper, though for ever expecting more good than occurs, does not always pay for its hopes by any proportionate depression. It soon flies over the present failure, and begins to hope again. For half an hour Mr. Weston was surprised and sorry: but then he began to perceive that Frank's coming two or three months later would be a much better plan, better time of year, better weather; and that he would be able, without any doubt, to stay considerably longer with them than if he had come sooner.

These feelings rapidly restored his comfort, while Mrs. Weston, of a more apprehensive disposition, foresaw nothing but a repetition of excuses and delays; and after all her concern for what her husband was to suffer, suffered a great deal more herself.

Emma was not at this time in a state of spirits to care really about Mr. Frank Churchill's not coming, except as a disappointment at Randalls. The acquaintance, at present, had no charm for her. She wanted, rather, to be quiet and out of temptation; but still, as it was desirable that she should appear, in general, like her usual self, she took care to express as much interest in the circumstance, and enter as warmly into Mr. and Mrs. Weston's disappointment as might naturally belong to their friendship.

She was the first to announce it to Mr. Knightley; and exclaimed quite as much as was necessary (or, being acting a part, perhaps rather more,) at the conduct of the Churchills in keeping him away. She then proceeded to say a good deal more than she felt of the advantage of such an addition to their confined society in Surrey; the pleasure of looking at somebody new; the gala-day to Highbury entire, which the sight of him would have made; and ending with reflections on the Churchills again, found herself directly involved in a disagreement with Mr. Knightley; and, to her great amusement, perceived that she was taking the other side of the question from her real opinion, and, making use of Mrs. Weston's arguments against herself.

"The Churchills are very likely in fault," said Mr. Knightley, coolly; "but I dare say he might come if he would."

"I do not know why you should say so. He wishes exceedingly to come; but his uncle and aunt will not spare him."

"I cannot believe that he has not the power of coming, if he made a point of it. It is too unlikely for me to believe it without proof."

"How odd you are! What has Mr. Frank Churchill done, to make you suppose him such an unnatural creature?"

"I am not supposing him at all an unnatural creature, in suspecting that he may have learned to be above his connections, and to care very little for any thing but his own pleasure, from living with those who have always set him the example of it. It is a great deal more natural than one could wish, that a young man, brought up by those who are proud, luxurious, and selfish, should be proud, luxurious, and selfish too. If Frank Churchill had wanted to see his father, he would have contrived it between September and January. A man at his age,—what is he?—three or four and twenty—cannot be without the means of doing as much as that. It is impossible."

"That's easily said, and easily felt by you, who have always been your own master. You are the worst judge in the world, Mr. Knightley, of the difficulties of dependence. You do not know what it is to have tempers to manage."

"It is not to be conceived that a man of three or four and twenty should not have liberty of mind or limb to that amount. He cannot want money, he cannot want leisure. We know, on the contrary, that he has so much of both, that he is glad to get rid of them at the idlest haunts in the kingdom. We hear of him for ever at some watering-place or other; a little while ago he was at Weymouth. This proves that he can leave the Churchills."

"Yes, sometimes he can."

"And those times are, whenever he thinks it worth his while; whenever there is any temptation of pleasure."

"It is very unfair to judge of any body's conduct, without an intimate knowledge of their situation. Nobody, who has not been in the interior of a family, can say what the difficulties of any individual of that family may be. We ought to be acquainted with Enscombe, and with Mrs. Churchill's temper, before we pretend to decide with what her nephew can do. He may, at times, be able to do a great deal more than he can at others."

"There is one thing, Emma, which a man can always do, if he chooses, and that is, his duty; not by manœuvering and finessing, but by vigour and resolution. It is Frank Churchill's duty to pay this attention to his father. He knows it to be so, by his promises and messages; but if he wished to do it, it might be done. A man who felt rightly would say at once, simply and resolutely, to Mrs. Churchill, 'Every sacrifice of mere pleasure you will always find me ready to make to your convenience; but I must go and see my father immediately. I know he would be hurt by my failing in such a mark of respect to him on the present occasion. I shall, therefore, set off to-morrow.' If he would say so to her at once, in the tone of decision becoming a man, there would be no opposition made to his going."

"No," said Emma, laughing; "but perhaps there might be some made to his coming back again. Such language for a young man entirely dependent to use! Nobody but you, Mr. Knightley, would imagine it possible: but you have not an idea of what is requisite in situations directly opposite to your own. Mr. Frank Churchill to be making such a speech as that to the uncle and aunt who have brought him up, and are to provide for him!—standing up in the middle of the room, I suppose, and speaking as loud as he could! How can you imagine such conduct practicable?"

"Depend upon it, Emma, a sensible man would find no difficulty in it. He would feel himself in the right; and the declaration,—made, of course, as a man of sense would make it, in a proper manner,—would do him more good, raise him higher, fix his interest stronger with the people he depended on, than all that a line of shifts and expedients can ever do. Respect would be added to affection. They would feel that they could trust him; that the nephew, who had done rightly by his father, would do rightly by them; for they know, as well as he does,—as well as all the world must know,—that he ought to pay this visit to his father; and while meanly exerting their power to delay it, are in their hearts not thinking the better of him for submitting to their whims. Respect for right conduct is felt by every body. If he would act in this sort of manner, on principle, consistently, regularly, their little minds would bend to his."

"I rather doubt that. You are very fond of bending little minds; but where little minds belong to rich people in authority, I think they have a knack of swelling out, till they are quite as unmanageable as great ones. I can imagine, that if you, as you are, Mr. Knightley, were to be transported and placed all at once in Mr. Frank Churchill's situation, you would be able to say and do just what you have been recommending for him; and it might have a very good effect. The Churchills might not have a word to say in return; but then, you would have no habits of early obedience and long observance to break through. To him who has, it might not be so easy to burst forth at once into perfect independence, and set all their claims on his gratitude and regard at nought. He may have as strong a sense of what would be right as you can have, without being so equal, under particular circumstances, to act up to it."

"Then, it would not be so strong a sense. If it failed to produce equal exertion, it could not be an equal conviction."

"Oh the difference of situation and habit! I wish you would try to understand what an amiable young man may be likely to feel in directly opposing those whom, as child and boy, he has been looking up to all his life."

"Your amiable young man is a very weak young man, if this be the first occasion of his carrying through a resolution to do right against the will of others. It ought to have been a habit with him, by this time, of following his duty, instead of consulting expediency. I can allow for the fears of the child, but not of the man. As he became rational, he ought to have roused himself, and shaken off all that was unworthy in their authority. He ought to have opposed the first attempt on their side to make him slight his father. Had he begun as he ought, there would have been no difficulty now."

"We shall never agree about him," cried Emma; "but that is nothing extraordinary. I have not the least idea of his being a weak young man: I feel sure that he is not. Mr. Weston would not be blind to folly, though in his own son; but he is very likely to have a more yielding, complying, mild disposition, than would suit your notions of man's perfection. I dare say he has; and though it may cut him off from some advantages, it will secure him many others."

"Yes; all the advantages of sitting still when he ought to move, and of leading a life of mere idle pleasure, and fancying himself extremely expert in finding excuses for it. He can sit down and write a fine flourishing letter, full of professions and falsehoods, and persuade himself that he has hit upon the very best method in the world of preserving peace at home, and preventing his father's having any right to complain. His letters disgust me."

"Your feelings are singular. They seem to satisfy every body else."

"I suspect they do not satisfy Mrs. Weston. They hardly can satisfy a woman of her good sense and quick feelings: standing in a mother's place, but without a mother's affection to blind her. It is on her account that attention to Randalls is doubly due, and she must doubly feel the omission. Had she been a person of consequence herself, he would have come, I dare say; and it would not have signified whether he did or no. Can you think your friend behindhand in these sort of considerations? Do you suppose she does not often say all this to herself? No, Emma; your amiable young man can be amiable only in French, not in English. He may be very 'amiable,' have very good manners, and be very agreeable; but he can have no English delicacy towards the feelings of other people,—nothing really amiable about him."

"You seem determined to think ill of him."

"Me! not at all," replied Mr. Knightley, rather displeased; "I do not want to think ill of him. I should be as ready to acknowledge his merits as any other man; but I hear of none, except what are merely personal,—that he is well-grown and good-looking, with smooth, plausible manners."

"Well, if he have nothing else to recommend him, he will be a treasure at Highbury. We do not often look upon fine young men, well bred and agreeable. We must not be nice, and ask for all the virtues into the bargain. Cannot you imagine, Mr. Knightley, what a *sensation* his coming will produce? There will be but one subject throughout the parishes of Donwell and Highbury; but one interest—one object of curiosity; it will be all Mr. Frank Churchill; we shall think and speak of nobody else."

"You will excuse my being so much overpowered. If I find him conversible, I shall be glad of his acquaintance; but if he is only a chattering coxcomb, he will not occupy much of my time or thoughts."

"My idea of him is, that he can adapt his conversation to the taste of every body, and has the power as well as the wish of being universally agreeable. To you, he will talk of farming; to me, of drawing or music; and so on to every body, having that general information on all subjects which will enable him to follow the lead, or take the lead, just as propriety may require, and to speak extremely well on each; that is my idea of him."

"And mine," said Mr. Knightley, warmly, "is, that if he turn out any thing like it, he will be the most insufferable fellow breathing! What! at three-and-twenty to be the king of his company—the great man—the practised politician, who is to read every body's character, and make every body's talents conduce to the display of his own superiority; to be dispensing his flatteries around, that he may make all appear like fools compared with himself! My dear Emma, your own good sense could not endure such a puppy when it came to the point."

"I will say no more about him," cried Emma,—"you turn every thing to evil. We are both prejudiced; you against, I for him; and we have no chance of agreeing till he is really here."

"Prejudiced! I am not prejudiced."

"But I am very much, and without being at all ashamed of it. My love for Mr. and Mrs. Weston gives me a decided prejudice in his favour."

"He is a person I never think of from one month's end to another," said Mr. Knightley, with a degree of vexation, which made Emma immediately talk of something else, though she could not comprehend why he should be angry.

To take a dislike to a young man, only because he appeared to be of a different disposition from himself, was unworthy the real liberality of mind which she was always used to acknowledge in him; for with all the high opinion of himself, which she had often laid to his charge, she had never before for a moment supposed it could make him unjust to the merit of another.

END OF THE FIRST VOLUME.

# Volume the Second.

# Chapter I.

Emma and Harriet had been walking together one morning, and, in Emma's opinion, been talking enough of Mr. Elton for that day. She could not think that Harriet's solace or her own sins required more; and she was therefore industriously getting rid of the subject as they returned;—but it burst out again when she thought she had succeeded, and after speaking some time of what the poor must suffer in winter, and receiving no other answer than a very plaintive—"Mr. Elton is so good to the poor!" she found something else must be done.

They were just approaching the house where lived Mrs. and Miss Bates. She determined to call upon them and seek safety in numbers. There was always sufficient reason for such an attention: Mrs. and Miss Bates loved to be called on; and she knew she was considered by the very few who presumed ever to see imperfection in her as rather negligent in that respect, and as not contributing what she ought to the stock of their scanty comforts.

She had had many a hint from Mr. Knightley and some from her own heart, as to her deficiency, but none were equal to counteract the persuasion of its being very disagreeable,—a waste of time—tiresome women—and all the horror of being in danger of falling in with the second rate and third rate of Highbury, who were calling on them for ever, and therefore she seldom went near them. But now she made the sudden resolution of not passing their door without going in; observing, as she proposed it to Harriet, that, as well as she could calculate, they were just now quite safe from any letter from Jane Fairfax.

The house belonged to people in business. Mrs. and Miss Bates occupied the drawing-room floor; and there, in the very moderate-sized apartment, which was every thing to them, the visiters were most cordially and even gratefully welcomed; the quiet neat old lady, who with her knitting was seated in the warmest corner, wanting even to give up her place to Miss Woodhouse, and her more active, talking daughter, almost ready to overpower them with care and kindness, thanks for their visit, solicitude for their shoes, anxious enquiries after Mr. Woodhouse's health, cheerful communications about her mother's, and sweet-cake from the buffet:—"Mrs. Cole had just been there, just called in for ten minutes, and had been so good as to sit an hour with them, and *she* had taken a piece of cake, and been so kind as to say she liked it very much; and, therefore, she hoped Miss Woodhouse and Miss Smith would do them the favour to eat a piece too."

The mention of the Coles was sure to be followed by that of Mr. Elton. There was intimacy between them, and Mr. Cole had heard from Mr. Elton since his going away. Emma knew what was coming: they must have the letter over again, and settle how long he had been gone, and how much he was engaged in company, and what a favourite he was wherever he went, and how full the Master of the Ceremonies' ball had been; and she went through it very well, with all the interest and all the commendation that could be requisite, and always putting forward to prevent Harriet's being obliged to say a word.

This she had been prepared for when she entered the house; but meant, having once talked him handsomely over, to be no farther incommoded by any troublesome topic, and to wander at large amongst all the mistresses and misses of Highbury, and their card-parties. She had not been prepared to have Jane Fairfax succeed Mr. Elton; but he was actually hurried off by Miss Bates; she jumped away from him at last abruptly to the Coles, to usher in a letter from her niece.

"Oh yes,—Mr. Elton, I understood,—certainly as to dancing,—Mrs. Cole was telling me that dancing at the rooms at

Bath was—Mrs. Cole was so kind as to sit some time with us, talking of Jane; for as soon as she came in, she began enquiring after her, Jane is so very great a favourite there. Whenever she is with us, Mrs. Cole does not know how to show her kindness enough; and I must say that Jane deserves it as much as any body can. And so she began enquiring after her directly, saying, 'I know you cannot have heard from Jane lately, because it is not her time for writing;' and when I immediately said, 'But indeed we have, we had a letter this very morning,' I do not know that I ever saw any body more surprised. 'Have you, upon your honour?' said she; 'well, that is quite unexpected. Do let me hear what she says.'"

Emma's politeness was at hand directly, to say, with smiling interest,—

"Have you heard from Miss Fairfax so lately? I am extremely happy. I hope she is well?"

"Thank you. You are so kind!" replied the happily deceived aunt, while eagerly hunting for the letter. "Oh, here it is. I was sure it could not be far off; but I had put my huswife* upon it, you see, without being aware, and so it was quite hid, but I had it in my hand so very lately that I was almost sure it must be on the table. I was reading it to Mrs. Cole, and, since she went away, I was reading it again to my mother, for it is such a pleasure to her—a letter from Jane—that she can never hear it often enough; so I knew it could not be far off, and here it is, only just under my huswife,—and since you are so kind as to wish to hear what she says; but, first of all, I really must, in justice to Jane, apologise for her writing so short a letter, only two pages you see, hardly two, and in general she fills the whole paper and crosses half.[8] My mother often wonders that I can make it out so well. She often says, when the letter is first opened, 'Well, Hetty, now I think you will be put to it to make out all that checker-work'—don't you, ma'am? And then I tell her, I am

---

*Small carrying case for needlework tools.

sure she would contrive to make it out herself, if she had nobody to do it for her, every word of it,—I am sure she would
pore over it till she had made out every word. And, indeed,
though my mother's eyes are not so good as they were, she
can see amazingly well still, thank God! with the help of spectacles. It is such a blessing! My mother's are really very good
indeed. Jane often says, when she is here, 'I am sure, grandmamma, you must have had very strong eyes to see as you
do—and so much fine work as you have done too!—I only
wish my eyes may last me as well.'"

All this spoken extremely fast obliged Miss Bates to stop
for breath; and Emma said something very civil about the excellence of Miss Fairfax's handwriting.

"You are extremely kind," replied Miss Bates highly gratified; "you who are such a judge, and write so beautifully
yourself. I am sure there is nobody's praise that could give us
so much pleasure as Miss Woodhouse's. My mother does not
hear; she is a little deaf, you know. Ma'am," addressing her,
"do you hear what Miss Woodhouse is so obliging to say
about Jane's handwriting?"

And Emma had the advantage of hearing her own silly
compliment repeated twice over before the good old lady
could comprehend it. She was pondering, in the meanwhile,
upon the possibility, without seeming very rude, of making
her escape from Jane Fairfax's letter, and had almost resolved on hurrying away directly under some slight excuse,
when Miss Bates turned to her again and seized her attention.

"My mother's deafness is very trifling, you see, just nothing at all. By only raising my voice, and saying any thing two
or three times over, she is sure to hear; but then she is used
to my voice. But it is very remarkable that she should always
hear Jane better than she does me. Jane speaks so distinct!
However, she will not find her grandmamma at all deafer
than she was two years ago; which is saying a great deal at my
mother's time of life, and it really is full two years, you know,
since she was here. We never were so long without seeing her

before, and as I was telling Mrs. Cole, we shall hardly know how to make enough of her now."

"Are you expecting Miss Fairfax here soon?"

"Oh, yes; next week."

"Indeed! That must be a very great pleasure."

"Thank you. You are very kind. Yes, next week. Every body is so surprised; and every body says the same obliging things. I am sure she will be as happy to see her friends at Highbury as they can be to see her. Yes, Friday or Saturday; she cannot say which, because Col. Campbell will be wanting the carriage himself one of those days. So very good of them to send her the whole way! But they always do, you know. Oh yes, Friday or Saturday next. That is what she writes about. That is the reason of her writing out of rule, as we call it; for, in the common course, we should not have heard from her before next Tuesday or Wednesday."

"Yes, so I imagined. I was afraid there could be little chance of my hearing any thing of Miss Fairfax to-day."

"So obliging of you! No, we should not have heard, if it had not been for this particular circumstance, of her being to come here so soon. My mother is so delighted! for she is to be three months with us at least. Three months, she says so, positively, as I am going to have the pleasure of reading to you. The case is, you see, that the Campbells are going to Ireland. Mrs. Dixon has persuaded her father and mother to come over and see her directly. They had not intended to go over till the summer, but she is so impatient to see them again;—for till she married, last October, she was never away from them so much as a week, which must make it very strange to be in different kingdoms, I was going to say, but however different countries, and so she wrote a very urgent letter to her mother, or her father,—I declare I do not know which it was, but we shall see presently in Jane's letter,— wrote in Mr. Dixon's name as well as her own, to press their coming over directly; and they would give them the meeting in Dublin, and take them back to their country-seat, Baly-craig,—a beautiful place I fancy. Jane has heard a great deal of its beauty,—from Mr. Dixon, I mean,—I do not know that she ever heard about it from any body else,—but it was very natural, you know, that he should like to speak of his own place while he was paying his addresses,—and as Jane used to be very often walking out with them,—for Colonel and Mrs. Campbell were very particular about their daughter's not walking out often with only Mr. Dixon, for which I do not at all blame them: of course she heard every thing he might be telling Miss Campbell about his own home in Ireland; and I think she wrote us word that he had shown them some drawings of the place, views that he had taken himself. He is a most amiable, charming young man, I believe. Jane was quite longing to go to Ireland, from his account of things."

At this moment, an ingenious and animating suspicion entering Emma's brain with regard to Jane Fairfax, this charming Mr. Dixon, and the not going to Ireland, she said, with the insidious design of further discovery,—

"You must feel it very fortunate that Miss Fairfax should be allowed to come to you at such a time. Considering the very particular friendship between her and Mrs. Dixon, you could hardly have expected her to be excused from accompanying Colonel and Mrs. Campbell."

"Very true, very true, indeed. The very thing that we have always been rather afraid of; for we should not have liked to have her at such a distance from us, for months together,— not able to come if any thing was to happen; but you see every thing turns out for the best. They want her (Mr. and Mrs. Dixon) excessively to come over with Colonel and Mrs. Campbell; quite depend upon it; nothing can be more kind or pressing than their *joint* invitation, Jane says, as you will hear presently. Mr. Dixon does not seem in the least backward in any attention. He is a most charming young man. Ever since the service he rendered Jane at Weymouth, when they were out in that party on the water, and she, by the sudden whirling round of something or other among the sails, would have been dashed into the sea at once, and actually was all but gone, if he had not, with the greatest presence of mind, caught hold of her habit,—I can never think of it without trembling!—but ever since we had the history of that day, I have been so fond of Mr. Dixon!"

"But, in spite of all her friends' urgency, and her own wish of seeing Ireland, Miss Fairfax prefers devoting the time to you and Mrs. Bates?"

"Yes—entirely her own doing, entirely her own choice; and Colonel and Mrs. Campbell think she does quite right, just what they should recommend; and indeed they particularly *wish* her to try her native air, as she has not been quite so well as usual lately."

"I am concerned to hear of it. I think they judge wisely; but Mrs. Dixon must be very much disappointed. Mrs. Dixon, I understand, has no remarkable degree of personal beauty,—is not by any means to be compared with Miss Fairfax."

"Oh no. You are very obliging to say such things, but certainly not. There is no comparison between them. Miss Campbell always was absolutely plain, but extremely elegant and amiable."

"Yes, that of course."

"Jane caught a bad cold, poor thing! so long ago as the 7th of November (as I am going to read to you), and has never been well since. A long time, is not it, for a cold to hang upon her? She never mentioned it before, because she would not alarm us. Just like her! so considerate!—But, however, she is so far from well, that her kind friends the Campbells think she had better come home, and try an air that always agrees with her: and they have no doubt that three or four months at Highbury will entirely cure her; and it is certainly a great deal better that she should come here than go to Ireland, if she is unwell. Nobody could nurse her as we should do."

"It appears to me the most desirable arrangement in the world."

"And so she is to come to us next Friday or Saturday, and

the Campbells leave town in their way to Holyhead the Monday following, as you will find from Jane's letter. So sudden!—You may guess, dear Miss Woodhouse, what a flurry it has thrown me in! If it was not for the drawback of her illness,—but I am afraid we must expect to see her grown thin, and looking very poorly. I must tell you what an unlucky thing happened to me as to that. I always make a point of reading Jane's letters through to myself first, before I read them aloud to my mother, you know, for fear of there being any thing in them to distress her. Jane desired me to do it, so I always do; and so I began to-day with my usual caution: but no sooner did I come to the mention of her being unwell, than I burst out, quite frightened, with 'Bless me! poor Jane is ill!'—which my mother, being on the watch, heard distinctly, and was sadly alarmed at. However, when I read on, I found it was not near so bad as I fancied at first; and I make so light of it now to her, that she does not think much about it: but I cannot imagine how I could be so off my guard! If Jane does not get well soon, we will call in Mr. Perry. The expense shall not be thought of; and though he is so liberal and so fond of Jane, that I dare say he would not mean to charge any thing for attendance, we could not suffer it to be so, you know. He has a wife and family to maintain, and is not to be giving away his time. Well, now I have just given you a hint of what Jane writes about, we will turn to her letter; and I am sure she tells her own story a great deal better than I can tell it for her."

"I am afraid we must be running away," said Emma, glancing at Harriet, and beginning to rise, "my father will be expecting us. I had no intention, I thought I had no power, of staying more than five minutes, when I first entered the house. I merely called, because I would not pass the door without enquiring after Mrs. Bates; but I have been so pleasantly detained! Now, however, we must wish you and Mrs. Bates good morning."

And not all that could be urged to detain her succeeded. She regained the street, happy in this, that though much had been forced on her against her will, though she had, in fact, heard the whole substance of Jane Fairfax's letter, she had been able to escape the letter itself.

# Chapter II.

Jane Fairfax was an orphan, the only child of Mrs. Bates's youngest daughter.

The marriage of Lieut. Fairfax, of the——regiment of infantry, and Miss Jane Bates, had had its day of fame and pleasure, hope and interest; but nothing now remained of it save the melancholy remembrance of him dying in action abroad—of his widow sinking under consumption and grief soon afterwards—and this girl.

By birth she belonged to Highbury: and when at three years old, on losing her mother, she became the property, the charge, the consolation, the fondling of her grandmother and aunt, there had seemed every probability of her being permanently fixed there; of her being taught only what very limited means could command, and growing up with no advantages of connection or improvement to be engrafted on what nature had given her in a pleasing person, good understanding, and warm-hearted, well-meaning relations.

But the compassionate feelings of a friend of her father gave a change to her destiny. This was Col. Campbell, who had very highly regarded Fairfax, as an excellent officer and most deserving young man; and farther, had been indebted to him for such attentions, during a severe camp-fever, as he believed had saved his life. These were claims which he did not learn to overlook, though some years passed away from the death of poor Fairfax before his own return to England put any thing in his power. When he did return, he sought out the child and took notice of her. He was a married man with only one living child, a girl, about Jane's age: and Jane became their guest, paying them long visits and growing a favourite with all; and, before she was nine years old, his daughter's great fondness for her, and his own wish of being a real friend, united to produce an offer from Col. Campbell of undertaking the whole charge of her education. It was accepted; and from that period Jane had belonged to Col. Campbell's family, and had lived with them entirely, only visiting her grandmother from time to time.

The plan was that she should be brought up for educating others; the very few hundred pounds which she inherited from her father making independence impossible. To provide for her otherwise was out of Col. Campbell's power; for though his income, by pay and appointments, was handsome, his fortune was moderate, and must be all his daughter's; but, by giving her an education, he hoped to be supplying the means of respectable subsistence hereafter.

Such was Jane Fairfax's history. She had fallen into good hands, known nothing but kindness from the Campbells, and been given an excellent education. Living constantly with right-minded and well-informed people, her heart and understanding had received every advantage of discipline and culture; and Col. Campbell's residence being in London, every lighter talent had been done full justice to, by the attendance of first-rate masters. Her disposition and abilities were equally worthy of all that friendship could do; and at eighteen or nineteen she was, as far as such an early age can be qualified for the care of children, fully competent to the office of instruction herself; but she was too much beloved to be parted with. Neither father nor mother could promote, and the daughter could not endure it. The evil day was put off. It was easy to decide that she was still too young; and

Jane remained with them, sharing, as another daughter, in all the rational pleasures of an elegant society, and a judicious mixture of home and amusement, with only the drawback of the future,—the sobering suggestions of her own good understanding to remind her that all this might soon be over.

The affection of the whole family, the warm attachment of Miss Campbell in particular, was the more honourable to each party from the circumstance of Jane's decided superiority both in beauty and acquirements. That nature had given it in feature could not be unseen by the young woman, nor could her higher powers of mind be unfelt by the parents. They continued together with unabated regard, however, till the marriage of Miss Campbell, who by that chance, that luck which so often defies anticipation in matrimonial affairs, giving attraction to what is moderate rather than to what is superior, engaged the affections of Mr. Dixon, a young man, rich and agreeable, almost as soon as they were acquainted; and was eligibly and happily settled, while Jane Fairfax had yet her bread to earn.

This event had very lately taken place; too lately for any thing to be yet attempted by her less fortunate friend towards entering on her path of duty; though she had now reached the age which her own judgment had fixed on for beginning. She had long resolved that one-and-twenty should be the period. With the fortitude of a devoted noviciate, she had resolved at one-and-twenty to complete the sacrifice, and retire from all the pleasures of life, of rational intercourse, equal society, peace and hope, to penance and mortification for ever.

The good sense of Col. and Mrs. Campbell could not oppose such a resolution, though their feelings did. As long as they lived, no exertions would be necessary, their home might be hers for ever; and for their own comfort they would have retained her wholly; but this would be selfishness:— what must be at last, had better be soon. Perhaps they began to feel it might have been kinder and wiser to have resisted the temptation of any delay, and spared her from a taste of such enjoyments of ease and leisure as must now be relinquished. Still, however, affection was glad to catch at any reasonable excuse for not hurrying on the wretched moment. She had never been quite well since the time of their daughter's marriage; and till she should have completely recovered her usual strength, they must forbid her engaging in duties, which, so far from being compatible with a weakened frame and varying spirits, seemed, under the most favourable circumstances, to require something more than human perfection of body and mind to be discharged with tolerable comfort.

With regard to her not accompanying them to Ireland, her account to her aunt contained nothing but truth, though there might be some truths not told. It was her own choice to give the time of their absence to Highbury; to spend, perhaps, her last months of perfect liberty with those kind relations to whom she was so very dear: and the Campbells, whatever might be their motive or motives, whether single, or double, or treble, gave the arrangement their ready sanction, and said, that they depended more on a few months spent in her native air, for the recovery of her health, than on any thing else. Certain it was that she was to come; and that Highbury, instead of welcoming that perfect novelty which had been so long promised it—Mr. Frank Churchill—must put up for the present with Jane Fairfax, who could bring only the freshness of a two years' absence.

Emma was sorry to have to pay civilities to a person she did not like through three long months!—to be always doing more than she wished, and less than she ought! Why she did not like Jane Fairfax might be a difficult question to answer: Mr. Knightley had once told her it was because she saw in her the really accomplished young woman, which she wanted to be thought herself; and though the accusation had been eagerly refuted at the time, there were moments of self-examination in which her conscience could not quite acquit her. But "she could never get acquainted with her: she did not know how it was, but there was such coldness and reserve—such apparent indifference whether she pleased or not—and then, her aunt was such an eternal talker!—and she was made such a fuss with by every body!—and it had been always imagined that they were to be so intimate—because their ages were the same, every body had supposed they must be so fond of each other." These were her reasons; she had no better.

It was a dislike so little just,—every imputed fault was so magnified by fancy,—that she never saw Jane Fairfax, the first time after any considerable absence, without feeling that she had injured her; and now, when the due visit was paid, on her arrival, after a two years' interval, she was particularly struck with the very appearance and manners, which for those two whole years she had been depreciating. Jane Fairfax was very elegant, remarkably elegant; and she had herself the highest value for elegance. Her height was pretty, just such as almost every body would think tall, and nobody could think very tall; her figure particularly graceful; her size a most becoming medium, between fat and thin, though a slight appearance of ill-health seemed to point out the likeliest evil of the two. Emma could not but feel all this; and then, her face—her features—there was more beauty in them all together than she had remembered; it was not regular, but it was very pleasing beauty. Her eyes, a deep grey, with dark eyelashes and eyebrows, had never been denied their praise; but the skin, which she had been used to cavil at, as wanting colour, had a clearness and delicacy which really needed no fuller bloom. It was a style of beauty, of which elegance was the reigning character, and as such, she must, in honour, by all her principles, admire it: elegance, which, whether of person or of mind, she saw so little in Highbury. There, not to be vulgar, was distinction and merit.

In short, she sat, during the first visit, looking at Jane Fairfax with twofold complacency,—the sense of pleasure and the sense of rendering justice, and was determining that she would dislike her no longer. When she took in her history, indeed, her situation, as well as her beauty; when she considered what all this elegance was destined to, what she was going to sink from, how she was going to live, it seemed impossible to feel any thing but compassion and respect; especially, if to every well-known particular, entitling her to interest, were added the highly probable circumstance of an attachment to Mr. Dixon, which she had so naturally started to herself. In that case, nothing could be more pitiable or more honourable than the sacrifices she had resolved on. Emma was very willing now to acquit her of having seduced Mr. Dixon's affections from his wife, or of any thing mischievous which her imagination had suggested at first. If it were love, it might be simple, single, successless love on her side alone. She might have been unconsciously sucking in the sad poison, while a sharer of his conversation with her friend; and from the best, the purest of motives, might now be denying herself this visit to Ireland, and resolving to divide herself effectually from him and his connections by soon beginning her career of laborious duty.

Upon the whole, Emma left her with such softened, charitable feelings, as made her look around in walking home, and lament that Highbury afforded no young man worthy of giving her independence,—nobody that she could wish to scheme about for her.

These were charming feelings, but not lasting. Before she had committed herself by any public profession of eternal friendship for Jane Fairfax, or done more towards a recantation of past prejudices and errors, than saying to Mr. Knightley, "She certainly is handsome; she is better than handsome!" Jane had spent an evening at Hartfield with her grandmother and aunt, and every thing was relapsing much into its usual state. Former provocations reappeared. The aunt was as tiresome as ever; more tiresome, because anxiety for her health was now added to admiration of her powers; and they had to listen to the description of exactly how little bread and butter she ate for breakfast, and how small a slice of mutton for dinner as well as to see exhibitions of new caps and new workbags for her mother and herself; and Jane's offences rose again. They had music: Emma was obliged to play; and the thanks and praise which necessarily followed appeared to her an affectation of candour, an air of greatness, meaning only to show off in higher style her own very superior performance. She was, besides, which was the worst of all, so cold, so cautious! There was no getting at her real opinion. Wrapt up in a cloak of politeness, she seemed determined to hazard nothing. She was disgustingly, was suspiciously reserved.

If any thing could be more, where all was most, she was more reserved on the subject of Weymouth and the Dixons than any thing. She seemed bent on giving no real insight into Mr. Dixon's character, or her own value for his company, or opinion of the suitableness of the match. It was all general approbation and smoothness; nothing delineated or distinguished. It did her no service, however. Her caution was thrown away. Emma saw its artifice, and returned to her first surmises. There probably *was* something more to conceal than her own preference; Mr. Dixon, perhaps, had been very near changing one friend for the other, or been fixed only to Miss Campbell, for the sake of the future twelve thousand pounds.

The like reserve prevailed on other topics. She and Mr. Frank Churchill had been at Weymouth at the same time. It was known that they were a little acquainted; but not a syllable of real information could Emma procure as to what he truly was. "Was he handsome?"—"She believed he was reckoned a very fine young man."—"Was he agreeable?"—"He was generally thought so."—"Did he appear a sensible young man; a young man of information?"—"At a watering-place, or in a common London acquaintance, it was difficult to decide on such points. Manners were all that could be safely judged of, under a much longer knowledge than they had yet had of Mr. Churchill. She believed every body found his manners pleasing." Emma could not forgive her.

## Chapter III.

Emma could not forgive her: but as neither provocation nor resentment were discerned by Mr. Knightley, who had been of the party, and had seen only proper attention and pleasing behavior on each side, he was expressing the next morning, being at Hartfield again on business with Mr. Woodhouse, his approbation of the whole; not so openly as he might have done had her father been out of the room, but speaking plain enough to be very intelligible to Emma. He had been used to think her unjust to Jane, and had now great pleasure in marking an improvement.

"A very pleasant evening," he began as soon as Mr. Woodhouse had been talked into what was necessary, told that he understood, and the papers swept away;—"particularly pleasant. You and Miss Fairfax gave us some very good music. I do not know a more luxurious state sir, than sitting at one's ease to be entertained a whole evening by two such young women; sometimes with music and sometimes with conversation. I am sure Miss Fairfax must have found the evening pleasant, Emma. You left nothing undone. I was glad you made her play so much for having no instrument at her grandmother's, it must have been a real indulgence."

"I am happy you approved," said Emma, smiling; "but I hope I am not often deficient in what is due to guests at Hartfield."

"No, my dear," said her father instantly; "*that* I am sure

you are not. There is nobody half so attentive and civil as you are. If any thing, you are too attentive. The muffin last night,—if it had been handed round once, I think it would have been enough."

"No," said Mr. Knightley, nearly at the same time; "you are not often deficient; not often deficient, either in manner or comprehension. I think you understand me, therefore."

An arch look expressed—"I understand you well enough;" but she said only, "Miss Fairfax is reserved."

"I always told you she was—a little; but you will soon overcome all that part of her reserve which ought to be overcome, all that has its foundation in diffidence. What arises from discretion must be honoured."

"You think her diffident. I do not see it."

"My dear Emma," said he, moving from his chair into one close by her, "you are not going to tell me, I hope, that you had not a pleasant evening."

"Oh no; I was pleased with my own perseverance in asking questions, and amused to think how little information I obtained."

"I am disappointed," was his only answer.

"I hope every body had a pleasant evening," said Mr. Woodhouse, in his quiet way. "I had. Once, I felt the fire rather too much; but then I moved back my chair a little, a very little, and it did not disturb me. Miss Bates was very chatty and good humoured, as she always is, though she speaks rather too quick. However, she is very agreeable, and Mrs. Bates, too, in a different way. I like old friends; and Miss Jane Fairfax is a very pretty sort of young lady; a very pretty and a very well behaved young lady indeed. She must have found the evening agreeable, Mr. Knightley, because she had Emma."

"True, sir; and Emma, because she had Miss Fairfax."

Emma saw his anxiety, and wishing to appease it, at least for the present, said, and with a sincerity which no one could question,—

"She is a sort of elegant creature that one cannot keep

one's eyes from. I am always watching her to admire; and I do pity her from my heart."

Mr. Knightley looked as if he were more gratified than he cared to express; and before he could make any reply, Mr. Woodhouse, whose thoughts were on the Bates's, said,—

"It is a great pity that their circumstances should be so confined! a great pity indeed! and I have often wished—but it is so little one can venture to do—small, trifling presents, of any thing uncommon. Now, we have killed a porker, and Emma thinks of sending them a loin or a leg; it is very small and delicate—Hartfield pork is not like any other pork—but still it is pork—and, my dear Emma, unless one could be sure of their making it into steaks, nicely fried, as ours are fried, without the smallest grease, and not roast it, for no stomach can bear roast pork—I think we had better send the leg—do not you think so, my dear?"

"My dear papa, I sent the whole hind-quarter. I knew you would wish it. There will be the leg to be salted, you know, which is so very nice, and the loin to be dressed directly, in any manner they like."

"That's right, my dear, very right. I had not thought of it before, but that was the best way. They must not over-salt the leg; and then, if it is not over-salted, and if it is very thoroughly boiled, just as Serle boils ours, and eaten very moderately of, with a boiled turnip, and a little carrot or parsnip, I do not consider it unwholesome."

"Emma," slid Mr. Knightley, presently, "I have a piece of news for you. You like news—and I heard an article in my way hither that I think will interest you."

"News! Oh yes, I always like news. What is it?—why do you smile so?—where did you hear it?—at Randalls?"

He had time only to say,—

"No, not at Randalls; I have not been near Randalls,"—when the door was thrown open, and Miss Bates and Miss Fairfax walked into the room. Full of thanks and full of news, Miss Bates knew not which to give quickest. Mr. Knightley soon saw that he had lost his moment, and that not another syllable of communication could rest with him.

"Oh, my dear sir, how are you this morning? My dear Miss Woodhouse—I come quite overpowered. Such a beautiful hind-quarter of pork! You are too bountiful! Have you heard the news? Mr. Elton is going to be married."

Emma had not had time even to think of Mr. Elton, and she was so completely surprised, that she could not avoid a little start, and a little blush, at the sound.

"There is my news:—I thought it would interest you," said Mr. Knightley, with a smile, which implied a conviction of some part of what had passed between them.

"But where could *you* hear it?" cried Miss Bates. "Where could you possibly hear it, Mr. Knightley? For it is not five minutes since I received Mrs. Cole's note—no, it cannot be more than five—or at least ten—for I had got my bonnet and spencer* on, just ready to come out—I was only gone down to speak to Patty again about the pork—Jane was standing in the passage—were not you, Jane?—for my mother was so afraid that we had not any salting-pan large enough. So I said, I would go down and see, and Jane said, 'Shall I go down instead? for I think you have a little cold, and Patty has been washing the kitchen.'—'Oh, my dear,' said I—well, and just then came the note. A Miss Hawkins—that's all I know—a Miss Hawkins of Bath. But, Mr. Knightley, how could you possibly have heard it? for the very moment Mr. Cole told Mrs. Cole of it, she sat down and wrote to me. A Miss Hawkins——"

"I was with Mr. Cole on business an hour and a half ago. He had just read Elton's letter as I was shown in, and handed it to me directly."

"Well! that is quite—I suppose there never was a piece of news more generally interesting. My dear sir, you really are too bountiful. My mother desires her very best compliments

---

*Short jacket.

and regards, and a thousand thanks, and says you really quite oppress her."

"We consider our Hartfield pork," replied Mr. Wood-house—"indeed it certainly is, so very superior to all other pork, that Emma and I cannot have a greater pleasure than——"

"Oh, my dear sir, as my mother says, our friends are only too good to us. If ever there were people who, without having great wealth themselves, had every thing they could wish for, I am sure it is us. We may well say, that 'our lot is cast in a goodly heritage.'[9] Well, Mr. Knightley, and so you actually saw the letter—well——"

"It was short, merely to announce—but cheerful, exulting of course." Here was a sly glance at Emma. "He had been so fortunate as to—I forget the precise words—one has no business to remember them. The information was, as you state, that he was going to be married to a Miss Hawkins. By his style, I should imagine it just settled."

"Mr. Elton going to be married!" said Emma, as soon as she could speak. "He will have every body's wishes for his happiness."

"He is very young to settle," was Mr. Woodhouse's observation. "He had better not be in a hurry. He seemed to me very well off as he was. We were always glad to see him at Hartfield."

"A new neighbour for us all, Miss Woodhouse!" said Miss Bates joyfully: "my mother is so pleased!—she says she cannot bear to have the poor old vicarage without a mistress. This is great news, indeed. Jane, you have never seen Mr. Elton:—no wonder that you have such a curiosity to see him."

Jane's curiosity did not appear of that absorbing nature as wholly to occupy her.

"No, I have never seen Mr. Elton," she replied, starting on this appeal: "is he—is he a tall man?"

"Who shall answer that question?" cried Emma. "My father would say, 'Yes;' Mr. Knightley, 'No;' and Miss Bates and I, that he is just the happy medium. When you have been here a little longer, Miss Fairfax, you will understand that Mr.

Elton is the standard of perfection in Highbury, both in person and mind."

"Very true, Miss Woodhouse, so she will. He is the very best young man;—but, my dear Jane, if you remember, I told you yesterday he was precisely the height of Mr. Perry. Miss Hawkins,—I dare say, an excellent young woman. His extreme attention to my mother—wanting her to sit in the vicarage-pew, that she might hear the better, for my mother is a little deaf, you know—it is not much, but she does not hear quite quick. Jane says that Col. Campbell is a little deaf. He fancied bathing might be good for it—the warm bath—but she says it did him no lasting benefit. Col. Campbell, you know, is quite our angel. And Mr. Dixon seems a very charming young man, quite worthy of him. It is such a happiness when good people get together—and they always do. Now, here will be Mr. Elton and Miss Hawkins; and there are the Coles, such very good people; and the Perrys—I suppose there never was a happier or a better couple than Mr. and Mrs. Perry. I say, sir," turning to Mr. Woodhouse, "I think there are few places with such society as Highbury. I always say, we are quite blessed in our neighbours. My dear sir, if there is one thing my mother loves better that another, it is pork—a roast loin of pork——"

"As to who, or what Miss Hawkins is, or how long he has been acquainted with her," said Emma, "nothing, I suppose, can be known. One feels that it cannot be a very long acquaintance. He has been gone only four weeks."

Nobody had any information to give; and, after a few more wonderings, Emma said,—

"You are silent, Miss Fairfax—but I hope you mean to take an interest in this news. You, who have been hearing and seeing so much of late on these subjects, who must have been so deep in the business on Miss Campbell's account—we shall not excuse your being indifferent about Mr. Elton and Miss Hawkins."

"When I have seen Mr. Elton," replied Jane, "I dare say I shall be interested—but I believe it requires *that* with me.

And as it is some months since Miss Campbell married, the impression may be a little worn off."

"Yes, he has been gone just four weeks, as you observe, Miss Woodhouse," said Miss Bates, "four weeks yesterday:—a Miss Hawkins:—well, I had always rather fancied it would be some young lady hereabouts; not that I ever—Mrs. Cole once whispered to me—but I immediately said, 'No, Mr. Elton is a most worthy young man—but——' In short, I do not think I am particulary quick at those sort of discoveries. I do not pretend to it. What is before me, I see. At the same time, nobody could wonder if Mr. Elton should have aspired——Miss Woodhouse lets me chatter on, so good humouredly. She knows I would not offend for the world. How does Miss Smith do? She seems quite recovered now. Have you heard from Mrs. John Knightley lately? Oh, those dear little children. Jane, do you know I always fancy Mr. Dixon like Mr. John Knightley? I mean in person—tall, and with that sort of look—and not very talkative."

"Quite wrong, my dear aunt; there is no likeness at all."

"Very odd! but one never does form a just idea of any body beforehand. One takes up a notion, and runs away with it. Mr. Dixon, you say, is not, strictly speaking, handsome."

"Handsome! Oh no—far from it—certainly plain. I told you he was plain."

"My dear, you said that Miss Campbell would not allow him to be plain, and that you yourself——"

"Oh, as for me, my judgment is worth nothing. Where I have a regard, I always think a person well looking. But I gave what I believed the general opinion, when I called him plain."

"Well, my dear Jane, I believe we must be running away. The weather does not look well, and grandmamma will be uneasy. You are too obliging, my dear Miss Woodhouse; but we really must take leave. This has been a most agreeable piece of news indeed. I shall just go round by Mrs. Cole's; but I shall not stop three minutes: and, Jane, you had better go home directly—I would not have you out in a shower! We think she is the better for Highbury already. Thank you, we do indeed. I shall not attempt calling on Mrs. Goddard, for I really do not think she cares for any thing but *boiled* pork: when we dress the leg it will be another thing. Good morning to you, my dear sir. Oh, Mr. Knightley is coming too. Well, that is so very!—I am sure if Jane is tired, you will be so kind as to give her your arm. Mr. Elton, and Miss Hawkins. Good morning to you."

Emma, alone with her father, had half her attention wanted by him, while he lamented that young people would be in such a hurry to marry—and to marry strangers too—and the other half she could give to her own view of the subject. It was to herself an amusing and a very welcome piece of news, as proving that Mr. Elton could not have suffered long; but she was sorry for Harriet: Harriet must feel it—and all that she could hope was, by giving the first information herself, to save her from hearing it abruptly from others. It was now about the time that she was likely to call. If she were to meet Miss Bates in her way!—and upon its beginning to rain, Emma was obliged to expect that the weather would be detaining her at Mrs. Goddard's, and that the intelligence would undoubtedly rush upon her without preparation.

The shower was heavy, but short; and it had not been over five minutes, when in came Harriet, with just the heated, agitated look which hurrying thither with a full heart was likely to give; and the "Oh, Miss Woodhouse, what do you think has happened?" which instantly burst forth, had all the evidence of corresponding perturbation. As the blow was given, Emma felt that she could not now show greater kindness than in listening; and Harriet, unchecked, ran eagerly through what she had to tell. "She had set out from Mrs. Goddard's half an hour ago—she had been afraid it would rain—she had been afraid it would pour down every moment—but she thought she might get to Hartfield first—she had hurried on as fast as possible; but then, as she was passing by the house where a young woman was making up a gown for her, she thought she would just step in and see how it went on; and though she did not seem to stay half a moment there, soon after she came out it began to rain, and she did not know what to do; so she ran on directly, as fast as she could, and took shelter at Ford's." Ford's was the principal woollen-draper, linen-draper, and haberdasher's shop united—the shop first in size and fashion in the place. "And so, there she had sat, without an idea of any thing in the world, full ten minutes, perhaps—where, all of a sudden, who should come in—to be sure it was so very odd!—but they always dealt at Ford's—who should come in, but Elizabeth Martin and her brother! Dear Miss Woodhouse! only think. I thought I should have fainted. I did not know what to do. I was sitting near the door—Elizabeth saw me directly; but he did not; he was busy with the umbrella. I am sure she saw me, but she looked away directly, and took no notice; and they both went to quite the farther end of the shop; and I kept sitting near the door. Oh dear; I was so miserable! I am sure I must have been as white as my gown. I could not go away, you know, because of the rain; but I did so wish myself any where in the world but there. Oh dear, Miss Woodhouse—well, at last, I fancy, he looked round and saw me; for, instead of going on with their buyings, they began whispering to one another. I am sure they were talking of me; and I could not help thinking that he was persuading her to speak to me—(do you think he was, Miss Woodhouse?)—for presently she came forward—came quite up to me, and asked me how I did, and seemed ready to shake hands, if I would. She did not do any of it in the same way that she used; I could see she was altered; but, however, she seemed to *try* to be very friendly, and we shook hands, and stood talking some time; but I know no more what I said—I was in such a tremble! I remember she said she was sorry we never met now; which I thought almost too kind! Dear Miss Woodhouse, I was absolutely miserable! By that time, it was beginning to hold up, and I was determined that nothing should stop me from getting away—and then—only think!—I found he was coming up towards me too—slowly, you know, and as if he did not quite know what to do; and so he came and spoke, and I answered—and I stood for a minute, feeling dreadfully, you know, one cannot tell how; and then I took courage, and said it did not rain, and I must go; and so off I set: and I had not got three yards from the door, when he came after me, only to say, if I was going to Hartfield, he thought I had much better go round by Mr. Cole's stables, for I should find the near way quite floated by this rain. Oh dear, I thought it would have been the death of me! So I said, I was very much obliged to him: you know I could not do less; and then he went back to Elizabeth, and I came round by the stables—I believe I did—but I hardly knew where I was, or any thing about it. Oh, Miss Woodhouse, I would rather have done any thing than had it happen; and yet, you know, there was a sort of satisfaction in seeing him behave so pleasantly and so kindly. And Elizabeth, too. Oh, Miss Woodhouse, do talk to me, and make me comfortable again."

Very sincerely did Emma wish to do so; but it was not immediately in her power. She was obliged to stop and think. She was not thoroughly comfortable herself. The young man's conduct, and his sister's, seemed the result of real feeling, and she could not but pity them. As Harriet described it, there had been an interesting mixture of wounded affection and genuine delicacy in their behaviour: but she had believed them to be well-meaning, worthy people, before; and what difference did this make in the evils of the connection? It was folly to be disturbed by it. Of course, he must be sorry to lose her,—they must be all sorry: ambition, as well as love, had probably been mortified. They might all have hoped to rise by Harriet's acquaintance; and besides, what was the value of Harriet's description? So easily pleased,—so little discerning,—what signified her praise?

She exerted herself, and did try to make her comfortable, by considering all that had passed as a mere trifle, and quite unworthy of being dwelt on.

"It might be distressing for the moment," said she, "but you seem to have behaved extremely well; and it is over,— and may never,—can never, as a first meeting,—occur again, and therefore you need not think about it."

Harriet said, "Very true," and she "would not think about it;" but still she talked of it—still she could talk of nothing else; and Emma, at last, in order to put the Martins out of her head, was obliged to hurry on the news, which she had meant to give with so much tender caution, hardly knowing herself whether to rejoice or be angry, ashamed or only amused, at such a state of mind in poor Harriet—such a conclusion of Mr. Elton's importance with her!

Mr. Elton's rights, however, gradually revived. Though she did not feel the first intelligence as she might have done the day before, or an hour before, its interest soon increased; and before their first conversation was over, she had talked herself into all the sensations of curiosity, wonder and regret, pain and pleasure, as to this fortunate Miss Hawkins, which could conduce to place the Martins under proper subordination in her fancy.

Emma learned to be rather glad that there had been such a meeting. It had been serviceable in deadening the first shock, without retaining any influence to alarm. As Harriet now lived, the Martins could not get at her, without seeking her, where hitherto they had wanted either the courage or the condescension to seek her; for since her refusal of the brother, the sisters had never been at Mrs. Goddard's; and a twelvemonth might pass without their being thrown together again, with any necessity, or even any power of speech.

## *Chapter IV.*

Human nature is so well disposed towards those who are in interesting situations, that a young person, who either marries or dies, is sure of being kindly spoken of.

A week had not passed since Miss Hawkins's name was first mentioned in Highbury, before she was, by some means or other, discovered to have every recommendation of person and mind,—to be handsome, elegant, highly accomplished, and perfectly amiable; and when Mr. Elton himself arrived to triumph in his happy prospects, and circulate the fame of her merits, there was very little more for him to do than to tell her Christian name, and say whose music she principally played.

Mr. Elton returned, a very happy man. He had gone away rejected and mortified, disappointed in a very sanguine hope, after a series of what had appeared to him strong encouragement; and not only losing the right lady, but finding himself debased to the level of a very wrong one. He had gone away deeply offended, he came back engaged to another; and to another as superior, of course, to the first, as under such circumstances what is gained always is to what is lost. He came back gay and self-satisfied, eager and busy, caring nothing for Miss Woodhouse, and defying Miss Smith.

The charming Augusta Hawkins, in addition to all the usual advantages of perfect beauty and merit, was in possession of an independent fortune, of so many thousands as would always be called ten,—a point of some dignity, as well as some convenience. The story told well: he had not thrown himself away—he had gained a woman of 10,000*l*., or thereabouts, and he had gained her with such delightful rapidity; the first hour of introduction had been so very soon followed by distinguishing notice; the history which he had to give Mrs. Cole of the rise and progress of the affair was so glorious; the steps so quick, from the accidental rencontre,* to the dinner at Mr. Green's, and the party at Mrs. Brown's,—smiles and blushes rising in importance,—with consciousness and agitation richly scattered; the lady had been so easily impressed,—so sweetly disposed;—had, in

---

*Encounter (French).

short, to use a most intelligible phrase, been so very ready to have him, that vanity and prudence were equally contented.

He had caught both substance and shadow, both fortune and affection, and was just the happy man he ought to be;—talking only of himself and his own concerns,—expecting to be congratulated,—ready to be laughed at,—and, with cordial, fearless smiles, now addressing all the young ladies of the place, to whom, a few weeks ago, he would have been more cautiously gallant.

The wedding was no distant event, as the parties had only themselves to please, and nothing but the necessary preparations to wait for; and when he set out for Bath again, there was a general expectation, which a certain glance of Mrs. Cole's did not seem to contradict, that when he next entered Highbury he would bring his bride.

During his present short stay, Emma had barely seen him; but just enough to feel that the first meeting was over, and to give her the impression of his not being improved by the mixture of pique and pretension now spread over his air. She was, in fact, beginning very much to wonder that she had ever thought him pleasing at all; and his sight was so inseparably connected with some very disagreeable feelings, that, except in a moral light, as a penance, a lesson, a source of profitable humiliation to her own mind, she would have been thankful to be assured of never seeing him again. She wished him very well; but he gave her pain; and his welfare twenty miles off would administer most satisfaction.

The pain of his continued residence in Highbury, however, must certainly be lessened by his marriage. Many vain solicitudes would be prevented—many awkwardnesses smoothed by it. A *Mrs. Elton* would be an excuse for any change of intercourse; former intimacy might sink without remark. It would be almost beginning their life of civility again.

Of the lady individually, Emma thought very little. She was good enough for Mr. Elton, no doubt; accomplished enough for Highbury—handsome enough—to look plain,

probably, by Harriet's side. As to connection, there Emma
was perfectly easy; persuaded, that after all his own vaunted
claims and disdain of Harriet, he had done nothing. On that
article, truth seemed attainable. *What* she was, must be uncertain; but *who* she was, might be found out; and setting aside
the 10,000*l.*, it did not appear that she was at all Harriet's
superior. She brought no name, no blood, no alliance. Miss
Hawkins was the youngest of the two daughters of a Bristol—
merchant, of course, he must be called; but, as the whole of
the profits of his mercantile life appeared so very moderate,
it was unfair to guess the dignity of his line of trade had been
very moderate also. Part of every winter she had been used
to spend in Bath; but Bristol was her home, the very heart of
Bristol; for though the father and mother had died some
years ago, an uncle remained—in the law line:—nothing
more distinctly honourable was hazarded of him, than that
he was in the law line; and with him the daughter had lived.
Emma guessed him to be the drudge of some attorney, and
too stupid to rise. And all the grandeur of the connection
seemed dependent on the elder sister, who was *very well married*, to a gentleman in a *great way,* near Bristol, who kept two
carriages! That was the wind-up of the history; that was the
glory of Miss Hawkins.

Could she but have given Harriet her feelings about it all!
She had talked her into love; but, alas! she was not so easily
to be talked out of it. The charm of an object to occupy the
many vacancies of Harriet's mind was not to be talked away.
He might be superseded by another; he certainly would, indeed; nothing could be clearer; even a Robert Martin would
have been sufficient; but nothing else, she feared, would
cure her. Harriet was one of those, who, having once begun,
would be always in love. And now, poor girl, she was considerably worse from this reappearance of Mr. Elton—she was
always having a glimpse of him somewhere or other. Emma
saw him only once; but two or three times every day Harriet
was sure *just* to meet with him, or *just* to miss him, *just* to
hear his voice, or see his shoulder, *just* to have something

occur to preserve him in her fancy, in all the favouring warmth of surprise and conjecture. She was, moreover, perpetually hearing about him; for, excepting when at Hartfield, she was always among those who saw no fault in Mr. Elton, and found nothing so interesting as the discussion of his concerns; and every report, therefore, every guess,—all that had already occurred, all that might occur in the arrangement of his affairs, comprehending income, servants, and furniture,—was continually in agitation around her. Her regard was receiving strength by invariable praise of him, and her regrets kept alive, and feelings irritated by ceaseless repetitions of Miss Hawkins's happiness, and continual observation of how much he seemed attached!—his air as he walked by the house—the very sitting of his hat, being all in proof of how much he was in love!

Had it been allowable entertainment, had there been no pain to her friend, or reproach to herself, in the waverings of Harriet's mind, Emma would have been amused by its variations. Sometimes Mr. Elton predominated, sometimes the Martins; and each was occasionally useful as a check to the other. Mr. Elton's engagement had been the cure of the agitation of meeting Mr. Martin. The unhappiness produced by the knowledge of that engagement had been a little put aside by Elizabeth Martin's calling at Mrs. Goddard's a few days afterwards. Harriet had not been at home; but a note had been prepared and left for her, written in the very style to touch,—a small mixture of reproach with a great deal of kindness; and till Mr. Elton himself appeared, she had been much occupied by it, continually pondering over what could be done in return, and wishing to do more than she dared to confess. But Mr. Elton, in person, had driven away all such cares. While he staid, the Martins were forgotten; and on the very morning of his setting off for Bath again, Emma, to dissipate some of the distress it occasioned, judged it best for her to return Elizabeth Martin's visit.

How that visit was to be acknowledged, what would be necessary, and what might be safest, had been a point of some doubtful consideration. Absolute neglect of the mother and sisters, when invited to come, would be ingratitude. It must not be; and yet the danger of a renewal of the acquaintance!

After much thinking, she could determine on nothing better than Harriet's returning the visit; but in a way that, if they had understanding, should convince them that it was to be only a formal acquaintance. She meant to take her in the carriage, leave her at the Abbey-Mill, while she drove a little farther, and call for her again so soon as to allow no time for insidious applications or dangerous recurrences to the past, and give the most decided proof of what degree of intimacy was chosen for the future.

She could think of nothing better; and though there was something in it which her own heart could not approve—something of ingratitude, merely glossed over—it must be done, or what would become of Harriet?

## Chapter V.

Small heart had Harriet for visiting. Only half an hour before her friend called for her at Mrs. Goddard's, her evil stars had led her to the very spot, where, at that moment, a trunk, directed to *The Rev. Philip Elton, White Hart, Bath*, was to be seen under the operation of being lifted into the butcher's cart, which was to convey it to where the coaches passed; and every thing in this world, excepting that trunk and the direction, was consequently a blank.

She went, however; and when they reached the farm, and she was to be put down, at the end of the broad, neat gravel walk, which led between espalier apple-trees to the front door, the sight of every thing which had given her so much pleasure the autumn before, was beginning to revive a little local agitation; and when they parted, Emma observed her to be looking around with a sort of fearful curiosity, which determined her not to allow the visit to exceed the proposed quarter of an hour. She went on herself, to give that portion of time to an old servant who was married, and settled in Donwell.

The quarter of an hour brought her punctually to the white gate again; and Miss Smith receiving her summons, was with her without delay, and unattended by any alarming young man. She came solitarily down the gravel walk—a Miss Martin just appearing at the door, and parting with her seemingly with ceremonious civility.

Harriet could not very soon give an intelligible account. She was feeling too much; but at last Emma collected from her enough to understand the sort of meeting, and the sort of pain it was creating. She had seen only Mrs. Martin and the two girls. They had received her doubtingly, if not coolly; and nothing beyond the merest common-place had been talked almost all the time—till just at last, when Mrs. Martin's saying, all of a sudden, that she thought Miss Smith was grown, had brought on a more interesting subject, and a warmer manner. In that very room she had been measured last September with her two friends. There were the pencilled marks and memorandums on the wainscot by the window. *He* had done it. They all seemed to remember the day, the hour, the party, the occasion,—to feel the same consciousness, the same regrets,—to be ready to return to the same good understanding; and they were just growing again like themselves (Harriet, as Emma must suspect, as ready as the best of them to be cordial and happy,) when the carriage re-appeared, and all was over. The style of the visit, and the shortness of it, were then felt to be decisive. Fourteen minutes to be given to those with whom she had thankfully passed six weeks not six months ago! Emma could not but picture it all, and feel how justly they might resent, how naturally Harriet must suffer. It was a bad business. She would have given a great deal, or endured a great deal, to have had the Martins in a higher rank of life. They were so deserving, that a *little* higher should have been enough; but as it was, how could she have done otherwise? Impossible! She could not repent. They must be separated; but there was a great deal of pain in the process—so much to herself at this time, that she soon felt the necessity of a little consolation, and resolved on going home by way of Randalls to procure it. Her mind was quite sick of Mr. Elton and the Martins. The refreshment of Randalls was absolutely necessary.

It was a good scheme; but on driving to the door they heard that neither "master nor mistress was at home:" they had both been out some time; the man believed they were gone to Hartfield.

"This is too bad," cried Emma, as they turned away. "And now we shall just miss them; too provoking: I do not know when I have been so disappointed." And she leaned back in the corner, to indulge her murmurs, or to reason them away; probably a little of both—such being the commonest process of a not ill-disposed mind. Presently the carriage stopt: she looked up; it was stopt by Mr. and Mrs. Weston, who were standing to speak to her. There was instant pleasure in the sight of them, and still greater pleasure was conveyed in sound; for Mr. Weston immediately accosted her with,—

"How d'ye do?—how d'ye do?—We have been sitting with your father—glad to see him so well. Frank comes to-morrow— I had a letter this morning—we see him to-morrow by dinner-time to a certainty—he is at Oxford to-day, and he comes for a whole fortnight; I knew it would be so. If he had come at Christmas he could not have staid three days: I was always glad he did not come at Christmas; now we are going to have just the right weather for him,—fine, dry, settled weather. We shall enjoy him completely; every thing has turned out exactly as we could wish."

There was no resisting such news, no possibility of avoiding the influence of such a happy face as Mr. Weston's, confirmed as it all was by the words and the countenance of his wife, fewer and quieter, but not less to the purpose. To know that *she* thought his coming certain was enough to make Emma consider it so, and sincerely did she rejoice in their joy. It was a most delightful re-animation of exhausted spirits. The worn-out past was sunk in the freshness of what was coming; and in the rapidity of half a moment's thought, she hoped Mr. Elton would now be talked of no more.

Mr. Weston gave her the history of the engagements at Enscombe, which allowed his son to answer for having an entire fortnight at his command, as well as the route and the method of his journey; and she listened, and smiled, and congratulated.

"I shall soon bring him over to Hartfield," said he, at the conclusion.

Emma could imagine she saw a touch of the arm at this speech, from his wife.

"We had better move on, Mr. Weston," said she; "we are detaining the girls."

"Well, well, I am ready;" and turning again to Emma, "but you must not be expecting such a *very* fine young man; you have only had *my* account, you know; I dare say he is really nothing extraordinary,"—though his own sparkling eyes at the moment were speaking a very different conviction.

Emma could look perfectly unconscious and innocent, and answer in a manner that appropriated nothing.

"Think of me to-morrow, my dear Emma, about four o'clock," was Mrs. Weston's parting injunction; spoken with some anxiety, and meant only for her.

"Four o'clock!—depend upon it he will be here by three," was Mr. Weston's quick amendment; and so ended a most satisfactory meeting. Emma's spirits were mounted quite up to happiness; every thing wore a different air; James and his horses seemed not half so sluggish as before. When she looked at the hedges, she thought the elder at least must soon be coming out; and when she turned round to Harriet she saw something like a look of spring, a tender smile even there.

"Will Mr. Frank Churchill pass through Bath as well as Oxford?" was a question, however, which did not augur much.

But neither geography nor tranquillity could come all at once; and Emma was now in a humour to resolve that they should both come in time.

The morning of the interesting day arrived, and Mrs. Weston's faithful pupil did not forget either at ten, or eleven, or twelve o'clock, that she was to think of her at four.

"My dear, dear, anxious friend," said she, in mental soliloquy, while walking down stairs from her own room, "always over-careful for every body's comfort but your own: I see you now in all your little fidgets, going again and again into his room, to be sure that all is right." The clock struck twelve as she passed through the hall. " 'Tis twelve,—I shall not forget to think of you four hours hence; and by this time to-morrow, perhaps, or a little later, I may be thinking of the possibility of their all calling here. I am sure they will bring him soon."

She opened the parlour door, and saw two gentlemen sitting with her father,—Mr. Weston and his son. They had been arrived only a few minutes; and Mr. Weston had scarcely finished his explanation of Frank's being a day before his time, and her father was yet in the midst of his very civil welcome and congratulations, when she appeared, to have her share of surprise, introduction, and pleasure.

The Frank Churchill so long talked of, so high in interest, was actually before her—he was presented to her; and she did not think too much had been said in his praise; he was a *very* good looking young man; height, air, address, all were unexceptionable, and his countenance had a great deal of the spirit and liveliness of his father's; he looked quick and sensible. She felt immediately that she should like him; and there was a well-bred ease of manner, and a readiness to talk, which convinced her that he came intending to be acquainted with her, and that acquainted they soon must be.

He had reached Randalls the evening before. She was pleased with the eagerness to arrive which had made him alter his plan, and travel earlier, later, and quicker, that he might gain half a day.

"I told you yesterday," cried Mr. Weston with exultation,—

"I told you all that he would be here before the time named. I remembered what I used to do myself. One cannot creep upon a journey: one cannot help getting on faster than one has planned; and the pleasure of coming in upon one's friends before the look-out begins is worth a great deal more than any little exertion it needs."

"It is a great pleasure where one can indulge in it," said the young man, "though there are not many houses that I should presume on so far; but in coming *home* I felt I might do any thing."

The word *home* made his father look on him with fresh complacency. Emma was directly sure that he knew how to make himself agreeable; the conviction was strengthened by what followed. He was very much pleased with Randalls, thought it a most admirably arranged house, would hardly allow it even to be very small, admired the situation, the walk to Highbury, Highbury itself, Hartfield still more, and professed himself to have always felt the sort of interest in the country, which none but one's *own* country gives, and the greatest curiosity to visit it. That he should never have been able to indulge so amiable a feeling before passed suspiciously through Emma's brain; but still if it were a falsehood, it was a pleasant one, and pleasantly handled. His manner had no air of study or exaggeration. He did really look and speak as if in a state of no common enjoyment.

Their subjects, in general, were such as belong to an opening acquaintance. On his side were the enquiries,—"Was she a horse-woman?—Pleasant rides?—Pleasant walks?—Had they a large neighbourhood?—Highbury, perhaps, afforded society enough?—There were several very pretty houses in and about it.—Balls—had they balls?—Was it a musical society?"

But when satisfied on all these points, and their acquaintance proportionately advanced, he contrived to find an opportunity, while their two fathers were engaged with each other, of introducing his mother-in-law, and speaking of her with so much handsome praise, so much warm admiration, so much gratitude for the happiness she secured to his father, and her very kind reception of himself, as was an additional proof of his knowing how to please—and of his certainly thinking it worth while to try to please her. He did not advance a word of praise beyond what she knew to be thoroughly deserved by Mrs. Weston; but, undoubtedly, he could know very little of the matter. He understood what would be welcome; he could be sure of little else. "His father's marriage," he said, "had been the wisest measure: every friend must rejoice in it; and the family from whom he had received such a blessing must be ever considered as having conferred the highest obligation on him."

He got as near as he could to thanking her for Miss Taylor's merits, without seeming quite to forget that, in the common course of things, it was to be rather supposed that Miss Taylor had formed Miss Woodhouse's character, than Miss Woodhouse Miss Taylor's. And at last, as if resolved to qualify his opinion completely for travelling round to its object, he wound it all up with astonishment at the youth and beauty of her person.

"Elegant, agreeable manners, I was prepared for," said he; "but I confess that, considering every thing, I had not expected more than a very tolerably well-looking woman of a certain age; I did not know that I was to find a pretty young woman in Mrs. Weston."

"You cannot see too much perfection in Mrs. Weston, for my feelings," said Emma: "were you to guess her to be *eighteen*, I should listen with pleasure; but *she* would be ready to quarrel with you for using such words. Don't let her imagine that you have spoken of her as a pretty young woman."

"I hope I should know better," he replied; "no, depend upon it (with a gallant bow), that in addressing Mrs. Weston I should understand whom I might praise without any danger of being thought extravagant in my terms."

Emma wondered whether the same suspicion of what might be expected from their knowing each other, which had taken strong possession of her mind, had ever crossed his; and whether his compliments were to be considered as marks of acquiescence, or proofs of defiance. She must see more of him to understand his ways; at present, she only felt they were agreeable.

She had no doubt of what Mr. Weston was often thinking about. His quick eye she detected again and again glancing towards them with a happy expression; and even, when he might have determined not to look, she was confident that he was often listening.

Her own father's perfect exemption from any thought of the kind, the entire deficiency in him of all such sort of penetration or suspicion, was a most comfortable circumstance. Happily, he was not farther from approving matrimony than from foreseeing it. Though always objecting to every marriage that was arranged, he never suffered beforehand from the apprehension of any; it seemed as if he could not think so ill of any two persons' understanding as to suppose they meant to marry till it were proved against them. She blessed the favouring blindness. He could now, without the drawback of a single unpleasant surmise, without a glance forward at any possible treachery in his guest, give way to all his natural kind-hearted civility in solicitous enquiries after Mr. Frank Churchill's accommodation on his journey, through the sad evils of sleeping two nights on the road, and express very genuine unmixed anxiety to know that he had certainly escaped catching cold,—which, however, he could not allow him to feel quite assured of himself, till after another night.

A reasonable visit paid, Mr. Weston began to move. "He must be going. He had business at the Crown about his hay, and a great many errands for Mrs. Weston at Ford's; but he need not hurry any body else." His son, too well bred to hear the hint, rose immediately also, saying,—

"As you are going farther on business, sir, I will take the opportunity of paying a visit, which must be paid some day or other, and therefore may as well be paid now. I have the honour of being acquainted with a neighbour of yours (turning to Emma), a lady residing in or near Highbury; a family of the name of Fairfax. I shall have no difficulty, I suppose, in finding the house; though Fairfax, I believe, is not the proper name,—I should rather say Barnes or Bates. Do you know any family of that name?"

"To be sure we do," cried his father: "Mrs. Bates—we passed her house—I saw Miss Bates at the window. True, true, you are acquainted with Miss Fairfax; I remember you knew her at Weymouth, and a fine girl she is. Call upon her, by all means."

"There is no necessity for my calling this morning," said the young man: "another day would do as well; but there was that degree of acquaintance at Weymouth which——"

"Oh, go to-day, go to-day. Do not defer it. What is right to be done cannot be done too soon. And, besides, I must give you a hint, Frank—any want of attention to her *here* should be carefully avoided. You saw her with the Campbells, when she was the equal of every body she mixed with, but here she is with a poor old grandmother, who has barely enough to live on. If you do not call early it will be a slight."

The son looked convinced.

"I have heard her speak of the acquaintance," said Emma: "she is a very elegant young woman."

He agreed to it, but with so quiet a "Yes," as inclined her almost to doubt his real concurrence; and yet there must be a very distinct sort of elegance for the fashionable world, if Jane Fairfax could be thought only ordinarily gifted with it.

"If you were never particularly struck by her manners before," said she, "I think you will to-day. You will see her to advantage; see her and hear her—no, I am afraid you will not hear her at all, for she has an aunt who never holds her tongue."

"You are acquainted with Miss Jane Fairfax, sir, are you?" said Mr. Woodhouse, always the last to make his way in conversation; "then give me leave to assure you, that you will find her a very agreeable young lady. She is staying here on a visit to her grandmamma and aunt, very worthy people; I have known them all my life. They will be extremely glad to see you, I am sure; and one of my servants shall go with you to show you the way."

"My dear sir, upon no account in the world; my father can direct me."

"But your father is not going so far; he is only going to the Crown, quite on the other side of the street, and there are a great many houses: you might be very much at a loss, and it is a very dirty walk, unless you keep on the footpath; but my coachman can tell you where you had best cross the street."

Mr. Frank Churchill still declined it, looking as serious as he could; and his father gave his hearty support, by calling out, "My good friend, this is quite unnecessary; Frank knows a puddle of water when he sees it, and as to Mrs. Bates's, he may get there from the Crown in a hop, step, and jump."

They were permitted to go alone; and with a cordial nod from one, and a graceful bow from the other, the two gentlemen took leave. Emma remained very well pleased with this beginning of the acquaintance, and could now engage to think of them all at Randalls any hour of the day, with full confidence in their comfort.

## Chapter VI.

The next morning brought Mr. Frank Churchill again. He came with Mrs. Weston, to whom and to Highbury he seemed to take very cordially. He had been sitting with her, it appeared, most companionably at home, till her usual hour of exercise; and on being desired to choose their walk, immediately fixed on Highbury. "He did not doubt there being very pleasant walks in every direction, but if left to him, he should always choose the same. Highbury, that airy, cheerful, happy-looking Highbury, would be his constant attraction." Highbury, with Mrs. Weston, stood for

Hartfield; and she trusted to its bearing the same construction with him. They walked thither directly.

Emma had hardly expected them: for Mr. Weston, who had called in for half a minute, in order to hear that his son was very handsome, knew nothing of their plans; and it was an agreeable surprise to her, therefore, to perceive them walking up to the house together, arm in arm. She was wanting to see him again, and especially to see him in company with Mrs. Weston, upon his behavior to whom her opinion of him was to depend. If he were deficient there, nothing should make amends for it. But on seeing them together, she became perfectly satisfied. It was not merely in fine words or hyperbolical compliment that he paid his duty; nothing could be more proper or pleasing than his whole manner to her,—nothing could more agreeably denote his wish of considering her as a friend and securing her affection. And there was time enough for Emma to form a reasonable judgment, as their visit included all the rest of the morning. They were all three walking about together for an hour or two,—first round the shrubberies of Hartfield, and afterwards in Highbury. He was delighted with every thing: admired Hartfield sufficiently for Mr. Woodhouse's ear; and when their going farther was resolved on, confessed his wish to be made acquainted with the whole village, and found matter of commendation and interest much oftener than Emma could have supposed.

Some of the objects of his curiosity spoke very amiable feelings. He begged to be shown the house which his father had lived in so long, and which had been the home of his father's father; and on recollecting that an old woman, who had nursed him, was still living, walked in quest of her cottage, from one end of the street to the other; and though in some points of pursuit or observation there was no positive merit, they showed, altogether, a good will towards Highbury in general, which must be very like a merit to those he was with.

Emma watched, and decided, that with such feelings as were now shown it could not be fairly supposed that he had been ever voluntarily absenting himself: that he had not been acting a part, or making a parade of insincere professions; and that Mr. Knightley certainly had not done him justice.

Their first pause was at the Crown Inn, an inconsiderable house, though the principal one of the sort, where a couple of pair of post-horses were kept, more for the convenience of the neighbourhood than from any run on the road; and his companions had not expected to be detained by any interest excited there: but in passing it they gave the history of the large room visibly added. It had been built many years ago for a ball-room, and while the neighbourhood had been in a particularly populous, dancing state, had been occasionally used as such: but such brilliant days had long passed away; and now the highest purpose for which it was ever wanted was to accommodate a whist club established among the gentlemen and half gentlemen of the place. He was immediately interested. Its character as a ball-room caught him; and instead of passing on, he stopt for several minutes at the two superior sashed windows which were open, to look in and contemplate its capabilities, and lament that its original purpose should have ceased. He saw no fault in the room; he would acknowledge none which they suggested. No; it was long enough, broad enough, handsome enough. It would hold the very number for comfort. They ought to have balls there at least every fortnight through the winter. Why had not Miss Woodhouse revived the former good old days of the room? She who could do any thing in Highbury! The want of proper families in the place, and the conviction that none beyond the place and its immediate environs could be tempted to attend, were mentioned; but he was not satisfied. He could not be persuaded that so many good-looking houses as he saw around him could not furnish numbers enough for such a meeting; and even when particulars were given and families described, he was still unwilling to admit that the inconvenience of such a mixture would be any thing, or that there would be the smallest difficulty in every body's returning into their proper place the next morning. He argued like a young man very much bent on dancing; and Emma was rather surprised to see the constitution of the Weston prevail so decidedly against the habits of the Churchills. He seemed to have all the life and spirit, cheerful feelings, and social inclinations of his father, and nothing of the pride or reserve of Enscombe. Of pride, indeed, there was, perhaps scarcely enough; his indifference to a confusion of rank bordered too much on inelegance of mind. He could be no judge, however, of the evil he was holding cheap. It was but an effusion of lively spirits.

At last he was persuaded to move on from the front of the Crown; and being now almost facing the house where the Bates's lodged, Emma recollected his intended visit the day before, and asked him if he had paid it.

"Yes, oh yes," he replied, "I was just going to mention it. A very successful visit. I saw all the three ladies; and felt very much obliged to you for your preparatory hint. If the talking aunt had taken me quite by surprise, it must have been the death of me. As it was, I was only betrayed into paying a most unreasonable visit. Ten minutes would have been all that was necessary, perhaps all that was proper; and I had told my father I should certainly be at home before him, but there was no getting away, no pause; and, to my utter astonishment, I found, when he (finding me no where else) joined me there at last, that I had been actually sitting with them very nearly three quarters of an hour. The good lady had not given me the possibility of escape before."

"And how did you think Miss Fairfax looking?"

"Ill, very ill;—that is, if a young lady can ever be allowed to look ill: but the expression is hardly admissible, Mrs. Weston, is it? Ladies can never look ill; and, seriously, Miss Fairfax is naturally so pale, as almost always to give the appearance of ill health—a most deplorable want of complexion."

Emma would not agree to this, and began a warm defence of Miss Fairfax's complexion. "It was certainly never brilliant, but she would not allow it to have a sickly hue in general; and there was a softness and delicacy in her skin which gave peculiar elegance to the character of her face."

He listened with all due deference; acknowledged that he had heard many people say the same: but yet he must confess, that to him nothing could make amends for the want of the fine glow of health. Where features were indifferent, a fine complexion gave beauty to them all; and where they were good, the effect was,—fortunately he need not attempt to describe what the effect was.

"Well," said Emma, "there is no disputing about taste. At least you admire her, except her complexion."

He shook his head and laughed. "I cannot separate Miss Fairfax and her complexion."

"Did you see her often at Weymouth? Were you often in the same society?"

At this moment they were approaching Ford's, and he hastily exclaimed, "Ha! this must be the very shop that every body attends every day of their lives, as my father informs me. He comes to Highbury himself, he says, six days out of the seven, and has always business at Ford's. If it be not inconvenient to you, pray let us go in, that I may prove myself to belong to the place,—to be a true citizen of Highbury. I must buy something at Ford's. It will be taking out my freedom. I dare say they sell gloves."

"Oh yes, gloves and every thing. I do admire your patriotism. You will be adored in Highbury. You were very popular before you came, because you were Mr. Weston's son; but lay out half-a-guinea at Ford's, and your popularity will stand upon your own virtues."

They went in; and while the sleek, well-tied parcels of "Men's Beavers" and "York Tan" were bringing down and displaying on the counter, he said,—"But I beg your pardon, Miss Woodhouse, you were speaking to me, you were saying something at the very moment of this burst of my *amor patriæ*.* Do not let me lose it; I assure you the utmost stretch of

---

*Love of one's country (Latin).

public fame would not make me amends for the loss of any happiness in private life."

"I merely asked, whether you had known much of Miss Fairfax and her party at Weymouth?"

"And now that I understand your question, I must pronounce it to be a very unfair one. It is always the lady's right to decide on the degree of acquaintance. Miss Fairfax must already have given her account. I shall not commit myself by claiming more than she may choose to allow."

"Upon my word, you answer as discreetly as she could do herself. But her account of every thing leaves so much to be guessed; she is so very reserved, so very unwilling to give the least information about any body, that I really think you may say what you like of your acquaintance with her."

"May I, indeed? Then I will speak the truth, and nothing suits me so well. I met her frequently at Weymouth. I had known the Campbells a little in town; and at Weymouth we were very much in the same set. Col. Campbell is a very agreeable man, and Mrs. Campbell a friendly, warm-hearted woman. I like them all."

"You know Miss Fairfax's situation in life, I conclude; what she is destined to be."

"Yes"—(rather hesitatingly)—"I believe I do."

"You get upon delicate subjects, Emma," said Mrs. Weston, smiling; "remember that I am here. Mr. Frank Churchill hardly knows what to say when you speak of Miss Fairfax's situation in life. I will move a little farther off."

"I certainly do forget to think of *her*," said Emma, "as having ever been any thing but my friend and my dearest friend."

He looked as if he fully understood and honoured such a sentiment.

When the gloves were bought, and they had quitted the shop again,—"Did you ever hear the young lady we were speaking of play?" said Frank Churchill.

"Ever hear her!" repeated Emma. "You forget how much she belongs to Highbury. I have heard her every year of our lives since we both began. She plays charmingly."

"You think so, do you? I wanted the opinion of some one who could really judge. She appeared to me to play well, that is, with considerable taste, but I know nothing of the matter myself. I am excessively fond of music, but without the smallest skill or right of judging of any body's performance. I have been used to hear hers admired; and I remember one proof of her being thought to play well: a man, a very musical man, and in love with another woman—engaged to her—on the point of marriage—would yet never ask that other woman to sit down to the instrument, if the lady in question could sit down instead—never seemed to like to hear one if he could hear the other. That I thought, in a man of known musical talent, was some proof."

"Proof, indeed!" said Emma, highly amused. "Mr. Dixon is very musical, is he? We shall know more about them all, in half an hour, from you, than Miss Fairfax would have vouchsafed in half a year."

"Yes, Mr. Dixon and Miss Campbell were the persons; and I thought it a very strong proof."

"Certainly, very strong it was; to own the truth, a great deal stronger than, if *I* had been Miss Campbell, would have been at all agreeable to me. I could not excuse a man's having more music than love—more ear than eye—a more acute sensibility to fine sounds than to my feelings. How did Miss Campbell appear to like it?"

"It was her very particular friend, you know."

"Poor comfort!" said Emma, laughing. "One would rather have a stranger preferred than one's very particular friend: with a stranger it might not recur again; but the misery of having a very particular friend always at hand, to do every thing better than one does one's self! Poor Mrs. Dixon! Well, I am glad she is gone to settle in Ireland."

"You are right. It was not very flattering to Miss Campbell; but she really did not seem to feel it."

"So much the better, or so much the worse: I do not know which. But be it sweetness, or be it stupidity in her— quickness of friendship, or dulness of feeling—there was one person, I think, who must have felt it—Miss Fairfax herself. *She* must have felt the improper and dangerous distinction."

"As to that—I do not——"

"Oh, do not imagine that I expect an account of Miss Fairfax's sensations from you, or from any body else. They are known to no human being, I guess, but herself; but if she continued to play whenever she was asked by Mr. Dixon, one may guess what one chooses."

"There appeared such a perfectly good understanding among them all——" he began rather quickly, but checking himself, added, "however, it is impossible for me to say on what terms they really were—how it might all be behind the scenes. I can only say that there was smoothness outwardly. But you, who have known Miss Fairfax from a child, must be a better judge of her character, and of how she is likely to conduct herself in critical situations, than I can be."

"I have known her from a child, undoubtedly: we have been children and women together; and it is natural to suppose that we should be intimate,—that we should have taken to each other whenever she visited her friends. But we never did. I hardly know how it has happened; a little, perhaps, from that wickedness on my side which was prone to take disgust towards a girl so idolised and so cried up as she always was, by her aunt and grandmother, and all their set. And then, her reserve; I never could attach myself to any one so completely reserved."

"It is a most repulsive quality, indeed," said he. "Oftentimes very convenient, no doubt, but never pleasing. There is safety in reserve, but no attraction. One cannot love a reserved person."

"Not till the reserve ceases towards one's self; and then the attraction may be the greater. But I must be more in want of a friend, or an agreeable companion, than I have yet been, to take the trouble of conquering any body's reserve to procure one. Intimacy between Miss Fairfax and me is quite out of the question. I have no reason to think ill of her—not the least—except that such extreme and perpetual cautiousness of word and manner, such a dread of giving a distinct idea about any body, is apt to suggest suspicions of there being something to conceal."

He perfectly agreed with her; and after walking together so long, and thinking so much alike, Emma felt herself so well acquainted with him, that she could hardly believe it to be only their second meeting. He was not exactly what she had expected; less of the man of the world in some of his notions, less of the spoiled child of fortune, therefore better than she had expected. His ideas seemed more moderate—his feelings warmer. She was particularly struck by his manner of considering Mr. Elton's house, which, as well as the church, he would go and look at, and would not join them in finding much fault with. No, he could not believe it a bad house; not such a house as a man was to be pitied for having. If it were to be shared with the woman he loved, he could not think any man to be pitied for having that house. There must be ample room in it for every real comfort. The man must be a blockhead who wanted more.

Mrs. Weston laughed, and said he did not know what he was talking about. Used only to a large house himself, and without ever thinking how many advantages and accommodations were attached to its size, he could be no judge of the privations inevitably belonging to a small one. But Emma, in her own mind, determined that he *did* know what he was talking about, and that he showed a very amiable inclination to settle early in life, and to marry, from worthy motives. He might not be aware of the inroads on domestic peace to be occasioned by no housekeeper's room, or a bad butler's pantry; but no doubt he did perfectly feel that Enscombe could not make him happy, and that whenever he were attached, he would willingly give up much of wealth to be allowed an early establishment.

## *Chapter VII.*

E mma's very good opinion of Frank Churchill was a little shaken the following day, by hearing that he was gone off to London, merely to have his hair cut. A sudden freak seemed to have seized him at breakfast, and he had sent for a chaise and set off intending to return to dinner, but with no more important view that appeared than having his hair cut. There was certainly no harm in his travelling sixteen miles twice over on such an errand; but there was an air of foppery and nonsense in it which she could not approve. It did not accord with the rationality of plan, the moderation in expense, or even the unselfish warmth of heart which she had believed herself to discern in him yesterday. Vanity, extravagance, love of change, restlessness of temper, which must be doing something, good or bad; heedlessness as to the pleasure of his father and Mrs. Weston, indifferent as to how his conduct might appear in general; he became liable to all these changes. His father only called him a coxcomb, and thought it a very good story; but that Mrs. Weston did not like it, was clear enough, by her passing it over as quickly as possible, and making no other comment than that "all young people would have their little whims."

With the exception of this little blot, Emma found that his visit hitherto had given her friend only good ideas of him. Mrs. Weston was very ready to say how attentive and pleasant a companion he made himself,—how much she saw to like in his disposition altogether. He appeared to have a very open temper,—certainly a very cheerful and lively one; she could observe nothing wrong in his notions, a great deal decidedly right; he spoke of his uncle with warm regard, was fond of talking of him; said he would be the best man in the world if he were left to himself; and though there was no being attached to the aunt, he acknowledged her kindness with gratitude, and seemed to mean always to speak of her with respect. This was all very promising; and, but for such an unfortunate fancy for having his hair cut, there was nothing to denote him unworthy of the distinguished honour which her imagination had given him; the honour, if not of being really in love with her, of being at least very near it, and saved only by her own indifference—(for still her resolution held of never marrying)—the honour, in short, of being marked out for her by all their joint acquaintance.

Mr. Weston, on his side, added a virtue to the account which must have some weight. He gave her to understand that Frank admired her extremely—thought her very beautiful and very charming; and with so much to be said for him altogether, she found she must not judge him harshly:—as Mrs. Weston observed, "all young people would have their little whims."

There was one person among his new acquaintance in Surrey not so leniently disposed. In general he was judged, throughout the parishes of Donwell and Highbury, with great candour; liberal allowances were made for the little excesses of such a handsome young man,—one who smiled so often and bowed so well; but there was one spirit among them not to be softened, from its power of censure, by bows or smiles,—Mr. Knightley. The circumstance was told him at Hartfield: for the moment, he was silent; but Emma heard him almost immediately afterwards say to himself, over a newspaper he held in his hand, "Hum! just the trifling, silly fellow I took him for." She had half a mind to resent; but an instant's observation convinced her that it was really said only to relieve his own feelings, and not meant to provoke; and therefore she let it pass.

Although in one instance the bearers of not good tidings, Mr. and Mrs. Weston's visit this morning was in another respect particularly opportune. Something occurred while they were at Hartfield to make Emma want their advice; and, which was still more lucky, she wanted exactly the advice they gave.

This was the occurrence:—The Coles had been settled some years in Highbury, and were very good sort of people, friendly, liberal, and unpretending; but, on the other hand, they were of low origin, in trade, and only moderately genteel. On their first coming into the country, they had lived in proportion to their income, quietly, keeping little company, and that little unexpensively; but the last year or two had brought them a considerable increase of means—the house in town had yielded greater profits, and fortune in general had smiled on them. With their wealth, their views increased; their want of a larger house, their inclination for more company. They added to their house, to their number of servants, to their expenses of every sort; and by this time were, in fortune and style of living, second only to the family at Hartfield. Their love of society, and their new dining-room, prepared every body for their keeping dinner-company; and a few parties, chiefly among the single men, had already taken place. The regular and best families Emma could hardly suppose they would presume to invite,—neither Donwell, nor Hartfield, nor Randalls. Nothing should tempt *her* to go, if they did; and she regretted that her father's known habits would be giving her refusal less meaning than she could wish. The Coles were very respectable in their way, but they ought to be taught that it was not for them to arrange the terms on which the superior families would visit them. This lesson, she very much feared, they would receive only from herself; she had little hope of Mr. Knightley, none of Mr. Weston.

But she had made up her mind how to meet this presumption so many weeks before it appeared, that when insult came at last, it found her very differently affected. Donwell and Randalls had received their invitation, and none had come for her father and herself; and Mrs. Weston's accounting for it with "I suppose they will not take the liberty with you; they know you do not dine out," was not quite sufficient. She felt that she should like to have had the power of refusal; and afterwards, as the idea of the party to be assembled there, consisting precisely of those whose society was dearest to her, occurred again and again, she did not know that she might not have been tempted to accept. Harriet was to be there in the evening, and the Bateses. They had been speaking of it as they walked about Highbury the day before, and Frank Churchill had most earnestly lamented her absence. Might not the evening end in a dance? had been a question of his. The bare possibility of it acted as a further irritation on her spirits; and her being left in solitary grandeur, even supposing the omission to be intended as a compliment, was but poor comfort.

It was the arrival of this very invitation, while the Westons were at Hartfield, which made their presence so acceptable; for though her first remark on reading it was that "of course it must be declined," she so very soon proceeded to ask them what they advised her to do, that their advice for her going was most prompt and successful.

She owned that, considering every thing, she was not absolutely without inclination for the party. The Coles expressed themselves so properly—there was so much real attention in the manner of it—so much consideration for her father. "They would have solicited the honour earlier, but had been waiting the arrival of a folding screen from London, which they hoped might keep Mr. Woodhouse from any draught of air, and therefore induce him the more readily to give them the honour of his company." Upon the whole, she was very persuadable; and it being briefly settled among themselves how it might be done without neglecting his comfort,—how certainly Mrs. Goddard, if not Mrs. Bates, might be depended on for bearing him company,—Mr. Woodhouse was to be talked into an acquiescence of his daughter's going out to dinner on a day now near at hand, and spending the whole evening away from him. As for *his* going, Emma did not wish him to think it possible; the hours would be too late, and the party too numerous. He was soon pretty well resigned.

"I am not fond of dinner-visiting," said he; "I never was. No more is Emma. Late hours do not agree with us. I am sorry Mr. and Mrs. Cole should have done it. I think it would be much better if they would come in one afternoon next summer, and take their tea with us; take us in their afternoon walk, which they might do, as our hours are so reasonable, and yet get home without being out in the damp of the evening. The dews of a summer evening are what I would not expose any body too. However, as they are so very desirous to have dear Emma dine with them, and as you will both be there, and Mr. Knightley too, to take care of her, I cannot wish to prevent it, provided the weather be what it ought, neither damp, nor cold, nor windy." Then turning to Mrs. Weston with a look of gentle reproach,—"Ah, Miss Taylor, if you had not married, you would have staid at home with me."

"Well, sir," cried Mr. Weston, "as I took Miss Taylor away, it is incumbent on me to supply her place, if I can; and I will step to Mrs. Goddard in a moment, if you wish it."

But the idea of any thing to be done in a *moment* was increasing, not lessening, Mr. Woodhouse's agitation. The ladies knew better how to allay it. Mr. Weston must be quiet, and every thing deliberately arranged.

With this treatment, Mr. Woodhouse was soon composed enough for talking as usual. "He should be happy to see Mrs. Goddard. He had a great regard for Mrs. Goddard; and Emma should write a line and invite her. James could take the note. But first of all, there must be an answer written to Mrs. Cole."

"You will make my excuses, my dear, as civilly as possible. You will say that I am quite an invalid, and go nowhere, and therefore must decline their obliging invitation; beginning with my *compliments*, of course. But you will do every thing right. I need not tell you what is to be done. We must remember to let James know that the carriage will be wanted on Tuesday. I shall have no fears for you with him. We have never been there above once since the new approach was made; but still I have no doubt that James will take you very safely: and when you get there, you must tell him at what time you would have him come for you again; and you had better name an early hour. You will not like staying late. You will get very tired when tea is over."

"But you would not wish me to come away before I am tired, papa?"

"Oh no, my love; but you will soon be tired. There will be a great many people talking at once. You will not like the noise."

"But, my dear sir," cried Mr. Weston, "if Emma comes away early, it will be breaking up the party."

"And no great harm if it does," said Mr. Woodhouse. "The sooner every party breaks up the better."

"But you do not consider how it may appear to the Coles. Emma's going away directly after tea might be giving offence. They are good-natured people, and think little of their own claims; but still they must feel that any body's hurrying away is no great compliment; and Miss Woodhouse's doing it would be more thought of than any other person's in the room. You would not wish to disappoint and mortify the Coles, I am sure, sir; friendly, good sort of people as ever lived, and who have been your neighbours these *ten* years."

"No, upon no account in the world. Mr. Weston, I am much obliged to you for reminding me. I should be extremely sorry to be giving them any pain. I know what worthy people they are. Perry tells me that Mr. Cole never touches malt liquor. You would not think it to look at him, but he is bilious—Mr. Cole is very bilious. No, I would not be the means of giving them any pain. My dear Emma, we must consider this. I am sure, rather than run the risk of hurting Mr. and Mrs. Cole, you would stay a little longer than you might wish. You will not regard being tired. You will be perfectly safe, you know, among your friends."

"Oh yes, papa. I have no fears at all for myself; and I should have no scruples of staying as late as Mrs. Weston, but on your account. I am only afraid of your sitting up for me. I am not afraid of your not being exceedingly comfortable with Mrs. Goddard. She loves piquet, you know; but when she is gone home, I am afraid you will be sitting up by yourself, instead of going to bed at your usual time; and the idea of that would entirely destroy my comfort. You must promise me not to sit up."

He did, on the condition of some promises on her side: such as that, if she came home cold, she would be sure to warm herself thoroughly; if hungry, that she would take something to eat; that her own maid should sit up for her; and that Serle and the butler should see that every thing were safe in the house as usual.

## Chapter VIII.

Frank Churchill came back again; and if he kept his father's dinner waiting it was not known at Hartfield; for Mrs. Weston was too anxious for his being a favourite with Mr. Woodhouse, to betray any imperfection which could be concealed.

He came back, had had his hair cut, and laughed at himself with a very good grace, but without seeming really at all ashamed of what he had done. He had no reason to wish his hair longer to conceal any confusion of face; no reason to wish the money unspent to improve his spirits. He was quite as undaunted and as lively as ever; and, after seeing him, Emma thus moralised to herself:—

"I do not know whether it ought to be so, but certainly silly things do cease to be silly if they are done by sensible people in an impudent way. Wickedness is always wickedness, but folly is not always folly. It depends upon the character of those who handle it. Mr. Knightley, he is *not* a trifling, silly young man. If he were, he would have done this differently. He would either have gloried in the achievement, or been ashamed of it. There would have been either the ostentation of a coxcomb, or the evasions of a mind too weak to defend its own vanities. No, I am perfectly sure that he is not trifling or silly."

With Tuesday came the agreeable prospect of seeing him again, and for a longer time than hitherto; of judging of his general manners, and, by inference, of the meaning of his manners towards herself; of guessing how soon it might be necessary for her to throw coldness into her air; and of fancying what the observations of all those might be, who were now seeing them together for the first time.

She meant to be very happy, in spite of the scene being laid at Mr. Cole's; and without being able to forget that among the failings of Mr. Elton, even in the days of his favour, none had disturbed her more than his propensity to dine with Mr. Cole.

Her father's comfort was amply secured, Mrs. Bates as well as Mrs. Goddard being able to come; and her last pleasing duty, before she left the house, was to pay her respects to them as they sat together after dinner; and while her father was fondly noticing the beauty of her dress, to make the two ladies all the amends in her power, by helping them to large slices of cake and full glasses of wine, for whatever unwilling self-denial his care of their constitution might have obliged them to practise during the meal. She had provided a plentiful dinner for them; she wished she could know that they had been allowed to eat it.

She followed another carriage to Mr. Cole's door; and was pleased to see that it was Mr. Knightley's; for Mr. Knightley keeping no horses, having little spare money and a great deal of health, activity, and independence, was too apt, in Emma's opinion, to get about as he could, and not use his carriage so often as became the owner of Donwell Abbey. She had an opportunity now of speaking her approbation while warm from her heart, for he stopped to hand her out.

"This is coming as you should do," said she; "like a gentleman. I am quite glad to see you."

He thanked her, observing, "How lucky that we should arrive at the same moment; for, if we had met first in the drawing-room, I doubt whether you would have discerned me to be more of a gentleman than usual. You might not have distinguished how I came by my look or manner."

"Yes I should; I am sure I should. There is always a look of consciousness or bustle when people come in a way which they know to be beneath them. You think you carry it off very well, I dare say; but with you it is a sort of bravado, an air of affected unconcern: I always observe it whenever I meet you under those circumstances. *Now* you have nothing to try for. You are not afraid of being supposed ashamed. You are not striving to look taller than any body else. *Now* I shall really be very happy to walk into the same room with you."

"Nonsensical girl!" was his reply, but not at all in anger.

Emma had as much reason to be satisfied with the rest of the party as with Mr. Knightley. She was received with a cordial respect which could not but please, and given all the consequence she could wish for. When the Westons arrived, the kindest looks of love, the strongest of admiration, were for her, from both husband and wife: the son approached her with a cheerful eagerness which marked her as his peculiar object, and at dinner she found him seated by her; and, as she firmly believed, not without some dexterity on his side.

The party was rather large, as it included one other family,—a proper unobjectionable country family, whom the Coles had the advantage of naming among their acquaintance,—and the male part of Mr. Cox's family, the lawyer of Highbury. The less worthy females were to come in the evening, with Miss Bates, Miss Fairfax, and Miss Smith; but already, at dinner, they were too numerous for any subject of conversation to be general; and, while politics and Mr. Elton were talked over, Emma could fairly surrender all her attention to the pleasantness of her neighbour. The first remote sound to which she felt herself obliged to attend was the name of Jane Fairfax. Mrs. Cole seemed to be relating something of her that was expected to be very interesting. She listened, and found it well worth listening to. That very dear part of Emma, her fancy, received an amusing supply. Mrs. Cole was telling that she had been calling on Miss Bates; and, as soon as she entered the room, had been struck by the sight of a piano-forte, a very elegant looking instrument; not a grand, but a large-sized square piano-forte: and the substance of the story, the end of all the dialogue which ensued of surprise, and enquiry, and congratulations on her side, and explanations on Miss Bates's, was, that this piano-forte had arrived from Broadwood's[10] the day before, to the great astonishment of both aunt and niece, entirely unexpected; that, at first, by Miss Bates's account, Jane herself was quite at a loss, quite bewildered to think who could possibly have ordered it; but now they were both perfectly satisfied that it could be from only one quarter,—of course it must be from Colonel Campbell.

"One can suppose nothing else," added Mrs. Cole; "and I was only surprised that there could ever have been a doubt. But Jane, it seems, had a letter from them very lately, and not a word was said about it. She knows their ways best; but I should not consider their silence as any reason for their not meaning to make the present. They might choose to surprise her."

Mrs. Cole had many to agree with her; every body who

spoke on the subject was equally convinced that it must come from Colonel Campbell, and equally rejoiced that such a present had been made; and there were enough ready to speak to allow Emma to think her own way, and still listen to Mrs. Cole.

"I declare, I do not know when I have heard any thing that has given me more satisfaction. It always has quite hurt me that Jane Fairfax, who plays so delightfully, should not have an instrument. It seemed quite a shame, especially considering how many houses there are where fine instruments are absolutely thrown away. This is like giving ourselves a slap, to be sure; and it was but yesterday I was telling Mr. Cole I really was ashamed to look at our new grand piano-forte in the drawing-room, while I do not know one note from another, and our little girls, who are but just beginning, perhaps may never make any thing of it; and there is poor Jane Fairfax, who is mistress of music, has not any thing of the nature of an instrument, not even the pitifulest old spinet* in the world, to amuse herself with. I was saying this to Mr. Cole but yesterday, and he quite agreed with me; only he is so particularly fond of music that he could not help indulging himself in the purchase, hoping that some of our good neighbours might be so obliging occasionally to put it to a better use than we can; and that really is the reason why the instrument was bought—or else I am sure we ought to be ashamed of it. We are in great hopes that Miss Woodhouse may be prevailed with to try it this evening."

Miss Woodhouse made the proper acquiescence; and finding that nothing more was to be entrapped from any communication of Mrs. Cole's, turned to Frank Churchill.

"Why do you smile?" said she.

---

*One of the smaller keyboard instruments that were manufactured in the course of the development of the modern piano; today the term refers specifically to a small and compact upright piano.

"Nay, why do you?"

"Me! I suppose I smile for pleasure at Colonel Campbell's being so rich and so liberal. It is a handsome present."

"Very."

"I rather wonder that it was never made before."

"Perhaps Miss Fairfax has never been staying here so long before."

"Or that he did not give her the use of their own instrument, which must now be shut up in London, untouched by any body."

"That is a grand piano-forte, and he might think it too large for Mrs. Bates's house."

"You may *say* what you choose, but your countenance testifies that your *thoughts* on this subject are very much like mine."

"I do not know. I rather believe you are giving me more credit for acuteness than I deserve. I smile because you smile, and shall probably suspect whatever I find you suspect; but at present I do not see what there is to question. If Colonel Campbell is not the person, who can be?"

"What do you say to Mrs. Dixon?"

"Mrs. Dixon! very true, indeed. I had not thought of Mrs. Dixon. She must know, as well as her father, how acceptable an instrument would be; and perhaps the mode of it, the mystery, the surprise, is more like a young woman's scheme than an elderly man's. It is Mrs. Dixon, I dare say. I told you that your suspicions would guide mine."

"If so, you must extend your suspicions, and comprehend *Mr.* Dixon in them."

"Mr. Dixon! very well. Yes, I immediately perceive that it must be the joint present of Mr. and Mrs. Dixon. We were speaking the other day, you know, of his being so warm an admirer of her performance."

"Yes, and what you told me on that head confirmed an idea which I had entertained before. 1 do not mean to reflect upon the good intentions of either Mr. Dixon or Miss Fairfax; but I cannot help suspecting either that, after making his proposals to her friend, he had the misfortune to fall in love with *her*, or that he became conscious of a little attachment on her side. One might guess twenty things without guessing exactly the right; but I am sure there must be a particular cause for her choosing to come to Highbury, instead of going with the Campbells to Ireland. Here, she must be leading a life of privation and penance; there, it would have been all enjoyment. As to the pretence of trying her native air, I look upon that as a mere excuse. In the summer it might have passed; but what can any body's native air do for them in the months of January, February, and March? Good fires and carriages would be much more to the purpose in most cases of delicate health, and I dare say in hers. I do not require you to adopt all my suspicions, though you make so noble a profession of doing it, but I honestly tell you what they are."

"And, upon my word, they have an air of great probability. Mr. Dixon's preference of her music to her friend's I can answer for being very decided."

"And then, he saved her life. Did you ever hear of that? A water party; and by some accident she was falling overboard. He caught her."

"He did. I was there—one of the party."

"Were you really? Well! But you observed nothing, of course, for it seems to be a new idea to you. If I had been there, I think I should have made some discoveries."

"I dare say you would; but I, simple I, saw nothing but the fact, that Miss Fairfax was nearly dashed from the vessel, and that Mr. Dixon caught her—it was the work of a moment. And though the consequent shock and alarm were very great, and much more durable—indeed I believe it was half an hour before any of us were comfortable again—yet that was too general a sensation for any thing of peculiar anxiety to be observable. I do not mean to say, however, that you might not have made discoveries."

The conversation was here interrupted. They were called on to share in the awkwardness of a rather long interval between the courses, and obliged to be as formal and as orderly as the others; but when the table was again safely covered, when every corner dish was placed exactly right, and occupation and ease were generally restored, Emma said,—

"The arrival of this piano-forte is decisive with me. I wanted to know a little more, and this tells me quite enough. Depend upon it, we shall soon hear that it is a present from Mr. and Mrs. Dixon."

"And if the Dixons should absolutely deny all knowledge of it, we must conclude it to come from the Campbells."

"No, I am sure it is not from the Campbells. Miss Fairfax knows it is not from the Campbells, or they would have been guessed at first. She would not have been puzzled, had she dared fix on them. I may not have convinced you, perhaps, but I am perfectly convinced myself that Mr. Dixon is a principal in the business."

"Indeed you injure me if you suppose me unconvinced. Your reasonings carry my judgment along with them entirely. At first, while I supposed you satisfied that Colonel Campbell was the giver, I saw it only as paternal kindness, and thought it the most natural thing in the world. But when you mentioned Mrs. Dixon, I felt how much more probable that it should be the tribute of warm female friendship. And now I can see it in no other light than as an offering of love."

There was no occasion to press the matter farther. The conviction seemed real; he looked as if he felt it. She said no more,—other subjects took their turn; and the rest of the dinner passed away; the dessert succeeded; the children came in, and were talked to and admired amid the usual rate of conversation; a few clever things said, a few downright silly, but by much the larger proportion neither the one nor the other—nothing worse than every-day remarks, dull repetitions, old news, and heavy jokes.

The ladies had not been long in the drawing-room, before the other ladies, in their different divisions, arrived. Emma watched the *entrée* of her own particular little friend; and if she could not exult in her dignity and grace, she could not only love the blooming sweetness and the artless manner, but could most heartily rejoice in that light, cheerful, unsentimental disposition which allowed her so many alleviations of pleasure in the midst of the pangs of disappointed affection. There she sat—and who would have guessed how many tears she had been lately shedding? To be in company, nicely dressed herself, and seeing others nicely dressed, to sit and smile and look pretty, and say nothing, was enough for the happiness of the present hour. Jane Fairfax did look and move superior; but Emma suspected she might have been glad to change feelings with Harriet,—very glad to have purchased the mortification of having loved—yes, of having loved even Mr. Elton in vain,—by the surrender of all the dangerous pleasure of knowing herself beloved by the husband of her friend.

In so large a party it was not necessary that Emma should approach her. She did not wish to speak of the piano-forte, she felt too much in the secret herself, to think the appearance of curiosity or interest fair, and therefore purposely kept at a distance; but by the others, the subject was almost immediately introduced, and she saw the blush of consciousness with which congratulations were received, the blush of guilt which accompanied the name of "my excellent friend Colonel Campbell."

Mrs. Weston, kind-hearted and musical, was particularly interested by the circumstance, and Emma could not help being amused at her perseverance in dwelling on the subject; and having so much to ask and to say as to tone, touch, and pedal, totally unsuspicious of that wish of saying as little about it as possible, which she plainly read in the fair heroine's countenance.

They were soon joined by some of the gentlemen; and the very first of the early was Frank Churchill. In he walked, the first and the handsomest; and after paying his compliments *en passant* to Miss Bates and her niece, made his way directly to the opposite side of the circle, where sat Miss Woodhouse; and till he could find a seat by her, would not sit at all. Emma divined what every body present must be thinking. She was his object, and every body must perceive it. She introduced him to her friend Miss Smith, and, at convenient moments afterwards, heard what each thought of the other. "He had never seen so lovely a face, and was delighted with her *naïveté*." And she,—"only to be sure it was paying him too great a compliment, but she did think there were some looks a little like Mr. Elton." Emma restrained her indignation, and only turned from her in silence.

Smiles of intelligence passed between her and the gentleman on first glancing towards Miss Fairfax; but it was most prudent to avoid speech. He told her that he had been impatient to leave the dining-room—hated sitting long—was always the first to move when he could—that his father, Mr. Knightley, Mr. Cox, and Mr. Cole, were left very busy over parish business—that as long as he had staid, however, it had been pleasant enough, as he found them in general a set of gentlemen-like, sensible men; and spoke so handsomely of Highbury altogether—thought it so abundant in agreeable families—that Emma began to feel she had been used to despise the place rather too much. She questioned him as to the society in Yorkshire, the extent of the neighbourhood about Enscombe, and the sort; and could make out from his answers that, as far as Enscombe was concerned, there was very little going on; that their visitings were among a range of great families, none very near; and that even when days were fixed, and invitations accepted, it was an even chance that Mrs. Churchill were not in health or spirits for going; that they made a point of visiting no fresh person; and that, though he had his separate engagements, it was not without difficulty without considerable address *at times*, that he could get away, or introduce an acquaintance for a night.

She saw that Enscombe could not satisfy, and that Highbury, taken in its best, might reasonably please a young man who had more retirement at home than he liked. His importance at Enscombe was very evident. He did not boast, but it naturally betrayed itself, that he had persuaded his aunt where his uncle could do nothing, and on her laughing and noticing it, he owned that he believed (excepting one or two points) he could *with time* persuade her to any thing. One of those points on which his influence failed he then mentioned. He had wanted very much to go abroad—had been very eager indeed to be allowed to travel—but she would not hear of it. This had happened the year before. *Now*, he said, he was beginning to have no longer the same wish.

The unpersuadable point, which he did not mention, Emma guessed to be good behaviour to his father.

"I have made a most wretched discovery," said he, after a short pause. "I have been here a week to-morrow—half my time. I never knew days fly so fast. A week to-morrow!—and I have hardly begun to enjoy myself. But just got acquainted with Mrs. Weston, and others. I hate the recollection."

"Perhaps you may now begin to regret that you spent one whole day, out of so few, in having your hair cut."

"No," said he, smiling, "that is no subject of regret at all. I have no pleasure in seeing my friends, unless I can believe myself fit to be seen."

The rest of the gentlemen being now in the room, Emma found herself obliged to turn from him for a few minutes, and listen to Mr. Cole. When Mr. Cole had moved away, and her attention could be restored as before, she saw Frank Churchill looking intently across the room at Miss Fairfax, who was sitting exactly opposite.

"What is the matter?" said she.

He started. "Thank you for rousing me," he replied. "I believe I have been very rude; but really Miss Fairfax has done her hair in so odd a way—so very odd a way—that I cannot keep my eyes from her. I never saw any thing so *outrée!*\* Those curls! This must be a fancy of her own. I see nobody else looking like her. I must go and ask her whether it is an

---

\*Extravagant.

Irish fashion. Shall I?—Yes, I will—I declare I will—and you shall see how she takes it;—whether she colours."

He was gone immediately; and Emma soon saw him standing before Miss Fairfax, and talking to her; but as to its effect on the young lady, as he had improvidently placed himself exactly between them, exactly in front of Miss Fairfax, she could absolutely distinguish nothing.

Before he could return to his chair, it was taken by Mrs. Weston.

"This is the luxury of a large party," said she: "one can get near every body, and say every thing. My dear Emma, I am longing to talk to you. I have been making discoveries and forming plans, just like yourself, and I must tell them while the idea is fresh. Do you know how Miss Bates and her niece came here?"

"How!—They were invited, were not they?"

"Oh yes—but how they were conveyed hither?—the manner of their coming?"

"They walked, I conclude. How else could they come?"

"Very true. Well, a little while ago it occurred to me how very sad it would be to have Jane Fairfax walking home again, late at night, and cold as the nights are now. And as I looked at her, though I never saw her appear to more advantage, it struck me that she was heated, and would therefore be particularly liable to take cold. Poor girl! I could not bear the idea of it; so, as soon as Mr. Weston came into the room, and I could get at him, I spoke to him about the carriage. You may guess how readily he came into my wishes; and having his approbation, I made my way directly to Miss Bates, to assure her that the carriage would be at her service before it took us home; for I thought it would be making her comfortable at once. Good soul! she was as grateful as possible, you may be sure. 'Nobody was ever so fortunate as herself!'—but with many, many thanks,—'there was no occasion to trouble us, for Mr. Knightley's carriage had brought, and was to take them home again.' I was quite surprised;—very glad, I am sure; but really quite surprised. Such a very kind attention—and so thoughtful an attention!—the sort of thing that so few men would think of. And, in short, from knowing his usual ways, I am very much inclined to think that it was for their accommodation the carriage was used at all. I do suspect he would not have had a pair of horses for himself, and that it was only as an excuse for assisting them."

"Very likely," said Emma, "nothing more likely. I know no man more likely than Mr. Knightley to do the sort of thing— to do any thing really good-natured, useful, considerate, or benevolent. He is not a gallant man, but he is a very humane one; and this, considering Jane Fairfax's ill health, would appear a case of humanity to him;—and for an act of unostentatious kindness, there is nobody whom I would fix on more than on Mr. Knightley. I know he had horses to-day—for we arrived together; and I laughed at him about it, but he said not a word that could betray."

"Well," said Mrs. Weston, smiling, "you give him credit for more simple, disinterested benevolence in this instance than I do; for while Miss Bates was speaking, a suspicion darted into my head, and I have never been able to get it out again. The more I think of it, the more probable it appears. In short, I have made a match between Mr. Knightley and Jane Fairfax. See the consequence of keeping you company!— What do you say to it?"

"Mr. Knightley and Jane Fairfax!" exclaimed Emma. "Dear Mrs. Weston, how could you think of such a thing?— Mr. Knightley!—Mr. Knightley must not marry!—You would not have little Henry cut out from Donwell?—Oh no, no,— Henry must have Donwell. I cannot at all consent to Mr. Knightley's marrying; and I am sure it is not at all likely. I am amazed that you should think of such a thing."

"My dear Emma, I have told you what led me to think of it. I do not want the match—I do not want to injure dear little Henry—but the idea has been given me by circumstances; and if Mr. Knightley really wished to marry, you would not have him refrain on Henry's account, a boy of six years old, who knows nothing of the matter?"

"Yes, I would. I could not bear to have Henry supplanted. Mr. Knightley marry! No, I have never had such an idea, and I cannot adopt it now. And Jane Fairfax, too, of all women!"

"Nay, she has always been a first favourite with him, as you very well know."

"But the imprudence of such a match!"

"I am not speaking of its prudence—merely its probability."

"I see no probability in it, unless you have any better foundation than what you mention. His good-nature, his humanity, as I tell you, would be quite enough to account for the horses. He has a great regard for the Bateses, you know, independent of Jane Fairfax—and is always glad to show them attention. My dear Mrs. Weston, do not take to match-making. You do it very ill. Jane Fairfax mistress of the Abbey! Oh no, no;—every feeling revolts. For his own sake, I would not have him do so mad a thing."

"Imprudent, if you please—but not mad. Excepting inequality of fortune, and perhaps a little disparity of age, I can see nothing unsuitable."

"But Mr. Knightley does not want to marry. I am sure he has not the least idea of it. Do not put it into his head. Why should he marry? He is as happy as possible by himself; with his farm, and his sheep, and his library, and all the parish to manage; and he is extremely fond of his brother's children. He has no occasion to marry, either to fill up his time or his heart."

"My dear Emma, as long as he thinks so, it is so; but if he really loves Jane Fairfax——"

"Nonsense! He does not care about Jane Fairfax. In the way of love, I am sure he does not. He would do any good to her, or her family; but—

"Well," said Mrs. Weston, laughing, "perhaps the greatest good he could do them would be to give Jane such a respectable home."

"If it would be good to her, I am sure it would be evil to himself—a very shameful and degrading connection. How would he bear to have Miss Bates belonging to him? To have her haunting the Abbey, and thanking him all day long for his great kindness in marrying Jane?—'So very kind and obliging! But he always had been such a very kind neighbour!' And then fly off, through half a sentence, to her mother's old petticoat. 'Not that it was such a very old petticoat either—for still it would last a great while,—and, indeed, she must thankfully say that their petticoats were all very strong.'"

"For shame, Emma! Do not mimic her. You divert me against my conscience. And, upon my word, I do not think Mr. Knightley would be much disturbed by Miss Bates. Little things do not irritate him. She might talk on; and if he wanted to say any thing himself, he would only talk louder, and drown her voice. But the question is not, whether it would be a bad connection for him, but whether he wishes it; and I think he does. I have heard him speak, and so must you, so very highly of Jane Fairfax! The interest he takes in her—his anxiety about her health—his concern that she should have no happier prospect! I have heard him express himself so warmly on those points! Such an admirer of her performance on the piano-forte, and of her voice! I have heard him say, that he could listen to her for ever. Oh, and I had almost forgotten one idea that occurred to me—this piano-forte that has been sent her by somebody—though we have all been so well satisfied to consider it a present from the Campbells, may it not be from Mr. Knightley? I cannot help suspecting him. I think he is just the person to do it, even without being in love."

"Then it can be no argument to prove that he is in love. But I do not think it is at all a likely thing for him to do. Mr. Knightley does nothing mysteriously."

"I have heard him lamenting her having no instrument repeatedly; oftener than I should suppose such a circumstance would, in the common course of things, occur to him."

"Very well; if he had intended to give her one, he would have told her so."

"There might be scruples of delicacy, my dear Emma. I have

a very strong notion that it comes from him. I am sure he was particularly silent when Mrs. Cole told us of it at dinner."

"You take up an idea, Mrs. Weston, and run away with it, as you have many a time reproached me with doing. I see no sign of attachment. I believe nothing of the piano-forte, and proof only shall convince me that Mr. Knightley has any thought of marrying Jane Fairfax."

They combated the point some time longer in the same way, Emma rather gaining ground over the mind of her friend; for Mrs. Weston was the most used of the two to yield; till a little bustle in the room showed them that tea was over, and the instrument in preparation; and at the same moment Mr. Cole approaching to entreat Miss Woodhouse would do them the honour of trying it. Frank Churchill, of whom, in the eagerness of her conversation with Mrs. Weston, she had been seeing nothing, except that he had found a seat by Miss Fairfax, followed Mr. Cole, to add his very pressing entreaties; and as, in every respect, it suited Emma best to lead, she gave a very proper compliance.

She knew the limitations of her own powers too well to attempt more than she could perform with credit; she wanted neither taste nor spirit in the little things which are generally acceptable, and could accompany her own voice well. One accompaniment to her song took her agreeably by surprise—a second, slightly but correctly taken by Frank Churchill. Her pardon was duly begged at the close of the song, and every thing usual followed. He was accused of having a delightful voice, and a perfect knowledge of music; which was properly denied; and that he knew nothing of the matter, and had no voice at all, roundly asserted. They sang together once more; and Emma would then resign her place to Miss Fairfax, whose performance, both vocal and instrumental, she never could attempt to conceal from herself, was infinitely superior to her own.

With mixed feelings, she seated herself at a little distance from the numbers round the instrument, to listen. Frank Churchill sang again. They had sung together once or twice, it appeared, at Weymouth. But the sight of Mr. Knightley among the most attentive soon drew away half Emma's mind; and she fell into a train of thinking on the subject of Mrs. Weston's suspicions, to which the sweet sounds of the united voices gave only momentary interruptions. Her objections to Mr. Knightley's marrying did not in the least subside. She could see nothing but evil in it. It would be a great disappointment to Mr. John Knightley, consequently to Isabella. A real injury to the children—a most mortifying change, and material loss to them all—a very great deduction from her father's daily comfort—and, as to herself, she could not at all endure the idea of Jane Fairfax at Donwell Abbey. A Mrs. Knightley for them all to give way to! No—Mr. Knightley must never marry. Little Henry must remain the heir of Donwell.

Presently Mr. Knightley looked back, and came and sat down by her. They talked at first only of the performance. His admiration was certainly very warm; yet she thought, but for Mrs. Weston, it would not have struck her. As a sort of touchstone, however, she began to speak of his kindness in conveying the aunt and niece; and though his answer was in the spirit of cutting the matter short, she believed it to indicate only his disinclination to dwell on any kindness of his own.

"I often feel concerned," said she, "that I dare not make *our* carriage more useful on such occasions. It is not that I am without the wish; but you know how impossible my father would deem it that James should put to for such a purpose."

"Quite out of the question, quite out of the question," he replied; "but you must often wish it, I am sure." And he smiled with such seeming pleasure at the conviction, that she must proceed another step.

"This present from the Campbells," said she—"this pianoforte is very kindly given."

"Yes," he replied, and without the smallest apparent embarrassment. "But they would have done better had they given her notice of it. Surprises are foolish things. The pleasure is not enhanced, and the inconvenience is often considerable. I should have expected better judgment in Colonel Campbell."

From that moment, Emma could have taken her oath that Mr. Knightley had had no concern in giving the instrument. But whether he were entirely free from peculiar attachment— whether there were no actual preference—remained a little longer doubtful. Towards the end of Jane's second song, her voice grew thick.

"That will do," said he, when it was finished, thinking aloud, "you have sung quite enough for one evening; now be quiet."

Another song, however, was soon begged for. "One more;—they would not fatigue Miss Fairfax on any account, and would only ask for one more." And Frank Churchill was heard to say, "I think you could manage this without effort; the first part is so very trifling. The strength of the song falls on the second."

Mr. Knightley grew angry.

"That fellow," said he, indignantly, "thinks of nothing but showing off his own voice. Thus must not be." And touching Miss Bates, who at that moment passed near,—"Miss Bates, are you mad, to let your niece sing herself hoarse in this manner? Go, and interfere. They have no mercy on her."

Miss Bates, in her real anxiety for Jane, could hardly stay even to be grateful, before she stepped forward and put an end to all further singing. Here ceased the concert part of the evening, for Miss Woodhouse and Miss Fairfax were the only young lady performers; but soon (within five minutes) the proposal of dancing—originating nobody exactly knew where—was so effectually promoted by Mr. and Mrs. Cole, that every thing was rapidly clearing away, to give proper space. Mrs. Weston, capital in her country-dances, was seated, and beginning an irresistible waltz; and Frank Churchill, coming up with most becoming gallantry to Emma, had secured her hand, and led her up to the top.

While waiting till the other young people could pair themselves off, Emma found time, in spite of the compliments she was receiving on her voice and her taste, to look about, and see what became of Mr. Knightley. This would be a trial. He was no dancer in general. If he were to be very

alert in engaging Jane Fairfax now, it might augur something. There was no immediate appearance. No; he was talking to Mrs. Cole—he was looking on unconcerned; Jane was
asked by somebody else, and he was still talking to Mrs. Cole.

Emma had no longer an alarm for Henry: his interest was
yet safe; and she led off the dance with genuine spirit and
enjoyment. Not more than five couple could be mustered;
but the rarity and the suddenness of it made it very delightful, and she found herself well matched in a partner. They
were a couple worth looking at.

Two dances, unfortunately, were all that could be allowed. It was growing late, and Miss Bates became anxious to
get home, on her mother's account. After some attempts,
therefore, to be permitted to begin again, they were obliged
to thank Mrs. Weston, look sorrowful, and have done.

"Perhaps it is as well," said Frank Churchill, as he attended Emma to her carriage. "I must have asked Miss Fairfax, and her languid dancing would not have agreed with
me, after yours."

## Chapter IX.

E mma did not repent her condescension in going to
the Coles. The visit afforded her many pleasant recollections the next day; and all that she might be supposed to have lost on the side of dignified seclusion must be
amply repaid in the splendour of popularity. She must have
delighted the Coles—worthy people, who deserved to be
made happy!—and left a name behind her that would not
soon die away.

Perfect happiness, even in memory, is not common; and

there were two points on which she was not quite easy. She doubted whether she had not transgressed the duty of woman by woman, in betraying her suspicions of Jane Fairfax's feelings to Frank Churchill. It was hardly right; but it had been so strong an idea, that it would escape her, and his submission to all that she told was a compliment to her penetration which made it difficult for her to be quite certain that she ought to have held her tongue.

The other circumstance of regret related also to Jane Fairfax, and there she had no doubt. She did unfeignedly and unequivocally regret the inferiority of her own playing and singing. She did most heartily grieve over the idleness of her childhood; and sat down and practised vigorously an hour and a half.

She was then interrupted by Harriet's coming in; and if Harriet's praise could have satisfied her, she might soon have been comforted.

"Oh, if I could but play as well as you and Miss Fairfax!"

"Don't class us together, Harriet. My playing is no more like hers than a lamp is like sunshine."

"O dear, I think you play the best of the two. I think you play quite as well as she does. I am sure I had much rather hear you. Every body last night said how well you played."

"Those who knew any thing about it must have felt the difference. The truth is, Harriet, that my playing is just good enough to be praised, but Jane Fairfax's is much beyond it."

"Well, I always shall think that you play quite as well as she does, or that if there is any difference nobody would ever find it out. Mr. Cole said how much taste you had, and Mr. Frank Churchill talked a great deal about your taste, and that he valued taste much more than execution."

"Ah, but Jane Fairfax has them both, Harriet."

"Are you sure? I saw she had execution, but I did not know she had any taste. Nobody talked about it; and I hate Italian singing: there is no understanding a word of it. Besides, if she does play so very well, you know, it is no more than she is obliged to do, because she will have to teach. The

Coxes were wondering last night whether she would get into any great family. How do you think the Coxes looked?"

"Just as they always do,—very vulgar."

"They told me something," said Harriet, rather hesitatingly, "but it is nothing of any consequence."

Emma was obliged to ask what they had told her, though fearful of its producing Mr. Elton.

"They told me that Mr. Martin dined with them last Saturday."

"Oh!"

"He came to their father upon some business, and he asked him to stay dinner."

"Oh!"

"They talked a great deal about him, especially Anne Cox. I do not know what she meant, but she asked me if I thought I should go and stay there again next summer."

"She meant to be impertinently curious, just as such an Anne Cox should be."

"She said he was very agreeable the day he dined there. He sat by her at dinner. Miss Nash thinks either of the Coxes would be very glad to marry him."

"Very likely; I think they are, without exception, the most vulgar girls in Highbury."

Harriet had business at Ford's. Emma thought it most prudent to go with her. Another accidental meeting with the Martins was possible, and, in her present state, would be dangerous.

Harriet, tempted by every thing, and swayed by half a word, was always very long at a purchase; and while she was still hanging over muslins, and changing her mind, Emma went to the door for amusement. Much could not be hoped from the traffic of even the busiest part of Highbury;—Mr. Perry walking hastily by; Mr. William Cox letting himself in at the office door; Mr. Cole's carriage-horses returning from exercise; or a stray letter-boy on an obstinate mule, were the liveliest objects she could presume to expect; and when her eyes fell only on the butcher with his tray, a tidy old woman

travelling homewards from shop with her full basket, two
curs quarrelling over a dirty bone, and a string of dawdling
children round the baker's little bow-window eyeing the gingerbread, she knew she had no reason to complain, and was
amused enough: quite enough still to stand at the door. A
mind lively and at ease can do with seeing nothing, and can
see nothing that does not answer.

She looked down the Randalls road. The scene enlarged;
two persons appeared; Mrs. Weston and her son-in-law. They
were walking into Highbury;—to Hartfield of course: they
were stopping, however, in the first place at Mrs. Bates's,
whose house was a little nearer Randalls than Ford's, and
had all but knocked when Emma caught their eye. Immediately they crossed the road and came forward to her; and the
agreeableness of yesterday's engagement seemed to give
fresh pleasure to the present meeting. Mrs. Weston informed her that she was going to call on the Bateses, in
order to hear the new instrument.

"For my companion tells me," said she, "that I absolutely
promised Miss Bates last night that I would come this morning. I was not aware of it myself. I did not know that I had
fixed a day; but as he says I did, I am going now."

"And while Mrs. Weston pays her visit, I may be allowed, I
hope," said Frank Churchill, "to join your party and wait for
her at Hartfield, if you are going home."

Mrs. Weston was disappointed.

"I thought you meant to go with me. They would be very
much pleased."

"Me! I should be quite in the way. But, perhaps, I may be
equally in the way here. Miss Woodhouse looks as if she did
not want me. My aunt always sends me off when she is shop-
ping. She says I fidget her to death; Miss Woodhouse looks as
if she could almost say the same. What am I to do?"

"I am here on no business of my own," said Emma, "I am
only waiting for my friend. She will probably have soon
done, and then we shall go home. But you had better go with
Mrs. Weston and hear the instrument."

"Well, if you advise it. But (with a smile) if Colonel Campbell should have employed a careless friend, and if it should prove to have an indifferent tone, what shall I say? I shall be no support to Mrs. Weston. She might do very well by herself. A disagreeable truth would be palatable through her lips, but I am the wretchedest being in the world at a civil falsehood."

"I do not believe any such thing," replied Emma; "I am persuaded that you can be as insincere as your neighbours, when it is necessary; but there is no reason to suppose the instrument is indifferent. Quite otherwise, indeed, if I understood Miss Fairfax's opinion last night."

"Do come with me," said Mrs. Weston, "if it be not very disagreeable to you. It need not detain us long. We will go to Hartfield afterwards. We will follow them to Hartfield. I really wish you to call with me: it will be felt so great an attention—and I always thought you meant it."

He could say no more; and, with the hope of Hartfield to reward him, returned with Mrs. Weston to Mrs. Bates's door. Emma watched them in, and then joined Harriet at the interesting counter, trying, with all the force of her own mind, to convince her that, if she wanted plain muslin, it was of no use to look at figured; and that a blue riband, be it ever so beautiful, would still never match her yellow pattern. At last it was all settled, even to the destination of the parcel.

"Should I send it to Mrs. Goddard's, ma'am?" asked Mrs. Ford.—"Yes—no—yes, to Mrs. Goddard's. Only my pattern gown is at Hartfield. No, you shall send it to Hartfield, if you please. But then, Mrs. Goddard will want to see it. And I could take the pattern gown home any day. But I shall want the riband directly; so it had better go to Hartfield—at least the riband. You could make it into two parcels, Mrs. Ford, could not you?"

"It is not worth while, Harriet, to give Mrs. Ford the trouble of two parcels."

"No more it is."

"No trouble in the world, ma'am," said the obliging Mrs. Ford.

"Oh, but indeed I would much rather have it only in one. Then, if you please, you shall send it all to Mrs. Goddard's— I do not know—no, I think, Miss Woodhouse, I may just as well have it sent to Hartfield, and take it home with me at night. What do you advise?"

"That you do not give another half-second to the subject. To Hartfield, if you please, Mrs. Ford."

"Ay, that will be much best," said Harriet, quite satisfied; "I should not at all like to have it sent to Mrs. Goddard's."

Voices approached the shop, or rather, one voice and two ladies; Mrs. Weston and Miss Bates met them at the door.

"My dear Miss Woodhouse," said the latter, "I am just run across to entreat the favour of you to come and sit down with us a little while, and give us your opinion of our new instrument—you and Miss Smith. How do you do, Miss Smith?— Very well, I thank you.—And I begged Mrs. Weston to come with me, that I might be sure of succeeding."

"I hope Mrs. Bates and Miss Fairfax are——"

"Very well, I am much obliged to you. My mother is delightfully well; and Jane caught no cold last night. How is Mr. Woodhouse? I am so glad to hear such a good account. Mrs. Weston told me you were here.—Oh, then, said I, I must run across; I am sure Miss Woodhouse will allow me just to run across and entreat her to come in: my mother will be so very happy to see her; and now we are such a nice party, she cannot refuse. 'Ay, pray do,' said Mr. Frank Churchill, 'Miss Woodhouse's opinion of the instrument will be worth having.'—But, said I, I shall be more sure of succeeding if one of you will go with me.—'Oh,' said he, 'wait half a minute, till I have finished my job:' for, would you believe it, Miss Woodhouse, there he is, in the most obliging manner in the world, fastening in the rivet of my mother's spectacles. The rivet came out, you know, this morning; so very obliging!— For my mother had no use of her spectacles—could not put them on. And, by the by, every body ought to have two pair of spectacles; they should indeed. Jane said so. I meant to take them over to John Saunders the first thing I did, but something or other hindered me all the morning; first one thing, then another, there is no saying what, you know. At one time, Patty came to say she thought the kitchen chimney wanted sweeping. Oh, said I, Patty, do not come with your bad news to me. Here is the rivet of your mistress's spectacles out. Then the baked apples came home;* Mrs. Wallis sent them by her boy; they are extremely civil and obliging to us, the Wallises, always. I have heard some people say that Mrs. Wallis can be uncivil and give a very rude answer; but we have never known any thing but the greatest attention from them. And it cannot be for the value of our custom now, for what is our consumption of bread, you know? only three of us. Besides, dear Jane, at present,—and she really eats nothing,—makes such a shocking breakfast, you would be quite frightened if you saw it. I dare not let my mother know how little she eats; so I say one thing, and then I say another, and it passes off. But about the middle of the day she gets hungry, and there is nothing she likes so well as these baked apples, and they are extremely wholesome; for I took the opportunity the other day of asking Mr. Perry; I happened to meet him in the street. Not that I had any doubt before. I have so often heard Mr. Woodhouse recommend a baked apple. I believe it is the only way that Mr. Woodhouse thinks the fruit thoroughly wholesome. We have apple dumplings, however, very often. Patty makes an excellent apple-dumpling. Well, Mrs. Weston, you have prevailed, I hope, and these ladies will oblige us."

Emma would be "very happy to wait on Mrs. Bates, &c.," and they did at last move out of the shop, with no further delay from Miss Bates than,—

"How do you do, Mrs. Ford? I beg your pardon; I did not

---

*It was customary to send food that needed to be cooked in an oven to the local bakery.

see you before. I hear you have a charming collection of new ribands from town. Jane came back delighted yesterday. Thank ye, the gloves do very well—only a little too large about the wrist; but Jane is taking them in."

"What was I talking of?" said she, beginning again when they were all in the street.

Emma wondered on what, of all the medley, she would fix.

"I declare I cannot recollect what I was talking of. Oh, my mother's spectacles. So very obliging of Mr. Frank Churchill! 'Oh!' said he, 'I do think I can fasten the rivet; I like a job of this kind excessively.' Which, you know, showed him to be so very—— Indeed I must say that, much as I had heard of him before, and much as I had expected, he very far exceeds any thing—— I do congratulate you, Mrs. Weston, most warmly. He seems every thing the fondest parent could—— 'Oh!' said he, 'I can fasten the rivet. I like a job of that sort excessively.' I never shall forget his manner. And when I brought out the baked apples from the closet, and hoped our friends would be so very obliging as to take some, 'Oh!' said he directly, 'there is nothing in the way of fruit half so good, and these are the finest looking home-baked apples I ever saw in my life.' That, you know, was so very—— And I am sure, by his manner, it was no compliment. Indeed they are very delightful apples, and Mrs. Wallis does them full justice, only we do not have them baked more than twice, and Mr. Woodhouse made us promise to have them done three times; but Miss Woodhouse will be so good as not to mention it. The apples themselves are the very finest sort for baking, beyond a doubt; all from Donwell—some of Mr. Knightley's most liberal supply. He sends us a sack every year; and certainly there never was such a keeping apple any where as one of his trees—I believe there is two of them. My mother says the orchard was always famous in her younger days. But I was really quite shocked the other day; for Mr. Knightley called one morning, and Jane was eating these apples, and we talked about them, and said how much she enjoyed them, and he

asked whether we were not got to the end of our stock. 'I am
sure you must be,' said he, 'and I will send you another supply; for I have a great many more than I can ever use.
William Larkins let me keep a larger quantity than usual this
year. I will send you some more, before they get good for
nothing.' So I begged he would not—for really as to ours
being gone, I could not absolutely say that we had a great
many left—it was but half a dozen indeed; but they should
be all kept for Jane; and I could not at all bear that he should
be sending us more, so liberal as he had been already; and
Jane said the same. And when he was gone, she almost quarrelled with me: no I should not say quarrelled, for we never
had a quarrel in our lives; but she was quite distressed that I
had owned the apples were so nearly gone; she wished I had
made him believe we had a great many left. Oh, said I, my
dear, I did say as much as I could. However, the very same
evening William Larkins came over with a large basket of apples, the same sort of apples, a bushel at least, and I was very
much obliged, and went down and spoke to William Larkins,
and said every thing, as you may suppose. William Larkins is
such an old acquaintance! I am always glad to see him. But,
however, I found afterwards from Patty, that William said it
was all the apples of *that* sort his master had; he had brought
them all—and now his master had not one left to bake or
boil. William did not seem to mind it himself, he was so
pleased to think his master had sold so many; for William,
you know, thinks more of his master's profit than any thing;
but Mrs. Hodges, he said, was quite displeased at their being
all sent away. She could not bear that her master should not
be able to have another apple-tart this spring. He told Patty
this, but bid her not mind it, and be sure not to say any thing
to us about it, for Mrs. Hodges *would* be cross sometimes,
and as long as so many sacks were sold, it did not signify who
ate the remainder. And so Patty told me, and I was excessively shocked, indeed! I would not have Mr. Knightley know
any thing about it for the world! He would be so very—I

wanted to keep it from Jane's knowledge; but, unluckily, I had mentioned it before I was aware."

Miss Bates had just done as Patty opened the door; and her visiters walked up stairs without having any regular narration to attend to, pursued only by the sounds of her desultory good will.

"Pray take care, Mrs. Weston, there is a step at the turning. Pray take care, Miss Woodhouse, ours is rather a dark staircase—rather darker and narrower than one could wish. Miss Smith, pray take care. Miss Woodhouse, I am quite concerned, I am sure you hit your foot. Miss Smith, the step at the turning."

## Chapter X.

The appearance of the little sitting-room as they entered was tranquillity itself; Mrs. Bates, deprived of her usual employment, slumbering on one side of the fire, Frank Churchill, at a table near her, most deedily* occupied about her spectacles, and Jane Fairfax, standing with her back to them, intent on her piano-forte.

Busy as he was, however, the young man was yet able to show a most happy countenance on seeing Emma again.

"This is a pleasure," said he, in rather a low voice, "coming at least ten minutes earlier than I had calculated. You find me trying to be useful; tell me if you think I shall succeed."

"What!" said Mrs. Weston, "have not you finished it yet?

---

*Busily, done with great attention.

you would not earn a very good livelihood as a working silversmith at this rate."

"I have not been working uninterruptedly," he replied, "I have been assisting Miss Fairfax in trying to make her instrument stand steadily; it was not quite firm; an unevenness in the floor, I believe. You see we have been wedging one leg with paper. This was very kind of you to be persuaded to come. I was almost afraid you would be hurrying home."

He contrived that she should be seated by him; and was sufficiently employed in looking out the best baked apple for her, and trying to make her help or advise him in his work, till Jane Fairfax was quite ready to sit down to the piano-forte again. That she was not immediately ready, Emma did suspect to arise from the state of her nerves; she had not yet possessed the instrument long enough to touch it without emotion; she must reason herself into the power of performance; and Emma could not but pity such feelings, whatever their origin, and could not but resolve never to expose them to her neighbour again.

At last Jane began, and though the first bars were feebly given, the powers of the instrument were gradually done full justice to. Mrs. Weston had been delighted before, and was delighted again; Emma joined her in all her praise; and the piano-forte, with every proper discrimination, was pronounced to be altogether of the highest promise.

"Whoever Colonel Campbell might employ," said Frank Churchill, with a smile at Emma, "the person has not chosen ill. I heard a good deal of Colonel Campbell's taste at Weymouth; and the softness of the upper notes I am sure is exactly what he and *all that party* would particularly prize. I dare say, Miss Fairfax, that he either gave his friend very minute directions, or wrote to Broadwood himself. Do not you think so?"

Jane did not look round. She was not obliged to hear. Mrs. Weston had been speaking to her at the same moment.

"It is not fair," said Emma, in a whisper; "mine was a random guess. Do not distress her."

He shook his head with a smile, and looked as if he had very little doubt and very little mercy. Soon afterwards he began again,—

"How much your friends in Ireland must be enjoying your pleasure on this occasion, Miss Fairfax. I dare say they often think of you, and wonder which will be the day, the precise day of the instrument's coming to hand. Do you imagine Colonel Campbell knows the business to be going forward just at this time? Do you imagine it to be the consequence of an immediate commission from him, or that he may have sent only a general direction, an order indefinite as to time, to depend upon contingencies and conveniences?"

He paused. She could not but hear; she could not avoid answering,—

"Till I have a letter from Colonel Campbell," said she, in a voice of forced calmness. "I can imagine nothing with any confidence. It must be all conjecture."

"Conjecture! Ay, sometimes one conjectures right, and sometimes one conjectures wrong. I wish I could conjecture how soon I shall make this rivet quite firm. What nonsense one talks, Miss Woodhouse, when hard at work, if one talks at all; your real workmen, I suppose, hold their tongues; but we, gentlemen labourers, if we get hold of a word—Miss Fairfax said something about conjecturing. There, it is done. I have the pleasure, madam, (to Mrs. Bates,) of restoring your spectacles, healed for the present."

He was very warmly thanked both by mother and daughter: to escape a little from the latter, he went to the pianoforte, and begged Miss Fairfax, who was still sitting at it, to play something more.

"If you are very kind," said he, "it will be one of the waltzes we danced last night; let me live them over again. You did not enjoy them as I did; you appeared tired the whole time. I believe you were glad we danced no longer; but I would have given worlds—all the worlds one ever has to give—for another half hour."

She played.

"What felicity it is to hear a tune again which *has* made one happy! If I mistake not, that was danced at Weymouth."

She looked up at him for a moment, coloured deeply, and played something else. He took some music from a chair near the piano-forte, and turning to Emma, said,—

"Here is something quite new to me. Do you know it? Cramer.[11] And here are a new set of Irish melodies. That, from such a quarter, one might expect. This was all sent with the instrument. Very thoughtful of Colonel Campbell, was not it? He knew Miss Fairfax could have no music here. I honour that part of the attention particularly; it shows it to have been so thoroughly from the heart. Nothing hastily done; nothing incomplete. True affection only could have prompted it."

Emma wished he would be less pointed, yet could not help being amused; and when, on glancing her eye towards Jane Fairfax, she caught the remains of a smile; when she saw that, with all the deep blush of consciousness, there had been a smile of secret delight, she had less scruple in the amusement, and much less compunction with respect to her. This amiable, upright, perfect Jane Fairfax was apparently cherishing very reprehensible feelings.

He brought all the music to her, and they looked it over together. Emma took the opportunity of whispering,—

"You speak too plain. She must understand you."

"I hope she does. I would have her understand me. I am not in the least ashamed of my meaning."

"But, really, I am half ashamed, and wish I had never taken up the idea."

"I am very glad you did, and that you communicated it to me. I have now a key to all her odd looks and ways. Leave shame to her. If she does wrong, she ought to feel it."

"She is not entirely without it, I think."

"I do not see much sign of it. She is playing *Robin Adair*[12] at this moment—*his* favourite."

Shortly afterwards Miss Bates, passing near the window, descried Mr. Knightley on horseback not far off.

"Mr. Knightley, I declare! I must speak to him, if possible, just to thank him. I will not open the window here; it would give you all cold; but I can go into my mother's room, you know. I dare say he will come in when he knows who is here. Quite delightful to have you all meet so! Our little room so honoured!"

She was in the adjoining chamber while she still spoke, and, opening the casement there, immediately called Mr. Knightley's attention, and every syllable of their conversation was as distinctly heard by the others as if it had passed within the same apartment.

"How d'ye do? How d'ye do? Very well, I thank you. So obliged to you for the carriage last night. We were just in time; my mother just ready for us. Pray come in; do come in. You will find some friends here."

So began Miss Bates; and Mr. Knightley seemed determined to be heard in his turn, for most resolutely and commandingly did he say,—

"How is your niece, Miss Bates? I want to enquire after you all, but particularly your niece. How is Miss Fairfax? I hope she caught no cold last night. How is she to day? Tell me how Miss Fairfax is."

And Miss Bates was obliged to give a direct answer before he would hear her in any thing else. The listeners were amused; and Mrs. Weston gave Emma a look of particular meaning. But Emma still shook her head in steady scepticism.

"So obliged to you!—so very much obliged to you for the carriage," resumed Miss Bates.

He cut her short with,—

"I am going to Kingston. Can I do any thing for you?"

"Oh dear, Kingston—are you? Mrs. Cole was saying the other day she wanted something from Kingston."

"Mrs. Cole has servants to send; can I do any thing for *you?*"

"No, I thank you. But do come in. Who do you think is here? Miss Woodhouse and Miss Smith; so kind as to call to hear the new piano-forte. Do put up your horse at the Crown, and come in."

"Well," said he, in a deliberating manner, "for five minutes, perhaps."

"And here is Mrs. Weston and Mr. Frank Churchill too! Quite delightful; so many friends!"

"No, not now, I thank you. I could not stay two minutes. I must get on to Kingston as fast as I can."

"Oh, do come in. They will be so very happy to see you."

"No, no; your room is full enough. I will call another day, and hear the piano-forte."

"Well, I am so sorry! Oh, Mr. Knightley, what a delightful party last night! how extremely pleasant! Did you ever see such dancing? Was not it delightful? Miss Woodhouse and Mr. Frank Churchill; I never saw any thing equal to it."

"Oh, very delightful, indeed: I can say nothing less, for I suppose Miss Woodhouse and Mr. Frank Churchill are hearing every thing that passes. And (raising his voice still more) I do not see why Miss Fairfax should not be mentioned too. I think Miss Fairfax dances very well; and Mrs. Weston is the very best country-dance player, without exception, in England. Now, if your friends have any gratitude, they will say something pretty loud about you and me in return; but I cannot stay to hear it."

"Oh, Mr. Knightley, one moment more; something of consequence—so shocked! Jane and I are both so shocked about the apples!"

"What is the matter now?"

"To think of your sending us all your store apples. You said you had a great many, and now you have not one left. We really are so shocked! Mrs. Hodges may well be angry. William Larkins mentioned it here. You should not have done it, indeed you should not. Ah, he is off. He never can bear to be thanked. But I thought he would have staid now, and it would have been a pity not to have mentioned——

Well (returning into the room), I have not been able to succeed. Mr. Knightley cannot stop. He is going to Kingston. He asked me if he could do any thing——"

"Yes," said Jane; "we heard his kind offers; we heard every thing."

"Oh yes, my dear, I dare say you might; because, you know, the door was open, and the window was open, and Mr. Knightley spoke loud. You must have heard every thing to be sure. 'Can I do any thing for you at Kingston?' said he; so I just mentioned—— Oh, Miss Woodhouse, must you be going? You seem but just come; so very obliging of you."

Emma found it really time to be at home; the visit had already lasted long; and, on examining watches, so much of the morning was perceived to be gone, that Mrs. Weston and her companion, taking leave also, could allow themselves only to walk with the two young ladies to Hartfield gates, before they set off for Randalls.

# Chapter XI.

It may be possible to do without dancing entirely. Instances have been known of young people passing many, many months successively, without being at any ball of any description, and no material injury accrue either to body or mind;—but when a beginning is made—when the felicities of rapid motion have once been, though slightly, felt—it must be a very heavy set that does not ask for more.

Frank Churchill had danced once at Highbury, and longed to dance again; and the last half hour of an evening which Mr. Woodhouse was persuaded to spend with his daughter at Randalls was passed by the two young people in schemes on the subject. Frank's was the first idea, and his the greatest zeal in pursuing it; for the lady was the best judge of the difficulties, and the most solicitous for accommodation and appearance. But still she had inclination enough for showing people again how delightfully Mr. Frank Churchill and Miss Woodhouse danced—for doing that in which she need not blush to compare herself with Jane Fairfax—and even for simple dancing itself, without any of the wicked aids of vanity—to assist him first in pacing out the room they were in to see what it could be made to hold—and then in taking the dimensions of the other parlour, in the hope of discovering, in spite of all that Mr. Weston could say of their exactly equal size, that it was a little the largest.

His first proposition and request, that the dance begun at Mr. Cole's should be finished there,—that the same party should be collected, and the same musician engaged,—met with the readiest acquiescence. Mr. Weston entered into the idea with thorough enjoyment, and Mrs. Weston most willingly undertook to play as long as they could wish to dance; and the interesting employment had followed, of reckoning up exactly who there would be, and portioning out the indispensable division of space to every couple.

"You and Miss Smith, and Miss Fairfax, will be three, and the two Miss Coxes five," had been repeated many times over. "And there will be the two Gilberts, young Cox, my father, and myself, besides Mr. Knightley. Yes, that will be quite enough for pleasure. You and Miss Smith, and Miss Fairfax, will be three, and the two Miss Coxes five; and for five couple there will be plenty of room."

But soon it came to be on one side,—

"But will there be good room for five couple?—I really do not think there will."

On another,—

"And after all, five couple are not enough to make it worth while to stand up. Five couple are nothing, when one thinks seriously about it. It will not do to *invite* five couple. It can be allowable only as the thought of the moment."

Somebody said that *Miss* Gilbert was expected at her brother's, and must be invited with the rest. Somebody else believed *Mrs.* Gilbert would have danced the other evening, if she had been asked. A word was put in for a second young Cox; and at last, Mr. Weston naming one family of cousins who must be included, and another of very old acquaintance who could not be left out, it became a certainty that the five couple would be at least ten, and a very interesting speculation in what possible manner they could be disposed of.

The doors of the two rooms were just opposite each other. "Might not they use both rooms, and dance across the passage?" It seemed the best scheme; and yet it was not so good but that many of them wanted a better. Emma said it would be awkward; Mrs. Weston was in distress about the supper; and Mr. Woodhouse opposed it earnestly on the score of health. It made him so very unhappy, indeed, that it could not be persevered in.

"Oh no," said he; "it would be the extreme of imprudence. I could not bear it for Emma!—Emma is not strong. She would catch a dreadful cold. So would poor little Harriet. So would you all. Mrs. Weston, you would be quite laid up; do not let them talk of such a wild thing; pray do not let them talk of it. That young man (speaking lower) is very thoughtless. Do not tell his father, but that young man is not quite the thing. He has been opening the doors very often this evening, and keeping them open very inconsiderately. He does not think of the draught. I do not mean to set you against him, but indeed he is not quite the thing."

Mrs. Weston was sorry for such a charge. She knew the importance of it, and said every thing in her power to do it away. Every door was now closed, the passage plan given up, and the first scheme, of dancing only in the room they were in, resorted to again; and with such good-will on Frank Churchill's part, that the space which a quarter of an hour before had been deemed barely sufficient for five couple, was now endeavoured to be made out quite enough for ten.

"We were too magnificent," said he. "We allowed unnecessary room. Ten couple may stand here very well."

Emma demurred. "It would be a crowd—a sad crowd; and what could be worse than dancing without space to turn in?"

"Very true," he gravely replied; "it was very bad." But still he went on measuring, and still he ended with,—

"I think there will be very tolerable room for ten couple."

"No, no," said she, "you are quite unreasonable. It would be dreadful to be standing so close. Nothing can be farther from pleasure than to be dancing in a crowd—and a crowd in a little room."

"There is no denying it," he replied. "I agree with you exactly. A crowd in a little room—Miss Woodhouse, you have the art of giving pictures in a few words. Exquisite, quite exquisite! Still, however, having proceeded so far, one is unwilling to give the matter up. It would be a disappointment to my father—and altogether—I do not know that—I am rather of opinion that ten couple might stand here very well."

Emma perceived that the nature of his gallantry was a little self-willed, and that he would rather oppose than lose the pleasure of dancing with her; but she took the compliment, and forgave the rest. Had she intended ever to *marry* him, it might have been worth while to pause and consider, and try to understand the value of his preference, and the character of his temper; but for all the purposes of their acquaintance he was quite amiable enough.

Before the middle of the next day he was at Hartfield; and he entered the room with such an agreeable smile as certified the continuance of the scheme. It soon appeared that he came to announce an improvement.

"Well, Miss Woodhouse," he almost immediately began, "your inclination for dancing has not been quite frightened away, I hope, by the terrors of my father's little rooms. I bring a new proposal on the subject—a thought of my father's, which waits only your approbation to be acted upon.

May I hope for the honour of your hand for the two first dances of this little projected ball, to be given, not at Randalls, but at the Crown Inn?"

"The Crown!"

"Yes; if you and Mr. Woodhouse see no objection, and I trust you cannot, my father hopes his friends will be so kind as to visit him there. Better accommodations he can promise them, and not a less grateful welcome than at Randalls. It is his own idea. Mrs. Weston sees no objection to it, provided you are satisfied. This is what we all feel. Oh, you were perfectly right! Ten couple, in either of the Randalls' rooms, would have been insufferable—dreadful! I felt how right you were the whole time, but was too anxious for securing *any thing* to like to yield. Is not it a good exchange? You consent—I hope you consent?"

"It appears to me a plan that nobody can object to, if Mr. and Mrs. Weston do not. I think it admirable; and, as far as I can answer for myself, shall be most happy——It seems the only improvement that could be. Papa, do you not think it an excellent improvement?"

She was obliged to repeat and explain it, before it was fully comprehended; and then, being quite new, further representations were necessary to make it acceptable.

"No; he thought it very far from an improvement—a very bad plan—much worse than the other. A room at an inn was always damp and dangerous; never properly aired, or fit to be inhabited. If they must dance, they had better dance at Randalls. He had never been in the room at the Crown in his life—did not know the people who kept it by sight. Oh no—a very bad plan. They would catch worse colds at the Crown than any where."

"I was going to observe, sir," said Frank Churchill, "that one of the great recommendations of this change would be the very little danger of any body's catching cold—so much less danger at the Crown than at Randalls! Mr. Perry might have reason to regret the alteration, but nobody else could."

"Sir," said Mr. Woodhouse, rather warmly, "you are very

much mistaken if you suppose Mr. Perry to be that sort of character. Mr. Perry is extremely concerned when any of us are ill. But I do not understand how the room at the Crown can be safer for you than your father's house."

"From the very circumstance of its being larger, sir. We shall have no occasion to open the windows at all—not once the whole evening; and it is that dreadful habit of opening the windows, letting in cold air upon heated bodies, which (as you well know, sir) does the mischief."

"Open the windows! but surely, Mr. Churchill, nobody would think of opening the windows at Randalls. Nobody could be so imprudent! I never heard of such a thing. Dancing with open windows! I am sure, neither your father nor Mrs. Weston (poor Miss Taylor that was) would suffer it."

"Ah! sir—but a thoughtless young person will sometimes step behind a window-curtain, and throw up a sash, without its being suspected. I have often known it done myself."

"Have you, indeed, sir? Bless me! I never could have supposed it. But I live out of the world, and am often astonished at what I hear. However, this does make a difference; and, perhaps, when we come to talk it over—but these sort of things require a good deal of consideration. One cannot resolve upon them in a hurry. If Mr. and Mrs. Weston will be so obliging as to call here one morning, we may talk it over, and see what can be done."

"But, unfortunately, sir, my time is so limited——"

"Oh," interrupted Emma, "there will be plenty of time for talking every thing over. There is no hurry at all. If it can be contrived to be at the Crown, papa, it will be very convenient for the horses. They will be so near their own stable."

"So they will, my dear. That is a great thing. Not that James ever complains; but it is right to spare our horses when we can. If I could be sure of the rooms being thoroughly aired—but is Mrs. Stokes to be trusted? I doubt it. I do not know her, even by sight."

"I can answer for every thing of that nature, sir, because

it will be under Mrs. Weston's care. Mrs. Weston undertakes to direct the whole."

"There, papa! Now you must be satisfied—our own dear Mrs. Weston, who is carefulness itself. Do not you remember what Mr. Perry said, so many years ago, when I had the measles? 'If *Miss Taylor* undertakes to wrap Miss Emma up, you need not have any fears, sir.' How often have I heard you speak of it as such a compliment to her!"

"Ay, very true. Mr. Perry did say so. I shall never forget it. Poor little Emma! You were very bad with the measles; that is, you would have been very bad, but for Perry's great attention. He came four times a-day for a week. He said, from the first, it was a very good sort—which was our great comfort; but the measles are a dreadful complaint. I hope whenever poor Isabella's little ones have the measles, she will send for Perry."

"My father and Mrs. Weston are at the Crown at this moment," said Frank Churchill, "examining the capabilities of the house. I left them there and came on to Hartfield, impatient for your opinion, and hoping you might be persuaded to join them and give your advice on the spot. I was desired to say so from both. It would be the greatest pleasure to them, if you could allow me to attend you there. They can do nothing satisfactorily without you."

Emma was most happy to be called to such a council; and, her father engaging to think it all over while she was gone, the two young people set off together without delay for the Crown. There were Mr. and Mrs. Weston; delighted to see her and receive her approbation, very busy and very happy in their different way; she, in some little distress; and he, finding every thing perfect.

"Emma," said she, "this paper is worse than I expected. Look! in places you see it is dreadfully dirty; and the wainscot is more yellow and forlorn than any thing could have imagined."

"My dear, you are too particular," said her husband. "What does all that signify? You will see nothing of it by candle-light. It will be as clean as Randalls by candle-light. We never see any thing of it on our club-nights."

The ladies here probably exchanged looks which meant, "Men never know when things are dirty or not;" and the gentlemen perhaps thought each to himself, "Women will have their little nonsenses and needless cares."

One perplexity, however, arose, which the gentlemen did not disdain: it regarded a supper room. At the time of the ball-room's being built, suppers had not been in question; and a small card-room adjoining was the only addition. What was to be done? This card-room would be wanted as a card-room now; or, if cards were conveniently voted unnecessary by their four selves, still was not it too small for any comfortable supper? Another room of much better size might be secured for the purpose; but it was at the other end of the house, and a long awkward passage must be gone through to get at it. This made a difficulty. Mrs. Weston was afraid of draughts for the young people in that passage; and neither Emma nor the gentlemen could tolerate the prospect of being miserably crowded at supper.

Mrs. Weston proposed having no regular supper: merely sandwiches, &c. set out in the little room; but that was scouted as a wretched suggestion. A private dance, without sitting down to supper, was pronounced an infamous fraud upon the rights of men and women; and Mrs. Weston must not speak of it again. She then took another line of expediency, and looking into the doubtful room, observed,—

"I do not think it *is* so very small. We shall not be many, you know."

And Mr. Weston at the same time, walking briskly with long steps through the passage, was calling out,—

"You talk a great deal of the length of this passage, my dear. It is a mere nothing after all; and not the least draught from the stairs."

"I wish," said Mrs. Weston, "one could know which arrangement our guests in general would like best. To do what would be most generally pleasing must be our object—if one could but tell what that would be."

"Yes, very true," cried Frank, "very true. You want your neighbours' opinions. I do not wonder at you. If one could ascertain what the chief of them—the Coles, for instance. They are not far off. Shall I call upon them? Or Miss Bates? She is still nearer.—And I do not know whether Miss Bates is not as likely to understand the inclinations of the rest of the people as any body. I think we do want a larger council. Suppose I go and invite Miss Bates to join us?"

"Well—if you please," said Mrs. Weston, rather hesitating, "if you think she will be of any use."

"You will get nothing to the purpose from Miss Bates," said Emma. "She will be all delight and gratitude, but she will tell you nothing. She will not even listen to your questions. I see no advantage in consulting Miss Bates."

"But she is so amusing, so extremely amusing! I am very fond of hearing Miss Bates talk. And I need not bring the whole family, you know."

Here Mr. Weston joined them, and on hearing what was proposed, gave it his decided approbation.

"Ay, do, Frank.—Go and fetch Miss Bates, and let us end the matter at once. She will enjoy the scheme, I am sure; and I do not know a properer person for showing us how to do away difficulties. Fetch Miss Bates. We are growing a little too nice. She is a standing lesson of how to be happy. But fetch them both. Invite them both."

"Both, sir! Can the old lady——?"

"The old lady! No, the young lady, to be sure. I shall think you a great blockhead, Frank, if you bring the aunt without the niece."

"Oh! I beg your pardon, sir. I did not immediately recollect. Undoubtedly, if you wish it, I will endeavour to persuade them both." And away he ran.

Long before he re-appeared, attending the short, neat, brisk-moving aunt, and her elegant niece,—Mrs. Weston, like a sweet-tempered woman and a good wife, had examined the passage again, and found the evils of it much less than she had supposed before—indeed very trifling; and here ended the difficulties of decision. All the rest, in speculation at least, was perfectly smooth. All the minor arrangements of table and chair, lights and music, tea and supper, made themselves; or were left as mere trifles, to be settled at any time between Mrs. Weston and Mrs. Stokes. Every body invited was certainly to come; Frank had already written to Enscombe to propose staying a few days beyond his fortnight, which could not possibly be refused. And a delightful dance it was to be.

Most cordially, when Miss Bates arrived, did she agree that it must. As a counsellor she was not wanted; but as an approver (a much safer character) she was truly welcome. Her approbation, at once general and minute, warm and incessant, could not but please; and for another half-hour they were all walking to and fro between the different rooms, some suggesting, some attending, and all in happy enjoyment of the future. The party did not break up without Emma's being positively secured for the first two dances by the hero of the evening, nor without her overhearing Mr. Weston whisper to his wife, "He has asked her, my dear. That's right. I knew he would!"

## Chapter XII.

One thing only was wanting to make the prospect of the ball completely satisfactory to Emma,—its being fixed for a day within the granted term of Frank Churchill's stay in Surrey; for, in spite of Mr. Weston's confidence, she could not think it so very impossible that the Churchills might not allow their nephew to remain a day beyond his fortnight. But this was not judged feasible. The preparations must take their time, nothing could be properly ready till the third week were entered on, and for a few days they must be planning, proceeding, and hoping in uncertainty—at the risk—in her opinion, the great risk of its being all in vain.

Enscombe, however, was gracious, gracious in fact, if not in word. His wish of staying longer evidently did not please; but it was not opposed. All was safe and prosperous; and as the removal of one solicitude generally makes way for another, Emma, being now certain of her ball, began to adopt as the next vexation Mr. Knightley's provoking indifference about it. Either because he did not dance himself, or because the plan had been formed without his being consulted, he seemed resolved that it should not interest him, determined against its exciting any present curiosity, or affording him any future amusement. To her voluntary communications Emma could get no more approving reply than,

"Very well. If the Westons think it worth while to be at all this trouble for a few hours of noisy entertainment, I have nothing to say against it, but that they shall not choose pleasures for me.—Oh, yes! I must be there; I could not refuse; and I will keep as much awake as I can; but I would rather be at home, looking over William Larkins's week's account; much rather, I confess.—Pleasure in seeing dancing!—not I, indeed,—I never look at it—I do not know who does.—Fine dancing, I believe, like virtue, must be its own reward. Those who are standing by are usually thinking of something very different."

This Emma felt was aimed at her; and it made her quite angry. It was not in compliment to Jane Fairfax, however, that he was so indifferent, or so indignant; he was not guided by *her* feelings in reprobating the ball, for *she* enjoyed the thought of it to an extraordinary degree. It made her animated—open-hearted: she voluntarily said,—

"Oh! Miss Woodhouse, I hope nothing may happen to

prevent the ball! What a disappointment it would be! I do look forward to it, I own, with *very* great pleasure."

It was not to oblige Jane Fairfax, therefore, that he would have preferred the society of William Larkins. No!—she was more and more convinced that Mrs. Weston was quite mistaken in that surmise. There was a great deal of friendly and of compassionate attachment on his side—but no love.

Alas! there was soon no leisure for quarrelling with Mr. Knightley. Two days of joyful security were immediately followed by the overthrow of every thing. A letter arrived from Mr. Churchill to urge his nephew's instant return. Mrs. Churchill was unwell—far too unwell to do without him; she had been in a very suffering state (so said her husband) when writing to her nephew two days before, though from her usual unwillingness to give pain, and constant habit of never thinking of herself, she had not mentioned it; but now she was too ill to trifle, and must entreat him to set off for Enscombe without delay.

The substance of this letter was forwarded to Emma, in a note from Mrs. Weston, instantly. As to his going, it was inevitable. He must be gone within a few hours, though without feeling any real alarm for his aunt, to lessen his repugnance. He knew her illnesses; they never occurred but for her own convenience.

Mrs. Weston added, "that he could only allow himself time to hurry to Highbury, after breakfast, and take leave of the few friends there whom he could suppose to feel any interest in him; and that he might be expected at Hartfield very soon."

This wretched note was the finale of Emma's breakfast. When once it had been read, there was no doing any thing, but lament and exclaim. The loss of the ball—the loss of the young man—and all that the young man might be feeling!—It was too wretched!—Such a delightful evening as it would have been!—Every body so happy! and she and her partner the happiest!—"I said it would be so," was the only consolation.

Her father's feelings were quite distinct. He thought principally of Mrs. Churchill's illness, and wanted to know how she was treated; and as for the ball, it was shocking to have dear Emma disappointed; but they would all be safer at home.

Emma was ready for her visiter some time before he appeared; but if this reflected at all upon his impatience, his sorrowful look and total want of spirits when he did come might redeem him. He felt the going away almost too much to speak of it. His dejection was most evident. He sat really lost in thought for the first few minutes; and when rousing himself, it was only to say,—

"Of all horrid things, leave-taking is the worst."

"But you will come again," said Emma. "This will not be your only visit to Randalls."

"Ah!—(shaking his head)—the uncertainty of when I may be able to return!—I shall try for it with a zeal! It will be the object of all my thoughts and cares!—and if my uncle and aunt go to town this spring—but I am afraid—they did not stir last spring—I am afraid it is a custom gone for ever."

"Our poor ball must be quite given up."

"Ah! that ball!—why did we wait for any thing?—why not seize the pleasure at once?—How often is happiness destroyed by preparation, foolish preparation!—You told us it would be so.—Oh! Miss Woodhouse, why are you always so right?"

"Indeed, I am very sorry to be right in this instance. I would much rather have been merry than wise."

"If I can come again, we are still to have our ball. My father depends on it. Do not forget your engagement."

Emma looked graciously.

"Such a fortnight as it has been!" he continued; "every day more precious and more delightful than the day before!—every day making me less fit to bear any other place. Happy those who can remain at Highbury!"

"As you do us such ample justice now," said Emma, laughing, "I will venture to ask, whether you did not come a little doubtingly at first? Do not we rather surpass your expectations? I am sure we do. I am sure you did not much expect to like us. You would not have been so long in coming, if you had had a pleasant idea of Highbury."

He laughed rather consciously; and though denying the sentiment, Emma was convinced that it had been so.

"And you must be off this very morning?"

"Yes; my father is to join me here: we shall walk back together, and I must be off immediately. I am almost afraid that every moment will bring him."

"Not five minutes to spare even for your friends Miss Fairfax and Miss Bates? How unlucky! Miss Bates's powerful, argumentative mind might have strengthened yours."

"Yes—I *have* called there; passing the door, I thought it better. It was a right thing to do. I went in for three minutes, and was detained by Miss Bates's being absent. She was out; and I felt it impossible not to wait till she came in. She is a woman that one may, that one *must* laugh at; but that one would not wish to slight. It was better to pay my visit, then—"

He hesitated, got up, walked to a window.

"In short," said he, "perhaps, Miss Woodhouse—I think you can hardly be quite without suspicion."—

He looked at her, as if wanting to read her thoughts. She hardly knew what to say. It seemed like the forerunner of something absolutely serious, which she did not wish. Forcing herself to speak, therefore, in the hope of putting it by, she calmly said,—

"You are quite in the right; it was most natural to pay your visit, then—"

He was silent. She believed he was looking at her; probably reflecting on what she had said, and trying to understand the manner. She heard him sigh. It was natural for him to feel that he had *cause* to sigh. He could not believe her to be encouraging him. A few awkward moments passed, and he sat down again; and in a more determined manner said,—

"It was something to feel that all the rest of my time might be given to Hartfield. My regard for Hartfield is most warm,"—

He stopped again, rose again, and seemed quite embarrassed.—He was more in love with her than Emma had supposed; and who can say how it might have ended, if his father had not made his appearance? Mr. Woodhouse soon followed; and the necessity of exertion made him composed.

A very few minutes more, however, completed the present trial. Mr. Weston, always alert when business was to be done, and as incapable of procrastinating any evil that was inevitable, as of foreseeing any that was doubtful, said, "It was time to go;" and the young man, though he might and did sigh, could not but agree, and rise to take leave.

"I shall hear about you all," said he; "that is my chief consolation. I shall hear of every thing that is going on among you. I have engaged Mrs. Weston to correspond with me. She has been so kind as to promise it. Oh! the blessing of a female correspondent, when one is really interested in the absent!—she will tell me every thing. In her letters I shall be at dear Highbury again."

A very friendly shake of the hand, a very earnest "Good bye," closed the speech, and the door had soon shut out Frank Churchill. Short had been the notice—short their meeting; he was gone; and Emma felt so sorry to part, and foresaw so great a loss to their little society from his absence as to begin to be afraid of being too sorry, and feeling it too much.

It was a sad change. They had been meeting almost every day since his arrival. Certainly his being at Randalls had given great spirit to the last two weeks—indescribable spirit; the idea, the expectation of seeing him which every morning had brought, the assurance of his attentions, his liveliness, his manners! It had been a very happy fortnight, and forlorn must be the sinking from it into the common course of Hartfield days. To complete every other recommendation, he had *almost* told her that he loved her. What strength, or what constancy of affection he might be subject to, was another point; but at present she could not doubt his having a decidedly warm admiration, a conscious preference of herself; and this persuasion, joined to all the rest, made her think that she *must* be a little in love with him, in spite of every previous determination against it.

"1 certainly must," said she. "This sensation of listlessness, weariness, stupidity, this disinclination to sit down and employ myself, this feeling of every thing being dull and insipid about the house!—I must be in love; I should be the oddest creature in the world if I were not—for a few weeks at least. Well, evil to some is always good to others. I shall have many fellow-mourners for the ball, if not for Frank Churchill; but Mr. Knightley will be happy. He may spend the evening with his dear William Larkins now if he likes."

Mr. Knightley, however, showed no triumphant happiness. He could not say that he was sorry on his own account; his very cheerful look would have contradicted him if he had; but he said, and very steadily, that he was sorry for the disappointment of the others, and with considerable kindness added:—

"You, Emma, who have so few opportunities of dancing, you are really out of luck; you are very much out of luck!"

It was some days before she saw Jane Fairfax, to judge of her honest regret in this woful change; but when they did meet, her composure was odious. She had been particularly unwell, however, suffering from headache to a degree, which made her aunt declare that, had the ball taken place, she did not think Jane could have attended it; and it was charity to impute some of her unbecoming indifference to the languor of ill health.

## Chapter XIII.

Emma continued to entertain no doubt of her being in love. Her ideas only varied as to the how much. At first, she thought it was a good deal; and afterwards, but little. She had great pleasure in hearing Frank Churchill talked of; and, for his sake, greater pleasure than ever in seeing Mr. and Mrs. Weston; she was very often thinking of him, and quite impatient for a letter, that she might know how he was, how were his spirits, how was his aunt, and what was the chance of his coming to Randalls again this spring. But, on the other hand, she could not admit herself to be unhappy, nor, after the first morning, to be less disposed for employment than usual; she was still busy and cheerful; and, pleasing as he was, she could yet imagine him to have faults; and farther, though thinking of him so much, and, as she sat drawing or working, forming a thousand amusing schemes for the progress and close of their attachment, fancying interesting dialogues, and inventing elegant letters; the conclusion of every imaginary declaration on his side was that she *refused him.* Their affection was always to subside into friendship. Every thing tender and charming was to mark their parting; but still they were to part. When she became sensible of this, it struck her that she could not be very much in love; for in spite of her previous and fixed determination never to quit her father, never to marry, a strong attachment certainly must produce more of a struggle than she could foresee in her own feelings.

"I do not find myself making any use of the word *sacrifice,*" said she. "In not one of all my clever replies, my delicate negatives, is there any allusion to making a sacrifice. I do suspect that he is not really necessary to my happiness. So much the better. I certainly will not persuade myself to feel more than I do. I am quite enough in love. I should be sorry to be more."

Upon the whole, she was equally contented with her view of his feelings.

"*He* is undoubtedly very much in love—every thing denotes it—very much in love indeed!—and when he comes again, if his affection continue, I must be on my guard not to encourage it. It would be most inexcusable to do otherwise, as my own mind is quite made up. Not that I imagine he can think I have been encouraging him hitherto. No; if he had believed me at all to share his feelings, he would not

have been so wretched. Could he have thought himself encouraged, his looks and language at parting would have
been different. Still, however, I must be on my guard. This is
in the supposition of his attachment continuing what it now
is; but I do not know that I expect it will; I do not look upon
him to be quite the sort of man—I do not altogether build
upon his steadiness or constancy. His feelings are warm, but
I can imagine them rather changeable. Every consideration
of the subject, in short, makes me thankful that my happiness is not more deeply involved. I shall do very well again
after a little while—and then, it will be a good thing over; for
they say every body is in love once in their lives, and I shall
have been let off easily."

When his letter to Mrs. Weston arrived, Emma had the
perusal of it; and she read it with a degree of pleasure and
admiration which made her at first shake her head over her
own sensations, and think she had undervalued their
strength. It was a long, well-written letter, giving the particulars of his journey and of his feelings, expressing all the affection, gratitude, and respect which was natural and
honourable, and describing every thing exterior and local
that could be supposed attractive, with spirit and precision.
No suspicious flourishes now of apology or concern; it was
the language of real feeling towards Mrs. Weston; and the
transition from Highbury to Enscombe, the contrast between the places in some of the first blessings of social life,
was just enough touched on to show how keenly it was felt,
and how much more might have been said but for the restraints of propriety.—The charm of her own name was not
wanting. *Miss Woodhouse* appeared more than once, and
never without a something of pleasing connection, either a
compliment to her taste, or a remembrance of what she had
said; and in the very last time of its meeting her eye, un-
adorned as it was by any such broad wreath of gallantry, she
yet could discern the effect of her influence, and acknowledge the greatest compliment perhaps of all conveyed. Com-
pressed into the very lowest vacant corner were these

words—"I had not a spare moment on Tuesday, as you know, for Miss Woodhouse's beautiful little friend. Pray make my excuses and adieus to her." This, Emma could not doubt, was all for herself. Harriet was remembered only from being *her* friend. His information and prospects, as to Enscombe, were neither worse nor better than had been anticipated; Mrs. Churchill was recovering, and he dared not yet, even in his own imagination, fix a time for coming to Randalls again.

Gratifying, however, and stimulative as was the letter in the material part, its sentiments, she yet found, when it was folded up and returned to Mrs. Weston, that it had not added any lasting warmth—that she could still do without the writer, and that he must learn to do without her. Her intentions were unchanged. Her resolution of refusal only grew more interesting, by the addition of a scheme for his subsequent consolation and happiness. His recollection of Harriet, and the words which clothed it,—the "beautiful little friend,"—suggested to her the idea of Harriet's succeeding her in his affections. Was it impossible?—No. Harriet undoubtedly was greatly his inferior in understanding; but he had been very much struck with the loveliness of her face and the warm simplicity of her manner; and all the probabilities of circumstance and connection were in her favour. For Harriet, it would be advantageous and delightful indeed.

"I must not dwell upon it," said she; "I must not think of it. I know the danger of indulging such speculations. But stranger things have happened; and when we cease to care for each other as we do now, it will be the means of confirming us in that sort of true disinterested friendship which I can already look forward to with pleasure."

It was well to have a comfort in store on Harriet's behalf, though it might be wise to let the fancy touch it seldom; for evil in that quarter was at hand. As Frank Churchill's arrival had succeeded Mr. Elton's engagement in the conversation of Highbury, as the latest interest had entirely borne down the first, so now, upon Frank Churchill's disappearance, Mr.

Elton's concerns were assuming the most irresistible form.—
His wedding-day was named. He would soon be among them
again—Mr. Elton and his bride. There was hardly time to
talk over the first letter from Enscombe, before "Mr. Elton
and his bride" was in every body's mouth, and Frank
Churchill was forgotten. Emma grew sick at the sound. She
had three weeks of happy exemption from Mr. Elton; and
Harriet's mind, she had been willing to hope, had been
lately gaining strength. With Mr. Weston's ball in view at
least, there had been a great deal of insensibility to other
things; but it was now too evident that she had not attained
such a state of composure as could stand against the actual
approach—new carriage, bell ringing and all.

Poor Harriet was in a flutter of spirits which required all
the reasonings, and soothings, and attentions of every kind
that Emma could give. Emma felt that she could not do too
much for her, that Harriet had a right to all her ingenuity
and all her patience; but it was heavy work to be for ever convincing without producing any effect; for ever agreed to,
without being able to make their opinions the same. Harriet
listened submissively, and said, "it was very true; it was just as
Miss Woodhouse described—it was not worth while to think
about them,—and she would not think about them any
longer." But no change of subject could avail, and the next
half hour saw her as anxious and restless about the Eltons as
before. At last Emma attacked her on another ground.

"Your allowing yourself to be so occupied and so unhappy
about Mr. Elton's marrying, Harriet, is the strongest reproach you can make *me*. You could not give me a greater reproof for the mistake I fell into. It was all my doing, I know. I
have not forgotten it, I assure you. Deceived myself, I did very
miserably deceive you; and it will be a painful reflection to me
for ever. Do not imagine me in danger of forgetting it."

Harriet felt this too much to utter more than a few words
of eager exclamation. Emma continued,—

"I have not said, exert yourself, Harriet, for my sake; think
less, talk less of Mr. Elton for my sake; because, for your own

sake rather, I would wish it to be done, for the sake of what is more important than my comfort,—a habit of self-command in you, a consideration of what is your duty, an attention to propriety, an endeavour to avoid the suspicions of others, to save your health and credit, and restore your tranquillity. These are the motives which I have been pressing on you. They are very important, and sorry I am that you cannot feel them sufficiently to act upon them. My being saved from pain is a very secondary consideration. I want you to save yourself from greater pain. Perhaps I may sometimes have felt that Harriet would not forget what was due,—or rather, what would be kind by me."

This appeal to her affections did more than all the rest. The idea of wanting gratitude and consideration for Miss Woodhouse, whom she really loved extremely, made her wretched for a while; and when the violence of grief was comforted away, still remained powerful enough to prompt to what was right, and support her in it very tolerably.

"You, who have been the best friend I ever had in my life!—Want gratitude to you!—Nobody is equal to you! I care for nobody as I do for you! Oh, Miss Woodhouse, how ungrateful I have been!"

Such expressions, assisted as they were by every thing that look and manner could do, made Emma feel that she had never loved Harriet so well, nor valued her affection so highly before.

"There is no charm equal to tenderness of heart," said she afterwards to herself. "There is nothing to be compared to it. Warmth and tenderness of heart, with an affectionate, open manner, will beat all the clearness of head in the world, for attraction: I am sure it will. It is tenderness of heart which makes my dear father so generally beloved—which gives Isabella all her popularity. I have it not; but I know how to prize and respect it. Harriet is my superior in all the charm and all the felicity it gives. Dear Harriet!—I would not change you for the clearest-headed, longest-sighted, best-judging female breathing. Oh, the coldness of a Jane Fairfax! Harriet is worth a hundred such: and for a wife—a sensible man's wife—it is invaluable. I mention no names; but happy the man who changes Emma for Harriet!"

## Chapter XIV.

Mrs. Elton was first seen at church: but though devotion might be interrupted, curiosity could not be satisfied by a bride in a pew, and it must be left for the visits in form which were then to be paid, to settle whether she were very pretty indeed, or only rather pretty, or not pretty at all.

Emma had feelings, less of curiosity than of pride or propriety, to make her resolve on not being the last to pay her respects; and she made a point of Harriet's going with her, that the worst of the business might be gone through as soon as possible.

She could not enter the house again; could not be in the same room to which she had with such vain artifice retreated three months ago, to lace up her boot, without *recollecting*. A thousand vexatious thoughts would recur. Compliments, charades, and horrible blunders; and it was not to be supposed that poor Harriet should not be recollecting too; but she behaved very well, and was only rather pale and silent. The visit was of course short; and there was so much embarrassment and occupation of mind to shorten it, that Emma would not allow herself entirely to form an opinion of the lady, and on no account to give one, beyond the nothing-meaning terms of being "elegantly dressed, and very pleasing."

She did not really like her. She would not be in a hurry to find fault, but she suspected that there was no elegance;—

ease, but not elegance. She was almost sure that for a young woman, a stranger, a bride, there was too much ease. Her person was rather good; her face not unpretty; but neither feature, nor air, nor voice, nor manner was elegant. Emma thought, at least, it would turn out so.

As for Mr. Elton, his manners did not appear—but no, she would not permit a hasty or a witty word from herself about his manners. It was an awkward ceremony at any time to be receiving wedding-visits; and a man had need be all grace to acquit himself well through it. The woman was better off; she might have the assistance of fine clothes, and the privilege of bashfulness; but the man had only his own good sense to depend on: and when she considered how peculiarly unlucky poor Mr. Elton was in being in the same room at once with the woman he had just married, the woman he had wanted to marry, and the woman whom he had been expected to marry, she must allow him to have the right to look as little wise, and to be as much affectedly, and as little really, easy as could be.

"Well, Miss Woodhouse," said Harriet, when they had quitted the house, and after waiting in vain for her friend to begin; "Well, Miss Woodhouse (with a gentle sigh), what do you think of her? Is not she very charming?"

There was a little hesitation in Emma's answer.

"Oh! yes—very—a very pleasing young woman."

"I think her beautiful, quite beautiful."

"Very nicely dressed, indeed; a remarkably elegant gown."

"I am not at all surprised that she should have fallen in love."

"Oh! no; there is nothing to surprise one at all;—a pretty fortune; and she came in his way."

"I dare say," returned Harriet, sighing again, "I dare say she was very much attached to him."

"Perhaps she might; but it is not every man's fate to marry the woman who loves him best. Miss Hawkins, perhaps, wanted a home, and thought this the best offer she was likely to have."

"Yes," said Harriet earnestly, "and well she might, nobody

could ever have a better. Well, I wish them happy with all my heart. And now, Miss Woodhouse, I do not think I shall mind seeing them again. He is just as superior as ever: but being married, you know, it is quite a different thing. No, indeed, Miss Woodhouse, you need not be afraid; I can sit and admire him now without any great misery. To know that he has not thrown himself away, is such a comfort!—She does seem a charming young woman, just what he deserves. Happy creature! He called her 'Augusta.' How delightful!"

When the visit was returned, Emma made up her mind. She could then see more and judge better. From Harriet's happening not to be at Hartfield, and her father's being present to engage Mr. Elton, she had a quarter of an hour of the lady's conversation to herself, and could composedly attend to her; and the quarter of an hour quite convinced her that Mrs. Elton was a vain woman, extremely well satisfied with herself, and thinking much of her own importance; that she meant to shine and be very superior, but with manners which had been formed in a bad school, pert and familiar; that all her notions were drawn from one set of people, and one style of living; that, if not foolish, she was ignorant, and that her society would certainly do Mr. Elton no good.

Harriet would have been a better match. If not wise or refined herself, she would have connected him with those who were; but Miss Hawkins, it might be fairly supposed from her easy conceit, had been the best of her own set. The rich brother-in-law, near Bristol, was the pride of the alliance, and his place and his carriages were the pride of him.

The very first subject, after being seated, was Maple Grove, "My brother Mr. Suckling's seat;" a comparison of Hartfield to Maple Grove. The grounds of Hartfield were small, but neat and pretty; and the house was modern and well-built; Mrs. Elton seemed most favourably impressed by the size of the room, the entrance, and all that she could see or imagine. "Very like Maple Grove indeed! She was quite struck by the likeness!—That room was the very shape and size of the morning-room at Maple Grove; her sister's favourite room." Mr. Elton was appealed to. "Was not it astonishingly like?—She could really almost fancy herself at Maple Grove."

"And the staircase.—You know, as I came in, I observed how very like the staircase was; placed exactly in the same part of the house. I really could not help exclaiming! I assure you, Miss Woodhouse, it is very delightful to me to be reminded of a place I am so extremely partial to as Maple Grove. I have spent so many happy months there! (with a little sign of sentiment.) A charming place, undoubtedly. Every body who sees it is struck by its beauty; but to me it has been quite a home. Whenever you are transplanted, like me, Miss Woodhouse, you will understand how very delightful it is to meet with any thing at all like what one has left behind. I always say this is quite one of the evils of matrimony."

Emma made as slight a reply as she could; but it was fully sufficient for Mrs. Elton, who only wanted to be talking herself.

"So extremely like Maple Grove! And it is not merely the house; the grounds, I assure you, as far as I could observe, are strikingly like. The laurels at Maple Grove are in the same profusion as here, and stand very much in the same way,—just across the lawn; and I had a glimpse of a fine large tree, with a bench round it, which put me so exactly in mind! My brother and sister will be enchanted with this place. People who have extensive grounds themselves are always pleased with any thing in the same style."

Emma doubted the truth of this sentiment. She had a great idea that people who had extensive grounds themselves cared very little for the extensive grounds of any body else; but it was not worth while to attack an error so doubledyed, and she therefore only said in reply,—

"When you have seen more of this country, I am afraid you will think you have over-rated Hartfield. Surrey is full of beauties."

"Oh! yes, I am quite aware of that. It is the garden of England, you know. Surrey is the garden of England."

"Yes; but we must not rest our claims on that distinction. Many counties, I believe, are called the garden of England, as well as Surrey."

"No, I fancy not," replied Mrs. Elton, with a most satisfied smile. "I never heard any county but Surrey called so."

Emma was silenced.

"My brother and sister have promised us a visit in the spring, or summer at farthest," continued Mrs. Elton; "and that will be our time for exploring. While they are with us, we shall explore a great deal, I dare say. They will have their barouche-landau,[13] of course, which holds four perfectly; and therefore, without saying any thing of *our* carriage, we should be able to explore the different beauties extremely well. They would hardly come in their chaise, I think, at that season of the year. Indeed, when the time draws on, I shall decidedly recommend their bringing the barouche-landau; it will be so very much preferable. When people come into a beautiful country of this sort, you know, Miss Woodhouse, one naturally wishes them to see as much as possible; and Mr. Suckling is extremely fond of exploring. We explored to King's-Weston twice last summer, in that way, most delightfully, just after their first having the barouche-landau. You have many parties of that kind here, I suppose, Miss Woodhouse, every summer?"

"No; not immediately here. We are rather out of distance of the very striking beauties which attract the sort of parties you speak of; and we are a very quiet set of people, I believe; more disposed to stay at home than engage in schemes of pleasure."

"Ah! there is nothing like staying at home, for real comfort. Nobody can be more devoted to home than I am. I was quite a proverb for it at Maple Grove. Many a time has Selina said, when she has been going to Bristol, 'I really cannot get this girl to move from the house. I absolutely must go in by myself, though I hate being stuck up in the barouche-landau without a companion; but Augusta, I believe, with her own good will, would never stir beyond the park paling.'* Many a time has she said so; and yet I am no advocate for entire seclusion. I think, on the contrary, when people shut themselves up entirely from society, it is a very bad thing; and that it is much more advisable to mix in the world in a proper degree, without living in it either too much or too little. I perfectly understand your situation, however, Miss Woodhouse (looking towards Mr. Woodhouse), your father's state of health must be a great drawback. Why does not he try Bath?—Indeed he should. Let me recommend Bath to you. I assure you I have no doubt of its doing Mr. Woodhouse good."

"My father tried it more than once, formerly, but without receiving any benefit; and Mr. Perry, whose name, I dare say, is not unknown to you, does not conceive it would be at all more likely to be useful now."

"Ah! that's a great pity; for I assure you, Miss Woodhouse, where the waters do agree,[14] it is quite wonderful the relief they give. In my Bath life, I have seen such instances of it! And it is so cheerful a place, that it could not fail of being of use to Mr. Woodhouse's spirits, which, I understand, are sometimes much depressed. And as to its recommendation to *you*, I fancy I need not take much pains to dwell on them. The advantages of Bath to the young are pretty generally understood. It would be a charming introduction for you, who have lived so secluded a life; and I could immediately secure you some of the best society in the place. A line from me would bring you a little host of acquaintance; and my particular friend, Mrs. Partridge, the lady I have always resided with when in Bath, would be most happy to show you any attentions, and would be the very person for you to go into public with."

It was as much as Emma could bear, without being impolite. The idea of her being indebted to Mrs. Elton for what was called an *introduction*—of her going into public under

---

*Fence.

the auspices of a friend of Mrs. Elton's,—probably some vulgar, dashing widow, who, with the help of a boarder, just made a shift to live!—The dignity of Miss Woodhouse, of Hartfield, was sunk indeed!

She restrained herself, however, from any of the reproofs she could have given, and only thanked Mrs. Elton coolly; "but their going to Bath was quite out of the question; and she was not perfectly convinced that the place might suit her better than her father." And then, to prevent further outrage and indignation, changed the subject directly.

"I do not ask whether you are musical, Mrs. Elton. Upon these occasions, a lady's character generally precedes her; and Highbury has long known that you are a superior performer."

"Oh! no, indeed; I must protest against any such idea. A superior performer!—very far from it, I assure you: consider from how partial a quarter your information came. I am doatingly fond of music—passionately fond;—and my friends say I am not entirely devoid of taste; but as to any thing else, upon my honour my performance is *médiocre* to the last degree. You, Miss Woodhouse, I well know, play delightfully. I assure you it has been the greatest satisfaction, comfort, and delight to me, to hear what a musical society I am got into. I absolutely cannot do without music; it is a necessary of life to me; and having always been used to a very musical society, both at Maple Grove and in Bath, it would have been a most serious sacrifice. I honestly said as much to Mr. E. when he was speaking of my future home, and expressing his fears lest the retirement of it should be disagreeable; and the inferiority of the house too—knowing what I had been accustomed to—of course he was not wholly without apprehension. When he was speaking of it in that way, I honestly said that *the world* I could give up—parties, balls, plays—for I had no fear of retirement. Blessed with so many resources within myself, the world was not necessary to *me*. I could do very well without it. To those who had no resources it was a different thing; but my resources made me quite independent. And as to smaller-sized rooms than I had been used to, I really could not give it a thought. I hoped I was perfectly equal to any sacrifice of that description. Certainly, I had been accustomed to every luxury at Maple Grove; but I did assure him that two carriages were not necessary to my happiness, nor were spacious apartments. 'But,' said I, 'to be quite honest, I do not think I can live without something of a musical society. I condition for nothing else; but, without music, life would be a blank to me.'"

"We cannot suppose," said Emma, smiling, "that Mr. Elton would hesitate to assure you of there being a *very* musical society in Highbury; and I hope you will not find he has outstepped the truth more than may be pardoned, in consideration of the motive."

"No, indeed, I have no doubts at all on that head. I am delighted to find myself in such a circle: I hope we shall have many sweet little concerts together. I think, Miss Woodhouse, you and I must establish a musical club, and have regular weekly meetings at your house, or ours. Will not it be a good plan? If *we* exert ourselves, I think we shall not be long in want of allies. Something of that nature would be particularly desirable for *me*, as an inducement to keep me in practice; for married women, you know—there is a sad story against them, in general. They are but too apt to give up music."

"But you, who are so extremely fond of it,—there can be no danger, surely."

"I should hope not; but really, when I look round among my acquaintance, I tremble. Selina has entirely given up music;—never touches the instrument, though she played sweetly. And the same may be said of Mrs. Jeffereys—Clara Partridge that was,—and of the two Milmans, now Mrs. Bird and Mrs. James Cooper; and of more than I can enumerate. Upon my word, it is enough to put one in a fright. I used to be quite angry with Selina; but, really, I begin now to comprehend that a married woman has many things to call her attention. I believe I was half an hour this morning shut up with my housekeeper."

"But every thing of that kind," said Emma, "will soon be in so regular a train——"

"Well," said Mrs. Elton, laughing, "we shall see."

Emma, finding her so determined upon neglecting her music, had nothing more to say; and, after a moment's pause, Mrs. Elton chose another subject.

"We have been calling at Randalls," said she, "and found them both at home; and very pleasant people they seem to be. I like them extremely. Mr. Weston seems an excellent creature—quite a first-rate favourite with me already, I assure you. And *she* appears so truly good,—there is something so motherly and kind-hearted about her, that it wins upon one directly.—She was your governess, I think."

Emma was almost too much astonished to answer; but Mrs. Elton hardly waited for the affirmative before she went on.

"Having understood as much, I was rather astonished to find her so very lady-like. But she is really quite the gentle-woman."

"Mrs. Weston's manners," said Emma, "were always particularly good. Their propriety, simplicity, and elegance would make them the safest model for any young woman."

"And who do you think came in while we were there?"

Emma was quite at a loss. The tone implied some old acquaintance, and how could she possibly guess?

"Knightley!" continued Mrs. Elton;—"Knightley himself! Was not it lucky? For, not being within when he called the other day, I had never seen him before; and of course, as so particular a friend of Mr. E.'s, I had a great curiosity. 'My friend Knightley' had been so often mentioned, that I was really impatient to see him; and I must do my cara sposo* the justice to say, that he need not be ashamed of his friend. Knightley is quite the gentleman; I like him very much. Decidedly, I think, a very gentlemanlike man."

Happily, it was now time to be gone. They were off, and Emma could breathe.

"Insufferable woman!" was her immediate exclamation.

---

*Dear husband (Italian).

"Worse than I had supposed. Absolutely insufferable! Knightley!—I could not have believed it. Knightley!—never seen him in her life before, and call him Knightley!—and discover that he is a gentleman! A little upstart, vulgar being, with her Mr. E. and her *caro sposo*, and her resources, and all her airs of pert pretension and underbred finery. Actually to discover that Mr. Knightley is a gentleman! I doubt whether he will return the compliment, and discover her to be a lady. I could not have believed it! And to propose that she and I should unite to form a musical club! One would fancy we were bosom friends! And Mrs. Weston!—Astonished that the person who had brought me up should be a gentlewoman! Worse and worse. I never met with her equal. Much beyond my hopes. Harriet is disgraced by any comparison. Oh! what would Frank Churchill say to her, if he were here? How angry and how diverted he would be! Ah! there I am—thinking of him directly. Always the first person to be thought of! How I catch myself out! Frank Churchill comes as regularly into my mind!"—

All this ran so glibly through her thoughts, that by the time her father had arranged himself, after the bustle of the Eltons' departure, and was ready to speak, she was very tolerably capable of attending.

"Well, my dear," he deliberately began, "considering we never saw her before, she seems a very pretty sort of young lady; and I dare say she was very much pleased with you. She speaks a little too quick. A little quickness of voice there is which rather hurts the ear. But I believe I am nice; I do not like strange voices; and nobody speaks like you and poor Miss Taylor. However, she seems a very obliging, pretty-behaved young lady, and no doubt will make him a very good wife. Though I think he had better not have married. I made the best excuses I could for not having been able to wait on him and Mrs. Elton on this happy occasion; I said that I hoped I *should* in the course of the summer. But I ought to have gone before. Not to wait upon a bride is very remiss. Ah! it shows what a sad invalid I am!—But I do not like the corner into Vicarage-lane."

"I dare say your apologies were accepted, sir. Mr. Elton knows you."

"Yes: but a young lady—a bride—I ought to have paid my respects to her if possible. It was being very deficient."

"But, my dear papa, you are no friend to matrimony; and therefore why should you be so anxious to pay your respects to a *bride*? It ought to be no recommendation to *you*. It is encouraging people to marry if you make so much of them."

"No, my dear, I never encouraged any body to marry, but I would always wish to pay every proper attention to a lady—and a bride, especially, is never to be neglected. More is avowedly due to *her*. A bride, you know, my dear, is always the first in company, let the others be who they may."

"Well, papa, if this is not encouragement to marry, I do not know what is. And I should never have expected you to be lending your sanction to such vanity-baits for poor young ladies."

"My dear, you do not understand me. This is a matter of mere common politeness and good-breeding, and has nothing to do with any encouragement to people to marry."

Emma had done. Her father was growing nervous, and could not understand *her*. Her mind returned to Mrs. Elton's offences, and long, very long, did they occupy her.

## Chapter XV.

Emma was not required, by any subsequent discovery, to retract her ill opinion of Mrs. Elton. Her observation had been pretty correct. Such as Mrs. Elton appeared to her on this second interview, such she appeared whenever they met again,—self-important, presuming, familiar, ignorant, and ill-bred. She had a little beauty and a little accomplishment, but so little judgment that she thought herself coming with superior knowledge of the world, to enliven and improve a country neighbourhood; and conceived Miss Hawkins to have held such a place in society as Mrs. Elton's consequence only could surpass.

There was no reason to suppose Mr. Elton thought at all differently from his wife. He seemed not merely happy with her, but proud. He had the air of congratulating himself on having brought such a woman to Highbury, as not even Miss Woodhouse could equal; and the greater part of her new acquaintance, disposed to commend, or not in the habit of judging, following the lead of Miss Bates's good-will, or taking it for granted that the bride must be as clever and as agreeable as she professed herself, were very well satisfied; so that Mrs. Elton's praise passed from one mouth to another as it ought to do, unimpeded by Miss Woodhouse, who readily continued her first contribution, and talked with a good grace of her being "very pleasant, and very elegantly dressed."

In one respect Mrs. Elton grew even worse than she had appeared at first. Her feelings altered towards Emma.—Offended, probably, by the little encouragement which her proposals of intimacy met with, she drew back, in her turn, and gradually became much more cold and distant; and though the effect was agreeable, the ill-will which produced it was necessarily increasing Emma's dislike. Her manners too—and Mr. Elton's, were unpleasant towards Harriet. They were sneering and negligent. Emma hoped it must rapidly work Harriet's cure; but the sensations which could prompt such behaviour sunk them both very much.—It was not to be doubted that poor Harriet's attachment had been an offering to conjugal unreserve, and her own share in the story, under a colouring the least favourable to her and the most soothing to him, had in all likelihood been given also. She was, of course, the object of their joint dislike.—When they had nothing else to say, it must be always easy to begin abusing Miss Woodhouse; and the enmity which they dared not show in open disrespect to her, found a broader vent in contemptuous treatment of Harriet.

Mrs. Elton took a great fancy to Jane Fairfax; and from the first. Not merely when a state of warfare with one young lady might be supposed to recommend the other, but from the very first; and she was not satisfied with expressing a natural and reasonable admiration—but without solicitation, or plea, or privilege, she must be wanting to assist and befriend her.—Before Emma had forfeited her confidence, and about the third time of their meeting, she heard all Mrs. Elton's knight-errantry on the subject.

"Jane Fairfax is absolutely charming, Miss Woodhouse.— I quite rave about Jane Fairfax.—A sweet, interesting creature. So mild and lady-like—and with such talents!—I assure you I think she has very extraordinary talents. I do not scruple to say that she plays extremely well. I know enough of music to speak decidedly on that point. Oh! she is absolutely charming. You will laugh at my warmth—but, upon my word, I talk of nothing but Jane Fairfax.—And her situation is so calculated to affect one!—Miss Woodhouse, we must exert ourselves and endeavour to do something for her. We must bring her forward. Such talents as hers must not be suffered to remain unknown.—I dare say you have heard those charming lines of the poet,

'Full many a flower is born to blush unseen,
'And waste its fragrance on the desert air.'[15]

We must not allow them to be verified in sweet Jane Fairfax."

"I cannot think there is any danger of it," was Emma's calm answer;—"and when you are better acquainted with Miss Fairfax's situation, and understand what her home has been, with Colonel and Mrs. Campbell, I have no idea that you will suppose her talents can be unknown."

"Oh! but, dear Miss Woodhouse, she is now in such retirement, such obscurity, so thrown away. Whatever advantages she may have enjoyed with the Campbells are so palpably at an end! And I think she feels it. I am sure she does. She is very timid and silent. One can see that she feels the want of encouragement. I like her the better for it. I must confess it is a recommendation to me. I am a great advocate for timidity—and I am sure one does not often meet with it. But in those who are at all inferior, it is extremely prepossessing. Oh! I assure you, Jane Fairfax is a very delightful character, and interests me more than I can express."

"You appear to feel a great deal—but I am not aware how you or any of Miss Fairfax's acquaintance here, any of those who have known her longer than yourself, can show her any other attention than——"

"My dear Miss Woodhouse, a vast deal may be done by those who dare to act. You and I need not be afraid. If *we* set the example, many will follow it as far as they can; though all have not our situations. *We* have carriages to fetch and convey her home; and *we* live in a style which could not make the addition of Jane Fairfax at any time the least inconvenient. I should be extremely displeased if Wright were to send us up such a dinner, as could make me regret having asked *more* than Jane Fairfax to partake of it. I have no idea of that sort of thing. It is not likely that I *should*, considering what I have been used to. My greatest danger, perhaps, in housekeeping, may be quite the other way, in doing too much, and being too careless of expense. Maple Grove will probably be my model more than it ought to be—for we do not at all affect to equal my brother, Mr. Suckling, in income. However, my resolution is taken as to noticing Jane Fairfax. I shall certainly have her very often at my house, shall introduce her wherever I can, shall have musical parties to draw out her talents, and shall be constantly on the watch for an eligible situation. My acquaintance is so very extensive, that I have little doubt of hearing of something to suit her shortly. I shall introduce her, of course, very particularly to my brother and sister when they come to us. I am sure they will like her extremely; and when she gets a little acquainted with them, her

fears will completely wear off, for there really is nothing in
the manners of either but what is highly conciliating. I shall
have her very often indeed while they are with me; and I
dare say we shall sometimes find a seat for her in the
barouche-landau in some of our exploring parties."

"Poor Jane Fairfax!" thought Emma,—"you have not deserved this. You may have done wrong with regard to Mr.
Dixon; but this is a punishment beyond what you can have
merited! The kindness and protection of Mrs. Elton!—'Jane
Fairfax and Jane Fairfax.' Heavens! let me not suppose that
she dares go about Emma Woodhouse-ing me! But, upon my
honour, there seem no limits to the licentiousness of that
woman's tongue!"

Emma had not to listen to such paradings again—to any
so exclusively addressed to herself—so disgustingly deco-
rated with a "dear Miss Woodhouse." The change on Mrs.
Elton's side soon afterwards appeared, and she was left in
peace—neither forced to be the very particular friend of
Mrs. Elton, nor, under Mrs. Elton's guidance, the very active
patroness of Jane Fairfax, and only sharing with others in a
general way, in knowing what was felt, what was meditated,
what was done.

She looked on with some amusement. Miss Bates's gratitude for Mrs. Elton's attentions to Jane was in the first style
of guileless simplicity and warmth. She was quite one of her
worthies—the most amiable, affable, delightful woman—just
as accomplished and condescending as Mrs. Elton meant to
be considered. Emma's only surprise was that Jane Fairfax
should accept those attentions and tolerate Mrs. Elton as she
seemed to do. She heard of her walking with the Eltons, sitting with the Eltons, spending a day with the Eltons! This was
astonishing! She could not have believed it possible that the
taste or the pride of Miss Fairfax could endure such society
and friendship as the Vicarage had to offer.

"She is a riddle, quite a riddle," said she.—"To choose to
remain here month after month, under privations of every
sort. And now to choose the mortification of Mrs. Elton's no-

tice, and the penury of her conversation, rather than return to the superior companions who have always loved her with such real, generous affection."

Jane had come to Highbury professedly for three months; the Campbells were gone to Ireland for three months; but now the Campbells had promised their daughter to stay at least till Midsummer, and fresh invitations had arrived for her to join them there. According to Miss Bates—it all came from her—Mrs. Dixon had written most pressingly. Would Jane but go, means were to be found, servants sent, friends contrived—no travelling difficulty allowed to exist; but still she had declined it.

"She must have some motive, more powerful than appears, for refusing this invitation," was Emma's conclusion. "She must be under some sort of penance, inflicted either by the Campbells or herself. There is great fear, great caution, great resolution somewhere. She is *not* to be with the *Dixons*. The decree is issued by somebody. But why must she consent to be with the Eltons? Here is quite a separate puzzle."

Upon her speaking her wonder aloud on that part of the subject, before the few who knew her opinion of Mrs. Elton, Mrs. Weston ventured this apology for Jane.

"We cannot suppose that she has any great enjoyment at the Vicarage, my dear Emma—but it is better than being always at home. Her aunt is a good creature; but, as a constant companion, must be very tiresome. We must consider what Miss Fairfax quits, before we condemn her taste for what she goes to."

"You are right, Mrs. Weston," said Mr. Knightley warmly; "Miss Fairfax is as capable as any of us of forming a just opinion of Mrs. Elton. Could she have chosen with whom to associate, she would not have chosen her. But (with a reproachful smile at Emma) she receives attentions from Mrs. Elton, which nobody else pays her."

Emma felt that Mrs. Weston was giving her a momentary glance, and she was herself struck by his warmth. With a faint blush, she presently replied,—

"Such attentions as Mrs. Elton's, I should have imagined, would rather disgust than gratify Miss Fairfax. Mrs. Elton's invitations I should have imagined any thing but inviting."

"I should not wonder," said Mrs. Weston, "if Miss Fairfax were to have been drawn on beyond her own inclination, by her aunt's eagerness in accepting Mrs. Elton's civilities for her. Poor Miss Bates may very likely have committed her niece, and hurried her into a greater appearance of intimacy than her own good sense would have dictated, in spite of the very natural wish of a little change."

Both felt rather anxious to hear him speak again; and, after a few minutes' silence, he said,—

"Another thing must be taken into consideration too— Mrs. Elton does not talk *to* Miss Fairfax as she speaks *of* her. We all know the difference between the pronouns he or she and thou, the plainest spoken amongst us; we all feel the influence of a something beyond common civility in our personal intercourse with each other—a something more early implanted. We cannot give any body the disagreeable hints that we may have been very full of the hour before. We feel things differently. And besides the operation of this, as a general principle, you may be sure that Miss Fairfax awes Mrs. Elton by her superiority both of mind and manner; and that, face to face, Mrs. Elton treats her with all the respect which she has a claim to. Such a woman as Jane Fairfax probably never fell in Mrs. Elton's way before—and no degree of vanity can prevent her acknowledging her own comparative littleness in action, if not in consciousness."

"I know how highly you think of Jane Fairfax," said Emma. Little Henry was in her thoughts, and a mixture of alarm and delicacy made her irresolute what else to say.

"Yes," he replied, "any body may know how highly I think of her."

"And yet," said Emma, beginning hastily, and with an arch look, but soon stopping—it was better, however, to know the worst at once—she hurried on, "and yet, perhaps, you may hardly be aware yourself how highly it is. The extent of your admiration may take you by surprise some day or other."

Mr. Knightley was hard at work upon the lower buttons of his thick leather gaiters, and either the exertion of getting them together, or some other cause, brought the colour into his face, as he answered,—

"Oh! are you there? But you are miserably behind-hand. Mr. Cole gave me a hint of it six weeks ago."

He stopped. Emma felt her foot pressed by Mrs. Weston, and did not herself know what to think. In a moment he went on,—

"That will never be, however, I can assure you. Miss Fairfax, I dare say, would not have me if I were to ask her; and I am very sure I shall never ask her."

Emma returned her friend's pressure with interest; and was pleased enough to exclaim—

"You are not vain, Mr Knightley. I will say that for you."

He seemed hardly to hear her; he was thoughtful, and, in a manner which showed him not pleased, soon afterwards said,—

"So you have been settling that I should marry Jane Fairfax."

"No, indeed, I have not. You have scolded me too much for match-making for me to presume to take such a liberty with you. What I said just now meant nothing. One says those sort of things, of course, without any idea of a serious meaning. Oh! no; upon my word I have not the smallest wish for your marrying Jane Fairfax, or Jane any body. You would not come in and sit with us in this comfortable way if you were married."

Mr. Knightley was thoughtful again. The result of his reverie was,—"No, Emma, I do not think the extent of my admiration for her will ever take me by surprise. I never had a thought of her in that way, I assure you." And, soon afterwards, "Jane Fairfax is a very charming young woman—but not even Jane Fairfax is perfect. She has a fault. She has not the open temper which a man would wish for in a wife."

Emma could not but rejoice to hear that she had a fault.

"Well," said she, "and you soon silenced Mr. Cole, I suppose."

"Yes, very soon. He gave me a quiet hint; I told him he was mistaken; he asked my pardon, and said no more. Cole does not want to be wiser or wittier than his neighbours."

"In that respect how unlike dear Mrs. Elton, who wants to be wiser and wittier than all the world! I wonder how she speaks of the Coles—what she calls them. How can she find any appellation for them, deep enough in familiar vulgarity? She calls you Knightley; what can she do for Mr. Cole? And so I am not to be surprised that Jane Fairfax accepts her civilities, and consents to be with her. Mrs. Weston, your argument weighs most with me. I can much more readily enter into the temptation of getting away from Miss Bates, than I can believe in the triumph of Miss Fairfax's mind over Mrs. Elton. I have no faith in Mrs. Elton's acknowledging herself the inferior in thought, word, or deed; or in her being under any restraint beyond her own scanty rule of good breeding. I cannot imagine that she will not be continually insulting her visiter with praise, encouragement, and offers of service; that she will not be continually detailing her magnificent intentions, from the procuring her a permanent situation to the including her in those delightful exploring parties which are to take place in the barouche-landau."

"Jane Fairfax has feeling," said Mr. Knightley; "I do not accuse her of want of feeling. Her sensibilities, I suspect, are strong, and her temper excellent in its power of forbearance, patience, self-control; but it wants openness. She is reserved; more reserved, I think, than she used to be: and I love an open temper. No; till Cole alluded to my supposed attachment, it had never entered my head. I saw Jane Fairfax, and conversed with her, with admiration and pleasure always; but with no thought beyond."

"Well, Mrs. Weston," said Emma, triumphantly, when he left them, "what do you say now to Mr. Knightley's marrying Jane Fairfax?"

"Why, really, dear Emma, I say that he is so very much occupied by the idea of *not* being in love with her, that I should not wonder if it were to end in his being so at last. Do not beat me."

## Chapter XVI.

Every body in and about Highbury, who had ever visited Mr. Elton, was disposed to pay him attention on his marriage. Dinner parties and evening parties were made for him and his lady; and invitations flowed in so fast that she had soon the pleasure of apprehending they were never to have a disengaged day.

"I see how it is," said she; "I see what a life I am to lead among you. Upon my word we shall be absolutely dissipated. We really seem quite the fashion. If this is living in the country, it is nothing very formidable. From Monday next to Saturday, I assure you we have not a disengaged day! A woman with fewer resources than I have need not have been at a loss."

No invitation came amiss to her. Her Bath habits made evening parties perfectly natural to her, and Maple Grove had given her a taste for dinners. She was a little shocked at the want of two drawing-rooms, at the poor attempt at rout-cakes,* and there being no ice in the Highbury card parties. Mrs. Bates, Mrs. Perry, Mrs. Goddard, and others, were a good deal behind hand in knowledge of the world, but *she* would soon show them how every thing ought to be arranged. In the course of the spring she must return their civilities by one very superior party; in which her card tables

---

*Sweet cakes made specifically for parties.

should be set out with their separate candles and unbroken packs in the true style, and more waiters engaged for the evening than their own establishment could furnish, to carry round the refreshments at exactly the proper hour, and in the proper order.

Emma, in the meanwhile, could not be satisfied without a dinner at Hartfield for the Eltons. They must not do less than others, or she should be exposed to odious suspicions, and imagined capable of pitiful resentment. A dinner there must be. After Emma had talked about it for ten minutes, Mr. Woodhouse felt no unwillingness, and only made the usual stipulation of not sitting at the bottom of the table himself, with the usual regular difficulty of deciding who should do it for him.

The persons to be invited required little thought. Besides the Eltons, it must be the Westons and Mr. Knightley; so far it was all of course: and it was hardly less inevitable that poor little Harriet must be asked to make the eighth; but this invitation was not given with equal satisfaction, and, on many accounts, Emma was particularly pleased by Harriet's begging to be allowed to decline it. "She would rather not be in *his* company more than she could help. She was not quite able to see him and his charming happy wife together, without feeling uncomfortable. If Miss Woodhouse would not be displeased, she would rather stay at home." It was precisely what Emma would have wished, had she deemed it possible enough for wishing. She was delighted with the fortitude of her little friend,—for fortitude she knew it was in her to give up being in company, and stay at home; and she could now invite the very person whom she really wanted to make the eighth, Jane Fairfax. Since her last conversation with Mrs. Weston and Mr. Knightley she was more conscience-stricken about Jane Fairfax than she had often been. Mr. Knightley's words dwelt with her. He had said that Jane Fairfax received attentions from Mrs. Elton which nobody else paid her.

"This is very true," said she, "at least as far as relates to me, which was all that was meant, and it is very shameful. Of the same age, and always knowing her, I ought to have been more her friend. She will never like me now. I have neglected her too long. But I will show her greater attention than I have done."

Every invitation was successful. They were all disengaged and all happy. The preparatory interest of this dinner, however, was not yet over. A circumstance rather unlucky occurred. The two eldest little Knightleys were engaged to pay their grandpapa and aunt a visit of some weeks in the spring, and their papa now proposed bringing them, and staying one whole day at Hartfield—which one day would be the very day of this party. His professional engagements did not allow of his being put off, but both father and daughter were disturbed by its happening so. Mr. Woodhouse considered eight persons at dinner together as the utmost that his nerves could bear—and here would be a ninth—and Emma apprehended that it would be a ninth very much out of humour at not being able to come even to Hartfleld for forty-eight hours without falling in with a dinner-party.

She comforted her father better than she could comfort herself, by representing that though he certainly would make them nine, yet he always said so little, that the increase of noise would be very immaterial. She thought it in reality a sad exchange for herself, to have him, with his grave looks and reluctant conversation, opposed to her instead of his brother.

The event was more favourable to Mr. Woodhouse than to Emma. John Knightley came; but Mr. Weston was unexpectedly summoned to town and must be absent on the very day. He might be able to join them in the evening, but certainly not to dinner. Mr. Woodhouse was quite at ease; and the seeing him so, with the arrival of the little boys and the philosophic composure of her brother on hearing his fate, removed the chief of even Emma's vexation.

The day came, the party were punctually assembled, and

Mr. John Knightley seemed early to devote himself to the business of being agreeable. Instead of drawing his brother off to a window while they waited for dinner, he was talking to Miss Fairfax. Mrs. Elton, as elegant as lace and pearls could make her, he looked at in silence—wanting only to observe enough for Isabella's information—but Miss Fairfax was an old acquaintance and a quiet girl, and he could talk to her. He had met her before breakfast as he was returning from a walk with his little boys, when it had been just beginning to rain. It was natural to have some civil hopes on the subject, and he said,—

"I hope you did not venture far, Miss Fairfax, this morning, or I am sure you must have been wet. *We* scarcely got home in time. I hope you turned directly."

"I went only to the post-office," said she, "and reached home before the rain was much. It is my daily errand. I always fetch the letters when I am here. It saves trouble, and is a something to get me out. A walk before breakfast does me good."

"Not a walk in the rain I should imagine."

"No; but it did not absolutely rain when I set out."

Mr. John Knightley smiled, and replied,—

"That is to say, you chose to have your walk, for you were not six yards from your own door when I had the pleasure of meeting you; and Henry and John had seen more drops than they could count long before. The post-office has a great charm at one period of our lives. When you have lived to my age, you will begin to think letters are never worth going through the rain for."

There was a little blush, and then this answer:—

"I must not hope to be ever situated as you are, in the midst of every dearest connection, and therefore I cannot expect that simply growing older should make me indifferent about letters."

"Indifferent! Oh no—I never conceived you could become indifferent. Letters are no matter of indifference; they are generally a very positive curse."

"You are speaking of letters of business; mine are letters of friendship."

"I have often thought them the worst of the two," replied he coolly. "Business, you know, may bring money, but friendship hardly ever does."

"Ah! you are not serious now. I know Mr. John Knightley too well—I am very sure he understands the value of friendship as well as any body. I can easily believe that letters are very little to you, much less than to me; but it is not your being ten years older than myself which makes the difference, it is not age, but situation. You have every body dearest to you always at hand, I, probably, never shall again; and therefore till I have out-lived all my affections, a post-office, I think, must always have power to draw me out, in worse weather than to-day."

"When I talked of your being altered by time, by the progress of years," said John Knightley, "I meant to imply the change of situation which time usually brings. I consider one as including the other. Time will generally lessen the interest of every attachment not within the daily circle—but that is not the change I had in view for you. As an old friend, you will allow me to hope, Miss Fairfax, that ten years hence you may have as many concentrated objects as I have."

It was kindly said, and very far from giving offence. A pleasant "thank you" seemed meant to laugh it off; but a blush, a quivering lip, a tear in the eye, showed that it was felt beyond a laugh. Her attention was now claimed by Mr. Woodhouse, who being, according to his custom on such occasions, making the circle of his guests, and paying his particular compliments to the ladies, was ending with her—and with all his mildest urbanity, said,—

"I am very sorry to hear, Miss Fairfax, of your being out this morning in the rain. Young ladies should take care of themselves. Young ladies are delicate plants. They should take care of their health and their complexion. My dear, did you change your stockings?"

"Yes, sir, I did indeed; and I am very much obliged by your kind solicitude about me."

"My dear Miss Fairfax, young ladies are very sure to be cared for.—I hope your good grandmamma and aunt are well. They are some of my very old friends. I wish my health allowed me to be a better neighbour. You do us a great deal of honour to-day, I am sure. My daughter and I are both highly sensible of your goodness, and have the greatest satisfaction in seeing you at Hartfield."

The kind-hearted, polite old man might then sit down and feel that he had done his duty, and made every fair lady welcome and easy.

By this time the walk in the rain had reached Mrs. Elton, and her remonstrances now opened upon Jane.

"My dear Jane, what is this I hear?—Going to the post-office in the rain!—This must not be I assure you. You sad girl, how could you do such a thing? It is a sign I was not there to take care of you."

Jane very patiently assured her that she had not caught any cold.

"Oh! do not tell *me*. You really are a very sad girl, and do not know how to take care of yourself. To the post-office indeed! Mrs. Weston, did you ever hear the like? You and I must positively exert our authority."

"My advice," said Mrs. Weston kindly and persuasively, "I certainly do feel tempted to give.—Miss Fairfax, you must not run such risks. Liable as you have been to severe colds, indeed you ought to be particularly careful, especially at this time of year. The spring I always think requires more than common care. Better wait an hour or two, or even half a day for your letters, than run the risk of bringing on your cough again. Now do not you feel that you had? Yes, I am sure you are much too reasonable. You look as if you would not do such a thing again."

"Oh! she *shall not* do such a thing again," eagerly rejoined Mrs. Elton. "We will not allow her to do such a thing again:"—and nodding significantly—"there must be some arrangement made, there must indeed. I shall speak to Mr. E. The man who fetches our letters every morning (one of our men, I forget his name) shall enquire for yours too and bring them to you. That will obviate all difficulties you know; and from *us* I really think, my dear Jane, you can have no scruple to accept such an accommodation."

"You are extremely kind," said Jane; "but I cannot give up my early walk. I am advised to be out of doors as much as I can; I must walk somewhere, and the post-office is an object; and, upon my word, I have scarcely ever had a bad morning before."

"My dear Jane, say no more about it. The thing is determined, that is (laughing affectedly) as far as I can presume to determine any thing without the concurrence of my lord and master. You know, Mrs. Weston. you and I must be cautious how we express ourselves. But I do flatter myself, my dear Jane, that my influence is not entirely worn out. If I meet with no insuperable difficulties, therefore, consider that point as settled."

"Excuse me," said Jane earnestly, "I cannot by any means consent to such an arrangement, so needlessly troublesome to your servant. If the errand were not a pleasure to me, it could be done, as it always is when I am not here, by my grandmamma's."

"Oh! my dear; but so much as Patty has to do!—And it is a kindness to employ our men."

Jane looked as if she did not mean to be conquered; but, instead of answering, she began speaking again to Mr. John Knightley.

"The post-office is a wonderful establishment!" said she. "The regularity and despatch of it! If one thinks of all that it has to do, and all that it does so well, it is really astonishing!"

"It is certainly very well regulated."

"So seldom that any negligence or blunder appears! So seldom that a letter, among the thousands that are constantly passing about the kingdom, is even carried wrong— and not one in a million, I suppose, actually lost! And when one considers the variety of hands, and of bad hands too, that are to be deciphered, it increases the wonder."

"The clerks grow expert from habit. They must begin with some quickness of sight and hand, and exercise improves them. If you want any further explanation," continued he, smiling, "they are paid for it. That is the key to a great deal of capacity. The public pays and must be served well."

The varieties of hand-writing were further talked of, and the usual observations made.

"I have heard it asserted," said John Knightley, "that the same sort of hand-writing often prevails in a family; and where the same master teaches, it is natural enough. But for that reason, I should imagine the likeness must be chiefly confined to the females, for boys have very little teaching after an early age, and scramble into any hand they can get. Isabella and Emma, I think, do write very much alike. I have not always known their writing apart."

"Yes," said his brother hesitatingly, "there is a likeness. I know what you mean—but Emma's hand is the strongest."

"Isabella and Emma both write beautifully," said Mr. Woodhouse; "and always did. And so does poor Mrs. Weston"—with half a sigh and half a smile at her.

"I never saw any gentleman's hand-writing"—Emma began, looking also at Mrs. Weston; but stopped, on perceiving that Mrs. Weston was attending to some one else—and the pause gave her time to reflect. "Now, how am I going to introduce him?—Am I unequal to speaking his name at once before all these people? Is it necessary for me to use any roundabout phrase?—Your Yorkshire friend—your correspondent in Yorkshire;—that would be the way, I suppose, if I were very bad. No, I can pronounce his name without the smallest distress. I certainly get better and better.—Now for it."

Mrs. Weston was disengaged, and Emma began again—"Mr. Frank Churchill writes one of the best gentlemen's hands I ever saw."

"I do not admire it," said Mr. Knightley. "It is too small—wants strength. It is like a woman's writing."

This was not submitted to by either lady. They vindicated him against the base aspersion. "No, it by no means wanted strength—it was not a large hand, but very clear and certainly strong. Had not Mrs. Weston any letter about her to produce?" No, she had heard from him very lately, but having answered the letter, had put it away.

"If we were in the other room," said Emma—"if I had my writing-desk, I am sure I could produce a specimen. I have a note of his.—Do not you remember, Mrs. Weston, employing him to write for you one day?"

"He chose to say he was employed."

"Well, well, I have that note; and can show it after dinner to convince Mr. Knightley."

"Oh! when a gallant young man, like Mr. Frank Churchill," said Mr. Knightley drily, "writes to a fair lady like Miss Woodhouse, he will, of course, put forth his best."

Dinner was on table. Mrs. Elton, before she could be spoken to, was ready; and before Mr. Woodhouse had reached her with his request to be allowed to hand her into the dining-parlour, was saying—

"Must I go first? I really am ashamed of always leading the way."

Jane's solicitude about fetching her own letters had not escaped Emma. She had heard and seen it all; and felt some curiosity to know whether the wet walk of this morning had produced any. She suspected that it *had;* that it would not have been so resolutely encountered but in full expectation of hearing from some one very dear, and that it had not been in vain. She thought there was an air of greater happiness than usual—a glow both of complexion and spirits.

She could have made an enquiry or two, as to the expedition and the expense of the Irish mails;—it was at her tongue's end—but she abstained. She was quite determined not to utter a word that should hurt Jane Fairfax's feelings;

and they followed the other ladies out of the room, arm in arm, with an appearance of good-will highly becoming to the beauty and grace of each.

## Chapter XVII.

When the ladies returned to the drawing-room after dinner, Emma found it hardly possible to prevent their making two distinct parties;—with so much perseverance in judging and behaving ill did Mrs. Elton engross Jane Fairfax and slight herself. She and Mrs. Weston were obliged to be almost always either talking together or silent together. Mrs. Elton left them no choice. If Jane repressed her for a little time, she soon began again; and though much that passed between them was in a half-whisper, especially on Mrs. Elton's side, there was no avoiding a knowledge of their principal subjects:—The post-office—catching cold—fetching letters—and friendship, were long under discussion; and to them succeeded one which must be at least equally unpleasant to Jane,—enquiries whether she had yet heard of any situation likely to suit her, and professions of Mrs. Elton's meditated activity.

"Here is April come!" said she; "I get quite anxious about you. June will soon be here."

"But I have never fixed on June or any other month—merely looked forward to the summer in general."

"But have you really heard of nothing?"

"I have not even made any enquiry; I do not wish to make any yet."

"Oh! my dear, we cannot begin too early; you are not

aware of the difficulty of procuring exactly the desirable thing."

"I not aware!" said Jane, shaking her head; "dear Mrs. Elton, who can have thought of it as I have done?"

"But you have not seen so much of the world as I have. You do not know how many candidates there always are for the *first* situations. I saw a vast deal of that in the neighbourhood round Maple Grove. A cousin of Mr. Suckling, Mrs. Bragge, had such an infinity of applications; every body was anxious to be in her family, for she moves in the first circle. Wax-candles in the school-room! You may imagine how desirable! Of all houses in the kingdom, Mrs. Bragge's is the one I would most wish to see you in."

"Colonel and Mrs. Campbell are to be in town again by midsummer," said Jane. "I must spend some time with them; I am sure they will want it;—afterwards I may probably be glad to dispose of myself. But I would not wish you to take the trouble of making any enquiries at present."

"Trouble! ay, I know your scruples. You are afraid of giving me trouble; but I assure you, my dear Jane, the Campbells can hardly be more interested about you than I am. I shall write to Mrs. Partridge in a day or two, and shall give her a strict charge to be on the look-out for any thing eligible."

"Thank you, but I would rather you did not mention the subject to her; till the time draws nearer, I do not wish to be giving any body trouble."

"But, my dear child, the time is drawing near; here is April, and June, or say even July, is very near, with such business to accomplish before us. Your inexperience really amuses me! A situation such as you deserve, and your friends would require for you, is no every-day occurrence, is not obtained at a moment's notice; indeed, indeed, we must begin enquiring directly."

"Excuse me, ma'am, but this is by no means my intention; I make no enquiry myself, and should be sorry to have any made by my friends. When I am quite determined as to the time, I am not at all afraid of being long unemployed. There are places in town, offices, where enquiry would soon produce something—offices for the sale, not quite of human flesh, but of human intellect."

"Oh! my dear, human flesh! You quite shock me; if you mean a fling at the slave-trade, I assure you Mr. Suckling was always rather a friend to the abolition."

"I did not mean, I was not thinking of the slave-trade," replied Jane; "governess-trade, I assure you, was all that I had in view; widely different certainly as to the guilt of those who carry it on; but as to the greater misery of the victims, I do not know where it lies. But I only mean to say that there are advertising offices, and that by applying to them I should have no doubt of very soon meeting with something that would do."

"Something that would do!" repeated Mrs. Elton. "Ay, *that* may suit your humble ideas of yourself;—I know what a modest creature you are; but it will not satisfy your friends to have you taking up with any thing that may offer, any inferior common-place situation, in a family not moving in a certain circle, or able to command the elegancies of life."

"You are very obliging; but as to all that I am very indifferent; it would be no object to me to be with the rich; my mortifications, I think, would only be the greater; I should suffer more from comparison. A gentleman's family is all that I should condition for."

"I know you, I know you; you would take up with any thing; but I shall be a little more nice, and I am sure the good Campbells will be quite on my side; with your superior talents, you have a right to move in the first circle. Your musical knowledge alone would entitle you to name your own terms, have as many rooms as you like, and mix in the family as much as you chose;—that is—I do not know—if you knew the harp, you might do all that, I am very sure; but you sing as well as play;—yes, I really believe you might, even without the harp, stipulate for what you chose;—and you must and shall be delightfully, honourably and comfortably settled before the Campbells or I have any rest."

"You may well class the delight, the honour, and the comfort of such a situation together," said Jane, "they are pretty sure to be equal; however, I am very serious in not wishing any thing to be attempted at present for me. I am exceedingly obliged to you, Mrs. Elton, I am obliged to any body who feels for me, but I am quite serious in wishing nothing to be done till the summer. For two or three months longer I shall remain where I am, and as I am."

"And I am quite serious too, I assure you," replied Mrs. Elton gaily, "in resolving to be always on the watch, and employing my friends to watch also, that nothing really unexceptionable may pass us."

In this style she ran on; never thoroughly stopped by any thing till Mr. Woodhouse came into the room; her vanity had then a change of object, and Emma heard her saying in the same half-whisper to Jane,—

"Here comes this dear old beau of mine, I protest!—Only think of his gallantry in coming away before the other men!—what a dear creature he is!—I assure you I like him excessively. I admire all that quaint, old-fashioned politeness; it is much more to my taste than modern ease; modern ease often disgusts me. But this good old Mr. Woodhouse, I wish you had heard his gallant speeches to me at dinner. Oh! I assure you I began to think my *cara sposa* would be absolutely jealous. I fancy I am rather a favourite; he took notice of my gown. How do you like it?—Selina's choice—handsome, I think, but I do not know whether it is not over-trimmed; I have the greatest dislike to the idea of being over-trimmed— quite a horror of finery. I must put on a few ornaments *now*, because it is expected of me. A bride, you know, must appear like a bride, but my natural taste is all for simplicity; a simple style of dress is so infinitely preferable to finery. But I am quite in the minority, I believe; few people seem to value simplicity of dress,—show and finery are every thing. I have some notion of putting such a trimming as this to my white and silver poplin. Do you think it will look well?"

The whole party were but just re-assembled in the drawing-room when Mr. Weston made his appearance among them. He had returned to a late dinner, and walked to Hartfield as soon as it was over. He had been too much expected by the best judges, for surprise—but there was great joy. Mr. Woodhouse was almost as glad to see him now, as he would have been sorry to see him before. John Knightley only was in mute astonishment. That a man who might have spent his evening quietly at home after a day of business in London, should set off again, and walk half-a-mile to another man's house, for the sake of being in mixed company till bed-time, of finishing his day in the efforts of civility and the noise of numbers, was a circumstance to strike him deeply. A man who had been in motion since eight o'clock in the morning, and might now have been still,—who had been long talking, and might have been silent,—who had been in more than one crowd, and might have been alone!—Such a man, to quit the tranquillity and independence of his own fire-side, and on the evening of a cold sleety April day rush out again into the world!—Could he, by a touch of his finger, have instantly taken back his wife, there would have been a motive; but his coming would probably prolong rather than break up the party. John Knightley looked at him with amazement, then shrugged his shoulders, and said, "I could not have believed it even of *him*."

Mr. Weston meanwhile, perfectly unsuspicious of the indignation he was exciting, happy and cheerful as usual, and with all the right of being principal talker, which a day spent any where from home confers, was making himself agreeable among the rest; and having satisfied the enquiries of his wife as to his dinner, convincing her that none of all her careful directions to the servants had been forgotten, and spread abroad what public news he had heard, was proceeding to a family communication, which, though principally addressed to Mrs. Weston, he had not the smallest doubt of being highly interesting to every body in the room. He gave her a letter—it was from Frank, and to herself; he had met with it in his way, and had taken the liberty of opening it.

"Read it, read it," said he,—"it will give you pleasure; only a few lines—will not take you long; read it to Emma."

The two ladies looked over it together; and he sat smiling and talking to them the whole time, in a voice a little subdued, but very audible to every body.

"Well, he is coming, you see; good news, I think. Well, what do you say to it? I always told you he would be here again soon, did not I? Anne, my dear, did not I always tell you so, and you would not believe me? In town next week, you see—at the latest, I dare say; for *she* is as impatient as the black gentleman* when any thing is to be done; most likely they will be there to-morrow or Saturday. As to her illness, all nothing, of course. But it is an excellent thing to have Frank among us again, so near as town. They will stay a good while when they do come, and he will be half his time with us. This is precisely what I wanted. Well, pretty good news, is not it? Have you finished it? Has Emma read it all? Put it up, put it up; we will have a good talk about it some other time, but it will not do now. I shall only just mention the circumstance to the others in a common way."

Mrs. Weston was most comfortably pleased on the occasion. Her looks and words had nothing to restrain them. She was happy, she knew she was happy, and knew she ought to be happy. Her congratulations were warm and open; but Emma could not speak so fluently. *She* was a little occupied in weighing her own feelings, and trying to understand the degree of her agitation, which she rather thought was considerable.

Mr. Weston, however, too eager to be very observant, too communicative to want others to talk, was very well satisfied with what she did say, and soon moved away to make the rest

---

*That is, the Devil.

of his friends happy by a partial communication of what the whole room must have overheard already.

It was well that he took every body's joy for granted, or he might not have thought either Mr. Woodhouse or Mr. Knightley particularly delighted. They were the first entitled, after Mrs. Weston and Emma, to be made happy. From them he would have proceeded to Miss Fairfax; but she was so deep in conversation with John Knightley, that it would have been too positive an interruption; and, finding himself close to Mrs. Elton, and her attention disengaged, he necessarily began on the subject with her.

## *Chapter XVIII.*

"I hope I shall soon have the pleasure of introducing my son to you," said Mr. Weston.

Mrs. Elton, very willing to suppose a particular compliment intended her by such a hope, smiled most graciously.

"You have heard of a certain Frank Churchill, I presume," he continued, "and know him to be my son, though he does not bear my name."

"Oh yes, and I shall be very happy in his acquaintance. I am sure Mr. Elton will lose no time in calling on him; and we shall both have great pleasure in seeing him at the Vicarage."

"You are very obliging. Frank will be extremely happy, I am sure. He is to be in town next week, if not sooner. We have notice of it in a letter to-day. I met the letters in my way this morning, and seeing my son's hand, presumed to open it, though it was not directed to me—it was to Mrs. Weston.

She is his principal correspondent, I assure you. I hardly ever get a letter."

"And so you absolutely opened what was directed to her! Oh, Mr. Weston (laughing affectedly), I must protest against that. A most dangerous precedent indeed! I beg you will not let your neighbours follow your example. Upon my word, if this is what I am to expect, we married women must begin to exert ourselves. Oh, Mr. Weston, I could not have believed it of you!"

"Ay, we men are sad fellows. You must take care of yourself, Mrs. Elton. This letter tells us—it is a short letter—written in a hurry, merely to give us notice: it tells us that they are all coming up to town directly, on Mrs. Churchill's account: she has not been well the whole winter, and thinks Enscombe too cold for her; so they are all to move southward without loss of time."

"Indeed! from Yorkshire, I think. Enscombe is in Yorkshire?"

"Yes, they are about 190 miles from London: a considerable journey."

"Yes, upon my word, very considerable. Sixty-five miles farther than from Maple Grove to London. But what is distance, Mr. Weston, to people of large fortune? You would be amazed to hear how my brother, Mr. Suckling, sometimes flies about. You will hardly believe me, but twice in one week he and Mr. Bragge went to London and back again with four horses."

"The evil of the distance from Enscombe," said Mr. Weston, "is, that Mrs. Churchill, *as we understand*, has not been able to leave the sofa for a week together. In Frank's last letter she complained, he said, of being too weak to get into her conservatory without having both his arm and his uncle's. This, you know, speaks a great degree of weakness; but now she is so impatient to be in town, that she means to sleep only two nights on the road—so Frank writes word. Certainly, delicate ladies have very extraordinary constitutions, Mrs. Elton; you must grant me that."

"No, indeed, I shall grant you nothing. I always take the part of my own sex; I do indeed. I give you notice, you will find me a formidable antagonist on that point. I always stand up for women; and I assure you, if you knew how Selina feels with respect to sleeping at an inn, you would not wonder at Mrs. Churchill's making incredible exertions to avoid it. Selina says it is quite horror to her; and I believe I have caught a little of her nicety. She always travels with her own sheets; an excellent precaution. Does Mrs. Churchill do the same?"

"Depend upon it, Mrs. Churchill does every thing that any other fine lady ever did. Mrs. Churchill will not be second to any lady in the land for——"

Mrs. Elton eagerly interposed with,—

"Oh, Mr. Weston, do not mistake me. Selina is no fine lady, I assure you. Do not run away with such an idea."

"Is not she? Then she is no rule for Mrs. Churchill, who is as thorough a fine lady as any body ever beheld."

Mrs. Elton began to think she had been wrong in disclaiming so warmly. It was by no means her object to have it believed that her sister was *not* a fine lady; perhaps there was want of spirit in the pretence of it; and she was considering in what way she had best retract, when Mr. Weston went on.

"Mrs. Churchill is not much in my good graces, as you may suspect; but this is quite between ourselves. She is very fond of Frank, and therefore I would not speak ill of her. Besides, she is out of health now; but *that* indeed, by her own account, she has always been. I would not say so to every body, Mrs. Elton; but I have not much faith in Mrs. Churchill's illness."

"If she is really ill, why not go to Bath, Mr. Weston? To Bath, or to Clifton?"

"She has taken it into her head that Enscombe is too cold for her. The fact is, I suppose, that she is tired of Enscombe. She has now been a longer time stationary there than she ever was before, and she begins to want change. It is a retired place. A fine place, but very retired."

"Ay—like Maple Grove, I dare say. Nothing can stand more retired from the road than Maple Grove. Such an immense plantation all round it! You seem shut out from every thing—in the most complete retirement. And Mrs. Churchill probably has not health or spirits like Selina to enjoy that sort of seclusion. Or, perhaps she may not have resources enough in herself to be qualified for a country life. I always say a woman cannot have too many resources—and I feel very thankful that I have so many myself as to be quite independent of society."

"Frank was here in February for a fortnight."

"So I remember to have heard. He will find an *addition* to the society of Highbury when he comes again; that is, if I may presume to call myself an addition. But perhaps he may never have heard of there being such a creature in the world."

This was too loud a call for a compliment to be passed by, and Mr. Weston, with a very good grace, immediately exclaimed,—

"My dear madam! Nobody but yourself could imagine such a thing possible. Not heard of you! I believe Mrs. Weston's letters lately have been full of very little else than Mrs. Elton."

He had done his duty, and could return to his son.

"When Frank left us," continued he, "it was quite uncertain when we might see him again, which makes this day's news doubly welcome. It has been completely unexpected. That is, *I* always had a strong persuasion he would be here again soon; I was sure something favourable would turn up—but nobody believed me. He and Mrs. Weston were both dreadfully desponding. 'How could he contrive to come? And how could it be supposed that his uncle and aunt would spare him again?' and so forth. I always felt that something would happen in our favour; and so it has, you see. I have observed, Mrs. Elton, in the course of my life, that if things are going untowardly one month, they are sure to mend the next."

"Very true, Mr. Weston, perfectly true. It is just what I used to say to a certain gentleman in company in the days of courtship, when, because things did not go quite right—did not proceed with all the rapidity which suited his feelings—he was apt to be in despair, and exclaim that he was sure at this rate it would be *May* before Hymen's saffron robe[16] would be put on for us! Oh! the pains I have been at to dispel those gloomy ideas, and give him cheerfuller views! The carriage—we had disappointments about the carriage—one morning, I remember, he came to me quite in despair."

She was stopped by a slight fit of coughing, and Mr. Weston instantly seized the opportunity of going on.

"You were mentioning May. May is the very month which Mrs. Churchill is ordered, or has ordered herself, to spend in some warmer place than Enscombe—in short, to spend in London; so that we have the agreeable prospect of frequent visits from Frank the whole spring—precisely the season of the year which one should have chosen for it: days almost at the longest; weather genial and pleasant, always inviting one out, and never too hot for exercise. When he was here before, we made the best of it; but there was a good deal of wet, damp, cheerless weather; there always is in February, you know; and we could not do half that we intended. Now will be the time. This will be complete enjoyment; and I do not know, Mrs. Elton, whether the uncertainty of our meetings, the sort of constant expectation there will be of his coming in to-day or to-morrow, and at any hour, may not be more friendly to happiness than having him actually in the house. I think it is so. I think it is the state of mind which gives most spirit and delight. I hope you will be pleased with my son; but you must not expect a prodigy. He is generally thought a fine young man, but do not expect a prodigy. Mrs. Weston's partiality for him is very great, and, as you may suppose, most gratifying to me. She thinks nobody equal to him."

"And I assure you, Mr. Weston, I have very little doubt that my opinion will be decidedly in his favour. I have heard so much in praise of Mr. Frank Churchill. At the same time it is fair to observe, that I am one of those who always judge for themselves, and are by no means implicitly guided by others. I give you notice, that as I find your son, so I shall judge of him. I am no flatterer."

Mr. Weston was musing.

"I hope," said he presently, "I have not been severe upon poor Mrs. Churchill. If she is ill, I should be sorry to do her injustice; but there are some traits in her character which make it difficult for me to speak of her with the forbearance I could wish. You cannot be ignorant, Mrs. Elton, of my connection with the family, nor of the treatment I have met with; and, between ourselves, the whole blame of it is to be laid to her. She was the instigator. Frank's mother would never have been slighted as she was but for her. Mr. Churchill has pride; but his pride is nothing to his wife's; his is a quiet, indolent, gentlemanlike sort of pride, that would harm nobody, and only make himself a little helpless and tiresome; but her pride is arrogance and insolence. And what inclines one less to bear, she has no fair pretence of family or blood. She was nobody when he married her, barely the daughter of a gentleman; but ever since her being turned into a Churchill, she has out-Churchill'd them all in high and mighty claims: but in herself, I assure you, she is an upstart."

"Only think! well, that must be infinitely provoking! I have quite a horror of upstarts. Maple Grove has given me a thorough disgust to people of that sort; for there is a family in that neighbourhood who are such an annoyance to my brother and sister from the airs they give themselves! Your description of Mrs. Churchill made me think of them directly. People of the name of Tupman, very lately settled there, and encumbered with many low connections, but giving themselves immense airs, and expecting to be on a footing with the old established families. A year and a half is the very utmost that they can have lived at West Hall; and how they got their fortune nobody knows. They came from Birmingham, which is not a place to promise much, you know, Mr. Weston. One has not great hopes from Birmingham. I always say there is something direful in the sound: but nothing more is positively known of the Tupmans, though a good many things, I assure you, are suspected; and yet by their manners they evidently think themselves equal even to my brother, Mr. Suckling, who happens to be one of their nearest neighbours. It is infinitely too bad. Mr. Suckling, who has been eleven years a resident at Maple Grove, and whose father had it before him—I believe, at least—I am almost sure that old Mr. Suckling had completed the purchase before his death."

They were interrupted. Tea was carrying round, and Mr. Weston, having said all that he wanted, soon took the opportunity of walking away.

After tea, Mr. and Mrs. Weston, and Mr. Elton, sat down with Mr. Woodhouse to cards. The remaining five were left to their own powers, and Emma doubted their getting on very well; for Mr. Knightley seemed little disposed for conversation; Mrs. Elton was wanting notice, which nobody had inclination to pay, and she was herself in a worry of spirits which would have made her prefer being silent.

Mr. John Knightley proved more talkative than his brother. He was to leave them early the next day; and he soon began with—

"Well, Emma, I do not believe I have any thing more to say about the boys; but you have your sister's letter, and every thing is down at full length there we may be sure. My charge would be much more concise than her's, and probably not much in the same spirit; all that I have to recommend being comprised in—Do not spoil them, and do not physic* them."

"I rather hope to satisfy you both," said Emma; "for I shall do all in my power to make them happy, which will be enough for Isabella; and happiness must preclude false indulgence and physic."

---

*To treat with medicine.

"And if you find them troublesome, you must send them home again."

"That is very likely. You think so, do not you?"

"I hope I am aware that they may be too noisy for your father; or even may be some incumbrance to you, if your visiting engagements continue to increase as much as they have done lately."

"Increase!"

"Certainly; you must be sensible that the last half-year has made a great difference in your way of life."

"Difference! No, indeed I am not."

"There can be no doubt of your being much more engaged with company than you used to be. Witness this very time. Here am I come down for only one day, and you are engaged with a dinner-party! When did it happen before? or any thing like it? Your neighbourhood is increasing, and you mix more with it. A little while ago, every letter to Isabella brought an account of fresh gaieties; dinners at Mr. Cole's, or balls at the Crown. The difference which Randalls, Randalls alone, makes in your goings-on is very great."

"Yes," said his brother quickly; "it is Randalls that does it all."

"Very well; and as Randalls, I suppose, is not likely to have less influence than heretofore, it strikes me as a possible thing, Emma, that Henry and John may be sometimes in the way. And if they are, I only beg you to send them home."

"No," cried Mr. Knightley; "that need not be the consequence. Let them be sent to Donwell. I shall certainly be at leisure."

"Upon my word," exclaimed Emma, "you amuse me! I should like to know how many of all my numerous engagements take place without your being of the party; and why I am to be supposed in danger of wanting leisure to attend to the little boys. These amazing engagements of mine—what have they been? Dining once with the Coles, and having a ball talked of, which never took place. I can understand you—(nodding at Mr. John Knightley)—your good fortune in meeting with so many of your friends at once here delights you too much to pass unnoticed.—But you, (turning to Mr. Knightley,) who know how very, very seldom I am ever two hours from Hartfield—why you should foresee such a series of dissipation for me, I cannot imagine. And as to my dear little boys, I must say, that if aunt Emma has not time for them, I do not think they would fare much better with uncle Knightley, who is absent from home about five hours where she is absent one; and who, when he is at home, is either reading to himself or settling his accounts."

Mr. Knightley seemed to be trying not to smile; and succeeded without difficulty, upon Mrs. Elton's beginning to talk to him.

END OF THE SECOND VOLUME.

# Volume the Third.

# Chapter I.

A very little quiet reflection was enough to satisfy Emma as to the nature of her agitation on hearing this news of Frank Churchill. She was soon convinced that it was not for herself she was feeling at all apprehensive or embarrassed—it was for him. Her own attachment had really subsided into a mere nothing—it was not worth thinking of; but if he, who had undoubtedly been always so much the most in love of the two, were to be returning with the same warmth of sentiment which he had taken away, it would be very distressing. If a separation of two months should not have cooled him, there were dangers and evils before her: caution for him and for herself would be necessary. She did not mean to have her own affections entangled again, and it would be incumbent on her to avoid any encouragement of his.

She wished she might be able to keep him from an absolute declaration. That would be so very painful a conclusion of their present acquaintance; and yet, she could not help rather anticipating something decisive. She felt as if the spring would not pass without bringing a crisis, an event, a something to alter her present composed and tranquil state.

It was not very long, though rather longer than Mr. Weston had foreseen, before she had the power of forming some opinion of Frank Churchill's feelings. The Enscombe family were not in town quite so soon as had been imagined, but he was at Highbury very soon afterwards. He rode down for a couple of hours; he could not yet do more; but as he came from Randalls immediately to Hartfield, she could then exercise all her quick observation, and speedily determine how he was influenced, and how she must act. They met with the utmost friendliness. There could be no doubt of his great pleasure in seeing her. But she had an almost instant doubt of his caring for her as he had done, of his feeling the same tenderness in the same degree. She watched him well. It was a clear thing he was less in love than he had been. Absence, with the conviction probably of her indifference, had produced this very natural and very desirable effect.

He was in high spirits; as ready to talk and laugh as ever; and seemed delighted to speak of his former visit, and recur to old stories; and he was not without agitation. It was not in his calmness that she read his comparative indifference. He was not calm; his spirits were evidently fluttered; there was restlessness about him. Lively as he was, it seemed a liveliness that did not satisfy himself: but what decided her belief on the subject, was his staying only a quarter of an hour, and hurrying away to make other calls in Highbury. "He had seen a group of old acquaintance in the street as he passed—he had not stopped, he would not stop for more than a word—but he had the vanity to think they would be disappointed if he did not call; and, much as he wished to stay longer at Hartfield, he must hurry off."

She had no doubt as to his being less in love, but neither his agitated spirits nor his hurrying away seemed like a perfect cure; and she was rather inclined to think it implied a dread of her returning power, and a discreet resolution of not trusting himself with her long.

This was the only visit from Frank Churchill in the course of ten days. He was often hoping, intending to come; but was always prevented. His aunt could not bear to have him leave her. Such was his own account at Randalls. If he were quite sincere, if he really tried to come, it was to be inferred that Mrs. Churchill's removal to London had been of no service to the wilful or nervous part of her disorder. That she was really ill was very certain; he had declared himself convinced of it, at Randalls. Though much might be fancy, he could not doubt, when he looked back, that she was in a weaker state of health than she had been half a year ago. He did not believe it to proceed from any thing that care and medicine might not remove, or at least that she might not have many years of existence before her; but he could not be prevailed on, by all his father's doubts, to say that her complaints were merely imaginary, or that she was as strong as ever.

It soon appeared that London was not the place for her. She could not endure its noise. Her nerves were under continual irritation and suffering; and by the ten days' end, her nephew's letter to Randalls communicated a change of plan. They were going to remove immediately to Richmond. Mrs. Churchill had been recommended to the medical skill of an eminent person there, and had otherwise a fancy for the place. A ready-furnished house in a favourite spot was engaged, and much benefit expected from the change.

Emma heard that Frank wrote in the highest spirits of this arrangement, and seemed most fully to appreciate the blessing of having two months before him of such near neighbourhood to many dear friends; for the house was taken for May and June. She was told that now he wrote with the greatest confidence of being often with them, almost as often as he could even wish.

Emma saw how Mr. Weston understood these joyous prospects. He was considering her as the source of all the happiness they offered. She hoped it was not so. Two months must bring it to proof.

Mr. Weston's own happiness was indisputable. He was quite delighted. It was the very circumstance he could have wished for. Now, it would be really having Frank in their neighbourhood. What were nine miles to a young man?—An hour's ride. He would be always coming over. The difference in that respect of Richmond and London, was enough to make the whole difference of seeing him always and seeing him never. Sixteen miles—nay, eighteen—it must be full eighteen to Manchester Street—was a serious obstacle. Were he ever able to get away, the day would be spent in coming and returning. There was no comfort in having him in London; he might as well be at Enscombe; but Richmond was the very distance for easy intercourse. Better than nearer!

One good thing was immediately brought to a certainty by this removal,—the ball at the Crown. It had not been forgotten before; but it had been soon acknowledged vain to attempt to fix a day. Now, however, it was absolutely to be; every preparation was resumed; and very soon after the Churchills had removed to Richmond, a few lines from Frank, to say that his aunt felt already much better for the change, and that he had no doubt of being able to join them for twenty-four hours at any given time, induced them to name as early a day as possible.

Mr. Weston's ball was to be a real thing. A very few to-morrows stood between the young people of Highbury and happiness.

Mr. Woodhouse was resigned. The time of year lightened the evil to him. May was better for every thing than February. Mrs. Bates was engaged to spend the evening at Hartfield; James had due notice, and he sanguinely hoped that neither dear little Henry nor dear little John would have any thing the matter with them while dear Emma were gone.

## Chapter II.

No misfortune occurred, again to prevent the ball. The day approached, the day arrived; and, after a morning of some anxious watching, Frank Churchill, in all the certainty of his own self, reached Randalls before dinner, and every thing was safe.

No second meeting had there yet been between him and Emma. The room at the Crown was to witness it; but it would be better than a common meeting in a crowd. Mr. Weston had been so very earnest in his entreaties for her early attendance, for her arriving there as soon as possible after themselves, for the purpose of taking her opinion as to the propriety and comfort of the rooms before any other person came, that she could not refuse him, and must therefore spend some quiet interval in the young man's company. She was to convey Harriet, and they drove to the Crown in good time, the Randalls party just sufficiently before them.

Frank Churchill seemed to have been on the watch; and though he did not say much, his eyes declared that he meant to have a delightful evening. They all walked about together, to see that every thing was as it should be; and within a few minutes were joined by the contents of another carriage, which Emma could not hear the sound of at first, without great surprise. "So unreasonably early!" she was going to exclaim; but she presently found that it was a family of old friends, who were coming, like herself, by particular desire, to help Mr. Weston's judgment; and they were so very closely followed by another carriage of cousins, who had been entreated to come early with the same distinguishing earnestness, on the same errand, that it seemed as if half the company might soon be collected together for the purpose of preparatory inspection.

Emma perceived that her taste was not the only taste on which Mr. Weston depended, and felt, that to be the favourite and intimate of a man who had so many intimates and confidants, was not the very first distinction in the scale of vanity. She liked his open manners, but a little less of open-heartedness would have made him a higher character.—General benevolence, but not general friendship, made a man what he ought to be.—She could fancy such a man.

The whole party walked about, and looked, and praised again; and then, having nothing else to do, formed a sort of half circle round the fire, to observe in their various modes, till other subjects were started, that, though *May*, a fire in the evening was still very pleasant.

Emma found, that it was not Mr. Weston's fault, that the number of privy counsellors was not yet larger. They had stopped at Mrs. Bates's door to offer the use of their carriage, but the aunt and niece were to be brought by the Eltons.

Frank was standing by her, but not steadily; there was a restlessness, which showed a mind not at ease. He was looking about, he was going to the door, he was watching for the sound of other carriages,—impatient to begin, or afraid of being always near her.

Mrs. Elton was spoken of. "I think she must be here soon," said he. "I have a great curiosity to see Mrs. Elton, I have heard so much of her. It cannot be long, I think, before she comes."

A carriage was heard. He was on the move immediately; but coming back, said,—

"I am forgetting that I am not acquainted with her. I have never seen either Mr. or Mrs. Elton. I have no business to put myself forward."

Mr. and Mrs. Elton appeared; and all the smiles and the proprieties passed.

"But Miss Bates and Miss Fairfax!" said Mr. Weston, looking about. "We thought you were to bring them."

The mistake had been slight. The carriage was sent for them now. Emma longed to know what Frank's first opinion of Mrs. Elton might be; how he was affected by the studied elegance of her dress, and her smiles of graciousness. He was immediately qualifying himself to form an opinion, by giving her very proper attention, after the introduction had passed.

In a few minutes the carriage returned.—Somebody talked of rain.—"I will see that there are umbrellas, sir," said Frank to his father: "Miss Bates must not be forgotten:" and away he went. Mr. Weston was following; but Mrs. Elton detained him, to gratify him by her opinion of his son; and so briskly did she begin, that the young man himself, though by no means moving slowly, could hardly be out of hearing.

"A very fine young man, indeed, Mr. Weston. You know I candidly told you I should form my own opinion; and I am happy to say that I am extremely pleased with him. You may believe me. I never compliment. I think him a very handsome young man, and his manners are precisely what I like and approve,—so truly the gentleman, without the least conceit or puppyism. You must know I have a vast dislike to puppies—quite a horror of them. They were never tolerated at Maple Grove. Neither Mr. Suckling nor me had ever any patience with them; and we used sometimes to say very cutting things. Selina, who is mild almost to a fault, bore with them much better."

While she talked of his son, Mr. Weston's attention was chained; but when she got to Maple Grove, he could recollect that there were ladies just arriving to be attended to, and with happy smiles must hurry away.

Mrs. Elton turned to Mrs. Weston. "I have no doubt of its being our carriage with Miss Bates and Jane. Our coachman and horses are so extremely expeditious! I believe we drive faster than any body. What a pleasure it is to send one's carriage for a friend! I understand you were so kind as to offer, but another time it will be quite unnecessary. You may be very sure I shall always take care of *them*."

Miss Bates and Miss Fairfax, escorted by the two gentlemen, walked into the room; and Mrs. Elton seemed to think it as much her duty as Mrs. Weston's to receive them. Her gestures and movements might be understood by any one who looked on like Emma; but her words, every body's words, were soon lost under the incessant flow of Miss Bates, who came in talking, and had not finished her speech under many minutes after her being admitted into the circle at the fire. As the door opened she was heard,—

"So very obliging of you!—No rain at all. Nothing to signify. I do not care for myself. Quite thick shoes. And Jane declares—Well! (as soon as she was within the door), well! This is brilliant indeed! This is admirable! Excellently contrived, upon my word. Nothing wanting. Could not have imagined it. So well lighted up! Jane, Jane, look! Did you ever see any thing? Oh! Mr. Weston, you must really have had Aladdin's lamp. Good Mrs. Stokes would not know her own room again. I saw her as I came in; she was standing in the entrance. 'Oh! Mrs. Stokes,' said I—but, I had not time for more." She was now met by Mrs. Weston. "Very well, I thank you, ma'am. I hope you are quite well. Very happy to hear it. So afraid you might have a headache! seeing you pass by so often, and knowing how much trouble you must have. Delighted to hear it indeed.—Ah! dear Mrs. Elton, so obliged to you for the carriage; excellent time; Jane and I quite ready. Did not keep the horses a moment. Most comfortable carriage. Oh! and I am sure our thanks are due to you, Mrs. Weston, on that score. Mrs. Elton had most kindly sent Jane a note, or we should have been. But two such offers in one day! Never were such neighbours. I said to my mother, 'Upon my word, ma'am.' Thank you, my mother is remarkably well. Gone to Mr. Woodhouse's. I made her take her shawl,—for the evenings are not warm,—her large new shawl, Mrs. Dixon's wedding present. So kind of her to think of my mother! Bought at Weymouth, you know; Mr. Dixon's choice. There were three others, Jane says, which they hesitated about some time. Colonel Campbell rather preferred an olive.—My dear Jane, are you sure you did not wet your feet? It was but a drop or two, but I am so afraid: but Mr. Frank Churchill was so extremely—and there was a mat to step upon. I shall never forget his extreme politeness. Oh! Mr. Frank Churchill, I must tell you my mother's spectacles have never been in fault since; the rivet never came out again. My mother often talks of your good-nature: does not she Jane? Do not we often talk of Mr. Frank Churchill? Ah! here's Miss Woodhouse. Dear Miss Woodhouse, how do you do? Very well, I thank you, quite well. This is meeting quite in fairy land. Such a transformation! Must not compliment, I know (eyeing Emma most complacently)—that would be

rude; but upon my word, Miss Woodhouse, you do look—
how do you like Jane's hair? You are a judge. She did it all
herself. Quite wonderful how she does her hair! No hair-
dresser from London, I think, could.—Ah! Dr. Hughes, I declare—and Mrs. Hughes. Must go and speak to Dr. and Mrs.
Hughes for a moment. How do you do? How do you do?
Very well I thank you. This is delightful, is not it? Where's
dear Mr. Richard? Oh! there he is. Don't disturb him. Much
better employed talking to the young ladies. How do you do,
Mr. Richard? I saw you the other day as you rode through the
town. Mrs. Otway, I protest! and good Mr. Otway, and Miss
Otway, and Miss Caroline. Such a host of friends! and Mr.
George and Mr. Arthur! How do you do? How do you all do?
Quite well, I am much obliged to you. Never better. Don't I
hear another carriage? Who can this be?—very likely the
worthy Coles. Upon my word, this is charming, to be standing about among such friends! And such a noble fire! I am
quite roasted. No coffee, I thank you, for me; never take coffee. A little tea, if you please, sir, by-and-by; no hurry. Oh!
here it comes. Every thing so good!"

Frank Churchill returned to his station by Emma; and as
soon as Miss Bates was quiet, she found herself necessarily
overhearing the discourse of Mrs. Elton and Miss Fairfax,
who were standing a little way behind her. He was thoughtful. Whether he were overhearing too, she could not determine. After a good many compliments to Jane on her dress
and look,—compliments very quietly and properly taken,—
Mrs. Elton was evidently wanting to be complimented herself—and it was, "How do you like my gown?—How do you
like my trimming?—How has Wright done my hair?" with
many other relative questions, all answered with patient politeness. Mrs. Elton then said,—

"Nobody can think less of dress in general than I do: but
upon such an occasion as this, when every body's eyes are so
much upon me, and in compliment to the Westons, who I
have no doubt are giving this ball chiefly to do me honour,—
I would not wish to be inferior to others: and I see very few

pearls in the room except mine.—So, Frank Churchill is a capital dancer, I understand. We shall see if our styles suit.— A fine young man certainly is Frank Churchill. I like him very well."

At this moment Frank began talking so vigorously, that Emma could not but imagine he had overheard his own praises, and did not want to hear more;—and the voices of the ladies were drowned for awhile, till another suspension brought Mrs. Elton's tones again distinctly forward. Mr. Elton had just joined them, and his wife was exclaiming,—

"Oh! you have found us out at last, have you, in our seclusion?—I was this moment telling Jane, I thought you would begin to be impatient for tidings of us."

"Jane!" repeated Frank Churchill, with a look of surprise and displeasure. "That is easy; but Miss Fairfax does not disapprove it, I suppose."

"How do you like Mrs. Elton?" said Emma, in a whisper.

"Not at all."

"You are ungrateful."

"Ungrateful!—What do you mean?" Then changing from a frown to a smile,—"No, do not tell me,—I do not want to know what you mean. Where is my father? When are we to begin dancing?"

Emma could hardly understand him: he seemed in an odd humour. He walked off to find his father, but was quickly back again with both Mr. and Mrs. Weston. He had met with them in a little perplexity, which must be laid before Emma. It had just occurred to Mrs. Weston that Mrs. Elton must be asked to begin the ball; that she would expect it; which interfered with all their wishes of giving Emma that distinction. Emma heard the sad truth with fortitude.

"And what are we to do for a proper partner for her?" said Mr. Weston. "She will think Frank ought to ask her."

Frank turned instantly to Emma, to claim her former promise; and boasted himself an engaged man, which his father looked his most perfect approbation of—and it then appeared that Mrs. Weston was wanting *him* to dance with Mrs. Elton himself, and that their business was to help to persuade him into it, which was done pretty soon. Mr. Weston and Mrs. Elton led the way; Mr. Frank Churchill and Miss Woodhouse followed. Emma must submit to stand second to Mrs. Elton, though she had always considered the ball as peculiarly for her. It was almost enough to make her think of marrying.

Mrs. Elton had undoubtedly the advantage, at this time, in vanity completely gratified; for though she had intended to begin with Frank Churchill, she could not lose by the change. Mr. Weston might be his son's superior. In spite of this little rub, however, Emma was smiling with enjoyment, delighted to see the respectable length of the set as it was forming, and to feel that she had so many hours of unusual festivity before her. She was more disturbed by Mr. Knightley's not dancing, than by any thing else. There he was, among the standers-by, where he ought not to be; he ought to be dancing,—not classing himself with the husbands, and fathers, and whist-players, who were pretending to feel an interest in the dance till their rubbers were made up,—so young as he looked! He could not have appeared to greater advantage perhaps any where, than where he had placed himself. His tall, firm, upright figure, among the bulky forms and stooping shoulders of the elderly men, was such as Emma felt must draw every body's eyes; and, excepting her own partner, there was not one among the whole row of young men who could be compared with him. He moved a few steps nearer, and those few steps were enough to prove in how gentlemanlike a manner, with what natural grace, he must have danced, would he but take the trouble. Whenever she caught his eye, she forced him to smile; but in general he was looking grave. She wished he could love a ball-room better, and could like Frank Churchill better. He seemed often observing her. She must not flatter herself that he thought of her dancing; but if he were criticising her behaviour, she did not feel afraid.

There was nothing like flirtation between her and her partner. They seemed more like cheerful easy friends, than
lovers. That Frank Churchill thought less of her than he
had done, was indubitable.

The ball proceeded pleasantly. The anxious cares, the incessant attentions of Mrs. Weston, were not thrown away.
Every body seemed happy; and the praise of being a delightful ball which is seldom bestowed till after a ball has
ceased to be, was repeatedly given in the very beginning of
the existence of this. Of very important, very recordable
events, it was not more productive than such meetings usually are. There was one, however, which Emma thought
something of.—The two last dances before supper were
begun, and Harriet had no partner;—the only young lady
sitting down;—and so equal had been hitherto the number
of dancers, that how there could be any one disengaged was
the wonder. But Emma's wonder lessened soon afterwards,
on seeing Mr. Elton sauntering about. He would not ask Harriet to dance if it were possible to be avoided: she was sure
he would not—and she was expecting him every moment to
escape into the card-room.

Escape, however, was not his plan. He came to the part of
the room where the sitters-by were collected, spoke to some,
and walked about in front of them, as if to show his liberty,
and his resolution of maintaining it. He did not omit being
sometimes directly before Miss Smith, or speaking to those
who were close to her. Emma saw it. She was not yet dancing;
she was working her way up from the bottom, and had therefore leisure to look around, and by only turning her head a
little she saw it all. When she was half way up the set, the
whole group were exactly behind her, and she would no
longer allow her eyes to watch; but Mr. Elton was so near,
that she heard every syllable of a dialogue which just then
took place between him and Mrs. Weston; and she perceived
that his wife, who was standing immediately above her, was
not only listening also, but even encouraging him by signifi-
cant glances. The kind-hearted, gentle Mrs. Weston had left

her seat to join him and say, "Do not you dance, Mr. Elton?" to which his prompt reply was, "Most readily, Mrs. Weston, if you will dance with me."

"Me!—oh! no—I would get you a better partner than myself. I am no dancer."

"If Mrs. Gilbert wishes to dance," said he, "I shall have great pleasure, I am sure; for, though beginning to feel myself rather an old married man, and that my dancing days are over, it would give me very great pleasure at any time to stand up with an old friend like Mrs. Gilbert."

"Mrs. Gilbert does not mean to dance, but there is a young lady disengaged whom I should be very glad to see dancing—Miss Smith."

"Miss Smith—oh!—I had not observed. You are extremely obliging—and if I were not an old married man,—but my dancing days are over, Mrs. Weston. You will excuse me. Any thing else I should be most happy to do, at your command—but my dancing days are over."

Mrs. Weston said no more; and Emma could imagine with what surprise and mortification she must be returning to her seat. This was Mr. Elton! the amiable, obliging, gentle Mr. Elton. She looked round for a moment; he had joined Mr. Knightley at a little distance, and was arranging himself for settled conversation, while smiles of high glee passed between him and his wife.

She would not look again. Her heart was in a glow, and she feared her face might be as hot.

In another moment a happier sight caught her—Mr. Knightley leading Harriet to the set!—Never had she been more surprised, seldom more delighted, than at that instant. She was all pleasure and gratitude, both for Harriet and herself, and longed to be thanking him; and though too distant for speech, her countenance said much, as soon as she could catch his eye again.

His dancing proved to be just what she had believed it, extremely good; and Harriet would have seemed almost too lucky, if it had not been for the cruel state of things before,

and for the very complete enjoyment and very high sense of
the distinction which her happy features announced. It was
not thrown away on her; she bounded higher than ever, flew
farther down the middle, and was in a continual course of
smiles.

Mr. Elton had retreated into the card-room, looking
(Emma trusted) very foolish. She did not think he was quite
so hardened as his wife, though growing very like her: *she*
spoke some of her feelings, by observing audibly to her partner,—

"Knightley has taken pity on poor little Miss Smith!—Very
good-natured, I declare."

Supper was announced. The move began; and Miss Bates
might be heard from that moment without interruption, till
her being seated at table and taking up her spoon.

"Jane, Jane, my dear Jane, where are you? Here is your
tippet. Mrs. Weston begs you to put on your tippet. She says
she is afraid there will be draughts in the passage, though
every thing has been done—one door nailed up—quanti-
ties of matting—my dear Jane, indeed you must. Mr.
Churchill, oh! you are too obliging!—How well you put it
on!—so gratified! Excellent dancing indeed!—Yes, my dear,
I ran home, as I said I should, to help grandmamma to bed,
and got back again, and nobody missed me. I set off without
saying a word, just as I told you. Grandmamma was quite
well, had a charming evening with Mr. Woodhouse, a vast
deal of chat, and backgammon. Tea was made down stairs,
biscuits and baked apples and wine before she came away:
amazing luck in some of her throws: and she enquired a
great deal about you, how you were amused, and who were
your partners. 'Oh!' said I, 'I shall not forestall Jane; I left
her dancing with Mr. George Otway; she will love to tell you
all about it herself to-morrow: her first partner was Mr.
Elton; I do not know who will ask her next, perhaps Mr.
William Cox.' My dear sir, you are too obliging. Is there nobody you would not rather?—I am not helpless. Sir, you are
most kind. Upon my word, Jane on one arm, and me on the

other! Stop, stop, let us stand a little back, Mrs. Elton is
going; dear Mrs. Elton, how elegant she looks—beautiful
lace!—Now we all follow in her train. Quite the queen of
the evening!—Well, here we are at the passage. Two steps,
Jane, take care of the two steps. Oh! no, there is but one.
Well, I was persuaded there were two. How very odd! I was
convinced there were two, and there is but one. I never saw
any thing equal to the comfort and style—candles every-
where. I was telling you of your grandmamma, Jane,—there
was a little disappointment. The baked apples and biscuits,
excellent in their way, you know; but there was a delicate
fricassee of sweetbread and some asparagus brought in at
first, and good Mr. Woodhouse, not thinking the asparagus
quite boiled enough, sent it all out again. Now there is nothing grandmamma loves better than sweetbread and asparagus—so she was rather disappointed; but we agreed we
would not speak of it to any body, for fear of its getting
round to dear Miss Woodhouse, who would be so very much
concerned!—Well, this is brilliant! I am all amazement!—
could not have supposed any thing!—such elegance and
profusion! I have seen nothing like it since. Well, where
shall we sit? Where shall we sit? Any where, so that Jane is
not in a draught. Where *I* sit is of no consequence. Oh! do
you recommend this side? Well, I am sure, Mr. Churchill—
only it seems too good—but just as you please. What you direct in this house cannot be wrong. Dear Jane, how shall we
ever recollect half the dishes for grandmamma. Soup too!
Bless me! I should not be helped so soon, but it smells most
excellent, and I cannot help beginning."

Emma had no opportunity of speaking to Mr. Knightley
till after supper; but, when they were all in the ball-room
again, her eyes invited him irresistibly to come to her and be
thanked. He was warm in his reprobation of Mr. Elton's conduct; it had been unpardonable rudeness; and Mrs. Elton's
looks also received the due share of censure.

"They aimed at wounding more than Harriet," said he.
"Emma, why is it that they are your enemies?"

He looked with smiling penetration; and, on receiving no answer, added, "*She* ought not to be angry with you, I suspect, whatever he may be.—To that surmise, you say nothing, of course: but confess, Emma, that you did want him to marry Harriet."

"I did," replied Emma, "and they cannot forgive me."

He shook his head; but there was a smile of indulgence with it, and he only said,—

"I shall not scold you. I leave you to your own reflections."

"Can you trust me with such flatterers? Does my vain spirit ever tell me I am wrong?"

"Not your vain spirit, but your serious spirit. If one leads you wrong, I am sure the other tells you of it."

"I do own myself to have been completely mistaken in Mr. Elton. There is a littleness about him which you discovered, and which I did not: and I was fully convinced of his being in love with Harriet. It was through a series of strange blunders!"

"And, in return for your acknowledging so much, I will do you the justice to say, that you would have chosen for him better than he has chosen for himself. Harriet Smith has some first-rate qualities, which Mrs. Elton is totally without. An unpretending, single-minded, artless girl—infinitely to be preferred by any man of sense and taste to such a woman as Mrs. Elton. I found Harriet more conversable than I expected."

Emma was extremely gratified. They were interrupted by the bustle of Mr. Weston calling on every body to begin dancing again.

"Come, Miss Woodhouse, Miss Otway, Miss Fairfax, what are you all doing? Come, Emma, set your companions the example. Every body is lazy! Every body is asleep!"

"I am ready," said Emma, "whenever I am wanted."

"Whom are you going to dance with?" asked Mr. Knightley.

She hesitated a moment, and then replied, "With you, if you will ask me."

"Will you," said he, offering his hand.

"Indeed I will. You have shown that you can dance, and you know we are not really so much brother and sister as to make it at all improper."

"Brother and sister!—no, indeed."

# Chapter III.

This little explanation with Mr. Knightley gave Emma considerable pleasure. It was one of the agreeable recollections of the ball, which she walked about the lawn the next morning to enjoy. She was extremely glad that they had come to so good an understanding respecting the Eltons, and that their opinions of both husband and wife were so much alike; and his praise of Harriet, his concession in her favour, was peculiarly gratifying. The impertinence of the Eltons, which for a few minutes had threatened to ruin the rest of her evening, had been the occasion of some of its highest satisfactions; and she looked forward to another happy result—the cure of Harriet's infatuation. From Harriet's manner of speaking of the circumstance before they quitted the ball-room, she had strong hopes. It seemed as if her eyes were suddenly opened, and she were enabled to see that Mr. Elton was not the superior creature she had believed him. The fever was over, and Emma could harbour little fear of the pulse being quickened again by injurious courtesy. She depended on the evil feelings of the Eltons for supplying all the discipline of pointed neglect that could be further requisite. Harriet rational, Frank Churchill not too much in love, and

Mr. Knightley not wanting to quarrel with her; how very happy a summer must be before her!

She was not to see Frank Churchill this morning. He had told her, that he could not allow himself the pleasure of stopping at Hartfield, as he was to be at home by the middle of the day. She did not regret it.

Having arranged all these matters, looked them through, and put them all to rights, she was just turning to the house, with spirits freshened up for the demands of the two little boys, as well as of their grandpapa, when the great iron sweep-gate opened, and two persons entered whom she had never less expected to see together—Frank Churchill, with Harriet leaning on his arm—actually Harriet! A moment sufficed to convince her that something extraordinary had happened. Harriet looked white and frightened, and he was trying to cheer her. The iron gates and the front door were not twenty yards asunder;—they were all three soon in the hall; and Harriet immediately sinking into a chair, fainted away.

A young lady who faints must be recovered; questions must be answered, and surprises be explained. Such events are very interesting; but the suspense of them cannot last long. A few minutes made Emma acquainted with the whole.

Miss Smith, and Miss Bickerton, another parlour boarder at Mrs. Goddard's, who had been also at the ball, had walked out together, and taken a road—the Richmond road, which, though apparently public enough for safety, had led them into alarm. About half a mile beyond Highbury, making a sudden turn, and deeply shaded by elms on each side, it became for a considerable stretch very retired; and when the young ladies had advanced some way into it, they had suddenly perceived, at a small distance before them, on a broader patch of greensward by the side, a party of gipsies. A child on the watch came towards them to beg; and Miss Bickerton, excessively frightened, gave a great scream, and calling on Harriet to follow her, ran up a steep bank, cleared a slight hedge at the top, and made the best of her way by a short cut back to Highbury. But poor Harriet could not follow. She had suffered very much from cramp after dancing, and her first attempt to mount the bank brought on such a return of it as made her absolutely powerless; and in this state, and exceedingly terrified, she had been obliged to remain.

How the trampers might have behaved, had the young ladies been more courageous, must be doubtful; but such an invitation for attack could not be resisted; and Harriet was soon assailed by half a dozen children, headed by a stout woman and a great boy, all clamorous, and impertinent in look, though not absolutely in word. More and more frightened, she immediately promised them money, and taking out her purse, gave them a shilling, and begged them not to want more, or to use her ill. She was then able to walk, though but slowly, and was moving away—but her terror and her purse were too tempting; and she was followed, or rather surrounded, by the whole gang, demanding more.

In this state Frank Churchill had found her, she trembling and conditioning, they loud and insolent. By a most fortunate chance, his leaving Highbury had been delayed so as to bring him to her assistance at this critical moment. The pleasantness of the morning had induced him to walk forward, and leave his horses to meet him by another road, a mile or two beyond Highbury; and happening to have borrowed a pair of scissors the night before of Miss Bates, and to have forgotten to restore them, he had been obliged to stop at her door, and go in for a few minutes: he was therefore later than he had intended; and being on foot, was unseen by the whole party till almost close to them. The terror which the woman and boy had been creating in Harriet was then their own portion. He had left them completely frightened; and Harriet eagerly clinging to him, and hardly able to speak, had just strength enough to reach Hartfield, before her spirits were quite overcome. It was his idea to bring her to Hartfield; he had thought of no other place.

This was the amount of the whole story,—of his communication and of Harriet's, as soon as she had recovered her senses and speech. He dared not stay longer than to see her well; these several delays left him not another minute to lose; and Emma engaging to give assurance of her safety to Mrs. Goddard, and notice of there being such a set of people in the neighbourhood to Mr. Knightley, he set off, with all the grateful blessings that she could utter for her friend and herself.

Such an adventure as this,—a fine young man and a lovely young woman thrown together in such a way,—could hardly fail of suggesting certain ideas to the coldest heart and the steadiest brain. So Emma thought, at least. Could a linguist, could a grammarian, could even a mathematician have seen what she did, have witnessed their appearance together, and heard their history of it, without feeling that circumstances had been at work to make them peculiarly interesting to each other? How much more must an imaginist, like herself, be on fire with speculation and foresight!— especially with such a ground-work of anticipation as her mind had already made.

It was a very extraordinary thing! Nothing of the sort had ever occurred before to any young ladies in the place, within her memory; no rencontre, no alarm of the kind: and now it had happened to the very person, and at the very hour, when the other very person was chancing to pass by to rescue her! It certainly was very extraordinary! And knowing, as she did, the favourable state of mind of each at this period, it struck her the more. He was wishing to get the better of his attachment to herself, she just recovering from her mania for Mr. Elton. It seemed as if every thing united to promise the most interesting consequences. It was not possible that the occurrence should not be strongly recommending each to the other.

In the few minutes' conversation which she had yet had

with him, while Harriet had been partially insensible, he had spoken of her terror, her *naïveté*, her fervor as she seized and clung to his arm, with a sensibility amused and delighted; and just at last, after Harriet's own account had been given, he had expressed his indignation at the abominable folly of Miss Bickerton in the warmest terms. Every thing was to take its natural course, however, neither impelled nor assisted. She would not stir a step, nor drop a hint. No, she had had enough of interference. There could be no harm in a scheme, a mere passive scheme. It was no more than a wish. Beyond it she would on no account proceed.

Emma's first resolution was to keep her father from the knowledge of what had passed, aware of the anxiety and alarm it would occasion: but she soon felt that concealment must be impossible. Within half an hour it was known all over Highbury. It was the very event to engage those who talk most, the young and the low; and all the youth and servants in the place were soon in the happiness of frightful news. The last night's ball seemed lost in the gipsies. Poor Mr. Woodhouse trembled as he sat, and, as Emma had foreseen, would scarcely be satisfied without their promising never to go beyond the shrubbery again. It was some comfort to him that many enquiries after himself and Miss Woodhouse (for his neighbours knew that he loved to be enquired after), as well as Miss Smith, were coming in during the rest of the day; and he had the pleasure of returning for answer, that they were all very indifferent; which, though not exactly true, for she was perfectly well, and Harriet not much otherwise, Emma would not interfere with. She had an unhappy state of health in general for the child of such a man, for she hardly knew what indisposition was; and if he did not invent illnesses for her, she could make no figure in a message.

The gipsies did not wait for the operations of justice; they took themselves off in a hurry. The young ladies of Highbury might have walked again in safety before their panic began, and the whole history dwindled soon into a matter of little importance but to Emma and her nephews: in her imagination it maintained its ground; and Henry and John were still asking every day for the story of Harriet and the gipsies, and still tenaciously setting her right if she varied in the slightest particular from the original recital.

## Chapter IV.

A very few days had passed after this adventure, when Harriet came one morning to Emma with a small parcel in her hand, and after sitting down and hesitating, thus began:—

"Miss Woodhouse—if you are at leisure, I have something that I should like to tell you; a sort of confession to make—and then, you know, it will be over."

Emma was a good deal surprised; but begged her to speak. There was a seriousness in Harriet's manner which prepared her, quite as much as her words, for something more than ordinary.

"It is my duty, and I am sure it is my wish," she continued, "to have no reserves with you on this subject. As I am, happily, quite an altered creature in *one respect*, it is very fit that you should have the satisfaction of knowing it. I do not want to say more than is necessary; I am too much ashamed of having given way as I have done, and I dare say you understand me."

"Yes," said Emma, "I hope I do."

"How I could so long a time be fancying myself——" cried Harriet, warmly. "It seems like madness! I can see nothing at all extraordinary in him now. I do not care whether I meet him or not, except that, of the two, I had rather not see him; and, indeed, I would go any distance round to avoid him; but I do not envy his wife in the least: I neither admire her nor envy her, as I have done. She is very charming, I dare say, and all that; but I think her very ill-tempered and disagreeable: I shall never forget her look the other night. However, I assure you, Miss Woodhouse, I wish her no evil. No; let them be ever so happy together, it will not give me another moment's pang; and, to convince you that I have been speaking truth, I am now going to destroy—what I ought to have destroyed long ago—what I ought never to have kept: I know that very well (blushing as she spoke). However, now I will destroy it all; and it is my particular wish to do it in your presence, that you may see how rational I am grown. Cannot you guess what this parcel holds?" said she, with a conscious look.

"Not the least in the world. Did he ever give you any thing?"

"No—I cannot call them gifts; but they are things that I have valued very much."

She held the parcel towards her, and Emma read the words "Most precious treasures" on the top. Her curiosity was greatly excited. Harriet unfolded the parcel, and she looked on with impatience. Within abundance of silver paper was a pretty little Tunbridge-ware box,[17] which Harriet opened: it was well lined with the softest cotton; but, excepting the cotton, Emma saw only a small piece of court-plaister.*

"Now," said Harriet, "you *must* recollect."

"No, indeed, I do not."

"Dear me! I should not have thought it possible you could forget what passed in this very room about court-plaister, one of the very last times we ever met in it. It was but a very few days before I had my sore throat—just before Mr. and Mrs. John Knightley came; I think the very evening. Do not

---

*Silk-based skin covering applied to minor cuts or bruises; an early form of what today we call an adhesive bandage.

you remember his cutting his finger with your new penknife, and your recommending court-plaister? But, as you had none about you, and knew I had, you desired me to supply him; and so I took mine out, and cut him a piece: but it was a great deal too large, and he cut it smaller, and kept playing some time with what was left before he gave it back to me. And so then, in my nonsense, I could not help making a treasure of it; so I put it by, never to be used, and looked at it now and then as a great treat."

"My dearest Harriet!" cried Emma, putting her hand before her face, and jumping up, "you make me more ashamed of myself than I can bear. Remember it? Ay, I remember it all now; all, except your saving this relic: I knew nothing of that till this moment,—but the cutting the finger, and my recommending court-plaister, and saying I had none about me.— Oh! my sins, my sins!—And I had plenty all the while in my pocket! One of my senseless tricks. I deserve to be under a continual blush all the rest of my life.—Well (sitting down again), go on: what else?"

"And had you really some at hand yourself? I am sure I never suspected it, you did it so naturally."

"And so you actually put this piece of court-plaister by for his sake," said Emma, recovering from her state of shame and feeling, divided between wonder and amusement; and secretly she added to herself, "Lord bless me! when should I ever have thought of putting by in cotton a piece of court-plaister that Frank Churchill had been pulling about! I never was equal to this."

"Here," resumed Harriet, turning to her box again, "here is something still more valuable,—I mean that *has been* more valuable,—because this is what did really once belong to him, which the court-plaister never did."

Emma was quite eager to see this superior treasure. It was the end of an old pencil, the part without any lead.

"This was really his," said Harriet. "Do not you remember one morning?—no, I dare say you do not. But one morning—I forget exactly the day,—but perhaps it was the Tuesday or Wednesday before *that evening*, he wanted to make a memorandum in his pocket-book; it was about spruce beer. Mr. Knightley had been telling him something about brewing spruce beer, and he wanted to put it down; but when he took out his pencil, there was so little lead that he soon cut it all away, and it would not do, so you lent him another, and this was left upon the table as good for nothing. But I kept my eye on it; and, as soon as I dared, caught it up, and never parted with it again from that moment."

"I do remember it," cried Emma; "I perfectly remember it. Talking about spruce beer. Oh! yes. Mr. Knightley and I both saying we liked it, and Mr. Elton's seeming resolved to learn to like it too. I perfectly remember it.—Stop; Mr. Knightley was standing just here, was not he? I have an idea he was standing just here."

"Ah! I do not know. I cannot recollect. It is very odd, but I cannot recollect. Mr. Elton was sitting here, I remember, much about where I am now."

"Well, go on."

"Oh! that's all. I have nothing more to show you, or to say, except that I am now going to throw them both behind the fire, and I wish you to see me do it."

"My poor dear Harriet! and have you actually found happiness in treasuring up these things?"

"Yes, simpleton as I was!—but I am quite ashamed of it now, and wish I could forget as easily as I can burn them. It was very wrong of me, you know, to keep any remembrances after he was married. I knew it was——but had not resolution enough to part with them."

"But, Harriet, is it necessary to burn the court-plaister? I have not a word to say for the bit of old pencil, but the court-plaister might be useful."

"I shall be happier to burn it," replied Harriet. "It has a disagreeable look to me. I must get rid of every thing. There it goes, and there is an end, thank Heaven! of Mr. Elton."

"And when," thought Emma, "will there be a beginning of Mr. Churchill?"

She had soon afterwards reason to believe, that the beginning was already made, and could not but hope that the gipsy, though she had *told* no fortune, might be proved to have made Harriet's. About a fortnight after the alarm, they came to a sufficient explanation, and quite undesignedly. Emma was not thinking of it at the moment, which made the information she received more valuable. She merely said, in the course of some trivial chat, "Well, Harriet, whenever you marry, I would advise you to do so and so"—and thought no more of it, till after a minute's silence she heard Harriet say, in a very serious tone, "I shall never marry."

Emma then looked up, and immediately saw how it was; and after a moment's debate, as to whether it should pass unnoticed or not, replied,—

"Never marry!—This is a new resolution."

"It is one that I shall never change, however."

After another short hesitation, "I hope it does not proceed from—I hope it is not in compliment to Mr. Elton?"

"Mr. Elton, indeed!" cried Harriet, indignantly.—"Oh! no"—and Emma could just catch the words, "so superior to Mr. Elton!"

She then took a longer time for consideration. Should she proceed no farther?—should she let it pass, and seem to suspect nothing?—Perhaps Harriet might think her cold or angry if she did; or, perhaps, if she were totally silent, it might only drive Harriet into asking her to hear too much; and against any thing like such an unreserve as had been, such an open and frequent discussion of hopes and chances, she was perfectly resolved. She believed it would be wiser for her to say and know at once, all that she meant to say and know. Plain dealing was always best. She had previously determined how far she would proceed, on any application of the sort; and it would be safer for both, to have the judicious law of her own brain laid down with speed. She was decided, and thus spoke,—

"Harriet, I will not affect to be in doubt of your meaning. Your resolution, or rather your expectation of never marrying, results from an idea that the person whom you might prefer would be too greatly your superior in situation to think of you, Is not it so?"

"Oh, Miss Woodhouse, believe me, I have not the presumption to suppose,—indeed I am not so mad. But it is a pleasure to me to admire him at a distance, and to think of his infinite superiority to all the rest of the world, with the gratitude, wonder, and veneration, which are so proper, in me especially."

"I am not at all surprised at you, Harriet. The service he rendered you was enough to warm your heart."

"Service! oh, it was such an inexpressible obligation! The very recollection of it, and all that I felt at the time, when I saw him coming,—his noble look, and my wretchedness before. Such a change! In one moment such a change! From perfect misery to perfect happiness!"

"It is very natural. It is natural, and it is honourable. Yes, honourable, I think, to choose so well and so gratefully. But that it will be a fortunate preference is more than I can promise. I do not advise you to give way to it, Harriet. I do not by any means engage for its being returned. Consider what you are about. Perhaps it will be wisest in you to check your feelings while you can: at any rate do not let them carry you far, unless you are persuaded of his liking you. Be observant of him. Let his behaviour be the guide of your sensations. I give you this caution now, because I shall never speak to you again on the subject. I am determined against all interference. Henceforward I know nothing of the matter. Let no name ever pass our lips. We were very wrong before; we will be cautious now. He is your superior, no doubt, and there do seem objections and obstacles of a very serious nature; but yet, Harriet, more wonderful things have taken place; there have been matches of greater disparity. But take care of yourself. I would not have you too sanguine; though, however it may end, be assured that your raising your thoughts to *him*, is a mark of good taste which I shall always know how to value."

Harriet kissed her hand in silent and submissive gratitude. Emma was very decided in thinking such an attachment no bad thing for her friend. Its tendency would be to raise and refine her mind—and it must be saving her from the danger of degradation.

## Chapter V.

In this state of schemes, and hopes, and connivance, June opened upon Hartfield. To Highbury, in general, it brought no material change. The Eltons were still talking of a visit from the Sucklings, and of the use to be made of their barouche-landau; and Jane Fairfax was still at her grandmother's; and as the return of the Campbells from Ireland was again delayed, and August, instead of Midsummer, fixed for it, she was likely to remain there full two months longer, provided at least she were able to defeat Mrs. Elton's activity in her service, and save herself from being hurried into a delightful situation against her will.

Mr. Knightley, who, for some reason best known to himself, had certainly taken an early dislike to Frank Churchill, was only growing to dislike him more. He began to suspect him of some double dealing in his pursuit of Emma. That Emma was his object appeared indisputable. Every thing declared it; his own attentions, his father's hints, his mother-in-law's guarded silence; it was all in unison; words, conduct, discretion, and indiscretion, told the same story. But while so many were devoting him to Emma, and Emma herself making him over to Harriet, Mr. Knightley began to suspect him of some inclination to trifle with Jane Fairfax. He could not understand it; but there were symptoms of intelligence between them—he thought so at least—symptoms of admiration on his side, which, having once observed, he could not persuade himself to think entirely void of meaning, however he might wish to escape any of Emma's errors of imagination. *She* was not present when the suspicion first arose. He was dining with the Randalls' family, and Jane at the Eltons'; and he had seen a look, more than a single look, at Miss Fairfax, which, from the admirer of Miss Woodhouse, seemed somewhat out of place. When he was again in their company, he could not help remembering what he had seen; nor could he avoid observations which, unless it were like Cowper and his fire at twilight,

Myself creating what I saw,[18]

brought him yet stronger suspicion of there being a something of private liking, of private understanding even, between Frank Churchill and Jane.

He had walked up one day after dinner, as he very often did, to spend his evening at Hartfield. Emma and Harriet were going to walk; he joined them; and, on returning, they fell in with a larger party, who, like themselves, judged it wisest to take their exercise early, as the weather threatened rain; Mr. and Mrs. Weston and their son, Miss Bates and her niece, who had accidentally met. They all united; and, on reaching Hartfield gates, Emma, who knew it was exactly the sort of visiting that would be welcome to her father, pressed them all to go in and drink tea with him. The Randalls' party agreed to it immediately; and after a pretty long speech from Miss Bates, which few persons listened to, she also found it possible to accept dear Miss Woodhouse's most obliging invitation.

As they were turning into the grounds, Mr. Perry passed by on horseback. The gentlemen spoke of his horse.

"By the bye," said Frank Churchill to Mrs. Weston presently, "what became of Mr. Perry's plan of setting up his carriage?"

Mrs. Weston looked surprised, and said, "I did not know that he ever had any such plan."

"Nay, I had it from you. You wrote me word of it three months ago."

"Me! Impossible!"

"Indeed you did. I remember it perfectly. You mentioned it as what was certainly to be very soon. Mrs. Perry had told somebody, and was extremely happy about it. It was owing to *her* persuasion, as she thought his being out in bad weather did him a great deal of harm. You must remember it now?"

"Upon my word I never heard of it till this moment."

"Never! really never!—Bless me! how could it be? Then I must have dreamt it—but I was completely persuaded—Miss Smith, you walk as if you were tired. You will not be sorry to find yourself at home."

"What is this?—What is this?" cried Mr. Weston, "about Perry and a carriage? Is Perry going to set up his carriage, Frank? I am glad he can afford it. You had it from himself, had you?"

"No, sir," replied his son, laughing, "I seem to have had it from nobody. Very odd! I really was persuaded of Mrs. Weston's having mentioned it in one of her letters to Enscombe, many weeks ago, with all these particulars—but as she declares she never heard a syllable of it before, of course it must have been a dream. I am a great dreamer. I dream of every body at Highbury when I am away; and when I have gone through my particular friends, then I begin dreaming of Mr. and Mrs. Perry."

"It is odd though," observed his father, "that you should have had such a regular connected dream about people whom it was not very likely you should be thinking of at Enscombe. Perry's setting up his carriage! and his wife's persuading him to it, out of care for his health—just what will happen, I have no doubt, some time or other; only a little premature. What an air of probability sometimes runs through a dream! And at others, what a heap of absurdities it is! Well, Frank, your dream certainly shows that Highbury is in your thoughts when you are absent. Emma, you are a great dreamer, I think?"

Emma was out of hearing. She had hurried on before her guests to prepare her father for their appearance, and was beyond the reach of Mr. Weston's hint.

"Why, to own the truth," cried Miss Bates, who had been trying in vain to be heard the last two minutes, "if I must speak on this subject, there is no denying that Mr. Frank Churchill might have—I do not mean to say that he did not dream it—I am sure I have sometimes the oddest dreams in the world—but if I am questioned about it, I must acknowledge that there was such an idea last spring: for Mrs. Perry herself mentioned it to my mother, and the Coles knew of it as well as ourselves—but it was quite a secret, known to nobody else, and only thought of about three days. Mrs. Perry was very anxious that he should have a carriage, and came to my mother in great spirits one morning because she thought she had prevailed. Jane, don't you remember grandmamma's telling us of it when we got home? I forget where we had been walking to—very likely to Randalls; yes, I think it was to Randalls. Mrs. Perry was always particularly fond of my mother—indeed I do not know who is not—and she had mentioned it to her in confidence; she had no objection to her telling us, of course, but it was not to go beyond: and, from that day to this, I never mentioned it to a soul that I know of. At the same time, I will not positively answer for my having never dropt a hint, because I know I do sometimes pop out a thing before I am aware. I am a talker, you know; I am rather a talker; and now and then I have let a thing escape me which I should not. I am not like Jane; I wish I were. I will answer for it *she* never betrayed the least thing in the world. Where is she? Oh! just behind. Perfectly remember Mrs. Perry's coming. Extraordinary dream indeed!"

They were entering the hall. Mr. Knightley's eyes had preceded Miss Bates's in a glance at Jane. From Frank Churchill's face, where he thought he saw confusion suppressed or laughed away, he had involuntarily turned to hers;

but she was indeed behind, and too busy with her shawl. Mr. Weston had walked in. The two other gentlemen waited at the door to let her pass. Mr. Knightley suspected in Frank Churchill the determination of catching her eye—he seemed watching her intently—in vain, however, if it were so. Jane passed between them into the hall, and looked at neither.

There was no time for further remark or explanation. The dream must be borne with, and Mr. Knightley must take his seat with the rest round the large modern circular table which Emma had introduced at Hartfield, and which none but Emma could have had power to place there and persuade her father to use, instead of the small sized Pembroke,* on which two of his daily meals had, for forty years, been crowded. Tea passed pleasantly, and nobody seemed in a hurry to move.

"Miss Woodhouse," said Frank Churchill, after examining a table behind him, which he could reach as he sat, "have your nephews taken away their alphabets—their box of letters? It used to stand here. Where is it? This is a sort of dull-looking evening, that ought to be treated rather as winter than summer. We had great amusement with those letters one morning. I want to puzzle you again."

Emma was pleased with the thought; and producing the box, the table was quickly scattered over with alphabets, which no one seemed so much disposed to employ as their two selves. They were rapidly forming words for each other, or for any body else who would be puzzled. The quietness of the game made it particularly eligible for Mr. Woodhouse, who had often been distressed by the more animated sort, which Mr. Weston had occasionally introduced, and who now sat happily occupied in lamenting, with tender melancholy, over the departure of the "poor little boys," or in fondly pointing out, as he took up any stray letter near him, how beautifully Emma had written it.

---

*Small drop-leaf table.

Frank Churchill placed a word before Miss Fairfax. She gave a slight glance round the table, and applied herself to it. Frank was next to Emma, Jane opposite to them; and Mr. Knightley so placed as to see them all; and it was his object to see as much as he could, with as little apparent observation. The word was discovered, and with a faint smile pushed away. If meant to be immediately mixed with the others, and buried from sight, she should have looked on the table instead of looking just across, for it was not mixed; and Harriet, eager after every fresh word, and finding out none, directly took it up, and fell to work. She was sitting by Mr. Knightley, and turned to him for help. The word was *blunder;* and as Harriet exultingly proclaimed it, there was a blush on Jane's cheek which gave it a meaning not otherwise ostensible. Mr. Knightley connected it with the dream; but how it could all be, was beyond his comprehension. How the delicacy, the discretion of his favourite could have been so lain asleep! He feared there must be some decided involvement. Disingenuousness and double dealing seemed to meet him at every turn. These letters were but the vehicle for gallantry and trick. It was a child's play, chosen to conceal a deeper game on Frank Churchill's part.

With great indignation did he continue to observe him; with great alarm and distrust, to observe also his two blinded companions. He saw a short word prepared for Emma, and given to her with a look sly and demure. He saw that Emma had soon made it out, and found it highly entertaining, though it was something which she judged it proper to appear to censure; for she said, "Nonsense! for shame!" He heard Frank Churchill next say, with a glance towards Jane, "I will give it to her,—shall I?" and as clearly heard Emma opposing it with eager laughing warmth,—"No, no, you must not, you shall not, indeed."

It was done, however. This gallant young man, who seemed to love without feeling, and to recommend himself without complaisance, directly handed over the word to Miss Fairfax, and with a particular degree of sedate civility entreated her to study it. Mr. Knightley's excessive curiosity to know what this word might be, made him seize every possible moment for darting his eye towards it, and it was not long before he saw it to be *Dixon*. Jane Fairfax's perception seemed to accompany his; her comprehension was certainly more equal to the covert meaning, the superior intelligence, of those five letters so arranged. She was evidently displeased; looked up, and seeing herself watched, blushed more deeply than he had ever perceived her, and saying only, "I did not know that proper names were allowed," pushed away the letters with even an angry spirit, and looked resolved to be engaged by no other word that could be offered. Her face was averted from those who had made the attack, and turned towards her aunt.

"Ay, very true, my dear," cried the latter, though Jane had not spoken a word: "I was just going to say the same thing. It is time for us to be going, indeed. The evening is closing in, and grandmamma will be looking for us. My dear sir, you are too obliging. We really must wish you good night."

Jane's alertness in moving, proved her as ready as her aunt had preconceived. She was immediately up, and wanting to quit the table; but so many were also moving, that she could not get away; and Mr. Knightley thought he saw another collection of letters,* anxiously pushed towards her, and resolutely swept away by her unexamined. She was afterwards looking for her shawl,—Frank Churchill was looking also: it was growing dusk, and the room was in confusion; and how they parted, Mr. Knightley could not tell.

He remained at Hartfield after all the rest, his thoughts full of what he had seen; so full, that when the candles came to assist his observations, he must,—yes, he certainly must, as a friend—an anxious friend—give Emma some hint, ask her some question. He could not see her in a situation of such danger, without trying to preserve her. It was his duty.

---

*Possibly the word "pardon."

"Pray, Emma," said he, "may I ask in what lay the great amusement, the poignant sting of the last word given to you and Miss Fairfax? I saw the word, and am curious to know how it could be so very entertaining to the one, and so very distressing to the other."

Emma was extremely confused. She could not endure to give him the true explanation; for though her suspicions were by no means removed, she was really ashamed of having ever imparted them.

"Oh!" she cried, in evident embarrassment, "it all meant nothing: a mere joke among ourselves."

"The joke," he replied, gravely, "seemed confined to you and Mr. Churchill."

He had hoped she would speak again, but she did not. She would rather busy herself about any thing, than speak. He sat a little while in doubt. A variety of evils crossed his mind. Interference—fruitless interference. Emma's confusion, and the acknowledged intimacy, seemed to declare her affection engaged. Yet he would speak. He owed it to her, to risk any thing that might be involved in an unwelcome interference, rather than her welfare; to encounter any thing, rather than the remembrance of neglect in such a cause.

"My dear Emma," said he at last, with earnest kindness, "do you think you perfectly understand the degree of acquaintance between the gentleman and lady we have been speaking of?"

"Between Mr. Frank Churchill, and Miss Fairfax? Oh! yes, perfectly. Why do you make a doubt of it?"

"Have you never at any time had reason to think that he admired her, or that she admired him?"

"Never, never!" she cried with a most open eagerness: "Never, for the twentieth part of a moment, did such an idea occur to me. And how could it possibly come into your head?"

"I have lately imagined that I saw symptoms of attachment between them; certain expressive looks, which I did not believe meant to be public."

"Oh! you amuse me excessively. I am delighted to find that you can vouchsafe to let your imagination wander; but it will not do—very sorry to check you in your first essay, but indeed it will not do. There is no admiration between them, I do assure you; and the appearances which have caught you, have arisen from some peculiar circumstances; feelings rather of a totally different nature: it is impossible exactly to explain; there is a good deal of nonsense in it; but the part which is capable of being communicated, which is sense, is, that they are as far from any attachment or admiration for one another, as any two beings in the world can be. That is, I *presume* it to be so on her side, and I can *answer* for its being so on his. I will answer for the gentleman's indifference."

She spoke with a confidence which staggered, with a satisfaction which silenced Mr. Knightley. She was in gay spirits, and would have prolonged the conversation, wanting to hear the particulars of his suspicions, every look described, and all the wheres and hows of a circumstance which highly entertained her; but his gaiety did not meet hers. He found he could not be useful, and his feelings were too much irritated for talking. That he might not be irritated into an absolute fever by the fire which Mr. Woodhouse's tender habits required almost every evening throughout the year, he soon afterwards took a hasty leave, and walked home to the coolness and solitude of Donwell Abbey.

## Chapter VI.

After being long fed with hopes of a speedy visit from Mr. and Mrs. Suckling, the Highbury world were obliged to endure the mortification of hearing that they could not possibly come till the autumn. No such importation of novelties could enrich their intellectual stores at present. In the daily interchange of news, they must be again restricted to the other topics, with which for a while the Sucklings' coming had been united, such as the last accounts of Mrs. Churchill, whose health seemed every day to supply a different report, and the situation of Mrs. Weston, whose happiness it was to be hoped might eventually be as much increased by the arrival of a child, as that of all her neighbours was by the approach of it.

Mrs. Elton was very much disappointed. It was the delay of a great deal of pleasure and parade. Her introductions and recommendations must all wait, and every projected party be still only talked of. So she thought at first;—but a little consideration convinced her that every thing need not be put off. Why should not they explore to Box Hill though the Sucklings did not come? They could go there again with them in the autumn. It was settled that they should go to Box Hill. That there was to be such a party had been long generally known: it had even given the idea of another. Emma had never been to Box Hill; she wished to see what every body found so well worth seeing, and she and Mr. Weston had agreed to choose some fine morning and drive thither. Two or three more of the chosen only were to be admitted to join them, and it was to be done in a quiet, unpretending, elegant way, infinitely superior to the bustle and preparation, the regular eating and drinking, and pic-nic parade of the Eltons and the Sucklings.

This was so very well understood between them, that Emma could not but feel some surprise, and a little displeasure, on hearing from Mr. Weston that he had been proposing to Mrs. Elton, as her brother and sister had failed her, that the two parties should unite, and go together; and that as Mrs. Elton had very readily acceded to it, so it was to be, if she had no objection. Now, as her objection was nothing but her very great dislike of Mrs. Elton, of which Mr. Weston must already be perfectly aware, it was not worth bringing forward again:—it could not be done without a reproof to him, which would be giving pain to his wife; and she found herself, therefore, obliged to consent to an arrangement which she would have done a great deal to avoid; an arrangement which would, probably, expose her even to the degradation of being said to be of Mrs. Elton's party! Every feeling was offended; and the forbearance of her outward submission left a heavy arrear* due of secret severity in her reflections, on the unmanageable good-will of Mr. Weston's temper.

"I am glad you approve of what I have done," said he, very comfortably. "But I thought you would. Such schemes as these are nothing without numbers. One cannot have too large a party. A large party secures its own amusement. And she is a good-natured woman after all. One could not leave her out."

Emma denied none of it aloud, and agreed to none of it in private.

It was now the middle of June and the weather fine; and Mrs. Elton was growing impatient to name the day, and settle with Mr. Weston as to pigeon-pies and cold lamb, when a lame carriage-horse threw every thing into sad uncertainty. It might be weeks, it might be only a few days, before the horse were useable; but no preparations could be ventured on, and it was all melancholy stagnation. Mrs. Elton's resources were inadequate to such an attack.

"Is not this most vexatious, Knightley?" she cried; "and such weather for exploring! these delays and disappointments are quite odious. What are we to do? The year will wear away at this rate, and nothing done. Before this time, last year, I assure you, we had a delightful exploring party from Maple Grove to Kings Weston."

"You had better explore to Donwell," replied Mr. Knightley. "That may be done without horses. Come, and eat my strawberries: they are ripening fast."

---

*Remainder.

If Mr. Knightley did not begin seriously, he was obliged to proceed so; for his proposal was caught at with delight; and the "Oh! I should like it of all things," was not plainer in words than manner. Donwell was famous for its strawberry-beds, which seemed a plea for the invitation: but no plea was necessary; cabbage-beds would have been enough to tempt the lady, who only wanted to be going somewhere. She promised him again and again to come—much oftener than he doubted—and was extremely gratified by such a proof of intimacy, such a distinguishing compliment as she chose to consider it.

"You may depend upon me," said she; "I certainly will come.—Name your day, and I will come.—You will allow me to bring Jane Fairfax?"

"I cannot name a day," said he, "till I have spoken to some others, whom I would wish to meet you."

"Oh, leave all that to me; only give me a carte-blanche.—I am Lady Patroness, you know. It is my party. I will bring friends with me."

"I hope you will bring Elton," said he; "but I will not trouble you to give any other invitations."

"Oh, now you are looking very sly;—but consider,—you need not be afraid of delegating power to *me*. I am no young lady on her preferment. Married women, you know, may be safely authorised. It is my party. Leave it all to me. I will invite your guests."

"No," he calmly replied, "there is but one married woman in the world whom I can ever allow to invite what guests she pleases to Donwell, and that one is—"

"Mrs. Weston, I suppose," interrupted Mrs. Elton, rather mortified.

"No,—Mrs. Knightley; and, till she is in being, I will manage such matters myself."

"Ah, you are an odd creature!" she cried, satisfied to have no one preferred to herself. "You are a humourist, and may say what you like. Quite a humourist. Well, I shall bring Jane with me—Jane and her aunt. The rest I leave to you, I have no objections at all to meeting the Hartfield family. Don't scruple, I know you are attached to them."

"You certainly will meet them, if I can prevail; and I shall call on Miss Bates in my way home."

"That is quite unnecessary; I see Jane every day;—but as you like. It is to be a morning scheme, you know, Knightley; quite a simple thing. I shall wear a large bonnet, and bring one of my little baskets hanging on my arm. Here,—proba-bly this basket with pink riband. Nothing can be more sim-ple, you see. And Jane will have such another. There is to be no form or parade—a sort of gipsy party. We are to walk about your gardens, and gather the strawberries ourselves, and sit under trees; and whatever else you may like to pro-vide, it is to be all out of doors; a table spread in the shade, you know. Every thing as natural and simple as possible. Is not that your idea?"

"Not quite. My idea of the simple and the natural will be to have the table spread in the dining-room. The nature and the simplicity of gentlemen and ladies, with their servants and furniture, I think is best observed by meals within doors. When you are tired of eating strawberries in the garden, there shall be cold meat in the house."

"Well, as you please; only don't have a great set-out. And, by the bye, can I or my housekeeper be of any use to you with our opinion? Pray be sincere, Knightley. If you wish me to talk to Mrs. Hodges, or to inspect any thing—"

"I have not the least wish for it, I thank you."

"Well,—but if any difficulties should arise, my house-keeper is extremely clever."

"I will answer for it, that mine thinks herself full as clever, and would spurn anybody's assistance."

"1 wish we had a donkey. The thing would be for us all to come on donkeys, Jane, Miss Bates, and me, and my caro sposo walking by. I really must talk to him about purchasing a donkey. In a country life I conceive it to be a sort of nec-essary; for, let a woman have ever so many resources, it is not possible for her to be always shut up at home; and very long walks, you know—in summer there is dust, and in winter there is dirt."

"You will not find either between Donwell and Highbury. Donwell-lane is never dusty, and now it is perfectly dry. Come on a donkey, however, if you prefer it. You can borrow Mrs. Cole's. I would wish every thing to be as much to your taste as possible."

"That I am sure you would. Indeed I do you justice, my good friend. Under that peculiar sort of dry, blunt manner, I know you have the warmest heart. As I tell Mr. E., you are a thorough humourist. Yes, believe me, Knightley, I am fully sensible of your attention to me in the whole of this scheme. You have hit upon the very thing to please me."

Mr. Knightley had another reason for avoiding a table in the shade. He wished to persuade Mr. Woodhouse, as well as Emma, to join the party; and he knew that to have any of them sitting down out of doors to eat would inevitably make him ill. Mr. Woodhouse must not, under the specious pretence of a morning drive, and an hour or two spent at Donwell, be tempted away to his misery.

He was invited on good faith. No lurking horrors were to upbraid him for his easy credulity. He did consent. He had not been at Donwell for two years. "Some very fine morning, he, Emma, and Harriet, could go very well; and he could sit still with Mrs. Weston while the dear girls walked about the gardens. He did not suppose they could be damp now, in the middle of the day. He should like to see the old house again exceedingly, and should be very happy to meet Mr. and Mrs. Elton, and any other of his neighbours. He could not see any objection at all to his and Emma's, and Harriet's, going there some very fine morning. He thought it very well done of Mr. Knightley to invite them; very kind and sensible; much cleverer than dining out. He was not fond of dining out."

Mr. Knightley was fortunate in every body's most ready concurrence. The invitation was every where so well received, that it seemed as if, like Mrs. Elton, they were all taking the scheme as a particular compliment to themselves. Emma and Harriet professed very high expectations of pleasure from it; and Mr. Weston, unasked, promised to get Frank over to join them, if possible; a proof of approbation and gratitude which could have been dispensed with. Mr. Knightley was then obliged to say that he should be glad to see him; and Mr. Weston engaged to lose no time in writing, and spare no arguments to induce him to come.

In the meanwhile the lame horse recovered so fast, that the party to Box Hill was again under happy consideration; and at last Donwell was settled for one day, and Box Hill for the next; the weather appearing exactly right.

Under a bright mid-day sun, at almost Midsummer, Mr. Woodhouse was safely conveyed in his carriage, with one window down, to partake of this *al fresco** party; and in one of the most comfortable rooms in the Abbey, especially prepared for him by a fire all the morning, he was happily placed, quite at his ease, ready to talk with pleasure of what had been achieved, and advise every body to come and sit down, and not to heat themselves. Mrs. Weston, who seemed to have walked there on purpose to be tired, and sit all the time with him, remained, when all the others were invited or persuaded out, his patient listener and sympathiser.

It was so long since Emma had been at the Abbey, that as soon as she was satisfied of her father's comfort, she was glad to leave him, and look around her; eager to refresh and correct her memory with more particular observation, more exact understanding of a house and grounds which must ever be so interesting to her and all her family.

She felt all the honest pride and complacency which her alliance with the present and future proprietor could fairly warrant, as she viewed the respectable size and style of the building, its suitable, becoming characteristic situation, low and sheltered; its ample gardens stretching down to mead-

---

*In the open air (Italian).

ows washed by a stream, of which the Abbey, with all the old neglect of prospect, had scarcely a sight,—and its abundance of timber in rows and avenues, which neither fashion nor extravagance had rooted up. The house was larger than Hartfield, and totally unlike it, covering a good deal of ground, rambling and irregular, with many comfortable and one or two handsome rooms. It was just what it ought to be, and it looked what it was; and Emma felt an increasing respect for it, as the residence of a family of such true gentility, untainted in blood and understanding. Some faults of temper John Knightley had; but Isabella had connected herself unexceptionably. She had given them neither men, nor names, nor places, that could raise a blush. These were pleasant feelings, and she walked about and indulged them till it was necessary to do as the others did, and collect round the strawberry beds. The whole party were assembled, excepting Frank Churchill, who was expected every moment from Richmond; and Mrs. Elton, in all her apparatus of happiness, her large bonnet and her basket, was very ready to lead the way in gathering, accepting, or talking. Strawberries, and only strawberries, could now be thought or spoken of. "The best fruit in England—every body's favourite—always wholesome. These the finest beds and finest sorts. Delightful to gather for one's self—the only way of really enjoying them. Morning decidedly the best time—never tired—every sort good—hautboy infinitely superior—no comparison—the others hardly eatable—hautboys very scarce—Chili preferred—white wood finest flavour of all—price of strawberries in London—abundance about Bristol—Maple Grove—cultivation—beds when to be renewed—gardeners thinking exactly different—no general rule—gardeners never to be put out of their way—delicious fruit—only too rich to be eaten much of—inferior to cherries—currants more refreshing—only objection to gathering strawberries the stooping—glaring sun—tired to death—could bear it no longer—must go and sit in the shade."

Such, for half an hour, was the conversation; interrupted

only once by Mrs. Weston, who came out, in her solicitude after her son-in-law, to enquire if he were come; and she was a little uneasy. She had some fears of his horse.

Seats tolerably in the shade were found; and now Emma was obliged to overhear what Mrs. Elton and Jane Fairfax were talking of. A situation, a most desirable situation, was in question. Mrs. Elton had received notice of it that morning, and was in raptures. It was not with Mrs. Suckling, it was not with Mrs. Bragge, but in felicity and splendour it fell short only of them: it was with a cousin of Mrs. Bragge, an acquaintance of Mrs. Suckling, a lady known at Maple Grove. Delightful, charming, superior, first circles, spheres, lines, ranks, every thing: and Mrs. Elton was wild to have the offer closed with immediately. On her side, all was warmth, energy, and triumph; and she positively refused to take her friend's negative, though Miss Fairfax continued to assure her that she would not at present engage in any thing—repeating the same motives which she had been heard to urge before. Still Mrs. Elton insisted on being authorised to write an acquiescence by the morrow's post. How Jane could bear it at all, was astonishing to Emma. She did look vexed; she did speak pointedly; and at last, with a decision of action unusual to her, proposed a removal. "Should not they walk? Would not Mr. Knightley show them the gardens—all the gardens? She wished to see the whole extent." The pertinacity of her friend seemed more than she could bear.

It was hot; and after walking some time over the gardens in a scattered, dispersed way, scarcely any three together, they insensibly followed one another to the delicious shade of a broad short avenue of limes, which, stretching beyond the garden at an equal distance from the river, seemed the finish of the pleasure grounds. It led to nothing; nothing but a view at the end over a low stone wall with high pillars, which seemed intended, in their erection, to give the appearance of an approach to the house, which never had been there. Disputable, however, as might be the taste of such a termination, it was in itself a charming walk, and the view which closed it extremely pretty. The considerable slope, at nearly the foot of which the Abbey stood, gradually acquired a steeper form beyond its grounds; and at half a mile distant was a bank of considerable abruptness and grandeur, well clothed with wood; and at the bottom of this bank, favourably placed and sheltered, rose the Abbey-Mill Farm, with meadows in front, and the river making a close and handsome curve around it.

It was a sweet view—sweet to the eye and the mind. English verdure, English culture,* English comfort, seen under a sun bright, without being oppressive.

In this walk Emma and Mr. Weston found all the others assembled; and towards this view she immediately perceived Mr. Knightley and Harriet distinct from the rest, quietly leading the way. Mr. Knightley and Harriet! It was an odd *tête-à-tête;* but she was glad to see it. There had been a time when he would have scorned her as a companion, and turned from her with little ceremony. Now they seemed in pleasant conversation. There had been a time also when Emma would have been sorry to see Harriet in a spot so favourable for the Abbey-Mill Farm; but now she feared it not. It might be safely viewed with all its appendages of prosperity and beauty, its rich pastures, spreading flocks, orchard in blossom, and light column of smoke ascending. She joined them at the wall, and found them more engaged in talking than in looking around. He was giving Harriet information as to modes of agriculture, &c.; and Emma received a smile which seemed to say, "These are my own concerns. I have a right to talk on such subjects, without being suspected of introducing Robert Martin." She did not suspect him. It was too old a story. Robert Martin had probably ceased to think of Harriet. They took a few turns together along the walk. The shade was most refreshing, and Emma found it the pleasantest part of the day.

---

*Agriculture.

The next remove was to the house; they must all go in and eat; and they were all seated and busy, and still Frank Churchill did not come. Mrs. Weston looked, and looked in vain. His father would not own himself uneasy, and laughed at her fears; but she could not be cured of wishing that he would part with his black mare. He had expressed himself as to coming, with more than common certainty. "His aunt was so much better, that he had not a doubt of getting over to them." Mrs. Churchill's state, however, as many were ready to remind her, was liable to such sudden variation as might disappoint her nephew in the most reasonable dependence; and Mrs. Weston was at last persuaded to believe, or to say, that it must be by some attack of Mrs. Churchill that he was prevented coming. Emma looked at Harriet while the point was under consideration; she behaved very well, and betrayed no emotion.

The cold repast was over, and the party were to go out once more to see what had not yet been seen, the old Abbey fish-ponds; perhaps get as far as the clover, which was to be begun cutting on the morrow, or, at any rate, have the pleasure of being hot, and growing cool again. Mr. Woodhouse, who had already taken his little round in the highest part of the gardens, where no damps from the river were imagined even by him, stirred no more; and his daughter resolved to remain with him, that Mrs. Weston might be persuaded away by her husband to the exercise and variety which her spirits seemed to need.

Mr. Knightley had done all in his power for Mr. Woodhouse's entertainment. Books of engravings, drawers of medals, cameos,* corals, shells, and every other family collection within his cabinets, had been prepared for his old friend, to while away the morning; and the kindness had perfectly answered. Mr. Woodhouse had been exceedingly well

---

*A cameo is normally a medallion made out of semiprecious stone or shell, with a figure or profile carved in raised relief; often set in a brooch, pendant, or ring.

amused. Mrs. Weston had been showing them all to him, and now he would show them all to Emma; fortunate in having no other resemblance to a child, than in a total want of taste for what he saw, for he was slow, constant, and methodical. Before this second looking over was begun, however, Emma walked into the hall for the sake of a few moments' free observation of the entrance and ground-plot of the house, and was hardly there, when Jane Fairfax appeared, coming quickly in from the garden, and with a look of escape. Little expecting to meet Miss Woodhouse so soon, there was a start at first; but Miss Woodhouse was the very person she was in quest of.

"Will you be so kind," said she, "when I am missed, as to say that I am gone home? I am going this moment. My aunt is not aware how late it is, nor how long we have been absent; but I am sure we shall be wanted, and I am determined to go directly. I have said nothing about it to any body. It would only be giving trouble and distress. Some are gone to the ponds, and some to the lime walk. Till they all come in I shall not be missed; and when they do, will you have the goodness to say that I am gone?"

"Certainly, if you wish it; but you are not going to walk to Highbury alone?"

"Yes; what should hurt me? I walk fast. I shall be at home in twenty minutes."

"But it is too far, indeed it is, to be walking quite alone. Let my father's servant go with you. Let me order the carriage. It can be round in five minutes."

"Thank you, thank you; but on no account; I would rather walk. And for *me* to be afraid of walking alone; I, who may so soon have to guard others!"

She spoke with great agitation; and Emma very feelingly replied,— "That can be no reason for your being exposed to danger now. I must order the carriage. The heat even would be danger. You are fatigued already."

"I am," she answered, "I am fatigued; but it is not the sort of fatigue—quick walking will refresh me. Miss Woodhouse, we all know at times what it is to be wearied in spirits. Mine, I confess, are exhausted. The greatest kindness you can show me, will be to let me have my own way, and only say that I am gone when it is necessary."

Emma had not another word to oppose. She saw it all; and entering into her feelings, promoted her quitting the house immediately, and watched her safely off with the zeal of a friend. Her parting look was grateful; and her parting words, "Oh! Miss Woodhouse, the comfort of being some-times alone!" seemed to burst from an overcharged heart, and to describe somewhat of the continual endurance to be practised by her, even towards some of those who loved her best.

"Such a home, indeed! such an aunt!" said Emma, as she turned back into the hall again. "I do pity you. And the more sensibility you betray of their just horrors, the more I shall like you."

Jane had not been gone a quarter of an hour, and they had only accomplished some views of St. Mark's Place, Venice, when Frank Churchill entered the room. Emma had not been thinking of him; she had forgotten to think of him; but she was very glad to see him. Mrs. Weston would be at ease. The black mare was blameless; *they* were right who had named Mrs. Churchill as the cause. He had been detained by a temporary increase of illness in her;—a nervous seizure, which had lasted some hours; and he had quite given up every thought of coming till very late; and had he known how hot a ride he should have, and how late, with all his hurry, he must be, he believed he should not have come at all. The heat was excessive; he had never suffered any thing like it—almost wished he had staid at home—nothing killed him like heat—he could bear any degree of cold, &c., but heat was intolerable; and he sat down, at the greatest possible distance from the slight remains of Mr. Woodhouse's fire, looking very deplorable.

"You will soon be cooler, if you sit still," said Emma.

"As soon as I am cooler I shall go back again. I could very

ill be spared; but such a point had been made of my coming! You will all be going soon, I suppose; the whole party breaking up. I met *one* as I came—Madness in such weather!—absolute madness!"

Emma listened, and looked, and soon perceived that Frank Churchill's state might be best defined by the expressive phrase of being out of humour. Some people were always cross when they were hot. Such might be his constitution; and as she knew that eating and drinking were often the cure of such incidental complaints, she recommended his taking some refreshment; he would find abundance of every thing in the dining-room; and she humanely pointed out the door.

"No; he should not eat. He was not hungry; it would only make him hotter." In two minutes, however, he relented in his own favour; and muttering something about spruce beer, walked off. Emma returned all her attention to her father, saying in secret,—

"I am glad I have done being in love with him. I should not like a man who is so soon discomposed by a hot morning. Harriet's sweet easy temper will not mind it."

He was gone long enough to have had a very comfortable meal, and came back all the better—grown quite cool, and, with good manners, like himself, able to draw a chair close to them, take an interest in their employment, and regret, in a reasonable way, that he should be so late. He was not in his best spirits, but seemed trying to improve them; and, at last, made himself talk nonsense very agreeably. They were looking over views in Swisserland.

"As soon as my aunt gets well, I shall go abroad," said he. I shall never be easy till I have seen some of these places. You will have my sketches, some time or other, to look at—or my tour to read—or my poem. I shall do something to expose myself."

"That may be—but not by sketches in Swisserland. You will never go to Swisserland. Your uncle and aunt will never allow you to leave England."

"They may be induced to go too. A warm climate may be prescribed for her. I have more than half an expectation of our all going abroad. I assure you I have. I feel a strong persuasion, this morning, that I shall soon be abroad. I ought to travel. I am tired of doing nothing. I want a change. I am serious, Miss Woodhouse, whatever your penetrating eyes may fancy—I am sick of England—and would leave it to-morrow, if I could."

"You are sick of prosperity and indulgence. Cannot you invent a few hardships for yourself, and be contented to stay?"

"*I* sick of prosperity and indulgence! You are quite mistaken. I do not look upon myself as either prosperous or indulged. I am thwarted in every thing material. I do not consider myself at all a fortunate person."

"You are not quite so miserable, though, as when you first came. Go, and eat and drink a little more, and you will do very well. Another slice of cold meat, another draught of Madeira* and water, will make you nearly on a par with the rest of us."

"No—I shall not stir. I shall sit by you. You are my best cure."

"We are going to Box Hill to-morrow: you will join us. It is not Swisserland, but it will be something for a young man so much in want of a change. You will stay, and go with us?"

"No, certainly not; I shall go home in the cool of the evening."

"But you may come again in the cool of to-morrow morning."

"No—It will not be worth while. If I come, I shall be cross."

"Then pray stay at Richmond."

"But if I do, I shall be crosser still. I can never bear to think of you all there without me."

---

*Type of wine.

"These are difficulties which you must settle for yourself. Choose your own degree of crossness. I shall press you no more."

The rest of the party were now returning, and all were soon collected. With some there was great joy at the sight of Frank Churchill; others took it very composedly; but there was a very general distress and disturbance on Miss Fairfax's disappearance being explained. That it was time for every body to go, concluded the subject; and with a short final arrangement for the next day's scheme, they parted. Frank Churchill's little inclination to exclude himself increased so much, that his last words to Emma were,—

"Well;—if *you* wish me to stay and join the party, I will."

She smiled her acceptance; and nothing less than a summons from Richmond was to take him back before the following evening.

## Chapter VII.

They had a very fine day for Box Hill; and all the other outward circumstances of arrangement, accommodation, and punctuality, were in favour of a pleasant party. Mr. Weston directed the whole, officiating safely between Hartfield and the vicarage, and every body was in good time. Emma and Harriet went together; Miss Bates and her niece, with the Eltons; the gentlemen on horseback. Mrs. Weston remained with Mr. Woodhouse. Nothing was wanting but to be happy when they got there. Seven miles were travelled in expectation of enjoyment, and every body had a burst of admiration on first arriving; but in the general amount of the day there was deficiency. There was a languor, a want of spirits, a want of union, which could not be got over. They separated too much into parties. The Eltons walked together; Mr. Knightley took charge of Miss Bates and Jane; and Emma and Harriet belonged to Frank Churchill. And Mr. Weston tried, in vain, to make them harmonise better. It seemed at first an accidental division, but it never materially varied. Mr. and Mrs. Elton, indeed, showed no unwillingness to mix, and be as agreeable as they could: but during the two whole hours that were spent on the hill, there seemed a principle of separation between the other parties, too strong for any fine prospects, or any cold collation, or any cheerful Mr. Weston, to remove.

At first it was downright dulness to Emma. She had never seen Frank Churchill so silent and stupid. He said nothing worth hearing—looked without seeing—admired without intelligence—listened without knowing what she said. While he was so dull, it was no wonder that Harriet should be dull likewise; and they were both insufferable.

When they all sat down it was better—to her taste a great deal better—for Frank Churchill grew talkative and gay, making her his first subject. Every distinguishing attention that could be paid, was paid to her. To amuse her, and be agreeable in her eyes, seemed all that he cared for,—and Emma, glad to be enlivened, not sorry to be flattered, was gay and easy too, and gave him all the friendly encouragement, the admission to be gallant, which she had ever given in the first and most animating period of their acquaintance; but which now, in her own estimation, meant nothing, though in the judgment of most people looking on it, must have had such an appearance as no English word but flirtation could very well describe. "Mr. Frank Churchill and Miss Woodhouse flirted together excessively." They were laying themselves open to that very phrase—and to having it sent off in a letter to Maple Grove by one lady, to Ireland by another. Not that Emma was gay and thoughtless from any real felicity; it was rather because she felt less happy than she had expected. She laughed because she was disappointed; and though she liked him for his attentions, and thought them all, whether in friendship, admiration, or playfulness, extremely judicious, they were not winning back her heart. She still intended him for her friend.

"How much I am obliged to you," said he, "for telling me to come to-day!—If it had not been for you, I should certainly have lost all the happiness of this party. I had quite determined to go away again."

"Yes, you were very cross; and I do not know what about, except that you were too late for the best strawberries. I was a kinder friend than you deserved. But you were humble. You begged hard to be commanded to come."

"Don't say I was cross. I was fatigued. The heat overcame me."

"It is hotter to-day."

"Not to my feelings. I am perfectly comfortable to-day."

"You are comfortable because you are under command."

"Your command?—Yes."

"Perhaps I intended you to say so, but I meant self-command. You had, somehow or other, broken bounds yesterday, and run away from your own management; but to-day you are got back again—and as I cannot be always with you, it is best to believe your temper under your own command rather than mine."

"It comes to the same thing. I can have no self-command without a motive. You order me, whether you speak or not. And you can be always with me. You are always with me."

"Dating from three o'clock yesterday. My perpetual influence could not begin earlier, or you would not have been so much out of humour before."

"Three o'clock yesterday! That is your date. I thought I had seen you first in February."

"Your gallantry is really unanswerable. But (lowering her voice) nobody speaks except ourselves, and it is rather too much to be talking nonsense for the entertainment of seven silent people."

"I say nothing of which I am ashamed," replied he, with

lively impudence. "I saw you first in February. Let every body on the Hill hear me if they can. Let my accents swell to Mickleham on one side, and Dorking on the other. I saw you first in February." And then whispering,—"Our companions are excessively stupid. What shall we do to rouse them? Any nonsense will serve. They *shall* talk. Ladies and gentlemen, I am ordered by Miss Woodhouse (who, where ever she is, presides,) to say, that she desires to know what you are all thinking of."

Some laughed, and answered good-humouredly. Miss Bates said a great deal; Mrs. Elton swelled at the idea of Miss Woodhouse's presiding; Mr. Knightley's answer was the most distinct.

"Is Miss Woodhouse sure that she would like to hear what we are all thinking of?"

"Oh, no, no!" cried Emma, laughing as carelessly as she could,—"upon no account in the world. It is the very last thing I would stand the brunt of just now. Let me hear any thing rather than what you are all thinking of. I will not say quite all. There are one or two, perhaps, (glancing at Mr. Weston and Harriet), whose thoughts I might not be afraid of knowing."

"It is a sort of thing," cried Mrs. Elton emphatically, "which *I* should not have thought myself privileged to enquire into. Though, perhaps, as the *chaperon** of the party—*I* never was in any circle—exploring parties—young ladies—married women—"

Her mutterings were chiefly to her husband; and he murmured, in reply,—

"Very true, my love, very true. Exactly so, indeed—quite unheard of—but some ladies say any thing. Better pass it off as a joke. Every body knows what is due to *you*."

"It will not do," whispered Frank to Emma, "they are most of them affronted. I will attack them with more address.

---

*Escort charged with preserving propriety.

Ladies and gentlemen, I am ordered by Miss Woodhouse to
say, that she waves her right of knowing exactly what you may
all be thinking of, and only requires something very entertaining from each of you, in a general way. Here are seven of
you, besides myself, (who, she is pleased to say, am very entertaining already,) and she only demands from each of you,
either one thing very clever, be it prose or verse, original or
repeated; or two things moderately clever, or three things
very dull indeed; and she engages to laugh heartily at them
all."

"Oh! very well," exclaimed Miss Bates; "then I need not
be uneasy. 'Three things very dull indeed.' That will just do
for me, you know. I shall be sure to say three dull things as
soon as ever I open my mouth, sha'n't I? (looking round
with the most good-humoured dependence on every body's
assent.) Do not you all think I shall?"

Emma could not resist.

"Ah! ma'am, but there may be a difficulty. Pardon me,
but you will be limited as to the number,—only three at
once."

Miss Bates, deceived by the mock ceremony of her manner, did not immediately catch her meaning; but, when it
burst on her, it could not anger, though a slight blush
showed that it could pain her.

"Ah! well—to be sure. Yes, I see what she means (turning
to Mr. Knightley), and I will try to hold my tongue. I must
make myself very disagreeable, or she would not have said
such a thing to an old friend."

"I like your plan," cried Mr. Weston. "Agreed, agreed. I
will do my best. I am making a conundrum. How will a conundrum reckon?"

"Low, I am afraid, sir, very low," answered his son; "but we
shall be indulgent, especially to any one who leads the way."

"No, no," said Emma, "it will not reckon low. A conundrum of Mr. Weston's shall clear him and his next neighbour. Come, sir, pray let me hear it."

"I doubt its being very clever myself," said Mr. Weston. "It is too much a matter of fact; but here it is.—What two letters of the alphabet are there that express perfection?"

"What two letters!—express perfection! I am sure I do not know."

"Ah! you will never guess. You (to Emma), I am certain, will never guess. I will tell you. M. and A. Em—ma. Do you understand?"

Understanding and gratification came together. It might be a very indifferent piece of wit; but Emma found a great deal to laugh at and enjoy in it; and so did Frank and Harriet. It did not seem to touch the rest of the party equally; some looked very stupid about it; and Mr. Knightley gravely said,—

"This explains the sort of clever thing that is wanted, and Mr. Weston has done very well for himself; but he must have knocked up every body else. *Perfection* should not have come quite so soon."

"Oh! for myself, I protest I must be excused," said Mrs. Elton. "*I* really cannot attempt—I am not at all fond of the sort of thing. I had an acrostic* once sent to me upon my own name, which I was not at all pleased with. I knew who it came from. An abominable puppy! You know who I mean (nodding to her husband). These kind of things are very well at Christmas, when one is sitting round the fire; but quite out of place, in my opinion, when one is exploring about the country in summer. Miss Woodhouse must excuse me. I am not one of those who have witty things at every body's service. I do not pretend to be a wit. I have a great deal of vivacity in my own way, but I really must be allowed to judge when to speak, and when to hold my tongue. Pass us, if you please, Mr. Churchill. Pass Mr. E., Knightley, Jane, and myself. We have nothing clever to say,—not one of us."

"Yes, yes, pray pass *me*," added her husband, with a sort of sneering consciousness; "*I* have nothing to say that can en-

---

*Poem in which the initial letters of each line spell out a word.

tertain Miss Woodhouse, or any other young lady. An old married man—quite good for nothing. Shall we walk, Augusta?"

"With all my heart. I am really tired of exploring so long on one spot. Come, Jane, take my other arm."

Jane declined it, however, and the husband and wife walked off. "Happy couple!" said Frank Churchill, as soon as they were out of hearing; "how well they suit one another! Very lucky—marrying as they did, upon an acquaintance formed only in a public place! They only knew each other, I think, a few weeks in Bath! Peculiarly lucky! for as to any real knowledge of a person's disposition that Bath, or any public place, can give—it is all nothing; there can be no knowledge. It is only by seeing women in their own homes, among their own set, just as they always are, that you can form any just judgment. Short of that, it is all guess and luck—and will generally be ill-luck. How many a man has committed himself on a short acquaintance, and rued it all the rest of his life!"

Miss Fairfax, who had seldom spoken before, except among her own confederates, spoke now.

"Such things do occur, undoubtedly." She was stopped by a cough. Frank Churchill turned towards her to listen.

"You were speaking," said he, gravely. She recovered her voice.

"I was only going to observe, that though such unfortunate circumstances do sometimes occur both to men and women, I cannot imagine them to be very frequent. A hasty and imprudent attachment may arise—but there is generally time to recover from it afterwards. I would be understood to mean, that it can be only weak, irresolute characters (whose happiness must be always at the mercy of chance), who will suffer an unfortunate acquaintance to be an inconvenience, an oppression for ever."

He made no answer; merely looked, and bowed in submission; and soon afterwards said, in a lively tone,—

"Well, I have so little confidence in my own judgment,

that whenever I marry, I hope somebody will choose my wife for me. Will you? (turning to Emma). Will you choose a wife for me? I am sure I should like any body fixed on by you. You provide for the family, you know (with a smile at his father). Find somebody for me. I am in no hurry. Adopt her; educate her."

"And make her like myself."

"By all means, if you can."

"Very well. I undertake the commission. You shall have a charming wife."

"She must be very lively, and have hazel eyes. I care for nothing else. I shall go abroad for a couple of years—and when I return, I shall come to you for my wife. Remember."

Emma was in no danger of forgetting. It was a commission to touch every favourite feeling. Would not Harriet be the very creature described? Hazel eyes excepted, two years more might make her all that he wished. He might even have Harriet in his thoughts at the moment; who could say? Referring the education to her seemed to imply it.

"Now, ma'am," said Jane to her aunt, "shall we join Mrs. Elton?"

"If you please, my dear. With all my heart. I am quite ready. I was ready to have gone with her, but this will do just as well. We shall soon overtake her. There she is—no, that's somebody else. That's one of the ladies in the Irish car party, not at all like her. Well, I declare——"

They walked off, followed in half a minute by Mr. Knightley. Mr. Weston, his son, Emma, and Harriet, only remained; and the young man's spirits now rose to a pitch almost unpleasant. Even Emma grew tired at last of flattery and merriment, and wished herself rather walking quietly about with any of the others, or sitting almost alone, and quite unattended to, in tranquil observation of the beautiful views beneath her. The appearance of the servants looking out for them to give notice of the carriages was a joyful sight; and even the bustle of collecting and preparing to depart, and the solicitude of Mrs. Elton to have *her* carriage first, were gladly endured, in the prospect of the quiet drive home which was to close the very questionable enjoyments of this day of pleasure. Such another scheme, composed of so many ill-assorted people, she hoped never to be betrayed into again.

While waiting for the carriage, she found Mr. Knightley by her side. He looked around, as if to see that no one were near, and then said,—

"Emma, I must once more speak to you as I have been used to do: a privilege rather endured than allowed, perhaps; but I must still use it. I cannot see you acting wrong, without a remonstrance. How could you be so unfeeling to Miss Bates? How could you be so insolent in your wit to a woman of her character, age, and situation? Emma, I had not thought it possible."

Emma recollected, blushed, was sorry, but tried to laugh it off.

"Nay, how could I help saying what I did? Nobody could have helped it. It was not so very bad. I dare say she did not understand me."

"I assure you she did. She felt your full meaning. She has talked of it since. I wish you could have heard how she talked of it—with what candour and generosity. I wish you could have heard her honouring your forbearance, in being able to pay her such attentions, as she was for ever receiving from yourself and your father, when her society must be so irksome."

"Oh!" cried Emma, "I know there is not a better creature in the world: but you must allow, that what is good and what is ridiculous are most unfortunately blended in her."

"They are blended," said he, "I acknowledge; and, were she prosperous, I could allow much for the occasional prevalence of the ridiculous over the good. Were she a woman of fortune, I would leave her every harmless absurdity to take its chance, I would not quarrel with you for any liberties of manner. Were she your equal in situation—but, Emma, consider how far this is from being the case. She is poor; she has sunk from the comforts she was born to; and if she live to old age, must probably sink more. Her situation should secure your compassion. It was badly done, indeed! You, whom she had known from an infant, whom she had seen grow up from a period when her notice was an honour,—to have you now, in thoughtless spirits, and the pride of the moment, laugh at her, humble her—and before her niece, too—and before others, many of whom (certainly *some*) would be entirely guided by *your* treatment of her. This is not pleasant to you, Emma—and it is very far from pleasant to me; but I must, I will,—I will tell you truths while I can; satisfied with proving myself your friend by very faithful counsel, and trusting that you will some time or other do me greater justice than you can do now."

While they talked, they were advancing towards the carriage; it was ready; and, before she could speak again, he had handed her in. He had misinterpreted the feelings which had kept her face averted, and her tongue motionless. They were combined only of anger against herself, mortification, and deep concern. She had not been able to speak; and, on entering the carriage, sunk back for a moment overcome; then reproaching herself for having taken no leave, making no acknowledgment, parting in apparent sullenness, she looked out with voice and hand eager to show a difference; but it was just too late. He had turned away, and the horses were in motion. She continued to look back, but in vain; and soon, with what appeared unusual speed, they were half way down the hill, and every thing left far behind. She was vexed beyond what could have been expressed—almost beyond what she could conceal. Never had she felt so agitated, mortified, grieved, at any circumstance in her life. She was most forcibly struck. The truth of his representation there was no denying. She felt it at her heart. How could she have been so brutal, so cruel to Miss Bates! How could she have exposed herself to such ill opinion in any one she valued! And how suffer him to leave her without saying one word of gratitude, of concurrence, of common kindness!

Time did not compose her. As she reflected more, she seemed but to feel it more. She never had been so depressed. Happily it was not necessary to speak. There was only Harriet, who seemed not in spirits herself, fagged, and very willing to be silent; and Emma felt the tears running down her cheeks almost all the way home, without being at any trouble to check them, extraordinary as they were.

# Chapter VIII.

The wretchedness of a scheme to Box Hill was in Emma's thoughts all the evening. How it might be considered by the rest of the party, she could not tell. They, in their different homes, and their different ways, might be looking back on it with pleasure; but in her view it was a morning more completely mis-spent, more totally bare of rational satisfaction at the time, and more to be abhorred in recollection, than any she had ever passed. A whole evening of backgammon with her father was felicity to it. *There*, indeed, lay real pleasure, for there she was giving up the sweetest hours of the twenty-four to his comfort; and feeling that, unmerited as might be the degree of his fond affection and confiding esteem, she could not, in her general conduct, be open to any severe reproach. As a daughter, she hoped she was not without a heart. She hoped no one could have said to her, "How could you be so unfeeling to your father?—I must, I will tell you truths while I can." Miss Bates should never again—no never! If attention, in future, could do away the past, she might hope to be forgiven. She had been often remiss, her conscience told her so; remiss, perhaps, more in thought than fact; scornful, ungracious.

But it should be so no more. In the warmth of true contrition, she would call upon her the very next morning, and it should be the beginning, on her side, of a regular, equal, kindly intercourse.

She was just as determined when the morrow came, and went early, that nothing might prevent her. It was not unlikely, she thought, that she might see Mr. Knightley in her way; or, perhaps, he might come in while she were paying her visit. She had no objection. She would not be ashamed of the appearance of the penitence, so justly and truly hers. Her eyes were towards Donwell as she walked, but she saw him not.

"The ladies were all at home." She had never rejoiced at the sound before, nor ever before entered the passage, nor walked up the stairs, with any wish of giving pleasure, but in conferring obligation, or of deriving it, except in subsequent ridicule.

There was a bustle on her approach; a good deal of moving and talking. She heard Miss Bates's voice; something was to be done in a hurry; the maid looked frightened and awkward; hoped she would be pleased to wait a moment, and then ushered her in too soon. The aunt and niece seemed both escaping into the adjoining room. Jane she had a distinct glimpse of, looking extremely ill; and, before the door had shut them out, she heard Miss Bates saying, "Well, my dear, I shall *say* you are laid down upon the bed, and I am sure you are ill enough."

Poor old Mrs. Bates, civil and humble as usual, looked as if she did not quite understand what was going on.

"I am afraid Jane is not very well," said she, "but I do not know; they *tell* me she is well. I dare say my daughter will be here presently, Miss Woodhouse. I hope you find a chair. I wish Hetty had not gone. I am very little able—have you a chair, ma'am? Do you sit where you like? I am sure she will be here presently."

Emma seriously hoped she would. She had a moment's fear of Miss Bates keeping away from her. But Miss Bates soon came—"Very happy and obliged,"—but Emma's conscience told her that there was not the same cheerful volubility as before,—less ease of look and manner. A very friendly enquiry after Miss Fairfax, she hoped, might lead the way to a return of old feelings. The touch seemed immediate.

"Ah, Miss Woodhouse, how kind you are! I suppose you have heard—and are come to give us joy. This does not seem much like joy, indeed, in me (twinkling away a tear or two); but it will be very trying for us to part with her, after having had her so long; and she has a dreadful headache just now, writing all the morning: such long letters, you know, to be written to Colonel Campbell and Mrs. Dixon. 'My dear,' said I, 'you will blind yourself,' for tears were in her eyes perpetually. One cannot wonder, one cannot wonder. It is a great change; and though she is amazingly fortunate,—such a situation, I suppose, as no young woman before ever met with on first going out; do not think us ungrateful, Miss Woodhouse, for such surprising good fortune (again dispersing her tears)—but, poor dear soul; if you were to see what a headache she has. When one is in great pain, you know one cannot feel any blessing quite as it may deserve. She is as low as possible. To look at her, nobody would think how delighted and happy she is to have secured such a situation. You will excuse her not coming to you, she is not able, she is gone into her own room. I want her to lie down upon the bed. 'My dear,' said I, 'I shall say you are laid down upon the bed:' but, however, she is not; she is walking about the room. But, now that she has written her letters, she says she shall soon be well. She will be extremely sorry to miss seeing you, Miss Woodhouse, but your kindness will excuse her. You were kept waiting at the door; I was quite ashamed; but somehow there was a little bustle; for it so happened, that we had not heard the knock; and, till you were on the stairs, we did not know anybody was coming. 'It is only Mrs. Cole,' said I, 'depend upon it; nobody else would come so early.'—'Well,' said she, 'it must be borne some time or other, and it may as well be now.' But then Patty came in, and said it was you. 'Oh!' said I, 'it is Miss Woodhouse, I am sure you will like to see her.'—'I can see nobody,' said she, and up she got, and would go away; and that was what made us keep you waiting; and extremely sorry and ashamed we were. 'If you must go, my dear,' said I, 'you must, and I will say you are laid down upon the bed.' "

Emma was most sincerely interested. Her heart had been long growing kinder towards Jane; and this picture of her present sufferings acted as a cure of every former ungenerous suspicion, and left her nothing but pity; and the remembrance of the less just and less gentle sensations of the past, obliged her to admit that Jane might very naturally resolve, on seeing Mrs. Cole, or any other steady friend, when she might not bear to see herself. She spoke as she felt, with earnest regret and solicitude; sincerely wishing that the circumstances which she collected from Miss Bates to be now actually determined on, might be as much for Miss Fairfax's advantage and comfort as possible. "It must be a severe trial to them all. She had understood it was to be delayed till Colonel Campbell's return."

"So very kind!" replied Miss Bates; "but you are always kind."

There was no bearing such an "always;" and to break through her dreadful gratitude, Emma made the direct enquiry of—

"Where, may I ask, is Miss Fairfax going?"

"To a Mrs. Smallridge,—charming woman,—most superior,—to have the charge of her three little girls,—delightful children. Impossible that any situation could be more replete with comfort; if we except, perhaps, Mrs. Suckling's own family, and Mrs. Bragge's; but Mrs. Smallridge is intimate with both, and in the very same neighbourhood:—lives only four miles from Maple Grove. Jane will be only four miles from Maple Grove."

"Mrs. Elton, I suppose, has been the person, to whom Miss Fairfax owes——"

"Yes, our good Mrs. Elton. The most indefatigable, true friend. She would not take a denial. She would not let Jane say, 'No;' for when Jane first heard of it, (it was the day before yesterday, the very morning we were at Donwell,) when Jane first heard of it, she was quite decided against accepting the offer, and for the reasons you mention; exactly as you say, she had made up her mind to close with nothing till Colonel Campbell's return, and nothing should induce her to enter into any engagement at present—and so she told Mrs. Elton over and over again—and I am sure I had no more idea that she would change her mind;—but that good Mrs. Elton, whose judgment never fails her, saw farther than I did. It is not every body that would have stood out in such a kind way as she did, and refuse to take Jane's answer; but she positively declared she would *not* write any such denial yesterday, as Jane wished her; she would wait—and, sure enough, yesterday evening, it was all settled that Jane should go. Quite a surprise to me! I had not the least idea!—Jane took Mrs. Elton aside, and told her at once, that upon thinking over the advantages of Mrs. Suckling's situation, she had come to the resolution of accepting it. I did not know a word of it till it was all settled."

"You spent the evening with Mrs. Elton?"

"Yes, all of us; Mrs. Elton would have us come. It was settled so, upon the hill, while we were walking about with Mr. Knightley. 'You *must all* spend your evening with us,' said she—'I positively must have you *all* come.'"

"Mr. Knightley was there too, was he?"

"No, not Mr. Knightley; he declined it from the first; and though I thought he would come, because Mrs. Elton declared she would not let him off, he did not; but my mother, and Jane, and I, were all there, and a very agreeable evening we had. Such kind friends, you know, Miss Woodhouse, one must always find agreeable, though every body seemed rather fagged after the morning's party. Even pleasure, you know, is fatiguing—and I cannot say that any of them seemed very much to have enjoyed it. However, *I* shall always think it a very pleasant party, and feel extremely obliged to the kind friends who included me in it."

"Miss Fairfax, I suppose, though you were not aware of it, had been making up her mind the whole day."

"I dare say she had."

"Whenever the time may come, it must be unwelcome to her and all her friends—but I hope her engagement will have every alleviation that is possible—I mean, as to the character and manners of the family."

"Thank you, dear Miss Woodhouse. Yes, indeed, there is every thing in the world that can make her happy in it. Except the Sucklings and Bragges, there is not such another nursery establishment, so liberal and elegant, in all Mrs. Elton's acquaintance. Mrs. Smallridge, a most delightful woman! A style of living almost equal to Maple Grove—and as to the children, except the little Sucklings and little Bragges, there are not such elegant sweet children any where. Jane will be treated with such regard and kindness! It will be nothing but pleasure, a life of pleasure. And her salary—I really cannot venture to name her salary to you, Miss Woodhouse. Even you, used as you are to great sums, would hardly believe that so much could be given to a young person like Jane."

"Ah, madam," cried Emma, "if other children are at all like what I remember to have been myself, I should think five times the amount of what I have ever yet heard named as a salary on such occasions dearly earned."

"You are so noble in your ideas."

"And when is Miss Fairfax to leave you?"

"Very soon, very soon, indeed; that's the worst of it. Within a fortnight. Mrs. Smallridge is in a great hurry. My poor mother does not know how to bear it. So then, I try to put it out of her thoughts, and say, 'Come, ma'am, do not let us think about it any more.'"

"Her friends must all be sorry to lose her; and will not Colonel and Mrs. Campbell be sorry to find that she has engaged herself before their return?"

"Yes; Jane says she is sure they will; but yet, this is such a situation as she cannot feel herself justified in declining. I was so astonished when she first told me what she had been saying to Mrs. Elton, and when Mrs. Elton at the same moment came congratulating me upon it. It was before tea—stay—no, it could not be before tea, because we were just going to cards—and yet it was before tea, because I remember thinking—oh no, now I recollect, now I have it; something happened before tea, but not that. Mr. Elton was called out of the room before tea, old John Abdy's son wanted to speak with him. Poor old John, I have a great regard for him; he was clerk to my poor father twenty-seven years; and now, poor old man, he is bed-ridden, and very poorly with the rheumatic gout in his joints—I must go and see him to-day; and so will Jane, I am sure, if she gets out at all. And poor John's son came to talk to Mr. Elton about relief from the parish: he is very well to do himself, you know, being head man at the Crown, ostler, and every thing of that sort, but still he cannot keep his father without some help; and so, when Mr. Elton came back, he told us what John ostler had been telling him, and then it came out about the chaise having been sent to Randalls to take Mr. Frank Churchill to Richmond. That was what happened before tea. It was after tea that Jane spoke to Mrs. Elton."

Miss Bates would hardly give Emma time to say how perfectly new this circumstance was to her; but as without supposing it possible that she could be ignorant of any of the particulars of Mr. Frank Churchill's going, she proceeded to give them all, it was of no consequence.

What Mr. Elton had learned from the ostler on the subject, being the accumulation of the ostler's own knowledge, and the knowledge of the servants at Randalls, was, that a messenger had come over from Richmond soon after the return of the party from Box Hill—which messenger, however, had been no more than was expected; and that Mr. Churchill had sent his nephew a few lines, containing, upon the whole, a tolerable account of Mrs. Churchill, and only wishing him not to delay coming back beyond the next morning early; but that Mr. Frank Churchill having resolved to go home directly, without waiting at all, and his horse seeming to have got a cold, Tom had been sent off immediately for the Crown chaise, and the ostler had stood out and seen it pass by, the boy going a good pace, and driving very steady.

There was nothing in all this either to astonish or interest, and it caught Emma's attention only as it united with the subject which already engaged her mind. The contrast between Mrs. Churchill's importance in the world, and Jane Fairfax's, struck her; one was every thing, the other nothing—and she sat musing on the difference of woman's destiny, and quite unconscious on what her eyes were fixed, till roused by Miss Bates's saying,—

"Ay, I see what you are thinking of, the piano-forte. What is to become of that? Very true. Poor dear Jane was talking of it just now. 'You must go,' said she. 'You and I must part. You will have no business here. Let it stay, however,' said she; 'give it house-room till Colonel Campbell comes back. I shall talk about it to him; he will settle for me; he will help me out of all my difficulties.'—And to this day, I do believe, she knows not whether it was his present or his daughter's."

Now Emma was obliged to think of the piano-forte; and the remembrance of all her former fanciful and unfair conjectures was so little pleasing, that she soon allowed herself to believe her visit had been long enough; and, with a repetition of every thing that she could venture to say of the good wishes which she really felt, took leave.

# Chapter IX.

Emma's pensive meditations, as she walked home, were not interrupted; but on entering the parlour, she found those who must rouse her. Mr. Knightley and Harriet had arrived during her absence, and were sitting with her father. Mr. Knightley immediately got up, and, in a manner decidedly graver than usual, said,—

"I would not go away without seeing you, but I have no time to spare, and therefore must now be gone directly. I am going to London, to spend a few days with John and Isabella. Have you any thing to send or say, besides the 'love,' which nobody carries?"

"Nothing at all. But is not this a sudden scheme?"

"Yes—rather—I have been thinking of it some little time."

Emma was sure he had not forgiven her; he looked unlike himself. Time, however, she thought, would tell him that they ought to be friends again. While he stood, as if meaning to go, but not going—her father began his enquiries.

"Well, my dear, and did you get there safely?—And how did you find my worthy old friend and her daughter?—I dare say they must have been very much obliged to you for coming. Dear Emma has been to call on Mrs. and Miss Bates, Mr. Knightley, as I told you before. She is always so attentive to them."

Emma's colour was heightened by this unjust praise; and with a smile and shake of the head, which spoke much, she looked at Mr. Knightley. It seemed as if there were an instantaneous impression in her favour, as if his eyes received the truth from hers, and all that had passed of good in her feelings were at once caught and honoured. He looked at her with a glow of regard. She was warmly gratified—and in another moment still more so, by a little movement of more than common friendliness on his part. He took her hand;—whether she had not herself made the first motion, she could not say—she might, perhaps, have rather offered it—but he took her hand, pressed it, and certainly was on the point of carrying it to his lips—when, from some fancy or other, he suddenly let it go. Why he should feel such a scruple, why he should change his mind when it was all but done, she could not perceive. He would have judged better, she thought, if he had not stopped. The intention, however, was indubitable; and whether it was that his manners had in general so little gallantry, or however else it happened, but she thought nothing became

him more. It was with him, of so simple, yet so dignified a
nature. She could not but recall the attempt with great satisfaction. It spoke such perfect amity. He left them immediately afterwards—gone in a moment. He always moved
with the alertness of a mind which could neither be unde-
cided nor dilatory, but now he seemed more sudden than
usual in his disappearance.

Emma could not regret her having gone to Miss Bates,
but she wished she had left her ten minutes earlier;—it
would have been a great pleasure to talk over Jane Fairfax's situation with Mr. Knightley. Neither would she regret
that he should be going to Brunswick Square, for she knew
how much his visit would be enjoyed—but it might have
happened at a better time—and to have had longer notice
of it, would have been pleasanter. They parted thorough
friends, however; she could not be deceived as to the
meaning of his countenance, and his unfinished gallantry;—it was all done to assure her that she had fully recovered his good opinion. He had been sitting with them
half an hour, she found. It was a pity that she had not come
back earlier.

In the hope of diverting her father's thoughts from the
disagreeableness of Mr. Knightley's going to London; and
going so suddenly; and going on horseback, which she knew
would be all very bad; Emma communicated her news of
Jane Fairfax, and her dependence on the effect was justified;
it supplied a very useful check,—interested, without disturb-
ing him. He had long made up his mind to Jane Fairfax's
going out as governess, and could talk of it cheerfully, but
Mr. Knightley's going to London had been an unexpected
blow.

"I am very glad, indeed, my dear, to hear she is to be so
comfortably settled. Mrs. Elton is very good-natured and
agreeable, and I dare say her acquaintance are just what they
ought to be. I hope it is a dry situation, and that her health
will be taken good care of. It ought to be a first object, as I
am sure poor Miss Taylor's always was with me. You know, my

dear, she is going to be to this new lady what Miss Taylor was to us. And I hope she will be better off in one respect, and not be induced to go away after it has been her home so long."

The following day brought news from Richmond to throw every thing else into the back-ground. An express arrived at Randalls to announce the death of Mrs. Churchill. Though her nephew had had no particular reason to hasten back on her account, she had not lived above six-and-thirty hours after his return. A sudden seizure, of a different nature from any thing foreboded by her general state, had carried her off after a short struggle. The great Mrs. Churchill was no more.

It was felt as such things must be felt. Every body had a degree of gravity and sorrow; tenderness towards the departed, solicitude for the surviving friends; and, in a reasonable time, curiosity to know where she would be buried. Goldsmith tells us, that when lovely woman stoops to folly,[19] she has nothing to do but to die; and when she stoops to be disagreeable, it is equally to be recommended as a clearer of ill fame. Mrs. Churchill, after being disliked at least twenty-five years, was now spoken of with compassionate allowances. In one point she was fully justified. She had never been admitted before to be seriously ill. The event acquitted her of all the fancifulness, and all the selfishness of imaginary complaints.

"Poor Mrs. Churchill! no doubt she had been suffering a great deal: more than any body had ever supposed—and continual pain would try the temper. It was a sad event—a great shock—with all her faults, what would Mr. Churchill do without her? Mr. Churchill's loss would be dreadful, indeed. Mr. Churchill would never get over it." Even Mr. Weston shook his head, and looked solemn, and said, "Ah, poor woman, who would have thought it!" and resolved, that his mourning should be as handsome as possible; and his wife sat sighing and moralising over her broad hems with a commiseration and good sense true and steady. How it would affect Frank was among the earliest thoughts of both. It was also a very early speculation with Emma. The character of Mrs. Churchill, the grief of her husband—her mind glanced over them both with awe and compassion—and then rested with lightened feelings on how Frank might be affected by the event, how benefited, how freed. She saw in a moment all the possible good. Now an attachment to Harriet Smith would have nothing to encounter. Mr. Churchill, independent of his wife, was feared by nobody; an easy, guidable man, to be persuaded into any thing by his nephew. All that remained to be wished was, that the nephew should form the attachment, as, with all her good will in the cause, Emma could feel no certainty of its being already formed.

Harriet behaved extremely well on the occasion, with great self-command. Whatever she might feel of brighter hope, she betrayed nothing. Emma was gratified to observe such a proof in her of strengthened character, and refrained from any allusion that might endanger its maintenance. They spoke, therefore, of Mrs. Churchill's death with mutual forbearance.

Short letters from Frank were received at Randalls, communicating all that was immediately important of their state and plans. Mr. Churchill was better than could be expected; and their first removal, on the departure of the funeral for Yorkshire, was to be to the house of a very old friend in Windsor, to whom Mr. Churchill had been promising a visit the last ten years. At present, there was nothing to be done for Harriet; good wishes for the future were all that could yet be possible on Emma's side.

It was a more pressing concern to show attention to Jane Fairfax, whose prospects were closing, while Harriet's opened, and whose engagements now allowed of no delay in any one at Highbury, who wished to show her kindness—and with Emma it was grown into a first wish. She had scarcely a stronger regret than for her past coldness; and the person, whom she had been so many months neglecting, was now the very one on whom she would have lavished every distinction of regard or sympathy. She wanted to be of use to her; wanted to show a value for her society, and testify respect and consideration. She resolved to prevail on her to spend a day at Hartfield. A note was written to urge it. The invitation was refused, and by a verbal message. "Miss Fairfax was not well enough to write;" and when Mr. Perry called at Hartfield, the same morning, it appeared that she was so much indisposed as to have been visited, though against her own consent, by himself, and that she was suffering under severe headachs, and a nervous fever to a degree, which made him doubt the possibility of her going to Mrs. Smallridge's at the time proposed. Her health seemed for the moment completely deranged—appetite quite gone—and though there were no absolutely alarming symptoms, nothing touching the pulmonary complaint, which was the standing apprehension of the family, Mr. Perry was uneasy about her. He thought she had undertaken more than she was equal to, and that she felt it so herself, though she would not own it. Her spirits seemed overcome. Her present home, he could not but observe, was unfavourable to a nervous disorder;—confined always to one room;—he could have wished it otherwise;—and her good aunt, though his very old friend, he must acknowledge to be not the best companion for an invalid of that description. Her care and attention could not be questioned; they were, in fact, only too great. He very much feared that Miss Fairfax derived more evil than good from them. Emma listened with the warmest concern; grieved for her more and more, and looked around eager to discover some way of being useful. To take her—be it only an hour or two—from her aunt, to give her change of air and scene, and quiet rational conversation, even for an hour or two, might do her good; and the following morning she wrote again to say, in the most feeling language she could command, that she would call for her in the carriage at any hour that Jane would name—mentioning that she had Mr. Perry's decided opinion, in favour of such exercise for his patient. The answer was only in this short note:—

"Miss Fairfax's compliments and thanks, but is quite unequal to any exercise."

Emma felt that her own note had deserved something better; but it was impossible to quarrel with words, whose tremulous inequality showed indisposition so plainly, and she thought only of how she might best counteract this unwillingness to be seen or assisted. In spite of the answer, therefore, she ordered the carriage, and drove to Mrs. Bates's, in the hope that Jane would be induced to join her—but it would not do;—Miss Bates came to the carriage door, all gratitude, and agreeing with her most earnestly in thinking an airing might be of the greatest service—and every thing that message could do was tried—but all in vain. Miss Bates was obliged to return without success; Jane was quite unpersuadable; the mere proposal of going out seemed to make her worse. Emma wished she could have seen her, and tried her own powers: but, almost before she could hint the wish, Miss Bates made it appear that she had promised her niece on no account to let Miss Woodhouse in. "Indeed, the truth was, that poor dear Jane could not bear to see any body—any body at all—Mrs. Elton, indeed, could not be denied—and Mrs. Cole had made such a point—and Mrs. Perry had said so much—but, except them, Jane would really see nobody."

Emma did not want to be classed with the Mrs. Eltons, the Mrs. Perrys, and the Mrs. Coles, who would force themselves any where; neither could she feel any right of preference herself—she submitted, therefore, and only questioned Miss Bates farther as to her niece's appetite and diet, which she longed to be able to assist. On that subject poor Miss Bates was very unhappy, and very communicative; Jane would hardly eat any thing:—Mr. Perry recommended nourishing food; but every thing they could command (and never had any body such good neighbours) was distasteful.

Emma, on reaching home, called the housekeeper directly to an examination of her stores; and some arrow-root of very superior quality was speedily despatched to Miss Bates with a most friendly note. In half an hour the arrow-root was returned, with a thousand thanks from Miss Bates, but "dear Jane would not be satisfied without its being sent back; it was a thing she could not take—and, moreover, she insisted on her saying, that she was not at all in want of any thing."

When Emma afterwards heard that Jane Fairfax had been seen wandering about the meadows, at some distance from Highbury, on the afternoon of the very day on which she had, under the plea of being unequal to any exercise, so peremptorily refused to go out with her in the carriage she could have no doubt—putting every thing together—that Jane was resolved to receive no kindness from *her*. She was sorry, very sorry. Her heart was grieved for a state which seemed but the more pitiable from this sort of irritation of spirits, inconsistency of action, and inequality of powers; and it mortified her that she was given so little credit for proper feeling, or esteemed so little worthy as a friend: but she had the consolation of knowing that her intentions were good, and of being able to say to herself, that could Mr. Knightley have been privy to all her attempts of assisting Jane Fairfax, could he even have seen into her heart, he would not, on this occasion, have found any thing to reprove.

## Chapter X.

One morning, about ten days after Mrs. Churchill's decease, Emma was called down stairs to Mr. Weston, who "could not stay five minutes, and wanted particularly to speak with her."—He met her at the parlour door, and hardly asking her how she did, in the natural key of his voice, sunk it immediately, to say, unheard by her father,—

"Can you come to Randalls at any time this morning?— Do, if it be possible. Mrs. Weston wants to see you. She must see you."

"Is she unwell?"

"No, no, not at all—only a little agitated. She would have ordered the carriage, and come to you, but she must see you *alone*, and that you know (nodding towards her father)— Humph! can you come?"

"Certainly. This moment, if you please. It is impossible to refuse what you ask in such a way, but what can be the matter? is she really not ill?"

"Depend upon me, but ask no more questions. You will know it all in time. The most unaccountable business! But hush, hush!"

To guess what all this meant was impossible even for Emma. Something really important seemed announced by his looks; but, as her friend was well, she endeavoured not to be uneasy, and settling it with her father, that she would take her walk now, she and Mr. Weston were soon out of the house together, and on their way at a quick pace for Randalls.

"Now," said Emma, when they were fairly beyond the sweep gates—"now, Mr. Weston, do let me know what has happened."

"No, no," he gravely replied. "Don't ask me. I promised my wife to leave it all to her. She will break it to you better than I can. Do not be impatient, Emma; it will all come out too soon."

"Break it to me," cried Emma, standing still with terror. "Good God! Mr. Weston, tell me at once. Something has happened in Brunswick Square. I know it has. Tell me, I charge you tell me this moment what it is."

"No, indeed, you are mistaken."

"Mr. Weston do not trifle with me. Consider how many of my dearest friends are now in Brunswick Square. Which of them is it? I charge you by all that is sacred not to attempt concealment."

"Upon my word, Emma."

"Your word! why not your honour! why not say upon your honour, that it has nothing to do with any of them? Good heavens! What can be to be *broke* to me, that does relate to one of that family?"

"Upon my honour," said he very seriously, "it does not. It is not in the smallest degree connected with any human being of the name of Knightley."

Emma's courage returned, and she walked on.

"I was wrong," he continued, "in talking of its being *broke* to you. I should not have used the expression. In fact, it does not concern you, it concerns only myself;—that is, we hope. Humph!—In short, my dear Emma, there is no occasion to be so uneasy about it. I don't say that it is not a disagreeable business, but things might be much worse. if we walk fast, we shall soon be at Randalls."

Emma found that she must wait; and now it required little effort. She asked no more questions therefore, merely employed her own fancy, and that soon pointed out to her the probability of its being some money concern,—something just come to light, of a disagreeable nature in the circumstances of the family; something which the late event at Richmond had brought forward. Her fancy was very active. Half a dozen natural children, perhaps, and poor Frank cut off! This, though very undesirable, would be no matter of agony to her. It inspired little more than an animating curiosity.

"Who is that gentleman on horseback?" said she, as they proceeded; speaking more to assist Mr. Weston in keeping his secret, than with any other view.

"I do not know. One of the Otways.—Not Frank; it is not Frank, I assure you. You will not see him. He is half way to Windsor by this time."

"Has your son been with you, then?"

"Oh! yes, did not you know? Well, well, never mind."

For a moment he was silent; and then added, in a tone much more guarded and demure,—

"Yes, Frank came over this morning, just to ask us how we did."

They hurried on, and were speedily at Randalls.—"Well, my dear," said he, as they entered the room,—"I have brought her, and now I hope you will soon be better. I shall leave you together. There is no use in delay. I shall not be far off, if you want me."—And Emma distinctly heard him add, in a lower tone, before he quitted the room,—"I have been as good as my word. She has not the least idea."

Mrs. Weston was looking so ill, and had an air of so much perturbation, that Emma's uneasiness increased; and the moment they were alone, she eagerly said,—

"What is it, my dear friend? Something of a very unpleasant nature, I find, has occurred;—do let me know directly what it is. I have been walking all this way in complete suspense. We both abhor suspense. Do not let mine continue longer. It will do you good to speak of your distress, whatever it may be."

"Have you, indeed, no idea?" said Mrs. Weston in a trembling voice. "Cannot you, my dear Emma—cannot you form a guess as to what you are to hear?"

"So far as that it relates to Mr. Frank Churchill, I do guess."

"You are right. It does relate to him, and I will tell you directly;" (resuming her work, and seeming resolved against looking up.) "He has been here this very morning, on a most extraordinary errand. It is impossible to express our surprise. He came to speak to his father on a subject,—to announce an attachment——"

She stopped to breathe. Emma thought first of herself, and then of Harriet.

"More than an attachment, indeed," resumed Mrs. Weston: "an engagement—a positive engagement. What will you

say, Emma—what will any body say—when it is known that
Frank Churchill and Miss Fairfax are engaged; nay, that they
have been long engaged?"

Emma even jumped with surprise; and, horror-struck, exclaimed,—

"Jane Fairfax! Good God! You are not serious? You do not
mean it?"

"You may well be amazed," returned Mrs. Weston, still
averting her eyes, and talking on with eagerness, that Emma
might have time to recover—"you may well be amazed. But
it is even so. There has been a solemn engagement between
them ever since October,—formed at Weymouth, and kept a
secret from every body. Not a creature knowing it but themselves—neither the Campbells, nor her family, nor his. It is
so wonderful, that, though perfectly convinced of the fact, it
is yet almost incredible to myself. I can hardly believe it. I
thought I knew him."

Emma scarcely heard what was said. Her mind was divided between two ideas: her own former conversations with
him about Miss Fairfax; and poor Harriet: and for some time
she could only exclaim, and require confirmation, repeated
confirmation.

"Well!" said she at last, trying to recover herself; "this is a
circumstance which I must think of at least half a day, before
I can at all comprehend it. What!—engaged to her all the
winter—before either of them came to Highbury?"

"Engaged since October,—secretly engaged. It has hurt
me, Emma, very much. It has hurt his father equally. *Some
part* of his conduct we cannot excuse."

Emma pondered a moment, and then replied,—"I will
not pretend *not* to understand you; and to give you all the relief in my power, be assured that no such effect has followed
his attentions to me, as you are apprehensive of."

Mrs. Weston looked up, afraid to believe; but Emma's
countenance was as steady as her words.

"That you may have less difficulty in believing this boast,
of my present perfect indifference," she continued, "I will

farther tell you, that there was a period in the early part of
our acquaintance, when I did like him—when I was very
much disposed to be attached to him; nay, was attached—
and how it came to cease, is perhaps the wonder. Fortunately, however, it did cease. I have really for some time
past, for at least these three months, cared nothing about
him. You may believe me, Mrs. Weston. This is the simple
truth."

Mrs. Weston kissed her with tears of joy; and when she
could find utterance, assured her, that this protestation
had done her more good than any thing else in the world
could do.

"Mr. Weston will be almost as much relieved as myself,"
said she. "On this point we have been wretched. It was our
darling wish that you might be attached to each other, and
we were persuaded that it was so. Imagine what we have been
feeling on your account."

"I have escaped; and that I should escape, may be a matter of grateful wonder to you and myself. But this does not
acquit *him*, Mrs. Weston; and I must say, that I think him
greatly to blame. What right had he to come among us with
affection and faith engaged, and with manners so *very* disengaged? What right had he to endeavour to please, as he
certainly did—to distinguish any one young woman with persevering attention, as he certainly did, while he really belonged to another? How could he tell what mischief he
might be doing?—How could he tell that he might not be
making me in love with him? Very wrong, very wrong indeed."

"From something that he said, my dear Emma, I rather
imagine——"

"And how could *she* bear such behaviour? Composure
with a witness! to look on, while repeated attentions were offering to another woman before her face, and not resent it.
That is a degree of placidity, which I can neither comprehend nor respect."

"There were misunderstandings between them, Emma;

he said so expressly. He had not time to enter into much explanation. He was here only a quarter of an hour, and in a state of agitation which did not allow the full use even of the time he could stay—but that there had been misunderstandings he decidedly said. The present crisis, indeed, seemed to be brought on by them; and those misunderstandings might very possibly arise from the impropriety of his conduct."

"Impropriety! Oh! Mrs. Weston, it is too calm a censure. Much, much beyond impropriety! It has sunk him—I cannot say how it has sunk him in my opinion. So unlike what a man should be! None of that upright integrity, that strict adherence to truth and principle, that disdain of trick and littleness, which a man should display in every transaction of his life."

"Nay, dear Emma, now I must take his part; for though be has been wrong in this instance, I have known him long enough to answer for his having many, very many good qualities; and——"

"Good God!" cried Emma, not attending to her.—"Mrs. Smallridge, too! Jane actually on the point of going as governess! What could he mean by such horrible indelicacy? To suffer her to engage herself—to suffer her even to think of such a measure!"

"He knew nothing about it, Emma. On this article I can fully acquit him. It was a private resolution of hers, not communicated to him, or at least not communicated in a way to carry conviction. Till yesterday, I know, he said he was in the dark as to her plans. They burst on him, I do not know how, but by some letter or message—and it was the discovery of what she was doing, of this very project of hers, which determined him to come forward at once, own it all to his uncle, throw himself on his kindness, and, in short, put an end to the miserable state of concealment that had been carrying on so long."

Emma began to listen better.

"I am to hear from him soon," continued Mrs. Weston.

"He told me at parting, that he should soon write; and he spoke in a manner which seemed to promise me many particulars that could not be given now. Let us wait, therefore, for this letter. It may bring many extenuations. It may make many things intelligible and excusable which now are not to be understood. Don't let us be severe; don't let us be in a hurry to condemn him. Let us have patience. I must love him; and now that I am satisfied on one point, the one material point, I am sincerely anxious for its all turning out well, and ready to hope that it may. They must both have suffered a great deal under such a system of secresy and concealment."

"*His* sufferings," replied Emma drily, "do not appear to have done him much harm. Well, and how did Mr. Churchill take it?"

"Most favourably for his nephew—gave his consent with scarcely a difficulty. Conceive what the events of a week have done in that family! While poor Mrs. Churchill lived, I suppose there could not have been a hope, a chance, a possibility; but scarcely are her remains at rest in the family vault, than her husband is persuaded to act exactly opposite to what she would have required. What a blessing it is, when undue influence does not survive the grave!—He gave his consent with very little persuasion."

"Ah!" thought Emma, "he would have done as much for Harriet."

"This was settled last night, and Frank was off with the light this morning. He stopped at Highbury, at the Bates's, I fancy, some time, and then came on hither; but was in such a hurry to get back to his uncle, to whom he is just now more necessary than ever, that, as I tell you, he could stay with us but a quarter of an hour. He was very much agitated—very much indeed—to a degree that made him appear quite a different creature from any thing I had ever seen him before. In addition to all the rest, there had been the shock of finding her so very unwell, which he had had no previous suspicion of, and there was every appearance of his having been feeling a great deal."

"And do you really believe the affair to have been carrying on with such perfect secrecy?—The Campbells, the Dixons—did none of them know of the engagement?"

Emma could not speak the name of Dixon without a little blush.

"None; not one. He positively said that it had been known to no being in the world but their two selves."

"Well," said Emma, "I suppose we shall gradually grow reconciled to the idea, and I wish them very happy. But I shall always think it a very abominable sort of proceeding. What has it been but a system of hypocrisy and deceit,—espionage, and treachery?—To come among us with professions of openness and simplicity; and such a league in secret to judge us all!—Here have we been the whole winter and spring completely duped, fancying ourselves all on an equal footing of truth and honour, with two people in the midst of us who may have been carrying round, comparing and sitting in judgment on sentiments and words that were never meant for both to hear.—They must take the consequence, if they have heard each other spoken of in a way not perfectly agreeable!"

"I am quite easy on that head," replied Mrs. Weston. "I am very sure that I never said any thing of either to the other, which both might not have heard."

"You are in luck.—Your only blunder was confined to my ear, when you imagined a certain friend of ours in love with the lady."

"True. But as I have always had a thoroughly good opinion of Miss Fairfax, I never could, under any blunder, have spoken ill of her; and as to speaking ill of him, there I must have been safe."

At this moment Mr. Weston appeared at a little distance from the window, evidently on the watch. His wife gave him a look which invited him in; and, while he was coming round, added,—"Now, dearest Emma, let me entreat you to

say and look every thing that may set his heart at ease and incline him to be satisfied with the match. Let us make the best
of it—and, indeed, almost every thing may be fairly said in
her favour. It is not a connection to gratify; but if Mr.
Churchill does not feel that, why should we? and it may be a
very fortunate circumstance for him,—for Frank, I mean,—
that he should have attached himself to a girl of such steadiness of character and good judgment as I have always given
her credit for—and still am disposed to give her credit for, in
spite of this one great deviation from the strict rule of right.
And how much may be said in her situation for even that
error!"

"Much, indeed!" cried Emma, feelingly. "If a woman can
ever be excused for thinking only of herself, it is in a situation like Jane Fairfax's.—Of such, one may almost say, that
'the world is not theirs, nor the world's law.' "[20]

She met Mr. Weston on his entrance, with a smiling countenance, exclaiming,—

"A very pretty trick you have been playing me, upon my
word! This was a device, I suppose, to sport with my curiosity, and exercise my talent of guessing. But you really frightened me. I thought you had lost half your property, at least.
And here, instead of its being a matter of condolence, it
turns out to be one of congratulation.—I congratulate you,
Mr. Weston, with all my heart, on the prospect of having one
of the most lovely and accomplished young women in England for your daughter."

A glance or two between him and his wife convinced him
that all was as right as this speech proclaimed; and its happy
effect on his spirits was immediate. His air and voice recovered their usual briskness: he shook her heartily and gratefully by the hand, and entered on the subject in a manner to
prove that he now only wanted time and persuasion to think
the engagement no very bad thing. His companions suggested only what could palliate imprudence or smooth objections; and by the time they had talked it all over together,
and he had talked it all over again with Emma, in their walk

back to Hartfield, he was become perfectly reconciled, and not far from thinking it the very best thing that Frank could possibly have done.

# *Chapter XI.*

"Harriet, poor Harriet!"—Those were the words; in them lay the tormenting ideas which Emma could not get rid of, and which constituted the real misery of the business to her. Frank Churchill had behaved very ill by herself—very ill in many ways,—but it was not so much *his* behaviour as her *own*, which made her so angry with him. It was the scrape which he had drawn her into on Harriet's account, that gave the deepest hue to his offence.—Poor Harriet! to be a second time the dupe of her misconceptions and flattery. Mr. Knightley had spoken prophetically, when he once said, "Emma, you have been no friend to Harriet Smith."—She was afraid she had done her nothing but disservice.—It was true that she had not to charge herself in this instance, as in the former, with being the sole and original author of the mischief; with having suggested such feelings as might otherwise never have entered Harriet's imagination; for Harriet had acknowledged her admiration and preference of Frank Churchill before she had ever given her a hint on the subject; but she felt completely guilty of having encouraged what she might have repressed. She might have prevented the indulgence and increase of such sentiments. Her influence would have been enough. And now she was very conscious that she ought to have prevented them.—She felt that she had been risking her friend's happiness on most insufficient grounds. Common sense would have directed her to tell Harriet that she must not allow herself to think of him, and that there were five hundred chances to one against his ever caring for her.—"But, with common sense," she added, "I am afraid I have had little to do."

She was extremely angry with herself. If she could not have been angry with Frank Churchill too, it would have been dreadful.—As for Jane Fairfax, she might at least relieve her feelings from any present solicitude on her account. Harriet would be anxiety enough; she need no longer be unhappy about Jane, whose troubles and whose ill health having, of course, the same origin, must be equally under cure.—Her days of insignificance and evil were over.—She would soon be well, and happy, and prosperous.—Emma could now imagine why her own attentions had been slighted. This discovery laid many smaller matters open. No doubt it had been from jealousy.—In Jane's eyes she had been a rival; and well might any thing she could offer of assistance or regard be repulsed. An airing in the Hartfield carriage would have been the rack, and arrow-root from the Hartfield store-room must have been poison. She understood it all; and as far as her mind could disengage itself from the injustice and selfishness of angry feelings, she acknowledged that Jane Fairfax would have neither elevation nor happiness beyond her desert. But poor Harriet was such an engrossing charge! There was little sympathy to be spared for any body else. Emma was sadly fearful that this second disappointment would be more severe than the first. Considering the very superior claims of the object, it ought; and judging by its apparently stronger effect on Harriet's mind, produce reserve and self-command, it would.—She must communicate the painful truth, however, and as soon as possible. An injunction of secresy had been among Mr. Weston's parting words. "For the present the whole affair was to be completely a secret. Mr. Churchill had made a point of it, as a token of respect to the wife he had so very recently lost; and every body admitted it to be no more than due decorum."—Emma had promised; but still Harriet must be excepted. It was her superior duty.

In spite of her vexation, she could not help feeling it almost ridiculous, that she should have the very same distressing and delicate office to perform by Harriet, which Mrs. Weston had just gone through by herself. The intelligence, which had been so anxiously announced to her, she was now to be anxiously announcing to another. Her heart beat quick on hearing Harriet's footstep and voice; so, she supposed, had poor Mrs. Weston felt when *she* was approaching Randalls. Could the event of the disclosure bear an equal resemblance!—But of that, unfortunately, there could be no chance.

"Well, Miss Woodhouse," cried Harriet, coming eagerly into the room, "is not this the oddest news that ever was?"

"What news do you mean?" replied Emma, unable to guess, by look or voice, whether Harriet could indeed have received any hint.

"About Jane Fairfax. Did you ever hear any thing so strange? Oh!—you need not be afraid of owning it to me, for Mr. Weston has told me himself. I met him just now. He told me it was to be a great secret; and, therefore, I should not think of mentioning it to any body but you, but he said you knew it."

"What did Mr. Weston tell you?" said Emma, still perplexed.

"Oh! he told me all about it; that Jane Fairfax and Mr. Frank Churchill are to be married, and that they have been privately engaged to one another this long while. How very odd!"

It was, indeed, so odd; Harriet's behaviour was so extremely odd, that Emma did not know how to understand it. Her character appeared absolutely changed. She seemed to propose showing no agitation, or disappointment, or peculiar concern in the discovery. Emma looked at her, quite unable to speak.

"Had you any idea," cried Harriet, "of his being in love

with her?—You, perhaps, might.—You (blushing as she spoke), who can see into every body's heart; but nobody else——"

"Upon my word," said Emma, "I begin to doubt my having any such talent. Can you seriously ask me, Harriet, whether I imagined him attached to another woman at the very time that I was—tacitly, if not openly—encouraging you to give way to your own feelings?—I never had the slightest suspicion, till within the last hour, of Mr. Frank Churchill's having the least regard for Jane Fairfax. You may be very sure that, if I had, I should have cautioned you accordingly."

"Me!" cried Harriet, colouring, and astonished. "Why should you caution me?—You do not think I care about Mr. Frank Churchill."

"I am delighted to hear you speak so stoutly on the subject," replied Emma, smiling; "but you do not mean to deny that there was a time—and not very distant either—when you gave me reason to understand that you did care about him?"

"Him!—never, never. Dear Miss Woodhouse, how could you so mistake me?" (turning away distressed.)

"Harriet," cried Emma, after a moment's pause, "what do you mean?—Good Heaven! what do you mean?—Mistake you!—Am I to suppose then——?"

She could not speak another word.—Her voice was lost; and she sat down, waiting in great terror till Harriet should answer.

Harriet, who was standing at some distance, and with face turned from her, did not immediately say any thing; and when she did speak, it was in a voice nearly as agitated as Emma's.

"I should not have thought it possible," she began, "that you could have misunderstood me! I know we agreed never to name him—but considering how infinitely superior he is to every body else, I should not have thought it possible that I could be supposed to mean any other person. Mr. Frank Churchill, indeed! I do not know who would ever look at him in the company of the other. I hope I have a better taste than to think of Mr. Frank Churchill, who is like nobody by his side. And that you should have been so mistaken, is amazing!—I am sure, but for believing that you entirely approved and meant to encourage me in my attachment, I should have considered it at first too great a presumption almost to dare to think of him. At first, if you had not told me that more wonderful things had happened; that there had been matches of greater disparity (those were your very words);— I should not have dared to give way to———I should not have thought it possible———But if *you*, who had always acquainted with him———"

"Harriet," cried Emma, collecting herself resolutely, "let us understand each other now, without the possibility of farther mistake. Are you speaking of—Mr. Knightley?"

"To be sure I am. I never could have an idea of any body else,—and so I thought you knew. When we talked about him, it was clear as possible."

"Not quite," returned Emma, with forced calmness; "for all that you then said appeared to me to relate to a different person. I could almost assert that you had *named* Mr. Frank Churchill. I am sure the service Mr. Frank Churchill had rendered you, in protecting you from the gipsies, was spoken of."

"Oh, Miss Woodhouse, how you do forget!"

"My dear Harriet, I perfectly remember the substance of what I said on the occasion. I told you that I did not wonder at your attachment; that, considering the service he had rendered you, it was extremely natural:—and you agreed to it, expressing yourself very warmly as to your sense of that service, and mentioning even what your sensations had been in seeing him come forward to your rescue. The impression of it is strong on my memory."

"Oh, dear," cried Harriet, "now I recollect what you mean; but I was thinking of something very different at the time. It was not the gipsies—it was not Mr. Frank Churchill that I meant. No! (with some elevation) I was thinking of a much more precious circumstance,—of Mr. Knightley's coming and asking me to dance, when Mr. Elton would not stand up with me, and when there was no other partner in the room. That was the kind action; that was the noble benevolence and generosity; that was the service which made me begin to feel how superior he was to every other being upon earth."

"Good God!" cried Emma, "this has been a most unfortunate—most deplorable mistake! What is to be done?"

"You would not have encouraged me, then, if you had understood me. At least, however, I cannot be worse off than I should have been, if the other had been the person; and now—it *is* possible——"

She paused a few moments. Emma could not speak.

"I do not wonder, Miss Woodhouse," she resumed, "that you should feel a great difference between the two, as to me or as to any body. You must think one five hundred million times more above me than the other. But I hope, Miss Woodhouse, that supposing—that if—strange as it may appear——But you know they were your own words, that *more* wonderful things had happened; matches of *greater* disparity had taken place than between Mr. Frank Churchill and me; and, therefore, it seems as if such a thing even as this may have occurred before;—and if I should be so fortunate, beyond expression, as to——if Mr. Knightley should really——if *he* does not mind the disparity, I hope, dear Miss Woodhouse, you will not set yourself against it, and try to put difficulties in the way. But you are too good for that, I am sure."

Harriet was standing at one of the windows. Emma turned round to look at her in consternation, and hastily said,—

"Have you any idea of Mr. Knightley's returning your affection?"

"Yes," replied Harriet modestly, but not fearfully; "I must say that I have."

Emma's eyes were instantly withdrawn; and she sat silently

meditating, in a fixed attitude, for a few minutes. A few minutes were sufficient for making her acquainted with her own heart. A mind like hers, once opening to suspicion, made rapid progress: she touched—she admitted—she acknowledged the whole truth. Why was it so much worse that Harriet should be in love wiih Mr. Knightley, than with Frank Churchill? Why was the evil so dreadfully increased by Harriet's having some hope of a return? It darted through her with the speed of an arrow, that Mr. Knightley must marry no one but herself!

Her own conduct, as well as her own heart, was before her in the same few minutes. She saw it all with a clearness which had never blessed her before. How improperly had she been acting by Harriet! How inconsiderate, how indelicate, how irrational, how unfeeling, had been her conduct! What blindness, what madness, had led her on! It struck her with dreadful force, and she was ready to give it every bad name in the world. Some portion of respect for herself, however, in spite of all these demerits—some concern for her own appearance, and a strong sense of justice by Harriet (there would be no need of *compassion* to the girl who believed herself loved by Mr. Knightley—but justice required that she should not be made unhappy by any coldness now)—gave Emma the resolution to sit and endure farther with calmness, with even apparent kindness. For her own advantage, indeed, it was fit that the utmost extent of Harriet's hopes should be enquired into; and Harriet had done nothing to forfeit the regard and interest which had been so voluntarily formed and maintained—or to deserve to be slighted by the person whose counsels had never led her right. Rousing from reflection, therefore, and subduing her emotion, she turned to Harriet again, and, in a more inviting accent, renewed the conversation; for as to the subject which had first introduced it, the wonderful story of Jane Fairfax, that was quite sunk and lost. Neither of them thought but of Mr. Knightley and themselves.

Harriet, who had been standing in no unhappy reverie,

was yet very glad to be called from it, by the now encouraging manner of such a judge, and such a friend, as Miss Woodhouse; and only wanted invitation to give the history of her hopes with great though trembling delight. Emma's tremblings, as she asked, and as she listened, were better concealed than Harriet's, but they were not less. Her voice was not unsteady; but her mind was in all the perturbation that such a development of self, such a burst of threatening evil, such a confusion of sudden and perplexing emotions, must create. She listened with much inward suffering, but with great outward patience, to Harriet's detail. Methodical, or well arranged, or very well delivered, it could not be expected to be; but it contained, when separated from all the feebleness and tautology of the narration, a substance to sink her spirit; especially with the corroborating circumstances which her own memory brought in favour of Mr. Knightley's most improved opinion of Harriet.

Harriet had been conscious of a difference in his behaviour ever since those two decisive dances. Emma knew that he had, on that occasion, found her much superior to his expectation. From that evening, or at least from the time of Miss Woodhouse's encouraging her to think of him, Harriet had begun to be sensible of his talking to her much more than she had been used to do, and of his having, indeed, quite a different manner towards her;—a manner of kindness and sweetness. Latterly, she had been more and more aware of it. When they had been all walking together, he had so often come and walked by her, and talked so very delightfully!—He seemed to want to be acquainted with her. Emma knew it to have been very much the case: she had often observed the change, to almost the same extent. Harriet repeated expressions of approbation and praise from him,—and Emma felt them to be in the closest agreement with what she had known of his opinion of Harriet. He praised her for being without art or affectation; for having simple, honest, generous feelings. She knew that he saw such recommendations in Harriet; he had dwelt on them to her more than once. Much that lived in Harriet's memory; many little particulars of the notice she had received from him; a look, a speech, a removal from one chair to another, a compliment implied, a preference inferred; had been unnoticed, because unsuspected, by Emma. Circumstances that might swell to half an hour's relation, and contained multiplied proofs to her who had seen them, had passed undiscerned by her who now heard them; but the two latest occurrences to be mentioned—the two of strongest promise to Harriet—were not without some degree of witness from Emma herself. The first was his walking with her apart from the others in the lime walk at Donwell, where they had been walking some time before Emma came, and he had taken pains (as she was convinced) to draw her from the rest to himself; and at first he had talked to her in a more particular way than he had ever done before,—in a very particular way indeed!—(Harriet could not recall it without a blush.) He seemed to be almost asking her whether her affections were engaged. But as soon as she (Miss Woodhouse) appeared likely to join them, he changed the subject, and began talking about farming. The second was his having sat talking with her nearly half an hour before Emma came back from her visit, the very last morning of his being at Hartfield,—though, when he first came in, he had said that he could not stay five minutes,—and his having told her, during their conversation, that though he must go to London, it was very much against his inclination that he left home at all, which was much more (as Emma felt) than he had acknowledged to *her*. The superior degree of confidence towards Harriet which this one article marked, gave her severe pain.

On the subject of the first of the two circumstances, she did, after a little reflection, venture the following question:—"Might he not?—Is not it possible, that when enquiring, as you thought, into the state of your affections, he might be alluding to Mr. Martin,—he might have Mr. Martin's interest in view?" But Harriet rejected the suspicion with spirit.

"Mr. Martin! No, indeed!—There was not a hint of Mr. Martin. I hope I know better now, than to care for Mr. Martin, or to be suspected of it."

When Harriet had closed her evidence, she appealed to her dear Miss Woodhouse, to say whether she had not good ground for hope.

"I never should have presumed to think of it at first," said she, "but for you. You told me to observe him carefully, and let his behaviour be the rule of mine—and so I have. But now I seem to feel that I may deserve him; and that if he does choose me, it will not be any thing so very wonderful."

The bitter feelings occasioned by this speech, the many bitter feelings, made the utmost exertion necessary on Emma's side, to enable her to say in reply,—

"Harriet, I will only venture to declare, that Mr. Knightley is the last man in the world who would intentionally give any woman the idea of his feeling for her more than he really does."

Harriet seemed ready to worship her friend for a sentence so satisfactory; and Emma was only saved from raptures and fondness, which at that moment would have been dreadful penance, by the sound of her father's footsteps. He was coming through the hall. Harriet was too much agitated to encounter him. "She could not compose herself—Mr. Woodhouse would be alarmed—she had better go;"—with most ready encouragement from her friend, therefore, she passed off through another door—and the moment she was gone, this was the spontaneous burst of Emma's feelings: "Oh God! that I had never seen her!"

The rest of the day, the following night, were hardly enough for her thoughts. She was bewildered amidst the confusion of all that had rushed on her within the last few hours. Every moment had brought a fresh surprise; and every surprise must be matter of humiliation to her.—How to understand it all! How to understand the deceptions she had been thus practising on herself, and living under!—The blunders, the blindness of her own head and heart!—She sat still, she walked about, she tried her own room, she tried the shrubbery—in every place, every posture, she perceived that she had acted most weakly; that she had been imposed on by others in a most mortifying degree; that she had been imposing on herself in a degree yet more mortifying; that she was wretched, and should probably find this day but the beginning of wretchedness.

To understand, thoroughly understand her own heart, was the first endeavour. To that point went every leisure moment which her father's claims on her allowed, and every moment of involuntary absence of mind.

How long had Mr. Knightley been so dear to her, as every feeling declared him now to be? When had his influence, such influence begun? When had he succeeded to that place in her affection, which Frank Churchill had once, for a short period, occupied?—She looked back; she compared the two—compared them, as they had always stood in her estimation, from the time of the latter's becoming known to her—and as they must at any time have been compared by her, had it—oh! had it, by any blessed felicity, occurred to her, to institute the comparison. She saw that there never had been a time when she did not consider Mr. Knightley as infinitely the superior, or when his regard for her had not been infinitely the most dear. She saw, that in persuading herself, in fancying, in acting to the contrary, she had been entirely under a delusion, totally ignorant of her own heart—and, in short, that she had never really cared for Frank Churchill at all!

This was the conclusion of the first series of reflection. This was the knowledge of herself, on the first question of enquiry, which she reached; and without being long in reaching it. She was most sorrowfully indignant; ashamed of every sensation but the one revealed to her—her affection for Mr. Knightley. Every other part of her mind was disgusting.

With insufferable vanity had she believed herself in the secret of every body's feelings; with unpardonable arrogance proposed to arrange every body's destiny. She was proved to have been universally mistaken; and she had not quite done nothing—for she had done mischief. She had brought evil on Harriet, on herself, and, she too much feared, on Mr. Knightley. Were this most unequal of all connections to take place, on her must rest all the reproach of having given it a beginning; for his attachment, she must believe to be produced only by a consciousness of Harriet's ;—and even were this not the case, he would never have known Harriet at all but for her folly.

Mr. Knightley and Harriet Smith!—It was an union to distance every wonder of the kind. The attachment of Frank Churchill and Jane Fairfax became commonplace, threadbare, stale in the comparison, exciting no surprise, presenting no disparity, affording nothing to be said or thought. Mr. Knightley and Harriet Smith! Such an elevation on her side! Such a debasement on his! It was horrible to Emma to think how it must sink him in the general opinion, to foresee the smiles, the sneers, the merriment it would prompt at his expense; the mortification and disdain of his brother, the thousand inconveniencies to himself. Could it be? No; it was impossible. And yet it was far, very far, from impossible.— Was it a new circumstance for a man of first-rate abilities to be captivated by very inferior powers? Was it new for one, perhaps too busy to seek, to be the prize of a girl who would seek him? Was it new for any thing in this world to be unequal, inconsistent, incongruous—or for chance and circumstance (as second causes)[21] to direct the human fate?

Oh! had she never brought Harriet forward! Had she left her where she ought, and where he had told her she ought! Had she not, with a folly which no tongue could express, prevented her marrying the unexceptionable young man who would have made her happy and respectable in the line of life to which she ought to belong, all would have been safe; none of this dreadful sequel would have been.

How Harriet could ever have had the presumption to raise her thoughts to Mr. Knightley!—How she could dare to fancy herself the chosen of such a man till actually assured of it! But Harriet was less humble, had fewer scruples than formerly. Her inferiority, whether of mind or situation, seemed little felt. She had seemed more sensible of Mr. Elton's being to stoop in marrying her, than she now seemed of Mr. Knightley's. Alas! was not that her own doing too? Who had been at pains to give Harriet notions of self-consequence but herself? Who but herself had taught her, that she was to elevate herself if possible, and that her claims were great to a high worldly establishment? If Harriet, from being humble, were grown vain, it was her doing too.

## Chapter XII.

T ill now that she was threatened with its loss Emma had never known how much of her happiness depended on being *first* with Mr. Knightley, first in interest and affection. Satisfied that it was so, and feeling it her due, she had enjoyed it without reflection; and only in the dread of being supplanted, found how inexpressibly important it had been. Long, very long, she felt she had been first; for, having no female connections of his own there had been only Isabella whose claims could be compared with hers, and she had always known exactly how far he loved and esteemed Isabella. She had herself been first with him for many years past. She had not deserved it; she had often been negligent or perverse, slighting his advice, or even wilfully opposing him, insensible of half his merits, and quarrelling with him because he would not acknowledge her false and insolent estimate of her own—but still, from family attachment and habit, and thorough excellence of mind, he had loved her, and watched over her from a girl, with an endeavour to improve her, and an anxiety for her doing right, which no other creature had at all shared. In spite of all her faults, she knew she was dear to him; might she not say, very dear? When the suggestions of hope, however, which must follow here, presented themselves, she could not presume to indulge them. Harriet Smith might think herself not unworthy of being peculiarly, exclusively, passionately loved by Mr. Knightley. *She* could not. She could not flatter herself with any idea of blindness in his attachment to *her*. She had received a very recent proof of its impartiality. How shocked had he been by her behaviour to Miss Bates! How directly, how strongly had he expressed himself to her on the subject! Not too strongly for the offence—but far, far too strongly to issue from any feeling softer than upright justice and clear-sighted good will. She had no hope, nothing to deserve the name of hope, that he could have that sort of affection for herself which was now in question; but there was a hope, (at times a slight one, at times much stronger,) that Harriet might have deceived herself, and be over-rating his regard for *her*. Wish it she must, for his sake—be the consequence nothing to herself, but his remaining single all his life. Could she be secure of that, indeed, of his never marrying at all, she believed she should be perfectly satisfied. Let him but continue the same Mr. Knightley to her and her father, the same Mr. Knightley to all the world; let Donwell and Hartfield lose none of their precious intercourse of friendship and confidence, and her peace would be fully secured. Marriage, in fact, would not do for her. It would be incompatible with what she owed to her father, and with what she felt for him. Nothing should separate her from her father. She would not marry, even if she were asked by Mr. Knightley.

It must be her ardent wish that Harriet might be disappointed; and she hoped, that when able to see them together again, she might at least be able to ascertain what the chances for it were. She should see them henceforward with the closest observance; and wretchedly as she had hitherto misunderstood even those she was watching, she did not know how to admit that she could be blinded here. He was expected back every day. The power of observation would be soon given—frightfully soon it appeared when her thoughts were in one course. In the meanwhile, she resolved against seeing Harriet. It would do neither of them good, it would do the subject no good, to be talking of it farther. She was resolved not to be convinced, as long as she could doubt, and yet had no authority for opposing Harriet's confidence. To talk would be only to irritate. She wrote to her, therefore, kindly, but decisively, to beg that she would not, at present, come to Hartfield; acknowledging it to be her conviction, that all farther confidential discussion of *one* topic had better be avoided; and hoping, that if a few days were allowed to pass before they met again, except in the company of others—she objected only to a *tête-à-tête*—they might be able to act as if they had forgotten the conversation of yesterday. Harriet submitted, and approved, and was grateful.

This point was just arranged, when a visiter arrived to tear Emma's thoughts a little from the one subject which had engrossed them, sleeping or waking, the last twenty-four hours—Mrs. Weston, who had been calling on her daughter-in-law elect, and took Hartfield in her way home, almost as much in duty to Emma as in pleasure to herself, to relate all the particulars of so interesting an interview.

Mr. Weston had accompanied her to Mrs. Bates's, and gone through his share of this essential attention most handsomely; but she having then induced Miss Fairfax to join her in an airing, was now returned with much more to say, and much more to say with satisfaction, than a quarter of an hour spent in Mrs. Bates's parlour, with all the incumbrance of awkward feelings, could have afforded.

A little curiosity Emma had; and she made the most of it while her friend related. Mrs. Weston had set off to pay the visit in a good deal of agitation herself; and in the first place had wished not to go at all at present, to be allowed merely to write to Miss Fairfax instead, and to defer this ceremoni-

ous call till a little time had passed, and Mr. Churchill could
be reconciled to the engagement's becoming known; as,
considering every thing, she thought such a visit could not
be paid without leading to reports: but Mr. Weston had
thought differently; he was extremely anxious to show his approbation to Miss Fairfax and her family, and did not conceive that any suspicion could be excited by it; or if it were,
that it would be of any consequence; for "such things," he
observed, "always got about." Emma smiled, and felt that Mr.
Weston had very good reason for saying so. They had gone,
in short; and very great had been the evident distress and
confusion of *the* lady. She had hardly been able to speak a
word, and every look and action had shown how deeply she
was suffering from consciousness. The quiet, heartfelt satisfaction of the old lady, and the rapturous delight of her
daughter, who proved even too joyous to talk as usual, had
been a gratifying, yet almost an affecting, scene. They were
both so truly respectable in their happiness, so disinterested
in every sensation; thought so much of Jane; so much of
every body, and so little of themselves, that every kindly feeling was at work for them. Miss Fairfax's recent illness had offered a fair plea for Mrs. Weston to invite her to an airing;
she had drawn back and declined at first, but, on being
pressed, had yielded; and, in the course of their drive, Mrs.
Weston had, by gentle encouragement, overcome so much
of her embarrassment, as to bring her to converse on the important subject. Apologies for her seemingly ungracious silence in their first reception, and the warmest expressions of
the gratitude she was always feeling towards herself and Mr.
Weston, must necessarily open the cause; but when these ef-
fusions were put by, they had talked a good deal of the present and of the future state of the engagement. Mrs. Weston
was convinced that such conversation must be the greatest
relief to her companion, pent up within her own mind as
every thing had so long been, and was very much pleased
with all that she had said on the subject.

"On the misery of what she had suffered, during the concealment of so many months," continued Mrs. Weston, "she was energetic. This was one of her expressions. 'I will not say, that since I entered into the engagement I have not had some happy moments; but I can say, that I have never known the blessing of one tranquil hour:'—and the quivering lip, Emma, which uttered it, was an attestation that I felt at my heart."

"Poor girl!" said Emma. "She thinks herself wrong, then, for having consented to a private engagement?"

"Wrong! No one, I believe, can blame her more than she is disposed to blame herself. 'The consequence,' said she, 'has been a state of perpetual suffering to me; and so it ought. But after all the punishment that misconduct can bring, it is still not less misconduct. Pain is no expiation. I never can be blameless. I have been acting contrary to all my sense of right; and the fortunate turn that every thing has taken, and the kindness I am now receiving, is what my conscience tells me ought not to be. Do not imagine, madam,' she continued, 'that I was taught wrong. Do not let any reflection fall on the principles or the care of the friends who brought me up. The error has been all my own; and I do assure you that, with all the excuse that present circumstances may appear to give, I shall yet dread making the story known to Colonel Campbell.'"

"Poor girl!" said Emma again. "She loves him, then, excessively, I suppose. It must have been from attachment only, that she could be led to form the engagement. Her affection must have overpowered her judgment."

"Yes, I have no doubt of her being extremely attached to him."

"I am afraid," returned Emma, sighing, "that I must often have contributed to make her unhappy."

"On your side, my love, it was very innocently done. But she probably had something of that in her thoughts, when alluding to the misunderstandings which he had given us hints of before. One natural consequence of the evil she had involved herself in," she said, "was that of making her *unrea-*

*sonable*. The consciousness of having done amiss, had exposed her to a thousand inquietudes, and made her captious and irritable to a degree that must have been—that had been—hard for him to bear. 'I did not make the allowances,' said she, 'which I ought to have done, for his temper and spirits—his delightful spirits, and that gaiety, that playfulness of disposition, which, under any other circumstances, would, I am sure, have been as constantly bewitching to me as they were at first.' She then began to speak of you, and of the great kindness you had shown her during her illness; and, with a blush which showed me how it was all connected, desired me, whenever I had an opportunity, to thank you—I could not thank you too much—for every wish and every endeavour to do her good. She was sensible that you had never received any proper acknowledgment from herself."

"If I did not know her to be happy now," said Emma, seriously, "which, in spite of every little drawback from her scrupulous conscience, she must be, I could not bear these thanks; for, oh, Mrs. Weston, if there were an account drawn up of the evil and the good I have done Miss Fairfax——Well (checking herself and trying to be more lively), this is all to be forgotten. You are very kind to bring me these interesting particulars: they show her to the greatest advantage. I am sure she is very good: I hope she will be very happy. It is fit that the fortune should be on his side, for I think the merit will be all on hers."

Such a conclusion could not pass unanswered by Mrs. Weston. She thought well of Frank in almost every respect; and, what was more, she loved him very much, and her defence was, therefore, earnest. She talked with a great deal of reason, and at least equal affection; but she had too much to urge for Emma's attention: it was soon gone to Brunswick Square or to Donwell: she forgot to attempt to listen; and when Mrs. Weston ended with, "We have not yet had the letter we are so anxious for, you know, but I hope it will soon come," she was obliged to pause before she answered, and at last obliged to answer at random, before she could at all recollect what letter it was which they were so anxious for.

"Are you well, my Emma?" was Mrs. Weston's parting question.

"Oh, perfectly. I am always well, you know. Be sure to give me intelligence of the letter as soon as possible."

Mrs. Weston's communications furnished Emma with more food for unpleasant reflection, by increasing her esteem and compassion, and her sense of past injustice towards Miss Fairfax. She bitterly regretted not having sought a closer acquaintance with her, and blushed for the envious feelings which had certainly been, in some measure, the cause. Had she followed Mr. Knightley's known wishes, in paying that attention to Miss Fairfax which was every way her due; had she tried to know her better; had she done her part towards intimacy; had she endeavoured to find a friend there instead of in Harriet Smith; she must, in all probability, have been spared from every pain which pressed on her now. Birth, abilities, and education had been equally marking one as an associate for her, to be received with gratitude; and the other—what was she? Supposing even that they had never become intimate friends; that she had never been admitted into Miss Fairfax's confidence on this important matter,—which was most probable,—still, in knowing her as she ought, and as she might, she must have been preserved from the abominable suspicions of an improper attachment to Mr. Dixon, which she had not only so foolishly fashioned and harboured herself, but had so unpardonably imparted; an idea which she greatly feared had been made a subject of material distress to the delicacy of Jane's feelings, by the levity or carelessness of Frank Churchill's. Of all the sources of evil surrounding the former, since her coming to Highbury, she was persuaded that she must herself have been the worst. She must have been a perpetual enemy. They never could have been all three together, without her having stabbed Jane Fairfax's peace in a thousand instances; and on Box

Hill, perhaps, it had been the agony of a mind that would bear no more.

The evening of this day was very long, and melancholy, at Hartfield. The weather added what it could of gloom. A cold stormy rain set in, and nothing of July appeared but in the trees and shrubs, which the wind was despoiling, and the length of the day, which only made such cruel sights the longer visible.

The weather affected Mr. Woodhouse; and he could only be kept tolerably comfortable by almost ceaseless attention on his daughter's side, and by exertions which had never caused her half so much before. It reminded her of their first forlorn *tête-à-tête*, on the evening of Mrs. Weston's wedding-day; but Mr. Knightley had walked in then, soon after tea, and dissipated every melancholy fancy. Alas! such delightful proofs of Hartfield's attraction, as those sort of visits conveyed, might shortly be over. The picture which she had then drawn of the privations of the approaching winter had proved erroneous; no friends had deserted them, no pleasures had been lost. But her present forebodings she feared would experience no similar contradiction. The prospect before her now was threatening to a degree that could not be entirely dispelled—that might not be even partially brightened. If all took place that might take place among the circle of her friends, Hartfield must be comparatively deserted; and she left to cheer her father with the spirits only of ruined happiness.

The child to be born at Randalls must be a tie there even dearer than herself; and Mrs. Weston's heart and time would be occupied by it. They should lose her; and probably, in great measure, her husband also. Frank Churchill would return among them no more; and Miss Fairfax, it was reasonable to suppose, would soon cease to belong to Highbury. They would be married, and settled either at or near Enscombe. All that were good would be withdrawn; and if to these losses the loss of Donwell were to be added, what would remain of cheerful or of rational society within their reach? Mr. Knightley to be no longer coming there for his evening comfort! No longer walking in at all hours, as if ever willing to change his own home for theirs! How was it to be endured? And if he were to be lost to them for Harriet's sake; if he were to be thought of hereafter, as finding in Harriet's society all that he wanted; if Harriet were to be the chosen, the first, the dearest, the friend, the wife to whom he looked for all the best blessings of existence; what could be increasing Emma's wretchedness but the reflection never far distant from her mind, that it had been all her own work?

When it came to such a pitch as this, she was not able to refrain from a start, or a heavy sigh, or even from walking about the room for a few seconds; and the only source whence any thing like consolation or composure could be drawn, was in the resolution of her own better conduct, and the hope that, however inferior in spirit and gaiety might be the following and every future winter of her life to the past, it would yet find her more rational, more acquainted with herself, and leave her less to regret when it were gone.

## Chapter XIII.

The weather continued much the same all the following morning; and the same loneliness, and the same melancholy, seemed to reign at Hartfield; but in the afternoon it cleared; the wind changed into a softer quarter; the clouds were carried off; the sun appeared; it was summer again. With all the eagerness which such a transition gives, Emma resolved to be out of doors as soon as possible.

Never had the exquisite sight, smell, sensation of nature, tranquil, warm, and brilliant after a storm, been more attractive to her. She longed for the serenity they might gradually introduce; and on Mr. Perry's coming in soon after dinner, with a disengaged hour to give her father, she lost no time in hurrying into the shubbery. There, with spirits freshened, and thoughts a little relieved, she had taken a few turns, when she saw Mr. Knightley passing through the garden door, and coming towards her. It was the first intimation of his being returned from London. She had been thinking of him the moment before, as unquestionably sixteen miles distant. There was time only for the quickest arrangement of mind. She must be collected and calm. In half a minute they were together. The "How d'ye do's" were quiet and constrained on each side. She asked after their mutual friends; they were all well. When had he left them? Only that morning. He must have had a wet ride. Yes! He meant to walk with her, she found. "He had just looked into the dining room, and as he was not wanted there, preferred being out of doors." She thought he neither looked nor spoke cheerfully; and the first possible cause for it, suggested by her fears, was, that he had perhaps been communicating his plans to his brother, and was pained by the manner in which they had been received.

They walked together. He was silent. She thought he was often looking at her, and trying for a fuller view of her face than it suited her to give. And this belief produced another dread. Perhaps he wanted to speak to her of his attachment to Harriet; he might be watching for encouragement to begin. She did not, could not, feel equal to lead the way to any such subject. He must do it all himself. Yet she could not bear this silence. With him it was most unnatural. She considered, resolved, and, trying to smile, began,—

"You have some news to hear, now you are come back, that will rather surprise you."

"Have I?" said he quietly, and looking at her; "of what nature?"

"Oh, the best nature in the world—a wedding."

After waiting a moment, as if to be sure she intended to say no more, he replied,—

"If you mean Miss Fairfax and Frank Churchill, I have heard that already."

"How is it possible?" cried Emma, turning her glowing cheeks towards him; for while she spoke, it occurred to her that he might have called at Mrs. Goddard's in his way.

"I had a few lines on parish business from Mr. Weston this morning, and at the end of them he gave me a brief account of what had happened."

Emma was quite relieved, and could presently say, with a little more composure,—

"*You* probably have been less surprised than any of us, for you have had your suspicions. I have not forgotten that you once tried to give me a caution. I wish I had attended to it—but (with a sinking voice and a heavy sigh) I seem to have been doomed to blindness."

For a moment or two nothing was said, and she was unsuspicious of having excited any particular interest, till she found her arm drawn within his, and pressed against his heart, and heard him thus saying, in a tone of great sensibility, speaking low,—

"Time, my dearest Emma, time will heal the wound. Your own excellent sense; your exertions for your father's sake; I know you will not allow yourself——" Her arm was pressed again, as he added, in a more broken and subdued accent, "The feelings of the warmest friendship—indignation—abominable scoundrel!" And in a louder, steadier tone, he concluded with, "He will soon be gone. They will soon be in Yorkshire. I am sorry for *her*. She deserves a better fate."

Emma understood him; and as soon as she could recover from the flutter of pleasure, excited by such tender consideration, replied,—

"You are very kind, but you are mistaken, and I must set you right. I am not in want of that sort of compassion. My blindness to what was going on led me to act by them in a way that I must always be ashamed of, and I was very foolishly tempted to say and do many things which may well lay me open to unpleasant conjectures, but I have no other reason to regret that I was not in the secret earlier."

"Emma," cried he, looking eagerly at her, "are you, indeed?"—but checking himself—"No, no, I understand you—forgive me—I am pleased that you can say even so much. He is no object of regret, indeed! and it will not be very long, I hope, before that becomes the acknowledgment of more than your reason. Fortunate that your affections were not farther entangled!—I could never, I confess, from your manners, assure myself as to the degree of what you felt—I could only be certain that there was a preference—and a preference which I never believed him to deserve. He is a disgrace to the name of man. And is he to be rewarded with that sweet young woman?—Jane, Jane, you will be a miserable creature."

"Mr. Knightley," said Emma, trying to be lively, but really confused,—"I am in a very extraordinary situation. I cannot let you continue in your error; and yet, perhaps, since my manners gave such an impression, I have as much reason to be ashamed of confessing that I never have been at all attached to the person we are speaking of, as it might be natural for a woman to feel in confessing exactly the reverse. But I never have."

He listened in perfect silence. She wished him to speak, but he would not. She supposed she must say more before she were entitled to his clemency; but it was a hard case to be obliged still to lower herself in his opinion. She went on, however.

"I have very little to say for my own conduct. I was tempted by his attentions, and allowed myself to appear pleased. An old story, probably,—a common case,—and no more than has happened to hundreds of my sex before; and yet it may not be the more excusable in one who sets up as I do for understanding. Many circumstances assisted the temptation. He was the son of Mr. Weston—he was continually here—I always found him very pleasant—and, in short, for (with a sigh) let me swell out the causes ever so ingeniously, they all centre in this at last—my vanity was flattered, and I allowed his attentions. Latterly, however, for some time, indeed, I have had no idea of their meaning any thing. I thought them a habit, a trick, nothing that called for seriousness on my side. He has imposed on me, but he has not injured me. I have never been attached to him. And now I can tolerably comprehend his behaviour. He never wished to attach me. It was merely a blind to conceal his real situation with another. It was his object to blind all about him; and no one, I am sure, could be more effectually blinded than myself—except that I was *not* blinded—that it was my good fortune—that, in short, I was somehow or other safe from him."

She had hoped for an answer here—for a few words to say that her conduct was at least intelligible; but he was silent; and, as far as she could judge, deep in thought. At last, and tolerably in his usual tone, he said,—

"I have never had a high opinion of Frank Churchill. I can suppose, however, that I may have under-rated him. My acquaintance with him has been but trifling. And even if I have not under-rated him hitherto, he may yet turn out well. With such a woman he has a chance. I have no motive for wishing him ill—and for her sake, whose happiness will be involved in his good character and conduct, I shall certainly wish him well."

"I have no doubt of their being happy together," said Emma; "I believe them to be very mutually and very sincerely attached."

"He is a most fortunate man," returned Mr. Knightley, with energy. "So early in life—at three-and-twenty—a period when, if a man chooses a wife, he generally chooses ill. At three-and-twenty to have drawn such a prize! What years of felicity that man, in all human calculation, has before him! Assured of the love of such a woman—the disinterested love for Jane Fairfax's character vouches for her disinterestedness; every thing in his favour,—equality of situation—I mean, as far as regards society, and all the habits and manners that are important; equality in every point but one— and that one, since the purity of her heart is not to be doubted, such as must increase his felicity, for it will be his to bestow the only advantages she wants. A man would always wish to give a woman a better home than the one he takes her from; and he who can do it, where there is no doubt of *her* regard, must, I think, be the happiest of mortals. Frank Churchill is, indeed, the favourite of fortune. Every thing turns out for his good. He meets with a young woman at a watering-place, gains her affection, cannot even weary her by negligent treatment—and had he and all his family sought round the world for a perfect wife for him, they could not have found her superior. His aunt is in the way. His aunt dies. He has only to speak. His friends are eager to promote his happiness. He has used every body ill—and they are all delighted to forgive him. He is a fortunate man, indeed!"

"You speak as if you envied him."

"And I do envy him, Emma. In one respect he is the object of my envy."

Emma could say no more. They seemed to be within half a sentence of Harriet, and her immediate feeling was to avert the subject, if possible. She made her plan; she would speak of something totally different—the children in Brunswick Square; and she only waited for breath to begin, when Mr. Knightley startled her, by saying,—

"You will not ask me what is the point of envy. You are determined, I see, to have no curiosity. You are wise—but *I* cannot be wise. Emma, I must tell what you will not ask, though I may wish it unsaid the next moment."

"Oh, then, don't speak it, don't speak it," she eagerly cried. "Take a little time, consider, do not commit yourself."

"Thank you," said he, in an accent of deep mortification, and not another syllable followed.

Emma could not bear to give him pain. He was wishing to confide in her—perhaps to consult her;—cost her what it would, she would listen. She might assist his resolution, or reconcile him to it; she might give just praise to Harriet, or, by representing to him his own independence, relieve him from that state of indecision, which must be more intolerable than any alternative to such a mind as his. They had reached the house.

"You are going in, I suppose," said he.

"No," replied Emma, quite confirmed by the depressed manner in which he still spoke, "I should like to take another turn. Mr. Perry is not gone." And, after proceeding a few steps, she added,—"I stopped you ungraciously, just now, Mr. Knightley, and, I am afraid, gave you pain. But if you have any wish to speak openly to me as a friend, or to ask my opinion of any thing that you may have in contemplation— as a friend, indeed, you may command me. I will hear whatever you like. I will tell you exactly what I think."

"As a friend!" repeated Mr. Knightley. "Emma, that I fear is a word—No, I have no wish. Stay, yes, why should I hesitate? I have gone too far already for concealment. Emma, I accept your offer, extraordinary as it may seem, I accept it, and refer myself to you as a friend. Tell me, then, have I no chance of ever succeeding?"

He stopped in his earnestness to look the question, and the expression of his eyes overpowered her.

"My dearest Emma," said he, "for dearest you will always be, whatever the event of this hour's conversation, my dearest, most beloved Emma—tell me at once. Say 'No,' if it is to be said." She could really say nothing. "You are silent," he cried, with great animation; "absolutely silent! at present I ask no more."

Emma was almost ready to sink under the agitation of this moment. The dread of being awakened from the happiest dream was perhaps the most prominent feeling.

"I cannot make speeches, Emma:"—he soon resumed, and in a tone of such sincere, decided, intelligible tenderness as was tolerably convincing. "If I loved you less, I might be able to talk about it more. But you know what I am. You hear nothing but truth from me. I have blamed you, and lectured you, and you have borne it as no other woman in England would have borne it. Bear with the truths I would tell you now, dearest Emma, as well as you have borne with them. The manner, perhaps, may have as little to recommend them. God knows, I have been a very indifferent lover. But you understand me. Yes, you see, you understand my feelings—and will return them if you can. At present, I ask only to hear, once to hear your voice."

While he spoke, Emma's mind was most busy, and, with all the wonderful velocity of thought, had been able—and yet without losing a word—to catch and comprehend the exact truth of the whole; to see that Harriet's hopes had been entirely groundless, a mistake, a delusion, as complete a delusion as any of her own—that Harriet was nothing; that she was every thing herself; that what she had been saying relative to Harriet had been all taken as the language of her own feelings; and that her agitation, her doubts, her reluctance, her discouragement, had been all received as discouragement from herself. And not only was there time for these convictions, with all their glow of attendant happiness; there was time also to rejoice that Harriet's secret had not escaped her, and to resolve that it need not and should not. It was all the service she could now render her poor friend; for as to any of that heroism of sentiment which might have prompted her to entreat him to transfer his affection from herself to Harriet, as infinitely the most worthy of the two—or even the more simple sublimity of resolving to refuse him at once and for ever, without vouchsafing any motive, because he could not marry them both, Emma had it not. She felt for Harriet, with pain and with contrition; but no flight of generosity run mad, opposing all that could be probable or reasonable, entered her brain. She had led her friend astray, and it would be a reproach to her for ever; but her judgment was as strong as her feelings, and as strong as it had ever been before, in reprobating any such alliance for him, as most unequal and degrading. Her way was clear, though not quite smooth. She spoke then, on being so entreated. What did she say? Just what she ought, of course. A lady always does. She said enough to show there need not be despair—and to invite him to say more himself. He *had* despaired at one period; he had received such an injunction to caution and silence, as for the time crushed every hope;—she had begun by refusing to hear him. The change had perhaps been somewhat sudden;—her proposal of taking another turn, her renewing the conversation which she had just put an end to, might be a little extraordinary. She felt its inconsistency; but Mr. Knightley was so obliging as to put up with it, and seek no farther explanation.

Seldom, very seldom, does complete truth belong to any human disclosure; seldom can it happen that something is not a little disguised, or a little mistaken; but where, as in this case, though the conduct is mistaken, the feelings are not, it may not be very material. Mr. Knightley could not impute to Emma a more relenting heart than she possessed, or a heart more disposed to accept of his.

He had, in fact, been wholly unsuspicious of his own influence. He had followed her into the shrubbery with no idea of trying it. He had come, in his anxiety to see how she bore Frank Churchill's engagement, with no selfish view, no view at all, but of endeavouring, if she allowed him an opening, to soothe or to counsel her. The rest had been the work of the moment, the immediate effect of what he heard, on his feelings. The delightful assurance of her total indifference towards Frank Churchill, of her having a heart completely disengaged from him, had given birth to the hope, that, in time, he might gain her affection himself;—but it had been no present hope—he had only, in the momentary conquest of eagerness over judgment, aspired to be told that she did not forbid his attempt to attach her. The superior hopes which gradually opened were so much the more enchanting. The affection which he had been asking to be allowed to create if he could, was already his. Within half an hour he had passed from a thoroughly distressed state of mind, to something so like perfect happiness, that it could bear no other name.

*Her* change was equal. This one half hour had given to each the same precious certainty of being beloved, had cleared from each the same degree of ignorance, jealousy, or distrust. On his side, there had been a long standing jealousy, old as the arrival, or even the expectation, of Frank Churchill. He had been in love with Emma, and jealous of Frank Churchill, from about the same period, one sentiment having probably enlightened him as to the other. It was his jealousy of Frank Churchill that had taken him from the country. The Box Hill party had decided him on going away. He would save himself from witnessing again such permitted, encouraged attentions. He had gone to learn to be indifferent. But he had gone to a wrong place. There was too much domestic happiness in his brother's house; woman wore too amiable a form in it; Isabella was too much like Emma—differing only in those striking inferiorities which always brought the other in brilliancy before him, for much to have been done, even had his time been longer. He had staid on, however, vigorously, day after day—till this very morning's post had conveyed the history of Jane Fairfax. Then, with the gladness which must be felt, nay, which he did not scruple to feel, having never believed Frank Churchill to be at all deserving Emma, was there so much fond solicitude, so much keen anxiety for her, that he could stay no longer. He had ridden home through the rain; and had walked up directly after dinner, to see how this sweetest and best of all creatures, faultless in spite of all her faults, bore the discovery.

He had found her agitated and low. Frank Churchill was a villain. He heard her declare that she had never loved him. Frank Churchill's character was not desperate. She was his own Emma, by hand and word, when they returned into the house; and if he could have thought of Frank Churchill then, he might have deemed him a very good sort of fellow.

## Chapter XIV.

What totally different feelings did Emma take back into the house from what she had brought out!—she had then been only daring to hope for a little respite of suffering;—she was now in an exquisite flutter of happiness, and such happiness, moreover, as she believed must still be greater when the flutter should have passed away.

They sat down to tea—the same party round the same table—how often it had been collected! and how often had her eyes fallen on the same shrubs in the lawn, and observed the same beautiful effect of the western sun! But never in such a state of spirits, never in any thing like it; and it was with difficulty that she could summon enough of her usual self to be the attentive lady of the house, or even the attentive daughter.

Poor Mr. Woodhouse little suspected what was plotting against him in the breast of that man whom he was so cordially welcoming, and so anxiously hoping might not have taken cold from his ride. Could he have seen the heart, he would have cared very little for the lungs; but without the most distant imagination of the impending evil, without the slightest perception of any thing extraordinary, in the looks or ways of either, he repeated to them very comfortably all the articles of news he had received from Mr. Perry, and talked on with much self-contentment, totally unsuspicious of what they could have told him in return.

As long as Mr. Knightley remained with them, Emma's fever continued; but when he was gone, she began to be a little tranquillised and subdued, and in the course of the sleepless night, which was the tax for such an evening, she found one or two such very serious points to consider, as made her feel, that even her happiness must have some alloy. Her father—and Harriet. She could not be alone without feeling the full weight of their separate claims; and how to guard the comfort of both to the utmost, was the question. With respect to her father, it was a question soon answered. She hardly knew yet what Mr. Knightley would ask; but a very short parley with her own heart produced the most solemn resolution of never quitting her father. She even wept over the idea of it, as a sin of thought. While he lived, it must be only an engagement; but she flattered herself, that if divested of the danger of drawing her away, it might become an increase of comfort to him. How to do her best by Harriet, was of more difficult decision; how to spare her from any unnecessary pain; how to make her any possible atonement; how to appear least her enemy. On these subjects, her perplexity and distress were very great—and her mind had to pass again and again through every bitter reproach and sorrowful regret that had ever surrounded it. She could only resolve at last, that she would still avoid a meeting with her, and communicate all that need be told by letter; that it would be inexpressibly desirable to have her removed just now for a time from Highbury, and—indulging in one scheme more—nearly resolve, that it might be practicable to get an invitation for her to Brunswick Square. Isabella had been pleased with Harriet; and a few weeks spent in London must give her some amusement. She did not think it in Harriet's nature to escape being benefited by novelty and variety, by the streets, the shops, and the children. At any rate, it would be a proof of attention and kindness in herself, from whom every thing was due; a separation for the present; an averting of the evil day, when they must all be together again.

She rose early, and wrote her letter to Harriet; an employment which left her so very serious, so nearly sad, that Mr. Knightley, in walking up to Hartfield to breakfast, did not arrive at all too soon; and half an hour stolen afterwards to go over the same ground again with him, literally and figuratively, was quite necessary to reinstate her in a proper share of the happiness of the evening before.

He had not left her long, by no means long enough for her to have the slightest inclination for thinking of any body else, when a letter was brought her from Randalls—a very thick letter; she guessed what it must contain, and deprecated the necessity of reading it. She was now in perfect charity with Frank Churchill; she wanted no explanations, she wanted only to have her thoughts to herself—and as for understanding any thing he wrote, she was sure she was incapable of it. It must be waded through, however. She opened the packet; it was too surely so;—a note from Mrs. Weston to herself, ushered in the letter from Frank to Mrs. Weston.

> "I have the greatest pleasure, my dear Emma, in forwarding to you the enclosed. I know what thorough justice you will do it, and have scarcely a doubt of its happy effect. I think we shall never materially disagree about the writer again; but I will not delay you by a long preface. We are quite well. This letter has been the cure of all the little nervousness I have been feeling lately. I did not quite like your looks on Tuesday, but it was an ungenial morning; and though you will never own being affected by weather, I think every body feels a north-east wind. I felt for your dear father very much in the storm of Tuesday afternoon and yesterday morning, but had the comfort of hearing last night, by Mr. Perry, that it had not made him ill.
>
> > "Yours ever,
> > A. W."

[*To Mrs. Weston.*]

Windsor,—July.

"My dear Madam,

"If I made myself intelligible yesterday, this letter will be expected; but, expected or not, I know it will be read with candour and indulgence. You are all goodness, and I believe there will be need of even all your goodness to allow for some parts of my past conduct. But I have been forgiven by one who had still more to resent. My courage rises while I write. It is very difficult for the prosperous to be humble. I have already met with such success in two applications for pardon, that I may be in danger of thinking myself too sure of yours, and of those among your friends who have had any ground of offence. You must all endeavour to comprehend the exact nature of my situation when I first arrived at Randalls; you must consider me as having a secret which was to be kept at all hazards. This was the fact. My right to place myself in a situation requiring such concealment is another question. I shall not discuss it here. For my temptation to *think* it a right, I refer every caviller* to a brick house, sashed windows below, and casements above, in Highbury. I dared not address her openly; my difficulties in the then state of Enscombe must be too well known to require definition; and I was fortunate enough to prevail, before we parted at Weymouth, and to induce the most upright female mind in the creation to stoop in charity to a secret engagement. Had she refused, I should have gone mad. But you will be ready to say, What was your hope in doing this? What did you look forward to? To any thing, every thing—to time, chance, circumstance, slow effects, sudden bursts, perseverance and weariness, health and sickness. Every possi-

---

*One who cavils—that is, raises petty objections.

bility of good was before me, and the first of blessings secured, in obtaining her promises of faith and correspondence. If you need farther explanation, I have the
honour, my dear madam, of being your husband's son,
and the advantage of inheriting a disposition to hope for
good, which no inheritance of houses or lands can ever
equal the value of. See me, then, under these circumstances, arriving on my first visit to Randalls; and here I
am conscious of wrong, for that visit might have been
sooner paid. You will look back, and see that I did not
come till Miss Fairfax was in Highbury; and as *you* were
the person slighted, you will forgive me instantly: but I
must work on my father's compassion, by reminding him,
that so long as I absented myself from his house, so long
I lost the blessing of knowing you. My behaviour, during
the very happy fortnight which I spent with you, did not,
I hope, lay me open to reprehension, excepting on one
point. And now I come to the principal, the only important part of my conduct, while belonging to you, which
excites my own anxiety, or requires very solicitous explanation. With the greatest respect, and the warmest friendship, do I mention Miss Woodhouse; my father, perhaps,
will think I ought to add, with the deepest humiliation. A
few words which dropped from him yesterday spoke his
opinion, and some censure I acknowledge myself liable
to. My behaviour to Miss Woodhouse indicated, I believe,
more than it ought. In order to assist a concealment so essential to me, I was led on to make more than an allowable use of the sort of intimacy into which we were
immediately thrown. I cannot deny that Miss Woodhouse
was my ostensible object; but I am sure you will believe
the declaration, that had I not been convinced of her indifference, I would not have been induced by any selfish
views to go on. Amiable and delightful as Miss Woodhouse is, she never gave me the idea of a young woman
likely to be attached; and that she was perfectly free from
any tendency to being attached to me, was as much my

conviction as my wish. She received my attentions with an easy, friendly, good-humoured playfulness, which exactly suited me. We seemed to understand each other. From our relative situation, those attentions were her due, and were felt to be so. Whether Miss Woodhouse began really to understand me before the expiration of that fortnight, I cannot say: when I called to take leave of her, I remember that I was within a moment of confessing the truth, and I then fancied she was not without suspicion; but I have no doubt of her having since detected me,—at least, in some degree. She may not have surmised the whole, but her quickness must have penetrated a part. I cannot doubt it. You will find, whenever the subject becomes freed from its present restraints, that it did not take her wholly by surprise. She frequently gave me hints of it. I remember her telling me at the ball, that I owed Mrs. Elton gratitude for her attentions to Miss Fairfax. I hope this history of my conduct towards her will be admitted by you and my father as great extenuation of what you saw amiss. While you considered me as having sinned against Emma Woodhouse, I could deserve nothing from either. Acquit me here, and procure for me, when it is allowable, the acquittal and good wishes of that said Emma Woodhouse, whom I regard with so much brotherly affection as to long to have her as deeply and as happily in love as myself. Whatever strange things I said or did during that fortnight, you have now a key to. My heart was in Highbury, and my business was to get my body thither as often as might be, and with the least suspicion. If you remember any queernesses, set them all to the right account. Of the piano-forte so much talked of, I feel it only necessary to say, that its being ordered was absolutely unknown to Miss F——, who would never have allowed me to send it, had any choice been given her. The delicacy of her mind throughout the whole engagement, my dear madam, is much beyond my power of doing justice to. You will soon, I earnestly hope, know her thoroughly yourself. No description can describe her. She must tell you herself what she is; yet not by word, for never was there a human creature who would so designedly suppress her own merit. Since I began this letter, which will be longer than I foresaw, I have heard from her. She gives a good account of her own health; but, as she never complains, I dare not depend. I want to have your opinion of her looks. I know you will soon call on her; she is living in dread of the visit. Perhaps it is paid already. Let me hear from you without delay; I am impatient for a thousand particulars. Remember how few minutes I was at Randalls, and in how bewildered, how mad a state: and I am not much better yet; still insane either from happiness or misery. When I think of the kindness and favour I have met with, of her excellence and patience, and my uncle's generosity, I am mad with joy: but when I recollect all the uneasiness I occasioned her, and how little I deserve to be forgiven, I am mad with anger. If I could but see her again! But I must not propose it yet: my uncle has been too good for me to encroach. I must still add to this long letter. You have not heard all that you ought to hear. I could not give any connected detail yesterday; but the suddenness and, in one light, the unseasonableness with which the affair burst out, needs explanation; for though the event of the 26th ult.,* as you will conclude, immediately opened to me the happiest prospects, I should not have presumed on such early measures, but from the very particular circumstances which left me not an hour to lose. I should myself have shrunk from any thing so hasty, and she would have felt every scruple of mine with multiplied strength and refinement: but I had no choice. The hasty engagement she had entered into with that woman—— Here, my dear madam, I was obliged to leave off abruptly, to recollect

---

*Abbreviation for *ultimo* (Latin), meaning "last"; indicates the month preceding the present.

and compose myself. I have been walking over the country, and am now, I hope, rational enough to make the rest of my letter what it ought to be. It is, in fact, a most mortifying retrospect for me. I behaved shamefully. And here I can admit, that my manners to Miss W., in being unpleasant to Miss F., were highly blamable. *She* disapproved them, which ought to have been enough. My plea of concealing the truth she did not think sufficient. She was displeased; I thought unreasonably so: I thought her, on a thousand occasions, unnecessarily scrupulous and cautious: I thought her even cold. But she was always right. If I had followed her judgment, and subdued my spirits to the level of what she deemed proper, I should have escaped the greatest unhappiness I have ever known. We quarrelled. Do you remember the morning spent at Donwell? *There* every little dissatisfaction that had occurred before came to a crisis. I was late; I met her walking home by herself, and wanted to walk with her, but she would not suffer it. She absolutely refused to allow me, which I then thought most unreasonable. Now, however, I see nothing in it but a very natural and consistent degree of discretion. While I, to blind the world to our engagement, was behaving one hour with objectionable particularity to another woman, was she to be consenting the next to a proposal which might have made every previous caution useless? Had we been met walking together between Donwell and Highbury, the truth must have been suspected. I was mad enough, however, to resent. I doubted her affection. I doubted it more the next day on Box Hill; when, provoked by such conduct on my side, such shameful, insolent neglect of her, and such apparent devotion to Miss W., as it would have been impossible for any woman of sense to endure, she spoke her resentment in a form of words perfectly intelligible to me. In short, my dear madam, it was a quarrel blameless on her side, abominable on mine; and I returned the same evening to Richmond, though I might have staid with you till the

next morning, merely because I would be as angry with
her as possible. Even then, I was not such a fool as not to
mean to be reconciled in time; but I was the injured person, injured by her coldness, and I went away, determined
that she should make the first advances. I shall always congratulate myself that you were not of the Box Hill party.
Had you witnessed my behaviour there, I can hardly suppose you would ever have thought well of me again. Its effect upon her appears in the immediate resolution it
produced: as soon as she found I was really gone from
Randalls, she closed with the offer of that officious Mrs.
Elton; the whole system of whose treatment of her, by the
by, has ever filled me with indignation and hatred. I must
not quarrel with a spirit of forbearance which has been so
richly extended towards myself; but, otherwise, I should
loudly protest against the share of it which that woman
has known. 'Jane,' indeed! You will observe that I have
not yet indulged myself in calling her by that name, even
to you. Think, then, what I must have endured in hearing
it bandied between the Eltons, with all the vulgarity of
needless repetition, and all the insolence of imaginary superiority. Have patience with me, I shall soon have done.
She closed with this offer, resolving to break with me entirely, and wrote the next day to tell me that we never
were to meet again. *She felt the engagement to be a source of re-*
*pentance and misery to each: she dissolved it.* This letter
reached me on the very morning of my poor aunt's
death. I answered it within an hour; but from the confusion of my mind, and the multiplicity of business falling
on me at once, my answer, instead of being sent with all
the many other letters of that day, was locked up in my
writing-desk; and I, trusting that I had written enough,
though but a few lines, to satisfy her, remained without
any uneasiness. I was rather disappointed that I did not
hear from her again speedily; but I made excuses for her,
and was too busy, and—may I add?—too cheerful in my
views to be captious. We removed to Windsor; and two

days afterwards I received a parcel from her—my own letters all returned!—and a few lines at the same time by the post, stating her extreme surprise at not having had the smallest reply to her last; and adding, that as silence on such a point could not be misconstrued, and as it must be equally desirable to both to have every subordinate arrangement concluded as soon as possible, she now sent me, by a safe conveyance, all my letters, and requested, that if I could not directly command hers, so as to send them to Highbury within a week, I would forward them after that period to her at——: in short, the full direction to Mr. Smallridge's, near Bristol, stared me in the face. I knew the name, the place, I knew all about it, and instantly saw what she had been doing. It was perfectly accordant with that resolution of character which I knew her to possess; and the secrecy she had maintained, as to any such design in her former letter, was equally descriptive of its anxious delicacy. For the world would not she have seemed to threaten me. Imagine the shock; imagine how, till I had actually detected my own blunder, I raved at the blunders of the post. What was to be done? One thing only. I must speak to my uncle. Without his sanction I could not hope to be listened to again. I spoke; circumstances were in my favour; the late event had softened away his pride, and he was, earlier than I could have anticipated, wholly reconciled and complying; and could say at last, poor man! with a deep sigh, that he wished I might find as much happiness in the marriage state as he had done. I felt that it would be of a different sort. Are you disposed to pity me for what I must have suffered in opening the cause to him, for my suspense while all was at stake? No; do not pity me till I reached Highbury, and saw how ill I had made her. Do not pity me till I saw her wan, sick looks. I reached Highbury at the time of day when, from my knowledge of their late breakfast hour, I was certain of a good chance of finding her alone. I was not disappointed; and at last I was not disappointed either in the object of my journey. A great deal of very reasonable, very just displeasure I had to persuade away. But it is done; we are reconciled, dearer, much dearer, than ever, and no moment's uneasiness can ever occur between us again. Now, my dear madam, I will release you; but I could not conclude before. A thousand and a thousand thanks for all the kindness you have ever shown me, and ten thousand for the attentions your heart will dictate towards her. If you think me in a way to be happier than I deserve, I am quite of your opinion. Miss W. calls me the child of good fortune. I hope she is right. In one respect, my good fortune is undoubted, that of being able to subscribe myself,

> "Your obliged and affectionate Son,
> F. C. WESTON CHURCHILL."

## *Chapter XV.*

This letter must make its way to Emma's feelings. She was obliged, in spite of her previous determination to the contrary, to do it all the justice that Mrs. Weston foretold. As soon as she came to her own name, it was irresistible: every line relating to herself was interesting, and almost every line agreeable; and when this charm ceased, the subject could still maintain itself, by the natural return of her former regard for the writer, and the very strong attraction which any picture of love must have for her at that moment. She never stopped till she had gone through the whole; and though it was impossible not to feel that he had been wrong, yet he had been less wrong than she had supposed; and he had suffered, and was very sorry; and he was so grateful to Mrs. Weston, and so much in love with Miss Fairfax, and she was so happy herself, that there was no being severe; and could he have entered the room, she must have shaken hands with him as heartily as ever.

She thought so well of the letter, that when Mr. Knightley came again, she desired him to read it. She was sure of Mrs. Weston's wishing it to be communicated; especially to one, who, like Mr. Knightley, had seen so much to blame in his conduct.

"I shall be very glad to look it over," said he, "but it seems long. I will take it home with me at night."

But that would not do. Mr. Weston was to call in the evening, and she must return it by him.

"I would rather be talking to you," he replied; "but as it seems a matter of justice, it shall be done."

He began—stopping, however, almost directly to say, "Had I been offered the sight of one of this gentleman's letters to his mother-in-law a few months ago, Emma, it would not have been taken with such indifference."

He proceeded a little farther, reading to himself; and then, with a smile, observed, "Humph!—a fine complimentary opening; but it is his way. One man's style must not be the rule of another's. We will not be severe."

"It will be natural for me," he added shortly afterwards, "to speak my opinion aloud as I read. By doing it, I shall feel that I am near you. It will not be so great a loss of time; but if you dislike it——"

"Not at all. I should wish it."

Mr. Knightley returned to his reading with greater alacrity.

"He trifles here," said he, "as to the temptation. He knows he is wrong, and has nothing rational to urge. Bad. He ought not to have formed the engagement. 'His father's disposition:'—he is unjust, however, to his father. Mr. Weston's sanguine temper was a blessing on all his upright and honourable exertions; but Mr. Weston earned every present comfort before he endeavoured to gain it. Very true; he did not come till Miss Fairfax was here."

"And I have not forgotten," said Emma, "how sure you were that he might have come sooner if he would. You pass it over very handsomely;—but you were perfectly right."

"I was not quite impartial in my judgment, Emma; but yet, I think, had *you* not been in the case, I should still have distrusted him."

When he came to Miss Woodhouse, he was obliged to read the whole of it aloud—all that related to her, with a smile, a look, a shake of the head, a word or two of assent, or disapprobation, or merely of love, as the subject required; concluding, however, seriously, and, after steady reflection, thus,—

"Very bad—though it might have been worse. Playing a most dangerous game. Too much indebted to the event for his acquittal. No judge of his own manners by you. Always deceived, in fact, by his own wishes, and regardless of little besides his own convenience. Fancying you to have fathomed his secret! Natural enough! his own mind full of intrigue, that he should suspect it in others. Mystery—finesse—how they pervert the understanding! My Emma, does not every thing serve to prove more and more the beauty of truth and sincerity in all our dealings with each other?"

Emma agreed to it, and with a blush of sensibility on Harriet's account, which she could not give any sincere explanation of.

"You had better go on," said she.

He did so, but very soon stopped again to say, "The pianoforte! Ah!—that was the act of a very, very young man, one too young to consider whether the inconvenience of it might not very much exceed the pleasure. A boyish scheme, indeed! I cannot comprehend a man's wishing to give a woman any proof of affection which he knows she would rather dispense with; and he did know that she would have prevented the instrument's coming if she could."

After this, he made some progress without any pause.

Frank Churchill's confession of having behaved shamefully was the first thing to call for more than a word in passing.

"I perfectly agree with you, sir," was then his remark. "You did behave very shamefully. You never wrote a truer line." And having gone through what immediately followed of the basis of their disagreement, and his persisting to act in direct opposition to Jane Fairfax's sense of right, he made a fuller pause to say, "This is very bad. He had induced her to place herself, for his sake, in a situation of extreme difficulty and uneasiness, and it should have been his first object to prevent her from suffering unnecessarily. She must have had much more to contend with in carrying on the correspondence than he could. He should have respected even unreasonable scruples, had there been such; but hers were all reasonable. We must look to her one fault, and remember that she had done a wrong thing in consenting to the engagement, to bear that she should have been in such a state of punishment."

Emma knew that he was now getting to the Box Hill party, and grew uncomfortable. Her own behaviour had been so very improper! She was deeply ashamed, and a little afraid of his next look. It was all read, however, steadily, attentively, and without the smallest remark; and, excepting one momentary glance at her, instantly withdrawn, in the fear of giving pain—no remembrance of Box Hill seemed to exist.

"There is no saying much for the delicacy of our good friends, the Eltons," was his next observation. "His feelings are natural. What! actually resolve to break with him entirely! She felt the engagement to be a source of repentance and misery to each—she dissolved it. What a view this gives of her sense of his behaviour! Well, he must be a most extraordinary——"

"Nay, nay, read on. You will find how very much he suffers."

"I hope he does," replied Mr. Knightley, coolly and resuming the letter.—"'Smallridge!'—What does this mean? What is all this?"

"She had engaged to go as governess to Mrs. Smallridge's children—a dear friend of Mrs. Elton's—a neighbour of Maple Grove; and, by the bye, I wonder how Mrs. Elton bears the disappointment."

"Say nothing, my dear Emma, while you oblige me to read—not even of Mrs. Elton. Only one page more. I shall soon have done. What a letter the man writes!"

"I wish you would read it with a kinder spirit towards him."

"Well, there *is* feeling here. He does seem to have suffered in finding her ill. Certainly, I can have no doubt of his being fond of her. 'Dearer, much dearer than ever.' I hope he may long continue to feel all the value of such a reconciliation. He is a very liberal thanker, with his thousands and tens of thousands.—'Happier than I deserve.' Come, he knows himself there. 'Miss Woodhouse calls me the child of good fortune.' Those were Miss Woodhouse's words, were they? And a fine ending—and there is a letter. 'The child of good fortune!' That was your name for him, was it?"

"You do not appear so well satisfied with his letter as I am; but still you must, at least I hope you must, think the better of him for it. I hope it does him some service with you."

"Yes, certainly it does. He has had great faults,—faults of inconsideration and thoughtlessness; and I am very much of his opinion in thinking him likely to be happier than he deserves: but still as he is, beyond a doubt, really attached to Miss Fairfax, and will soon, it may be hoped, have the advantage of being constantly with her, I am very ready to believe his character will improve, and acquire from hers the steadiness and delicacy of principle that it wants. And now, let me talk to you of something else. I have another person's interest at present so much at heart, that I cannot think any longer about Frank Churchill. Ever since I left you this morning, Emma, my mind has been hard at work on one subject."

The subject followed; it was in plain, unaffected, gentleman-like English, such as Mr. Knightley used even to the woman he was in love with, how to be able to ask her to marry him, without attacking the happiness of her father. Emma's answer was ready at the first word. "While her dear father lived, any change of condition must be impossible for her. She could never quit him." Part only of this answer, however, was admitted. The impossibility of her quitting her father, Mr. Knightley felt as strongly as herself; but the inadmissibility of any other change he could not agree to. He had been thinking it over most deeply, most intently; he had at first hoped to induce Mr. Woodhouse to remove with her to Donwell; he had wanted to believe it feasible, but his knowledge of Mr. Woodhouse would not suffer him to deceive himself long; and now he confessed his persuasion, that such a transplantation would be a risk of her father's comfort, perhaps even of his life, which must not be hazarded. Mr. Woodhouse taken from Hartfield!—No, he felt that it ought not to be attempted. But the plan which had arisen on the sacrifice of this, he trusted his dearest Emma would not find in any respect objectionable; it was, that he should be received at Hartfield! that so long as her father's happiness—in other words his life—required Hartfield to continue her home, it should be his likewise.

Of their all removing to Donwell, Emma had already had her own passing thoughts. Like him, she had tried the scheme and rejected it; but such an alternative as this had not occurred to her. She was sensible of all the affection it evinced. She felt that, in quitting Donwell, he must be sacrificing a great deal of independence of hours and habits; that in living constantly with her father, and in no house of his own, there would be much, very much, to be borne with. She promised to think of it, and advised him to think of it more; but he was fully convinced, that no reflection could alter his wishes or his opinion on the subject. He had given it, he could assure her, very long and calm consideration; he had been walking away from William Larkins the whole morning to have his thoughts to himself.

"Ah! there is one difficulty unprovided for," cried Emma.

"I am sure William Larkins will not like it. You must get his consent before you ask mine."

She promised, however, to think of it; and pretty nearly promised, moreover, to think of it, with the intention of finding it a very good scheme.

It is remarkable, that Emma, in the many, very many, points of view in which she was now beginning to consider Donwell Abbey, was never struck with any sense of injury to her nephew Henry, whose rights as heir expectant had formerly been so tenaciously regarded. Think she must of the possible difference to the poor little boy; and yet she only gave herself a saucy conscious smile about it, and found amusement in detecting the real cause of that violent dislike of Mr. Knightley's marrying Jane Fairfax, or any body else, which at the time she had wholly imputed to the amiable solicitude of the sister and the aunt.

This proposal of his, this plan of marrying and continuing at Hartfield—the more she contemplated it the more pleasing it became. His evils seemed to lessen, her own advantages to increase, their mutual good to outweigh every drawback. Such a companion for herself in the periods of anxiety and cheerlessness before her! Such a partner in all those duties and cares to which time must be giving increase of melancholy!

She would have been too happy but for poor Harriet; but every blessing of her own seemed to involve and advance the sufferings of her friend, who must now be even excluded from Hartfield. The delightful family-party which Emma was securing for herself, poor Harriet must, in mere charitable caution, be kept at a distance from. She would be a loser in every way. Emma could not deplore her future absence as any deduction from her own enjoyment. In such a party, Harriet would be rather a dead weight than otherwise; but for the poor girl herself, it seemed a peculiarly cruel necessity that was to be placing her in such a state of unmerited punishment.

In time, of course, Mr. Knightley would be forgotten, that

is, supplanted; but this could not be expected to happen very early. Mr. Knightley himself would be doing nothing to assist the cure; not like Mr. Elton. Mr. Knightley, always so kind, so feeling, so truly considerate for every body, would never deserve to be less worshipped than now; and it really was too much to hope even of Harriet, that she could be in love with more than *three* men in one year.

## Chapter XVI.

It was a very great relief to Emma to find Harriet as desirous as herself to avoid a meeting. Their intercourse was painful enough by letter. How much worse had they been obliged to meet!

Harriet expressed herself very much, as might be supposed, without reproaches, or apparent sense of ill usage; and yet Emma fancied there was a something of resentment, a something bordering on it in her style, which increased the desirableness of their being separate. It might be only her own consciousness; but it seemed as if an angel only could have been quite without resentment under such a stroke.

She had no difficulty in procuring Isabella's invitation; and she was fortunate in having a sufficient reason for asking it, without resorting to invention. There was a tooth amiss. Harriet really wished, and had wished some time, to consult a dentist. Mrs. John Knightley was delighted to be of use: any thing of ill-health was a recommendation to her— and though not so fond of a dentist as of a Mr. Wingfield, she was quite eager to have Harriet under her care. When it was thus settled on her sister's side, Emma proposed it to her friend, and found her very persuadable. Harriet was to go;

she was invited for at least a fortnight; she was to be conveyed in Mr. Woodhouse's carriage. It was all arranged, it was
all completed, and Harriet was safe in Brunswick Square.

Now Emma could, indeed, enjoy Mr. Knightley's visits;
now she could talk, and she could listen with true happiness,
unchecked by that sense of injustice, of guilt, of something
most painful, which had haunted her when remembering
how disappointed a heart was near her, how much might at
that moment, and at a little distance, be enduring by the
feelings which she had led astray herself.

The difference of Harriet at Mrs. Goddard's, or in London, made perhaps an unreasonable difference in Emma's
sensations; but she could not think of her in London without objects of curiosity and employment, which must be
averting the past, and carrying her out of herself.

She would not allow any other anxiety to succeed directly
to the place in her mind which Harriet had occupied. There
was a communication before her, one which *she* only could
be competent to make—the confession of her engagement
to her father; but she would have nothing to do with it at
present. She had resolved to defer the disclosure till Mrs.
Weston were safe and well. No additional agitation should be
thrown at this period among those she loved—and the evil
should not act on herself by anticipation before the appointed time. A fortnight, at least, of leisure and peace of
mind, to crown every warmer, but more agitating, delight,
should be hers.

She soon resolved, equally as a duty and a pleasure, to
employ half an hour of this holiday of spirits in calling on
Miss Fairfax. She ought to go—and she was longing to see
her; the resemblance of their present situations increasing
every other motive of good will. It would be a *secret* satisfaction; but the consciousness of a similarity of prospect would
certainly add to the interest with which she should attend to
any thing Jane might communicate.

She went—she had driven once unsuccessfully to the
door, but had not been into the house since the morning

after Box Hill, when poor Jane had been in such distress as had filled her with compassion, though all the worst of her sufferings had been unsuspected. The fear of being still unwelcome determined her, though assured of their being at home, to wait in the passage, and send up her name. She heard Patty announcing it; but no such bustle succeeded as poor Miss Bates had before made so happily intelligible. No; she heard nothing but the instant reply of, "Beg her to walk up;" and a moment afterwards she was met on the stairs by Jane herself, coming eagerly forward as if no other reception of her were felt sufficient. Emma had never seen her look so well, so lovely, so engaging. There was consciousness, animation, and warmth; there was every thing which her countenance or manner could ever have wanted. She came forward with an offered hand; and said, in a low, but very feeling tone,—

"This is most kind, indeed! Miss Woodhouse, it is impossible for me to express——I hope you will believe——Excuse me for being so entirely without words."

Emma was gratified, and would soon have shown no want of words if the sound of Mrs. Elton's voice from the sitting-room had not checked her, and made it expedient to compress all her friendly and all her congratulatory sensations into a very, very earnest shake of the hand.

Mrs. Bates and Mrs. Elton were together. Miss Bates was out, which accounted for the previous tranquillity. Emma could have wished Mrs. Elton elsewhere; but she was in a humour to have patience with every body; and as Mrs. Elton met her with unusual graciousness, she hoped the rencontre would do them no harm.

She soon believed herself to penetrate Mrs. Elton's thoughts, and understand why she was, like herself, in happy spirits; it was being in Miss Fairfax's confidence, and fancying herself acquainted with what was still a secret to other people. Emma saw symptoms of it immediately in the expression of her face; and while paying her own compliments to Mrs. Bates, and appearing to attend to the good old lady's replies, she saw her with a sort of anxious parade of mystery fold up a letter which she had apparently been reading aloud to Miss Fairfax, and return it into the purple and gold reticule* by her side, saying, with significant nods,—

"We can finish this some other time, you know. You and I shall not want opportunities; and, in fact, you have heard all the essential already. I only wanted to prove to you that Mrs. S. admits our apology, and is not offended. You see how delightfully she writes. Oh, she is a sweet creature! You would have doated on her, had you gone.—But not a word more. Let us be discreet—quite on our good behaviour.—Hush!—You remember those lines—I forget the poem at this moment:—

> 'For when a lady's in the case,
> You know, all other things give place.'[22]

Now I say, my dear, in *our* case, for *lady*, read——mum! a word to the wise. I am in a fine flow of spirits, an't I? But I want to set your heart at ease as to Mrs. S. *My* representation, you see, has quite appeased her."

And again, on Emma's merely turning her head to look at Mrs. Bates's knitting, she added, in a half whisper,—

"I mentioned no *names*, you will observe. Oh no! cautious as a minister of state. I managed it extremely well."

Emma could not doubt. It was a palpable display, repeated on every possible occasion. When they had all talked a little while in harmony of the weather and Mrs. Weston, she found herself abruptly addressed with,—

"Do not you think, Miss Woodhouse, our saucy little friend here is charmingly recovered? Do not you think her cure does Perry the highest credit? (here was a side glance of great meaning at Jane.) Upon my word, Perry has restored her in a wonderful short time! Oh, if you had seen

_____

*Woman's drawstring bag.

her, as I did, when she was at the worst!" And when Mrs.
Bates was saying something to Emma, whispered farther, "We
do not say a word of any *assistance* that Perry might have; not
a word of a certain young physician from Windsor. Oh no,
Perry shall have all the credit.

"I have scarce had the pleasure of seeing you, Miss
Woodhouse," she shortly afterwards began, "since the party
to Box Hill. Very pleasant party. But yet I think there was
something wanting. Things did not seem—that is, there
seemed a little cloud upon the spirits of some. So it appeared
to me, at least, but I might be mistaken. However, I think it
answered so far as to tempt one to go again. What say you
both to our collecting the same party, and exploring to Box
Hill again, while the fine weather lasts? It must be the same
party, you know, quite the same party, not *one* exception."

Soon after this Miss Bates came in, and Emma could not
help being diverted by the perplexity of her first answer to
herself, resulting, she supposed, from doubt of what might
be said, and impatience to say every thing.

"Thank you, dear Miss Woodhouse, you are all kindness.
It is impossible to say—Yes, indeed, I quite understand—
dearest Jane's prospects—that is, I do not mean. But she is
charmingly recovered. How is Mr. Woodhouse? I am so
glad.—Quite out of my power.—Such a happy little circle as
you find us here.—Yes, indeed.—Charming young man!—
that is—so very friendly; I mean good Mr. Perry!—such attention to Jane!" And from her great, her more than
commonly thankful delight towards Mrs. Elton for being
there, Emma guessed that there had been a little show of resentment towards Jane, from the vicarage quarter, which was
now graciously overcome.—After a few whispers, indeed,
which placed it beyond a guess, Mrs Elton, speaking louder,
said,—

"Yes, here I am, my good friend; and here I have been so
long, that any where else I should think it necessary to apologise: but, the truth is, that I am waiting for my lord and

master. He promised to join me here, and pay his respects to you."

"What! are we to have the pleasure of a call from Mr. Elton? That will be a favour indeed! for I know gentlemen do not like morning visits, and Mr. Elton's time is so engaged."

"Upon my word it is, Miss Bates. He really is engaged from morning to night. There is no end of people's coming to him, on some pretence or other. The magistrates, and overseers, and churchwardens, are always wanting his opinion. They seem not able to do any thing without him. 'Upon my word, Mr. E., I often say, rather you than I. I do not know what would become of my crayons and my instrument, if I had half so many applicants.' Bad enough as it is, for I absolutely neglect them both to an unpardonable degree. I believe I have not played a bar this fortnight. However, he is coming, I assure you: yes, indeed, on purpose to wait on you all." And putting up her hand to screen her words from Emma—"A congratulatory visit, you know. Oh! yes, quite indispensable."

Miss Bates looked about her, so happily.

"He promised to come to me as soon as he could disengage himself from Knightley; but he and Knightley are shut up together in deep consultation. Mr. E. is Knightley's right hand."

Emma would not have smiled for the world, and only said, "Is Mr. Elton gone on foot to Donwell? He will have a hot walk."

"Oh no, it is a meeting at the Crown—a regular meeting. Weston and Cole will be there too; but one is apt to speak only of those who lead. I fancy Mr. E. and Knightley have every thing their own way."

"Have not you mistaken the day?" said Emma. "I am almost certain that the meeting at the Crown is not till to-morrow. Mr. Knightley was at Hartfield yesterday, and spoke of it as for Saturday."

"Oh no, the meeting is certainly to-day," was the abrupt

answer, which denoted the impossibility of any blunder on Mrs. Elton's side. "I do believe," she continued, "this is the most troublesome parish that ever was. We never heard of such things at Maple Grove."

"Your parish there was small," said Jane.

"Upon my word, my dear, I do not know, for I never heard the subject talked of."

"But it is proved by the smallness of the school, which I have heard you speak of, as under the patronage of your sister and Mrs. Bragge; the only school, and not more than five and twenty children."

"Ah! you clever creature, that's very true. What a thinking brain you have! I say, Jane, what a perfect character you and I should make, if we could be shaken together. My liveliness and your solidity would produce perfection. Not that I presume to insinuate, however, that *some* people may not think *you* perfection already. But hush!—not a word, if you please."

It seemed an unnecessary caution; Jane was wanting to give her words, not to Mrs. Elton, but to Miss Woodhouse, as the latter plainly saw. The wish of distinguishing her, as far as civility permitted, was very evident, though it could not often proceed beyond a look.

Mr. Elton made his appearance. His lady greeted him with some of her sparkling vivacity.

"Very pretty, sir, upon my word; to send me on here, to be an encumbrance to my friends, so long before you vouchsafe to come. But you knew what a dutiful creature you had to deal with. You knew I should not stir till my lord and master appeared. Here have I been sitting this hour, giving these young ladies a sample of true conjugal obedience; for who can say, you know, how soon it may be wanted?"

Mr. Elton was so hot and tired, that all this wit seemed thrown away. His civilities to the other ladies must be paid; but his subsequent object was to lament over himself, for the heat he was suffering, and the walk he had had for nothing.

"When I got to Donwell," said he, "Knightley could not be found. Very odd! very unaccountable! after the note I sent him this morning, and the message he returned, that he should certainly be at home till one."

"Donwell!" cried his wife. "My dear Mr. E., you have not been to Donwell; you mean the Crown; you come from the meeting at the Crown."

"No, no, that's to-morrow; and I particularly wanted to see Knightley to-day on that very account. Such a dreadful broiling morning! I went over the fields too (speaking in a tone of great ill usage), which made it so much the worse. And then not to find him at home! I assure you I am not at all pleased. And no apology left, no message for me. The housekeeper declared she knew nothing of my being expected. Very extraordinary! And nobody knew at all which way he was gone. Perhaps to Hartfield, perhaps to the Abbey Mill, perhaps into his woods. Miss Woodhouse, this is not like our friend Knightley. Can you explain it?"

Emma amused herself by protesting that it was very extraordinary indeed, and that she had not a syllable to say for him.

"I cannot imagine," cried Mrs. Elton, (feeling the indignity as a wife ought to do,) "I cannot imagine how he could do such a thing by you, of all people in the world! The very last person whom one should expect to be forgotten! My dear Mr. E., he must have left a message for you, I am sure he must. Not even Knightley could be so very eccentric;— and his servants forgot it. Depend upon it that was the case: and very likely to happen with the Donwell servants, who are all, I have often observed, extremely awkward and remiss. I am sure I would not have such a creature as his Harry stand at our sideboard for any consideration. And as for Mrs. Hodges, Wright holds her very cheap indeed. She promised Wright a receipt, and never sent it."

"I met William Larkins," continued Mr. Elton, "as I got near the house, and he told me I should not find his master at home, but I did not believe him. William seemed rather out of humour. He did not know what was come to his master lately, he said, but he could hardly ever get the speech of him. I have nothing to do with William's wants, but it really is of very great importance that *I* should see Knightley today; and it becomes a matter, therefore, of very serious inconvenience that I should have had this hot walk to no purpose."

Emma felt that she could not do better than go home directly. In all probability she was at this very time waited for there; and Mr. Knightley might be preserved from sinking deeper in aggression towards Mr. Elton, if not towards William Larkins.

She was pleased, on taking leave, to find Miss Fairfax determined to attend her out of the room, to go with her even down stairs; it gave her an opportunity which she immediately made use of, to say,—

"It is as well, perhaps, that I have not had the possibility. Had you not been surrounded by other friends, I might have been tempted to introduce a subject, to ask questions, to speak more openly than might have been strictly correct. I feel that I should certainly have been impertinent."

"Oh!" cried Jane, with a blush and an hesitation which Emma thought infinitely more becoming to her than all the elegance of all her usual composure—"there would have been no danger. The danger would have been of my wearying you. You could not have gratified me more than by expressing an interest——. Indeed, Miss Woodhouse, (speaking more collectedly,) with the consciousness which I have of misconduct, very great misconduct, it is particularly consoling to me to know that those of my friends, whose good opinion is most worth preserving, are not disgusted to such a degree as to—I have not time for half that I could wish to say. I long to make apologies, excuses, to urge something for myself. I feel it so very due. But, unfortunately—in short, if your compassion does not stand my friend——"

"Oh! you are too scrupulous, indeed you are," cried Emma, warmly, and taking her hand. "You owe me no apologies; and every body to whom you might be supposed to owe them, is so perfectly satisfied, so delighted even—"

"You are very kind, but I know what my manners were to you. So cold and artificial! I had always a part to act. It was a life of deceit! I know that I must have disgusted you."

"Pray say no more. I feel that all the apologies should be on my side. Let us forgive each other at once. We must do whatever is to be done quickest, and I think our feelings will lose no time there. I hope you have pleasant accounts from Windsor?"

"Very."

"And the next news, I suppose, will be, that we are to lose you—just as I begin to know you."

"Oh! as to all that, of course nothing can be thought of yet. I am here till claimed by Colonel and Mrs. Campbell."

"Nothing can be actually settled yet, perhaps," replied Emma, smiling—"but, excuse me, it must be thought of."

The smile was returned as Jane answered,—

"You are very right; it has been thought of. And I will own to you (I am sure it will be safe), that so far as our living with Mr. Churchill at Enscombe, it is settled. There must be three months, at least, of deep mourning; but when they are over, I imagine there will be nothing more to wait for."

"Thank you, thank you. This is just what I wanted to be assured of. Oh! if you knew how much I love every thing that is decided and open!—Good bye, good bye."

# Chapter XVII.

Mrs. Weston's friends were all made happy by her safety; and if the satisfaction of her well-doing could be increased to Emma, it was by knowing her to be the mother of a little girl. She had been decided in wishing for a Miss Weston. She would not acknowledge that it was with any view of making a match for her, hereafter, with either of Isabella's sons; but she was convinced that a daughter would suit both father and mother best. It would be a great comfort to Mr. Weston, as he grew older—and even Mr. Weston might be growing older ten years hence—to have his fireside enlivened by the sports and the nonsense, the freaks and the fancies of a child never banished from home;* and Mrs. Weston—no one could doubt that a daughter would be most to her; and it would be quite a pity that any one who so well knew how to teach, should not have their powers in exercise again.

"She has had the advantage, you know, of practising on me," she continued—"like La Baronne d'Almane on La Comtesse d'Ostalis, in Madame de Genlis' Adelaide and Theodore,[23] and we shall now see her own little Adelaide educated on a more perfect plan."

"That is," replied Mr. Knightley, "she will indulge her even more than she did you, and believe that she does not indulge her at all. It will be the only difference."

"Poor child!" cried Emma; "at that rate, what will become of her?"

"Nothing very bad. The fate of thousands. She will be disagreeable in infancy, and correct herself as she grows older. I am losing all my bitterness against spoiled children, my dearest Emma. I, who am owing all my happiness to *you*, would not it be horrible ingratitude in me to be severe on them?"

Emma laughed, and replied: "But I had the assistance of all your endeavours to counteract the indulgence of other people. I doubt whether my own sense would have corrected me without it."

"Do you?—I have no doubt. Nature gave you understanding:—Miss Taylor gave you principles. You must have

---

*Sent to boarding school, as a son would be.

done well. My interference was quite as likely to do harm as good. It was very natural for you to say, what right has he to lecture me? and I am afraid very natural for you to feel that it was done in a disagreeable manner. I do not believe I did you any good. The good was all to myself, by making you an object of the tenderest affection to me. I could not think about you so much without doating on you, faults and all; and by dint of fancying so many errors, have been in love with you ever since you were thirteen at least."

"I am sure you were of use to me," cried Emma. "I was very often influenced rightly by you—oftener than I would own at the time. I am very sure you did me good. And if poor little Anna Weston is to be spoiled, it will be the greatest humanity in you to do as much for her as you have done for me, except falling in love with her when she is thirteen."

"How often, when you were a girl, have you said to me, with one of your saucy looks,—'Mr. Knightley, I am going to do so and so; papa says I may,' or, 'I have Miss Taylor's leave'—something which, you knew, I did not approve. In such cases my interference was giving you two bad feelings instead of one."

"What an amiable creature I was! No wonder you should hold my speeches in such affectionate remembrance."

"'Mr. Knightley.' You always called me, 'Mr. Knightley;' and, from habit, it has not so very formal a sound. And yet it is formal. I want you to call me something else, but I do not know what."

"I remember once calling you 'George,' in one of my amiable fits, about ten years ago. I did it because I thought it would offend you; but, as you made no objection, I never did it again."

"And cannot you call me 'George' now?"

"Impossible! I never can call you any thing but 'Mr. Knightley.' I will not promise even to equal the elegant terseness of Mrs. Elton, by calling you Mr. K. But I will promise," she added presently, laughing and blushing, "I will promise to call you once by your Christian name. I do not say when, but perhaps you may guess where;—in the building in which N. takes M. for better, for worse."[24]

Emma grieved that she could not be more openly just to one important service which his better sense would have rendered her, to the advice which would have saved her from the worst of all her womanly follies—her wilful intimacy with Harriet Smith; but it was too tender a subject. She could not enter on it. Harriet was very seldom mentioned between them. This, on his side, might merely proceed from her not being thought of; but Emma was rather inclined to attribute it to delicacy, and a suspicion, from some appearances, that their friendship were declining. She was aware herself, that, parting under any other circumstances, they certainly should have corresponded more, and that her intelligence would not have rested, as it now almost wholly did, on Isabella's letters. He might observe that it was so. The pain of being obliged to practise concealment towards him, was very little inferior to the pain of having made Harriet unhappy.

Isabella sent quite as good an account of her visiter as could be expected; on her first arrival she had thought her out of spirits, which appeared perfectly natural, as there was a dentist to be consulted; but, since that business had been over, she did not appear to find Harriet different from what she had known her before. Isabella, to be sure, was no very quick observer; yet if Harriet had not been equal to playing with the children, it would not have escaped her. Emma's comforts and hopes were most agreeably carried on, by Harriet's being to stay longer; her fortnight was likely to be a month at least. Mr. and Mrs. John Knightley were to come down in August, and she was invited to remain till they could bring her back.

"John does not even mention your friend," said Mr. Knightley. "Here is his answer, if you like to see it."

It was the answer to the communication of his intended

marriage. Emma accepted it with a very eager hand, with an impatience all alive to know what he would say about it, and not at all checked by hearing that her friend was unmentioned.

"John enters like a brother into my happiness," continued Mr. Knightley, "but he is no complimenter; and though I well know him to have, likewise, a most brotherly affection for you, he is so far from making flourishes, that any other young woman might think him rather cool in her praise. But I am not afraid of your seeing what he writes."

"He writes like a sensible man," replied Emma, when she had read the letter. "I honour his sincerity. It is very plain that he considers the good fortune of the engagement as all on my side, but that he is not without hope of my growing, in time, as worthy of your affection, as you think me already. Had he said any thing to bear a different construction, I should not have believed him."

"My Emma, he means no such thing. He only means——"

"He and I should differ very little in our estimation of the two,"—interrupted she, with a sort of serious smile—"much less, perhaps; than he is aware of, if we could enter without ceremony or reserve on the subject."

"Emma, my dear Emma——"

"Oh!" she cried with more thorough gaiety, "if you fancy your brother does not do me justice, only wait till my dear father is in the secret, and hear his opinion. Depend upon it, he will be much farther from doing *you* justice. He will think all the happiness, all the advantage, on your side of the question; all the merit on mine. I wish I may not sink into 'poor Emma' with him at once. His tender compassion towards oppressed worth can go no farther."

"Ah!" he cried, "I wish your father might be half as easily convinced as John will be, of our having every right that equal worth can give, to be happy together. I am amused by one part of John's letter—did you notice it?—where he says, that my information did not take him wholly by surprise, that he was rather in expectation of hearing something of the kind."

"If I understand your brother, he only means so far as your having some thoughts of marrying. He had no idea of me. He seems perfectly unprepared for that."

"Yes, yes—but I am amused that he should have seen so far into my feelings. What has he been judging by? I am not conscious of any difference in my spirits or conversation that could prepare him at this time for my marrying any more than at another. But it was so, I suppose. I dare say there was a difference when I was staying with them the other day. I believe I did not play with the children quite so much as usual. I remember one evening the poor boys saying, 'Uncle seems always tired now.'"

The time was coming when the news must spread farther, and other persons' reception of it tried. As soon as Mrs. Weston was sufficiently recovered to admit Mr. Woodhouse's visits, Emma having it in view that her gentle reasonings should be employed in the cause, resolved first to announce it at home, and then at Randalls. But how to break it to her father at last! She had bound herself to do it, in such an hour of Mr. Knightley's absence, or when it came to the point her heart would have failed her, and she must have put it off; but Mr. Knightley was to come at such a time, and follow up the beginning she was to make. She was forced to speak, and to speak cheerfully too. She must not make it a more decided subject of misery to him, by a melancholy tone herself. She must not appear to think it a misfortune. With all the spirits she could command, she prepared him first for something strange, and then, in few words, said, that if his consent and approbation could be obtained—which, she trusted, would be attended with no difficulty, since it was a plan to promote the happiness of all—she and Mr. Knightley meant to marry; by which means Hartfield would receive the constant addition of that person's company, whom she knew he loved, next to his daughters and Mrs. Weston, best in the world.

Poor man!—it was at first a considerable shock to him, and he tried earnestly to dissuade her from it. She was reminded, more than once, of her having always said she would never marry, and assured that it would be a great deal better for her to remain single; and told of poor Isabella, and poor Miss Taylor. But it would not do. Emma hung about him affectionately, and smiled, and said it must be so; and that he must not class her with Isabella and Mrs. Weston, whose marriages taking them from Hartfield had, indeed, made a melancholy change: but she was not going from Hartfield; she should be always there; she was introducing no change in their numbers or their comforts but for the better; and she was very sure that he would be a great deal the happier for having Mr. Knightley always at hand, when he were once got used to the idea. Did not he love Mr. Knightley very much? He would not deny that he did, she was sure. Whom did he ever want to consult on business but Mr. Knightley? Who was so useful to him, who so ready to write his letters, who so glad to assist him? Who so cheerful, so attentive, so attached to him? Would not he like to have him always on the spot? Yes. That was all very true. Mr. Knightley could not be there too often; he should be glad to see him every day: but they did see him every day as it was. Why could not they go on as they had done?

Mr. Woodhouse could not be soon reconciled; but the worst was overcome, the idea was given; time and continual repetition must do the rest. To Emma's entreaties and assurances succeeded Mr. Knightley's, whose fond praise of her gave the subject even a kind of welcome; and he was soon used to be talked to by each on every fair occasion. They had all the assistance which Isabella could give, by letters of the strongest approbation; and Mrs. Weston was ready, on the first meeting, to consider the subject in the most serviceable light; first, as a settled, and, secondly, as a good one—well aware of the nearly equal importance of the two recommendations to Mr. Woodhouse's mind. It was agreed upon, as what was to be; and every body by whom he was used to be guided assuring him that it would be for his happiness; and having some feelings himself which almost admitted it, he began to think that some time or other, in another year or two, perhaps, it might not be so very bad if the marriage did take place.

Mrs. Weston was acting no part, feigning no feelings in all that she said to him in favour of the event. She had been extremely surprised, never more so, than when Emma first opened the affair to her; but she saw in it only increase of happiness to all, and had no scruple in urging him to the utmost. She had such a regard for Mr. Knightley, as to think he deserved even her dearest Emma; and it was in every respect so proper, suitable, and unexceptionable a connection, and in one respect, one point of the highest importance, so peculiarly eligible, so singularly fortunate, that now it seemed as if Emma could not safely have attached herself to any other creature, and that she had herself been the stupidest of beings in not having thought of it, and wished it long ago. How very few of those men in a rank of life to address Emma would have renounced their own home for Hartfield! And who but Mr. Knightley could know and bear with Mr. Woodhouse, so as to make such an arrangement desirable! The difficulty of disposing of poor Mr. Woodhouse had been always felt in her husband's plans and her own, for a marriage between Frank and Emma. How to settle the claims of Enscombe and Hartfield had been a continual impediment—less acknowledged by Mr. Weston than by herself—but even he had never been able to finish the subject better than by saying,—"Those matters will take care of themselves; the young people will find a way." But here there was nothing to be shifted off in a wild speculation on the future. It was all right, all open, all equal. No sacrifice on any side worth the name. It was a union of the highest promise of felicity in itself, and without one real, rational difficulty to oppose or delay it.

Mrs. Weston, with her baby on her knee, indulging in

such reflections as these, was one of the happiest women in the world. If any thing could increase her delight, it was perceiving that the baby would soon have outgrown its first set of caps.

The news was universally a surprise wherever it spread; and Mr. Weston had his five minutes' share of it; but five minutes were enough to familiarise the idea to his quickness of mind. He saw the advantages of the match, and rejoiced in them with all the constancy of his wife; but the wonder of it was very soon nothing; and by the end of an hour, he was not far from believing that he had always foreseen it.

"It is to be a secret, I conclude," said he. "These matters are always a secret, till it is found out that every body knows them. Only let me be told when I may speak out. I wonder whether Jane has any suspicion."

He went to Highbury the next morning and satisfied himself on that point. He told her the news. Was not she like a daughter, his eldest daughter?—he must tell her; and Miss Bates being present, it passed, of course, to Mrs. Cole, Mrs. Perry, and Mrs. Elton, immediately afterwards. It was no more than the principals were prepared for; they had calculated from the time of its being known at Randalls, how soon it would be over Highbury; and were thinking of themselves, as the evening wonder in many a family circle, with great sagacity.

In general, it was a very well approved match. Some might think him, and others might think her, the most in luck. One set might recommend their all removing to Donwell, and leaving Hartfield for the John Knightleys; and another might predict disagreements among their servants; but yet, upon the whole, there was no serious objection raised, except in one habitation—the vicarage. There, the surprise was not softened by any satisfaction. Mr. Elton cared little about it, compared with his wife; he only hoped "the young lady's pride would now be contented;" and supposed "she had always meant to catch Knightley if she could;" and, on the point of living at Hartfield, could daringly exclaim,

"Rather he than I!" But Mrs. Elton was very much discomposed indeed. "Poor Knightley! poor fellow!—sad business for him. She was extremely concerned; for, though very eccentric, he had a thousand good qualities. How could he be so taken in? Did not think him at all in love—not in the least. Poor Knightley! There would be an end of all pleasant intercourse with him. How happy he had been to come and dine with them whenever they asked him! But that would be all over now. Poor fellow! No more exploring parties to Donwell made for *her*. Oh no; there would be a Mrs. Knightley to throw cold water on every thing. Extremely disagreeable! But she was not at all sorry that she had abused the housekeeper the other day. Shocking plan, living together. It would never do. She knew a family near Maple Grove who had tried it, and been obliged to separate before the end of the first quarter."

# Chapter XVIII.

T ime passed on. A few more to-morrows, and the party from London would be arriving. It was an alarming change; and Emma was thinking of it one morning, as what must bring a great deal to agitate and grieve her, when Mr. Knightley came in, and distressing thoughts were put by. After the first chat of pleasure, he was silent; and then, in a graver tone, began with,—

"I have something to tell you, Emma; some news."

"Good or bad?" said she, quickly, looking up in his face.

"I do not know which it ought to be called."

"Oh, good I am sure. I see it in your countenance. You are trying not to smile."

"I am afraid," said he, composing his features, "I am very much afraid, my dear Emma, that you will not smile when you hear it."

"Indeed! but why so?—I can hardly imagine that any thing which pleases or amuses you should not please and amuse me too."

"There is one subject," he replied, "I hope but one, on which we do not think alike." He paused a moment, again smiling, with his eyes fixed on her face. "Does nothing occur to you? Do not you recollect? Harriet Smith."

Her cheeks flushed at the name, and she felt afraid of something, though she knew not what.

"Have you heard from her yourself this morning?" cried he. "You have, I believe, and know the whole."

"No, I have not: I know nothing; pray tell me."

"You are prepared for the worst, I see; and very bad it is. Harriet Smith marries Robert Martin."

Emma gave a start, which did not seem like being prepared; and her eyes, in eager gaze, said, "No, this is impossible!" but her lips were closed.

"It is so, indeed!" continued Mr. Knightley; "I have it from Robert Martin himself. He left me not half an hour ago."

She was still looking at him with the most speaking amazement.

"You like it, my Emma, as little as I feared—I wish our opinions were the same. But in time they will. Time, you may be very sure, will make one or the other of us think differently; and, in the meanwhile, we need not talk much on the subject."

"You mistake me, you quite mistake me," she replied, exerting herself. "It is not that such a circumstance would now make me unhappy, but I cannot believe it. It seems an impossibility! You cannot mean to say, that Harriet Smith has accepted Robert Martin. You cannot mean that he has even proposed to her again—yet. You only mean, that he intends it."

"I mean that he has done it," answered Mr. Knightley, with smiling but determined decision, "and been accepted."

"Good God!" she cried. "Well!"—Then having recourse to her work-basket, in excuse for leaning down her face, and concealing all the exquisite feelings of delight and entertainment which she knew she must be expressing, she added, "Well, now tell me every thing; make this intelligible to me. How, where, when? Let me know it all. I never was more surprised—but it does not make me unhappy, I assure you. How—how has it been possible?"

"It is a very simple story. He went to town on business three days ago, and I got him to take charge of some papers which I was wanting to send to John. He delivered these papers to John, at his chambers, and was asked by him to join their party the same evening to Astley's.[25] They were going to take the two eldest boys to Astley's. The party was to be our brother and sister, Henry, John——, and Miss Smith. My friend Robert could not resist. They called for him in their way; were all extremely amused; and my brother asked him to dine with them the next day, which he did, and in the course of that visit (as I understand) he found an opportunity of speaking to Harriet; and certainly did not speak in vain. She made him, by her acceptance, as happy even as he is deserving. He came down by yesterday's coach, and was with me this morning, immediately after breakfast, to report his proceedings, first on my affairs, and then on his own. This is all that I can relate of the how, where, and when. Your friend Harriet will make a much longer history when you see her. She will give you all the minute particulars, which only woman's language can make interesting. In our communications we deal only in the great. However, I must say, that Robert Martin's heart teemed for *him*, and to *me*, very overflowing; and that he did mention, without its being much to the purpose, that after quitting their box at Astley's, my brother took charge of Mrs. John Knightley and little John, and he followed with Miss Smith and Henry; and that at one time they were in such a crowd, as to make Miss Smith rather uneasy."

He stopped. Emma dared not attempt any immediate reply. To speak, she was sure would be to betray a most unreasonable degree of happiness. She must wait a moment, or he would think her mad. Her silence disturbed him; and after observing her a little while, he added,—

"Emma, my love, you said that this circumstance would not now make you unhappy; but I am afraid it gives you more pain than you expected. His situation is an evil; but you must consider it as what satisfies your friend: and I will answer for your thinking better and better of him as you know him more: his good sense and good principles would delight you. As far as the man is concerned, you could not wish your friend in better hands. His rank in society I would alter if I could; which is saying a great deal, I assure you, Emma. You laugh at me about William Larkins; but I could quite as ill spare Robert Martin."

He wanted her to look up and smile; and having now brought herself not to smile too broadly, she did, cheerfully answering,—

"You need not be at any pains to reconcile me to the match. I think Harriet is doing extremely well. *Her* connections may be worse than *his:* in respectability of character, there can be no doubt that they are. I have been silent from surprise merely, excessive surprise. You cannot imagine how suddenly it has come on me! how peculiarly unprepared I was! for I had reason to believe her very lately more determined against him, much more than she was before."

"You ought to know your friend best," replied Mr. Knightley; "but I should say she was a good-tempered, soft-hearted girl, not likely to be very, very determined against any young man who told her he loved her."

Emma could not help laughing as she answered, "Upon my word, I believe you know her quite as well as I do. But, Mr. Knightley, are you perfectly sure that she has absolutely and downright *accepted* him? I could suppose she might in time, but can she already? Did not you misunderstand him? You were both talking of other things; of business, shows of cattle, or new drills; and might not you, in the confusion of so many subjects, mistake him? It was not Harriet's hand that he was certain of—it was the dimensions of some famous ox."

The contrast between the countenance and air of Mr. Knightley and Robert Martin was, at this moment, so strong to Emma's feelings, and so strong was the recollection of all that had so recently passed on Harriet's side, so fresh the sound of those words spoken with such emphasis, "No, I hope I know better than to think of Robert Martin," that she was really expecting the intelligence to prove, in some measure, premature. It could not be otherwise.

"Do you dare say this?" cried Mr. Knightley. "Do you dare to suppose me so great a blockhead, as not to know what a man is talking of? What do you deserve?"

"Oh! I always deserve the best treatment, because I never put up with any other; and, therefore, you must give me a plain, direct answer. Are you quite sure that you understand the terms on which Mr. Martin and Harriet now are?"

"I am quite sure," he replied, speaking very distinctly, "that he told me she had accepted him; and that there was no obscurity, nothing doubtful, in the words he used; and I think I can give you a proof that it must be so. He asked my opinion as to what he was now to do. He knew of no one but Mrs. Goddard to whom he could apply for information of her relations or friends. Could I mention any thing more fit to be done, than to go to Mrs. Goddard? I assured him that I could not. Then, he said, he would endeavour to see her in the course of this day."

"I am perfectly satisfied," replied Emma, with the brightest smiles, "and most sincerely wish them happy."

"You are materially changed since we talked on this subject before."

"I hope so—for at that time I was a fool."

"And I am changed also; for I am now very willing to grant you all Harriet's good qualities. I have taken some pains for your sake, and for Robert Martin's sake (whom I have always had reason to believe as much in love with her as ever), to get acquainted with her. I have often talked to her a good deal. You must have seen that I did. Sometimes, indeed, I have thought you were half suspecting me of pleading poor Martin's cause, which was never the case: but, from all my observations, I am convinced of her being an artless, amiable girl, with very good notions, very seriously good principles, and placing her happiness in the affections and utility of domestic life. Much of this, I have no doubt, she may thank you for."

"Me!" cried Emma, shaking her head. "Ah, poor Harriet!"

She checked herself, however, and submitted quietly to a little more praise than she deserved.

Their conversation was soon afterwards closed by the entrance of her father. She was not sorry. She wanted to be alone. Her mind was in a state of flutter and wonder, which made it impossible for her to be collected. She was in dancing, singing, exclaiming spirits; and till she had moved about, and talked to herself, and, laughed and reflected, she could be fit for nothing rational.

Her father's business was to announce James's being gone out to put the horses to, preparatory to their now daily drive to Randalls; and she had, therefore, an immediate excuse for disappearing.

The joy, the gratitude, the exquisite delight of her sensations may be imagined. The sole grievance and alloy thus removed in the prospect of Harriet's welfare, she was really in danger of becoming too happy for security. What had she to wish for? Nothing, but to grow more worthy of him, whose intentions and judgment had been ever so superior to her own. Nothing but that the lessons of her past folly might teach her humility and circumspection in future.

Serious she was, very serious, in her thankfulness and in her resolutions; and yet there was no preventing a laugh, sometimes in the very midst of them. She must laugh at such a close—such an end of the doleful disappointment of five weeks back—such a heart—such a Harriet!

Now there would be pleasure in her returning; every thing would be a pleasure: it would be a great pleasure to know Robert Martin.

High in the rank of her most serious and heartfelt felicities was the reflection that all necessity of concealment from Mr. Knightley would soon be over. The disguise, equivocation, mystery, so hateful to her to practise, might soon be over. She could now look forward to giving him that full and perfect confidence which her disposition was most ready to welcome as a duty.

In the gayest and happiest spirits, she set forward with her father, not always listening, but always agreeing, to what he said; and, whether in speech or silence, conniving at the comfortable persuasion of his being obliged to go to Randalls every day, or poor Mrs. Weston would be disappointed.

They arrived. Mrs. Weston was alone in the drawing-room. But hardly had they been told of the baby, and Mr. Woodhouse received the thanks for coming, which he asked for, when a glimpse was caught through the blind of two figures passing near the window.

"It is Frank and Miss Fairfax," said Mrs. Weston. "I was just going to tell you of our agreeable surprise in seeing him arrive this morning. He stays till to-morrow, and Miss Fairfax has been persuaded to spend the day with us. They are coming in, I hope."

In half a minute they were in the room. Emma was extremely glad to see him; but there was a degree of confusion, a number of embarrassing recollections, on each side. They met readily and smiling, but with a consciousness which at first allowed little to be said; and having all sat down again, there was for some time such a blank in the circle that Emma began to doubt whether the wish now indulged, which she had long felt, of seeing Frank Churchill once more, and of seeing him with Jane, would yield its proportion of pleasure. When Mr. Weston joined the party, however, and when the baby was fetched, there was no longer a want of subject or animation, or of courage and opportunity for Frank Churchill to draw near her and say,—

"I have to thank you, Miss Woodhouse, for a very kind, forgiving message, in one of Mrs. Weston's letters. I hope time has not made you less willing to pardon: I hope you do not retract what you then said."

"No, indeed," cried Emma, most happy to begin; "not in the least. I am particularly glad to see and shake hands with you, and to give you joy in person."

He thanked her with all his heart, and continued some time to speak with serious feeling of his gratitude and happiness.

"Is not she looking well?" said he, turning his eyes towards Jane,—"better than she ever used to do? You see how my father and Mrs. Weston doat upon her."

But his spirits were soon rising again; and, with laughing eyes, after mentioning the expected return of the Campbells, he named the name of Dixon. Emma blushed, and forbade its being pronounced in her hearing.

"I can never think of it," she cried, "without extreme shame."

"The shame," he answered, "is all mine, or ought to be. But is it possible that you had no suspicion? I mean of late: early, I know, you had none."

"I never had the smallest, I assure you."

"That appears quite wonderful. I was once very near,— and I wish I had; it would have been better. But though I was always doing wrong things, their were very *bad* wrong things, and such as did me no service. It would have been a much better transgression, had I broken the bond of secrecy and told you every thing."

"It is now not worth a regret," said Emma.

"I have some hope," resumed he, "of my uncle's being persuaded to pay a visit at Randalls; he wants to be introduced to her. When the Campbells are returned, we shall meet them in London, and continue there, I trust, till we may carry her northward; but now, I am at such a distance from her—is not it hard, Miss Woodhouse? Till this morning, we have not once met since the day of reconciliation. Do not you pity me?"

Emma spoke her pity so very kindly, that, with a sudden accession of gay thought, he cried,—

"Ah! By the by,"—then sinking his voice, and looking demure for the moment,—"I hope Mr. Knightley is well?" He paused. She coloured and laughed. "I know you saw my letter, and think you may remember my wish in your favour. Let me return your congratulations. I assure you that I have heard the news with the warmest interest and satisfaction. He is a man whom I cannot presume to praise."

Emma was delighted, and only wanted him to go on in the same style; but his mind was the next moment in his own concerns and with his own Jane, and his next words were,—

"Did you ever see such a skin? such smoothness, such delicacy, and yet without being actually fair. One cannot call her fair. It is a most uncommon complexion, with her dark eyelashes and hair—a most distinguishing complexion! So peculiarly the lady in it. Just colour enough for beauty."

"I have always admired her complexion," replied Emma, archly; "but do not I remember the time when you found fault with her for being so pale? When we first began to talk of her. Have you quite forgotten?"

"Oh no!—what an impudent dog I was!—how could I dare——"

But he laughed so heartily at the recollection, that Emma could not help saying,—

"I do suspect that in the midst of your perplexities at that time, you had very great amusement in tricking us all. I am sure you had. I am sure it was a consolation to you."

"Oh no, no, no!—how can you suspect me of such a thing? I was the most miserable wretch."

"Not quite so miserable as to be insensible to mirth. I am sure it was a source of high entertainment to you, to feel that you were taking us all in. Perhaps I am the readier to suspect, because, to tell you the truth, I think it might have been some amusement to myself in the same situation. I think there is a little likeness between us."

He bowed.

"If not in our dispositions," she presently added, with a look of true sensibility, "there is a likeness in our destiny; the destiny which bids fair to connect us with two characters so much superior to our own."

"True, true," he answered, warmly. "No, not true on your side. You can have no superior, but most true on mine. She is a complete angel. Look at her. Is not she an angel in every gesture? Observe the turn of her throat. Observe her eyes, as she is looking up at my father. You will be glad to hear (inclining his head, and whispering seriously) that my uncle means to give her all my aunt's jewels. They are to be new set. I am resolved to have some in an ornament for the head. Will not it be beautiful in her dark hair?"

"Very beautiful, indeed," replied Emma; and she spoke so kindly, that he gratefully burst out,—

"How delighted I am to see you again! and to see you in such excellent looks! I would not have missed this meeting for the world. I should certainly have called at Hartfield had you failed to come."

The others had been talking of the child, Mrs. Weston giving an account of a little alarm she had been under the evening before, from the infant's appearing not quite well. She believed she had been foolish, but it had alarmed her, and she had been within half a minute of sending for Mr. Perry. Perhaps she ought to be ashamed, but Mr. Weston had been almost as uneasy as herself. In ten minutes, however, the child had been perfectly well again. This was her history; and particularly interesting it was to Mr. Woodhouse, who commended her very much for thinking of sending for Perry, and only regretted that she had not done it. "She should always send for Perry, if the child appeared in the slightest degree disordered, were it only for a moment. She could not be too soon alarmed, nor send for Perry too often. It was a pity, perhaps, that he had not come last night; for, though the child seemed well now, very well considering, it would probably have been better if Perry had seen it."

Frank Churchill caught the name.

"Perry!" said he to Emma, and trying, as he spoke, to catch Miss Fairfax's eye. "My friend Mr. Perry! What are they saying about Mr. Perry? Has he been here this morning? And how does he travel now? Has he set up his carriage?"

Emma soon recollected, and understood him; and while she joined in the laugh, it was evident from Jane's countenance that she too was really hearing him, though trying to seem deaf.

"Such an extraordinary dream of mine!" he cried. "I can never think of it without laughing. She hears us, she hears us, Miss Woodhouse. I see it in her cheek, her smile, her vain attempt to frown. Look at her. Do not you see that, at this instant, the very passage of her own letter, which sent me the report, is passing under her eye; that the whole blunder is spread before her; that she can attend to nothing else, though pretending to listen to the others?"

Jane was forced to smile completely, for a moment; and the smile partly remained as she turned towards him, and said in a conscious, low, yet steady voice,—

"How you can bear such recollections, is astonishing to me! They *will* sometimes obtrude: but how can you *court* them?"

He had a great deal to say in return, and very entertainingly; but Emma's feelings were chiefly with Jane in the argument: and on leaving Randalls, and falling naturally into a comparison of the two men, she felt, that, pleased as she had been to see Frank Churchill, and really regarding him as she did with friendship, she, had never been more sensible of Mr. Knightley's high superiority of character. The happiness of this most happy day received its completion in the animated contemplation of his worth which this comparison produced.

# Chapter XIX.

If Emma had still, at intervals, an anxious feeling for Harriet, a momentary doubt of its being possible for her to be really cured of her attachment to Mr. Knightley, and really able to accept another man from unbiased inclination, it was not long that she had to suffer from the recurrence of any such uncertainty. A very few days brought the party from London; and she had no sooner an opportunity of being one hour alone with Harriet, than she became perfectly satisfied, unaccountable as it was, that Robert Martin had thoroughly supplanted Mr. Knightley, and was now forming all her views of happiness.

Harriet was a little distressed—did look a little foolish at first; but having once owned that she had been presumptuous and silly, and self-deceived, before, her pain and confusion seemed to die away with the words, and leave her without a care for the past, and with the fullest exultation in the present and future; for, as to her friend's approbation, Emma had instantly removed every fear of that nature, by meeting her with the most unqualified congratulations. Harriet was most happy to give every particular of the evening at Astley's, and the dinner the next day; she could dwell on it all with the utmost delight. But what did such particulars explain? The fact was, as Emma could now acknowledge, that Harriet had always liked Robert Martin; and that his continuing to love her had been irresistible. Beyond this, it must ever be unintelligible to Emma.

The event, however, was most joyful; and every day was giving her fresh reason for thinking so. Harriet's parentage became known. She proved to be the daughter of a trades-man, rich enough to afford her the comfortable mainte-nance which had ever been hers, and decent enough to have always wished for concealment. Such was the blood of gen-tility which Emma had formerly been so ready to vouch for! It was likely to be as untainted, perhaps, as the blood of many a gentleman; but what a connection had she been preparing for Mr. Knightley, or for the Churchills, or even for Mr. Elton! The stain of illegitimacy, unbleached by nobility or wealth, would have been a stain indeed.

No objection was raised on the father's side; the young man was treated liberally; it was all as it should be: and as Emma became acquainted with Robert Martin, who was now introduced at Hartfield, she fully acknowledged on him all the appearance of sense and worth which could bid fairest for her little friend. She had no doubt of Harriet's happiness with any good-tempered man; but with him, and in the home he offered, there would be the hope of more, of secu-rity, stability, and improvement. She would be placed in the midst of those who loved her, and who had better sense than herself; retired enough for safety, and occupied enough for cheerfulness. She would be never led into temptation, nor left for it to find her out. She would be respectable and happy; and Emma admitted her to be the luckiest creature in the world, to have created so steady and persevering an af-fection in such a man; or, if not quite the luckiest, to yield only to herself.

Harriet, necessarily drawn away by her engagements with the Martins, was less and less at Hartfield, which was not to be regretted. The intimacy between her and Emma must sink; their friendship must change into a calmer sort of good-will; and, fortunately, what ought to be, and must be, seemed already beginning, and in the most gradual, natural manner.

Before the end of September, Emma attended Harriet to church, and saw her hand bestowed on Robert Martin with so complete a satisfaction, as no remembrances, even connected with Mr. Elton as he stood before them, could impair. Perhaps, indeed, at that time, she scarcely saw Mr. Elton, but as the clergyman whose blessing at the altar might next fall on herself. Robert Martin and Harriet Smith, the latest couple engaged of the three, were the first to be married.

Jane Fairfax had already quitted Highbury, and was restored to the comforts of her beloved home with the Campbells. The Mr. Churchills were also in town; and they were only waiting for November.

The intermediate month was the one fixed on, as far as they dared, by Emma and Mr. Knightley. They had determined that their marriage ought to be concluded, while John and Isabella were still at Hartfield, to allow them the fortnight's absence in a tour to the sea-side, which was the plan. John and Isabella, and every other friend, were agreed in approving it. But Mr. Woodhouse—how was Mr. Woodhouse to be induced to consent?—he, who had never yet alluded to their marriage but as a distant event.

When first sounded on the subject, he was so miserable, that they were almost hopeless. A second allusion, indeed, gave less pain. He began to think it was to be, and that he could not prevent it—a very promising step of the mind on its way to resignation. Still, however, he was not happy. Nay, he appeared so much otherwise, that his daughter's courage failed. She could not bear to see him suffering, to know him fancying himself neglected; and though her understanding almost acquiesced in the assurance of both the Mr. Knightleys, that when once the event were over, his distress would be soon over too, she hesitated—she could not proceed.

In this state of suspense, they were befriended, not by any sudden illumination of Mr. Woodhouse's mind, or any wonderful change of his nervous system, but by the operation of the same system in another way. Mrs. Weston's poultry-house was robbed one night of all her turkeys,—evidently by the ingenuity of man. Other poultry-yards in the neighbourhood also suffered. Pilfering was *house-breaking* to Mr. Woodhouse's fears. He was very uneasy; and but for the sense of his son-in-law's protection, would have been under wretched alarm every night of his life. The strength, resolution, and presence of mind of the Mr. Knightleys, commanded his fullest dependence. While either of them protected him and his, Hartfield was safe. But Mr. John Knightley must be in London again by the end of the first week in November.

The result of this distress was, that, with a much more voluntary, cheerful consent, than his daughter had ever presumed to hope for at the moment, she was able to fix her wedding-day; and Mr. Elton was called on, within a month from the marriage of Mr. and Mrs. Robert Martin, to join the hands of Mr. Knightley and Miss Woodhouse.

The wedding was very much like other weddings, where the parties have no taste for finery or parade; and Mrs. Elton, from the particulars detailed by her husband, thought it all extremely shabby, and very inferior to her own. "Very little white satin, very few lace veils; a most pitiful business! Selina would stare when she heard of it." But, in spite of these deficiencies, the wishes, the hopes, the confidence, the predictions of the small band of true friends who witnessed the ceremony, were fully answered in the perfect happiness of the union.

THE END.

# Endnotes

1. (p. 26) *he would read something aloud out of the Elegant Extracts. . . . Children of the Abbey:* Elegant Extracts was one of a number of popular anthologies for younger readers first published during the 1780s and reprinted during the early decades of the nineteenth century. *The Vicar of Wakefield,* by Oliver Goldsmith, was published in 1766; *The Romance of the Forest* (1791) is by Ann Radcliffe; Regina Maria Dalton Roche wrote the tale *The Children of the Abbey* (1796). Although Martin has read the universally popular novel by Goldsmith, he remains untouched by the Gothic romances, whose original audiences were said to be very largely composed of women.

2. (p. 66) *My first doth affliction . . . to soften and heal:* The answer is woman—that is, woe + man. Riddles, charades, and conundrums, popularly used as pastimes, combine verse and wordplay.

3. (p. 71) *"The course of true love never did run smooth":* Emma is quoting a line from William Shakespeare's *A Midsummer Night's Dream* (act 1, scene 1).

4. (p. 71) *"to speak to him, at Michaelmas":* Harriet is referring to the season surrounding the feast of Saint Michael, celebrated on September 29.

5. (p. 74) *"Kitty, a fair but frozen maid . . . So fatal to my suit before":* This is the first stanza of a well-known riddle, said to have been written by actor David Garrick (1717–1779). The answer is chimney-sweeper.

6. (p. 90) *Cobham:* This small Surrey town in the south of England is, some readers have claimed, the model for Highbury. However, no positive attribution of an actual village has ever been convincingly demonstrated.

7. (p. 99) *philippics:* Originally this term referred to the heated orations delivered by the Greek statesman Demosthenes (384–322 B.C.) against Philip II, the leader of Mace-

donia. Now "philippic" is used to indicate any bitter, goading invective.

8. (p. 147) *"she fills the whole paper and crosses half"*: To conserve paper, a letter in Jane Austen's time would be written with script running both horizontally and either vertically or diagonally on the same sheet.

9. (p. 164) *"our lot is cast in a goodly heritage"*: This is a slightly inaccurate reference to the Bible, Psalm 16:5–7 (King James Version).

10. (p. 202) *this piano-forte had arrived from Broadwood's*: Broadwood's, a London manufacturer renowned for the quality of its piano-fortes, was a pioneer in the technological development of the modern instrument. Beethoven used one of the instruments that they sent him.

11. (p. 229) *Cramer*: Johann Baptist Cramer (1771–1858), a leading pianist and prolific composer, founded a successful London music publishing firm in 1824.

12. (p. 229) *"She is playing* Robin Adair"*: This romantic song, written in the 1750s by Lady Caroline Keppel, describes the singer's heartbreak at having lost her love, Robin Adair.

13. (p. 257) *"They will have their barouche-landau"*: This four-seat carriage had a collapsible top, making it convenient for exploring the countryside or for taking a turn in the park. Mrs. Elton mentions her brother's barouche-landau in order to identify him as a person of wealth and social distinction.

14. (p. 258) *"where the waters do agree"*: The mineral waters of the resort town Bath, in Somerset, England, were taken as a restorative for every conceivable ailment. Bath, as a setting, features prominently in the literature of Austen's time.

15. (p. 265) *"Full many a flower . . . on the desert air"*: Emma would have been familiar with these lines from the well-known poem "Elegy Written in a Country Churchyard," by Thomas Gray (1716–1771). This is not the only occasion on which Mrs. Elton inappropriately introduces a quotation.

16. (p. 291) *"before Hymen's saffron robe"*: In Greek mythology, Hymen is the god of marriage. John Milton refers to Hymen's saffron robe in "L'Allegro" (1631).

17. (p. 321) *a pretty little Tunbridge-ware box:* In the eighteenth and nineteenth centuries, resident artisans in the region of Tunbridge Wells, Kent, produced wooden boxes, tables, and toys notable for their detailed wood mosaic inlays.

18. (p. 327) *Myself creating what I saw:* This is a reference to William Cowper's (1731–1800) best-known poem, "The Task."

19. (p. 369) *Goldsmith tells us, that when lovely woman stoops to folly:* The narrator is referring to Oliver Goldsmith's novel *The Vicar of Wakefield* (1766).

20. (p. 382) *"the world is not theirs, nor the world's law":* Emma is recalling a line from Shakespeare's *Romeo and Juliet* (act 5, scene 1), in which Romeo says, "The world is not thy friend, nor the world's law; / The world affords no law to make thee rich."

21. (p. 394) *for chance and circumstance (as second causes):* The first cause is God or religion, in this context a heavenly design. The second cause, in this case, is chance or circumstance, decidedly undesigned. Austen's lines echo Alexander Pope's *The Dunciad* IV.

22. (p. 433) *"For when a lady's in the case, . . . things give place":* These lines are from the satirical fable "The Hare and Many Friends," by John Gay (1685–1732). At the end of the tale, the hounds eat the hare (lady).

23. (p. 440) *"in Madame de Genlis' Adelaide and Theodore":* Emma, like Austen, probably read the novel *Adelaide and Theodore*, by Stéphanie Félicité Brulart de Genlis, marchioness De Sillery, in its 1783 English translation.

24. (p. 442) *"in the building in which N. takes M. for better, for worse":* The building referred to is the wedding chapel; Emma will use Mr. Knightley's first name only during the wedding ceremony. "For better, for worse" are words taken from that ceremony as it is printed in the Book of Common Prayer of the Anglican Church.

25. (p. 450) *"join their party the same evening to Astley's":* They are going to a circus founded by trick rider and theatrical manager Philip Astley (1742–1814) and held in the Royal Amphitheater of Arts.

# *Inspired by* Emma

## FILM

In 1995 four of Jane Austen's novels were made into films: Ang Lee's *Sense and Sensibility*; Simon Langton's four-and-a-half-hour miniseries *Pride and Prejudice*; the BBC's production of *Persuasion*; and *Clueless*, a modernization of *Emma*.

*Clueless* is particularly innovative in its adaptation of Jane Austen. Written and directed by Amy Heckerling, the film shifts the story to a modern-day Beverly Hills high school and an environment furnished with liposuction, drug abuse, and Starbucks. Alicia Silverstone is irresistible as the charismatic Cher, the rich, spoiled, and totally irresponsible matchmaking character based on Emma. She is inviting, affectionate, warm-hearted, and well-intentioned as she wanders through her plastic world, always aiming to improve the lives of others. She acts a matchmaker for her teachers, makes over a coarse Brooklyn transplant, and keeps her stressed father's cholesterol at acceptable levels. The film reproduces the confused romances of the novel, and the change in period allows for humorous translations: In the novel, gypsies harass Harriet; in the movie, boys at the mall hang Tai over the railing. Both subtle and self-mocking, *Clueless* was such a hit that it led to a television series—though one that largely ignored its origins in Jane Austen.

Douglas McGrath's *Emma* (1996) is a stricter adaptation of Austen. In this light and finely toned version, Gwyneth Paltrow shines in the title role, supported by Toni Collette as Harriet, Jeremy Northam as Mr. Knightley, Alan Cumming as Mr. Elton, and Ewan McGregor in the role of Frank Churchill. Paltrow brings to life the nuances of gesture, facial expression, and manner of Austen's Emma. The film's production design is subtle and precise: in one scene, potted orange trees in a lush room frame a posing Emma; the lace, curtains, and croquet sets adorning the estates are pitch-perfect. In the opening sequence, a globe of the world spins amid the stars as the credits roll by, an ironic gesture that underscores the unimportance of village life in the grand scheme of things.

## A ROOM OF ONE'S OWN

Virginia Woolf invokes Jane Austen with reverence in her landmark feminist tract *A Room of One's Own* (1929). Lamenting the paucity of great woman writers in history, Woolf ascribes the phenomenon partially to the fact that writers need privacy to compose their works—a room of their own, which Austen lacked. Woolf describes the remarkable conditions in which Austen composed her masterpieces: in the family sitting-room, subject to frequent interruption, hiding her works with blotting paper whenever visitors entered. Yet despite these impediments and the confining patriarchal society in which she lived, Austen was, as Woolf put it, able to compose "without hate, without bitterness, without fear, without protest, without preaching. That was how Shakespeare wrote."

# Comments & Questions

*In this section, we aim to provide the reader with an array of perspectives on the text, as well as questions that challenge those perspectives. The commentary has been culled from sources as diverse as reviews contemporaneous with the work, letters written by the author, literary criticism of later generations, and appreciations written throughout the work's history. Following the commentary, a series of questions seeks to filter Jane Austen's* Emma *through a variety of points of view and bring about a richer understanding of this enduring work.*

## COMMENTS

### SIR WALTER SCOTT

We . . . bestow no mean compliment upon the author of *Emma*, when we say that, keeping close to common incidents, and to such characters as occupy the ordinary walks of life, she has produced sketches of such spirit and originality, that we never miss the excitation which depends upon a narrative of uncommon events, arising from the consideration of minds, manners, and sentiments, greatly above our own. In this class she stands almost alone; for the scenes of Miss Edgeworth are laid in higher life, varied by more romantic incident, and by her remarkable power of embodying and illustrating national character. But the author of *Emma* confines herself chiefly to the middling classes of society; her most distinguished characters do not rise greatly above well-bred country gentlemen and ladies; and those which are sketched with most originality and precision, belong to a class rather below that standard. The narrative of all her novels is composed of such common occurrences as may have fallen under the observation of most folks; and her dramatis personæ conduct themselves upon the motives and princi-

ples which the readers may recognize as ruling their own
and that of most of their acquaintances. The kind of moral,
also, which these novels inculcate, applies equally to the
paths of common life.

—from *Quarterly Review* (October 1815)

**CHARLOTTE BRONTË**

I have likewise read one of Miss Austen's works "Emma"—
read it with interest and with just the degree of admiration
which Miss Austen herself would have thought sensible and
suitable—anything like warmth or enthusiasm; anything energetic, poignant, heart-felt, is utterly out of place in com-
mending these works: all such demonstration the authoress
would have met with a well-bred sneer. . . . Her business is
not half so much with the human heart as with the human
eyes, mouth, hands and feet; what sees keenly, speaks aptly,
moves flexibly, it suits her to study, but what is the unseen
seat of Life and the sentient target of Death—*this* Miss
Austen ignores.

—from a letter to W. S. Williams (April 12, 1850)

**GEORGE HENRY LEWES**

Jane Austen [is] the greatest artist that has ever written,
using the term to signify the most perfect mastery over the
means to her end. There are heights and depths in human
nature Miss Austen has never scaled nor fathomed, there are
worlds of passionate existence into which she has never set
foot; but although this is obvious to every reader, it is equally
obvious that she has risked no failures by attempting to de-
lineate that which she had not seen. Her circle may be restricted, but it is complete. Her world is a perfect orb, and
vital. Life, as it presents itself to an English gentlewoman
peacefully yet actively engaged in her quiet village, is mir-
rored in her works with a purity and fidelity that must endow
them with interest for all time. To read one of her books is
like an actual experience of life: you know the people as if
you have lived with them. The marvellous reality and subtle

distinctive traits noticeable in her portraits has led Macaulay
to call her a prose Shakspeare. If the whole force of the distinction which lies in that epithet *prose* be fairly appreciated,
no one, we think, will dispute the compliment; for out of
Shakspeare it would be difficult to find characters so typical
yet so nicely demarcated within the limits of their kind.

—from *Westminster Review* (July 1852)

**MARGARET OLIPHANT**
*Emma*, perhaps, is the work upon which most suffrages would
meet as the most perfect of all [Miss Austen's] performances.

—from *The Literary History of England* (1895)

**WILLIAM LYON PHELPS**
Emma has more actual faults than any other of Miss Austen's
persons who are intended to gain the reader's sympathy. She
is something of a snob, understands perfectly the privileges
of her social rank, and means to have others understand
them as well. She thinks she understands human nature, and
delights to act in the role of match-maker, in which capacity
she is a failure. Best of all, she is ignorant of her own heart,
as the most charming heroines in fiction are wont to be. She
does not realise that she loves Knightley until the spark of
jealousy sets her soul aflame. The curious thing is, that before we finish the book we actually like her all the better for
her faults, and for her numerous mistakes; her heart is pure,
sound, and good, and her sense of principle is as deeply
rooted as the Rock of Gibraltar. She is, however, a snob; and
this is the only instance in fiction that I can remember at this
moment where a snob is not only attractive, but lovable.

—from *Essays on Books* (1914)

**REGINALD FARRER**
'Emma' is the very climax of Jane Austen's work; and a real
appreciation of 'Emma' is the final test of citizenship in her
kingdom. For this is not an easy book to read; it should never
be the beginner's primer, nor be published without a prefa-

tory synopsis. Only when the story has been thoroughly as-
similated, can the infinite delights and subtleties of its work-
manship begin to be appreciated, as you realise the manifold
complexity of the book's web, and find that every sentence,
almost every epithet, has its definite reference to equally un-
emphasised points before and after in the development of
the plot. Thus it is that, while twelve readings of 'Pride and
Prejudice' give you twelve periods of pleasure repeated, as
many readings of 'Emma' give you that pleasure, not repeated only, but squared and squared again with each perusal, till at every fresh reading you feel anew that you never
understood anything like the widening sum of its delights.
But, until you know the story, you are apt to find its movement dense and slow and obscure, difficult to follow, and not
very obviously worth the following.

For this is *the* novel of character, and of character alone,
and of one dominating character in particular. And many a
rash reader, and some who are not rash, have been shut out
on the threshold of Emma's Comedy by a dislike of Emma
herself. Well did Jane Austen know what she was about, when
she said, 'I am going to take a heroine whom nobody but myself will much like.' And, in so far as she fails to make people
like Emma, so far would her whole attempt have to be
judged a failure, were it not that really the failure, like the
loss, is theirs who have not taken the trouble to understand
what is being attempted. Jane Austen loved tackling problems; her hardest of all, her most deliberate, and her most
triumphantly solved, is Emma.

—from *Quarterly Review* (July 1917)

**VIRGINIA WOOLF**

Jane Austen is . . . a mistress of much deeper emotion than
appears upon the surface. She stimulates us to supply what is
not there. What she offers is, apparently, a trifle, yet is composed of something that expands in the reader's mind and
endows with the most enduring form of life scenes which are
outwardly trivial. Always the stress is laid upon character.

How, we are made to wonder, will Emma behave when Lord Osborne and Tom Musgrave make their call at five minutes before three, just as Mary is bringing in the tray and the knife-case? It is an extremely awkward situation. The young men are accustomed to much greater refinement. Emma may prove herself ill-bred, vulgar, a nonentity. The turns and twists of the dialogue keep us on the tenterhooks of suspense. Our attention is half upon the present moment, half upon the future. And when, in the end, Emma behaves in such a way as to vindicate our highest hopes of her, we are moved as if we had been made witnesses of a matter of the highest importance.

—from *The Common Reader* (1925)

**E. M. FORSTER**

I am a Jane Austenite, and therefore slightly imbecile about Jane Austen. My fatuous expression and airs of personal immunity—how ill they set on the face, say, of a Stevensonian! But Jane Austen is so different. She is my favorite author! I read and re-read, the mouth open and the mind closed. Shut up in measureless content, I greet her by the name of most kind hostess, while criticism slumbers.

—from *Abinger Harvest* (1936)

## QUESTIONS

1. Speaking of *Emma*, Jane Austen said "I am going to take a heroine whom nobody but myself will like much." What would you say is likeable and what is hard to like about the character Emma?

2. "One half of the world cannot understand the pleasures of the other," says Emma. Do gender differences constitute an important theme in *Emma*? Beyond individual differences in personality among the characters, how do men and women differ in *Emma*?

3. At the end of the novel, do Emma and Knightley deserve each other? Why or why not?

4. Even Jane Austen's most devoted fans agree that she does not directly deal with extreme passions, heroic tragedies, or world-historical events. What is it in her work that can appeal to street-tough guys, jaded sophisticates, and over-educated academics?

# For Further Reading

## LETTERS

Le Faye, Deirdre. *Jane Austen's Letters.* Third edition. Oxford: Oxford University Press, 1995.

## BIOGRAPHY

Honan, Park. *Jane Austen: Her Life.* New York: St. Martin's Press, 1987.

Austen-Leigh, James Edward. *A Memoir of Jane Austen and Other Family Recollections.* 1870. Edited by Kathryn Sutherland. Oxford and New York: Oxford University Press, 2002.

Tomalin, Claire. *Jane Austen: A Life.* New York: Alfred A. Knopf, 1997.

## COMMENTARY AND CRITICISM

Brown, Julia Prewitt. *Jane Austen's Novels: Social Change and Literary Form.* Cambridge, MA: Harvard University Press, 1979.

Butler, Marilyn. *Jane Austen and the War of Ideas.* Oxford: Clarendon Press, 1975.

Copeland, Edward, and McMaster, Juliet, eds. *The Cambridge Companion to Jane Austen.* Cambridge and New York: Cambridge University Press, 1997.

Lynch, Deidre, ed. *Janeites: Austen's Disciples and Devotees.* Princeton, NJ: Princeton University Press, 2000.

Johnson, Claudia L. *Jane Austen: Women, Politics, and the Novel.* Chicago: University of Chicago Press, 1988.

Poovey, Mary. *The Proper Lady and the Woman Writer: Ideology as Style in the Works of Mary Wollstonecraft, Mary Shelley, and Jane Austen.* Chicago: University of Chicago Press, 1984.

Southam, B. C., ed. *Jane Austen: The Critical Heritage.* Vol. 1: 1811–1870; Vol. 2: 1870–1940. London and New York: Routledge and K. Paul, 1968, 1987.

Tanner, Tony. *Jane Austen.* Cambridge, MA: Harvard University Press, 1986.

Trilling, Lionel. "*Emma* and the Legend of Jane Austen." In *Beyond Culture.* New York: Viking, 1965.